THE
PARADISE
TRILOGY

teddekker.com

DEKKER FANTASY

Immanuel's Veins
House (WITH FRANK PERETTI)

BOOKS OF HISTORY CHRONICLES

THE LOST BOOKS (YOUNG ADULT)
Chosen
Infidel
Renegade
Chaos
Lunatic (WITH KACI HILL)
Elyon (WITH KACI HILL)
The Lost Books Visual Edition

THE CIRCLE SERIES
Black
Red
White
Green
The Circle Series Visual Edition

THE PARADISE BOOKS
Showdown
Saint
Sinner

DEKKER MYSTERY

Kiss (WITH ERIN HEALY)
Burn (WITH ERIN HEALY)

THE HEAVEN TRILOGY
Heaven's Wager
When Heaven Weeps
Thunder of Heaven

The Martyr's Song

THE CALEB BOOKS
Blessed Child
A Man Called Blessed

DEKKER THRILLER

THR3E
Obsessed
Adam
Skin
Blink of an Eye

THE
PARADISE
TRILOGY

TED DEKKER

THOMAS NELSON
Since 1798

NASHVILLE   DALLAS   MEXICO CITY   RIO DE JANEIRO

Published in Nashville, Tennessee, by Thomas Nelson. Thomas Nelson is a registered trademark of Thomas Nelson, Inc.

Published in association with Thomas Nelson and Creative Trust, 5141 Virginia Way, Suite 320, Brentwood, TN, 37027.

Thomas Nelson, Inc., titles may be purchased in bulk for educational, business, fund-raising, or sales promotional use. For information, please email SpecialMarkets@ThomasNelson.com.

Publisher's Note: This novel is a work of fiction. Names, characters, places, and incidents are either products of the author's imagination or used fictitiously. All characters are fictional, and any similarity to people living or dead is purely coincidental.

ISBN 978-1-4016-8698-7

Printed in the United States of America

12 13 14 15 16 17 QG 6 5 4 3 2 1

Dear Reader,

I STILL REMEMBER the day I first conceived of *Showdown*, the first novel in the Paradise saga. Any story in which the power of words can reshape reality and become flesh to dwell among mortal beings is naturally irresistible to wordsmiths of my ilk. Emboldened by unrestrained creative energy, I sat down and breathed life into a character named Marsuvees Black, little knowing that his name would become a trademark for me; never guessing that fans would begin showing up at events dressed like Marsuvees, muttering by then the all too familiar words: "Wanna trip, Baby?" Who could have guessed that a villain with a proclivity for eyeballs and worms would connect with so many readers?

But the path to Paradise didn't go so smoothly for me. I first penned *Showdown*—then titled *Storytellers*—before any of my novels were published, only to have it soundly rejected by every publisher my agent sent it to. It was too dark, they said. Too disturbing. Too much like Stephen King and not enough like Beverly Lewis or something along those lines. I didn't understand. The story is a hugely rewarding telling of love and passion that snatches desperate characters from a valley of despair and takes them to a place of great hope.

Defeated, I went on to pen another story. And another. And then many others, always believing that the story of Paradise would one day find its way into the hearts of many. It wasn't until I sat across the lunch table from my publisher Allen Arnold with tears in my eyes as I told him about *Showdown* that I found my first champion for Paradise. It became a defining moment for what would become a tremendously rewarding partnership.

Showdown was first published a couple years later and immediately found its way into the hearts of readers across the country. Naturally, some were taken aback, but no truly gripping story is without its detractors. *Saint* soon continued the story of Paradise, which found its consummation in *Sinner*.

They say the trilogy in your hands is core Dekker, something even I don't fully understand yet. I only hope it's also core you as well. Dive into the story and find yourself. If you can't, you'll surely find your friends, your children, your spouse, or the killer next door.

Enjoy

CONTENTS

SHOWDOWN

PROLOGUE

"HOW MANY children?" Marsuvees Black asked, examining his finger-nails. Strange behavior for a man interviewing for such a lofty position.

"Thirty-seven," David said. "And they may be only thirteen or fourteen years old, but I wouldn't call them children. They are students, yes, but most of them already have the intelligence of a postgraduate. Believe me, you've never met anyone like them."

Black settled back in the tall leather chair and pressed his thumbs and fingers together to form a triangle. He sighed. The monk from the Nevada desert was a strange one, to be sure. But David Abraham, director of the monastery's project, had to admit that genius was often accompanied by eccentric behavior.

"Thirty-seven special children who could one day change humanity's understanding of the world," Black said. "I think I could pull myself from my desert solitude for such a noble task. Wouldn't you agree? God knows I've been in solitude for three years now."

"You'll have to take that up with God," David said. "With or without you, our project will one day change the world. I can guarantee you that."

"Then why do you need me? You're aware of my"—he hesitated—"that I'm not exactly your typical monk."

"Naturally. I would say you're hardly a monk at all. You've spent a few years atoning for rather gratuitous sins, and for that I think you possess a unique appreciation for our struggle with evil."

"What makes you think I've beaten my demons?"

"Have you?"

"Do we ever?"

"Yes, we do," David said.

"If any man has truly beaten his demons, I have. But the struggle isn't over. There are new battles every day. I don't know why you need a conflicted man like me."

David thought a moment. "I don't need you. But God might. I think he does."

Black raised an eyebrow. "No one knows, you say? No one at all?"

"Only the few who must."

"And the project is sponsored by Harvard University?"

"That is correct."

David had spent months narrowing his search for the right teacher to fill the vacant post. Marsuvees Black brought certain risks, but the job was his if he chose to take the vow of secrecy and sequester himself in the Colorado mountains with them for the next four years.

The monk stared at his fingernail again. Scratched at it. A soft smile crossed his face.

"I'll let you know," he said.

CHAPTER ONE

PARADISE, COLORADO

One year later
Wednesday

THE SOUND of boots crunching into gravel carried across the blacktop while the man who wore them was still a shimmering black figure approaching the sign that read *Welcome to Paradise, Colorado. Population 450.*

Cecil Marshal shifted his seat on the town's only public bench, shaded from the hot midsummer sun by the town's only drinking establishment, and measured the stranger strutting along the road's shoulder like some kind of black-caped superhero. It wasn't just the man's black broad-brimmed hat, or his dark trench coat whipped about by a warm afternoon breeze, but the way he carried himself that made Cecil think, *Jiminy Cricket, Zorro's a-coming.*

The town sat in a small valley with forested mountains that butted up against the buildings on all four sides. One road in and the same road out. The road in descended into the valley around a curve half a mile behind the stranger. The road out was a "snaker" that took to the back country, headed north.

Paradise was a typical small mountain town, the kind with one of most things and none of many things.

One convenience store/gas station/video store/grocery store. One bar/restaurant. One old theater that had closed its doors long ago. One church. One mechanic—Paul Bitters, who fixed broken tractors and cars in his barn a mile north of town. One of a few other establishments that hardly counted as establishments.

No hospital. No arcade. No real grocery store other than the convenience store—everyone shopped in Delta, twenty miles west. No police station or bowling alley or car dealer or bike shop or choice of cuisine . . .

The only thing there was more than none or one of was hairdressers. There were three hairdressers, one on Main Street and two who worked out of their homes, which didn't really count.

"Looks lost," Johnny Drake said.

Cecil turned to the blond boy beside him. Johnny slouched back, legs dangling off the bench, watching the stranger.

His mother, Sally Drake, had come to town after being abandoned by some worthless husband when Johnny was a baby, thirteen years earlier. Sally's father, Dillon Drake, had passed away, leaving her the house that she and Johnny now lived in.

She'd decided to stay in Paradise for the house, after unsuccessfully trying to sell it. The decision was mighty courageous, considering the scandal Sally suffered shortly after her arrival. The thought of it still made Cecil angry. As far as he was concerned, the town hadn't found its soul since. They were a sick lot, these Paradise folk. If he could speak, he would stand up in that monstrosity they called a church and say so.

But Cecil couldn't speak. He was a mute. Had been since his birth, eighty-one years ago.

Johnny watched the stranger and rolled a large red marble between his fingers. He was born with a crooked leg, which was one thing that had bonded him to Cecil. The Children's Hospital in Denver corrected his leg surgically, and even though he still limped now and then, he was pretty much an ordinary boy now.

No, not ordinary. Extraordinary. A bona fide genius, they would all see that soon enough. Cecil loved the boy as his own. It was probably a good thing Johnny didn't know about the mess that had followed his birth.

Cecil turned back to the stranger, who'd left the graveled shoulder and now clacked down the middle of the road in black, steel-toed cowboy boots like a freshly shoed quarter horse. Black boots, black pants, black trench coat, black hat, white shirt. A real city slicker. On foot, three miles from the nearest highway. *I'll bet he's sporting a black mustache to boot.*

Cecil dropped his eyes to the leather-bound copy of *Moby Dick* in his lap. Today he would give Johnny the book that had filled his world with wonder when he was fourteen.

He looked at the boy. Kid was growing up fast. The sweetest, biggest-hearted boy any man could ever want for a son.

Johnny suddenly gasped. He had those big light brown eyes fixed in the direction of the city slicker, and his mouth lay open as if he'd swallowed a fly.

Cecil lifted his head and followed the boy's eyes. The black-cloaked stranger strutted down Main Street's yellow dashes now, arms swinging under the folds of a calf-length duster, silver-tipped boots stabbing the air with each step. His head turned to face Cecil and Johnny.

The brief thought that Zorro might be wearing a disguise—a Halloween mask of a skull—flashed through Cecil's mind. But this was no mask. The head jutting from the stranger's white shirt was all bone. Not a lick of skin or flesh covered the bleached jaw. It smiled at them with a wide set of pearl teeth. Two eyes stared directly at Cecil, suspended in their deep bone sockets, like the eyes down at the butcher shop in Junction: too big, too round, and never blinking.

Cecil's pulse spiked. The ghostly apparition strode on, right up the middle of the street as if it owned Paradise, like a cocky gunslinger. And then the stranger veered from his course and headed directly toward them.

Cecil felt his book drop. His hands shook in his lap like the stranger's eyes, shaking in their sockets with each step, above a grinning face full of teeth. Cecil scanned the man's body, searched for the long bony fingers. There, at the end of long black sleeves, dangling limp, the stranger's hands swung to his gait.

Flesh. Strong, bronzed, fleshy hands, curving gently with a gold ring flashing in the sun. Cecil jerked his eyes back to the stranger's face and felt an ice-cold bucket of relief cascade over his head.

The face staring at him smiled gently with a full set of lips, parted slightly to reveal white teeth. A tanned nose, small and sharp but no doubt stiff with cartilage like any other nose. A thick set of eyebrows curved above the man's glinting eyes—jet-black like the color of his shoulder-length hair.

The stranger was twenty feet from them now. Cecil clamped his mouth shut and swallowed the pooled saliva. *Did I see what I just thought I saw?* He glanced down at young Johnny. The boy still gaped. Yep, he'd seen it too.

Cecil remembered the book. He bent over and scanned the dusty boards at his feet and spotted it under the bench. He reached way down so his rump raised off the bench, steadied his tipping torso with his left hand on the boardwalk, and swung his right arm under the seat. His fingers touched the book. He clasped it with bony fingers, jerked it to safety, and shoved himself up.

When his head cleared the bench, the stranger stopped in front of them. Cecil mostly saw the black pants. A zipper and two pockets. *A crotch. A polyester crotch.* He hesitated a brief moment and lifted his head.

For a moment the man just stood there, arms hanging loosely, long hair lifting from his shoulders in the breeze, black eyes staring directly into Cecil's, lips drawn tight as if to say, *Get a grip, old fool. Don't you know who I am?*

He towered, over six foot, dressed in the spotless getup with silver flashing on his boots and around his belt like one of those country-western singers on cable. Cecil tried to imagine the square chin and high cheekbones bared of flesh, stripped dry like a skull in the desert.

He couldn't.

The stranger's eyes shifted to the boy. "Hello, my friend. Mighty fine town you have here. Can you tell me where I would find the man in charge?"

Johnny's Adam's apple bobbed. But he didn't answer. The man waited, eyebrows raised like he expected a quick answer. But Johnny wasn't answering.

The man turned back to Cecil. "How about you, old man? Can you tell me who's in charge here? The mayor? Chief of police?"

"He . . . he can't speak," Johnny said.

"That right? Well, you obviously can. You may not be much to look at, but your mouth works. So speak up."

Johnny hesitated. "A . . . about what?"

The man casually slipped his right hand into the pocket of his slacks and moved his fingers as if he were playing with coins. "About fixin' things around here."

Move on, stranger. You're no good. Just move on and find some other town. He should tell the stranger that. He should stand right up and point to the edge of town and tell the man where he should take his bones.

But Cecil didn't stand up and say anything. Couldn't. Besides, his throat was still in knots, which made it difficult to breathe much less stand up and play marshal.

"Yordon?" Johnny said.

The man in black pulled his hand from his pocket and stared at it. A translucent gel of some kind smothered his fingers, a fact that seemed to distract him for a moment. His eyes shifted to Johnny.

"Yordon?" The man began to lick the gel from his hand. "And who's Yordon?" He sucked at his fingers, cleaning them. "Now you're mute, boy? Speak up."

"The father?"

The man ran his wet fingers under his nose and drew a long breath through his nostrils. "You have to love the sweet smell of truth. Care for a sniff?"

He lowered his hand and ran it under Johnny's nose. The boy jerked away, and the man swept his hand in front of Cecil's face. Smelled musty, like dirty socks. Cecil pulled back.

"What did I tell you?" the man said, grinning. "This stuff will make you see the world in a whole new way, guaranteed."

Eyes back on Johnny. "Who else?"

Johnny stared at him.

"I said *who else*? Besides the father."

Johnny glanced at the bar, thirty yards to their right. "Maybe Steve?"

"Steve. That's the owner of the bar?" The man studied Smither's Saloon.

Cecil looked at the establishment's flaking white frontage. It needed a few coats of paint, but then so did half the buildings in Paradise. A plaque hung at an odd angle behind the swinging screen door. Faded red letters spelled *Open*. A dead neon Budweiser sign hung in one of the saloon's three windows.

He looked back at the stranger, who still faced the bar.

But the man's eyes weren't looking at the saloon; they were twisted down, fixed on Cecil. Crooked smile.

He cocked his arm up to his shoulder as if it were spring-loaded and formed a prong with two fingers, like a cobra poised to strike. Slowly, he brought the hand toward Cecil and then stopped, a foot from his face.

What on earth was the man doing? What did he think—

The stranger moved his hand closer, closer. Cecil's vision blurred and he instinctively clamped his eyes shut. Hot and cold flashes ripped up and down his spine like passing freight trains. He wanted to scream. He wanted to yell for help. *Help me, boy! Can't you see what he's doing? Help me, for heaven's sake!*

But he could do nothing more than open his mouth wide and suck in air, making little gasping sounds—*hach, hach*—like a plunger working in a toilet.

A long second crawled by. Then two. Cecil stopped sucking air and jerked his eyes open.

Pink filled his vision—the fuzzy pink of two fingers hovering like a wishbone an inch from his eyes. The fingers rushed at him. Cecil didn't have the time to close his lids this time. The man's pink pointers jabbed straight into his eye sockets.

Red-hot fire exploded in his skull. He saw an image of a cowboy branding a calf's hide with a burning iron. Only this was no calf's hide. This was eyeballs. *His* eyeballs.

Cecil's mouth strained wide in a muted scream.

The fingers dug right to the back of his sockets, wiggled deep. Waves of nausea washed through Cecil's gut. He thought he was going to throw up.

Then he could see he wasn't throwing up, because he could see everything. From a vantage point ten feet above the bench he saw it all. He saw Johnny cowering in horror at the far end of the short bench. He saw the black cowboy hat almost hiding the stranger's excited black eyes.

The man planted his feet wide, grinning with glee, right arm extended toward Cecil's face, fingers plugged into his eye sockets like an electric cord as if to say, *Here, you old bat, let me juice you up a little.*

Cecil's head tilted back with those two bloody prongs quivering above his nose. His whole body shook on the bench.

Pain swept to the ends of his bones and then was gone, as if it had leaked right out his heels. *Maybe that's what happens when you die. Maybe that's why I'm floating up here.*

The stranger's arm jerked back, and Cecil saw his eyeballs tear free from their sockets, cupped in the stranger's fingers. A loud, wet sucking sound filled the afternoon air. Little Johnny threw his arms over his head.

With his left hand, the stranger reached for his own face. Jabbed at his eyes. Plucked out his own black eyeballs.

Now he held a set of round, marblelike organs in each hand, a blue pair and a black pair. From above, Cecil caught a quick glimpse of the stranger's empty sockets, black holes drilled into his skull.

They weren't bleeding.

His own, on the other hand, began to ooze thick red streams down his cheeks. The stranger chuckled once and slapped the two black-marble eyes into Cecil's sockets in one smooth motion, as if plucking and replacing eyeballs was an art long ago perfected by his kind. He flung Cecil's blue eyes into his own skull and then wiped the blood running down the old man's cheeks with his palms. The bleeding stopped, but his eyelids had flapped closed, so Cecil couldn't see what his new eyes looked like.

The man wiped his own eyes as if brushing away tears and adjusted his collar. "Now I have their eyes," he mumbled. He turned to his left and strode toward Steve Smither's saloon.

The black-clad stranger had taken three steps when he stopped and turned back to Johnny, who was still fixed in shock. For one horrifying moment Cecil believed the stranger was considering another victim.

"You ever see a trick like that, boy?"

Johnny couldn't have answered if he'd wanted to.

The stranger winked, spun on his heels, and walked toward the saloon.

The pain was back. It washed over Cecil's cranium and spread like a fire, first through his eyes and then directly down his back.

Oh, God Almighty, help me!

Cecil's world began to spin in crazy circles. From somewhere in the dark he heard a *thump* echo through his mind. *My book*, he thought. *I've dropped my book again.*

JOHNNY CRINGED in horror. He gaped at the stranger, who appeared frozen on the steps to Smither's Saloon. Everything had stopped. Everything except for his heart, which was crashing in his ears.

The saloon door slammed.

He tore himself from the bench, tripped on a rock, and sprawled to the dirt. Pain knifed into his palm. He scrambled to his feet and spun. The old man was slumped on the bench, eyes closed, mouth open.

"Cecil?" Johnny whispered. Nothing. A little louder. "Cecil!"

He stepped forward cautiously, put a hand on Cecil's knee, and shook it. Still nothing.

Johnny lifted a trembling thumb to the old man's left eye and pulled up the eyelid. Cecil's blue eyes, not the stranger's black eyes. And there was no blood.

He released the eyelid and stood back. It occurred to him that Cecil's chest wasn't moving. He leaned forward and put his ear against his shirt. No heartbeat.

He bolted, nearly toppling again, and ran for home, ignoring the pain in his leg.

CHAPTER TWO

PARADISE
Wednesday

STEVE SMITHER stood behind his cherry bar and polished a tall Budweiser glass. Paula Smither, his wife, sat at the end of the bar, next to Katie Bowers and the minister's secretary, Nancy. Behind the women, Chris Ingles and his friend Mark had herded six others into a poker game. Waylon Jennings's mournful baritone leaked out from the old jukebox. But it wasn't the poker or the beer or the music that had brought the crowd today.

It was the fact that the town's one and only mayor/marshal, Frank Marsh, had run off with his "secretary" three days ago.

Katie Bowers pulled a string of gum from her mouth, balled it into a wad, and dropped it into the ashtray. She lifted her beer and glared at Steve. Strange how a pretty valley girl like Katie, who wore her makeup loud and talked even louder, could be so unattractive.

Katie set her bottle down. "Lighten up, Paula. It's not like we haven't been here before."

"That was different," Paula shot back.

"Was it?" Katie glanced at Steve. "Be a doll and give us some peanuts."

"She's right, that was different," he said, reaching under the counter for the Planters tin. The air had thickened with the last exchange.

Katie's husband, Claude Bowers, spoke without looking at his wife. "Go easy, Katie. It's not like *nothing* happened here." The huge Swede sat at the bar, running his forefinger around the rim of his mug.

"Oh, lighten up. I'm not actually endorsing what he did. I'm just saying that it's not that big a deal, and I think most of us agree. Last I heard, 50 percent of marriages in this country end in divorce. So that's the world we

13

live in. We might as well get used to it." She took another sip of her beer and
dipped her hand into the peanut bowl.

Steve caught his wife's eyes and winked. She might not be as slender as
Katie, or have her magazine looks, but to him Paula was the prettier woman
by far. They met in high school, two immigrants trying to make their way
in a country insensitive to both of them. The Colorado mountains proved
to be the perfect refuge for their wild romance.

"Frank didn't do anything right by Cynthia," Steve said.

That silenced them for a moment.

"Well, as far as I'm concerned, it takes two," Katie said. "I doubt Cynthia's
totally innocent in all this. What goes around, comes around."

Paula stared Katie down. "How can you say that? Cynthia's only crime
is that she's twenty years older than that bimbo Frank ran off with. And
what about little Bobby? He's seven, for heaven's sake! What did he do to
deserve this?"

"What did Johnny Drake do to deserve the scandal his mother caused?"

Steve glanced at Nancy and rolled his eyes. "What's Stanley saying
about this?"

"Yeah," Katie said with a twinkle in her eye. "What's good old Stanley say
about all this?"

Nancy shrugged, making her heavyset body jiggle. "Not much. Life can
be rough."

Steve could have told them that much. It was a stupid question, all things
considered.

"All I'm saying is we shouldn't get our panties in a wad as if this thing's
the black plague sent by God to punish our little village," Katie said.

Chris and Mark both broke into a chuckle.

Steve walked over to Paula and kissed her on the forehead. "It'll be okay,"
he said softly. Their eyes met and Paula softened. She always defended victims and underdogs, regardless of the cause.

The screen door creaked open and then slammed shut.

Steve turned, grateful for the interruption. A stranger stood at the door,
eyeing the room.

"Afternoon," Steve said.

The stranger was dressed in a crisp black getup that looked like it had come off a Macy's rack only this morning. Clean-cut. A bit like Johnny Cash. Waylon Jennings ended his song on a sad note, and the jukebox hissed silently.

The man removed his hat and shed his coat. What was he doing wearing a coat in the middle of summer anyway? And a black coat at that.

The man threw his coat over a chair and stepped up to the bar. Strong, sharp, tanned face. "You wouldn't happen to have a drink in this place, would you?"

"Last time I checked," Steve said with a grin.

The stranger slid onto a stool two down from Claude and smiled warmly. "Good. Soda water will be fine."

Steve dug a bottle from the ice chest, popped its cap under the bar, and slid it to the man. "One dollar," he said.

The others stared at the stranger, and although the poker game continued, Steve doubted the players were as fixed on their cards as a moment ago. It wasn't every day that a character like this walked into town.

A pool ball clicked across the room. The stranger tossed a silver dollar onto the counter. "So. This is Paradise." He shoved a hand toward Steve. "Name's Black," he said. "Marsuvees Black. You can call me Preacher if you want."

Steve took the hand. A preacher, huh? Figured. A preacher named Black dressed like an urban cowboy. A cowboy with blue eyes rimmed in red as if they hadn't slept in a while.

"Smither. Steve Smither. So where you headed, Preacher?"

The preacher took a sip of the water and followed it with a satisfied *aaahh*.

"Well, I'm headed here, Steve. Right here to Paradise, Colorado." He set the bottle on the bar. "Funny thing happened to me this afternoon."

Black looked at Paula and Katie for a moment and then shifted his gaze to the poker players, who ignored the cards for the moment and returned his stare.

"I was coasting down the highway with my window rolled down, enjoying the mountain air, thinking how blessed I was to have a life filled with hope and grace when, *pow*, the engine bangs in front of me and the front wheels lock up solid. By the time I get Mr. Buick over to the shoulder, she's smokin' like hell's gateway. Motor was gone."

The preacher took another swig from the bottle of soda and swallowed hard. The room listened. No one bothered to restart the jukebox.

"Soon as I climbed out, I knew it was God," Black said.

Steve felt a burning in his ear at the word. Not that there was anything unusual about the word *God* in Paradise. Practically the whole town packed the Episcopal church every Sunday. But the way the theatrical man *said* the word sent waves of heat through Steve's ears. Formal and hollow, like it came from a deep drum. *Gauuwwdd.*

"God?" Steve said.

The preacher nodded. "God. God was saying something. And the second I saw the sign that my '78 Buick had nearly run over, I knew what he was saying."

Black lifted the bottle to his lips again. Steve glanced at Claude and smiled one of those can-you-believe-this-guy smiles. "And what was that?"

"The sign said, *Paradise 2 Miles.* And then the voice popped in my head. *Go 2 Paradise*, it said." Black drew a two in the air as he spoke. "Bring grace and hope to the lost town of Paradise."

Steve picked up another glass and rubbed it with the towel at his waist. Grace and hope. Paradise had enough religion for a town twenty times its size. The church already dominated the community's social life.

The man named Marsuvees Black drilled Steve with a blue stare. "But there was more," he said.

Steve felt his gut tighten at the look and stopped rubbing the glass.

"God said he'd give us a sign." Black reached over to the peanut bowl without removing his eyes from Steve and brought a nut to his lips.

"A sign?"

"A sign. A wart. A man with a wart. Said there's something ugly hidden under this town's skin. Said I was to bring grace and hope with a capital *G* and a capital *H*."

Steve looked at the others. They were no longer smiling, which was odd, because he figured Chris at least would be snickering. But there was something in Black's voice. Something like Freon, chilling to the bone. Paula and Katie sat wide-eyed now. Claude fidgeted. By the pool table, Case Donner leaned on his stick and stared at Chris.

Black looked at the poker table. "Any of you have a wart?"

Mark smiled and uttered a nervous chuckle. He shifted his gaze to Chris, wooden next to him.

"No?" The preacher popped another peanut into his mouth and crunched down. "None of you has a wart over there?"

Still no response. Steve felt his heart pick up its pace.

"How about you there?" Marsuvees asked, nodding at Chris. "You sure you don't have a wart behind your right ear?"

Chris opened his mouth slowly, and Steve believed that the man had a wart precisely where the stranger suggested. He turned back to Black, who continued chewing on a peanut.

"No? Well, I know it's there. A redhead with a wart. That would be the sign. Now, if you're not a redhead with a wart, I'll eat my hat and walk right out of here."

Chris sat dumbfounded.

"This is your day," Black said. "Because there's always two sides to a sign. My side and your side. For me to know that God did indeed bring me to Paradise, and for you to know that I was sent." The man stood from his stool and strolled toward Chris.

"Do you mind if I touch it?" Black asked softly.

"Touch it?" Chris stammered.

"Yes, touch it. Do you mind if I touch the wart behind your ear?"

Chris swung his stricken eyes to Steve, but Steve felt just as much surprise. For a while they held their places, frozen in the scene, totally unprepared for this surreal script. All except the preacher. He seemed to know how this play would end.

"It's okay." He placed a gentle hand on Chris's right shoulder and brushed imaginary dandruff from the blue mechanic's shirt that read *Chris* over the left pocket. "I can help you. A sign, remember?" And then he reached for Chris's ear like a magician doing a disappearing coin trick. His fingers brushed the side of Chris's skull, just behind his right ear. Black turned around, walked back to his stool, sat, and popped another peanut into his mouth.

"Now we will see what God meant when he said bring grace and hope to Paradise," Black said. "You ready, Chris?"

The stranger faced the redhead. "Feel your head there, son." Chris made no move.

"Go ahead, feel the wart."

Now Chris raised a hand to his cheek and then let his fingers creep up behind his right ear, keeping his eyes on the preacher. He reached his ear. Felt behind.

His fingers froze.

"It's . . ."

Silence.

"It's what?" Steve asked.

"It's . . . it's gone."

"What do you mean, it's gone?" Steve said.

"I swear. I had a wart here just like he said, and now it's gone!" Chris stared at the preacher with wide eyes.

Steve spun to the preacher, who was now grinning, big pearlies gleaming white. His front teeth gripped a single nut.

The glass in Steve's hand trembled. The brown knob between Black's teeth looked somewhat like a peanut, but he knew it couldn't be a peanut because peanuts did not bleed. And this thing was bleeding a thin trail of red down Black's lower teeth while the preacher sat there with his lips peeled back and his eyes wide, proudly displaying his catch.

To a person they all gaped at the man, slack-jawed.

Then, like a gulping fish, Black sucked the wart into his mouth, crunched twice deliberately, and swallowed hard.

He slowly surveyed the patrons, his eyes sparkling blue. *Face the music,* they were saying. *This is how you do grace and hope. You got a problem with that? Well, suck it up. I'm the real thing, honey.*

And he was, wasn't he? He had to be.

"Am I getting through?" Black scanned the crowd.

"God have mercy," Katie Bowers muttered.

"*God* is right, my sweetness. The rest we'll see about. Now that I have your attention, I'm going to make a demand. With this kind of power comes great responsibility—I'm sure you understand. My responsibility is to make sure that each and every one of you, those here and those not here, attend tonight's meeting."

What meeting?

"Seven o'clock sharp, in the church," Black said. "No excuses, no exceptions."

He snatched his hand up by his shoulder as if to keep everyone seated. He cocked his head to one side, faced the street outside.

"Another sign," he said, listening to the silence. "An old man. A deaf mute. Wasn't going to come to the meeting tonight. Thought I was too pushy."

Black lowered his hand slowly and faced them. "Seems as though he's dead now. Had a heart attack as I spoke."

Nancy gasped.

"You sure about that?" Steve asked. He was surprised he even asked the question, as if this man had the power to heal *and* kill. What kind of spiritual power was that? A moment ago, he thought Black might be the real deal, but this talk about Cecil cast a shadow over that possibility.

Black ignored his question. "This is serious business, my friends. I suggest you get back to your homes and wherever it is you waste away your lives and think hard and long about coming out tonight."

Tricks, tricks. He's manipulating us with tricks. The monotony of Paradise has been interrupted by a traveling trickster.

Black turned and drilled Steve with a stare. "You going to check outside, Steve, or are you going to just sit there thinking I'm nothing but a bag of tricks?"

Steve blinked.

Claude was up already, heading for the door. He shoved it open and stared outside.

"Steve . . ."

The big Swede stood gaping at the street. He faced them. "You'd better have a look. Something's wrong with Cecil."

CHAPTER THREE

THE MONASTERY
Wednesday

DEEP IN a monastery hidden in the mountain canyons not so far from Paradise, Colorado, an orphaned boy named Billy hurried to class, letting his gaze wander over the bas-relief pictographs inscribed in the rough-hewn stone around him. The pictures peered from their graven settings with fixed eyes. He could rarely look directly at the pictographs without it raising gooseflesh, and he wasn't sure why. Now proved no exception.

He pushed a heavy door open and squinted in the sunlight that filled the library. The monastery was laid out like an old wagon wheel, cut in half and buried into a wedge-shaped gap in the cliff so that its spokes ran into the mountain. At the center lay the one room that had a direct view of the sky through the top of the canyon—the hub of this half wheel, though it wasn't quite symmetrical.

A large, reinforced glass canopy bridged the opening—one of the only truly modern things about this otherwise ancient monastery. Sunlight poured into the expansive atrium. The library's wood floors encircled a large lawn where three oak trees and a myriad of shrubs grew. A welcome half-acre of escape from the Gothic halls.

Billy ran through the empty library and shuffled down a stone hallway leading to one of the monastery's many classrooms. He was late for writing class. In fact, he might have missed it. Not that it really mattered. He'd made the rest of his classes this week—what was one small writing class out of twenty-one subjects? There was mathematics, there was history, there was theology, there was geography, there was a whole line of other disciplines, and

Billy excelled in all of them, including writing. One missed class, although highly unusual, wouldn't mar his record.

He ran a hand through loose red curls and stopped to catch his breath before a door near the end of the hall. The soft whisper of voices floated through the oak door. And then a deep one, above the others.

Raul?

Yes, there it was again. Raul, the head overseer, was teaching this evening. A warm flutter ran through Billy's gut. Then again, any of the twelve overseers would have triggered the same response.

His hand trembled slightly as he reached for the door. He could handle this. He would just pull himself together and handle this like he'd handled everything else.

He twisted the knob and stepped into the room.

Raul stood at one end of the room next to a bubbling stone fountain. The other students—thirty-six in all if they were all here—sat at desks in two large semicircles with their backs to Billy, facing the tall, white-bloused overseer. A few glanced Billy's way, but most seemed intent on whatever nugget of truth the teacher had just tossed out.

Raul eyed him. *You're late.* Most overseers had to restrain their pleasure with the students, easy as it was to pound their backs with accolades or lift them from their feet in big bear hugs. But Raul's idea of a compliment was a slight nod.

Billy took a seat behind the others.

"Peace, my dear students, is the gateway to harmony," Raul said, his eyes still on Billy. "It is also the gateway to destruction. War and peace. Darcy, remind us of our first rule in writing."

"Write an extraordinary story that will leave your reader gasping," the pretty brunette said, taking liberty in paraphrasing the rules as they were all encouraged to do.

The four rules of writing were as familiar to the students as milk was to a baby.

1. Write to discover.
2. There is no greater discovery than love.

3. All love comes from the Creator.

4. Write what you will.

The rules reflected the students' purpose in their studies, certainly, but even more so in their lives as a whole. They were often encouraged to substitute the word *live* for the word *write*. Live to discover, as long as discovery leads to a love that comes from the Creator. One could only write what one knew, because to write well one must know well, as the teachers said, and to know well you must live well. None of the students' other classes made much sense without writing, because in this monastery, writing was the mirror of life.

Billy glanced at Darcy and saw that she looked his way. He winked at her. *You leave me gasping.* She smiled and he turned back to Raul, hoping the teacher hadn't caught the exchange.

"That's right," Raul said. "Forget the foolish notion that there are really only a handful of stories to be told. Write new stories and new characters, embarking on grand, unique journeys with twists and turns that will leave the reader wondering."

The overseer paused. "Now does that sound like peace? Twists and turns and gasping? Not really, does it?"

Except for the water's gurgling, the room fell silent. Students who were gazing at the lifelike murals surrounding the room brought their focus back to Raul. Billy felt a small twinge of excitement at the base of his neck.

"How can there be peace unless there is first conflict?" Raul dropped the statement like a small seed into the freshly tilled ground of thirty-seven young minds.

"Hear, hear," one of the students said. "We could use a little more twisting and turning around here."

Several chuckled.

A boy to Billy's left cleared his throat, and a dozen heads turned his way. The blond-haired boy with blue eyes had long ago earned the right to be heard. At thirteen Samuel was perhaps the most accomplished student in the monastery. Besides Billy, of course. They could both discuss most subjects with any teacher on any day and do it well. At one time Billy would have considered Samuel his best friend. Birds of a feather flock together, as the old cliché said. Until a month ago.

"Or how can there be conflict unless there is first peace?" Samuel returned in a light, polite voice. "We've always known that peace precedes conflict, that conflict disturbs the discovery of love, which is the heart of the second rule."

Approval rumbled through the class.

"Very good, Samuel." Raul stroked his chin. "But how can you write about peace or love unless you first subject the reader to ugly conflict? Wouldn't you minimize peace by minimizing conflict?"

"Unless the reader begins with the knowledge of peace. Why should we demonstrate peace through conflict if the reader already knows peace?"

Raul nodded. "But wouldn't you want to heighten the reader's understanding of peace by drawing him into conflict?"

"Conflict can just as easily compromise peace as amplify it," Samuel said.

The two volleyed as if in a tennis match. Though Raul was four times Samuel's elder, the boy was no ordinary thirteen-year old. Like the rest of them, he had never been beyond the monastery's walls, where the world waited with all of its compromise. They'd been sequestered their whole lives, learning of virtue and love and all that threatened both. The teachers said they had developed the intellects of adults.

"Yes, but such a story can amplify peace, can't it?" Raul said. "It can make one's understanding of peace as vivid as the conflict. That is the point, isn't it?"

"Makes sense to me," Dan, a short Hungarian boy, said.

Billy smiled. He wasn't surprised that Raul's argument made sense to many of the students, whose questions had grown increasingly bold this year thanks to the teachings of Marsuvees Black. It was difficult to tell exactly where Raul stood on the issue, however, because the overseers often taught with questions. He was either secretly laughing or sweating bullets, depending on who he really was under that Socratic mask of his.

"Would you need to place your hand in a fire to understand a cool breeze?" Samuel asked.

"No, but you might appreciate a cool breeze much more after standing in the fire for a day. What is a cool breeze unless there is also heat?"

"And why not avoid the heat altogether? Move to a milder climate, say. Or stay out of the sun. There's no use in exposing yourself to a lot of hot air when you already have the cool truth."

Raul smiled as laughter erupted around the room. He dipped his head in respect. "Yes, of course, Samuel. Well said. Well said, indeed. And I think on that note we will end our session."

The students began to rise and chatter about the discussion.

Billy snatched up his writing book.

"Billy." Raul motioned for him to wait.

As the last student filed out, Raul donned a long brown cloak with a hood. He lifted the hood to cover his head.

"Having interests outside of class gives you no excuse for being late."

He knew? No, not necessarily. The interests Raul spoke of could be an innocent reference to almost anything. Unless Raul was the masked man from the dungeons. Billy couldn't tell by the voice alone—not distorted as it was by the mask down below.

"I'm sorry, sir."

The teacher acknowledged the apology with a nod. But his eyes pierced Billy's conscience.

Billy slipped from the room, shivering. Raul's look had seemed too knowing, as if he meant to say, "I know you've been below, boy. I know that you're going there now. The dungeons will kill you."

Maybe I want to die, Raul. Maybe I just want to die.

THE ROUTE to the dungeons took Billy back past the library into a dark hall lit only by the flaming torch that he carried. He'd been down the hall a hundred times, but he'd entered the staircase only once, not twelve hours ago.

The memory was fresh enough to send a chill through his bones as he approached the forbidden door. He couldn't possibly resist it—not after his first exploration last night. The dungeon was dark and it was evil, but it was also wonderful, something he'd never dreamed of before, much less experienced.

His cryptic and overcautious journey from the classroom to this remote place had taken him at least thirty minutes. No one had seen him, he was sure of it.

Billy looked up and down the hall one last time, twisted the door's corroded handle, and pulled. The hinges squealed in protest. He slipped in, eased the heavy door shut, and stood breathless on the stone landing.

Before him, a winding stone stairway descended into shadows that moved in the torchlight. Billy walked to the edge of the landing, paused to still his heart, and stepped down. One step at a time.

A single question echoed through his skull. Was the monk here?

Billy assumed the masked man was a monk, having narrowed his identity down to three possibilities. If he was right, this person who'd lured him here earlier was either Raul, the head overseer whose class he left not half an hour ago, or the director himself, David Abraham.

Both were the right height. Both had low bass voices. Both spoke with the same accent and used similar verbiage.

Whomever it was, Billy took comfort in knowing that he wasn't the instigator of this dark sin. And he had no illusion that what he was doing was anything less than evil. Thirteen years under the tutelage of a dozen kind and faithful monks had made their intended impression. He did indeed know the difference between good and evil, love and hate, obedience and sin. And this was an irresistibly dark sin.

But he also now knew that he'd been created for this sin. He'd been born into evil, and now evil insisted that he understand it. For thirteen years the monks did their best to shield him from the truth of his nature, but his God-given desire to explore had won the battle.

Never mind that his decision might cost him the war.

The last thought surprised him. He was in a war between good and evil, and what lay ahead was evil, wasn't it? Yes, it had to be. And yet, if Marsuvees Black was right, he was destined to explore it.

Billy descended slowly, aware now of the flame's faint crackle. He eased off the last stair and stepped into the lower level's ten-by-twelve vestibule.

The black door that led into the dungeons was open! He was sure he'd closed—

"Hello, Billy."

He spun with a whoosh of flame. A tall hooded man emerged from the corner shadows, face obscured by the shiny black mask.

The room smelled mossy and wet. Billy felt an urge to run back up the stairs and slam the door shut on whoever hid in the brown cloak. But he couldn't. The tunnels on the other side of the black door called.

Billy swallowed. "Are you Raul?"

"Who I am is of no concern to you. What I offer you, on the other hand, is. I take it you went in last night?"

Billy didn't answer.

"How far did you get?"

"Just inside the door."

"You didn't enter the tunnels?"

"No."

Billy couldn't see the man's eyes, couldn't make any judgment about his emotions. He didn't know what frightened him more, the tunnels or the man.

"I see you found the desk."

It was the only piece of furniture outside the six tunnel entrances. How the man knew he'd spent some time at the desk was beyond him.

"Yes."

Billy saw the extinguished lamp hanging from the sconce beside the masked man. He must have entered through the tunnels, using that torch. But how did he know Billy would be here at this time?

"Today you'll go into the tunnels?"

"I don't know."

"You must. If you weren't meant to enter these tunnels, they wouldn't be available for you, now would they?"

The musty smell seemed to enter Billy's head, prompting him to agree. The tunnels were like a drug, and his desire to enter them had kept him awake all night. He'd fought the urge to come down here since the first time he found the note in his locker urging him to do so, nearly three months ago.

The dungeons contained discoveries wildly beyond any child's imagination, the note said. And the children had been brought to the monastery with those discoveries in mind. It was only a matter of time before each had an opportunity to enter and experience.

Billy turned toward the black doors. "How many tunnels are there?"

"Too many to count."

"How deep do they go?"

No response. Billy faced him. "Why do you want me to go in? And why won't you show yourself to me?"

"I won't show myself to you because this is a secret matter. I chose you from among the other students; you didn't choose me. Let's keep it that way. And I want you to go in because I want you to discover the kind of power you were made for. As I've said, it's why you were brought here in the first place. The only question is whether you have what it takes to fulfill your purpose."

The odor from the open door grew stronger. Billy wasn't sure what power the monk meant, but he'd felt enough last night to make his skin tingle with excitement. For the first time in his life, he had felt himself— truly himself. Could that be evil?

Billy stepped toward the door and peered in. Nothing had changed. Same damp cobblestones, same tall arching walls, same small desk off to the right.

Same six tunnels, gaping black beyond.

"Go deeper, Billy. And remember what I told you about Marsuvees Black."

Marsuvees Black? And what was that?

The tunnels seemed to suck him toward their yawning mouths with a magnetic force.

Oh yes. He remembered what the man had told him about Marsuvees Black. That the teacher was closer to truth than any of the others. That Billy must consider Black's teaching on exploring the furthest reaches of good and evil.

Billy took one last look at the cloaked man and then stepped into the forbidden dungeon. The door closed with a *thunk* behind him.

ALMOST IMMEDIATELY the musty odor went to work on his mind, dimming or accentuating or what, he didn't know, but time seemed to stall. It was a lovely feeling.

After an indiscernible amount of hazy deliberation, Billy decided that of the six primary tunnels he should enter the tunnel to his far right first, maybe because he was right-handed. Or maybe because the torch flamed in his right hand, dispelling more shadows there. He wasn't even sure why it mattered. He only knew that he had to enter one of these tunnels, and he had to do it now, before his chest burst.

Billy approached the tunnel slowly, torch arm extended. The flame's light lapped at the wall's moss-covered stones. Moisture seeped through the rock and dripped unevenly on the cobblestones, sending echoes down the black hall. He swallowed, set his right foot through the entry, and glanced back at the small desk where he'd stopped last night.

Don't be a weasel, Billy.

Billy entered the forbidden tunnel. He crept forward, one short step at a time, scanning the walls with peeled eyes. A cool draft kissed his cheeks. How deep was this thing? *Go deeper, Billy.*

He'd taken about ten steps when he first saw the pink pipe running along the wall to his right. It was roughly four inches in diameter, and it ran for ten feet before tapering to a head.

The pipe moved. Billy yelped and sprang back, striking his elbow on the wall. His cry echoed down the tunnel. The pipe bunched slowly, like an accordion, then stretched out and slid forward, and then paused.

Rubbing his elbow, Billy glanced back and saw not moss but another worm, resting on the opposite wall.

He leapt to safety and waved his light in an arch. No fewer than a dozen worms inched along the tunnel's walls and ceiling, each trailing a thick band of milky mucus. It smelled like old damp socks.

For several long minutes he remained rooted to the floor, quaking, gripping the torch with both hands. But the worms didn't threaten him, and his courage returned.

The gargantuan worms expanded and contracted silently past him, seemingly on a mission to nowhere. Like the worms of hell in the gospel according to Mark. *Worms that do not die. Those worms would grow to this size,* he thought. But they seemed harmless enough.

He walked deeper. Then even deeper. Water dripped incessantly, and the worms slid along moist walls made slimy by their mucus. Beyond thirty feet, the tunnel faded into blackness. Behind him, the same now.

How deep could this tunnel really go? A hundred yards? Five hundred yards? A mile?

Had it been constructed by human hands? It seemed more likely to him that this forbidden tunnel hidden below the monastery where they'd all been raised to love virtue was nothing less than a shaft into the heart of darkness itself.

And he was the lone warrior sent out to defeat that darkness.

But that was rubbish. Even through the fog that clouded his mind, he knew that much. Or at least suspected it.

Billy stopped and breathed deep. The intoxicating smell filled his mind with flowers, so to speak. It squeezed his heart with warmth. He looked at a large worm on his right, slithering through the translucent mucus. It struck him with sudden clarity that the odor was coming from the worms, not the tunnel itself.

A smattering of gel plopped to the ground two feet in front of his shoes. Seemed harmless. He bent down, touched it with his forefinger. Like thick oil or thin Vaseline. He brought it to his nose. His sense of well-being blossomed. Odd.

Billy wiped the stuff on one of the few dry stones at his feet and resumed his push, deeper.

He walked for a short time in numb contentedness until a large iron gate broke the wall on his right. What was this?

He shifted the torch into his left hand and approached it. The gate was made of iron bars, long ago rusted and covered in moss. By his torch's light he could make out a dusty earth floor and the faint outline of furniture beyond.

Billy raised a hand to the iron gate. A sudden scurrying startled him and he withdrew his hand. An obscenely large rat ran from the room, through Billy's spread legs, and down the hall, where it disappeared.

Billy pushed against the bars. The gate opened with a screech. *That was easy. Easy peasy.* He stepped forward on weak legs.

His torch flooded the room with yellow light, revealing three walls filled with antique hangings. Paintings that looked European and old, mostly portraits of historical figures he didn't recognize. Candleholders made of corroded metals and some woods. Masks.

More masks than he could count at the moment. The kind he envisioned at a masquerade ball in Venice, though he'd only seen pictures.

Weapons were mounted on one of the walls. Chains with nasty spiked balls, large pointed mallets, double-edged swords, helmets with slits for eyes.

Billy approached the wall and ran his hand along several of the weapons. Why such simple displays of antiquity pleased him as much as they did, he couldn't guess. Maybe it was the setting. The sludge. But every surface his finger touched seemed to be magical. Surely forces hid deep in every angle, every form, every shape, every color in this room.

Or, at the least, in his imagination, which was being pried wide open.

In one corner stood a skeleton, one of those he'd seen in museum picture books. Beside the skeleton was an open wardrobe filled with costumes, presumably to go with the masks. Long black trench coats and flashy silver belts and broad-brimmed hats. Boots.

Billy looked at the wall of masks again. He was sure the monk had been here.

After some time, Billy left the room and headed deeper.

Another room dawned on his right, this one empty except for some large rusted chests and shelves filled with small bottles. The milky contents of some bottles looked like the worm sludge but could just as easily be dirty water. Fascinating, but there was more, he could feel it.

He walked on. He couldn't walk forever, naturally. He had to find a place to rest. Not that his feet were tired, but his mind was overloaded and groggy with satisfaction.

A third room loomed on his right. Once again he pulled the gate open, at ease now with the squeal it made.

The scene illuminated by the wavering torch brought a warm flutter to his belly. On his right, a bookshelf rose to the stone cavern's ceiling, stacked with scores of books. Directly ahead, two matching chairs flanked a large, dusty Queen Anne sofa. A large boar head glared from the wall above the sofa, its long, dirty tusks jutting from an angry snarl. A wagon-wheel chandelier hovered above an antique desk on his left.

He'd found a study, carved here in the subterranean corridors.

Billy walked to the bookshelf and lifted the torch to reveal the titles. A thin film of dust covered the books, and he ran his finger down one of the spines. *Antonio's Ball.* He pulled the volume out and flipped it open. Old English.

"Huh."

He smiled and blew along the spines. Dust puffed into the air. They were all old titles he'd never heard of before. Except one: *Moby Dick* by Melville. He backed to the center of the room and turned in a circle. Fascinating. Even more than the room of art and theater, this study seemed to glow with mystery and magic.

Why was this place forbidden? Because evil resided here? According to whom? It seemed to him that the director himself would encourage the students to explore these magical halls. What harm was there in a little milky worm sludge?

It occurred to Billy then, standing in the middle of the small study below the monastery's foundation, that he had to bring someone else down here.

Billy turned to the desk and approached its tall, wooden chair. Several dust-covered books lay on one side, similar to the book he found last night on the desk outside the tunnels. That one was blank. Probably journals. The quill and inkwell looked surprisingly fresh.

He set his torch in an iron sconce and sat on the sofa.

This was a place of mold and moss and dripping water and massive worms. It was a heaven of mystery and books and art and . . . well, he couldn't describe it exactly, but he could feel it.

Billy laid his head back and smiled. He could sit here in dumb pleasure for the rest of his life.

ANDREW JACKMAN hurried down the dim hall, panting from the climb up through the monastery's innumerable stairs. Flames licked at the rock walls on both sides, one torch every twenty feet. Parts of the monastery were powered by electricity, but they wasted their precious light in none of the halls. An electric light bulb was far less expensive to keep lit than an oil torch, but that would mean upgrading the monastery, and upgrading wasn't a priority for David. Besides, it increased their risk of exposure.

David Abraham would never risk exposure. The number of people who knew of this mountain's secret could be counted on one page, and all went to great lengths to keep it that way. The fact that the large monastery was carved out of a wedge-shaped canyon no more than twenty meters wide at the top aided them in keeping its existence unnoticed, but even the best camouflage had its flaws. The school could be found, if one knew where to look.

Today the risk of their discovery had grown. No, not only of being found. Worse.

Andrew rounded a corner, hefted his robe with one hand to give his feet more room, and broke into a run.

He always knew that the project could fail, yes, but he'd given a dozen years of his life to the hope that it wouldn't. Now, the entire project teetered on the precipice of failure.

Why? Because one boy had defied them all.

He reached the tall door that led to the director's study and banged hard. "David!"

"Come."

He shoved the handle down and pushed the door in. Light streamed in from the large windows that faced the west, out of the canyon. David Abraham looked up from his large ironwood desk. A ten-by-ten-foot map of the world made of pearl and jade was built into the wall adjacent the long row of floor-to-ceiling bookcases. Leather and clothbound books only. A large crystal chandelier hung over a thick cross section cut from a redwood. Eight leather chairs surrounded it.

"We have a problem," Andrew said.

The director leaned back in his chair and tapped his hand with his pencil. "And what would that be?"

How should he say this? David might be unshakable, but Andrew had little doubt the news would send an earthquake through his bones.

"Billy's entered the dungeons."

David stared at him.

Andrew walked in. "He's down there now."

"How do you know?"

"He entered the staircase two hours ago and he hasn't emerged."

"That doesn't necessarily mean he's entered the tunnels."

"Of course he has; we both know that. We have to put a stop to it! He's not the only one who's been showing curiosity in the dark side lately. I've warned against this! I demand we put a stop to it. Immediately."

David set down his pen. "No."

He was a big man, more than six feet, and powerful. His blond hair rested on broad shoulders, which were covered by a brown hooded cloak. When he wasn't wearing billowing white shirts and black slacks, he favored the common dress of the teachers. It had been his insistence that they wear clothing befitting of a monastery, as he put it. But in Andrew's eyes he looked more like a Viking than a monk. Not that David pretended to be a monk—he was a world-renowned collector of antiquities and a professor of both psychology and history, tenured at Harvard, before he left it all for the project.

"Absolutely not, we can't interfere, you know that."

"But, sir—"

"I said no!" David stood. He glanced out the window at black storm clouds gathering in the valley near the canyon. "We knew this moment would come. Don't overreact."

"We knew? I certainly didn't know! I feared, but it was never a foregone conclusion. This wasn't part of the plan." Andrew was taken aback by the director's lack of outrage. How could the prospect of failure not ruin him?

"The storm clouds always eventually come," David said. "We always knew the children would be tested. The only question is how they will weather the storm."

"Billy's failed already, by going in. The subterranean tunnels will ruin him."

The director stared at him without speaking for a few seconds. His jaw-line bunched with tightened muscles. "Or give him the kind of power that you and I only dream about."

Project Showdown had been a highly controversial concept from the beginning. Its stated purpose was appealing enough to attract some of the world's best-educated and pious men of faith, but if the less discerning public knew what was happening here in this mountain, they might cry foul. Even David's decision, however reluctantly made, to exclude female teachers and thereby any maternal influence in the monastery would come under fire. But in David's mind, single-mindedness of the male teachers was paramount. It was a monastery after all, not a college. Andrew agreed.

The proposal that Dr. Abraham sent out to a select group of clergy was simple: Harvard University was conducting a closely guarded and some-what speculative examination of faith and human nature. The study sought to test the limits of mankind's capacity to affect nature through faith. In simple terms, Project Showdown meant to discover the extent to which a man could indeed move mountains (metaphorically or materially) through faith. A showdown of faith and natural laws, so to speak.

Put another way, the experiment was nothing less than an attempt to test the speculation that a noble savage—a child unspoiled by the rampant effects of evil in society, struggling only with the evil within themselves—might be taught skills that the rest of humanity could not learn. Certainly spiritual skills, perhaps even physical skills. If a person had no reason to doubt, and as such possessed unadulterated faith, they surely would be able to wield the power of their faith to humankind's advantage.

There was one problem, of course. Noble savages did not roam the streets of America or any other country in droves. So David Abraham intended to rear the noble savages from birth.

He took possession of this ancient Jesuit monastery hidden deep in the Colorado mountains and spent millions of dollars transforming it into an ideal setting for his study. He then selected thirty-seven orphans, most from disadvantaged parts of Europe, and arranged for them to be brought to the monastery, where they would be raised in community under specific guidelines. A lone child would not do because the children would be required to enter society one day, a prospect that could render them useless unless they had grown up in a functioning, if different, soci-ety of their own.

Perhaps the most important element in the study were the teachers. Twelve monks and priests had each agreed to a four-year commitment, but most remained after they were free to go home. The money paid to their families and various charities only partially justified their commitments. Their desire to see the effects of a noble savage's faith was motivation enough for most of them.

For nearly twelve years they carefully taught each child in the ways of truth, virtue, and faith, and they meticulously recorded every move of every child. Other than morning prayers, conducted before breakfast, the faith was stripped of liturgy and focused on simple teachings from both Old and New Testaments. Religious, doctrinal jargon in particular had been abandoned.

Naturally, they faced many challenges—arguments, jealousy, hurt feelings of one kind or another. But without the smothering influence of a world swimming in faithlessness, the children had matured remarkably well. There had been no overt acts of rebellion.

Until now.

Andrew believed David had always kept secrets. He walked with the air of a man plagued by more than the eyes could see. His understated reaction to the news that Billy had broken a cardinal rule made Andrew wonder if it really was news to the director at all. And now David claimed that good could come of this fall from grace. *A power we only dream of.*

David averted his eyes. "We can't rescue him, Andrew. We've poured our lives into him and we've taught him the way of faith and virtue, but he must choose."

"Then the end may be upon us."

David walked to a large bookcase lined with hundreds of clothbound volumes. Two masks rested on one of the shelves, one black and one white, signifying the basic struggle between good and evil faced by every man and woman and child who lived. The director's eyes lingered on the black mask before returning to Andrew. His eyes revealed deep emotion, whether fear or concern or resolve, Andrew couldn't tell.

"It's the power of the children's choice that we're after, isn't it?" David said. "The power that resides deep in those spirits is staggering. But only when it's tested will we see that power."

"They've been tested, a thousand times."

"Tested? Not really. Not the way they will be now."

Andrew paced, hands on hips. David made sense, but not enough to satisfy him. The tunnels had always been a mystery to the teachers, but from what Andrew knew, they were filled with evil. Raw evil. David repeatedly stated that the tunnels would dramatically alter the life of anyone who entered. The dungeons were off-limits to all.

Andrew faced David. "What precisely will Billy face down there? I certainly have the right to know that much."

David studied him, and for a moment Andrew thought he would break. "You'll know soon enough. Know this, the tunnels will open the mind. The heart." He tapped his chest. "The will. This is where the battle resides, and this is where true power waits."

His vague answers were maddening.

"It's rather strange that this occurs a week after the departure of Marsuvees Black."

No response.

The monk from the deserts of Nevada claimed to have lived there in isolation for three years. David preferred clergy that had lived in solitude, he said. They had the character required for this confining assignment.

But Marsuvees Black didn't strike Andrew as a monk who'd spent three years alone. He seemed more like a one-man Vegas show who had finished his penance in the desert and was reclaiming the glory of his previous life. After nine months, he began to act strangely and was given to outbursts and wild discourses on relativism and man's free will. When David reined him in, Marsuvees withdrew almost completely. Then, without warning, he left the monastery.

"Not that I'm accusing him, mind you. I would expect to see him twisting the ear of some poor parish somewhere, not plotting to affect Billy's good sense. But maybe his departure has undermined Billy's confidence in us. Marsuvees was rather outspoken about free will and grace. For all we know, he told Billy to go down there."

The monk's unscheduled departure caused a stir among the staff. Never had a teacher left without fulfilling his four-year commitment. Where he'd gone was of considerable concern, but the project had little contact with the outside world, and information was scarce.

The closest town was a small pit stop called Paradise, which in theory could provide a link to society beyond the electronic communications that the director reserved for himself. But even when the teachers left the monastery for brief reprieves, contact with this town was strictly prohibited. It was simply too close to risk any interaction.

David didn't seem interested in pursing this tangent on Marsuvees Black.

"What if the rebellion spreads?" Andrew asked. "Others have been questioning as well. What if Billy challenges the rules in an open debate?"

No response. The debate was by design the proverbial apple that David had set before them all. If any student was able to challenge the principles that governed the monastery and win the majority support of the other students, all existing rules would be subject to that student's interpretation until another clear majority overturned him or her.

David had ultimately placed the whole project in the hands of children. The rules guided them, but they had authority to determine the rules. If this incident spiraled out of control, the whole monastery could be run by Billy. It would be a disaster.

Then again, Billy *was* the project. He and the other thirty-six students.

"We do have risk," David finally said. "But the others aren't questioning like Billy has been."

"Risk? You don't throw a child in the pit of death and refer to it as risk."

"The pit of death, as you call it, resides *in* them! They were born with it." David stretched his arm out and pointed at the monastery wall. "Do you think Billy wasn't born evil? This study isn't about protecting them from evil, but teaching them as children to overcome it in the way Christ did."

He lowered his arm, face pink from his outburst. "'Yea, though I walk through the valley of the shadow of death, I will fear no evil.' Should we avoid the valley of death? No! We walk through it and conquer it and then turn back and face it without fear. For the joy set before him, Christ endured the cross. That's what we are doing, Andrew. I've given my life to that, not to false piety!"

"You're suggesting that to be genuine conquerors they *must* face the horrors of evil?"

"I'm suggesting that the horrors of sin will only be flushed out of hiding when the power of faith confronts them."

"Should we sin so that grace may abound?" Andrew demanded. "The children already face evil in their own hearts, as you say. I don't see the value in subjecting them to the pit of hell itself. Isn't it better to deal with this in the classroom?"

For a long moment David stared at him. Then he walked to the bookshelf, withdrew a large ancient Bible, and dropped it on a reading table beside the bookcase. He tapped the cover pointedly.

"Tell me why the Gospel writers gave us so much detail about the passion of Christ? Never mind, I'll tell you: so that we wouldn't forget his suffering. How dare a child of God look away from the pain of evil—doing so undermines the grace that conquers that evil. Of course we don't sin for the sake of grace, but neither do we sweep evil under a rug and pretend it doesn't exist. The consequence of evil must be faced by the students if we have any hope of success here."

Andrew knew that the director was right, but he couldn't help throwing out one last sentimental argument. "But they are only children. What if they don't conquer? What if they are conquered?"

"These students have been capable of abstract thought since age ten, sooner in many cases. They know how to question good and evil. *Billy* has chosen the time, not we. And if they are conquered, so be it. It is out of our hands. Now is the time for more prayer, not interference. Our future is in God's hands."

"I agree, but God has given us responsibility for the students. Our hands matter too."

"And our hands are tied!" David said. "I suggest we double the morning prayer times and leave Billy's heart to God."

The finality in his tone silenced Andrew. David strode to his desk, picked up an eight-by-ten photograph of his son, Samuel, who was among those students, and looked at the smiling face.

The room stilled to the sound of their breathing. The connection between David and Samuel had always been a source of profound respect for Andrew. At times like this, he felt oddly compelled to remove his gaze and leave the father to his thoughts, but today he watched. Love, respect, remorse.

No, not remorse. There was no reason for remorse, not in the case of his son.

"Where is Samuel?" David asked, eyes still on the picture.

"I don't know, sir."

David laid the frame down and set a brisk pace toward the door. "If you see him, tell him I'm looking for him."

"Yes, sir."

David left the room.

CHAPTER FOUR

PARADISE

Wednesday afternoon

JOHNNY PEERED out the front window, down the street, where half a dozen people gathered around Cecil on the bench.

The kitchen phone clattered into the cradle behind him. "Gotta go," his mother said. "They want me to take him to Junction."

Johnny dropped the curtain.

Sally swept up some papers from the counter and grabbed a light windbreaker. "They say a bad storm is hitting Montrose, headed north. Don't worry, I'll be back by dark."

"You have to listen to me, Mom."

"Stop it, Johnny. This is crazy. You live in those comics and games, and God help me, you can't come in here and tell me you saw someone kill Cecil by poking his eyes out."

"I didn't imagine the stranger. He was real. If I didn't imagine the man, what makes you think I imagined what he did?"

Sally closed her eyes and took a breath. Eyes open. "Cecil had his own eyes, Johnny—I saw them myself. Blue eyes, not black eyes. How could the stranger poke his eyes out if Cecil still has them?"

Good point.

"If I'm right, Cecil had a heart attack." She used a gentle tone now. "I'm sorry, I shouldn't have snapped, but you have to see how crazy this sounds, right?" She plucked the ambulance keys from the hutch. "The mind can do strange things when it's under a lot of stress. I think seeing someone die of a heart attack qualifies, don't you?"

Johnny chewed on his fingernail.

"Right?"

"I guess. Can't someone else take him?"

"No. This is what I'm paid for." She smoothed his hair, then pulled his head against her shoulder. "Come on, Johnny, everything's fine. I know you were close to Cecil. It has to hurt. I'm sorry. We'll all miss him."

He didn't know what to do, so he just stood still.

"You'll be okay," she said, pulling back.

"Sure."

But he wasn't sure. Not at all. The image of the man in black jabbing Cecil in the eyes refused to budge from his mind.

"I'll call you from Junction." Sally ruffled his hair and stepped toward the door. "There's food in the refrigerator. We're out of milk, maybe you could get some from the store for me."

"Okay."

"What did I say?"

"Get milk."

She smiled. "Maybe you should do something to occupy your mind— clean your room."

"Can I come with you?"

She shook her head. "State regs. I'll be back tonight, I promise."

He nodded.

"And you might want to keep the bit about the eyes to yourself."

Sally let the screen door slam and ran across the lawn toward the crowd.

Five minutes later she pulled the red Bronco-turned-ambulance onto Main Street and headed for Junction.

Johnny sighed and retreated to his room to let his nerves settle.

But they didn't settle so quick. Not for an hour. He had to get out.

"I DON'T care what you think, Katie," Paula Smither said, staring down the California blonde with her best angry eyes. "He's a man of God, not some sex object."

"Who said anything about sex? I said he was handsome. There a sin against that?"

They lounged in Katie's Nails and Tan, and honestly Paula didn't know why she subjected herself to Katie's nonstop crap. *Forgive the thought, Reverend.*

She sat in one of the dryer chairs, which was a bit small for her, but Chrissy and Mary had already taken the yellow vinyl guest seats. Katie was pouring a cup of coffee by the sales counter. The town's only official salon was hardly large enough to turn around in, and more gossip than styling went on in it. Most men went to Clipper Dan, the town's local barber. The women mostly went to Martha or Beatrice, who both cut hair out of their homes. Paula wondered how she'd ended up with this crowd.

Katie put the coffeepot down and turned. "Were you born this way?"

"Meaning what?" But Paula knew what Katie meant.

"You live to make everyone else's life miserable? So what if I think the preacher's good-looking?"

"Good-looking? I think the word you used was *hot.*"

"Okay, *hot* then. You didn't think he's hot?"

"Of course not. He's a *preacher,* for heaven's sake!"

"He's a man. Preacher or circus clown, he's a man." Katie faced Chrissy and Mary. "He was hot, trust me."

Chrissy grinned. "Just what we need around here. A hot preacher."

"Fire and brimstone," Mary said. "You ever date a preacher?"

"Not yet," Katie said with a wink.

Katie was digging for a comeback. Paula refused. This was their regular nonsense, and Katie's latest cutting remark stuck in Paula's mind. Born to make everyone else's life miserable?

Not everyone, Katie, just you. Only those who need it.

At least that's what Paula tried to tell herself. But was that how the others saw her? The goody-goody who walked around making everyone else's life miserable? The ugly, fat prude who compensated for her own failures by making sure others were fully aware of theirs?

Was there truth to that?

"Think about it," Katie was saying. "Cecil kicked the bucket this afternoon, and people are more interested in Chris's wart. What does that tell you? You watch, that church will be packed tonight. And they won't be there for Cecil's funeral."

"Hello, ladies."

Paula hadn't heard the door open. There in the frame stood Marsuvees Black, long black trench coat sucked back by the wind.

They stared as one.

He tipped his Stetson hat. "Lovely afternoon." He grinned. "God is merciful and kind and full of hope and grace. Putting four such lovely women on this earth is all the evidence I need."

Katie smiled. "Good afternoon, Preacher." She glided to him and held out her hand. "My name's Katie."

He took the hand, lifted it to his lips, and kissed it gently. "Katie. Such a ravishing name."

"Thank you."

"I assume I'll see you in the church tonight."

"Of course."

Black's eyes moved to Chrissy and Mary. He winked. It wasn't the kind of wink that was necessarily sensual—perhaps just a father-to-son kind of wink. Then again, Paula couldn't be sure.

His eyes settled on her. It was the first time his deep blue eyes had stared into her own, and she found the attention unnerving. Katie's remarks may have been inappropriate, but her friend was right. Black was handsome.

Beautiful. Intoxicating.

She felt completely flustered by his stare and desperately wanted to break off, but he seemed to have a hold on her. The realization only made it worse.

Black stepped past Katie and strode across the room, eyes fixed on Paula. He stopped in front of her and held out his hand.

She started to lift her hand to him before she realized what she was doing, and by then it was too late to stop without looking like a fool. His fingers gently took hers. He bent and kissed them lightly, letting his warm lips rest on her knuckles for a beat more than she thought necessary. When he straightened, she could feel his hot breath on the back of her hand. He hesitated, looking to her fingers, and for a brief moment she thought he was thinking about licking them.

Paula blinked away the thought, horrified that it had passed through her mind.

Black pulled her in with his blue gaze again. "And what is your name, my dear?"

"Paula," she said in a light voice.

"Paula. Paula, Paula." He seemed to be tasting her name. "Such a . . . beautiful name."

Black withdrew his other hand from his pocket, fingers closed in a fist. "Have you ever been anointed with oil, Paula?"

He opened his hand. A gel-like substance filled his palm—oil, she presumed. It smelled odd. Stale and musty. What he thought he was going to do with this smudge he called oil, she wasn't sure, but she wasn't about to be anointed or anything—

Black lifted his hand and applied it to her head, as if smoothing her hair back. "I anoint you with oil. As a sign of my purity to all who see you, a light shall shine from you."

Black removed his hand from her head and said so that none of the others could hear, "You are lovely, dear Paula. Your purity is a light on a hill for all to admire."

For a long moment he held her eyes. Then he walked toward the door. He turned and smiled at all of them.

"Thank you for such a warm welcome. I'm sure we'll be seeing each other tonight, but now I have to gather the flock. Make the rounds, so to speak. Ladies." He tipped his hat again and was gone.

"Paula?" Katie was staring at her head.

She lifted her hand to feel the spot on her head where Black had rubbed his hand.

"Was that bleach?" Mary asked.

Paula's hair was moist. She pulled her fingers away, smelled them. Same musty smell. "What?" she asked absently.

"Your hair's white!" Katie said. "He have bleach in his hand?" She crossed the salon in two steps. "Bleach couldn't do that, not that quick."

Paula faced the mirror behind her. A streak of white hair ran from her forehead back toward her crown, where Marsuvees Black had wiped his anointing.

Then Katie had her hands on Paula's head and was examining her hair up close. "That's no color, Paula. And if it's bleach, it's no bleach I've seen. Anything that strong would've burned your hair."

Paula pushed her away. Her head was tingling.

For a while they all stared at her in silence. She felt oddly satisfied by the boldness of this one white streak where she parted her dark brown hair, slightly to the right. What was it he had said? A light of purity for everyone to see.

It occurred to her that she hated the man. He'd forced this anointing of his on her without consent. And she was quite sure that the streak wouldn't wash out.

Black was trouble, more than any of them could guess.

Then why wasn't she fuming with rage? Why was she just looking at her hair in the mirror, thinking that it looked quite good? And she was the purest of this bunch, that was no secret.

"He's the devil," Paula said.

"Well, he sure has a strange way of showing it," Katie said.

Paula turned and walked toward the door. "He's the devil."

CHAPTER FIVE

PARADISE

Wednesday night

THE PARADISE Episcopal Church was packed to the gills by six forty-five Wednesday evening. Stanley Yordon scanned the restless crowd from the door that led to the baptismal. People milled in the aisles, leaned over pews swatting at each other playfully, snapped at children. They had come out of the woodwork, dressed in jeans and muddy boots—some wearing cowboy hats, others packing holsters. Goodness, who did they think this man was? Wyatt Earp?

Some of the community's more influential residents were dressed for church, in coats and ties and dresses and the whole bit. Well, good for them. Showing the house of God a little respect never hurt anyone.

He stared out at his congregation, which had been turned inside out by this preacher who claimed to be sent by God. Marsuvees Black. Claimed God pulled his car off the road and told him to bring grace and hope to Paradise. The problem was, God didn't speak to people like that anymore. Maybe he used to, to Abraham or Moses or the apostle Paul, but not now, and certainly not here in Paradise, Colorado.

In Paradise, God spoke through Sunday services and potluck and bingo. God spoke through community, even communities like this one, which looked like it might split at the seams.

He held out a hand to Blitzer's boy, Matthew. "Whoa, slow down there, son!" The kid ignored him and ran past, then down the far aisle, yelping like a native.

Coming apart at the seams. Thank God he was leaving for a quarterly board meeting in the morning. He could use a break from this bunch.

He stepped toward the platform. This was his church. He didn't care if the pope himself was coming. No one would trash his house. He leapt to the podium and flashed that preacher's smile he'd learned back in seminary. He leaned into the mic.

"Okay." Feedback squealed through the auditorium. He flinched and backed off. Of the two hundred men, women, and children stuffed into the church, fewer than half turned their attention to the podium, feedback and all.

"Is this better? Okay, let's settle down, folks." The clock on the back wall read six fifty-nine. Black planned to arrive at seven. "Seven o'clock sharp, Stan," the preacher had said. "I'll be here and you can bet your pension on that." For starters, no one called him Stan—his name was Stanley. He didn't care if Black didn't know; he hadn't liked the flash in Black's eyes when he said *Stan*, standing there on the church steps like he owned the place.

"Let's have some quiet here." His voice rang across the sanctuary.

Most of the adults complied, hushing at the sound of his deep voice. Nancy once told him his voice was commanding. Like a general's voice. He lifted a hand to the crowd.

"Let's take our seats, friends." A flurry of movement across the room signaled their obedience. Within ten seconds most of the flock faced him attentively, waiting for his next words.

Most, but not all. Small, scattered groups yammered on as if his request meant nothing at all to them. These were the unchurched. Uneducated, unchurched heathens. *You have to either beat them over the head with a tire iron to get their attention, or ignore them entirely.*

How could a man just waltz into town and have these sheep eating out of his hands so easily? Black had supposedly pulled off this miracle of his in Steve's bar, but that wouldn't account for such a crowd, would it? On any other day the seasoned farmers sitting in the pews would scoff at such a tale. But not today. Today they had flocked here to see more. It made no sense.

He glanced down at Chris Ingles. The man had run around town like a plucked goose, showing off that stupid ear of his. Yordon didn't know how it was that Chris had grown and lost a wart, but there had to be some trick to it. The man sat there with an open mouth, like an idiot. *If Chris came to my door looking like that, I might want to check things out too. The man's flipped his lid.*

Stanley Yordon smiled on, showing none of the anger that rose in him. "Okay, people . . ."

The baptismal door on his right swung open, and before he could say another word, the scene before him changed.

For starters, every eye jerked to his right and stared wide, as if an apparition of the Virgin Mary had just lit the wall. And with the shifting of eyes came a sudden and complete silence.

Black had arrived.

Yordon turned his head to the right, aware that his mouth still lay open, readied to deliver its blow to the heathens.

Marsuvees Black stood in the doorway dressed in black. Yordon's tongue dried up. *Goodness gracious, he's the devil.* He shut his mouth and swallowed.

Black's deep blue eyes slowly scanned the crowd. His feet were spread wide, his hands hung loosely like a man ready to draw. When the preacher's eyes reached Yordon, they stopped and stared for a long moment. And then his mouth lifted into a smile—*a preacher smile*, Yordon thought. The man stepped toward the platform.

Yordon cleared his throat, scrambled for words. "Ah . . . thank you," he said.

Feedback screamed through the sanctuary again. He winced. *Ah . . . thank you? Thank you for what? Compose yourself, man.*

"Sorry." He grinned stupidly. "Let's all give Mr. Minister Black a round of applause."

Mr. Minister?

He stepped away from the pulpit and began to clap as Black took the stage, beaming that plastic devil smile of his.

Marsuvees Black stepped up to the pulpit and dismissed him with a nod. Yordon felt one of the guest chairs at the back of his knees. He sat heavily.

The congregation stared. Then someone started with the clapping that spread through the building.

Black absorbed it, spreading his arms like a rock star at the end of a show. A cool wind from the air conditioner lifted thin wisps of black hair off his shoulders.

"Thank you," Black finally said. His bass voice rumbled over the crowd. "Thank you very much." He raised a hand and the sanctuary fell silent.

"Funny thing happened this afternoon," Black said. "I was driving my '83 Buick along the highway, thinking how good it was to be alive on God's beautiful green earth, wondering where I should go, when my engine locked up, right out there by the sign that says, *Paradise 2 Miles*. And then I heard God's voice speak clear and loud. *Go 2 Paradise*, he said." Black drew a two in the air. "*Bring grace and hope to the lost town of Paradise*, he said."

Eighty-three Buick, huh? That's not what Chris Ingles said.

Steve Smither sat on the front row, leaning forward in his seat. His wife, Paula, sat stiff like a board. There was an unattractive white streak in her hair—undoubtedly one of Katie's experiments.

Steve had served as a deacon since Yordon suggested he take the post two years ago, Paula had run the Sunday-school program for—what?—three years now. She had a heart for the children,

Claude Bowers sat down the bench from Steve. Now there was a leader Big, conservative, and quiet, but when he did speak, people listened. Except for Katie, of course. Funny how he ended up with Katie, who didn't have a conservative bone in her body. Big Claude and beautiful Katie.

Yordon thought all of this on the fly, in the same way all preachers think a thousand thoughts on the fly while looking out at their congregations.

Black lowered his voice a notch and continued. "So here I am, my friends. Here I am. And I assure you not one of you will remain unchanged when we're through here. Not a one."

The preacher let the words ring through the auditorium. At first no one responded. They just stared at him, some skeptical, some eager.

"How do we know what kind of power you really have?" Steve asked. His voice rumbled through the silence.

Black did not respond.

"Or if it's really real?" someone else shouted.

This time a chorus of *that's rights* and *amens* filled the room. Good. As Yordon knew they would, most of his people weren't buying Black's nonsense.

"Shut . . . your worthless traps," Black bit off. Not loudly, but distinctly and with a slight quaver.

The words took the breath out of the room.

"And consider it a warning, because the man of God can only take so much doubt."

Silence.

Black softened. "Chris Ingles, rise."

Chris jumped to his feet.

"Show them your ear."

Ingles jerked his right ear forward and those closest to him strained for a view. "You had a wart behind your ear?" Black asked.

"Yes."

"And now it's gone, isn't that right?"

"That's right."

Black put both hands on the podium and studied the congregation. Chris sat.

"Did I tell you to sit, Chris?" Black's voice was low, deep. Threatening.

Chris stood.

"Stick out your tongue, Chris."

Chris blinked, as if he hadn't heard right.

"Go on, son. Stick out your tongue for everyone to see."

Chris hesitated then thrust his tongue out.

Yordon leaned to his right for a better view.

Gasps filled the pews nearest Chris, who jerked his hand to his mouth and felt his tongue.

"Ahhhh!" Chris jerked his hand away. "Ahhhh!"

"He's got a huge wart on his tongue!" someone blurted. Cries of alarm filled the auditorium.

"Whadth happen?" Chris slurred, and Yordon wondered how large this supposed wart was.

"Shut up! Sit down."

Chris was feeling his tongue again. "What—"

"I said shut up! Sit down!"

Chris dropped to his seat.

"What I give, I can take, see?" Black let that settle in.

Yordon was sure the preacher hadn't actually healed Chris. Now he had his proof. He should be standing about now and confronting Black head-on. But he didn't.

"Do I have your attention?" Black asked.

No one answered.

"I said, *do I have your attention?*"

Dozens of *yeses* came at once.

"Good. Now, when I say that I've come to bring grace and hope, I may mean something altogether different than what you think. My kind of grace and hope is full of life, my friends. A real trip. Not that you have to agree with my definitions of these two most holy words. I'm not here to ram anything down your throats, no sir. But we're on dangerous ground here, and I strongly suggest you pay attention."

Black walked to his right where a pewter goblet that he'd requested sat on the altar. No bread or crackers, just a goblet filled with wine. For communion, he'd said.

Yordon had filled the goblet with grape juice.

"Before we learn how grace and hope will change your lives," Black said, lifting the goblet, "we're going to remember." He held the cup out. "Remember how things were before grace and hope came to town."

He sniffed the contents, paused for a moment, then seemed to accept Yordon's insubordination and walked back to the pulpit.

The man held the cup just below the pulpit. He was wiping his fingers on the edge of the goblet as if . . .

Yordon leaned forward with surprise. If he wasn't mistaken, Black was wiping a gel-like substance into the goblet! What on earth did the man think he was doing? Surely he didn't expect anyone to actually drink . . .

Unless he was poisoning them.

Black plunged his hand into the cup, causing some of the grape juice to spill at his feet. He swirled his fingers around a few times, then extracted his hand and flicked juice from his fingers back into the goblet.

Yordon came to his feet, terrified and outraged at once. "That's enough! No more theatrics." He stepped forward but didn't have the resolve to toss Black aside by the collar, as he fleetingly envisioned.

"I'm going to have to ask you to step down," Yordon said. "I don't know who you think –"

Black brought his hands together with a thunderclap. He lifted his right hand for all to see. There in his palm sat a large red apple.

No goblet.

Yordon groped for his seat.

"Do you remember?" Black asked the congregation, ignoring Yordon. "First there was an apple. The fruit of pleasure. All was good. Do you remember?"

Stony silence.

"Do you remember, Stan?" Black snapped without turning.

"Yes." The question and his own response caught Yordon off guard.

Black tossed the red apple into the air. "And then there came . . ."

When he caught the apple, it wasn't an apple.

It was a brown snake.

"The snake," Black said.

A gasp filled the room. Some shouts of alarm. Black held the three-foot snake by its midsection as the serpent lifted its head, testing the air with a long flickering tongue.

"But we know what happened to the snake, don't we?"

Slick as a magician, Black slid his hand to the reptile's tail and cracked the snake like a whip.

Crack!

The blurred snake became a rigid object roughly two feet in height. A dark wooden cross.

"The snake was defeated."

The congregation was evidently too stunned to react this time. You could stuff an apple up the sleeve. You could hide a snake past the cuff. But not this hefty cross.

"And that defeat gave us the fruit of the vine once again." Black slammed the cross against the pulpit, where it vanished in a horrendous crash. Wobbling on the surface was an apple, which he held up for all to see.

The same red apple he'd started with.

"Do you remember?" Black called out.

With his free hand, he lifted the goblet of grape juice. Yordon hadn't seen it reappear. He held the apple above the goblet and squeezed it. The fruit compressed like a sponge, and juice flowed into the cup.

Black opened a dry hand for all to see—apple gone. He lifted the cup high. "Do this in remembrance."

The congregation responded in an indistinct, astounded chorus. "Drink from this cup, the hope of my gospel." Black paced, goblet extended to all. "Drink, Chris. Drink, my friend. Show them."

Chris hesitated only a brief second before stumbling into the aisle and hurrying to the front. He took the goblet from Black and waited for some kind of encouragement.

"Just a sip. Don't be greedy. There are a lot of thirsty souls in this place."

Chris tilted the cup, sipped, then handed it back to the preacher.

"Go on, show them your tongue."

Yordon didn't have to look to know what had happened. But the cries of approval confirmed his guess. The wart was gone from Chris's tongue.

Chris was feeling his tongue with both sets of fingers.

Black addressed the congregation. "I want all of you to take a sip of this wine in remembrance. If you think for a second that you'll catch something, I can assure you that the only thing you'll catch is God's wrath if you don't drink."

He held the cup out to Ben Holden on the first pew. The man hurried forward, took the goblet.

"Pass it and drink!" Black said, spreading his arms wide. "Drink the living water and embrace hope."

Ben sipped, then passed the cup. It wound its way down the line.

"That's right. Drink, drink, drink, drink, drink."

Stanley Yordon stared at his congregation, struck by his own powerlessness to stop this incredible charade. His earlier wonder at Black's miracles had been replaced by a firm belief that the man was nothing but a bag of tricks after all.

Who would use such obvious gimmicks to impress a crowd? Please. An apple, a serpent, a cross, an apple. A Vegas entertainer could pull that off. He wondered how much Black paid Chris to play along with the wart business.

But watching Claude and Steve and Paula and the rest drink from the goblet, Yordon lacked conviction that he had the power to do anything other than make a fool of himself.

Black was saying something, but Yordon wasn't hearing. A few members let the cup pass by. But far more drank. Out of fear? Out of hope? Out of fear. Mostly fear. It had to be fear.

". . . have the choice to follow my way or his way."

Yordon froze at the last two words: *his way*. Unless Yordon was mistaken, Black had motioned *his* way when he spoke those two words. *His way*. But then he could have been mistaken, because he hadn't actually seen it. Still, a cold sweat replaced the heat under his collar.

"And believe me," Black continued, "many of you will be tempted to go the old way. I don't blame you really. You've been stuck in the same old ruts for so long, you wouldn't know grace or hope if they both smacked you upside the head at the same time."

Someone chuckled in the back.

"Well, let me tell you something, when I say *grace*, I am talking *Grace*, with a capital *G*, not some ambiguous theological term that preachers throw at you to impress the snot out of you. I mean GRACE. Capital G-R-A-C-E. Liberty. Freedom."

Black stepped out from the podium and opened his huge hands wide.

"And when I say *hope*, I mean *HOPE*, like, 'Man, I really hope I can have that. I *want* that.'" He closed both hands into fists. "I *have to* have that." Black's voice swelled to a crescendo. "Hope like, 'Get out of the way, that's *mine!*' hope!"

Black breathed heavily. Yordon stared, at a loss, still not sure what the preacher was driving at, still wondering if the man really had meant *him* when he said *his way*.

"Now, if any of you are looking for that kind of grace and hope, I'm bringing them to you. Grace and hope are here." He stood perfectly still, glaring at two hundred frozen faces. "You follow me and I'll rock your world, baby. I'll show you how to trip. Things will never be the same again."

Yordon scanned the auditorium. The silence seemed to drift on a bit long. He looked over at Black and blinked.

The man was trembling.

Black faced the crowd, slowly scanning it from left to right, trembling from head to toe.

"I want you to think about that. I need the leaders to understand the message for Paradise. I need you to follow me, baby." His voice intensified. "I need you to let go and let God. I need you to drop the sickening let's-play-church act and start slamming!"

Yordon's skin rippled with gooseflesh. *Slamming?*

An image of some rock star peering from a jewel case popped into Yordon's mind. Gene Simmons, right here in his church.

"Paula," Black said slowly, staring at her. "Katie, Nancy, Mary. I really do like those names. Suck up a little grace-juice, ladies."

His eyes shifted to Steve. "You hear me, Steve? And you, Claude. All of you. Trip with me, baby. Breathe deep and let it go where it wants to. If you let me, I'll show you. I'll show you all."

Yordon caught sight of the man's eyes from the side. Bloodshot.

When Black spoke again, his voice was low and biting. "You have a choice to make. When I come to you, you better not run scared. You just choose the real thing and maybe things will work out for you."

Yordon forced his eyes around the room. To a head they were glued on Black.

"You're going to have to decide," Black said, voice swelling. His trembling had subsided. "Are you going to follow me, the man God sent to Paradise with a new message of grace and hope? Hmm? Or are you going to follow *his* way?"

Yordon jerked his head to the pulpit. This time Black left no room for interpretation. This time, standing alone up on the platform, he stabbed his finger at Stanley.

For the first time since Marsuvees Black's entrance, the flock turned its attention back to Yordon. A sea of eyes gazed at him—some quizzical, some glaring, most big and round.

Johnny Drake stood in the foyer behind them all, hiding behind the door frame, staring directly at him. Yordon held his breath and looked back at the pulpit. Black had dropped his finger, thank God. He peeked out at the crowd again. They had returned their stares to the preacher.

"So you listen and you watch and you prepare your heart for a little change. And if you're lucky, you'll live to tell of the day that Paradise found grace and hope."

Black turned and strode from the podium without the slightest acknowledgment of Yordon. He walked off the stage and through the baptismal door. Twenty minutes after it had started, the service was over.

Yordon began to wonder how foolish he looked up there by himself. But they weren't looking at him. Not paying him the least bit of attention. And why should they?

There was a new preacher in town.

"YOU DRINK it?" Johnny asked.

"No," Roland Smither said. "You?"

"Are you kidding?"

They sat in Johnny's room, Johnny still stunned by what they'd both seen with their own eyes at the church half an hour earlier; Roland toggling the controller for Johnny's PlayStation, throwing tricks in Snowboard Madness.

Johnny couldn't quite bring himself to tell his friend about Black walking into town and killing Cecil. He hated the fact that his mother was still gone.

Roland tossed the control on the bed. "He's a fake. I've seen better stuff on magic shows."

"This isn't a show."

"How do you know? David Copperfield could make an elephant disappear on stage, so why couldn't this guy make a snake appear?"

"Could Copperfield grow a wart on someone's tongue?"

"Course he could, if Chris was in on it. Come on, don't be such a sucker."

What could he say? Maybe the eye thing with Cecil was a trick too. But Cecil was dead.

"You ever hear a preacher talk that way? 'Suck up some grace-juice'? This isn't just some magician on the road. You see the way he was shaking?"

The smile faded from Roland's face. "That's part of his gig, man. Lighten up, you're talking like an idiot."

Johnny stood and walked to his window. The leaves whipped by nearly horizontal. Such a strong wind for the middle of summer. "He put something in the drink."

"Course he did," Roland said. "Part of the show. Pretty cool too, if you ask me. He isn't afraid of Yordon, that's for sure."

Johnny faced his friend. "What if I'm right? What if he's dangerous?"

"My dad's got a gun. And before he used it, he'd call the cops." Roland sighed. "You really have to lighten up, Johnny."

The phone on his desk chirped. Johnny crossed the room and snatched it up. "Hello?"

"Hi, Johnny."

Relief swept over him. "Hey, Mom."

"You okay?"

"Well. Actually I don't know . . ."

"What do you mean? Something happen?"

"The preacher freaked everyone out at the service."

"Like what?"

"Like . . ." Running through the string of magic tricks felt stupid. Johnny condensed. "Like turning an apple into a snake. But it was the way he was talking. He threatened the whole town if they didn't listen to him."

"It'll be fine, Johnny. Listen, it's raining cats and dogs here. I wanted to get to the mall but ran out of time. I was hoping I could stay over and pick up some things in the morning."

Dread passed through his gut.

"Johnny? He died from a heart attack, Johnny. Okay? The doctor here all but confirmed it. There's no sign of any trauma to Cecil's eyes—I made sure of that, just for you. He's an illusionist or something, end of story." She paused. "Maybe Roland could spend the night with you."

"Roland's here." He looked at his friend, who'd returned to the video game, and felt some comfort.

"Ask him."

Johnny covered the phone and asked. Roland nodded. "Sure."

"He says he can do that."

"Okay. I'll be home about noon tomorrow. Lock the doors and make sure you get to bed by midnight. You'll be okay, Johnny. There's plenty to eat in the fridge. I'm at the Super Eight in Junction if you need me, okay? I love you, Johnny."

"I love you too."

He hung up the phone and suppressed an urge to cry. *Easy, Johnny. They're right. You're letting your imagination go wild.*

Roland scrambled from the bed. "I'll call my mom."

Five minutes later it was all settled. Roland was spending the night. They raided the refrigerator and hauled Cheez-Its, four Snickers bars, Planters peanuts, and two tall glasses of milk back to Johnny's room.

"Score," Roland said. "We still hanging out with Fred and Peter at the Starlight tomorrow?"

In the afternoon's excitement Johnny had forgotten about their customary summer gathering at the old theater. "I guess."

Roland jerked his head up. "What was that?"

"What was what?"

Roland stood slowly. "Was that an earthquake?"

They waited. Nothing.

Johnny was about to ask his friend to elaborate when the floor under his feet shifted, ever so slightly.

"Whoa!" He jumped onto the bed. "You feel that?"

Roland looked at him. His lips formed a twisted grin. "No. I didn't feel it the first time either. You see what I mean? Now you're feeling things."

Johnny blinked. He could have sworn . . .

Roland laughed and grabbed the peanuts. "You gotta lighten up, man."

It took Johnny an hour to fall asleep after they turned the lights off at midnight. When he finally drifted off, he dreamed of Marsuvees Black.

A nightmare.

THE TOWN of Paradise slipped into a deep slumber.

Before that, and after the service, the Malones went to Steve and Paula's house for coffee. They were divided on Black's theatrics. None of them could say they were real or an illusion, at least not definitively. Neither could they agree on the intent of his harsh talk. But in the end even Paula agreed that the man was captivating. Maybe too captivating, she said. Steve said she was overstating things, which earned him a glare.

They'd all sipped from the communion goblet, which earned a chuckle from Steve in retrospect. What people would do in the heat of religious fervor. No doubt about it, Black could handle a crowd. As far as Steve was concerned, Paradise could use some excitement.

Steve fell asleep easily enough, at about eleven, and drifted through a dreamless night.

The clock read eight when Steve jolted upright in his bed, wide awake, soaked with sweat, breathing heavily. A loud ringing filled his ears, a buzzing with a high-pitched whine that made him shake his head. He blinked in the morning light and gazed about the room, lost for a moment.

Paula was gone.

He swung his legs from the bed, thinking he should throw on a robe.

"Paula?"

No response.

Steve shuffled from the bedroom into the living room.

"Paula!"

Nothing.

She might be in the small garden she'd planted behind the house. Cost twice as much to grow tomatoes as purchase them at this altitude, but she found the hobby relaxing.

He headed for the back door. Morning light streamed through the windows. A beautiful day. He felt as contented as he could remember feeling. It was going to be a good day in Paradise.

Steve grabbed the doorknob and twisted. The air was perfectly calm and the grass was perfectly green and the sky was perfectly blue.

And Paradise was perfectly quiet.

"Paula?"

The garden was deserted. She was probably over talking someone's ear off about Black. Steve paused, thinking through yesterday's events. Had all that really happened? Sure it had. Chris had grown a wart, then lost it, then grown it, then lost it. The apple had become a snake, the snake had become a cross, the cross had become an apple. And more than half the town had tasted the sweet juice from that apple.

Including him.

A nervous excitement fluttered through his gut. Black sure knew how to get the heart moving.

A giggle turned his attention toward the tool shed. He studied the shed. Was that Paula's voice?

A dark hat broke the shed's vertical corner line. A man. But that hadn't been a man's voice giggling.

Steve was about to call out when the laughter came again, shrill this time.

The man stepped backward into Steve's line of sight.

Black.

Steve couldn't see who the preacher was holding behind the shed wall, but Black was turning to face him . . . had turned . . . was staring right at Steve, wearing a grin that Steve couldn't quite interpret.

"Hello, Steve."

Black's low and gravelly voice, hardly more than a whisper, carried clearly in the morning stillness.

"Good morning, Rev—"

"Do you know what I have back here, Steve?" His right arm was still hidden from view.

Paula? Steve's mind began to spin. No, that was ridiculous.

Marsuvees Black withdrew his arm. He gripped a wooden stake, about two feet in length and roughly three inches in diameter.

"Do you know what this is, Steve?" Still grinning. Another giggle behind the shed. Steve barely heard it, having fixed his mind on that stake in Black's hand.

He swallowed. "No."

"This is pleasure on a stick, Steve. This is what you skewer meat with before you eat it. This is what you stick apples on before dipping them in caramel. Can you fathom that, my friend?"

Black touched his lips to the stake's sharp point, kissed it, and sighed.

"This is grace and hope in Paradise," Black said.

Saliva had pooled under Steve's tongue. He swallowed it. The stick looked smooth, lovely, well shaped, beautiful.

But it was just a stick. What was Black's point?

The stake's point is his point, you idiot.

"And do you know what *this* is?" Black asked. He'd reached behind the shed and yanked a woman out by her hair.

Paula.

Black looked into Paula's eyes and jerked her head back. "Do you want your grace-juice, baby?"

She laughed shrilly.

"She's been a naughty wife, Steve."

Black leaned over Paula and kissed her on the lips. She returned his kiss. "A very naughty wife."

Rage swelled in Steve's chest. He sucked at the still air but couldn't seem to get enough oxygen into his lungs.

"What do we do to naughty wives?" Black demanded. "We stick them like caramel apples, that's what we do."

The reverend whirled Paula around so that her back faced Steve. It occurred to him that Paula's shrill laugh wasn't a laugh anymore. It was a scream. Or was it?

Steve clenched his hands. "Get away from her!" He took a step forward.

Paula threw her head back, cocked it at an odd angle, like a bent paper clip. She laughed hysterically. No scream at all, just this frenzied expression of delight. Her eyes opened and she drilled him with a mocking stare. He could see her neck, white in the sunlight. Smooth. Her hair fell to her shoulders.

The last thread of reason that moored Steve's mind snapped. He felt himself drift into a sea of incoherent fury.

"What do we do, Steve?" Black asked, still grinning.

Steve hesitated, confused by Black's question.

The preacher repeated himself, yelling this time. "What do we do?"

"Stake them?"

His wife's shrill laughter ceased. For a moment Paradise was still again.

Then she howled with horror. It was a scream now for sure. No laughter for Paula. But fact was, she deserved it. He would do . . .

You don't mean that, Steve.

. . . it himself if he was a little closer. Maybe he still could . . .

What on earth are you thinking?

. . . do it, teach her to . . .

Stop this! Stop this right now!

The preacher winked at Steve and thrust the stick forward.

Steve lunged up, gasping. It was dark. A fan swished slowly overhead.

He was in bed?

Rumpled bed sheets covered his legs. He grasped the covers on his left and felt his wife's sleeping form. She grunted. No harm.

Steve looked at the clock. Midnight. Steve exhaled and dropped back to his pillow. A nightmare.

Something was in his right hand. He lifted his arm.

A bloody stake.

MARSUVEES BLACK stood on the cliff overlooking Paradise, boots planted on the rock like two sledgehammers. Most of Paradise had slipped into dreams.

A hot wind blew into his face, but he didn't blink, did not feel the urge to blink. He stood with his arms cocked on his hips, his trench coat flying back in the breeze so that if Katie were to wake and peer up the mountain she might think a huge bat had landed on the cliff. But Katie wasn't waking up, not tonight, not with all that euphoria in her blood.

If they only knew what lay in store for them. A part of him wanted to go down there, wake them all from their slumber, and tell them the truth, all of it. But he had to bide his time. If he rushed things, they might not understand, and that could get nasty.

He had to help them understand their true makeup. He had to help them feel the horror, just enough to understand the truth of who they really were. Too fast and the plan could backfire. Too slow and they might never reach the maturity required to face the truth.

His legs were tired, so he folded them under himself and sat on the rock ledge. Crossed his arms.

It had been a good day. An even better night. They bought the whole thing without hardly a protest. It was hard for Black not to feel pride in what he'd done, but that wasn't the point. Pride could lead to a mistake. When it was all done and he'd set this town free, then he'd grant himself pride.

Someone coughed behind and to his right. Black knew who it was, but he didn't feel the need to acknowledge the man.

A tall figure dressed in a long hooded robe stepped from the shadows and stood beside him. For a minute the sight of the sleeping town seemed to hold them in a trance. The others in the monastery would undoubtedly crawl out of their skins if they knew these two met here, and why.

Then again, depending on how this all turned out, they might shout their praises.

Black could feel the weight of the man's eyes on him now.

"How does it feel?" the man asked.

"Incredible," Black said.

"Tell me what you did. I want to know everything."

"I did what was expected."

"Details."

Black supposed he owed the man at least that much. The telling took fifteen minutes, interrupted occasionally by questions and requests for further elaboration.

When he finished, silence engulfed them. Above, the black clouds boiled, visible even in the night sky like a claw reaching down from the heavens to crush this little victim nestled in the Colorado mountains.

But the clouds didn't tell the whole story. Not even half of it.

"You've done well." A hand settled on Black's shoulder, rested there for a moment, then withdrew.

"It's hard to believe we actually have this much power."

"We aren't the only ones with power," Black said.

"No. But we're ahead now. I think we will succeed."

"Yes, we will."

The wind howled.

"You need to rest."

Black smiled softly in the darkness. "Do I?"

"A little power doesn't make you immortal, now does it?"

"No, I suppose it doesn't."

The man turned and vanished into the black night behind them.

Marsuvees Black stared into the wind, barely breathing. Tomorrow was coming. He needed rest.

CHAPTER SIX

PARADISE

Thursday morning

REVEREND STANLEY Yordon crawled out of bed, surprised to find the little hand cocked past the ten.

Ten? Heavens, it had been years since he slept so late. Even when he drank with the boys, which he rarely did these days, he woke by eight at the latest. And here it was, past ten o'clock Thursday morning, the day after the big service.

The big service. The one in which a stranger had basically told the town to choose between his way or Stanley's way. By the looks of the flock after the meeting, they chose Black's way. They chose a message of so-called grace and hope that sounded more like the gospel according to Hugh Hefner than the gospel according to Luke.

Yordon walked into the bathroom and splashed water on his face. This cowboy preacher had waltzed into town and shown Paradise a party, all right. Forget bingo night, we're having us a real party. What'll you have? Some grace? Some hope? Let's throw in some magic to boot. We can grow and ungrow warts on demand.

They loved the entertainer! He'd have to talk to the bishop about this. Stanley shaved, dressed, ate a slice of dry toast. Hopefully, by the time he returned from Denver on Saturday, this fool would be gone and they could get back to church and the old reliable pig-roast potlucks that never failed to draw a crowd.

Yordon walked outside and immediately noticed the wind. A warm breeze blew down the road, almost hot. Dark clouds boiled overhead—the news had mentioned a coming rain storm, but here there was only wind. Wind and dust.

Main Street was deserted. At least Black wasn't holding a rally.

He walked briskly to the church, skirting a few dust devils as he went. The auditorium was still a mess from the previous night. Visitor cards and hymnals lay strewn about the pews and floor. *Those unchurched . . .* Yordon grunted. Wouldn't know respect if it hit them upside the head.

"Nancy?" He walked into the offices. "Nancy?"

"Here."

"Where?"

"In the kitchen."

He found his secretary with her head stuck in the church refrigerator. Her wide body all but obscured it. "I have to get going," he said, reaching for a coffee mug.

Nancy straightened and looked at him. "Going where?"

"Denver. Bishop Fraiser? Quarterly meeting?"

"Oh."

He poured hot coffee into his cup. "Frankly, it couldn't have come at a better time. With our mayor running off and that preacher coming in, I believe we have us a class-one mess on our hands."

"Come on, Father, the preacher's harmless. It's good for the town to get a little spice now and then."

Some of the coffee missed the cup. "A little spice? That's what you call last night? The man threatened me."

"Please. You can't take that seriously. Do you know what we did with those leftover danishes?"

"What danishes? I'm worried about the church and you're worried about danishes?"

"The danishes from Sunday's potluck. The cherry-apple ones with frosting. There was a whole rack of them right here yesterday."

Yordon sighed. "I'll be back Saturday."

"Oh, here they are!"

Nancy grabbed a tin plate from the top of the refrigerator and dug at the shrink-wrap that covered the old danishes. She pried a gooey pastry out and took a large bite.

"Personally, I think you're overreacting, but you go right on ahead. We'll be here when you get back." She smacked at the danish. "You're back Saturday? Why not tomorrow?"

"I always go for three days."

She shoved the rest of the pastry into her mouth.

Yordon wasn't sure what to think of this. Nancy lost fifty pounds in the last six months, thanks to a no-sugar diet. But here she was, stuffing her face with enough sugar to fuel the church for a week.

He thought about asking her but decided it would do more harm than good.

"I'll call you from Denver."

She nodded and dug out another pastry.

Yordon left the church, walked to a blue Chevy Caprice parked in the church lot, slid behind the driver's wheel, started the engine, and was past the old theater before it occurred to him that he'd forgotten his shaving kit. Never mind, he would pick up the basics at a convenience store.

Honestly, he couldn't get out of town fast enough.

Ten minutes later he approached the highway and slowed the old Caprice to a stop. The road was empty—as quiet as the road leading up to Paradise behind him.

An image popped into his mind. An image of an old Buick—Marsuvees Black's '83 Buick—sitting on the shoulder with its front bumper stuck into a buckled road sign. *Funny thing happened to me this afternoon*, Black had said.

But there was no car.

The sign was there, but no '83 Buick. When a car broke down on this strip of highway, it usually remained on the roadside for at least four or five days before the cops towed it away.

Curious, Yordon climbed out and walked toward the sign. A ringing lodged in his ears, and he whacked the side of his head to no avail. The air was still and cool down here. Amazing how the mountains play with weather. Hot in one valley and cool in the next. Seemed like it should be the other way around though. Hot down here and cool higher up, in Paradise. His boots crunched on the gravel as he rounded the sign.

Go 2 Paradise, Black had said. *Paradise 2 Miles*, drawing that stupid two in the air as if that was how to drive a point home.

Yordon shielded the sun from his eyes and gazed up at the green sign. *Paradise 3 Miles.*

That's what he thought. The sign read three, not two. The ringing in Stanley's ear grew a little louder. He looked down the road again. Three miles instead of two miles, and no car.

The man was a fake. But he already knew that.

He thought about turning the car around and heading back. The town had no mayor, no law enforcement. Only the Episcopal father. Stanley Yordon.

He slid into the Caprice, and with a last look down the deserted highway, he pulled the car into the road, bound for Denver, two hundred some-odd miles east.

JOHNNY AWOKE late Thursday morning, and for a full ten seconds he didn't think about the previous day's events. It was just another summer day after a sleepover.

He sat up. Mom was probably . . .

Mom was gone. Cecil had died. Marsuvees Black had poisoned the town.

He flung the covers off and stumbled into the hall. "Mom?"

But she was still in Junction, shopping—he already knew that. She wouldn't be home until noon at the earliest. And knowing her, it would be closer to late afternoon.

"What's up?" Roland asked, leaning out of the room. "You yelling?"

"Nothing. Just seeing if my mom's back."

Roland turned back into the room, dropped facedown on Johnny's bed. Johnny walked past him and peered out the window. Wind howled. Roland lay as if dead.

"You okay?" Johnny asked.

Roland groaned, pushed himself up on both elbows. "How late did we stay up?"

"Midnight. You want to see what's happening?"

Roland glanced at the clock, rolled off the bed, and grabbed his jeans. "Sheesh, it's ten o'clock! I have to mow. I'll see you at the Starlight later."

"You sure you don't want to see what's up?"

"What do mean, what's up? Nothing's up."

"After what happened last night? Trust me, something's up."

"My mom's going to kill me if I don't mow this morning," Roland said, pulling a worn yellow T-shirt over his head.

"In this wind?"

"Gotta go, trust me. See ya."

Roland left. Except for the wind moaning occasionally through the rafters, the house was quiet.

Too quiet for Johnny's peace of mind.

STEVE SMITHER pulled himself from a groggy sleep late Thursday morning, dressed in blue jeans and a red plaid shirt, and headed out to the kitchen.

Not until he passed the picture window that looked over the back lawn did he remember the dream.

The details fell into his mind. Black, stakes, Paula, *stakes*, shed, *STAKES*, screaming. A gust of wind whipped at the shed—no sign of Black or Paula. He had half a mind to check behind it. For stakes.

Steve swallowed, unnerved by the strong impulse. Then he remembered the stake in his hand. He ran back into the room and scanned the bed, the floor.

No bloody stake. That had been part of the dream too?

He headed back into the living room. Where was Paula?

Maybe he was still in the dream. Or maybe it *hadn't* been a dream.

He took a step toward the back door.

"Steve?"

"Hmm?" Steve stopped and turned toward Paula's voice. His head swam and for a second he thought he might fall, but the dizziness passed, leaving him with a headache.

And a lingering case of grogginess.

Paula leaned against the kitchen door frame, arms crossed. She looked a bit fuzzy to him. A bit loose. Her bathrobe draped over her body, untied, and her hair hung in tangles, straddling that terrible-looking white streak—God only knew why she'd let Katie do that to her.

Looked like a worn-out mutt.

He chided himself for the thought.

"What are you doing?" she asked.

He headed for the front door. "What does it look like I'm doing? The saloon doesn't open by itself."

She let him go without comment.

Steve paused in the wind, noticing it only as a faint distraction from an uncommon drive to check out the shed. Just to be sure. He had a dream, sure, but this feeling wasn't a dream. He had to check out the shed.

Steve rounded the house, approached the shed, and stopped three feet from the corner. His heart was hammering with an almost palpable desire to turn the corner and find the very stakes Black had used in his dream. Maybe even with blood on them. *Why?*

He took a deep breath and stuck his head around the corner.

Nothing.

"For the love of . . ." He clenched his teeth. "I can't believe he'd do this."

Do what, Steve? Who would do what?

What was he thinking? He put his hand on the fence, patted it once, and turned to leave.

Pain shot through his palm. He swore and jerked his hand away from the fence. A splinter the size of his little finger had sliced into the heel of his palm. He stared at it, speechless. Pain throbbed and his hand began to tremble. The thing was in deep, buried at an angle.

Steve dug at it with his fingernails but couldn't get a grip on the wood. He gripped his wrist and held his hand for a better view.

A stake. There was a stake in his palm. For crying—

"Hello, Steve."

Steve spun. Black stood by the shed, smiling warmly. His eyes dropped to Steve's hand, and his smile faded, replaced by a shadow of concern.

"You okay?"

Black moved forward, seemingly intent on examining him. But Steve wasn't sure he wanted the man to examine him.

"Do you mind?" Black asked, searching his eyes. Blue eyes. Comforting eyes. Genuinely concerned. The man looked different today than he had looked yesterday. He looked . . . kind.

Steve turned his hand for Black to inspect.

The man's fingers were warm. "Pretty deep," he said, digging in his pocket. He brought out one of those multipurpose pocketknives with small pliers.

"I think I can get it. Do you mind?"

Steve felt disconnected from the scene, despite the intensity of the pain and the sudden appearance of Black.

"Okay."

Black opened the knife and gently worked at freeing the sliver. The stake. Steve turned his eyes away and let him work.

The moment wasn't awkward, something that surprised him.

"Everything will make sense to you soon, Steve," Black said softly. A burst of pain made Steve flinch. When he looked at his hand, the sliver was gone. Black held it up in the pliers, smiling.

"You see, it hurts coming out, but in the end you wouldn't have it any other way." He let the sliver fall to the grass. "Just like this town. After a bit of pain it will all make sense. My ways are a bit unconventional, but you'll thank me, Steve. The whole town will thank me."

He lifted a hand and tipped his hat.

"Where are you going?" Steve asked.

"I was on my way to speak to the father when I saw you down here. I'm sure he's all messed up about now. It's not every day that someone comes into town and pulls the stunt I did yesterday. I think he deserves an explanation, don't you?"

Black walked away.

Steve wanted an explanation too, but he felt stupid calling out again. *What's that explanation, mister? And why did I dream what I dreamed?*

He was talking before he could stop himself. "What about my dream?" he called out.

Black stopped and turned back. "What dream?"

It was clear by his blank stare the Black really didn't know of any dream.

"Never mind," Steve said.

"Your dreams are your own, Steve." Black tipped his hat again and left.

Steve rubbed his palm with a thumb, relieved that the pain was gone. He stuck his hands into his pockets and headed for the saloon.

His head felt heavy.

STEVE SPENT the first thirty minutes by himself, wandering aimlessly around the bar, setting up shop. Wiping the counters down. Putting out glasses. Setting out peanuts. All without a thought.

His thoughts were elsewhere, on the stakes.

Claude came in about eleven, shirt untucked but buttoned up tight around his neck. He grunted and sat down in his regular spot along the bar. Early for Claude, who often came in for lunch, but never before noon.

"You open today?" Steve asked.

The big Swede didn't seem to hear.

Steve looked out the window and saw that Katie and Mary were angling for the saloon from across the street. Early for them too. It meant that others would see them coming and join them. That's how it always worked. Word spread fast in a small town. The lunch crowd was coming in early today.

"Sure," Claude said.

"Sure what?" Then Steve remembered his question.

"Sure I was open. Closed for lunch. Traffic's dead. Can I have a drink?"

"Lemonade?"

"Actually, I wouldn't mind something stronger if you have it." Claude rubbed his temples. "Head's throbbing."

"Beer?"

"Jack and Coke?"

Odd for a nondrinking man. Steve made the drink and served Claude. His mind drifted again.

The door banged and Katie walked in with Mary. Both ordered drinks. They were as quiet as Claude. Others started wandering in then, each entry punctuated by the slam of his screen door.

In some ways the stupor that clouded Steve's mind felt like the effects of the strong painkiller prescribed to him after some fool tourist's Doberman tried to rip off his hand.

Steve was normally a controlled fellow, ask anyone. But that hadn't stopped him from hauling out his shotgun with his unshredded hand and sending the Doberman to mutt hell with enough buckshot to splatter its head over a ten-foot-square section of the back wall.

Paula walked in. She was dressed for Sunday in a navy blue cotton dress with white piping on the neckline and pockets. Black leather flats. Who was she trying to impress? She sat at the end of the bar, and Steve ignored her.

Two fans swished overhead, and no one bothered turning on the jukebox. Steve stopped whatever he'd been doing, which was already a distant memory, and looked around at the "in" crowd of Paradise, Colorado. Without counting, he'd say about twenty.

The silence grew uncomfortable. Awkward. Downright infuriating.

Steve slammed his fist on the bar. "What's the problem?"

Katie looked up at him, blinking. "What do you think you're doing?"

He wasn't rightly sure, actually. He just didn't like the silence. A person can hide in a cacophony of noise, but everyone stands out in this kind of melancholic silence, and Steve wasn't in the mood to stand out.

"You think he poisoned us?" someone asked.

Katie faced Bob, an older farmer who raised the question. "Right."

Bob looked at one of his fingernails as if deciding whether it needed cleaning.

Once again silence stretched through the bar. A fly buzzed by Steve's ear.

"Could be," Claude said after a while. "We all drank his communion. Could be he poisoned us. I feel . . ." He stopped, either distracted or unsure how he felt.

"Well, if he did poison us, bring it on, medicine man," Katie said. "I feel pretty relaxed."

"Don't be stupid," Paula said. "The man's a devil, not a medicine man."

"You think a devil got up there and turned water into wine?" Katie challenged, coming to life.

"What water into wine?"

"Okay, then an apple into wine. Whatever. You get my point."

"No, Katie, I don't think I do. What is your point?"

"My point is if he wanted to kill us, he'd have done it last night."

They stared at her, uncomprehending. Steve didn't know what she was driving at either. Maybe she'd had a dream like his about a killing.

"Who said anything about killing?" Claude asked. "He's off his rocker maybe. He might be playing us for some reason, but I doubt a killer would be so obvious."

"What in the world are you all talking about?" Katie demanded. "He's no killer. He's a preacher."

"Come to bring grace and hope to Paradise," Bob said, still inspecting his fingernails.

"You're the one who brought up killer, Katie. And frankly it wouldn't surprise me. Either way, he's a devil," Paula said. "No man of God would talk the way he talked. I say we have our way with him before he has his way with us."

"Has his way with you?" Mary asked. "You holding out on us?"

A lone voice spoke out loudly from the rear door. "Paula's right. You should get rid of him or call the cops in Delta."

They turned as one to face Johnny Drake. The boy had come in the back and stood facing them with a fixed face.

"You eighteen, boy?" Steve asked. "Get out."

Paula stood. "Shut up, Steve." She walked toward the boy. "What makes you say that, Johnny?"

Johnny eyed them. "He may not be the devil, but he's not right." He hesitated. "And he's a killer."

Surprisingly, no one jumped on the boy. They were too lethargic to be jumping. Johnny seemed encouraged by this and continued.

"I watched him walk into town yesterday. Me and Cecil were on the bench. I know this may sound crazy, but Black killed Cecil."

Steve wasn't sure what to think about that, except to notice that the notion didn't seem preposterous. On the other hand, he doubted the boy had a clue what he was talking about. Probably dreamed Black had killed Cecil, just like he'd dreamed Black kissed and skewered Paula.

"You saying he actually killed Cecil?" Steve asked. "Or that Cecil died when Black was there, which is what he said."

"I mean he killed him."

"And how was that?"

"He . . ." Johnny shifted on his feet. "He jabbed his fingers into Cecil's eyes. Deep, maybe into his brains. I watched the whole thing. He killed him, and last night he threatened the whole town."

Did I hear that? I can't remember. I remember the stakes, but do I actually remember Black threatening . . .

"I remember it," a soft voice said. The rest of them were staring past Steve. He turned to the front door.

Marsuvees Black stood in the doorway, smiling at them. How'd he get in so quiet?

"It seems that Father Yordon has taken a leave of absence, so I suppose I should explain myself to the rest of you."

The man walked up to the bar. "Smart boy, Johnny. The rest of you should listen to him." He chuckled.

Black's sudden appearance had stunned them all. Steve had no doubt about his earlier judgment; there was something profoundly different about Black today. His eyes, though still blue, seemed a softer smiling blue rather than the drilling blue. His mouth had no mocking twist or angry snarl. He seemed almost earthy.

Black dug into his breast pocket and withdrew two objects, which he held, one in each hand.

"These look familiar?" he asked Johnny.

They were plastic or glass eyeballs, Steve saw. Smeared with paint to look like blood. Black rolled them down the bar toward Paula, who stepped back, repulsed. The eyeballs rolled off the bar and over to Johnny.

"Cecil's eyeballs," Black said gently.

Johnny stared wide-eyed as the balls stopped three feet from his shoes. He looked up. "But . . . that's not what I—"

"You saw what I wanted you to see. You saw me stick my fingers into Cecil's eye sockets and pull those eyes from his face. But those eyes are glass. Go on, pick them up."

Johnny bent, touched, then picked up the eyeballs. "Glass."

"Glass," Black said. "This, on the other hand"—he pulled an apple from his other breast pocket—"is a real apple. The same one you all saw last night. And this"—the preacher tossed the apple into the air, and when it landed in his hand it was a mug of lemonade—"is sleight of hand."

Steve was sure he'd seen an extra movement in there somewhere. "An illusion," he said. "You're a magician?"

"More than a magician. I'm a preacher who uses illusions to make a point, and I don't mind telling you that I've never had a town so wholly swallow my nonsense as this town did yesterday. You, my dear friends, have been like putty in the devil's hands."

They stared.

"But Cecil's dead!" Johnny said.

The glint left Black's eyes. He looked at the bar. "Yes, that was unfortunate." Eyes on Johnny. "Cecil had a heart attack, Johnny. Plain and simple. My trick sent him over the cliff he was already headed for. The only reason I didn't stop to pay him respects and administer rights was because I have been called to this town and I do have a message from God. I couldn't compromise for the sake of one man. I know it sounds crass, but doing anything else would have compromised my mission."

He let the statement rest. No one challenged him.

"And believe me, if you knew what I know about this town, you wouldn't want me to compromise my mission."

He held out a fist, then opened it. There lay a small clear bottle containing a milky translucent substance. "This look familiar? It's aloe vera mixed with a strong hallucinogen called peetock moss, which really isn't a moss at all, but something excreted by a rare worm. It was often used by Indians to call up images of what they thought were spirits."

Black set the four-inch-tall bottle on the bar. *Clunk.* A red ring circled the neck, otherwise there were no markings on the glass.

"It's potent but harmless. Forty-eight hours ago, I introduced quite a bit of this into the town's water supply. That was enough to soften up your susceptibility yesterday. Last night I put more into the communion glass. Most of you saw what I wanted you to see. Do any of you feel groggy?"

They didn't answer.

"The side effects. You've been duped, my friends. And in so doing, I've revealed the depravity of your hearts. Which is important if you know what I know about this town."

"Which is what?" someone asked.

"Which is that something very bad is coming. Without me, you poor folk don't stand a chance. Consider this training."

Steve's mind was still working a bit slow, but if he was catching all of this, Black was claiming to be nothing more than a magician who'd employed some drug called peacock or peetook or something or other, and he'd done it to make a point. Something bad was coming, and Black had a mission to protect the town from whatever that was.

Steve grunted. "Huh. You do this often?"

"On occasion. But not like this. Paradise is special. That's all you need to know. From here you'll have to trust me. Trust me, my friends, or die."

They stared at him, half in dumb wonderment.

"You drugged us?" the Swede asked.

"No, not really. I cleared your minds by feeding them something they wanted. Like feeding the body bread—no different. No lasting effect. No harm. I know it's a bit unorthodox, but it's the only way for the dumb saps in these parts to get a grasp on hope and grace, which is essential for what lies ahead."

"What's that?"

Black eyed Claude. "You're not only dense, you're deaf? I told you, that's it for now. Please try to concentrate when I speak. We don't have enough time to repeat every last thing I say."

A bit of the old Black was back. Frankly, Steve didn't mind.

"So they were tricks, right?" Katie said. "I knew it." She eyed the bottle on the bar and bit her lip. "I knew it."

It occurred to Steve that tricks or not, the stuff in that bottle was the real magic.

"So what's your point?" Paula asked. Her tone was harsh. She cleared her throat. "I mean how does this show us hope and grace? You're saying that you frightened Cecil into a heart attack with a trick, and you don't have a problem with that?"

"Paula, the pure one. That's good, I *want* you to question me. Of course I have a problem with Cecil's heart attack, but there was nothing I could do about it. I do magic, not miracles. Anything could have made that old heart of his stop."

"Still doesn't seem like anything a preacher would do," she said. "Neither does doping up a whole town."

Black studied her for too long, then put both palms on the bar and rubbed the wood gently. "Lovely," he said. "So lovely. Not all is as it seems, my friends. But the things that appear to us in everyday life are so compelling that we have a hard time looking past them to a greater reality. Sometimes it takes a very heavy dose of the other reality to get our attention. Think of me as the sword of truth, dividing bone from marrow."

He looked up and scanned them. "Preachers these days aren't willing to hand out heavy doses of that greater reality. They talk in old clichés that mean nothing to real people with real problems. I use a different language, and believe me, I am ready to dispense a heavy dose of a greater reality. You'll have to choose between your old way and my new way. The old way is to talk . . . all talk and no juice. My way is to show. All juice. Not everything I said yesterday is a sham. I have every intention of rocking your world. I will show you true grace and hope, and it won't look like the world's version of grace and hope. I'll show you a world swimming in the reality of God himself, but you'll have to allow me."

Black drilled Steve with a blue stare. "Let go and let God. Do you want to do that?"

Steve wasn't sure the preacher wanted an answer. But he *did* want to let go and let God, whatever that meant. He nodded.

"You'll have to give up your doubts. You'll have to trust me to remove the sliver that's worked its way under your skin, the stake that's been driven into your heart." Black's eyes shifted to Katie and the others at the end of the bar. "But in the end I will rock your world. Can I do that?"

"Yes," Katie said.

Black looked at the Swede. "Claude? I need agreement."

Claude glanced at his wife. "I guess."

"Then I would like to have dinner with you and your lovely wife tonight."

The preacher was looking at Claude, but Katie answered. "We'd love to have you."

Black faced her and bowed his head. "A wise choice, ma'am." He put his hand on the bottle, hesitated a moment, then slid it down the bar toward her.

"A little more won't hurt you," he said.

Then Marsuvees Black tipped his broad-rimmed hat, turned around, and walked out the door.

For a moment no one moved. Except Johnny. The boy slipped out the back the moment the screen door slammed shut.

"Wow," someone said.

Yeah, wow. Steve's eyes lingered on the bottle. They were all staring at Katie. She took the bottle and held it up to the light. Steve eased down the bar toward her.

Without further hesitation she spun the lid off and set it on the counter. Smelled the contents as if it were perfume.

"Seems harmless."

Katie splashed a little in her beer, swirled the drink around with her finger, and sipped at it.

Ten minutes later they had all tasted Black's concoction, some more than others. Although to say Paula tasted it might be an overstatement. She sniffed it then finally touched her tongue to the inside of the lid.

Tasted like nothing, she said.

But to Steve it tasted like wood.

Like wood stakes.

CHAPTER SEVEN

THE MONASTERY
Thursday morning

BILLY STROLLED into the cafeteria for a late breakfast, feeling self-conscious without knowing why. He'd missed the morning prayers, but that was no cause for guilt. He had violated the most sacred of monastery rules by entering the caverns below, but none of his classmates suspected anything.

Besides, if they knew what he knew, they would probably do the same. Marsuvees Black had been right. The impulse was in them for a reason. An animal created to be fed.

He'd spent half the night in the one tunnel, feeding the animal, and in the end it felt more like an hour. Maybe half an hour. He wasn't even sure what he'd done to eat up so much time. He had explored deeper—didn't matter. He could have sat on the couch and been just as happy.

Everything down there was exhilarating. He'd been awake less than an hour, and the thought of going back was already driving him crazy.

Half the kids had finished eating and vacated the cafeteria, but Darcy sat next to Paul at the far table. Billy went through the line, politely wishing the two overseers on serving duty a good morning, and shuffled to the table.

"Morning, Billy," Darcy said, smiling sheepishly. "You sleep well?"

Billy plopped his tray down and arranged his silverware. "Sure."

Paul shoved a piece of meat into his mouth. "Running a little late, are we?"

"Yeah." Billy nibbled on some eggs.

"You've been late a lot."

"Leave him alone," Darcy said. "So he's late now and then. So what?"

"I'm not saying it's a big deal. I'm just making conversation. I never said it was in any way significant. Although now that you mention it, being late repeatedly, as our Billy has been, is indicative of distraction, don't you think?"

The Brit's highfalutin tone irritated Billy. Always had. He ate his eggs without looking up. In writing class they'd memorized a quote from the philosopher Søren Kierkegaard, who'd once described writers as "spies who kept their eyes on suspicious characters, working on espionage, taking notes, observing particulars that everyone else overlooked, scouring the world for clues of meaning." The monastery was brimming with petty spies, because they were all writers.

"Yes, you're probably right," Darcy replied. "But just because a distraction is indicated doesn't mean it actually exists. Either way, his being late isn't necessarily significant."

"Stop it, both of you," Billy said. "You sound like two stuffed shirts from a university book." He raised his head and saw both staring at him with raised eyebrows. "I'm serious. You guys barely know the meaning of puberty, and here you are, discussing the fine points of a student's tardiness. Doesn't that strike you as odd?"

"Not really." Darcy's eyes flashed with mischief.

"It does me. We're too young for so much responsibility. We should be out playing baseball and splashing in the ocean. Not discussing tardiness and speaking like we're graduate students of the English language."

"I don't consider my life here that way," Paul said. "I rather enjoy it."

"Listen to you. *I rather enjoy it*," Billy mocked, wagging his head. Paul was black and British by birth. Although he'd grown up in the monastery without the accent, he fancied his heritage and practiced it whenever he could. By contrast, Darcy was the perfect Dutch blonde who tended to lift her language only when in Paul's company. They were the perfect pair, black and white, spouting high English.

"You sound like you've eaten a barrel of pickles," Billy said.

Darcy laughed.

"I rather like pickles, actually," Paul returned without missing a beat. "We were just talking about Marsuvees Black before you sat down, Billy. I think his sudden vacancy wasn't planned. What do you think?"

Billy had a spoonful of eggs lifted halfway to his mouth. He stopped, then finished the bite. "I don't know. What's your reasoning?"

"He seemed a bit off at the end there, encouraging the class to reach for the edges and such," Paul said. "To go out and search for the limits. Nothing wrong technically. It was just the look in his eyes when he talked about it. He seemed more interested in pushing us into the darkness than into the light." He turned to Darcy. "You saw it, right?"

"At times, yes. But the desire to explore boundaries is part of the human condition. Maybe it's better to explore them here, in the confines of the monastery, than out there."

"Maybe, within the context of the rules," Paul said.

Billy glanced around the cafeteria and saw that only a handful of students remained. "Please, Paul, don't tell me you never feel like blowing the rules. Take the rules of writing, which mirror all of our other rules. Who decided those particular rules should be the rules of writing anyway? Who erected those walls and said, 'Here, you be a good boy and only write stories that lead to love'?"

Paul looked thrown off. "Why would any writer want to go beyond the four rules?"

"Because they just want to, that's why. Because this little voice in their head keeps whispering that there's more out there than this," Billy said, waving his hand to the ceiling. "Believe me, there is."

The smile left Darcy's face. "Come on, Billy. Don't be like this. You're not making a lot of sense."

The same desire that had propelled Billy to explore the tunnels rose in his chest, urging him to tell. If Darcy could just see what he had seen. Touch what he'd touched.

Only one student remained bent over his meal on the far side of the room.

Billy turned to Darcy and Paul. "I not only think there's more, I *know* there is more." He whispered, looking directly into Darcy's eyes. "I know there's more because I've seen more."

Neither responded to that, so he continued, watching her eyes. "I've been below. I've seen the subterranean levels."

Darcy's mouth opened in shock. She glanced around. Paul sat unmoving, bug-eyed.

"Below?" Darcy asked in a whisper. "You've been to the forbidden levels?"

Billy nodded. "Yes, and they are more wonderful than you could ever imagine. Ever."

"But . . . you can't, Billy! It's forbidden!"

"Why? Have you ever asked that? You have no idea what the lower levels contain. I, on the other hand, do know what they contain, and I'm telling you that they'll expand your mind like nothing else you know."

"But it's prohibited," Paul said.

"By whom?"

"By David. By the overseers."

"And who are they?"

"Who are they? They *built* this place! They're our . . . teachers."

"Yes, but do they run your mind, Paul? Maybe Marsuvees was right. Think about what he's been saying here for the last few months. It's in the fourth rule of writing. There *are* no boundaries. Why? Because each of us makes our own way."

"The rules of writing aren't the only rules we live by," Darcy said.

"Yes, but they do make my point. Consider our writing, for example. We create our *own* stories. Don't you see it? We are *writers*. We choose our own stories. No one forces us to write this plot or that plot. No one insists we do or don't do this or that. It's for *us* to choose! And as long as we have the free will to choose, we have an obligation to explore those choices."

"You stop this talk right now, Billy!" Darcy whispered harshly. "You've lost your senses. Talk like this will get you thrown out of here."

"Talk like this got me to the subterranean levels. And I found the most wonderful halls imaginable there, filled with images and powers that took my breath away and left me shaking."

"But what of the third rule of writing?" Paul asked.

The simpleton was still too shocked to take any of this seriously.

Paul continued. "How can any of this lead to love, or to the Creator? It's all in the third rule, remember? Like Samuel said in class yesterday."

Billy's snarl surprised even him. "Forget Samuel! Samuel's a dope!" He sat back and took a breath. "If you understand that we create our stories, then technically we *do* abide by the third rule because we *are* creators. We discover love by discovering ourselves."

There, he'd said it. He'd repeated the theory that someone left in his locker, encouraging him to descend into the tunnels.

They stared at him, blinking.

"And Raul is right. Stories without proper conflicts are boring. In the real world, the story of life starts with conflict. I could challenge the prevailing rules here and win with my arguments. Maybe I will."

They didn't respond to that. How could they, blinded by denial?

"So when did you go below?" Darcy asked, glancing around nervously.

"Last two nights."

"Two times?"

"I had to, Darcy. The dungeons call. It's as if they know my name and call to me. None of the halls up here speaks to me like the dungeons. None of them calls me."

"Dungeons?"

"Figure of speech. Tunnels. Subterranean halls. I've found a study that contains hundreds of books to be read. I'm telling you, take the enjoyment of reading or writing or eating or anything you do up here, and down there it's ten times better. Try it once and you'll see."

"If you think Paul or I would go down there, you've lost your mind. Proof positive that the 'dungeons,' as you appropriately call them, have rotted your mind."

Billy just grinned.

"What you're doing isn't only prohibited, it sounds nasty, and I for one will have no part in it." Darcy scooted her chair back and stood.

Paul followed her lead. "Sorry, Billy. I do believe she's right."

"Well, don't either of you forget what I said. We have no boundaries, so don't go and flap your jaws about this. I'm entitled to do whatever I choose." He caught Darcy's eye. "I'll be waiting for you."

Billy watched them go, past the tray table toward the entry. *Idiots. Stupid fools.* And yet he had resisted the impulse at first, hadn't he, just like Darcy and Paul were doing now.

A voice spoke behind him. "Good morning, Billy." Billy twisted to face Samuel. The last student eating across the cafeteria while he'd spouted off about Samuel being a dope had been none other than Samuel himself.

Billy turned back to the table and clenched his eyes for a moment, hoping that Samuel hadn't been listening.

"Morning, Samuel."

Samuel stepped around the table and sat down. "You okay, Billy?"

"Sure, Samuel. I'm just fine. And you?"

"I'm good. Are you sure you're okay? You've seemed a bit upset lately."

Upset? And when had he looked upset? Billy's face grew a little hotter. "Well, I haven't been upset."

"You're struggling with something, Billy. It's written all over you. Part of me wants to tell you to snap out of it. Quit licking the floor and stand up." He paused. "But most of me just wants to tell you that we all go through struggles. We can help each other."

"What do you care, Samuel? What difference does it make to you?"

A few seconds passed before the answer came. "Everything each of us does affects the others. None of us lives in a vacuum. We're simply children on a quest to gain the highest forms of wisdom without being compromised in the process. But when one is compromised, the others are compromised. You see that, don't you?"

Billy waved his fork at the blond boy. "Each of us can do whatever he or she wants. You can't take that away."

"You're right. But do you think there aren't consequences to what you say or do?"

"And what would the consequence be if I told you to shut up, Samuel?"

Samuel just looked at him. There was something in his eyes, a look Billy could have identified a week ago, but which now just looked vague. Maybe it was hurt.

Billy thought of the halls below, running with worm gel. He had to get back.

"Just shut up," he said.

CHAPTER EIGHT

PARADISE

Thursday afternoon

JOHNNY'S PREDICAMENT had gone from bad to worse.

Now he wasn't sure what he'd seen yesterday. Actually he was sure—he'd seen Black kill Cecil, but he wasn't sure why he'd seen it. Didn't feel right, but it was possible that Black's explanation in the bar was the truth. The others were swallowing it, hook, line, and sinker. Didn't feel right, but that was supposedly Black's point.

Maybe he'd misjudged the man. His ways were strange to be sure, but again, that was his point. He didn't smell right, look right, or talk right. But he did look and talk more normal this morning than he had yesterday.

And all of that was his point.

Johnny's mother still hadn't returned from Junction. No surprise there. She'd be home this afternoon. She hadn't taken any of the stuff Black was handing out. Her exposure, like his own, was limited to whatever the preacher had put in the water supply. She'd be able to tell him what was up.

And maybe Roland and Fred would be straight in the mind. He'd know in a few minutes when they met behind the old theater.

Johnny glanced at the clock. Time to go. He was dressed in a blue Nike T-shirt with a faded brown button-down shirt hanging unbuttoned and tails out over his thin frame. Good to go.

The minute the door slammed shut behind him, he reconsidered taking the trek down Main Street to the Starlight, which loomed two hundred yards off. He'd been so eager to get home from the bar that he hadn't noticed just how odd the town looked.

For starters it was deserted. Not a soul.

Somewhere a screen door was banging in the wind. Wind-blown silt smothered the town in a dull gray-brown haze. Leaves danced by.

Bang, bang, bang. Whose door was that? Across the street stood the church. Closed. No cars in front of Smither's Saloon or All Right Convenience. Didn't mean no one was at either place, just no visitors.

Johnny walked deliberately, ignoring his throbbing leg. Off the sidewalk, under the large maple that shaded their house, down the side of Main Street. He crossed it.

When he reached the middle, at the point Black had turned toward him and Cecil yesterday, he again thought that the alley would have been a better choice. He was alone out here. Stranded. The wind tore at his hair and the dust whipped his pants and he was sure that at any moment something impossible would happen.

Paradise had become the town of impossibilities.

That was yesterday. That was the preacher's point.

Johnny picked up his pace, staring straight ahead, and then ran the last few steps along the old theater's wall. He rounded the back corner and pulled up in front of Roland, Fred Mars, and Peter Bowers, all sitting in a circle, protected from the wind by the large building.

They stared at him as if he'd come out of a snowstorm.

"Hey," he said.

They wore blue jeans and ratty T-shirts, except Fred, who wore a sun-bleached plaid farmer's shirt that looked like it had been found on a rocky riverbank.

"Hey," Roland said.

Johnny walked forward.

"Hey, Johnny," Peter said. The Bowers boy was big, like his father, Claude.

Johnny stopped. There was something out of whack with Fred and Peter. Dark circles under their eyes. Tired faces, as if they hadn't slept a wink last night.

"You gonna sit down?" Fred asked.

"You get any sleep last night, Fred?"

He shrugged. "Sure." But he didn't look so sure.

"What do you think about the preacher?" Fred asked.

Johnny settled to the ground next to Roland.

"I think . . ." Johnny stopped. Actually, he didn't know what to think anymore. "He's pretty weird, that's for sure." No one disagreed.

The mood was gloomy, which was strange because Johnny figured they'd find a way to rip the preacher to shreds with feeble attempts at humor.

"They say Chris was dying before the preacher healed him," Fred said. "Nothing like that's ever happened around here. The preacher's probably pretty close to God. Like Moses. That's what my parents think, anyway."

"Moses?" Peter said. "Moses was a prophet, not some preacher who walked into town growing warts in people's mouths."

"What do you call the plagues?"

"It doesn't matter anyway," Roland said. "Just because someone does something great doesn't make them a great person. Look at Hitler. Everybody liked him in Germany at one time, and look what he did to the Jews."

"What do you mean everybody liked Hitler?" Fred demanded, face red. "Nobody liked Hitler."

"Settle down," Peter said. "What gives, man?"

"If Roland wouldn't be so stupid—"

"I'm not being stupid! I'm just saying that Moses wasn't Hitler. And that maybe this guy isn't Moses either. He could be, I'm just saying he might not be."

Watching Fred, Johnny felt uneasy. He spoke as much to stop their bickering as to fill them in.

"I saw him this morning." They looked at him. "He was in the bar with the others."

Roland pushed. "And?"

"And he was . . . different. He said that he put something in the drinking water to make us all loopy. And that everything he did was just a trick."

"He said that?" Fred's eyes widened. "Why would he do that?"

"Loopy?" Peter Bowers said. He pulled a bottle from his pants. "You mean this?"

It was the bottle that Black had showed them in the bar, only now it was empty. Peter was grinning.

Johnny reached for it. "Where'd you get that?"

"My mom." He snatched it out of Johnny's reach, twirled off the lid, and lifted the bottle to his nose. "She said it was some good stuff."

"Good stuff? She tell you it came from Black?"

"Course she did. Why, does that scare you?" He stuck his tongue into the narrow neck and made a show of trying to lick the inside, but his tongue was too fat for the bottle.

"That's the stuff?" Roland asked.

Peter pulled the bottle off his tongue and licked his lips. "Tastes like toe sludge."

"*Sick!*" Fred grabbed the bottle from Peter's hand and shoved it up to his nose. "Doesn't smell bad. You taste this?"

"Course I did. It tastes like toe sludge."

"Yeah, right." Fred put his finger into the bottle, withdrew some of the residue, and touched it to his tongue. Satisfied it wasn't as disgusting as his friend had insisted, he licked his finger clean.

"Tastes like nothing."

"Let me see," Roland said, reaching for the bottle.

"I wouldn't," Johnny said.

"Come on, Johnny, don't be such a wimp. It's probably just water."

Peter dove for the bottle, but Fred rolled out of his way, laughing. He came to his feet and jumped back, sticking his finger in for another sample.

"Knock it off!" Peter yelled. By the looks of the vein sticking out of his neck, he wasn't too happy. He stood, brushing dust from his shirt. "Give it back."

"What for?"

They faced off, Fred taunting, Peter scowling. But in a flash, that changed. For no apparent reason, both Fred and Peter spun toward the theater's back wall and stared at it wide-eyed.

Their mouths dropped open.

"What?" Roland said, looking at the wall with Johnny. Weathered, once white boards ran vertically in bad need of fresh paint, but nothing seemed out of place.

"Holy . . ." Peter was whispering. He took a step back and Fred followed suit.

"What is it?" Roland demanded again.

Peter's mouth twisted, formed a grin. He stared at the wall. "Wow . . ."

"Wow," Fred echoed.

Johnny scrambled to his feet. *It's the bottle. Black was right, the stuff in the bottle makes people see things. That's what was . . .*

Peter was yelling in terror. He stumbled backward.

Fred screamed, white-faced. He whirled and ran. Straight into Peter. The boys crashed to the ground with grunts and yells. But both were too distracted by whatever they had seen to make anything of the collision. They scrambled to their feet, cast a quick glance at the wall, and ran for the corner, where they disappeared behind the theater.

They weren't screaming anymore. They were just running. The wind swallowed the sound of their feet.

Roland looked at Johnny, then back at the wall. "You see anything?"

"I'm telling you, it was the stuff in that bottle. What did I say? It makes people loopy."

Roland grinned crooked and walked to the wall. He put his hand on the boards. "What do you think they saw?"

Johnny kicked at the bare dirt behind the Starlight. He didn't want to be here and he didn't want to go home alone. Black might be good, Black might be bad, but whatever was happening in this town was officially terrifying.

"The preacher talked about helping people see another reality. Maybe they saw . . ." A thought occurred to him. "Maybe we should leave."

Roland turned back. "What? Like a ghost or something?"

"I don't know. Whatever it was, it wasn't good. I think we should go."

Roland slapped the boards. "There's nothing here, man. That's freaky. What's the world coming to?"

"Good question. You notice anything strange around here today?"

"Yeah, Fred and Peter."

"Not just Fred and Peter. You have any nightmares last night?"

That caught Roland off guard. "What do you mean, nightmares?"

"I mean did you dream about Black?"

"What makes you say that?"

Johnny shrugged. "I did."

"So did I."

"You ever see clouds like that this time of year?" Johnny asked, looking up. Flat clouds hung abnormally low, like someone had painted the sky dark gray just above the town.

Roland's gaze followed Johnny's. "Yeah. Pretty strange."

"There wasn't a cloud in the sky yesterday."

"You really think Black has anything to do with the weather?"

"Have you seen him today?"

"Actually, I did. My mom left her watch on the sink at Nails and Tan and wanted me to get it. Didn't want to talk to Katie. They had an argument yesterday or something. Maybe you didn't hear this, did you? I told Fred and Peter about it before you got here."

"Black was at Nails and Tan? When was this?"

"On my way here." Roland grinned. "He was there all right. He practically had his tongue down Katie's throat. Freaked me out, man."

The revelation stunned Johnny. "He was kissing her?"

"Okay, maybe that's an exaggeration. I couldn't actually see her because his back was to the door, but they were definitely close. Laughing."

"You tell anyone else about this?"

"Just Fred and Peter. I guarantee you my mom would flip."

"And you don't find that just a little bit strange, for a preacher to do that?"

Roland looked at the wall again. "Like you said, he's trying to get people's attention. Look at what just happened to Fred and Peter. The whole thing is pretty freaky, but you have to admit, it's kinda cool."

"Maybe. And maybe not," Johnny said.

"What do you mean, maybe or maybe not? It's either cool or it's not."

"Maybe. But that doesn't mean it's good."

"Has he done anything bad yet?"

Johnny thought about that. Fact was, scaring people to make a point wasn't a bad thing. All preachers did that at times, right? The Bible did that. What do you call God sending a whale to swallow Jonah? Maybe Black was that whale, going to towns to swallow them up so they would change their minds.

"Maybe not," Johnny said. "But we can't tell."

"Well, Peter said Black's gonna be at his house tonight." A thin smile tugged at Roland's lips. "You ever spy?"

"Spy on Black?"

"Come on, you know that half the people around here leave their shades open at night. You just sneak up and look in. You've done it."

"Not for a few years I haven't. And not on Black. What if we get caught?"

"We won't get caught."

"I don't know . . . he's . . ."

"He's Marsuvees Black. Come on, Johnny. He's just a crazy preacher who's messing with people's heads a bit. So we check him out."

Johnny glanced at the sky. Black, black, everything was black. "When?"

Roland shrugged. "Eight? After dark."

"Okay."

Roland grinned. "Cool."

"Cool," Johnny said.

But it didn't feel cool. Nothing about Black felt cool.

CHAPTER NINE

THE MONASTERY

Thursday afternoon

DARCY SAT in the rear of the class, looking at thirty-six heads covered with blond and brown and black hair. And one covered in red hair. Billy stuck out three rows over on her left, the monastery's cherry.

Billy glanced over with those green eyes of his, and she turned her head back to Raul, who was rambling on about the second rule.

Rambling? Not rambling as in *boring*. Rambling as in *We've heard this a million times, old man. Get on with some good stuff*. In truth, he was speaking eloquently about greatness in purity. On the other hand, it *was* rather boring. It bothered her that she thought so.

She stole a quick look at Billy and saw that he was fidgeting, probably bored out of his skull, waiting for class to end so he could sneak down to the dungeons and play with his ghosts. She was surprised to be thrilled at the idea and turned back to Raul. She pinched the bridge of her nose to concentrate on the overseer's words.

"So, someone tell me why," Raul said. "Why is an adventure which leads to purity so grand? Come on, we've been over this in our sleep."

Tyler raised his hand.

The overseer motioned to the brown-headed Indian boy, the youngest in the class.

"The Creator is pure. Therefore, a life that leads us to purity leads us to the Creator. And no man could possibly find an adventure grander than one that leads to the Creator."

A soft chorus of agreement rippled through the room.

"Yes," Darcy whispered as the approval died down. But her mind was on Billy. Had he also said *yes*, just to be proper?

"Someone else? Yes, Paul?"

Darcy wondered what was running through his head after their talk with Billy at breakfast.

"A path leading to purity will cross enough challenges to make the human head spin." The class chuckled. "It's not only arriving at the conclusion of purity which is so thrilling, but it's the journey to that conclusion. Overcoming the challenges. Each obstacle passed, each challenge met and won. This presents a new level of satisfaction."

Brilliant. Judging by their response, the rest of the class agreed with her assessment. *Brilliant indeed, but old hat, brother. Give me something new.*

The moment she thought it, Darcy knew Billy had gotten to her. Not that she had any intention of actually doing what Billy suggested. Heavens, no. But she wasn't thinking the same, and she wondered why. A little tick had burrowed into her skull, and every time she heard one of the old truths, the insect began to chew on her brain.

She looked at Billy again. He was staring at her, and this time she stared back. He was awfully cute with his auburn hair and green eyes. He was certainly one of the brightest students. Maybe second to Samuel.

Raul was speaking again, but she didn't hear him. Something in Billy's eyes pulled at her. Something that said, *You and I are the same.* And she liked that. It felt good.

Maybe Billy *was* on to something.

She had a responsibility to look after him, didn't she? At the very least she should check up on him. The poor soul was heading for a cliff without the slightest clue.

How did one get to the subterranean levels anyway?

CHAPTER TEN

PARADISE
Thursday night

AS FAR as Johnny could tell, nothing in Paradise changed that afternoon. Other than the wind, which was blowing harder, and the sky, which was growing darker. He spent the hours in his room, waiting for his mother to return.

Roland hung out for an hour but wanted to go home because, as he put it, his own mother and father were behaving a bit strange, and Johnny was making him nervous with all his talk about Black.

Johnny thumbed the toggle and blasted his way through one of his older PlayStation games, Red Alert IV. He paused the game every fifteen or twenty minutes to check the front window. The streets were empty. Paradise was too far off the beaten track to become a hotbed for tourism, but that didn't keep the odd traveler from braving the mountains to find this fruit-farming community. Maybe the storm discouraged visitors; it was raining hard along the Highway 50 corridor.

Johnny resumed his game and killed a few more bad guys without thinking through the steps. He tried to call his mother on the cell phone but couldn't find her signal. It happened up here, enough to make his mother swear on occasion.

Back to the game.

The front door slammed at six o'clock.

"Mom?"

Johnny ran out to the living room to greet his mother, who held several bulging bags. She was wearing new black jeans with a red and white blouse. Her blonde hair was windblown but she beamed, clearly not bothered by the weather.

"Finally," Johnny exclaimed. "What took you so long? I've been . . ."

He stopped short. Something about his mother's brown eyes scared him more than the horror movie he and Roland rented last weekend. They were . . . distracted. Dull. Not unlike the eyes of the rest in the bar.

"Hello, Johnny. Am I?"

"Are you what?"

"Late?"

"It's . . . it's six o'clock."

"Well, I've been home for an hour. I just stopped in to update the others." She walked past him. "Boy, is it raining down the mountain. Highway 50's a river! I half-expected to find the town washed away." She dropped her bags and faced him. "I tried calling on the cell, but the service is out. The storm's knocked everything out. I'm surprised we still have power."

"Where have you been?"

"I told you, I stayed in Grand Junction to shop."

"But you've been talking to the others?"

Her smile faded. "Well, of course, honey. What's wrong? You look like a ghost."

Johnny swallowed. "Nothing's wrong. It's just that nothing's right around here. The wind, the clouds, the preacher—"

"Of course nothing's normal. We're in the middle of a storm." She walked up to him and ruffled his hair, a habit of hers that he was losing interest in.

"I guess I owe you an apology. They told me about the eyes. I'm sorry for doubting you saw what you thought you saw. I just couldn't imagine anybody actually doing what you claimed the preacher did. I was right about that, but I had no right to dismiss you."

"It's okay." Johnny turned away and sat on the sofa. They'd stolen his thunder. "What did they tell you?"

"You mean Katie? The service, her dreams, the meeting this morning— pretty much everything, I suppose." She opened the refrigerator and studied the contents. "Why? You know something else?"

"So you believe him?"

Sally withdrew a bottle of cranberry juice and flipped open the cupboard for a glass. "Makes sense to me. Sure it's all a bit strange, but this world is half-full of strange people."

They were welcome words. If his mother thought Black was legit, then he probably *was* legit.

"If I'd gone to Junction and the medical examiner told me that Cecil died of trauma to the head or eyes, I would think differently. Actually, it's all a bit exciting, don't you think?"

"Unless he turns out to be a liar," Johnny said.

She poured her drink. "He was a liar. Yesterday, right? Katie said you were in the saloon. You heard him yourself. He did it to make a point."

"And what about this thing that's coming to Paradise? Katie tell you about that?"

"What thing?"

"Black said he's doing all this to help prepare us for something that's coming."

"He said that?" For the first time since she'd entered, a shadow of concern crossed his mother's face. "Hmm. Now that's weird. You hungry?"

His mother had a way of letting the steam out of his concerns. At least she was keeping an open mind.

"Sure. I'm starved."

They made small talk while Sally cooked up some spaghetti and prepared a green salad with tomatoes, Johnny's favorite. For an hour they were the normal small-family unit that Johnny had grown accustomed to since his grandfather's death. His mother was a bit distracted, but he wrote it off to a good shopping day. Funny how buying clothes and shoes could make someone so happy.

As the eight o'clock spying mission approached, his concern made a comeback. He thought about calling Roland and telling him he couldn't go out, but the fact of the matter was, he wanted to find out what Black was up to as much as Roland did. Maybe more.

Sally pushed her plate away. "Boy, that was delicious if I don't say so myself."

She picked up the bottle of oily Italian dressing and eyed it. "The preacher's stuff looks a bit like this. Don't you think?"

The comment caught Johnny off guard. She'd seen the bottle? "What do you mean?"

"Katie had a bottle—"

"You didn't taste it, did you?"

Sally looked up at Johnny, held his eyes. "It was harmless, Johnny." She set the bottle down. "She said it was aloe vera and some kind of mild sedative."

"Mild? It's got half the town seeing things!"

"Well, I haven't seen anything. Besides, I wouldn't mind knowing what all the hoopla's about." Sally stood and took her plate into the kitchen. "It'll be fine, Johnny. Paradise could use a little excitement now and then."

A question ballooned in his mind. Why were the rest so eager to taste Black's concoction while he had no interest? At least not enough interest to give in. They'd supposedly all been exposed to the water. Had he drunk any water in the last couple days? Yes, he had. So then why were they different from him? Maybe they really weren't.

His mother didn't think it was a big deal. So then it probably wasn't.

He looked at the clock—two minutes to eight. He had to meet Roland.

Maybe they were all just questioning things because that's exactly what the preacher wanted them to do. He was thinking pretty hard about things he'd hardly ever thought about, right? Maybe Black was an angel who'd come to save Paradise.

Then who was coming to kill them all?

JOHNNY LOOKED around the old theater and studied the street. He could just see the outline of the Bowerses' house. Like a ghost across the street, barely glowing in the night, shifting behind a thin curtain of blowing dust. The blinds were open.

He pulled his head back.

"Anything?" Roland asked.

"No. Were your parents around this afternoon?"

Roland hesitated. "My mom was. She forgot to make dinner."

"But you didn't see your dad?"

Another hesitation. "He was probably busy. Are we going to do this? I'm getting a headache."

Johnny took a deep breath. "Okay, we see if the preacher's over there. If he is, we watch him and see what he does. If we don't see him, we knock on the door and ask for Peter. That's the plan."

"Sounds good." Roland headed around the corner. He didn't seem bothered by the darkness, so Johnny followed, dismissing the inner voices that suggested caution.

A scrub-oak hedge surrounded the house. The barrier gave them perfect cover up to a height of three feet. They wedged themselves between the hedge and house, and Roland peered into the first dark window. After a moment, he shrugged and motioned them on.

Johnny began to settle. Seemed simple enough.

They crawled three quarters of the way around the house without seeing a single soul. The Bowerses had either left the house or occupied one of three remaining rooms—Claude Bowers's study, the master bedroom, or the main-floor bathroom.

Roland reached the study window and waited for Johnny to squat next to him. "Okay, you go up first this time," Roland whispered.

"Me?" Roland had led thus far.

"Sure. Just go up slow and peek in."

Johnny looked up. Seemed harmless enough, despite the fact that the window glowed faintly.

"You think he's going to poke your eyes out?" Roland asked, wiggling his eyebrows.

Johnny ignored the jab and slowly lifted his head to the window sill. He peered into the study, saw Claude sitting at his desk, and immediately jerked his head down.

"What?" Roland whispered. "They in there?"

"Claude." First contact. Adrenaline coursed through his veins. They hadn't exactly snuck into Fort Knox or anything, but his heart didn't seem to know the difference.

"What's he doing?"

"I don't know."

This time Roland eased up to the sill, held his nose there for a moment and then retreated. "He's . . . he's watching television."

This time both Roland and Johnny eased up to the window.

The room began to flash with blinding white strobes that ignited scenes on a monitor that sat on Claude's desk. Johnny couldn't see the images, but they seemed to mesmerize Claude. His mouth hung open dumbly.

The white strobes yielded to red and blues that lit his face. Johnny could hear music now, the bass thudding low. A music video. An intense music video that had turned Claude into a useless lump of a man.

A bottle of booze slipped from Claude's fingers and fell on the floor with a *thump*. He didn't seem to notice.

Claude blinked. He swallowed and began to chuckle. But he still hadn't moved.

Johnny craned for a better view. He caught a fleeting image of Black's head on the set, flapping back and forth as if on a spring. Then a red image that Johnny couldn't make out.

Claude lunged forward, twisted a knob, and sat back. The music pounded louder. Metal, head-banging music. Claude bent for the fallen bottle on the carpet and chuckled again.

The images popped relentlessly without breaking cadence. Claude took a swig from the bottle, half of which dripped off his chin onto his stomach, and began to giggle.

Johnny felt a tug on his sleeve. "He's not in there. Come on."

He dropped down. "You see that?"

"Lost his marbles. Black's not in there. Come on."

Johnny followed Roland to the next window. Master bedroom.

"Go," Roland whispered.

Johnny pulled himself up and looked through blinds that were closed but not properly, leaving slits he could see through if he pushed his eye flat against the glass.

A figure moved by the mirror above the double dresser. Katie was there, leaning into the mirror.

Johnny shifted for a better view.

"Anything?" Roland whispered.

She was dressed in a red skirt, too short and too tight, unless she was headed for a party. He could see Katie's face in the mirror, chin tilted up as she carefully applied a fresh coat of lipstick. She rubbed her lips together and turned her head for a side view. Maybe she and Claude were going to Delta. To a dance or something.

Roland's face came up next to his. Their breath fogged the glass, and Roland wiped the moisture off with his palm.

Johnny watched Katie fix something at the corner of her mouth. Satisfied, she tilted her head down and smiled into the mirror. She traced her freshly painted lips with a slow tongue.

Katie tried another look, this one with one finger on her cheek and her hip cocked as if to say, *Hey there, stranger*. She shifted into another look, this one tracing her open mouth with her tongue and a single finger along her neckline.

Roland dropped down and Johnny followed.

"You see that?" Roland whispered through his cockeyed smile.

"Well, it is Katie." Johnny glanced back at the office window, still glowing from the lighted computer screen inside. "Pretty weird, though. Both Claude and Katie. I wonder where Black is."

"Basement? We haven't tried the window wells."

"And where's Peter? Maybe we should just knock on the door and ask for Peter."

"Try the next window," Roland said.

Roland edged his way around the corner toward the bathroom window, waited for Johnny to catch up, then rose slowly. Wind howled through the eaves. Light seeped past the blinds, illuminating the hazy dust that filled the air. Johnny shielded his eyes and followed Roland to the windowsill.

The low blind provided only a three-inch gap at the bottom. Something blocked their view—a towel or something that made the window dark. Maybe a closet or . . .

The darkness shifted. He squinted. And then the darkness walked away from the window.

Johnny flinched. He stood there staring at Marsuvees Black's polyester trousers, less than three feet away.

The preacher had been leaning against the window. Right in front of Johnny's face, a pane of glass separating them. Now Black stood at the mirror.

A black, coverless DVD case rested on the white sink. Maybe for the DVD that Claude was watching this very moment in his office.

Johnny couldn't see what Black was doing, because the bottom of the blinds cut the man off at the shoulders. He would have to crouch a little to see Black's face and that meant moving. If he moved, Black might see him.

Roland breathed heavily. The window started to fog. Not good.

Johnny pulled back a fraction to allow circulation between his lips and the glass. Then down a little so that his eyes cleared the blinds.

Black was picking his teeth.

The man's fingernails were long, but well shaped, as if he recently had a manicure. The preacher valued cleanliness. He retracted his lips and studied his large white teeth.

He began rubbing a section of his lower teeth with his tongue. Unsuccessful with a mere tongue, the man's lips attacked his teeth. They moved furiously around his lower jaw. If lips could be double-jointed, the preacher owned a pair.

Still aggravated by something in his teeth, Black went after them with his fingernail. Johnny could see his clean-shaven jaw jutting out toward the mirror as he angled for whatever it was.

Roland had moved down for a better view and was breathing harder. Seeing the man go to work on his teeth was a mesmerizing sight. Not exactly the kind of evidence that revealed anything good or bad about him, but fascinating, nonetheless. The man really was getting worked up about whatever was stuck in his—

Black howled with rage.

The man lost his cool so suddenly that both Johnny and Roland yelped. If not for Black's own howl, he would've heard them for sure.

The preacher grabbed his lower lip with his right hand and yanked it down hard. It peeled cleanly off his jaw as if it were a mask. Long white teeth buried in three inches of pink flesh jutted into a gaping mouth. His lower lip slipped a good four or five inches below his chin.

With his other hand, Black wrenched a single tooth from his jaw and spit angrily into the mirror. A small chunk of white meat stuck to the glass.

The stranger shoved his tooth down into place. He released his lower lip. It snapped up over his teeth, and he rubbed his jaw like a man who'd just been slapped, but no worse for the wear.

Johnny's eyes dried in the wind. And then Black straightened his coat and turned toward the door.

Now, Johnny. Move now, while his back's turned. He dropped to his knees. The jar must have started his stalled heart, because he could hear the blood rushing through his ears now. He was hyperventilating.

Roland was beside him, also on his knees. "You . . . you see that?" He stared up at the window, stupefied.

Johnny tore through the hedge. He ran for the Starlight, across the street, a hundred yards off. His leg was bothering him, but adrenaline pushed him beyond the pain. He ran fast, maybe faster than he had in his life. Thankfully, the streetlight was out.

He broke into the clearing behind the theater and doubled over, wheezing. Roland slid to a stop beside him.

"You see that?" Roland said, panting. "Man, did we really see that?"

Johnny didn't answer.

"We have to tell someone." Roland began to pace.

"We could talk to our parents."

"They'll just say we're seeing things. That's what everyone'll say now."

Johnny hesitated, thinking. "And maybe they're right."

Roland scratched his head. "Man, that looked real. I wonder what Fred and Peter saw."

"Maybe we should go to the cops," Johnny said.

"Cops? In Delta? Now you think it was real?"

"I don't know what to think anymore."

CHAPTER ELEVEN

THE MONASTERY
Thursday night

BILLY WAS having a difficult time remembering exactly how many times he'd been to the dungeons in the last couple days. Well, yes, he knew, of course. Three times. Roughly. No, closer to five times. His memory was foggy.

His fascination with the dungeons, on the other hand, was less foggy. Crystal clear, in fact. Like a shaft of light in a pitch-black room, except that the tunnels were actually black, so if you could have a shaft of darkness in a room full of light . . .

Billy left the class in which Paul spouted off as if he owned wisdom itself, and he spent an hour easing his way closer to the east side of the monastery, past the library, to the dark hall. He didn't think he cared whether the others knew what he was up to, but he skirted the students and the teachers with great care anyway.

Raul knew, he thought. He hadn't run into the masked monk again, but upon rather fuzzy reflection, he narrowed the man's identity further. Yesterday he was confident it was either Raul or Marsuvees Black or David Abraham. Now he was quite sure it was either Raul or David Abraham, because the man had spoken about Marsuvees Black as if he was a third party.

The man could have been tricking him, of course. He could be Marsuvees Black, living in the tunnels, driven mad by the worm gel. But why would he wear a mask? He lacked the same motivation as Raul, an active teacher, and David, the director, both of whom would need to conceal their identity to continue their activities.

Simple deduction. The kind of simple deduction Darcy and Paul obviously lacked, at least when it came to considering the tunnels.

Billy took a deep breath, satisfied himself that the coast was clear, stepped into the staircase, grabbed a torch, and ran down the steps with the ease of familiarity. When he stepped up to the blackened doors he was breathing as hard from the excitement of what lay ahead as from the rapid descent.

The dead silence down here was broken only by a faint crackling from the torch. Billy stared at the tunnel doors, and in that moment he didn't care if Darcy or Paul or anybody followed him into the caverns. As long as he could enter himself.

Billy stepped forward and was reaching for the door when the unmistakable sound of a shoe scraping on stone filtered down the stairwell behind him. He jerked his hand back and scanned the room quickly, looking for a place to hide. Nothing.

Feet rounded the staircase. White tennis shoes, the kind students wore. A girl descended into view. Her skirt hung above trembling knees and her eyes were round like saucers.

"Darcy?" His voice echoed around the chamber.

"Billy?" Her voice trembled.

"You . . . you came."

Darcy looked around in dazed wonderment. Billy was too stunned to move. So then he wasn't the only one to come to his senses when presented with the right argument.

"It's . . . it's so gloomy," she said.

She needed encouragement. Billy walked up to her and reached out his hand. This was almost too good to be true. "Don't worry, you'll get used to it."

She took his hand, but her eyes remained on the walls. Throbbing flame light cast an eerie orange hue on the mossy rock walls; the black door seemed to absorb and swallow the light. It *was* rather gloomy.

"Wait till you see the inside."

She looked at him with some astonishment. "I'm not going inside. I just wanted to see what it looks like."

"Okay, but this is not *it*. *It* is through that door." He motioned toward the black doors. "You have to go in there to see *it*."

She shook her head. "No. I can't go in there." She paused. "Aren't you frightened?"

Billy released her hand and walked to the door. When the torch's circle of light moved with him, Darcy followed. He turned to her. "Frightened, Darcy? Tell me, what do you feel like right now?"

"I'm frightened."

"Yes, frightened. But what does frightened *feel* like? Tell me how you feel without using those old words. Say something a writer might write, like *I feel a chill down my spine* or something. Tell me exactly how you *feel.*"

She hesitated and glanced at the floor. "I feel . . . awful, Billy. I'm scared."

"Come on, Darcy. Those are the old words. Use the real words. How would you write it? Describe your feeling. *Show* me! What do *awful* and *scared* mean?"

"I think I should go now. This isn't right. This place is . . . it's evil." She took a step backward.

A thought crossed Billy's mind. She had no torch. In fact, she had no torch coming down the stairs, which meant she'd followed the light from his torch.

"It's too dark to go back, Darcy. You wouldn't catch me going up those stairs without a torch to keep whatever's hiding in the dark from stepping out. Will you just tell me what you feel, for Pete's sake? I've got a point to make here."

She looked back at the stairwell. When she turned around, her face was drawn tight and he knew he'd won, for the moment. She stood like a frail doll, dressed in her white cotton blouse and plaid skirt, hugging herself. She looked like she might start crying.

"I'm cold," she said. "My stomach is tied in knots. My legs are trembling, and I want to leave this place. To turn and run up the stairs. But you have the torch. What do you mean 'keep whatever's hiding'? Is there something in the stairwell?"

"Never mind. That's good, Darcy. And I feel like you too. My hands are shaking a little and my heart is beating a hundred miles an hour. See? We're the same here. Only I don't want to run up those stairs because I've been here before. Instead I want to run through that door."

"Well, I don't. Now give me the torch. You can go in there and find another one."

"Oh no, I can't. There aren't any torches in there. Besides, I think you're wrong. I don't think you feel fear at all. When someone tells me their stomach is tied in knots and their knees are knocking, I might guess they were about to step onto a thrilling roller-coaster ride, or maybe meet someone they're in love with. I think that's what you feel, Darcy, only you've never quite felt this way because you've never been *allowed* to ride a roller coaster, and so you're misinterpreting the feelings. You're mistaking something that's good for something that's bad."

Judging by her stare she thought he'd flipped his lid. And maybe he had.

"That's crazy. I'm scared, not thrilled. This isn't a thrill ride I'm feeling—you think I don't know the difference?" She shifted her eyes to the blackened doors.

"Then there is no difference between fear and excitement," Billy said. "Because they both feel the same to me, and they would feel the same to you if you just relaxed a little." He shifted on his feet. "Look, I've been down here several times now. Do I look any worse off? Am I a walking corpse? Do I look dead? I'm more *alive* than I've ever been! I feel like I've just been born into a big incredible world that's dying for me to gobble it up."

"I still don't want to go in. You're trying to lure me and frighten me—you think I can't see what you're doing? What do you take me for?"

"I take you for someone who thinks the way I do. Someone born to know all things well. And here's one thing you don't know so well: if you don't know this"—he motioned to the black door—"you can't even write about it intelligently. That's not trickery. It's common sense."

She stared at the doors. "It's trickery." She shivered and held her arms a little closer to her body. Billy let the silence lengthen.

"I don't have to go in to know what it's like in there. Just tell me what it's like."

"It's new. It's wonderful. There's . . . there's this odor and this salve on the walls . . ." He stopped, thinking his awkward description might deter her. "I can't really describe it."

"Yes, but what does it *feel* like? You made me tell you what I felt, now you tell me."

"Okay. It's dark. Everywhere it's dark. And maybe a little wet. But apart from that the halls are beautiful. They're the most wonderful things I've seen in my entire life. Mysterious, breathtaking. Every nook is packed with a history of its own, Darcy. You take one look at the bones"—he caught himself there; no sense in being too descriptive yet—"at the artifacts there, and you know it fills a hole in your soul."

"Bones? There're bones in there?"

"Not bones really. Just replicas, like carvings or sculptures that could look like bones. But they're wonderful, Darcy. Beautiful. Come in with me and I'll show you."

"There's a reason why this place is prohibited. Have you ever thought about that? The overseers aren't stupid, Billy. If they think it's wrong, then it's wrong."

"Unless they know something we don't. You thought about *that*? I have and it's a fact. They know that whoever enters these halls learns things that can't be learned up there. That's essentially what Marsuvees Black was trying to say before he left. And what's more, I think the director agrees."

"Don't be ridiculous."

"Then who first convinced me to come down here?"

"The director?" she said incredulously.

"Either him or Raul. They know we'll eventually stumble into an evil path too wide to ignore. Unless we face it now, how can we possibly face it later, when it matters more?"

Darcy put one hand on each side of her head, frustrated. "I don't know."

Billy blinked. *I don't know.* Not *yes* but not *no*, which was much better than *no*.

"But you do feel a little excited about the whole thing, don't you?"

"A little maybe."

"Consider this. We are taught to embrace life, right? To read and write and paint and speak and love and to embrace all forms of communication with passion. I mean, the entire purpose of our life here at the monastery is to become exceptional people. Well, I can tell you everything down here is greater than upstairs. Double the pleasure, double the satisfaction, double everything. My exploration down here is mind-numbing. The stories I've read—and I've only had time to read two short ones—were intoxicating. Even my writing takes on a new urgency and meaning." He stopped to catch his breath. "You can pick up a stone in there and find the dead granite in your hands utterly fascinating."

She didn't respond. She was mesmerized, he thought. And so she should be—he excited even himself.

"It's the final step, Darcy. This is what we were meant for. *This!*" He thrust his hand toward the blackened doors.

Billy lowered his arm and stepped toward her. "I'll tell you what. There's one room in there—a room built like a study, full of books and a sofa—very pleasant. Go with me there. Only there. Straight to the study, take a quick look around, and if you don't want to stay, I swear we'll come right back. But you have to at least see if I'm right. See if this isn't really meant for you, or for everyone, for that matter. You *have* to come!"

Darcy stared at the doors. Billy remembered a story they'd studied years ago, a true story in which an executioner had offered his victims the choice between the guillotine or some unknown fate that waited behind an ominous door. Most chose the guillotine. But one chose the door. He walked through, quaking in his boots, terrified, only to discover freedom.

"Just the study," he said. "No more."

She blinked once and then spoke in a thin voice. "I guess."

Billy began to tremble with excitement. "Okay. Okay, give me your hand."

He reached out, and she finally took his hand. He felt her weight leaning away from him, and he gave her a little tug. "I'm right here. I've got the light."

She followed reluctantly.

Billy stepped toward the door, praying under his breath that she wouldn't change her mind at the last second and bolt for the stairs. Shadows shifted on the charred wood, ebbing with the torch's flame. Darcy's breathing deepened at his shoulder, like an old man struggling against black lungs. He raised a hand to the rough cross brace and pushed. The massive doors squealed open. She withdrew at the sound, but he was finished with his reassurances. He wanted in.

Then they were inside and the doors closed behind them with a *thump*. Darcy jerked again and Billy turned around, his mind buzzing with excitement. Her mouth gaped. She tried to speak. At least he thought she tried to speak, but the sound that came out was like a soft groan, so he couldn't know for sure. He tugged at her arm.

"Come on."

He pulled her into the dark shaft on his far right. The sweet musty odor he'd come to love filled his nostrils.

"Billy!"

"Huh?" He stopped and followed her gaze. Yellow light from his torch splashed on the walls, illuminating one of the worms writhing slowly on the stone face.

"It's okay. Just a worm. They're everywhere down here. They don't bite, promise. Come on."

"But—"

"Come on!" He yanked her forward.

Darcy whimpered and then followed willingly enough—she had little choice. He began to jog, past dozens of the long pink worms slithering on the walls, past the two gated rooms he first discovered. Darcy staggered twice, and he yanked her back to her feet. She seemed to follow more willingly as they ran deeper into the tunnel.

And then the gated study loomed ahead to their right. Billy slowed to a walk, panting. He'd left the gate open. Should close it better next time, just in case. Just in case *what*, he didn't know, but just in case anyway.

He released Darcy and shifted the torch to his right hand. It slipped a little in his sweating palm, and he tightened his grip.

"Here it is."

Billy reached for the gate and pulled it open. Darcy bumped his elbow, causing the light to waver in the open study. He felt a surge of anger. Maybe he shouldn't have brought her. She might mess everything up—poke into his stuff and get in his way.

"Careful!" he snapped. They stepped into the small study.

On his right the shelves, stuffed with books, reached the ceiling. Except for a few he'd brushed off and pulled out, the books were still covered by a thin layer of dust.

He looked at the desk on his left. A journal lay on the desk, tilted just so, his pen resting on its cover. He'd filled the first few pages during his more recent visits.

A smile of wonder dawned on Darcy's face. "It's beautiful," she said. That was quick. "It's so beautiful, Billy."

She walked to the bookcase and reached out for a book. "What are these?"

"Classics. Storybooks. Journals. Who knows. I haven't had time to open many of them."

"There're so many."

"And there may be more. It's like a whole new world, Darcy. What did I tell you? Now how does it feel?"

She turned to him. "Stimulating?"

He winked at her, glad she'd come after all. "Yes, stimulating."

They held their gaze for a moment, and Billy thought she was the most beautiful creature he'd seen. His heart began to pick up its pace as he gazed into her eyes.

"Can you smell that?" he asked.

"Yes. It's sweet." She drew a deep breath and grinned.

"I think it comes from the worms."

She looked out at the darkened hall. "Really?"

"From their . . . from the stuff that comes from them. I think it makes everything down here . . . I don't know, maybe magical or something. It's almost like a drug that doubles or triples sensation. Course, I don't know, I'm just guessing."

Billy pulled a plum from his pocket. "See this? Just a plum, right?"

"Right."

"I brought it down to eat. To see if it tastes better here." He grinned and held it up between his thumb and forefinger. "I guarantee you it'll be different. Everything down here is different."

Billy brought the fruit to his lips, winked at Darcy again, and bit deep. Juice flooded his mouth.

The taste wasn't what he'd hoped for. He smacked his lips and let the flavor swirl around his tongue. But that was just it—there was no real flavor. It was bland, similar to nothing.

"Well?" she asked.

"Must be a bad fruit," he said, tossing the plum through the gate. "But everything else down here will knock your socks off. I can guarantee you that."

The failure bothered Billy for a moment. But almost immediately his hazy contentedness returned. The tunnels were working on him now. They certainly were. He was in the tunnels, right? Yes. In the nasty forbidden dungeon, God bless them, thank you very much.

Darcy really was beautiful. He'd never really noticed.

He took her by the hand. "Look at this." He led her to the journal on the desk.

"What is it?"

He touched it. "You can't tell?"

"It looks like a journal." Her voice held more wonder than any journal should engender. She laid a hand on his. "Can I see?"

He didn't respond immediately. He just stood there suspended in the moment with her hand touching his. She looked at him and gently lifted his hand from the book. She opened the cover, keeping her eyes on him. She dropped her gaze to the pages, and he followed her eyes.

"Do you like it?" he asked.

"What is this?"

"Just some doodling."

"I love it," she murmured. "I love it, Billy." She looked up at him, eyes wide. "Can I write?"

"In this book?"

"Are there others?"

"Sure. But maybe we can work on something together." He looked at her and swallowed, knowing that this was exactly what he wanted.

"A collaboration. You think that might be good?"

"I would like that. I would like that very much." And again he thought she must be the most beautiful woman he'd seen, never mind that she was only thirteen. So was he.

She raised a hand to his cheek. "I think you're very kind, Billy." Her fingers pulled his collar back. "You have a rash on your neck. Did you know that?"

The rash had started yesterday, but it wasn't important. What was important was Darcy.

"I think you're very kind too," he said.

She removed her hand. Time drifted by.

She looked at the book. "What kind of story should we write?"

Billy fanned through the pages. "You want to begin now?"

"We're writers aren't we? It's my favorite thing to do. What kind of story?"

Billy thought about that. "A story about discovering everything new. Like the dungeons. Frightful truths and breaking rules." He closed the book. "But there's other stuff to see. Let's explore first."

Darcy walked around the sofa, mesmerized by everything she saw. "I can't believe this place has been here this whole time. It's magical. I love it, Billy. I just love it."

"And I love you, Darcy."

She looked back at him. "You do?"

What was he saying? "I feel like I do."

"Well, I'm not sure I would go that far," she said. "I'm not even sure we should trust our feelings down here."

"But you're glad you came down."

"Yes." She walked toward the gate and peered back down the tunnel. "Yes, I am."

Billy withdrew the torch and walked into the dark hall. "Let's look around."

CHAPTER TWELVE

PARADISE

Friday morning

PAULA SMITHER awoke late in the morning, feeling sluggish, almost dead. Her mind crawled from the gray haze of another world, where it had been trapped for the last—she glanced at the clock—fifteen hours now. Eleven o'clock? What was she thinking sleeping in so late? And for two days in a row.

She slid off the mattress and walked toward the bathroom. What a dream. Wow, what a dream.

It came back to her in little chunks, and she caught her step at an image that flashed through her mind—a scene she didn't think she was capable of imagining. She lifted a hand to her stringy brown hair and ruffled it.

But it had felt so real. Not like a dream at all. More like she'd actually been there with him, letting him touch her face like that.

Amazing. Repulsive. Lovely. She didn't know which. Maybe all three.

There was something wrong with Marsuvees. Something demonic and evil and snakelike. He was finding a way to slither into her mind and whisper things that made her hate him.

Unless, of course, he was really her guiding angel, revealing her true inner self to her false outer self. Purifying her. Cleansing her with the delicious, ugly, brutal, lovely truth.

Which was what? That she wanted to be loved? That she hated herself? That she despised wickedness because she knew that deep inside her bones there was the marrow of wickedness, and the only way to deal with that evil was to draw it out of the bones?

The sword of truth was dividing bone from marrow.

She brought her fingers up to her lips and stroked them gently, the way he had. *If* he had. She turned to the mirror. The woman who stared out at her was short and pudgy. But her hair was long and her complexion shimmered in the glass, smooth and tanned from the summer sun. Her eyes glistened above a small nose. Not too bad really.

Paula looked at her body in profile, draped in one of Steve's old T-shirts. Shapely if you looked just right. At least not huge like Nancy. The one small blessing of giving birth to only one child after three miscarriages.

She moved toward the shower, keeping her eyes on her figure as she walked—no, slinked—across the room, like one of those young models walking down the street in slow motion. Paula's shin slammed into the side of the tiled bath, and she doubled over. She grasped her leg.

"Crap!"

The shock of pain brought her mind out of its lazy spin. *Listen to you, Paula. Using language like that. What's gotten into you?*

Marsuvees, a small voice whispered. *Marsuvees Black.*

She stood up and stared at the mirror again. Another chunk of her dream came to her, the part about meeting the tall preacher in the church basement, right in her own Sunday-school room.

She looked back at her bed—the sheets had been kicked to the floor. It was a dream. Just a dream. Still, she had no business even dreaming things like that. She'd best forget the man altogether, push him right from her mind and pretend she'd never even seen him.

Marsuvees filled in her mind's eye, blue eyes flashing. *Wanna trip like I do, baby?* He licked his lips. She clenched her eyes and shook the vision from her head. What had become of her?

Bone from marrow, that's what had become of her.

Where was Steve? Come to think of it, he hadn't slept in their bed last night, had he? In fact, he hadn't been home for supper either, but he often ate at the bar. He hadn't bothered to call, though. He'd been gone all day, the least he could do was call. She was too preoccupied with her inner dividing of bone and marrow to worry about Steve, but now her mind buzzed with the realization that he hadn't come home. What was going on?

Paula took a quick shower, going through the routines of washing and drying, distracted by the thoughts that peppered her mind.

Steve was gone and she didn't know to where.

Marsuvees was here, in her mind, and he refused to leave.

Her memories of yesterday afternoon were fuzzy. The preacher had come to the bar, she remembered that, but her mind regarded the rest hazily. It was almost as if she'd slept through the afternoon. Maybe she had. Maybe she slept for a full day.

But that couldn't be—she remembered walking through that wind to the church and finding Nancy there, pigging out on Twinkies. Unless *that* had been a dream too. All this nonsense brought on by Black's bland, intoxicating . . . syrup.

Paula slipped into a pink shirt, ran a quick comb through her hair, and walked out into the living room.

"Steve?"

The house was silent.

And where was Roland? Heaven only knew. The boy rarely spent the summer days indoors.

"Steve!" she yelled. She walked past the kitchen to his study, which was really just a place he messed around in. Empty. She checked the rest of the house quickly, now thinking she must be missing some event that the rest of the town was attending, like another meeting at the saloon with Marsuvees. The minister. Not "Marsuvees," but "the minister." *Come on, Paula, get a grip.*

Wanna trip like I do, baby?

She hurried to the front door, opened it, and stepped onto the porch. Dark cumulus clouds hovered low over the town, and a warm wind whipped through the trees, carrying stray leaves and dust through the street.

Summer wind. She loved the wind. Especially when the sun was out like it was now.

She glanced first up and then down Main Street. Deserted. That was odd. Paula walked to the sidewalk. She took three steps toward Nails and Tan and stopped. No, she didn't want to go to the witch's palace.

Katie might think of herself as the one woman in Paradise who really knew about life, but under all that talk she was still nothing more than a small-town girl with a broken tanning bed.

Paula turned and walked toward the church. Leaves flew by. She could barely see the church for all the dust in the air.

Wanna trip like I do, baby?

The base of her brain tingled.

That's the most ridiculous thing I've heard in my life, "wanna trip," like I'm some kind of druggie or something.

Then she heard the first sound of life since waking. A *thump*. Not a wood-against-wood *thump*, as if a branch fell, but a metal-against-wood *thump*. Almost a *crack*. The sound triggered a memory. Her father used to cut the heads off chickens with an ax like that. On a stump. Right through those thin necks in one blow.

She turned to her right. If she wasn't mistaken, the sound had come from behind her own house. She glanced at the church that was still swirling in the thin mask of dust, then veered toward the alley that led behind the house.

The gate to the white picket fence Steve put in last year swung in the wind. She stepped through the opening and headed for the back lawn.

The *thump* came again, closer now, definitely from the backyard, she thought. And then three times in a row—*thump, thump, thump.*

Wind banging something? But it sounded deliberate.

Paula approached the corner of the house and decided at the last minute that a little discretion might be in order. No telling what was happening back there.

Thump!

She stepped up to the gravel that surrounded the house, edged up to the corner, and peered into the backyard. The some-assembly-required shed that had taken Steve three days to assemble stood next to the back fence, its door flapping in the wind. She would have to shut that before the storm came.

An ax head rose past the shed's low roofline and swung back down, out of view.

Thump!

Someone was back there with an ax!

Paula pressed her body against the wall, out of the shed's view. Steve? Sure, it had to be Steve. Who else would be cutting wood behind their shed?

This was ridiculous. She was just going to have to walk over there and find out what he was up to, wasn't she? Paula looked around the corner again, saw that the yard was empty, and stepped out into the open.

Her first two steps were normal, but then she crouched and shuffled quickly to the shed wall without really knowing why she should feel creeped out about Steve chopping wood.

The wind moaned around the shed.

What if he catches me like this? What if Steve stands up and sees me creeping up on him like this? He'll think I'm nuts. But what if it isn't Steve at all? Or Roland? What if it's Marsuvees? She froze at the thought.

That was absurd, of course. No matter how unorthodox his ways, he was a minister of the gospel. Grace and hope. Not some crazy woodsman.

The thought surprised her. Just yesterday, she was quite sure he was the devil. Now she was not only giving him the benefit of the doubt, but defending his sacred mission. Dividing bone from marrow.

She stepped forward, brought her head to the corner, and looked behind the shed.

Steve knelt on the ground with a hatchet raised above his tangled dark hair. He brought the ax down.

Thump.

Paula winced. A long stake rested against the chopping block at his knees, shaved to a sharp point by the ax.

Steve was sharpening a stake. No, not just *a* stake. A dozen stakes. At least twelve of the things leaned against the fence beside him, all pointy sharp. What could he possibly be thinking, turning branches into short fat spears?

The sweaty shirt clinging to his back was the same shirt he'd worn yesterday, only now it was streaked with dried dust. His hair was matted with sweat and speckled with small woodchips.

Thump!

He mumbled something, and for a moment Paula thought he'd seen her. She eased back.

He spoke again. "Shut up . . ." The rest was lost in the wind.

What was he doing, kneeling there like an idiot, whacking at those sticks? She was half-tempted to grab him by the ear. *Get up, you useless*

good-for-nothing. Get to work and make us some money or something. And
where were you last night, anyway?

You wanna trip like I do, baby?

Paula spun from the shed and ran toward the sidewalk. If the fool
wanted to make tent pegs or whatever he was making back there, let him.
She had this bone-and-marrow business to attend to.

The street was still empty. Dust swirls danced on the blacktop like a troop
of Tasmanian devils. A thin layer of the stuff covered the street and sidewalk.
She ran a finger over the top of the mailbox, clearing a swath of dust. She
glanced in, saw the box was empty, slammed it shut, and jumped at the *bang.*

Wanna trip, huh? Wanna trip?

Sure, baby, I'll show you how to trip.

Please, Paula, you're downright loose when you want to be.

Did that mean she *wanted* to be loose? Was that what her marrow was
telling her?

There was something she was supposed to be doing, but she couldn't
remember. Steve was back there making sticks.

"What's the world coming to?" She walked back into the house.

IF A visitor had driven through Paradise that Friday, he might have wondered if it was a deserted Colorado ghost town. So thought Johnny Drake
as he stared out the front window.

If the visitor hung around long enough, he might see a stray soul or a
dog braving the hot gusting winds, darting from one building to another.
But in five minutes of staring, Johnny hadn't seen either. From what he
could tell, the shops were closed. Their windowsills were filling with dust,
and the streetlight was out. Boiling black clouds kept the valley in a perpetual dusk.

There were no visitors. Not even a lost magpie.

Johnny had awakened late, sat up groggily, and forced his mind to clear.
The events of last night crashed through his mind.

Roland had agreed to come by his room when he woke up. But a quick
check of his bedroom window showed no Roland.

He pulled on the same shirt he'd worn yesterday and hurried out to the living room. "Mom?"

But she wasn't there. Johnny ran to his mother's room and cracked the door. She was still sleeping under the sheets.

"Mom?"

Sally moaned, made a halfhearted attempt to lift her head, then collapsed back on the pillow.

Johnny stepped in. "Mom, wake up."

"Go."

The way she said it sent a sliver of fear through his chest.

It was Black's poison—had to be.

At a loss, Johnny had come here, to the front window, pulled the curtain back, and stared at the ghost town called Paradise.

A thought occurred to him. The streetlight was out. What about the phones?

Johnny ran to the kitchen and picked up the phone. If they were going to call . . .

No dial tone. Not even a hiss.

He tapped the disconnect twice.

Nothing. The wind had blown over one of the poles or something. Unless it was Black.

Johnny stood in the kitchen, phone in hand, mind numb. Black was either an angel or the devil, and Johnny was completely confused about which. Or why. Or what, if anything, he could do about it. Or if he even *should* do anything about it. He didn't know how to drive, and with the storm blowing . . .

A bang sounded at the back of the house. Roland. He dropped the phone into the cradle and ran to his bedroom.

Roland stood at his window, freckled face pressed against the glass. Johnny hurried to the window, flung it open. His friend looked at him over bags that darkened his eyes.

"Hey."

"You okay?"

"Sure."

Roland climbed inside and looked around. "A bit . . . tired maybe but okay."

Johnny shut the window. "You look sick."

Roland faced him. "Peter came by. You should have seen what *he* looked like."

"Peter? What did he say?"

"He said we had to meet him and Fred at the theater."

"What for?"

"He didn't say. Just said to come."

"I don't know."

"You got a better idea?"

Johnny didn't have a better idea, because he didn't have any ideas.

"When? Now?"

"Sure, now."

Johnny looked at the dark clouds. "Okay," he finally said.

THEY HEADED out into the wind five minutes later. The trees bent under strong gusts, and Johnny had to cover his eyes to keep the dust out. They walked down the alley behind All Right Convenience, toward the Starlight.

They rounded the theater, glad to be out of the wind. "Man, this stuff's really blowing," Roland said.

"So where are Peter and Fred?"

Roland looked around—no sign of them.

"Maybe they already left."

A *thump* sounded on the wind, close.

Johnny spun. "What was that?"

"Something probably blew into the building."

Another thud shook the wall.

"That . . . that came from the far end."

"Or inside," Roland said. His own suggestion dawned on him belatedly and his eyes grew round. He ran to the wall and pressed his ear flat.

"Someone's inside!" He spun around and ran for the corner.

"Where you going?"

"Come on!"

Johnny rounded the corner cautiously. Knee-high grass swayed like a shifting sea. The carcasses of several rusty cars rose from the grass. A dilapidated wooden windmill leaned against the wall, creaking in the wind.

The wind gusted and lifted a board from the wall, then dropped it with a loud *thud*.

Roland strode for the loose siding. He was going in.

Now Johnny was confronted with a decision. On one hand, he knew without a doubt that whatever waited inside the old theater couldn't be good. On the other hand, he couldn't just run from whatever was happening to this town. Particularly not when he had nowhere to run to.

"Hold on."

"They're in there, I heard them."

"Just hold on!" Johnny caught up to him and grabbed his shoulder. "How do you know it's them? You can't just barge in there like you own it."

"I heard music, man. You know anyone else who would be listening to music in the Starlight?"

"Just"—he nudged Roland to one side—"let me take a look."

He gripped the board by the bottom edge and lifted it.

Nothing jumped out at him or bowled him over, and the board was loose enough, so he lifted it higher. The nails had been pulled. Whoever was in there had taken a hammer or a crowbar to the wall to get in.

Together Roland and he shoved the board high, then eased their heads into the dark foot-wide gap.

The first thing Johnny saw were the theater's arching rafters, flickering with white light. Fire? Then he heard the music, pounding from somewhere inside. A wall stood between them and whoever was inside the main hall.

"That's Peter and Fred for sure," Roland said.

"Just stay behind me. And if I run, you run."

"Okay. Lighten up, sheesh."

Johnny squeezed through the opening. Roland followed. The board clunked closed. Protected from the howling wind, he could hear the music loudly now. An eerie, melancholic, thumping rock and roll. Gothic. Evil.

He edged forward—stage door on the right. Carefully, fighting every ounce of good reason, Johnny turned the knob and pulled the door open a crack.

The volume escalated. White light sputtered on the walls inside. No monsters. He pulled the door wider and eased his head through.

Light flashed from a box set on the stage, splashing white across the auditorium in staccato pulses. Three figures jerked in the strobe.

Dancing? More like writhing.

Johnny's heart climbed into his throat.

The auditorium had been ransacked. The place was dirty when he last saw it, two years earlier, but not trashed like this. It took a few seconds for the images to register, because they came at him in flashes of light. The long curtains hanging on the walls were shredded from top to bottom, and the old wooden seats had been torn from their anchors and scattered like a box of spilled jacks. Bottles and cans littered the floor—dozens of them, spilling liquid that sparkled in the light. Someone had spray-painted haphazard lines across the walls and huge Gothic letters on the torn screen.

Screw Hope!

In the middle of it all, the three figures jerked about, like stoned teenagers in a mosh pit.

Roland's head pushed past his arm.

The identity of the largest figure was clear. The bulky body teetering and twitching like a tortured penguin could only belong to Peter's father, Claude Bowers. He faced the flashing box, which Johnny now saw was actually a television set. His hands swayed to the music, creating the strange illusion that his arms were electric cords delivering shocks that convulsed his body.

Ten feet behind and to the left, the second man jerked back and forth like a bebopping bowling pin. He had an ax in his hands, and for one terrifying moment Johnny thought the man might be Roland's father. But then a flash lit the face and Johnny saw Chris Ingles, smiling like a vampire with bulging eyes.

He heard a gasp from Roland. Then he saw what Roland was looking at. The third figure was a boy his size, jumping up and down like a pogo stick.

Peter.

He tugged at Roland's collar, jerked him back through the door.

"You see that?" Roland whispered and stuck his head back in. Johnny hesitated a moment and then took another look.

The whole scene looked like something he might expect from a dream—a nightmare or a scene from an MTV music video—but this wasn't any of those. This was Peter and his father and Chris Ingles in the Starlight Theater in Paradise, Colorado, population 450. Writhing to headbanging music. And by the looks of it, they'd been at it awhile.

The ax man, Chris Ingles, spun and let loose a scream. He jumped from the stage, swung his ax above his head like a tomahawk, and took a swipe at one of the toppled theater seats. The chair cracked and flew across the room. Chris let out another whoop and resumed his lurching dance in front of the stage.

The smaller form—Peter—scooped up a bottle at his feet, cocked his arm back like a pitcher, and hurled the object at the television set. With a loud pop the tube exploded. Just like that, *boom*, and the room fell into darkness and total silence.

A flame from a lighter flickered to life, highlighting Claude Bower's sweaty face. The three stood dumbstruck, arms hanging limp, chests rising and falling.

"Who did that?" Claude asked with a heaving voice.

Peter took a step back.

"You do that, Peter?" Claude spoke as if the boy had just slapped him for no reason. "What . . . what you do that for?"

Johnny could hear his own breathing now. He shut his mouth and drew air through his nose. They should have left already, but Johnny teetered in that awful place between *must* run and *can't* run.

Claude stared at his son through the wavering flame, and for a moment Johnny thought he might actually take after him.

Then he did. He shrieked obscenities and lunged forward.

Peter spun and let out a yelp. He took three steps before his father's hand caught him and together they tumbled to the floor, crushing the lighter's flame under them. The room went black. Piercing shrieks echoed through the theater.

Roland bolted forward. "You sick son of . . ."

Johnny swiped at him, grabbing shirt, then air.

The room was too dark to see Roland running, and Peter's wails covered the sound of his feet.

Now Johnny was faced with another critical decision: to save Roland from sharing Peter's fate or to make a quick escape now, while he could.

He took off after Roland.

Problem was, he couldn't see.

And then he could. Light flared from a rag Chris Ingles had stuffed into a bottle. Johnny heard the sound of swishing liquid.

Johnny pulled up a third of the way down the right aisle. Roland took three more steps, placing him near the front. He slid to a stop.

Claude must have seen the boy, because he froze, fist raised over Peter, head turned toward the auditorium.

The intrusion seemed to disorient Claude. Chris Ingles was a statue—legs spread wide, torch licking the air beside his face, eyes ogling Roland.

Johnny and Roland were rooted in the aisle.

Peter wailed.

Claude released his son and stood up. Peter was still screaming bloody murder. Claude slapped his head with an open hand. "Shut up."

Peter whimpered and then shut up. Out of obedience or unconsciousness, Johnny couldn't tell.

Claude stepped over his son's body. "You guys bring anything?"

What?

"Yeah, we're looking for more stuff," Chris said.

"You have a TV?" Claude asked.

"Yeah, do you have a TV?" Ingles repeated.

Claude looked at Roland. "How about the TV from your dad's bar. You think he'd mind if we borrowed it?"

Roland wasn't responding.

"Listen, you little creep!" Ingles snapped. "He's asking you a question. It's a simple question. Just answer the stupid question, you dope. If you don't tell us, we're going to come down there and slap some sense into you. So shut your trap and just tell us what—"

"Shut up, Chris," Claude said.

Ingles looked at the big Swede. "I was just—"

"I said, shut up!" He was yelling. "Shut up, shut up, shut up!"

Chris looked like he'd been slapped. He swallowed. "Sheesh. I'm trying to get us a TV. If you want—ahhh!" Ingles screamed and jerked his hand from the bottle which had evidently gotten hot enough to burn him. The flame blinked out when the bottle hit the floor.

Darkness.

Johnny ran forward, grabbed Roland by his shirt, and tugged. "Come on," he whispered.

"Get that light back on!" Claude thundered.

"I burned my hand."

"It's dark," Peter said.

Johnny ran for the thin crack of light below the exit door. He slammed into the door. Yanked it open.

Claude yelled behind them. "Hey!"

They rushed through the service hall, crashed through the plank and out of the theater into the wind.

Johnny rounded the corner and pulled up, panting.

Roland looked back the way they'd come. "You see him hit Peter?" A crooked smile nudged his lips.

"You find that funny?"

"What are they doing?"

Good question. Or rather, why were they trashing the theater and going nuts over that television? It was crazy, plain and simple.

"What are we going to do?" Roland asked when Johnny didn't respond.

"I don't know. Maybe we should go get some help."

"How?"

A bang sounded inside the theater. Johnny glanced back. Coast was still clear. He headed for the street.

"Where you going?"

"Home. I have to get my mom up."

CHAPTER THIRTEEN

THE MONASTERY
Friday morning

SAMUEL STARED out of his father's study window at the black clouds roiling over the small town far below. "All because of one silly boy," he said.

"Not one silly boy," his father said.

Samuel turned, arms clasped behind his back. "Billy and Darcy. Two."

Dark rings circled his father's eyes, and his flesh seemed to sag around his cheeks. Samuel had never seen his father in such a state. He wanted to run over and hug him.

"Billy's called for a debate."

His father exposed his true concern, something he would guard even from the teachers. But he trusted his son, which made Samuel proud. "You yourself said that you expected it, Father. You told me that a month ago and again, last week, when Marsuvees Black left us. But you were sure that the power we have would all play to our advantage. You still believe that, don't you?"

David stared past him, his gaze distant and aimless. Samuel noticed that they were both standing with hands clasped behind their backs. Like father, like son.

"Yes," David said. "I've staked everything on that belief. You're right, the power in this place has always threatened to wreak havoc. And I've always believed good would prevail—it's why I left the university after your mother's death. But what if I'm wrong? And if I'm right, what will the cost be?"

Samuel walked up to his father and took his hand. When David had taken him for a long walk behind the monastery three days earlier and told him what was happening, without even the teachers' knowledge, Samuel thought his father was playing some sort of game with him. It took a full twenty-four hours for the implications to settle in. Billy had no real idea what he'd done.

But Samuel had the same power. An incredible fact. Then again, all of the children had the same power. And that was a bit frightening.

His father's eyes were glassy. "Can you imagine what would happen if this got out to the world, Samuel?"

"But it won't! We won't let it."

"It's not something we can control. Not now."

"My whole life you've taught me the power of Christ's love to overthrow evil. I know this is difficult for you, Father, but you have to believe what you've taught me."

David looked at his son. "Evil can be very powerful, Samuel."

"And so can love."

The door behind them opened. Samuel held his father's eyes one moment longer, then released his hand. He wasn't used to being the encourager in their relationship, but it felt right now. He was becoming a man, and his father needed him. The realization was both daunting and satisfying.

Two teachers and two students walked into the study. Raul and Andrew ushered the children through the door.

"Hey, Tyler. Hey, Christine."

"Hey, Samuel." They'd both been here before, but a trip to the director's study was an unusual occurrence. Their eyes took in the setting.

David smiled, cloaking all traces of concern. "Thank you for coming. Have a seat, please." He indicated the chairs around the redwood table.

"Thank you, sir," Christine said.

Tyler let Christine sit first. "Thank you, sir."

They grinned at Samuel. Tyler and Christine were both orphans from India and they, like some of the others, had taken to speaking in accents from their mother countries.

"Excuse us for just a moment." David walked toward the adjacent conference room. "Raul, Andrew, please follow me."

They walked into the room and closed the door.

Samuel sat and looked at his friends. Were they strong enough to stand up to Billy? No doubt. His father's concerns were overstated. "You guys eat already?"

"Yes," Tyler said. "Have you guys noticed how quickly they shut down the cafeteria these last two days?"

"No," Christine said. "Two o'clock like always."

"But two sharp?" Tyler snuck a look at the conference-room door and lowered his voice. "The overseers just seem a bit rushed. In fact, I'm not sure they aren't a bit uptight in general. I snapped Christian's boxers in the bathroom this morning, and Andrew happened to be walking by. He told me to grow up. That sound like Andrew to you?"

"Boys," Christine said, rolling her eyes. "How does snapping boxers translate to fun in that lofty mind of yours?"

"It translates as easily as pinning back your hair or painting your nails," Tyler said.

"I paint my nails for beauty. Beauty is intrinsically valuable."

"And I snapped Christian's boxers for humor. Humor's also intrinsically valuable."

Christine thought about that. "Point made."

"I still think the overseers need to lighten up a bit."

"I'll be sure to mention this to the director the moment he steps back in," Christine said with a smirk. "All overseers to ease up on the fun-seekers of our cherished clan."

She turned to Samuel. "So what's this all about?"

The enormity of her ignorance struck him as tragic. This was about the end of all things as they knew it. About the beginning of something either very good or very bad. How could he explain this to two kids who were for the moment preoccupied with snapping shorts and painting nails?

The door opened, saving Samuel from an answer. One look at Andrew and Samuel's gut tightened. The man's face was white. Raul looked concerned as well, but not like Andrew. Perhaps Raul had more faith in Christine than Andrew did.

They crossed the room and sat opposite Christine and Tyler. His father regarded them with unusual gravity.

Christine glanced at Samuel, any trace of a smile now gone. "What's wrong?"

"At least that much is obvious," David said. He drew a deep breath. "Christine, Tyler . . . We are very proud of you both. In fact it's my confidence in you that brings you here. I've watched you both and I see that your character is strong." He smiled.

Christine folded her hands. "Thank you, sir."

Tyler followed her example. "Thank you, sir."

"Good. Then let me tell you what I just told Andrew and Raul. Billy has challenged the school's prevailing rule of love in the first debate of its kind in the history of Project Showdown." He let the statement settle in.

"A debate?" Tyler asked. "Billy's arguing against love? What on earth would make him do that?"

"He and Darcy have entered the forbidden tunnels below the monastery," David said.

"They've what?" Christine demanded. "How could they do that?"

"Oh, it's quite simple, really. There's no lock on the door. Billy was the first to go in. He convinced Darcy to follow. This morning Billy issued his challenge. He'll argue against our assertion that love leads to the Creator and that the discovery of love is the point of our lives. It seems he's found something besides love to satisfy him. The debate will be held tomorrow before all the students. In the end, a two-thirds vote by the students will determine the course we will take. If Billy wins, he will determine what is taught here and who teaches it. He will also establish new rules, which can be overthrown only by a similar challenge and a two-thirds vote."

Christine jumped up. "He's a fool!" She relaxed her fists and sat. "Forgive me, I meant no disrespect, but he's the biggest fool. Not only for entering the tunnels, but for thinking that he can persuade two or three much less two-thirds of us to side with any twisted philosophy he tosses out."

"Why can't we just lock Billy up?" Tyler asked.

Samuel watched his father. Not even the teachers knew the real reason, though what the overseers accepted as truth was compelling enough. What good would it do to create a monastery full of noble savages with the potential to reshape society, and then, having failed, to lock them up? If they ultimately failed, then they would be put back into society to continue with the rest of spoiled humankind.

But if the children survived tests like this one, they would be even stronger in their faith, and their impact on society would be even greater. This is what the teachers believed. And part of it was true.

But only part of it.

Samuel's father finally spoke. "We can't, Tyler. You'll have to trust me on that. No one is forced here. The effects of forcing Billy's hand could be far more devastating than any of us imagines."

Samuel wondered if the two teachers caught his father's insinuation that the stakes were higher than they knew. Andrew stared at him with searching eyes. Raul looked at the bookshelf, expression blank.

"Who will he debate?" Christine asked.

"By rule it has to be a student. I have—"

"What kind of rule is that? Excuse the interruption."

"Not only a student, but one of five that he chooses," David said. "It's a rule that places the ultimate responsibility in any one of the students' hands. We are only as strong as our weakest links, both in life and in here. Billy put five students' names forward. I have chosen you, Christine."

"Me? It should be Samuel!"

"Samuel wasn't an option. It will be you."

Raul cleared his throat. "I must express my objection. I think we're going too fast. Having this debate tomorrow is premature. She needs time to prepare."

"No, no, that's not our call," Andrew responded. "I've looked up the rules. The debate must be held within twenty-four hours." It was odd that even the teachers were foggy on the rules of debate, Samuel thought. Then again, they'd never had to know.

"What on earth for?" Raul demanded. "If the future of the monastery is at hand, we should all tread carefully."

David held up a hand. "We've been treading carefully for twelve years. As it is now, Billy hardly stands a chance. The more time we give him, the stronger his argument will become. Time favors him, not us. The debate will be held tomorrow morning."

"And Billy will debate me?" Christine asked, still unconvinced.

"You know what he's going to argue," Samuel said. "I say throw it back in his face. Make him grovel and cry for mercy."

That earned him a few smiles.

"Oh, you can bet I will. Trying to argue that love has no trajectory, much less one set for our Maker, is like trying to argue that we are nothing more than a sea of slugs, inching aimlessly about in the dark. You're sure this is the basis of his argument?"

"I doubt he'll cast it in those terms," David said. "But in the end all arguments end there. You'll do fine, Christine."

She nodded. "And what happens to Billy when he's defeated?"

"Nothing."

"Nothing? Could he cast another challenge?"

"Not for three days."

"I think it's too soon," Raul said. "They're still children, for heaven's sake. They could drag us all down."

"Then, in the eyes of some, our project will have failed," David said.

"And not in the eyes of others?" Andrew asked.

David didn't respond.

CHAPTER FOURTEEN

PARADISE

Friday morning

PAULA WANDERED around her house without really knowing what she was doing. Oh, she did the dishes and made the bed, but she knew there was something else she should be doing. Problem was figuring it out.

It came to her out of nowhere. A blue streak of desire so deep that she gasped right there in her hallway.

Wanna trip, baby?

She left the house and walked up the street toward the church. The streets were still deserted, and the thumping sound was still coming from behind the house. *Get a clue, Steve. Please.*

Wanna trip?

Her pulse quickened and she quickened her pace. Steve could rot in hell for all she cared.

She found the front doors to the church locked. They were never locked. She walked to the side and entered through the office, hoping that Stanley and that fat secretary of his had left for lunch early or something.

Now come on, Paula, you have no right calling people fat. That could be you in twenty years.

But she is fat. Paula walked through the kitchen to the back stairs. *Fat as a cow.*

"Hello, Paula."

Paula gasped, startled. Nancy stood in the back-office doorway holding a large brown grocery bag. She wore a yellow cotton dress that made Paula think of a gunny sack with two holes cut out for those pudgy arms and another for her thick neck. A white substance that must be butter or frosting had dried on Nancy's left cheek.

"Don't scare me like that," Paula said. "Where is everybody?"

Nancy stared at her and held up the bag as though apologetic. "I just had to run to the store." She walked into the office without another word.

Paula breathed a quick sigh of relief and turned down the stairwell. See, now there was another weird thing. Nancy was fat enough as it is. No need to clean out Claude's store.

Wanna trip, huh? Like I do?

Paula stopped halfway down the stairs, her heart in her throat. What was she doing? Where was she going, anyway?

Down to the basement. To divide bone and marrow. Down to her office to trip.

Or at least to check on her Sunday-school room, just to make sure that everything was in order for Sunday service. Never could take the responsibility of teaching the children too seriously, right? Never.

When she landed on the gray carpet and rounded the corner to the all-purpose room, tingles were sweeping through her belly. Goose bumps fanned out at the base of her skull. *You shouldn't be here, Paula.*

Trip, trip, trip. Say it like that, baby. Say it like you mean it.

The room yawned vacant and still. She stepped across it lightly, barely breathing. The door to her office was cracked, but she often left it open. It was her office all right, given to her as the Sunday-school coordinator. The sign on the door said it in brass.

Paula reached the office, ran her sleeve over the brass plate, glanced back to the empty stairwell once, and pushed the door open.

The room was shrouded in darkness. Empty? Of course it was empty. What did she expect? She reached in and flipped the light switch. Four fluorescents stuttered to life.

Her desk sat as she had left it, neat and tidy with her little gray chair shoved under. The room was indeed empty, and an awful sense of disappointment ran through her chest. *Yeah, I'll show you how to trip, you freak show.* Her anger surprised her. *Trip this!* She flicked the air with her tongue.

Now that was forward. She did it again. Goodness, she was a regular sex bomb.

Paula stepped into her office and sighed. What had she come here for again?

A large black body moved to her left and she yelped.

Then she saw the whole of him, and her peripheral vision clouded. He stood there, tall, dressed in the same black trench coat he seemed never to take off, smiling under those sapphire eyes.

"Marsuvees!"

The initial shock fell away, and a cold wave of relief washed down her back. She smiled sheepishly.

He raised his shoulders in a shrug and chuckled. A low, empty chuckle that echoed through the room and bounced around in her skull. Paula felt a stab of fear.

"Paula . . . ha." He ended her name with air, and then clacked his teeth shut, as if taking a small bite out of the air.

Her name came to her like a soothing salve. An image of him standing up at the pulpit, commanding the attention of every last soul in town, ran through her mind.

"Hi." Her voice sounded like a squeak.

"I didn't mean to startle you. I just thought you might come here and . . ." He smiled warmly. "Well, I wanted to show you something."

See? He's so gentle, really. Just like in my dreams.

He looked at her without moving for a long time, until she thought she could feel the heat coming to her from those blue eyes.

"You know the story about the woman caught in adultery?" he asked.

Her heart skipped a beat. "Yes."

He took a step toward her. "You know, now there's a story of grace, Paula. I mean real grace. Don't you think?"

Wanna trip, baby, huh? Wanna, wanna?

"I guess." She took a step backward.

"Do you want to know what the truth of it was, Paula? I'll tell you. The truth of it was that the woman was no worse than the rest of them. They were all the same. All covered by grace. That's the truth of it, Paula. You have any bad thoughts toward anybody lately? Like Steve maybe? Because if you have, you are no better than that woman there in the story."

What was he saying? Of course she knew what he was saying. He was saying that if you think it, you might as well do it. The consequences are the same.

"The consequences are the same, Paula," Marsuvees said. "Either way, you don't get stoned."

She was feeling that tingle in her belly again.

Wanna trip with me? Wanna, baby?

"Yes," she said.

She wasn't sure whom she had said yes to then. Maybe to herself. She had stayed faithful to Steve for fifteen years without so much as looking at another man. Not that there was much to look at around here, but she'd never even had the desire. Now a man sent from God was hitting on her, telling her there was plenty of grace to go around, and Steve was sitting in the backyard losing his mind. Maybe she was losing hers as well.

He'd said that he was here to prepare them to withstand something bad. Something evil that would kill them if they didn't see things his way. He'd come to bring them the sword of truth.

Marsuvees walked toward her.

A wave of heat broke over her crown and cascaded down her shoulders. She could feel tiny beads of sweat popping from the pores on her forehead. It occurred to her that she wasn't wearing any makeup. *If he gets too close, he'll see the pimple on my jaw.* Thank goodness she'd taken a shower.

Wanna trip with me?

"Yes," she said again, and this time she knew she was answering that voice in her head. *Yes, yes, yes!*

No, Paula. No, no, no. This isn't grace and hope.

It's love. Love, love, love.

Love?

Do you want to trip? Do you want love?

Yes.

Marsuvees came within a foot of her and reached a hand to her face. She stood there trembling, wanting his touch unlike she had wanted anything in her memory.

She looked into his eyes, deep, where they became sapphire pools of safety. His hand rose to her cheek and then ever so lightly he touched her, at the corner of her parted lips.

She closed her eyes and let her mind fall.

"Meet me here," he whispered into her ear. She caught a faint whiff of his breath. It smelled sanitized. Like rubbing alcohol.

"After the meeting," he whispered. And then she felt his warm wet tongue on her neck. It ran up her cheek, past her ear, and right up into her hair. She shivered with pleasure and edged forward, wanting to feel his body more than she imagined possible.

"Tomorrow night, precious. Then everything will make sense." He pulled back.

"Yes," she said. His saliva began to dry cool on her cheek.

Tomorrow night?

She opened her eyes.

He was gone.

Gone! Her heart crashed to the ground, as if it had been held in a glass that someone dropped. She hurried to the door and scanned the outer room.

Empty.

Paula walked shakily to her desk and sat down heavily. What was she thinking? Bile rose to her throat and she felt she might throw up, right here on the desk.

Paula set her head in her hands and began to sob. But they really weren't sobs of horror or remorse anymore. They were sobs of self-pity.

She wanted to trip. She really, really did.

CHAPTER FIFTEEN

THE MONASTERY

Friday morning

"YOU'RE PUTTING words in my mouth," Paul cried. "Did I say I *want* to go down?"

"Sure you did," Darcy replied. "Want is part of curiosity. We all know you want. Now it's only a matter of your rights."

He looked confused, Billy thought. But he was caving already. It had been Darcy's idea to pursue the other students so soon. "If *I* went for it, then Paul will go for it. And if Paul goes for it, there's no telling how many we can get."

It had been her idea, but Billy made it his task. They would approach students strategically, beginning with Paul. *Well, swallow this, Paul.*

Darcy pressed. "As you said, Paul—and you're quite correct in saying—you possess full control over what is yours. Such as your will. And your rights. See, and you were prepared for a long drawn out argument. But it's very simple, really. You *do* have the right to do whatever you wish."

"But it's wrong."

"Says who?"

"Says them."

"But it's your right to decide what's right. Right?"

"My right?"

"Yes," Billy said. "And we know what you want. You want to go to the lower levels and have a peek. Like Darcy did. Because you look at Darcy here, and you think she looks quite well for one who's done the forbidden. And now you want to know what it feels like."

Paul's hesitation told Billy that he had his third convert. It took another twenty minutes of discussion, slowly whittling down Paul's increasingly meager objections, to get to the final point.

"So there you have it," Darcy said, grinning.

"So there I have it? Just like that?"

"Just like that. Let's go."

Paul balked. "Go? What do you mean go? Just go?"

"Yes. You exercise your will and you just go. Anything less would be denial of what your heart and your mind are telling you." Darcy stood. "Come on."

Paul stood shakily. "I don't know."

"Of course you don't. How can you know what you haven't tried? Look at me, do I look worse off?"

She scratched her neck, and Billy wondered if Paul noticed her light rash.

"Just a peek?"

"Just a peek."

"Okay, but just a peek."

Billy chuckled and slapped Paul on the back. "Just a peek. Don't worry, this will all be moot tomorrow anyway."

"How's that?"

Billy glanced at Darcy and winked. "I've challenged the monastery rules. No one knows yet, but tomorrow I'll defeat Christine in a debate and open the lower tunnels for all the students."

Paul was back to his bug eyes. "You're serious? Tomorrow?"

"Tomorrow."

"Well, what if you don't win?"

"I will." Billy stood to his feet and brushed off his pants. "You ready?"

"Now?"

"Why not? Just a peek, Paul. That's all you owe yourself. One small peek."

THEY STOOD in the vestibule, facing the huge black doors, three wide-eyed children.

"It's so dark down here," Paul said.

Billy pushed the black doors open.

"Don't be a wuss, Paul. You'll love it. The fear you're feeling is part of the fun. You'll see, I promise."

Billy and Darcy stepped past the door and waved Paul in. "Come on."

He walked toward them as if each step might set off a land mine. Funny how terrified he was. Billy's longing for the study was already mushrooming. *Hurry up, you spineless brat!*

Then Paul's head was in, craning for a view.

"Don't just stand there gawking. Come in!"

Paul stepped all the way in. But his heart remained outside, bouncing around the vestibule like a Super Ball. The thought made Billy chuckle.

He pushed the door closed behind Paul. *Clunk.*

They were in. Paul's words to Darcy rang in Billy's ears. *You went in there?* As if he thought she had tasted death itself.

Open your mouth, Paul boy. How does it taste?

Three thick pink worms writhed slowly under the torch's light on their right. Glistening bands of mucus trailed behind them. Billy could feel Paul trembling beside him.

"Wow . . ."

Darcy giggled. "Yeah, wow. I told you you'd like it." A faint rash had flowered on Darcy's lily-white Dutch neck—the same rash he'd developed. The tunnels had this effect. It was probably some kind of atmospheric thing.

"Wow."

The worms' pungent odor filled Billy's nostrils and made him impatient. He didn't have time for this nonsense.

"Come on." He turned and walked into the far right tunnel, leading the way with the torch. And then he was running toward the study, with Darcy at his side and Paul stumbling behind them, saucer-eyed.

They spent twenty minutes with Paul in the study, putting up with his foolishness. The dark passage sent him around a bend. He literally bounced off the walls of the small study, touching the books and examining the furniture—enough to make Billy wonder if they'd made a mistake in bringing him. Billy wanted to spend their time here exploring or

writing, not bouncing around like a lunatic. The distraction was annoying. Infuriating.

"What's this?" Paul asked. "You're writing a story together?"

Billy turned to the desk where Paul held his journal open, reading.

He and Darcy had stayed below deep into the night, exploring and reading and writing. In the end, mostly writing, a continuation of the story he'd
begun on his own. Darcy insisted on writing the women in it. "It takes a
woman to know a woman's true desires," she said. He chuckled and she lost
herself, bent over the book, intoxicated by her own creative power as much
as anything else in the dungeon.

"Put the book down. Mind your own business."

"Jiminy Cricket, Billy." Paul dropped the book onto the desk where it
landed with a slap. "I was thinking maybe I could write with you, but you've
turned into a raging monster."

"We're not saying you can't do things with us," Darcy said. "But you
have to take a deep breath and calm down. All your questions are getting
a bit annoying."

Paul seemed to shrug off her rebuke. He looked past the gate at the tunnel. "You want to go exploring."

Billy and Darcy exchanged a glance. "We've already explored."

"Well, maybe I'll find another bedroom or something. Or maybe I can
try one of the other halls."

Billy faced him, angered by the suggestion without knowing why. His
privacy was being trampled, though it had been at his insistence that Paul
had come.

"We have only one torch," Darcy said.

"Then come with me."

Billy did want to explore, but the thought of spending any more time
with the walking mouth called Paul made him nauseated.

"No, and the torch stays here."

Paul wasn't put off. "Then we'll make another." Without waiting for their
approval, he stripped off his shirt.

Billy watched as he tied it into a knot, thrust it onto the end of an old
broom handle he'd found in the corner, and turned the old torch upside

down over his contraption. Fuel leaked in flaming drips, igniting Paul's shirt. He laughed with delight and jumped aside to avoid a thin line of flame dripping to the floor.

"You won't have long," Billy said. "Maybe half an hour before that thing burns out and leaves you in the dark. Trust me, you don't want to get caught in those tunnels without a light."

Paul left the study without another word.

Billy glared after him and turned to find Darcy staring at him. "What?"

"You have a problem with him suddenly?" she asked.

"He just irritates me suddenly," he said.

"It's the tunnels."

"Yeah, well I hope he runs out of fuel and a bunch of centipedes get to him or something."

"Yeah, wouldn't that be something."

The idea grew on Billy. Maybe, if they were so fortunate, one of the big worms or a big leech or something would suck the blood from his head.

"We should follow him and lock him into a tunnel," Darcy said. "Let him starve."

"What? You have a problem with him suddenly?"

She smiled. "He just irritates me suddenly."

"Touché. What do we do?"

She looked at the desk. "Write?"

Billy sighed and walked to the book. He sat down, picked up his pen, and let his mind fall into the story. The world around him faded. Every word he wrote swallowed his senses entirely, leaving nothing left for distraction. He forgot about Paul; about the monastery; about the study; even about Darcy, until she plopped down beside him, knocking his arm.

He grunted and looked at her. *Oh, it's Darcy.* And then he went back to drawing his pen across the paper.

For a long time the only sounds he heard were sounds of heavy breathing and the scratching of pens. Those and the voices from his story in which he'd lost himself.

Billy filled a page and turned to the next, dabbing his pen in the inkwell as he did. He used red because red was the color of blood and blood brought life. And death.

A scream echoed faintly in his mind and he thought, *The people in my story are screaming.* He pressed his pen more firmly into the paper. The screaming grew louder, and he absently wondered if it was from pleasure or pain, because he couldn't tell by the sound alone. He would have to see their faces. He smiled at that.

The scream ripped through his skull like a blaring siren and he jerked upright. He swung to Darcy and saw her wide eyes. She'd heard it too. As one they spun to the door.

Paul stumbled up to the gate and pulled up, panting. He'd lost his torch. Black streaks ran down his bared chest. He gawked at them with round eyes.

Then, as if a film director had called "cut!" he straightened, grinned, and walked into the study.

Paul stood there in the flickering light, breathing hard and smiling stupidly. Something wet matted his hair and leaked down onto his face.

"Hey," he said.

Billy just stared. He should be writing instead of babysitting this hyperactive punk.

"Where you been?" Darcy asked. Billy heard annoyance in her demand too.

"Around."

Billy felt his mind drifting back to the story he'd been writing, but then he remembered that Paul had come screaming down the hall like a maniac, and he thought maybe it would be interesting to find where the bugger had been. "What did you find?"

"I found some stuff to eat," Paul said, holding out his hand.

Billy and Darcy stepped forward and looked into the outstretched hand. The same gooey substance on his chest filled his palm.

"What is it?" Darcy asked.

"It's like honey," he said, raising his hand to his mouth. He licked at his palm slowly, not bothering to remove his eyes from them as his tongue dipped into the mucus and withdrew back into his mouth. He swallowed and smiled.

"Honey." He held out his hand. "Try some."

Looked familiar, but Billy couldn't place it. He impulsively reached out, rolled his index finger through Paul's open palm, and brought the honey to his lips.

Only it wasn't honey. Tasted like nothing. He swallowed it, wondering where Paul had found the stuff. It didn't taste too bad, really. He reached for another helping as Darcy went for her first.

The room seemed to shift around him. He blinked and stared around. The furniture moved to the dancing flames.

"Wow. It's like a drug." He looked at Darcy who was smiling and nodding like a reflection in a distorted carnival mirror.

He turned back to Paul. "You lost your torch."

"Yeah. Can I write with you guys?"

Billy was too amiable to disagree. He shrugged.

There wasn't enough room for three at the small writing table, so they made Paul move to the coffee table, where he dropped to his haunches and opened one of the journals. They answered his questions about the story but finally told him to shut his mouth and just write something. He frowned in protest. But he did shut his mouth.

An hour passed before Darcy's voice interrupted Billy's stupor.

"The light's dying."

He jerked his head up. The flame was indeed waning. Billy grabbed the torch from the wall.

"Okay, let's go."

He led them back down the hall at a jog. If the flame died, there would be no way to relight it, and he didn't fancy stumbling through pitch-black tunnels.

He glanced at the wall and saw one of the worms throbbing in the light. *Worm hall. We'll call it Worm Hall.* He looked at another oozing that familiar gel.

An image of Paul smiling, holding out an open palm, popped into his mind and he slid to a halt. Paul and Darcy ran past and then pulled up.

"What?" Darcy asked, breathing hard.

Billy brought the flame closer to one of the worms. Its excretions oozed down the wall, a thick mucus reeking of week-old socks. That same odor he'd come to love. But something else tugged at his mind.

"Paul?"

Paul stood smiling at the worm, eyes flashing in the flickering flame. He walked past Billy and scraped his fingers along the wall, through the worm's trail. His hand came away dripping with the mucus. He sniffed his hand, sampled the creamy gel, and stuffed what remained into his right pocket.

He looked up to Billy. "We should take some of this up with us, don't you think?"

For a moment Billy didn't know what to think. On one hand, the mere thought that he had ingested these gargantuan slugs' droppings revolted him. On the other, he felt an odd craving for the taste. And then Darcy walked over to the wall, swiped a wad of goo from the worm's trail, and shoved it into her blouse.

"I suppose it would be okay."

CHAPTER SIXTEEN

PARADISE
Friday

FOR THE first time since Marsuvees Black came to town, Johnny began to feel the deadening effects of the poison.

The sluggishness hit him as he ran behind Smither's Saloon and angled for home by way of the back alley. On his right, Katie's Nails and Tan shifted. He pulled up and caught his breath.

The building looked normal, but he could have sworn . . .

The wall on his right shimmered, then returned to its solid state.

Johnny began to run. His head pounded with a dull ache. What was happening to them? Whatever it was, things were getting worse. Why wasn't anyone coming in from Delta? They might still be in some kind of storm, but wouldn't anyone notice that there were no calls or anything coming out of Paradise?

Then again, hardly anything ever came out of Paradise.

He stopped by the back door, settled himself, and looked back toward the alley. Seemed normal enough now. Except for the wind and dust and leaves and the constant dusk, even though it was midday—but at least he was seeing normal.

He pushed into the house and stood stock-still. Howling wind outside, total silence inside.

"Mom?"

He hurried to her room, dreading what he might find.

Sally was still in bed, sheet pulled over her head. He had to make another decision. Either Black was who he claimed to be, a minister of truth sent by God to save Paradise, or he wasn't. If he wasn't . . .

Johnny stared at his mother's prone form and thought about that. If Black wasn't who he claimed to be, then he was the opposite. A liar, a snake, the devil himself maybe.

Whoever he was, the people of Paradise were following him like lambs, either to safer pastures or to the slaughter. But which?

A shaft of pain ran through his head. Johnny pressed a hand against the spot and strode up to his mother's bed. The frustration pent up in his chest boiled over. He tightened both hands into fists and yelled at her.

"Mom!"

Sally groaned.

Again, long-winded this time.

"Mommmm!"

This time she jerked her head up and twisted it around. "What?" Her eyes were round and lost, surrounded by dark circles.

"What are you doing?" she asked.

Looking at her haggard face, Johnny was at a loss for words.

"What do you think you're doing standing at the end of my bed like some crazy bat?"

But?

"Get out of here, Johnny!" She thrust her finger at the door. "Get out of my room."

"It's going crazy, Mom. Do you know what time—"

"What's going crazy? You're going crazy, boy. Out!"

Johnny felt trapped. Betrayed. Frantic. He nearly turned and ran.

Nearly.

"Listen to yourself." He stepped forward, not back. "I'm your son and you're yelling at me like I'm a crazy bat! You were dreaming of bats, weren't you? Only it was Black who was the bat, not me." He tapped his chest. "This is Johnny, not a bat. You've been sleeping for over fourteen hours and your eyes are glazed over and you're yelling at me when all I'm trying to do is wake you up because the world is falling down around our ears!"

Sally stared at him, taken aback. Then she turned and dropped on her back, hands on her face. She exhaled forcefully and groaned. "Sorry . . . I don't know what my problem is. I . . ." She stalled.

"I do. It's that stuff Katie gave you yesterday. And I don't think that's all. Black's destroying our town."

"Please, Johnny, not this again."

"Take a look. Just look outside and tell me it's all fine."

She propped herself on her elbows, stared at him with dazed eyes, and finally agreed. "Fine."

Thirty seconds later they stood at the front door peering out into the dust-whipped dusk-at-midday. She'd see it now, Johnny was sure of it.

His head hammered with pain, then settled into a numb buzz. The sky brightened. The wind eased; the dust settled; the sun broke through. For a few inexplicable moments Paradise seemed less in the clutches of a dark storm than weathering a common summer wind. Johnny lost track of time.

A musty scent filled his nose. *Tastes like nothing.* He wouldn't mind tasting that nothing.

"And?" Sally said. "So we have a storm."

Johnny swallowed and his vision cleared. More accurately, he cleared his vision. Or had he? Somewhere in the back of his mind his mother's voice echoed softly.

And . . . So we have a storm.

Not the response he was looking for. But this new mystery swallowed his mind.

He blinked and stared out at the street, relaxing, searching for what he'd just seen. Again the air cleared. Again the wind eased. Again the sky lightened. His concentration faded, but he forced himself to focus.

The facade vanished. Dark clouds hung low overhead.

Was that what his mom was seeing?

This is what his mom was seeing.

They didn't see what he saw! They were somehow blinded to the true nature of the darkness that had settled over Paradise. So then Black's drug not only opened their eyes to things that weren't really happening, but it blinded them from seeing what *was* happening!

Unless all of it really was happening. Worst case.

Or unless Johnny was seeing Paradise as dark and terrible when it really wasn't.

"A little wind never hurt anyone," Sally said, leaving Johnny by the door.

He turned inside. "How dark is it out there? I mean . . . are the clouds black?"

"Dark? It's a windstorm, not a rainstorm."

"But there's clouds in the sky, right?"

"Sure. So what?"

"How many clouds?"

"Johnny, please . . ."

"I just want to know what you're seeing. Because when I look out I see endless low black clouds, worse than I've ever seen."

Her eyebrows met. "You're not serious, right?"

"That's what I see."

"Then you're seeing things again. It's overcast, but not black."

So, he was right.

Then again, who was seeing the sky as it really was, he or his mom?

"Mom, would you do something for me if I begged you to do it? Something that may seem stupid but to me is real important?"

She sat on the couch and leaned her head back. "What?"

"Don't drink any more water. And don't leave the house or touch any more of that stuff Katie's drinking."

She closed her eyes and took a deep breath. But she didn't answer. Johnny thought she might be going back to sleep.

"Mom?"

"What?"

"Did you hear me?"

"Hear what?"

Wind whistled by outside. He closed the door and repeated himself.

"Sure, Johnny. Whatever you say."

Johnny's head began to throb again, but he kept focus.

"Promise me."

Sally's eyes closed and her mouth parted slightly. She was lost to the world.

Fine. Johnny would just make sure she didn't drink any water. They had enough pop and milk to hold them for a couple days if they were careful.

He left his mother sprawled on the couch and went in search of the water main.

THE MUSIC drummed through his mind. That incredible, haunting music that Peter and his father and Chris had been lurching to.

Roland had seen his mother leave the house and make her way in the direction of the church. His father was gone—probably at the bar. That left him alone in the house.

Last night he was frightened by all of Johnny's talk and seeing Black pull his lip off his face. This morning he felt a continuing sense of dread as they headed out in search of Peter. But something had changed in the theater.

He was furious when Claude took after Peter and beat him. But when he got so close to them, and when he heard Claude ask if he'd brought anything, his anger changed to curiosity. So freaky.

Cool freaky.

Peter's father didn't look mean or angry. He just wanted something and he wanted it bad. He looked like a boy asking for an ice-cream cone.

Only it wasn't an ice-cream cone he wanted. He wanted what was on that TV. And Roland had seen what was on that TV. He couldn't really remember the details, but he thought he might want it too.

Roland watched the street for nearly an hour after Johnny headed home, thinking things through, working up his courage. They hadn't come out of the old theater yet. At least not that he'd seen, and he'd only gone for a drink once and to the bathroom once, and even then he'd been watching as best he could.

What they could possibly be doing in there, he had no idea, but he was vacillating between sneaking back to the theater for a look and staying put. His dilemma had cost him three fingernails so far.

The weather was starting to ease up. Less wind, not so dark.

Johnny was right about one thing—that juice of Black's did something to people. It had done something to Fred and Peter, and frankly he wouldn't mind knowing a little more firsthand.

Still no sign of his mom or dad. They were probably out getting juiced up. What if he was the only one out of luck? He thought about going to Johnny's but immediately decided that was the last thing he wanted. No, he wanted to find out exactly—and by that he really did mean precisely, as in *been there, done that*—what Peter was up to.

Roland let his mind drift. Time seemed hazy. Once he looked at his watch and it was one o'clock and the next time it was two, but he was sure a whole hour hadn't gone by.

Three ghosts walked out in the waning dust storm. Three blind mice, wandering from the big building to the small building. One big mouse, one medium-sized mouse, and one—

Roland jerked his eyes wide. Claude, Chris, and Peter had come forth. They seemed to float from the old theater toward his father's saloon.

All alive. All pretty mellow. All walking straight.

Roland lost sight of them as they exited the front window's field of view. He ran to the bathroom and picked them up again. They walked right up the steps, pulled open the saloon door, and disappeared inside.

For a long time Roland just stared at the empty landing. An image of Claude pouncing on Peter skipped through his brain. He swallowed. Freaky, man. Just plain freaky.

He began to pace. His head buzzed. He could/should just go and check it out, of course. But he shouldn't/wouldn't just go and check it out.

Johnny was yelling in one ear telling him to go bury his head under a pillow and not drink the water.

Roland was yelling in his other ear telling him he wasn't Johnny.

Could/should shouldn't/wouldn't freaky. Way freaky.

Another hour passed. He had to go. Could/would. He was missing out.

STEVE SMITHER walked along the back alley toward his saloon, carrying five more sticks under his arm. He'd already taken eight stakes into the saloon and hidden them under the bar. He wasn't sure when he'd taken them there—the hours were running together now like the letters of a foreign alphabet. Like Chinese letters. But he knew it was way past noon now, and he thought it must be Thursday. Or Friday. Maybe even Saturday. No, it couldn't be Saturday.

His dream kept popping in his mind, like a jack-in-the-box. Only it was Black-in-the-box, jumping up to say, *Surprise, Stevie! Oh, I'm sorry, is this your wife?*

Yeah, well, I've got a little surprise for you myself. He smiled wryly. Somewhere out there Paula was probably wondering where he was. But she would find out soon enough, wouldn't she? And then she would thank him.

He reached the saloon, mounted the steps, and dug for his keys. One of the stakes dropped to the ground and he swore. He fumbled in his pocket, pulled the key ring out, and bent for the fallen stake. A muffled bang filtered through the door, and he snapped upright.

What was that?

Someone's in your saloon, Stevie.

He froze there in the wind with one hand holding his keys and the other stretching over five cockeyed sticks ready to fall with the slightest movement. Muted laughter drifted through the door. He fingered through the ten or so keys, found the big brass one, and shoved it into the lock.

He pushed the door open. A loud crash. Howling laughter.

Yes, sirree, some fool was in his saloon. Well, he'd better not be. This saloon was closed, locked, off-limits to all fools, which meant *everybody*.

Another crash sounded, loud now. He glanced about the storeroom, set the stakes carefully on the floor with trembling hands. He reached the inner door and placed his hand on the knob.

Black-in-the-box popped up in his mind. *Not thinking too clearly are you?* It cackled past that plastic smile. *Not too clearly at all. You can't just walk in there unprepared.*

Another laugh peeled through the saloon, a shrill one that reminded Steve of Claude Bowers from down the street. He let go of the handle, shuffled back to where he'd set the stakes, and picked up the largest one. He swung it through the air, pleased at the small *whoosh* it made.

Wanna trip, baby? Here, let me help you trip.

Steve walked back to the door and shoved it open.

The three fools were there in the middle of his saloon, sitting on the only table left standing. Claude Bowers, Chris Ingles, and Peter, Claude's squirt kid. They looked at him with wide grins, like Black-in-the-boxes only without a box. He looked around the saloon.

The tables and chairs had been splintered into a hundred pieces that littered the floor like kindling. The large Coors chandelier over the pool table hung twisted and smashed so that only the white fluorescent housing looked familiar to him. The pool table glistened with a liquid. Maybe vomit. The heat began to rise up his body like an erupting volcano. Dozens of empty bottles stood along the windowsills and in groups around the floor, like bowling pins waiting to be toppled.

Steve felt his eyes bulge, felt the surge of blood in his temples. He looked to the right. The bar had been hacked at with a sharp tool of some kind. A large knife or an ax maybe. The bar stools were gone. Just gone.

Then he realized that they were on the floor, only they were splinters, not stools anymore. The front door had been ripped from its hinges and lay on its side.

"What in the fiery blazes is going on?"

He heard his voice asking the question, but he was thinking, *Where's Black-in-the-box*, because he knew this was really his doing.

Claude and gang were looking at him like he was a ghost who'd walked in on them.

"Hi, Steve," Chris said. "We didn't think you'd mind. Just having a little fun."

Black-in-the-box grinned in his mind. *Have a heart. They're not doing anything you wouldn't do. Let 'em trip, baby.*

"Didn't think I'd mind? What do you mean you didn't think I'd mind?"

Good for you, Stevie. You tell 'em.

"You little stinkin' weasels! How about I have a little fun with you?" He raised the stake in his hand like a bat. "How'd you like that?"

Peter—the little squirt who was picking his jaw with Steve's furniture—had an ax in his hand, and he laid it carefully on the table. *Clunk.*

You think putting that thing down somehow makes all this okay?

"Take it easy, Steve," Chris said. "We'll clean it up. Promise."

"Oh, I know you will, Chris. That's why I'm gonna let you live. If I didn't think you were gonna clean this up, I'd kill you." He lowered the stick and twirled it in his hand. "I'd run this stake right through your heart."

Now that would be a trip.

Chris chuckled. "Yeah. But we're gonna clean it up, right guys?" Neither Claude nor Peter answered and Chris glanced their way. "Right boys?"

"Of course, Chris," Claude answered, but he wore a crooked grin and Steve wasn't sure he liked the look of the fat man's smile.

"How about I give you exactly fifteen minutes to clean it up?" Steve said. "How about I come back in a quarter hour, and if you make this picture perfect I won't run this stake through your hearts?"

"Yeah," Chris said, chuckling nervously. "What's the use of living if you can't have a little fun now and then, right? We all have our kinds of fun, right, Steve? I mean you have yours"—he motioned toward the stick in Steve's hand—"and we have ours. But we'll clean it up. Swear it."

It was then, just as he was thinking that Chris had a point, that Steve remembered the eight stakes he'd hidden under the bar. He scanned the floor, searching for a sign of them. But wood was everywhere, broken into splinters.

A tiny sliver of fresh oak jumped into his vision. The rest of the wood faded into the floor and just that one little piece screamed up at him.

Here I am. And yes, I am one of your sticks. What do you think of that?

A dozen other splinters seemed to materialize. Steve's forehead began to throb. A sickening weight thudded into his gut like a bowl of thick oatmeal.

He jumped over to the bar. Rounded it. They had done it, hadn't they? They'd destroyed his sticks! He ripped the velvet draping away from the back of the bar.

The shelves were empty!

With a horrendous growl, Steve leaped over the bar and faced Chris. Black-in-the-box screamed in the back of his mind. *Do it, Stevie! Do him!*

Steve rushed.

The weasel raised an arm to protect himself. Steve stopped two feet from Chris, raised his stake high above his head, and swung it down with all of his strength.

Crack! Chris's forearm snapped like a twig. The man howled in pain and rolled into a ball. His right arm flopped onto the pool table at an unnatural angle. Steve raised the shaft again and beat down again.

Surprise, Chris! Say hello to my stake!

He brought the stick down again, and again, and again, feeling power rush through him like a drug that filled him with a hot pleasure.

Wanna trip, baby?

He hesitated and brought the stick down one last time. Chris crumpled, draped over the pool table, still.

Steve looked up at Claude and Peter, whose faces seemed carved of soap. He ran a hand along his stick and tried to wipe off the blood.

"Clean this up," he said and walked out the back, into the alley.

What a trip.

A boy stood in the alley, staring at him. He knew this boy. A rascal named Roland. This was his son.

"Beat it, boy."

Roland just stared at him with round eyes.

He almost said "beat it" again, but he decided not to bother. Roland was a big boy and could fend for himself. He probably didn't have the guts not to beat it.

Steve headed into the forest behind the bar. He looked back five paces past the first row of trees.

Roland wasn't beating it after all. He was already at the back door, peering in. Steve chuckled.

What a very major trip.

CHAPTER SEVENTEEN

PARADISE

Saturday morning

MOM WAS holding her own, Johnny thought, but that wasn't exactly encouraging considering what her own was. His mother had already half-lost it. She wasn't like Claude or Chris, but she wasn't her old self either. And no amount of prodding convinced her to explain herself to him.

She'd spent most of Friday afternoon on the couch, picking through the refrigerator and reading a novel by Dean Koontz. At least Johnny finally convinced her to stay away from the water, a promise she tried to break once only to discover that water no longer flowed into the Drake house. Johnny had found the main and turned it off.

She retired just after seven, and Johnny finally drifted off to sleep around midnight, still battling that throb that kept trying to latch itself onto his head. He'd actually become pretty good about deflecting the distortions when they came.

Why was he able to do this, but not everyone else? The best he could figure was that he had been terrified by Black when the preacher killed Cecil, and the moment put him on guard.

That and the fact that Johnny stayed clear of Black's poison, despite having undoubtedly ingested some in the water.

He awoke at ten o'clock Saturday. The clouds that he either saw or thought he saw were now so dark that he could hardly see across the dust-blown street.

Phone was still dead. He considered climbing into his mother's four-wheel drive and taking a shot at driving out of the valley. Sally had refused to take him out yesterday. Probably a good thing in retrospect, considering her condition. But he'd never driven, and the conditions were anything but decent for a trial run. There were too many cliffs bordering the two-lane road out.

Johnny stood in the kitchen and squinted against another headache. Stars popped to life, then faded. A musty smell drifted by. The tastes-like-nothing taste filled his mouth. He wanted it, sure he did.

But he also hated it.

He grunted and decided then that he couldn't just sit here without a plan. He had to talk to someone sane, at the very least. He had to talk to Roland even if it did mean leaving his mother for a few minutes and braving the dark wind.

Johnny poked his head into his mother's room, satisfied himself that she was still dead to the world, pulled on a hoodie for protection, and headed down the back alley.

The town was dark and windy and dusty and dead. Hot though.

He couldn't shake the possibility that he was actually only seeing this in his mind's eye. If so, then Black was probably a messenger from God after all. But after all he'd seen, Johnny couldn't make that fit.

A lone howl drifted above the wind. Johnny froze. What was that? A loud crash on his left, nearby in the forest. Then a loud grunt.

He began to run, straight toward Roland's house.

When he got there, he quickly came to the awful conclusion that the house was deserted. At least no one was stirring. Roland's shade was open and his bed was made, but no Roland. The lights were off in the whole place. Not a soul to be seen.

Main Street was just as empty.

Buffeted by fresh fear, Johnny sprinted back to his house, ignoring an ache in his weaker leg. Things were worse than yesterday, much worse. Where was everyone? And where was Black?

He had to get home.

Inside, the back door slammed shut behind him. Then again, things were no better in here. He stood alone in the hall for a few moments, soaking in the silence.

He wanted to cry. He was alone, wasn't he? And he had no place to go. Maybe it would be easier to walk over to the saloon and ask them for some of Black's crud. Maybe he should just walk out into the street and scream his surrender to the black sky, let the black angel administer some of his grace and hope.

Johnny checked on his mother again. No movement other than the rise and fall of the sheets with her breathing. No sense in waking her up.

He walked into his room, sat on his bed, and was about to lie down when the one-inch marble he had with him the day Cecil died rolled slowly toward the edge of his dresser.

Johnny blinked at the sight. The red shooter stopped, then rolled back the way it had come. It stopped in its original position.

Johnny's pulse quickened. Had he really seen that? What could have caused a marble to roll like that? No wind in here. No tremors, no tilting. But things rolled on their own sometimes, didn't they? The slightest force could . . .

The marble vanished.

Johnny stood, amazed. The space where the round red marble had sat just a moment ago was empty. Nothing but an oak dresser top.

He ran his hand over the varnished wood grain. He'd seen eyes poked out and an apple turned into a snake. He'd seen warts come and go. He'd even seen Black pull his lip off his face. But this was different.

This was the first time he'd seen something impossible happen without the magician on hand to execute his magic.

Fred and Peter saw something on the old theater wall, but only after they'd taken some of Black's slimy concoction. And he hadn't seen that himself. They'd all seen the clouds darkening overhead and dust blowing along the streets, but Johnny was quite sure that was real.

So what did that make this disappearance of the red marble? Real?

A *thunk* sounded behind him. He spun, but there was nothing he could . . .

He caught his breath. The red shooter sat on the wall, halfway up, near the door frame. Johnny lowered himself to his bed unsteadily. What was going on here? He watched it for a minute, waiting for it to move. The marble just sat there as if stuck to the wall with glue.

Johnny rose and approached the red shooter. Slowly, ever so slowly, he reached out. Touched it. Gripped it between his forefinger and thumb. Pulled it off the wall.

The glass shooter was smooth and weighty, exactly as it always had been. He let it rest in his palm and opened his fingers. The ball trembled and rose from his hand as if suspended on an invisible string.

Incredible! Johnny moved his hand to the right. The marble followed, precisely equaling the movement of his hand. He jerked his hand to the left. Again the marble followed precisely. No lag.

He moved his hand in a quick circle. The red orb followed every move without falling behind even a fraction of a second. A crooked smile formed on his face. This was absolutely . . .

The marble broke form, drifting toward the dresser. Like an unidentified flying object, the orb hovered two feet above the dresser for a long moment, then sunk slowly to the oak surface and touched down in its original resting place without a sound.

Johnny sat hard on the bed. The box springs squeaked. He didn't know what to think, other than it wasn't a trick. Black wasn't up in the attic floating the ball on an invisible string. He wasn't crouched behind the bed using magical magnets that worked on glass. Johnny had touched the marble. Held it in his hand. What he'd just seen had to be real.

The marble did not move.

Johnny just watched.

STEVE SMITHER had spent the night under the saloon's back porch, where he intended to keep an ear tuned to destruction. He awoke close to noon, although he wouldn't have known it by the sky, because the sun was obscured by dark clouds.

He had only four sticks left—Claude and gang destroyed eight, and he ruined one on Chris. He needed more sticks.

Steve walked home, past the shed, looking for any wood that might work. No wood.

He returned to the saloon and struck out for the forest, gripping one of the sharpened stakes in his left hand. His mind was foggy and he couldn't see too well, but he lurched toward the grove of saplings from which he'd harvested his other stakes.

The leaves were coming off the trees, an early fall in the middle of summer. What a trip.

Steve stumbled into a small clearing and paused, dazed. Had he forgotten something? His destination maybe. No, he was going to the grove of aspens to make some more sticks.

Or he would cut down some little trees and then haul them to his shed where he would make some more sticks. Unless Paula was there—then he would stay out at the grove where she couldn't ask him any questions, like why he was making so many sticks.

He looked down at the stake in his right hand and then at his left hand, hanging there, limp, empty. Of course! He'd forgotten the ax. Stupid, stupid!

Steve lifted his hand and stared at the dried blood on his forearm. Chris's blood. He wondered if he'd killed the man. An image of Chris lying there on the pool table all curled up filled his mind. He grinned and forgot about the ax for the moment.

Beat that man good, hadn't he? Should've beat the other two while he was at it. In fact, it was probably Claude's punk kid who'd found his sticks in the first place. Kids were like that, poking their noses in where they didn't belong.

Maybe they would come back for some more fun and he could have some more of *his* fun. He flexed his fingers around the crusted blood. This time he might stick the sharp end into them. They would sure howl about that!

The thought of making more sticks struck him as senseless. Why make more stakes when he had four perfectly good sticks? He should start learning how to *use* the stakes, shouldn't he? Like graduating from boot camp. It was time to learn how these things worked for real. He could always make more stakes. But learning how to *use* them, now that would be something.

And not just the blunt end either.

Steve stood in the small clearing, swaying on his feet, left hand clamped around a three-foot stake and the other bloody hand palm up by his chest. He looked around at the trees.

Well, I can't just go around poking people for practice. They'd never understand. So then what? What can I stick my stakes into?

A chipmunk scurried across the clearing, and Steve watched it go. Now here was a thought. Course, the critter was a bit small, but it could make for good practice. It could be like a mission: *Pursue and kill all the chipmunks. And any other bigger animals you encounter.*

Yes, sir. Now *bigger* animals might be something. He could jab them good with his stakes. *Jab, jab, jab.*

Steve clenched the stake with both hands and stalked into the forest.

WHILE STEVE was stumbling through the woods, discovering bloodlust, Claude Bowers was down by the Starlight Theater grinning up at the big sign. Beside him stood a badly bruised and bloodied Chris Ingles. Roland, Peter, and Fred stood to one side, watching his every move.

They'd fixed a crude splint to Chris's broken arm, but he'd complained for the last thirty minutes about the pain, and Claude was getting sick of telling him to shut up.

"Take some more of those painkillers and just shut your trap, Chris! Here, drink some of this." He shoved his bottle of Jack Daniels at the man.

"We're gonna ransack this entire town," Claude said, looking at his son with a wide grin. "What do you think of that?" He snatched the bottle back from Chris and took a slug. Chris had almost emptied it, but Peter had another bottle in his pocket, and they knew where Steve kept the rest.

Stevie Smither hadn't seen nothin' yet! They were going to teach that slime bucket what happened to anybody who messed with them.

"Neat," Peter said. A crooked grin twisted his face, and Claude thought maybe he shouldn't have beat him so hard yesterday. His right eye was swollen shut and his lip was still cracked with blood.

But he'd had it coming, smashing the television like that.

"Yeah, neat," Roland said, looking up.

Claude bent to the pile of axes at his feet, snatched up a large splitting ax, and handed his bottle to Peter. "Here, hold this. And don't go drinking it all."

He swaggered up to one of the two wooden posts that supported the sign swaying in the wind thirty feet above. "Ready?" He gripped the ax with both hands. A strong gust of wind hit him and he staggered back a step.

"Do it, Claude!" Chris said, still holding his right arm gingerly.

Claude raised the ax and put every one of his 280 pounds into the swing. The blade buried itself in the post with a loud *smack*, and Peter let out a *whoop*.

"Do it, Dad!"

"Yeah, do it!" Roland mimicked.

Claude tugged at the ax. It budged, but barely. He placed a foot on the pole for leverage. The blade came loose, and he tumbled to his rear end, cursing loudly. Chris howled with laughter.

"Shut up, Chris! I'll come over there and break your other arm!"

That settled him a bit. Chris snickered as Claude struggled to his feet and lined the ax up for another swing.

Smack!

The watching evidently proved too much for Peter. He set the bottles of booze on the ground, snatched up a hatchet. In his eagerness, his right foot knocked Claude's bottle over. The thirsty dust swallowed the amber liquid.

Claude stared at the bottle, ax just raised for a third swing.

Their eyes met—Claude's glaring, Peter's wide. "You'll pay for that," Claude rasped and swung angrily at the pole. *Smack!*

"I'm sorry. I swear. Can't Chris hold the bottles? He's a lame duck anyway."

"Shut up, Peter," Chris said. "Can't you see I'm hurt here? You think I just want to be a lame duck? I can hardly move here, man!"

"Shut up, Chris," Claude said. "Peter's right. Take the bottles."

Peter helped his dad hack at the large pole with his small hatchet. Roland joined him from the opposite side, swinging sporadically between Peter's continuous warnings not to miss and hit him by mistake.

It took the trio ten minutes of palm-blistering chops and nonstop bickering before the mighty sign at the south end of Paradise began to lean toward the street.

"Watch out!" Chris yelled. "It's coming down! It's gonna hit the car!"

Claude's old blue 310 Datsun was parked on the shoulder fifteen feet from the sign. None of them had considered the sign's trajectory. The sound of splintering wood rose above the wind, and the thirty-foot beacon began its descent.

If Claude had parked his Datsun seven feet to the right, the two support-ing poles would have straddled the car. Instead, the massive timber smashed onto the sedan's canopy, crushing it into the driver's seat. The huge Starlight sign slammed into the pavement beyond.

Claude raised his ax above his head, spread his legs wide, tilted his head to the black clouds, and let out a roar of approval.

Peter and Roland hopped up and down, ecstatic. Chris instinctively raised his broken arm in victory and then winced with pain. But the accomplish-ment was too great to be thwarted by a little pain, and he shouted anyway.

The sign's plastic casing lay shattered on the blacktop. The car sat buck-led like a fortune cookie. Claude's gang celebrated their first major feat of destruction.

"I'll drink to that!" Chris shouted.

They slammed the bottles of Jack Daniels together in a toast. Unfor-tunately, Chris's bottle proved to be a bit too brittle for his enthusiasm. It shattered on impact, spilling more amber liquid into the dust.

It was the last bottle, and none of the others were in a sharing mood. He shuffled off toward the saloon for more, cursing.

"What did I tell you?" Claude said, ignoring Chris. "Now was that a trip or was that a trip?"

"That was a trip," Peter answered.

"Yeah, well, we're gonna show this whole town how to trip. We're gonna do this town, boys!"

WHILE CLAUDE was busy plotting the trashing of Paradise by the Starlight Theater, Nancy was taking a screwdriver to the rear door of his store, All Right Convenience.

Nancy shoved the flat end into the keyhole and pried to the left. She'd never actually broken a lock before, and she didn't know what actually made them open other than a key. Perhaps a sledgehammer.

She doubted a screwdriver was the right tool for breaking into the local convenience store. But it was the only tool she could readily find when she finally made the decision to brave the wind for some food.

Her small indiscretion was Claude's fault. If the fat pig would open his doors for business, she wouldn't have to break in, now would she? The front doors had been locked for over forty-eight hours, and she was out of things to eat.

To make matters worse, the father had called and told her he wasn't coming back until Sunday morning, just in time for church. "I've got a message for the people," he'd said. "And I think the impact would be most powerful if I just walked in while they were already assembled for Sunday morning service. It's going to be powerful, Nancy. Powerful."

"Well, I hope people come," she said.

"What do you mean, come? They always come on Sunday."

"I don't know, Father. I haven't seen a soul all day. Are you going to a Sam's Club?"

"Why would I be going to a Sam's Club? What do you mean you haven't seen a soul all day? You mean in the church?"

"If you went by a Sam's Club, you could get me a large pack of those pastries I like so much. The cherry ones with glaze. Maybe a dozen packs, so we have them for church functions when we need them. And no, I don't mean the church. I mean the town. It's pretty quiet around here."

"But nothing's wrong, right? As far as you can tell everything's okay?"

"Yes, Father. It's just fine. Maybe you'd better get a couple dozen of those packs. They're pretty cheap at Sam's, you know?"

"I'm not going to Sam's," he said. "You weigh enough as it is. The last thing you need are glazed pastries."

Now what was he so rankled about? That jab was entirely unnecessary. But one of the advantages of weighing enough was the pressure you could bring to bear on a lock if you leaned on it hard enough.

The screwdriver bent as she brought her 270 pounds to bear. Something snapped, and she plowed into the white door frame, nose first. A warmth immediately ran down her lip.

I've broken the screwdriver. She pulled back, wiped her face, and brought her forearm away bloody. *Goodness.* She reached out to test the doorknob. *I've broken my nose too.*

The handle turned easily in her hand and the door swung away from her. What do you know? She stepped in, went straight to the bathroom, and flipped the lights on. The face staring at her in the mirror looked like an onion. An onion with two raisins for eyes and a red mustache.

The blood flowed freely over her mouth and down her chin. The white blouse she wore was already wet with blood, so she thought that maybe she looked more like a red-breasted robin. Either way, she was intrigued by the fact that the blood did not bother her. *I'm turning into a regular sinner.*

She grabbed some paper towels and wiped the blood from her chin, not bothering with the shirt for the moment. She had just broken into Claude's store, for heaven's sake. Getting out quickly wouldn't be such a stupid idea.

She snatched up some toilet paper and stuffed two little bullets of it into her nostrils. As long as the blood didn't flood her nasal cavities and drown her, she would be fine. The two red spikes sticking out of her nose didn't look too glamorous, but she was here for food, not a beauty contest.

Nancy hustled from the toilet and entered the store. The stocked shelves beckoned in the dim light. She smiled absently and scanned the goodies sitting faithfully in their little shiny wrappers.

So much food, so little time. Saliva began to gather in her jowls and she swallowed.

Nancy grabbed a bag from the counter and filled it with a single sweep of her arm. The paper sack tore and the goodies crashed to the floor. She swore and snatched up a plastic bag.

Nancy filled six of the bags before reluctantly deciding to retreat to the church to sort through her spoil. It had been a good trip.

She exited through the back without closing the door.

A good trip indeed.

WHILE NANCY was robbing Claude blind to feed her food lust, Katie waited impatiently in her beauty salon, fixing her hair, dreaming of a rendezvous with the preacher. No, not the preacher—for her it was Marsuvees. To others he may be *the minister* or *the preacher*, but she had stepped past that point, gaining access to the inner man.

Marsuvees, darling, could you hand me my dress?

She had this effect on most if not all men, of course. They all wanted her. And she never blamed a single one of them. If she'd been born male, she too would choose a woman with her body rather than one of those pudges like Paula.

Now there was a case. Paula. She recalled an image of Claude sitting in the third pew once, ogling Paula as she gave her annual Sunday-school report. She knew he'd been ogling and not just looking because when she elbowed him he jerked his eyes from the woman—guilty as sin. At the time, she thought the whole incident was rather silly.

But sometime between then and now, the memory had soured in her mind like week-old milk. Not that she cared much whether Claude eyed a woman or two now and then. But she just couldn't believe that he found Paula sexy, of all women. She was the Sunday-school coordinator, for goodness' sake, and you couldn't play Sunday-school coordinator and strut your stuff up there while talking about how many kids were participating in the Easter play. Sunday school and sexy didn't mix.

Katie glanced at her watch. One thirty. Marsuvees said he would meet her here at one.

Wanna trip like I do, Katie? Wanna trip with me?

His words burned in her ears. She closed her eyes and leaned against the wall, savoring the heat. The door opened and she jerked off the wall. She softened her look, cocked her head just a tad, and turned to the front.

Paula stood in the door frame, frowning. Katie's heart fell and she dropped the kiss-me look.

"What in blazes are you doing here?" she demanded, surprised at the revulsion that ripped through her throat. The white strip in the pudge's hair looked ridiculous!

"What am I doing here? What are you yelling at me for?"

"I'm not yelling at you. I'm just asking you what you're doing here. Last time I checked this shop did have my name on it. What do you want?"

Katie grabbed a pack of smokes from the counter and lit one up. Paula's response was coming slow. Marsuvees could show up at any moment, and she certainly didn't want Goody Two-shoes standing here looking so prissy when he walked in.

She blew a smoke ring. "So?"

Paula rested a hand on her waist and cocked her hips. "So I'll be leaving, that's what's *so*. Have you seen Marsuvees?"

Marsuvees? Not *the preacher* or *the minister*, but *Marsuvees*?

Katie raised an eyebrow. "Marsuvees? We're calling him Marsuvees now, are we?" She noticed Paula's black skirt and wondered when Miss Pudge had taken up wearing tight, short skirts. Certainly not while planning Sunday-school lessons.

"So what if I am?"

Heat began to warm Katie's face. A sickening heat, the kind that sometimes builds to fury. But there was no way Marsuvees and Paula were anything like her and Marsuvees. Not intimate and close and ready to take things to the moon.

"You're on a first-name basis with the preacher now? I'll bet Steve would be tickled to hear that."

Katie said it casually, with the intent of dousing any misplaced flames licking at Paula's heart, but she felt like jumping over there and sticking her cigarette into the woman's eyes.

Ordinarily the veiled threat would have earned a gasp of feigned disapproval. Maybe an about-face and a grand exit as an encore for good measure.

Ordinarily.

Things weren't so ordinary in Paradise these days.

Paula lowered her head like a cat intent on guarding her territory. "Stuff it, Katie! You think you're such a hot number? I've got news for you, honey. You're not the only one men find attractive around here. Just because Marsuvees has the hots for me doesn't mean you have to play jealous bimbo, you slug!"

Katie felt her jaw fall, as though someone had tied a ten-pound weight to her lower teeth and shoved it from her mouth. She was having difficulty understanding all of Paula's words, but a few were crystal clear.

Like *slug*.

Paula was calling her a slug and claiming to be having something in the works with Marsuvees in the same breath. She was lying through her teeth, of course. Marsuvees would never lay a hand on that squat tub, not when he knew he could have Katie any time he wanted. She'd made that abundantly clear to him.

"In your wildest fantasy. Marsuvees can't keep his eyes off me. And you have the gall to come into *my* shop and talk about *my* man that way? I oughta rip your tongue from your throat, you Neanderthal!"

She wanted nothing more than to do just that, maybe rip that head off while she was at it. She stuffed the cigarette between her lips and sucked hard.

Paula's face was turning beet red, and a thought dawned on Katie. *She means it. She's actually got something going with Black!*

"It may be your shop," Paula said, "but Marsuvees told me to meet him here at one thirty."

"In your dreams!"

"And it ain't the first time we've met, honey doll."

Katie launched herself at Paula, who took the rush head-on. They met in the center of the tiny shop, fingernails extended. Both managed to draw blood on the first pass—Katie from Paula's right shoulder, and Paula from Katie's left cheek. They attacked again, yowling like cats in heat, flailing their arms.

Within the space of thirty seconds both women looked like the victims of gang violence. The last thing Paula did was clamp her bony fist around a lock of Katie's strawberry hair and yank it cleanly from her skull before running, screaming for the door, her prize flying from her hand like a captured flag.

Katie jerked a hand to her head and pulled it down, wet with blood.

"I'll kill you, you witch! I'll kill you if it's the last thing I do!"

She collapsed to the chair and grabbed her pack of smokes.

What a trip.

WHILE KATIE and Paula were fighting, Johnny was watching the marble on his dresser.

Just watching.

CHAPTER EIGHTEEN

THE MONASTERY
Saturday morning

ACCORDING TO the rules of a debate, the official announcement detailing Billy's debate with Christine could not be made until the same morning. It was simply posted on the announcement board in the breakfast hall:

> An Official Debate has been issued
> and will be heard at
> 10:00 a.m. in the main lecture hall.
> All students must be present.

The intention was to let the actual debate frame the challenge, rather than a string of endless debates that would surely erupt sooner if the announcement was posted. But it would have been virtually impossible to live in the monastery during the last twenty-four hours and not know what was afoot.

The teachers wore worried looks, and the student's questions about Billy, Darcy, and Paul were answered in oblique terms. Billy and Darcy weren't s/ guarded, and Friday evening the halls echoed with soft whispers. Samı huddled with Tyler and Christine, twice in the library and once in Samı bedroom, late at night.

By morning, a strange silence had gripped Project Showdown.

Now the students hurried to the Hall of Truth, as they called th lecture hall, armed with the understanding that something profo about to alter their lives.

Samuel had questioned his father at length about the rules of debate, and the minute he stepped into the auditorium he saw they were being followed to the letter.

The room sloped like a theater to a large platform, accommodating long wooden pews that faced the stage. A single aisle divided the seating into two sections of fifteen pews each. Behind the stage, long maroon curtains hung from a domed ceiling, where indirect lighting cast a yellow hue throughout the room. Seven golden lamp stands stood on the platform, set in a semicircle behind ten high-back chairs. The overseers had seated themselves in the chairs. Two wood podiums, slightly angled toward each other, waited for the debaters. A single large chair was centered behind the podiums. His father's chair.

Samuel scanned the auditorium and took a deep breath. The monastery was about to see its first debate. More important, his father was about to watch Billy openly refute him in an attempt to undermine his life's aim. And by all Samuel could see, his father wasn't taking it well.

They spent an hour alone in his father's study the previous evening. He could still see his father's drawn face, often looking away, lost in deep thought.

"Don't worry, Father. Once Billy is brought to his senses, everything will change."

His father smiled. "You know, you and Billy used to play together often when you were young. Billy was the mischievous one. He would sneak up behind you and stick a thin blade of grass in your ear and then run away, squealing. You always overtook him, of course; no one could ever run like you. You would end up rolling around laughing on the grass with him."

"I'd forgotten," Samuel said. "You're right. We were always together, weren't we? What happened?"

"Project Showdown happened. It's always been about this moment."

They prayed for God's wisdom and above all the power of Christ to open the eyes of Billy's heart. But they both knew that the choice was Billy's alone.

Most of the children had taken their seats. They wore their customary uniforms—blue shorts and white shirts—most neatly groomed and giving the left side of the auditorium both a wide berth and numerous stares.

Darcy sat on the left, near the back, shifting on her pew. A red rash covered her face. Paul's as well. Stevie sat with them . . .

Stevie had gone down as well? So Billy had found three converts in just over one day. Samuel felt bumps rise on his neck. But the rules were clear—a two-thirds majority was required to prevail. Twenty-four students would have to vote against Christine for Billy's debate to succeed.

Samuel eased into a seat near the back, across the room from Darcy. Murmurs filled the hall. The monks whispered one to the other. Two dusty shafts of light descended from skylights, highlighting the podiums.

The curtain to the stage's left moved, and the room quieted. The heavy maroon cloth parted and his father walked into the light. Samuel's heart jumped at the sight. *That's my father! To them he is the director, but to me he is Father.* He felt like standing up and yelling, *Hey, Billy, that's my father and you'd better do what he says!*

Of course that would be out of order, but Samuel let the pride swell unchecked.

David walked to the center of the platform wearing a long black robe with a white collar, like a schoolmaster might wear at graduation ceremonies. He looked over the children for a moment. Stillness descended on the auditorium. The overseers sat, rigid; the children stared at David, scarcely breathing. Samuel's father had the air of authority that insisted on stillness.

And then his father's voice filled the auditorium. He spoke without a microphone. None was required in the hall. "Good morning, scholars, teachers. Thank you for coming. As you know, we are gathered for a debate."

He measured each of the students as he spoke, showing no visible reaction to the division in the class, but Samuel knew his father's heart was pained.

"This is our first debate. It's the first time a student has openly questioned my authority and rejected the rules. Some of you are wondering why we don't just put these dissidents out. Why not expel them, you ask? That's how it works in the world. When a man commits a crime, he is put away. When a child is disobedient, he is reprimanded. But here, we groom children not to follow the world's systems, but to change the world."

He cleared his throat. "The power each of you wield is beyond your comprehension. Within this room we indeed have the power to turn this world upside down. It's a great dream I have given everything for."

He raised a finger into the air. "But one rule of Project Showdown supersedes even that desire of mine, and that is the rule that you yourselves be given the complete freedom to choose your own ways. And this, my friends, brings us to today's debate."

He paused and scanned the room. "Billy has questioned the integrity of the third rule and will now debate the matter with Christine. You, my young scholars, will decide today whose argument you will follow. Listen carefully. Remember your lessons well. Think of your purpose. Measure all that you hear against the standard of truth you have always known. The future of this monastery is in your hands."

He stepped back and sat in the chair reserved for him.

The curtains on both ends of the stage parted. Billy stepped from the left; Christine from the right. A few coughs disturbed the auditorium. His father crossed his legs and looked at Darcy and the small band of dissidents.

Billy and Christine stepped up onto footstools that allowed them to stand tall behind the podiums. They were dressed in the blue robes they all wore for choir. The debate had no set structure but would not exceed an hour. At the end of the hour, the debaters and all overseers would be ushered from the room, and the students would be left alone to determine their own fate.

Samuel drew a slow breath, and as he did Christine brought her hand up, level with her shoulder. She extended her index finger to Billy.

"Billy," Christine cried shrilly, and some children flinched. "I accuse you of distorting the meaning of the third rule, the foundational rule by which all in the monastery live, the undeniable truth that all love comes from our Creator. I accuse you of heresy, and I challenge you to argue your heresy here, before the assembly, so that we may know what is the truth."

This was the track they had decided on last night. Christine would control the debate from the start by framing the third rule of writing: All love comes from the Creator, which in turn meant it would lead *to* the Creator. Surely the students wouldn't question the necessity of following God's will.

Identifying his will was the question. Was it found in the monastery rules, or was Billy right in forsaking those rules? This was the real issue.

Samuel was proud of Christine already. She was using strong words, worthy of any overseer.

Christine kept her hand outstretched, waiting Billy's response. But he said nothing.

She spoke again, distinctly, biting off each word. "Tell us, Billy, what is the precise meaning of the third rule?" She lowered her arm.

Billy rolled his eyes in exasperation and let his head loll Christine's way. "The third rule, please. You say that, *the third rule*, as if you spoke about the earth's end."

He chuckled. "The precise meaning? Yes, well, that's the whole problem, isn't it? There *is* no precise meaning. Only vague ambiguities that leave a dozen doors wide open for interpretation. And everyone in this room knows it. We've hinged our lives on the ambiguities of another man's word. Even the Bible, on which all of our rules are supposedly based, requires human interpretation, which is subject to ambiguous conclusions." He looked out at the students and grinned. "That's right, my fellow scholars. If you ask me, it's clear that ambiguity does indeed exist in the rules they've been shoving down our throats all these years."

Samuel glanced at a student near him, Sharon, who was listening intently.

"*Ambiguous*," Christine said, smiling. "A clever word. But let's be a little more specific, shall we? Surely you don't expect such intelligent children to fall for your cute phrasing. We need some content. Give us some content that we can weigh and measure. Perhaps you could answer one simple question directly?"

Billy flashed a patronizing grin. Samuel had half a mind to walk up there and smack it from his face.

Christine pressed. "The third rule emphatically states that all love comes from the Creator, leading directly to the implicit assertion that all love *leads* to the Creator. After all, if the Creator is the sole source of love, then how can one show any love which doesn't in turn lead to the Creator? Answer— he can't. I believe even you, Billy, will agree with the face value of this statement. Am I correct?"

Samuel was surprised to see the boy nod. Although he still wore that stupid grin.

"Good. Then we can at least begin in the arms of sanity," Christine said. "Trying to argue that love does not come from the Creator would be rather stupid, unless of course you don't believe in a Creator at all, in which case we would have to educate you by slogging through the preponderance of evidence that long ago settled this small-minded position."

"Sounds boring," Billy said. "And I can assure you I'm not into boring. Of course there is a Creator." Billy winked at his partners in crime.

"Then is it the Creator's character that's in question? Surely you don't—"

"Who is the Creator?" Billy asked.

In that moment, Samuel understood Billy's tack. The whole thing fell into his mind like a finished puzzle, and he knew rough waters lay ahead.

"The Creator is he who created," Christine said.

Billy faced the students. "You see, this is where we see the first point of ambiguity in the rules. Because we all create, don't we? We are all creators. We create meals and drawings and stories and such every day. The question that I posed to myself when this thought first crossed my mind was, *Well now, which creator does the third rule reference?* Hmm? Is it the Creator with a capital *C*, as they are written? Perhaps. Or perhaps not. After all, who first wrote that word with a capital letter? And who decided that it should refer to this creator or that creator?"

"Don't patronize us," Christine said. "We all know that David Abraham set the rules for the monastery. It's *his* project. How simple can you get? Your words will bury you!"

"David Abraham? I don't dispute the fact that the director does indeed run this project. I take to issue, however, our narrow understanding of the meaning of *creator*. We are all creators. We should live and love to discover ourselves as creators."

"Nonsense. That's not the meaning the director intended, and every last student knows it. You're arguing empty semantics. The Creator, with a capital *C*, as written, is God."

"Believe me, more than one of your precious students has been persuaded by virtue of these very semantics. But if you wish for a stronger argument, then consider this. When God, the Creator with a big *C*, created us, he created us as *creators*. And he purposefully gave us the power and resolve to choose what we would create, correct?"

No argument came from Christine.

"Well then, he has given us permission to live and love as creative beings, guided by our own creative power. How can you have a rule that prohibits you from doing something the Creator, with a big *C*, has specifically given you *permission* to do? Can our director overrule God with his rules?"

Billy faced the students. "Are you confused? Of course you're confused. And why? Because the rule is indeed ambiguous!"

Whispers scurried around the room. Samuel followed the argument. Apart from several well-hidden flaws, the argument seemed convincing. But it didn't matter. The concepts were heady enough to cast confusion in even the best minds.

He looked at his father and saw that he sat still, eyes closed. What if the vote swung against them? What if Christine's debate backfired and forced the prevailing doctrine into reclusion?

It would be a disaster! It would be the death of the monastery! Samuel straightened. *We've got to stop this, Father!*

"How does love fit into this?" Christine asked sharply.

The room grew quiet once again.

Christine continued. "The inclusion of love in the third rule trumps any ambiguity that may exist as a result of your semantic twists and turns. The meaning of love is crystal clear. Wouldn't you agree?"

"Is it?" Billy grinned as widely as before. "And what is that meaning, Christine?"

"Love is the purest expression of selflessness. It is the desire to please at the expense of one's own sense of need. It's looking for another to betray their desire so you can fulfill it. And there's your problem, Billy. You've told us today that the identity of the Creator is in question. Ambiguous, you said. We are all creators, you said. And indeed we *are*, in a sense. But we can't be the Creator as expressed in the rules because we can't love like the Creator. All love comes from the Creator, the third rule reads. Surely you don't hold that *all* love comes from any of us."

"I don't know, Christine. I don't think it's so clear. It's in your definition of love that I and the students find confusion."

"The students haven't expressed an opinion yet. Please refrain from begging the question."

Billy ignored the reprimand. "You say love is the purest expression of selflessness. And you assume that the one who made the universe has somehow expressed this form of love and therefore must be the one referred to in the rule, correct?"

"Yes."

"And how is God's act of creation so selfless? You see, I don't think the Creator is so selfless. I think he created the world for his pleasure. In fact, I don't believe the kind of love you speak of—this completely selfless nonsense—even exists."

A rumbling spread through the auditorium.

"That's blasphemy," Christine said.

"You show me a single act on the part of the Creator that doesn't benefit himself, Christine, and I daresay I will recant. I will withdraw every argument. It would indeed win your case. It would trump my entire premise."

"How is it possible for God to do anything that does not benefit pure goodness, which is, in fact, himself?" Christine shot back. "To say he must be selfless would be to demand that he not be God!"

"So then you agree. God cannot be selfless. And neither, my friends, can we." Billy stepped out from behind his podium. "You see, we are bound to be selfish. We are creators who will and must find love, which serves us as creators."

"Nonsense! You're saying that Christ's sacrifice was selfish?"

"I'm saying that, as Paul's epistle tells us, Christ endured the cross for the joy set before him. Sounds like he was at least thinking about what it would gain him, doesn't it?"

He eyed the children, avoiding Samuel. "At the very least it's a reasonable argument that leaves us with some ambiguity. Ambiguity, my friends. It's my only case. It's my whole case. Because in the face of ambiguity comes not only the *permission* to investigate, but the *responsibility* to investigate. To make forays into the unknown with the intent to discover what might lie there, hidden in the dark corners. I suggest to you today that anything less would be inexcusable for children of the great Creator."

Samuel closed his eyes. His face tingled. Christine was losing this debate. And not by such a small margin.

Christine spoke again, but not as confidently. "Investigate, you say? Then you'd best do it slowly and carefully, lest you inadvertently plunge into a hole from which there is no escape."

"Yes, carefully," Billy agreed. "But one cannot dissect a frog without cutting its flesh."

"I would say that there is a difference between God's rights and the rights of those he created," Christine said.

"And I would say he created us in his image, with the desire and right to investigate ambiguities, something that can be done only by getting your hands into both sides of an argument. Even Jesus Christ went into the desert to be tempted. This was how he discovered the true meaning of love." Billy sighed. "Which brings me to my second point. The second rule, that there is no discovery greater than love, is suspect too. The discovery of love may not be the most exciting thing after all. Dissecting the frog is pretty cool too, trust me on that. Since I'm a creator myself, I've altered the rules to allow for a little discovery of fun now and then, or maybe all the time."

The room fell silent. Christine paled. Billy leaned against his podium, grinning. Samuel looked at Darcy and saw that the girl had fallen asleep. Paul was smiling stupidly, scratching his rash. Samuel turned back to the stage. His father was looking directly at him.

"You're misinterpreting!" Christine snapped.

"Then you've made my case for me," Billy returned. "If something can be misinterpreted, then it is subject to interpretation. It is by nature ambiguous. And we, creatures created to create, must interpret. I am only doing what I was created to do."

The hour wasn't up, but the argument seemed to have stalled. Christine glanced around the room and turned to Billy. "In the end you will see, Billy," she said softly, as if the words were intended for Billy only. But the entire room heard them. "Your confusion will be your own undoing. This interpretation will bring a pain you can't imagine."

"That is for me to discover," he said, scratching the sores on his arm. "So far I don't regret one moment."

Christine looked briefly at David and then turned from the podium.

Leaving? She wasn't finished! There must be a way to put Billy back on his heels. Was further argument that pointless?

Taking the cue, Billy turned, walked to the curtains, and disappeared behind them.

That was it then. Samuel watched as first his father and then the line of overseers rose and walked from the room. The Hall of Truth now awaited the students' verdict.

For a moment no one moved. And then Samuel and Darcy stood simultaneously and made their way to the platform. Someone must have woken the sleeper. With a glance at each other they climbed the stage and walked to the opposing podiums.

So it all came to this. A single vote. No argument. No lengthy discussion. The argument had been cast. Only a single statement for each side of the debate remained. Samuel stepped to the side and allowed Darcy to speak first.

The girl raised a hand to her neck and scratched the rash. Darcy seemed oblivious to the fact, and she brought her hand away red with blood. She ran her fingers through matted hair, leaving thin trails of red in her bangs, then stuffed her hands into her pockets.

Darcy's speech was strained. "Hey," she began. "We all know what Billy said is true. Let's face it, we may not like it, but there's plenty of confusion out there. If you want to escape confusion, you should reapply as a horse or something, 'cause all humans have enough brains to be confused. Heck, *I'm* confused. It's why I decided to investigate. Like Billy said."

She broke into a wide grin. "And trust me, it's very cool. I listened to the holy robed ones for twelve years without questioning their rules. Well, now I've earned the right to spend a few days checking out the competition, just to round out my education, if you know what I mean."

She glanced over at Samuel. "Holy-boy here may not want you to vote for Billy, and that's okay, because he's confused too. He just won't admit it. But you owe it to yourselves, to all that is right, to vote for Billy if you're the least bit confused or even suspect there may be some ambiguity in the rules."

She stepped aside.

The students stared at Samuel with blank expressions. He caught an encouraging nod from Tyler and began his rebuttal.

"Hello, my friends. Two simple questions should be considered in all this mess. One, Billy speaks of ambiguity. Did any ambiguity rest with the rules before you heard him speak this morning? Not for me. In fact, I can't think of anything I am so certain of as the third rule. The rules are the basis for everything at the monastery. Without them, we're just orphans from the street. Your vote may return us there—to the streets."

He waited for any sign of approval. None.

"And second, if you want to judge the words of Billy, just look at the product of his words." He lifted an arm to Darcy. "Do you notice anything strange in this girl? Anything wrong or repelling? You'll have to judge for yourselves, but as I see it, whatever's eating at her flesh should remain in the dungeons where it belongs."

He lowered his hand. It was time to vote.

"All those who side with Christine in this matter should follow me, through the curtains to my left," Samuel said. "All those who side with Billy should follow Darcy to your left. Choose carefully." He turned and walked through the curtains.

The back room was empty except for several stacks of chairs against one wall. Samuel lifted his hands and saw that his fingers trembled. He clenched them and pushed his damp bangs from his forehead. He wanted to leave this place—to run and find his father and hug him and tell him it had all worked out after all.

The curtains brushed open behind him and he spun around. "Tyler!" He reached out for him, and they clasped hands. "Thank God!" he breathed. He looked to the curtains anxiously. "What do you think?"

Tyler took a deep breath. "I don't know, Samuel."

The curtains parted again and Marie walked in, followed by Kevin and Brandon. One by one Samuel grabbed them by the shoulders. "Good!

Good!" he said. Then they came in. Three more, in a group. Then two. "Good! Good!" Samuel felt a great weight begin to lift.

Another child walked in, smiling. And another. And then the curtains hung still. "Good," Samuel said, expecting at any second for the long, pleated fabric to move—to part and allow another child to pass.

But it hung still.

He spun around and counted the children with a shaking finger. ". . . ten, eleven."

Eleven!

Himself and Christine. Thirteen! He spun back to the curtains. That left twenty-four, and twenty-four would constitute a binding two-thirds majority. But that couldn't be!

His chest felt tight, suffocating. The musty air made slow passage through his nostrils while he willed the curtain to move. *Just move. Please move. Please just one more and we can pretend that this never happened. Just one!*

But the curtains hung straight, and long seconds crept by like snails along a razor, headed toward certain death.

FIFTEEN OF the twenty-four dissenters agreed to follow Billy, Darcy, and Paul down to the lower levels right then, after the vote was finalized. The rest would quickly follow. Like the rest, they entered the main door with tentative steps, trembling like tiny high-strung dogs.

"Move it, you fools!" Billy snapped at the huddling newcomers. Their eyes bugged white from taut faces. They stopped when he yelled at them, and he realized they were so terrified they couldn't process his request. He adopted a different tack.

"Come on, you guys. Everything will be fine. I promise."

Within ten minutes they were running through the dark passage, intent on their discovery.

The entourage of defectors had been underground for about an hour when one of the boys yanked Billy from the study and insisted that a monk wanted to meet with him. "In that last tunnel," he said breathlessly. "The one on the far end."

A monk? The masked monk had shown himself to this boy?

Billy brought a hand to his chest and scratched the blistering skin under his tunic. The rash was spreading. Something that sounded like an Indian war cry echoed down the dark hallway, and he spun to see a flame round the corner, bent back in the wind, held by a running girl. He stepped aside and she rushed by him, yelping.

Idiots! Behind him six students slouched around his study. If they tore up his library, he would have their necks. He turned up the tunnel toward the main entrance.

He would have to leave them because the boy said the monk wanted to see him. Who did they think he was, some monk's little puppy? And in the first tunnel to boot.

The worms seemed to have multiplied. They were thick on the walls, sliding around like massive hot dogs. They'd come from deeper in the tunnels, presumably attracted to the humans.

He left the study tunnel, as they were now calling it, passed four other large tunnel openings, shifted the flaming torch to his left palm, and stepped into the far hall. He'd stuck his head in here once but was so taken by the study since that he hadn't returned. Maybe he should have come back sooner.

The tunnel bored into the cliff for twenty feet and then veered to the left. Yellow stones the size of his fingernails glittered on the rough walls. Billy wondered if this tunnel might actually be a mining shaft running through a gold vein. A large worm slid across the ceiling, and he passed under it.

He walked down the hall, amazed at the number of gems flashing from the walls. Not just gold nuggets, but gold chains and trinkets buried among the gems. It looked as if the cavern had been a vault for jewels before a huge blast ripped through the place, driving the precious stones and metal into the wall.

"Billy."

He jumped and swung his torch to the left. The monk stood in a darkened doorway, black mask reflecting Billy's wavering light. If he had used a torch to get here, he'd extinguished it.

"I have something to show you, my friend." The tall man seemed unaware of the large worm that slid down the wall two inches from his right arm.

"What?" Billy felt quite confident, all things considered. He really didn't need this man now that he knew the tunnels and had won his debate. He wasn't even sure why the monk—assuming he was a monk—unnerved him.

"You did well," the man said, making no move to show Billy anything.

"Who are you?"

"I am the man who made you."

"And does this man have a name? What do you have to lose now? We've won!"

A pause. "I have more at stake here than the persuasion of a few students. Far more than one little valley or one small country. You'll see soon enough, my little friend."

"Don't call me your little friend. For all I know, you are my enemy."

Something about the man really did frighten Billy. What could he possibly mean by all this talk? Surely he didn't think he could control the students just because they'd come down here. Even if he did, he couldn't take over the world with them or anything so stupid.

"You don't control us," Billy said.

No response.

"So what did you want to show me?"

The man turned and walked into the darkness behind him. Billy hesitated and then followed, staying clear of the worm that started to squirm when the overseer left. The monk pushed through a side door.

A large room opened up before them, lit by a dozen flaming torches mounted about the walls. They stood on a second-story balcony overlooking a long row of towering bookcases and round tables surrounded by chairs.

Billy caught his breath. The discussion out in the dark hall left his mind. The scene made his heart race. The bookshelves were filled with books. Even from his perch up on the balcony Billy could see they were all the same size, like the books in his study.

He swung to his right and dashed for the stairs that led down to the large library. He hurried out to the center of the room and ran a hand along the nearest round table. Amazing. The furniture looked like it had been hewn from mahogany, a thousand years ago before power tools made shaping wood so easy. He touched the spindles on a chair before him. Tiny chisel marks ebbed in the torchlight. And the cases!

He walked to the closest case. At first he thought the shelves were constructed of a blackened hardwood, but one touch and he knew these were made of iron. Black iron.

He stepped to the front of the cases. The books were firmly secured to the shelving by small chains. He gripped the spine of one and pulled, but he couldn't extract it past the links that held it.

Billy scrunched his brow and replaced the book, wondering how he could read books that couldn't be removed from their shelves. Maybe the man had a key. He ran his hand along the rough iron, captivated by the grandeur of the tall cases.

Billy stepped back to the tables and looked up at the balcony where the man overlooked the rail. "You like it?" the monk asked.

"Like it? I love it. Is it for us?"

"It is for them."

"*Them?*"

"The other children, Billy. So that you may continue in your study without being disturbed."

Billy didn't know if he liked the idea. He gazed about again and imagined a dozen students strewn about this place. Then he imagined the same students running up and down the tunnels, yelling. Maybe the man had a point.

He would make the rest leave the study hall and come here, to the library, so he and Darcy could find some peace.

"When?"

"Tonight. Tell them to eat from the worms."

Yes, of course, the worm sludge. He'd known all along that it held some great significance. "They already are."

"Then have them eat more. And encourage them to write."

"Write?"

"It feeds their minds and keeps them out of trouble. Write your story. All of you."

"It's *my* story."

"You will make it theirs."

"It's bad enough that Paul has—"

"Do it, boy. We need the children occupied. Nothing occupies the mind down here like writing. But even with writing, one requires a focus. Tell them what your story is and have them write. It will keep them quiet."

CHAPTER NINETEEN

PARADISE

Saturday afternoon

THE RED marble didn't budge for two hours, at least not that Johnny had seen, and he'd watched it pretty close. It wasn't that he was still so fascinated by the shooter, but that he was out of alternatives. He should be doing something to fix the predicament they were in, but he was at a loss.

He couldn't phone out. He didn't want to go out. He didn't want to stay in either, but that was all there was to do now. Stay in his room, a ball of frayed nerves, and watch the marble while his head spun through possibilities.

He thought he heard his mother stirring down the hall once, but he couldn't be sure with all the wind banging things against the house. And he wasn't sure he wanted to confront her now.

Black was bad.

Black was good.

Black was a demon from hell who'd come to destroy and kill and do whatever demons do.

Black was an angel sent from heaven to expose the evil in the hearts of Paradise and give them all a message of hope and grace.

No. Black was bad, period. Nothing good could possibly cause any of this, unless of course Paradise was a modern Sodom and Gomorrah and this was all a new kind of fire and brimstone.

Either way, Johnny was a boy caught in the middle, powerless to do anything about Black, regardless of whether he was a demon or an angel or just a psycho preacher who had drugged the town.

"What ya doin'?"

Johnny's eyes jerked away from the marble. Sally stood in the hall, staring at him. She wore one of the new outfits she'd bought in Grand Junction, brown slacks and yellow silky-looking blouse. She'd done her makeup and brushed her hair, even put on a gold necklace and hoop earrings.

"Nothing."

She walked forward, smirking. "Is that so?" Her eyes weren't right. They were glassy and slightly bloodshot.

"Did you drink any more of the water?"

"Don't be silly, Johnny. Why wouldn't I drink the water, hmm? Because you turned it off, that's why. How do you expect me to flush the toilet?"

"You turned it back on?"

"Why not? Tastes just fine to me."

Johnny felt nauseated. If his mother was gone . . .

"Why are you staring at the marble?" she asked, crossing slowly toward the dresser. "Hmm?"

"It . . . I don't know; I think it moved."

Sally picked the red shooter up. "It did, did it?" She turned it around in her fingers. Then she lifted it up, pressed it against her right eye, and faced him.

She looked like a red-eyed dress-up doll.

Sally released the marble and let it fall to the carpet. It landed with a *thump*.

"Looks like a regular marble to me," she said, walking toward the door.

"Where are you going?"

"I have to go," she said.

Johnny scooted to the edge of his bed and dropped his feet to the floor. "Where? Outside?"

She turned around and curtsied. "I have a date, Johnny. You like?"

A date?

"With who?"

Sally winked, then turned and disappeared down the hall.

Johnny sat frozen to his bed. He didn't want to think anymore. The room shifted out of focus for a moment—the water was speaking. Or Black was speaking. Whatever it was, he thought that maybe he should just start listening because he didn't want to be alone anymore.

Black is bad.

Black is not good.

Black is a psycho preacher, not an angel sent from heaven.

And you, Johnny, are not powerless.

Wind howled through the front door. The screen door slammed shut. He knew that there was no way to stop her, but he had to try—he had to do something!

Johnny ran for the hall and had just stepped past his doorway when a loud *plunk* sounded behind him.

He seized up, midstride. He turned back to his bedroom.

The first thing Johnny saw was that the red marble wasn't lying on the floor. The second was that it had embedded itself in the wall above his headboard.

Plunk.

The marble shot out of the wall and came to a halt six inches from his nose.

He jumped back, but the marble jumped with him, staying exactly six inches from his nose. Johnny turned and ran down the hall, too panicked to scream.

He'd only taken four steps before realizing that the marble wasn't behind him. It was zooming through the air, still six inches in front of his nose.

He yelped and instinctively swatted at it like he might swat a bee doggedly pursuing him. Amazingly he made contact, and the ball flew into the wall, then fell to the floor. And lay still.

For one moment.

It returned to the air and came to rest six inches in front of his nose. This time it started to bounce in little one-inch hops.

If the marble was dangerous, wouldn't it have hit him by now? Didn't matter. Johnny couldn't accept this impossibility, bouncing in the air right in front of his nose.

He backed up. The marble hesitated, then bounced forward.

On the other hand, Johnny *had* to accept this impossibility in front of his nose. It was real, it was here, and it was bouncing like a pet, daring him to play.

Play?

Or daring him to hit it again, so that it would have sufficient justification to smash a neat round hole through his forehead.

Why would a marble bounce in front of him? And how?

The marble stopped bouncing. It slowly floated wide, then down the hall. Johnny watched in fascination.

The red shooter came to rest just in front of the rear door. It began to bounce again. He couldn't help thinking that the marble was like a dog, begging him.

The back door opened. Wind howled. The screen door squealed. The marble slid outside.

The screen door remained still in the face of the wind, unaffected by gusts that whipped into the house and down the hall.

The marble began to bounce again.

Johnny felt like he was being led into a decision. The marble seemed to want him to follow.

To what? A trap set by Black? But if Black wanted him, why didn't he just come and get him? Johnny could hardly believe that he was thinking like this. He'd always doubted the supernatural, mostly because his mother didn't believe in it. She hated the church and convinced him over the years that everything the church stood for was nonsense. That included the miraculous—everything from a virgin birth to blind eyes being opened.

So what would she say about floating marbles?

Well, his mother had been wrong. This was no hallucination, no magic trick. That marble bouncing outside their back door was supernatural.

If he didn't follow, then what?

Johnny turned into the short hall that led to his mother's room. He stepped past the wall. Waited.

The marble zoomed into view. And waited.

Johnny took a step toward it and the red sphere moved away, back down the hall and out of view. Johnny stepped out and faced the back door. The marble had taken up its bouncing just outside the house again.

Completely out of alternatives, Johnny walked down the hall and, when the marble flew into the alley, out of the house.

Gusts of hot wind tore at his clothes, but Johnny hardly cared about anything as insignificant as wind. His eyes were on the marble, which now rose a good ten feet into the air where it hovered, oblivious, like Johnny, to the wind.

Then it moved. At an angle. Gaining speed. Over the trees. It streaked out of sight in the direction of the steep slopes that rose to the south.

And it didn't return.

The sky was empty except for black clouds and blowing leaves. The marble was gone. Johnny felt stranded. Maybe even betrayed. He waited a full minute. Nothing. He couldn't just walk up the mountain.

Strange how badly he wanted that marble to return.

Johnny turned back to the door and saw that it was still open. He took a step toward the house. The door slammed shut.

Okay, so maybe he was supposed to go the other way, up the mountain. There was only one way that he knew of—a path that headed up behind the old theater, and that was rarely used because it traversed property owned by some corporation out east who frowned on trespassing. More than one hefty fine had been paid over the years.

Johnny faced the alley, gathered his courage, and struck out against the wind.

CHAPTER TWENTY

THE MONASTERY
Saturday afternoon

TEN OF the eleven teachers were seated around the thick mahogany conference table when David Abraham stepped into the room from his office. Ten. Raul was still missing.

The teachers looked crestfallen by the monumental defeat they'd been handed two hours earlier. A dozen white candles suspended from a golden chandelier lit their faces. Heavy navy blue velvet drapes imported from Spain lined the entire conference room except for the south wall, where a large painting of two children tickling each other's noses with daisies served as a constant reminder of why they'd all given so many years of their lives to Project Showdown.

"Where is Raul?" David asked, crossing to the head of the table.

"He's checking on the students," Andrew said.

As if on cue, Raul walked in, robe swirling. He walked to the table quickly.

"Fifteen more have followed the others into the tunnels," he said. "That makes nineteen below and eighteen above. I can hardly imagine a worse scenario."

Raul reached the table, but didn't sit. He paced, ran an arm across his wet brow, pushing his locks to the side as he did. "I understand this principle of testing them by fire to harden the steel of their wills, but it appears those wills have melted. At least most of them, and I imagine others will follow."

"Sit down, Raul."

The head overseer sat.

"Where is Samuel?" David asked.

"He's retreated to his room. To write, he said."

David nodded. He had always known that this moment would come, and upon reflection his decision to withhold the truth from these good-hearted men seemed right. Certainly necessary.

Now they would learn what he told Samuel four days earlier, when Billy first entered the forbidden places below.

"Evil has conquered the students," Andrew said.

David pulled out his chair and sat. "Has it, Andrew? Our risk has increased, but can there be life without risk? Did God take a risk by creating man with a free will? Did he know of the horrors that would follow?"

"God knew the outcome. We do not," Andrew said.

"True, but allowed evil to test that outcome. Did you all think this day would never come?"

"Don't get me wrong," Raul said. "God allowing evil and us jeopardizing our life's work strike me as two different things. Just because God allowed evil doesn't mean we should. These are children, David! They're contracting a disease down there!"

David looked around the table. "The rest of you feel the same?"

To a man they looked desperate. Several nodded. The rest didn't respond.

Mark Anthony, the forthright monk who'd come to them from a little-known New Mexico monastery, Christ in the Desert, spoke. "Correct me if I'm misunderstanding the situation, but there are only three ways out of our current predicament. One, the children come to their senses on their own, through a second challenge perhaps. Two, the children remain in the tunnels and disintegrate into an unholy mess, perhaps ending in death. Or three, we intervene."

"I think that summarizes it well enough," David said. "Assuming we can stop what has started. And of these outcomes, which conforms to the purpose of this project?"

Raul responded from the far end. "Certainly not death."

"Then what, Raul, is your suggestion?"

The head overseer hesitated. No matter how much they protested, surely none of them would suggest throwing in the towel until every possible alternative had been explored. David was counting on it.

"We cast another challenge immediately," Raul said. "This time Samuel can argue—"

"The rules require us to wait three days."

"Then change the rules!" Andrew said. "It's the rules that have put us here."

"So you're suggesting we pull the plug on the monastery now? Send the children back to the orphanages and count our project as a failure?"

No response. Good. He would build on this position of strength.

"Excuse me for the interruption." Francis Matthew, the quiet priest from Ireland, looked up at David. "But do we know what is causing their disease?"

David eyed the man. "The worms," he said.

"Worms?" Andrew said. "What worms?"

"There are worms in the dungeons. Their excretions seem to have a harmful effect on . . . certain children."

The teachers stared at him, clearly taken aback by this revelation.

"How long have you known about these . . . these worms?" Andrew asked.

David put his elbows on the table and gently pressed his palms together. "Bear with me for a moment. Mark, please remind us why we are here."

The overseer looked around the table, searching for the catch. They all knew why they were here. Why would David ask?

"We are twelve teachers—now eleven—gathered from around the world for this project sponsored by Harvard University. The project's purpose is to examine innocence and the effects of evil upon that innocence. We are sworn to follow strict guidelines in the instruction of thirty-seven children, which you brought to this monastery nearly thirteen years ago. The children have been carefully isolated from influences that might corrupt them. When they are sixteen, they will be reinserted into society, and we will see what effects the children and society have upon each other."

Mark stopped. In a nutshell that was it. Or, more correctly, that was what they all thought.

"And how have they been instructed?"

"They have been instructed in all disciplines. We have carefully taught them to distinguish right from wrong according to a monotheistic world-view that follows the teachings of Christ."

"Good. And what else?"

"I'm not sure how specific you want me to be. You determined from the beginning that we should focus all of their learning through writing. We've taught the children to understand the best of all human experiences and to pen them eloquently. They are arguably the world's finest writers at this age."

"An understatement, wouldn't you say?"

"I would. To a student, they are brilliant writers, regardless of their age."

David nodded slowly. "You've each done a masterful job with admirable dedication. I couldn't have found more loving and honorable men if I'd spent a decade scouring the earth."

They sat in silence. The air felt heavy.

"What I'm about to tell you will come as a shock. When you've heard, I think you'll understand my decision not to tell you sooner."

For twelve years, he'd dreaded this moment. Now that it was upon him, he was eager for it.

"You all know of me as a historian and psychologist. You also know that I was and am an avid collector of antiquities. My collection was well known before I left Harvard University."

"Left Harvard?" Andrew asked. "You're no longer with the university?"

"No, my friend, I am not." He took a deep breath. "In truth, Project Showdown has nothing whatsoever to do with Harvard. Or, for that matter, any other institution. It is funded and run solely by me. The sale of my collection was quite lucrative."

He paused and studied them. They would need a minute to absorb that he'd been feeding them a bald-faced lie for the past thirteen years. They were in shock. Either that or exceptionally even mannered.

He seized on their silence.

"Nearly twenty years ago, an antiquities dealer from Iran sent me a rather large shipment of unspecified and unverified artifacts for a tidy sum. Mostly clay pots, for which I quickly determined I'd overpaid. But there was one item of interest.

"The shipment contained a crate of ancient books, mostly diaries kept by mullahs and such. Among the books was one particularly old leather-bound volume that was unique for two reasons. One, it appeared to be from a time period earlier than its binding would suggest, like finding a steel sword from the bronze age. Two, it contained only one entry. The rest of the book was blank, which I could not make sense of, because the title was *The Stories of History*. I analyzed the single entry and discovered that it was written in a unique kind of charcoal whose use was discontinued long before the kind of paper in the book was ever discovered. Very odd. Do you follow this?"

They stared at him without responding, but these anomalies weren't lost on such scholars.

"For two years the book sat in my study, a mystery to me. Then one day my eldest son, Christopher, when he was five years old, wrote in the book. Yes, he was a very bright boy."

They all knew that his eldest son had been killed in an automobile accident when he was six.

"How he got the book from the shelf I don't know, but he had the book on the desk behind me. It was a secretary I reserved for paying bills and attending personal business. An oak desk. Stained, not painted. But you see, that was a problem, because when I glanced back to see my son with the book, I saw that the desk was red, not a stained oak as it had been only minutes earlier. I was stunned. Here sat a bright red desk in my office, and I had no idea how it got there."

They stared, uncomprehending. And who could comprehend such a thing?

"It was only after I'd circled the desk twice in disbelief that I looked at what Christopher had written. 'The desk is red.' Those were the words on the page written in his distinctive chicken scratch. He'd written 'the desk is red,' and now I was looking at a red desk."

"Surely you aren't suggesting that it had anything to do with his writing," Andrew said.

"Exactly my thoughts. I was inclined to think that my mind was playing tricks on me. That I'd had someone paint the desk red and forgotten about it, and that my son was simply writing what he saw. But my wife assured me that the desk had indeed been stained oak. She thought I'd painted it that hideous color and was outdoing myself by making up some nonsense about forgetting."

"That could have been."

"But it wasn't. It took me three days to accept the fact that my son's writing had somehow changed the desk. You have to understand, I wasn't a religious man at the time. This desk turning red because it was written red was tantamount to words becoming real, something that I wasn't able to accept. I took a chip off the desk and had it analyzed—trust me, my friends, the desk was red. Candy-apple red, to be exact. It was only then that I formed my hypothesis. This book from Iran was a history book with the power to *create* history. The power to create fact. My son had written 'the desk is red,' and so the desk was red."

"Impossible!" Mark said.

David stood and paced at the end of the table. "Impossible? For me, at the time, yes, it was impossible. But for religious men like you, it should be commonplace!"

He leveled his argument with animated gestures now. "Think of it! Holy Scripture is *full* of references to the power of words. A disciple cries, 'Rise up and walk,' and a man rises up and walks. Christ calls to the storm, 'Be still,' and the waves become still."

David strode to the shelf, pulled out the black leather-bound Bible, and thumped it with his knuckles. "Recorded in this book are scores and scores of events that are no less impossible than my desk turning red. Speaking donkeys, writing on the wall, people rising from the dead. These impossibilities, my friends, are the word becoming real. The word becoming flesh. This is the common ground which all such events share."

He set the Bible down. "'In the beginning was the Word . . . and the Word became flesh and dwelt among us.' That which is supernatural becomes natural—this is the incarnation, not only of Christ, but of all supernatural events. Satan reveals himself as what? A dragon, a snake, through an antichrist who is raised from the dead. Now how do those compare to my desk turning red?"

"They have spiritual significance," someone said.

"And so does this, as you will clearly see." Sweat beaded David's face. He took a calming breath.

"Why would God allow such a book to—"

"Why would God allow Hitler his chapter in history? Why would God send a whale to swallow Jonah or turn a woman into a pillar of salt? Surely there were other ways. But I'll leave the particular methods of God to God."

They could hardly argue. No one attempted to.

"What happened to the book?" Andrew asked.

CHAPTER TWENTY-ONE

PARADISE

Saturday afternoon

IT TOOK Johnny twenty minutes at a steady climb to reach the lookout over Paradise. He'd been up to the large rock slab that jutted out from the mountain a dozen times with Roland and the others—this far and no farther, their parents warned.

From this vantage, the buildings lining Main Street looked like play blocks strung along a nearly obscured street, black beneath the dust. Other than the Starlight Theater and the church, both of which looked too large for the town, the buildings were proportionate and evenly spaced. Behind the town, homes scattered across the valley, and long dirt roads wandered between a couple dozen fruit farms.

Johnny looked at it all through a haze kicked up by the wind. He'd been delayed by a scene of carnage as he left town. Someone had taken an ax to the south side of a building. Claude and company. Other than the toppled theater sign and several busted-up telephone poles, he couldn't see the damage through the dust from this distance.

Above him, the clouds roiled. They seemed to be lower today. The air was thinner up here. His right leg ached.

He faced the mountain. From here, a game trail led to only God knew where. This was it. This was the end of the line, and no red marble.

Which meant that he'd been mistaken. Deceived. Stranded. He scanned the trees for the red orb. Anything to suggest the red orb had been here. Anything at all out of the ordinary.

But the only thing that was clearly out of the ordinary was the fact that he'd come up here because a floating red marble had led him up here.

Johnny faced the valley feeling like an imbecile. Maybe he'd imagined the whole thing after all. Maybe this was what the others were doing down in Paradise right now. Chasing little red marbles around. Or other things that had worked themselves into their minds. Things like Black.

He stared out at the clouds, swamped with desperation. Something bad was happening, and no one could stop it. His vision clouded, then distorted with tears. Black and gray swirled. There was nothing to do. Nothing to see besides a hazy blur and the red sun floating low . . .

Johnny blinked.

It was a red sun floating low on the horizon. It was the red marble, hovering over the cliff ten feet from him. His heart jumped.

The marble streaked past him and he whirled. It stopped momentarily at the trailhead, then plunged into the brush.

He didn't need any more encouragement. He didn't care if he was being led into a trap. A voice in his head urged him to follow that marble, so he did. Branches broke and fell limp as he passed.

He began to run, stumbled once, caught himself, and continued his pursuit up the trail.

He wasn't sure how long he'd been following the marble when the trees ended and he found himself facing a huge canyon. He pulled up, panting.

The canyon yawned before him like a mouth cluttered with broken teeth. Dozens of rock formations cast shadows along the sandy floor. Boulders the size of small cars squatted at the base of a dozen landslides.

Blue sky, not black clouds, arched above him. The sunlight was bright enough to make him squint after four days of dusk. He started forward, elated.

The red marble moved deeper into the canyon.

Johnny followed.

CHAPTER TWENTY-TWO

THE MONASTERY
Saturday afternoon

"WHAT HAPPENED to the book?" David said. "Yes, that's the question, isn't it? I'll spare you the tedious details, but suffice it to say that I confidentially tested the book in every way I knew how. My first discovery was that the book didn't work for me. Only for Christopher. If I wrote, 'I have a million dollars in my account,' and then checked my bank balance, I had no more than before. But if I told Christopher to write, 'Daddy has a million dollars in his account . . .' Well, you get the point."

"You did that?"

"Did what?"

"Had your son write a million dollars into your account?"

"Wouldn't you?" He winked at Raul. "I reported it as an error, though not for a few days, I'll admit."

Several soft chuckles.

"Why only children?" Matthew asked.

"Belief. I am quite sure that an adult who possesses the faith of a child would also be able to write history."

"Do you still have this book?"

David held up his hand. "Let me finish. I also learned that the dealer who sold me the crate containing the book had a whole cache of them. Blank, every one of them. I immediately acquired all of them."

"How many?"

"One thousand four hundred and forty-three. Which is—"

"So many!"

"—significant. Yes, so many. I had them sent express delivery at considerable expense. I was a mess those days. Every waking moment was consumed by the book. I knew I had in my possession the most powerful tool in history. I could do anything, make anything. My power was mind-boggling. Or I should say, my son's power was mind-boggling. Fortunately he was willing to write whatever I wanted him to write. Then one day, three weeks after Christopher wrote my desk red, he wrote three simple words about our cat in a fit of frustration. 'Snuffles is dead.' And Snuffles was dead."

"Dead?" Andrew said.

"Dead. Right there in the hallway with no apparent cause of death. This terrible side of the books kept me awake that night. And the next. Imagine what one evil man could do with such a weapon. To make matters worse, Christopher was catching on. He played some havoc with his best friend following a heated argument. He broke the boy's arm. The next morning I made a decision to rid the world of the books. I asked Christopher to write a notation which is permanently etched on my mind into the book:

"'The books of histories are hiding deep in a Colorado canyon, in a home consistent with their nature, where they will remain until the day they are meant to be found by those destined to bring love into the world.'"

"Here?" Andrew said.

"You're getting ahead of me." He picked up his pace, eager to tell them the whole truth. "The books vanished, all of them. One year later, my son Christopher was killed, as you know. It crushed me. I spent months trying to convince my wife, Andrea, to conceive—"

"Another child for the books," one of them said.

"No, the books were gone. I simply wanted another child. She did conceive, and Samuel was born into the world. But the pregnancy was difficult, and my wife died giving birth. This you also know."

David slipped into his seat and leaned back.

"What you don't know is the depth of my depression at her death. I took a sabbatical and set out to find the books. I was desperate to bring my wife back, you see. My sorrow clouded my judgment. For a full year I methodically searched every canyon in the Colorado mountains. But I'd written them into hiding until the day they were meant to be found, and I gradually became convinced that I had done so wisely."

"So then you didn't find them. You want the children to find them."

"Patience, Nathan. One night I had a dream. An epiphany that introduced me to God in a way that haunts me still. I was thoroughly convinced that I should raise my son, Samuel, in total innocence, so that if he were to have the books, he would use them only for good. This, I determined, was the reason God had allowed the events in my life."

"I thought—"

"I found the books the next day. Which only confirmed my vision. The books were meant to be found, and meant to be found by me. To be used, not by me, but by Samuel. Or perhaps more than one Samuel."

Understanding dawned on the overseers' faces.

"I found them here, in this monastery hidden from the world. All 1,443 of them. I found 666 of them in the dungeons below, which I promptly sealed. And I found 777 of them in the library above—though I don't believe there is any difference between the books above and those below except in their symbolic placement. You see, the books had found themselves in a place consistent with their nature, exactly as Christopher had written. My friends, we are sitting on more raw power than has been known by any mortal man in all of history."

"They . . . you're saying that the books are here now?" Andrew demanded. "Where?"

David drilled them with a stare. He rose to his feet, crossed the room, and pushed the wall. It gave way under his weight. Slowly a large bookcase rotated into view. Hundreds of books lined the shelves.

Leather-bound books.

David extracted one and brought it to them. He sat down and placed it on the table.

They leaned in as one. Ancient black leather, roughly an inch thick. No title.

"The rest are in the dungeons. To the best of my knowledge they are the source of the worms in the dungeons. It's not the disease on Billy's skin that worries me most, it's the deception brought on by the worms."

"But nothing you, or we, or any adult writes in these books will occur," Nathan said. "Unless they have the belief of a child."

"That is my belief."

"But if the children, these thirty-seven that we've raised, were to write in the books, their words would actually change history?"

"To a point. As I understand it, the books can't force a person's will any more than God can force a person's will. But they can do almost everything else."

Andrew leaped out of his chair, sending it skidding across the stone floor behind him. "The books in the dungeons—Billy's writing in them?"

David lifted a hand. "Please, Andrew, sit."

He did, but slowly, fearfully.

"The answer is yes. I don't think the children are aware of the books' power, but they are writing a story."

It was too much information in too short a time, but David was confident that if he guided them methodically through the meat of his choice, they would come around to seeing the wisdom of it.

"They are writing a story about a town called Paradise."

"Not the town in the valley below us?" Mark said.

"Yes, that Paradise."

"Is . . . What's happening?"

"The town is coming apart at the seams," David said. "Apart from one man who had a heart attack, I don't think there's been any death, but there is certainly a mess brewing in Paradise."

A cacophony of protest filled the room. He let it run until a single question rose above the rest. "How do we know this?"

"I have my ways. Trust me, Paradise is falling under Billy's pen."

"You said he doesn't know the power of his words," Raul said.

"No, but he knows plenty about the town. He can see what's happening in his characters' minds. Although he can't force their wills, this bunch is influenced easily enough."

David decided against telling them about Marsuvees Black at the moment. The fate of their old colleague, though interesting, wouldn't help them understand the overall picture.

"It must be stopped!" Andrew cried. "This has gone too far!"

"And how would you propose we stop it, Andrew?"

"Pull the children out of the dungeons! Burn the books!"

"And risk interfering with the path the books have put us on? We are here *because* of the books; I believe only they will show us the way out. Project Showdown isn't a benign experiment to test the effects of children raised in isolation. It's about life pitted against death. It's about good in conflict with evil on a grand scale. I launched this project knowing full well that one day we would be seated at this table facing this very dilemma. But I'm convinced that it will lead to good, to love entering the world, *otherwise the books would never have been found.*"

He opened the book in front of him and raised his index finger. "But just to be safe, I had Samuel write another entry into Christopher's book, after we found it in the monastery library. Naturally he was too young to know what or why he was writing."

David read. "'As of this date, any word written in this book or any similar book so described'—I'll spare you the tedious description—'that is written by any person not currently residing in the monastery, and/or that does not lead to the discovery of love will be powerless. This rule is irrevocable.' It goes on to describe in detail this summary. I also had Samuel write the names of every student."

They didn't know how to respond.

"I knew from my tests with Christopher that making something irrevocable seems to bind the books. So you see, I have taken every precaution. The books are now limited to only those who were in the monastery on the date that this rule was written. And their power is limited to the discovery of love."

He shut the cover. Samuel had written another entry on that day, but it would only confuse them at this point. God help him if Samuel's final entry ever came into play.

"And if you require other assurances, I will only say that I have other safeguards."

David said this with far more conviction than he felt, and he prayed that his conviction would prove him right. But anything could happen, regardless of Christopher's or Samuel's entries. For all he knew, those destined to bring love to the world, presumably those in this monastery, wouldn't do so for another fifty years, and then only after destroying only God knew what.

"We are on dangerous ground," Andrew said. The others nodded.

"Without question," David said. "But we can no more pretend that the books don't exist than we can pretend evil doesn't exist. We entered dangerous territory the day Adam and Eve ate the apple."

"But even they had a choice," Andrew said. "You're saying that the whole town is following these evil impulses from Billy? That he simply writes and they listen and follow him, correct?"

"Pretty much, yes."

"Are they nothing but sheep?"

"No more than Eve was a sheep in the garden of good and evil. Do you think that if God had put a Jane or a Betsy in the garden, she would have made a different choice? Given the hearts of the people in Paradise and the powerful nature of Billy's writing, the fall from what grace they had is practically wholesale."

For a while no one spoke. The idea of a *story* wreaking so much havoc daunted them.

"We've assisted the children up to this point. I don't see why we can't nudge them now," Daniel said.

"On the contrary, we must let the children find their own way now, because it's what they've chosen. What is the greatest virtue?"

"Love."

"Yes. Love. From the beginning we've agreed that we must give the children the freedom to choose their own way. Should that change now that the stakes appear to be higher? Love can only be found in freedom of choice. And for choice to exist, there must be an alternative to choose. Something as compelling as love. Something that is evil, yes?"

"Yes," Raul said.

"We must allow our students the opportunity to love the truth in the face of alternatives. We've effectively put Paradise in the hands of the children, as intended by whatever force allowed me to find the books in the first place. Nothing we do can reverse that."

Andrew leaned forward again. "But to let them stay in the *dungeons—*"

"Let me tell you something, Andrew. The world *lives* in a dungeon. It's dark and cold and full of the worst, but it's where the world lives. Most well-meaning books do little to illuminate the way. What we're doing here requires a view of the dungeon. Do you understand? It's the only way to bring hope to that dungeon."

"And in the meantime whatever Billy and the others write will continue to bring destruction."

"To a point, yes."

"I still don't think—"

David slammed his palms on the table. "Then stop thinking, Andrew, at least for a moment! You've believed in me this far; you must believe that I've applied enough reason to Project Showdown to cover a week's worth of argument. You must believe me when I say that if we interfere with the children, we may pay a price far more devastating than Billy's writings."

He drew a deep breath. "We must trust in God. Which in this case means trusting in the books that surely he has given us. To betray the books is nothing less than a betrayal of the creative power that God has entrusted us which in turn is a betrayal of the children! We must trust the books to deliver us love in the end."

David couldn't remember being so forceful, but it was the only way he knew to bring them quickly up to speed with a matter that he'd lived with for twelve years.

Andrew broke the silence. "Can the damage be corrected by another student's writing? Samuel and Christine and some of the others could write."

David took a deep breath. "Samuel is writing," he said. "He's been writing for four days now."

CHAPTER TWENTY-THREE

PARADISE
Saturday afternoon

THE CANYON was deep and long, but the marble moved slowly enough for Johnny to keep up. He could see that the canyon ended ahead, maybe a hundred yards off. When he'd walked half of it, the red marble veered to the left and disappeared behind a towering gray boulder.

Johnny stopped. The sun was high, but the sheer rock rose so high that even now long gloomy shadows filled the canyon. He walked to the boulder and made his way around the stone.

Here, the canyon wall gaped to reveal another, smaller canyon. Johnny stopped and squinted, trying to make sense of the shadows moving across the granite face.

No marble.

The smaller canyon was wedge-shaped, like a teepee. It ended in a wall that rose roughly fifty feet. Nothing but rock.

He walked toward the wall. His mind was evenly divided, one half insisting that he had no business being here, the other calling him forward. He realized he was holding his breath. He exhaled.

He was ten feet from the cliff when something caught his eye. An irregularity on the surface. A straight, vertical line. Like someone had cut into the stone with a saw.

He ran his hand along the crack.

But it wasn't just a crack. It was the edge of a door. He saw the latch a foot lower. Johnny jerked his hand back. He stood frozen for three loud heartbeats, then turned and ran toward the safety of the boulder.

CHAPTER TWENTY-FOUR

THE MONASTERY
Saturday afternoon

SAMUEL HURRIED down the hall, eager to tell his father this plan that filled his mind in the hours since the debate.

He'd been writing in one of the blank books for four days now, carefully and with tempered purpose, but the time for caution had passed. Frankly, he couldn't wait to begin writing again, but this time with a new purpose.

He discovered on the first day that his writing connected with the characters of Paradise in a unique way. This storytelling experience was more enthralling than any he'd experienced. When he wrote into Paradise, he felt like he was really there, with the characters, speaking into their minds and hearing their thoughts. Thus he could extrapolate Billy's actions by reading the minds of the characters that Billy was influencing.

He also learned from these people what was happening in Paradise, at least to the extent that they actually knew what was happening. He could see the town in his imagination almost as clearly as if he were there.

He also experienced unique limitations. Unlike in his other stories, he couldn't force the characters to follow his every whim. He could play a game of wits with them, interjecting thoughts and suggestions, but in the end the characters did what they chose to do.

Samuel had written hundreds, maybe thousands of suggestions into the minds of Paradise's residents, and although each time he felt at least some influence on them, nearly every character he wrote into chose Billy's way. It made him wonder how Billy was able to influence the people so effectively.

Samuel couldn't write more than one character at a time, so he focused on the most responsive character he found—Johnny. There was something unique about the boy, and Samuel was sure it had something to do with the fact that Johnny had seen Black for who he was when he first walked into town.

Oddly enough, Samuel couldn't enter the mind of Marsuvees Black, the monk who betrayed them all. In a way that Samuel couldn't yet understand, Billy and Black were working together. As an active and willing accomplice, the monk's power was stunning. Samuel couldn't tell where Black ended and where Billy's writing began.

Either way, nothing happening in Paradise was a figment of the citizens' imaginations. It was all real. All except the sludge that Black had persuaded them was hallucinogenic, which, although real enough, was nothing more than starchy water. Billy's writing, not a hallucinogenic sludge, had deceived the people of Paradise. Black had merely distracted them long enough for Billy to sink his claws deep into their minds.

But now Samuel had a plan that he was quite sure would take Billy and company by storm. And for that plan to succeed, he needed his own accomplice.

Johnny.

He knocked on his father's office door. After a second attempt returned no response, he walked in. Vacant. But he could hear muffled voices from the conference room next door.

Samuel crossed to the door, knocked, and waited.

"Come."

He walked into a meeting of the overseers, who all wore dazed expressions.

David rose from the table. "Hello, Samuel."

Samuel hurried to him, eager. At the last second, he second-guessed his intention to hug his father and instead took David's arm.

"Hello, Father."

An awkward moment passed.

David glanced at the teachers. "Excuse me." He stepped away with Samuel. "What is it? You have something?"

"I have a plan."

David patted his hand and lowered his voice. "Nothing to them about Marsuvees yet."

Samuel nodded. "Okay."

Turning back to the table, David reassumed his usual volume. "My son has something he wants to share with us." David looked at him. "Go ahead, Samuel."

"Then they know about the writing?" Samuel asked.

"They know," his father said.

"And you know that I've been writing for several days now."

"Yes, they know everything."

Except about Marsuvees Black.

He let go of David's arm. "Among many things I've learned about how the books work is this fact: though I can't make people do things, I can do whatever I want with objects and animals—anything that doesn't have the capacity for moral choice, I would say. Billy's done some very interesting things . . ."

He decided now wasn't the time for details.

"If I were to write, 'The red marble on Johnny's dresser rises into the air and floats,' for example, then that's precisely what happens. But if I write, 'Johnny grabs the marble,' Johnny only has that thought. The decision to grab or not to grab is his. Has my father explained this?"

"Some, but go on," David said. "Hearing it from you is different."

Samuel addressed his father. "The bottom line is, I can't make ordinary people do things, but I doubt the rule applies to unordinary people."

"Unordinary, meaning what?"

"Fictional characters."

A light filled his father's eyes.

"I'm quite sure that I could write a character into existence, and it would have no will of its own."

"Turning an idea into reality," his father said.

"No different than turning an idea of a marble floating into reality when you think about it."

"That could work?" Andrew asked.

"You haven't tried it?" his father asked.

"No. Not without talking to you. But I'm sure it will work."

"So you want to write a fictional character into Paradise."

"Yes. We have three days before we can challenge Billy here. But his mind is in Paradise. If we can defeat him in Paradise, I think he'll fail here."

"Excellent!" David thundered. "Excellent thinking!" He grabbed Samuel by both shoulders. "I knew I could count on you." He beamed at the overseers. "You see?" Back to Samuel. "Have you given any thought to this character?"

"I would like to write a cop," Samuel said. "The law. And not just an ordinary lawman, but a gunslinger who has the skill and power to bring some order to Paradise."

"The law. I like it. I like it."

"Why only one?" one of the teachers asked. "Why not five, or ten?"

"I think prudence would dictate caution," David said. "Assuming this all works, we don't know what will happen to such a character."

"If you write them into existence, then surely you can write them out."

"So it would seem. But we don't know, do we? We can't very well populate the world with fictitious characters."

"The character that I write will have the strength of five," Samuel said. "I've decided to call him Thomas."

"Thomas?" Raul asked, eyebrow arched. "As in Doubting Thomas?"

"No, Thomas, after Thomas Hunter." Samuel looked at the history book. "In honor of the first entry."

David picked up the book and flipped it open. "I told you there was a single entry when I first received this book. It's a very short entry about Thomas Hunter and Monique de Raison—I'm sure you all know their names from the Raison Strain. It appears that this book is tied directly to him."

He faced Samuel. "So, when will your Thomas bring the law to the streets of Paradise?"

"As soon as I can bring Johnny up to speed."

"Johnny?"

Samuel hurried for the door. "He's a boy from Paradise who's going to help me."

"He agreed to this?"

Samuel turned back. "Not yet. But he will soon enough."

He left the teachers staring after him and hurried for the stairs. It was time to meet Johnny.

THE RED marble hadn't shown itself again. Had it come from behind that door?

Johnny waited ten minutes on the far side of the boulder before concluding that the marble was gone for good. At least for now.

He sneaked around the corner and peered at the box end of the smaller canyon. Nothing had changed. The marble had led him here, that much he knew for certain. He couldn't just run home now. Home was where things were going very, very wrong.

He stared at the door's faint outline for a full minute, working up his courage, assuring himself that, even if it was a door, it probably just led to an old mine shaft or something.

He walked up to the latch. Put his hand on it. Rusted metal. He pushed down. It moved with a creaking sound. The door gaped, four inches at first, then Johnny pushed it all the way open.

At first he wasn't sure what he was seeing beyond the door. Shadows. Another cliff wall. No, a man-made wall. Huge stone blocks were stacked in a brick pattern, rising five stories. A large cross topped two massive wooden doors, dead center. Rows of windows broke the building's flat lines. The space between the old rusted door that Johnny had opened and the large wooden doors was a stone courtyard, covered with sand in a scattered pattern.

An old mining operation? Looked more like something built by Indians. Something ancient. Amazing how well hidden it was. He'd never heard a word of this place.

The large door moved. Then stopped. But he was sure he'd seen it move. Johnny would have turned and run, but his legs refused to budge.

The door opened. A boy about his height, with blond hair and clear blue eyes, stepped out. He wore a white short-sleeved button-down shirt and blue shorts. White socks, brown shoes. The boy's hands hung loosely at his sides.

The boy walked halfway across the courtyard and stopped. "Hello, Johnny."

The boy knew his name? Johnny still couldn't move.

"Did you like the marble?"

"I . . . How did you know my name?"

The boy smiled. "That's a long story." He walked forward and held out his hand. "My name is Samuel."

Johnny took the hand. Real flesh, real eyes, real hair. Real boy.

Samuel walked by. "Follow me."

Johnny finally got his legs working. He followed the boy out into the canyon, where Samuel stopped and stared north, in the direction of Paradise.

"What's it like?" Samuel asked.

Johnny stepped to his side and faced the gaping canyon. "What's what like?"

"Life out there. You know, in the real world. Looking at it out here, it seems like a whole different reality."

"You don't come from the real world?"

Samuel looked at him with those bright blue eyes. "Real? Sure. But as you can see, it's pretty isolated up here. Did the marble scare you?"

"At first. You did that. How did you do that?"

"That's part of the story. But it's a wild story. I'm not sure you're ready for it."

"After what I've seen? I can't think of anything that would surprise me. Do you know what's been happening in Paradise?"

"I know some things, but I need to know more, which is why I brought you up here."

Johnny looked back at the hidden door. Still there. And when he turned his head, the boy was still there.

"How did you make the marble move?"

"I wrote it in a book. Not your typical writing book, but a book that makes whatever you write in it happen. Most things, anyway—I can't make people do things they don't want to do."

Johnny didn't know what to say. This was as unbelievable as Black pulling his lip off his chin. He wasn't dreaming, was he?

Samuel grinned. "I told you it was wild. You're not ready for it."

"I am ready," Johnny said, not sure why he would claim any such thing. "It's just . . . I've never heard of anything like it."

"You haven't? You don't go to church then. You ever hear of the Bible?"

"Yeah."

"It's full of stories that are as crazy as this one. And do you know why they sound crazy? Because they break all the rules that nature sets. They're supernatural. Crazy, unless you understand the rules of the supernatural, then they're not crazy at all. Then they're everyday life, and that's what we have here."

"Everyday life?"

"Everyday life."

Johnny recalled the afternoon when Black walked into town. "So men walking around without flesh on their faces, and apples turning into snakes, and marbles floating through the air are just everyday life?"

"They can be. They will be. They are, aren't they? You tell me. You saw it all with your own eyes. I have to rely on my mind."

"So it's all real. Everything happening down there is real?" Johnny asked.

"As real as anything you've ever touched or smelled or tasted or seen or heard."

"Then who is Marsuvees Black? He's the cause of all this, isn't he?"

"Only a small part of the cause," Samuel said. "There's Billy, and mostly there's the people of Paradise. But to answer your question, Black used to be a monk from Nevada. Before that a performer in Las Vegas. He was on the staff here at the monastery before he disappeared last week. He found the books in the dungeon, discovered their power, and decided to wreak a little havoc. My theory."

"So if he's, whatever, dealt with—"

"Then you still have Billy and the people of Paradise. Black's only one man with a few tricks up his sleeve. Maybe that's an understatement, but Marsuvees depends on Billy, because Billy has the books. See, grown-ups can't write in them. But Billy—he can do a lot of damage so long as the people follow his suggestions. We have to get to the people, Johnny."

Johnny pressed his hands against his temples and closed his eyes. "Okay, maybe you're right. Maybe this is too much for me. None of it makes any sense. You're talking about Billy and dungeons and books with supernatural power . . . It's crazy!"

Samuel smiled. "So we're back to that word again." He clasped his hands behind his back and paced slowly. Johnny had never heard a kid talk the way Samuel talked, walking about like a miniature monk. Not that he minded—it gave him more confidence in the boy.

"I need your help, Johnny. That's why you're here. And in order for you to help me, you're going to have to understand what's really happening in Paradise. And why."

Samuel faced him. "But nothing I tell you will make any sense unless you believe in the supernatural. You have to believe that God not only exists but that life is ultimately about an epic battle over the hearts of mankind. Good versus evil, not only as theological constructs or ideas, but as real forces at work wherever they are permitted to work. Do you follow?"

What choice did he have? His whole world had been turned topsy-turvy in four days, and short of a better explanation, the supernatural worked just fine.

"I guess."

"Not good enough."

"I mean yes. How can I not believe after what I've seen?"

"Trust me, seeing has very little to do with believing. Belief is a matter of the heart, not the eyes. Although I will admit, these books make the struggle between good and evil pretty visible in Paradise."

For the first time Johnny began to feel a sense of hope. He wasn't a lost soul in the hell that was swallowing Paradise. He was the person that Samuel had brought up to the mountains with a red marble.

His mind grappled briefly with that image.

But he had to believe. He would believe.

"I believe," he said. "If this isn't a dream—"

"No ifs."

"Okay then. I believe."

"Good. I think you're ready to hear the whole story," Samuel said.

AN HOUR later, Johnny sat on a boulder next to Samuel, stunned. It made sense, of course. Seeing it through Samuel's eyes, it made perfect sense.

All except for where the books had come from in the first place, but Samuel had no answer for that.

Samuel seemed content to let the silence stretch.

"So you want me to tell them all this at the meeting tonight," Johnny finally said. "Tell them that they've been deceived by Black and that a cop is coming to town tomorrow morning to set things straight."

"Exactly. Don't tell them how you know and don't say a word about Billy, but throw the book at Black."

Johnny frowned, nervous already. "And you want me to help this cop. Show him around and report back to you."

"That's it." Samuel grinned. "I need eyes on the ground, not only for Thomas, but for me. Billy's got Marsuvees Black; I have you."

"Sounds like a mismatch," Johnny said.

"Billy's no match for me."

"But I'm not sure how well I stack up against Black."

"Trust me, Johnny. This will work."

"What if this fictional character you write doesn't work? I mean, it's never been done before, so how can you be so sure?"

"Well, we'll just have to see, won't we? I'm open to suggestions."

Johnny couldn't think of any.

"So, it's a deal then?" Samuel stretched out his hand.

Johnny took it. "Okay. It's a deal."

"I'll be with you all the way."

"Could Black hurt me?"

Samuel hesitated. "If we don't stop them, yes. And that's what we're trying to do here. That's why I need you."

"Why me? I mean, why are the rest being led along by Billy so easily while I'm not? I mean, I know I started to believe the lies a few times, but I resisted, right? Why don't the rest?"

"My father says that all of you should have fallen to Black's lies. Eve ate the apple, right? He says that no matter who was in that garden at that time, they would have done the same. All the suffering and evil the world has ever seen wasn't because God made a mistake by putting Eve in there instead of someone else. Everyone would have done the same in her place. Follow?"

"Makes sense. Never thought about it that way. Then why not me?"

"Simple. You and Cecil saw Black for what he was before he started playing tricks. Why Billy let you see him, I don't know, but seeing Black as a bag of bones was enough to put the fear of God in you. Then I came along and began to counter Billy's nonsense. You felt it, but not as convincingly as the rest. And there's still Stanley Yordon. When he gets back, he could turn out to be a friend in all of this."

Johnny looked back into the smaller canyon. It was all amazing. Hardly believable. But he did believe. He really did.

"You want to take a look?" Samuel asked.

"At the monastery?"

"Yes!" Samuel jumped up, excited. "Just inside. I can't take you around, but it won't hurt to look."

"Sure."

Samuel grabbed his hand and pulled him to the gaping door. "The whole monastery is hidden by the cliffs except for a few places, where my father's camouflaged it. The glass on top, the front, some windows and doors. I've never seen, but they say it's hidden from the air."

Johnny looked up at the towering face, then at the large door beneath a huge old cross. "How long has it been here?"

"As long as the books at least—that's almost twenty years."

"Incredible."

Samuel led him to the double doors, poked his head in, then pushed one open. The foyer was dark, but there was enough light to reveal old paintings on stone walls on either side. A thick wooden table sat at the center of the area, shiny with layers of dried resin. Tall stained-glass windows peered in from above. No sign of lights. The stone floor was slick and shiny with wear.

It certainly looked ancient.

"It's huge," Johnny said.

"This? This is nothing. Go to the right and you find the library. Go up one floor and you'll find the cafeteria. The main hall straight ahead leads to the upper levels. The residences and the classrooms."

"And what about the basement?"

Samuel gestured. "Off the main hall to the left. A long series of stairs take you down. Not a place anyone in his right mind would want to go."

"Incredible."

Samuel put an arm around Johnny's shoulder and pulled him around. He walked with him back out. "We're a team, Johnny. You and me. We'll fix this mess for sure."

In some strange ways, Samuel seemed much younger than thirteen. In other ways, like in the way he reasoned, he seemed more like an adult. A strange mixture of innocence and education. Probably because he was isolated in the monastery his whole life.

Johnny faced the boy. "I need something from you."

"Say it."

"It's my mom. She's . . ." He hesitated. "Black's after her."

"You have to remember, we can't make people do things."

"But can you help?"

He looked at the monastery and spoke as much to himself as to Johnny. "I'll talk to Christine and Tyler. They can help." He slapped Johnny on the back. "Good idea. But you have to promise to talk to the whole town."

"I will."

Samuel grinned. "Prophet Johnny."

"Trust me, I don't feel like a prophet."

"I'll help you. Listen for me."

"I'm counting on it."

CHAPTER TWENTY-FIVE

PARADISE
Saturday night

TOTAL DARKNESS slid over Paradise early that night, before seven, which was abnormal this time of year. Clouds clamped down on the town like a blackened steel lid. Johnny looked for his mother when he stumbled into town at last light, but he couldn't find her.

He couldn't find anyone. No surprise.

He ran straight for the church with one thought on his mind: Black. He had to reach the church before Black did, so he could figure things out in his head before he did what he was about to do.

Which was what?

Johnny eased to a walk. Which was confronting Black head-on. Which was telling the whole town that they'd been deceived. Which was that the law was coming in force first thing in the morning.

Which was, having successfully completed his duties as prophet, to get to a safe place until morning.

He had rehearsed a hundred stinging one-liners while descending the mountain. He couldn't remember any at the moment, but they would come to him.

Johnny mounted the stairs, thankful that he'd beat the town to the service, assuming there was a service. If Billy found out what he and Samuel were up to, he might change things up on them.

He slid into the church and crept across the foyer to the auditorium doors. No sound. He nudged the doors open a crack, peered into the sanctuary, and caught his breath.

A sea of still heads faced an empty pulpit. Several dozen candles lined the stage. The sanctuary flickered in the shifting flames, absolutely silent.

Johnny felt his heart skip a beat and then knock into double time, just like that: *boom*, and then nothing, and then *boom-ba boom-ba boom!*

All four-hundred-some residents sat in the pews, motionless, staring as though seated for a séance. He wanted to run from the church, but the scene glued his feet to the carpet. Nobody seemed to notice him. He craned for a better view.

Children sat obediently by their parents, legs hanging from the pews. No twitching here, much less running and screaming through the rows. For a brief moment Johnny wondered if they were all dead, stuck here in rows like trophies, forced to sit while Black force-fed them his twisted version of grace and hope.

He imagined Black standing tall behind the podium, a monk from Vegas doped up on worm sludge. His eyes were gone and his lips opened wide. His white face mouthed the word *hope*, only it came out long and raspy.

Hhouuuppe.

His lower jaw fell from his face and gaped open to a black throat. His tongue wagged like a worm freshly yanked from the garden.

Johnny blinked and the image vanished.

A woman he recognized as Louise Timbers sat directly ahead of him in the last pew. Her blonde hair sat on her head like a twisted bird's nest, complete with pieces of straw and clumps of sand. Streaks of dried mud ran down her neck, disappearing below a blouse torn at the collar to reveal half of her left shoulder. A gash already scabbed over glared rusty red on her white skin.

They didn't all look as bad as Louise, but a lot did. The bad ones were here and there throughout the church, wearing sores like a new fad.

Johnny looked down the aisle where Claude Bowers sat next to Chris Ingles on the front pew. Peter and Fred sat on one side of them. Roland sat on the other. All five looked as if they had just engaged in hand-to-hand combat on a battlefield. Claude sagged in his seat, hands folded between his knees, mouth hanging open, spittle running down his chin.

Steve Smither sat with blood-spattered cheeks. He'd butchered a cow or something and not bothered to clean up. His wife, Paula, sat five rows behind and to his right. Unlike the others, she was cleaned up pretty, smiling at the empty podium. And beside her . . .

Sally. Even from this distance, Johnny could see that his mother was gone.

Johnny began to tremble with fear.

Crinkling paper disturbed the quiet, and Johnny glanced at the sound. Father Yordon's secretary sat at the far left, carefully unwrapping a Twinkie, shifting her eyes to see if anyone had heard that first loud tear. She wore a beard of blood, dried and cracking over her lips and chin.

The door to the church opened and a couple hurried in. The Jacksons, only they hardly looked like the Jacksons. They walked by Johnny without noticing him and entered the sanctuary.

Johnny stood back from the sanctuary doors. Paradise was hell.

But Black hadn't taken the stage yet.

Prophet Johnny.

Now, Johnny. Do it now, before Black comes to feed them his lies.

He had no choice. If someone didn't do something . . .

I'm with you, Johnny.

He took a deep breath and moved toward the door.

Another voice cackled in his mind. *Wanna trip, boy? How about a stake between your toes? Or a new set of eyes?*

His Adam's apple lodged in his throat, and he had to swallow to free it. He entered the sanctuary.

The people were like wooden dolls. The pulpit still stood vacant. The clock on the wall read 6:55.

I'm with you, Johnny.

A rattling chuckle echoed through his mind. Billy? Or Black.

Johnny forced his foot forward and lowered his head. He pushed himself up the aisle.

I can do this—it's just carpet passing under my feet, that's all. The church is really empty and I'm just rehearsing graduation or something. And even if it isn't really empty, the people in the pews aren't really looking at me. People always think people are looking at them when they're not.

Then he reached the platform. He stepped up. The candles glowed bright in long rows—short candles, tall candles, some thin and some fat, all flickering on the platform.

Any minute now someone's going to yank me back by the shoulders. A dizzying weakness washed over him, and for a moment he thought he was falling, but he grabbed the pulpit and held himself upright.

He pulled himself to the podium. Looked up.

He expected to see a thousand black holes staring at him. Instead he saw their eyes, blank, drained, and drooping. But eyes, not holes. They were all there staring at him, as if wondering what *he* was doing there.

Who is this interesting little boy in front of us? Some kid's up at the podium. Isn't that Sally's kid? What's he doing up at the podium?

They looked half-dead, as if they'd all just spent two sleepless days harvesting fruit and hadn't bothered to wash before coming to church. The candles lit their pupils, hundreds of miniature flames flickering in their skulls.

Speak the truth, Johnny. Tell them.

He swallowed and cleared his throat. "Hey." He immediately realized that only those in the first few rows could hear him. He shifted to his left and bent the microphone down.

"Hey"—his voice rang out over the speakers—"has anyone noticed that something strange is happening in Paradise?"

Not a soul moved.

"Has anybody noticed that the town is falling apart? The wind blowing without moving the clouds? The dust piled high like in a desert? People acting strange?"

"Yeah," a voice said.

Johnny looked toward the back. Old Man Peterson stood. The man wasn't like the others. "I've noticed all right," the man croaked. "Someone did some damage all right."

"Shut up, Bo," a woman said from across the auditorium. "Sit down and shut up."

A cackle rippled through the crowd. Old Man Peterson sat.

I believe, Johnny. Shout it from the rooftops.

In that moment, Johnny knew what he had to do. It didn't make any sense to him, and it had nothing to do with Bo or his wife yelling at him to shut up. It was just for him. He needed strength.

Johnny clenched his eyes shut. "I believe," he said. Then again, "I believe. I believe."

Louder, Johnny.

He felt a dam burst in his chest. "I believe!" He screamed it with all of his might. "I believe. I believe!" His voice reverberated through the room. He opened his eyes. The congregation just stared at him. But it didn't matter now.

"Bo's right," he said loudly. "Paradise is falling apart at the seams, and most of you are too blinded to see it. Wake up!"

"Hello, boy."

Johnny froze. Black's voice, ahead and on the left. He scanned the pews. Marsuvees Black sat next to Steve, arms folded across his chest, grinning at Johnny.

Johnny gripped the podium to steady himself.

Black stood. "You think anyone here cares what a whippersnapper rabble-rouser says?"

Johnny spoke before he lost his nerve. "Say what you want, but you're not a prophet from God with a message of hope and grace. You're a monk from the Nevada desert full of death and destruction."

Black took that in, and Johnny could see him change strategy on the fly, watched a new approach register on his bronzed face. The man stepped up to the platform and smiled sweetly at Johnny. Johnny thought Black might take his hand and pat it condescendingly.

"Death and destruction?" He swept a hand out at the crowd. "Do you see any death and destruction? No, you see a church full of souls who have tasted life and freedom like they've never tasted it before."

Johnny looked down at Claude Bowers sitting like an overstuffed mummy with drooping eyes. A half-empty bottle nestled in his crotch. He didn't look a bit affected by Johnny's accusations. Nor did anyone else.

"I'll tell you what," Black said. "Let's let the people tell us what they think."

Black brought his hands together. A thick finger of blazing white light crackled to life on the ceiling. Johnny watched in amazement as it slowly elongated, reaching down about six feet, as if God himself had stuck his finger through the roof and was now pointing at the congregation.

The people craned their necks in wonder.

Black chuckled. "Belieeeeeve," he said in a low, soft voice. He clapped his hands again.

A thunderclap shook the building from the inside out. The light ballooned and sent a jagged bolt of lightning to the floor. The lightning crashed into the aisle and was gone, leaving smoke from a six-foot hole in the carpet snaking toward a charred ceiling.

Cries of alarm erupted. Those who'd been dozing or even thinking of dozing were now on their feet, shouting in startled terror.

Marsuvees Black lifted both arms wide and pointed his chin to the ceiling. He sang one long note. The note grew and echoed and swallowed the church. The cries were overwhelmed and then silenced altogether. There was just Black on the stage with his one-note solo, inhumanly loud and deeply troubling.

At least for Johnny.

The rest seemed to find it calming.

Black ended abruptly and lowered his head, keeping his hands outstretched. "Do I have your attention? I think I do. Are you right, Johnny? Am I a demon from hell come to kill your old men?"

He snapped his fingers. Yellow flames hissed to life in each hand and licked six inches of air. "Or have I come to lick the fires of hell from your wounds with pleasure and grace, and with hope for more pleasure and grace?"

Black kept his eyes on the congregation and brought both hands to his face. He began to lick the fire with a long pink tongue. Faster, ravenous, sucking his fingers. It reminded Johnny of a dog going after meat. Black jabbed his right hand into his mouth, past the knuckles. The fire hissed out. He did the same with his left hand.

Black sighed with satisfaction, and then motioned to the people with his wet hands. "You tell me. Have I come to kill you, or have I come to heal your wounds?"

"You've come to heal our wounds!" a voice called from Johnny's right. Katie stood. She looked as though she were going to a dance, all made up and pretty except for a few scratches on her face.

She winked at Black. "I don't know about the rest of you, but I've never felt more alive in all my life."

But look at you, Katie! You're dying! Johnny opened his mouth to say it when Steve jumped to his feet.

"We're being set free!" Steve yelled. "We're learning what it means to be alive. Nobody's going to take that from us. No one!"

A dozen excited parishioners stood to their feet with Steve, all speaking at once, shouting out their agreement in a muddled mess of noise.

Sally watched the whole thing with wide eyes. She seemed confused, caught between Black and her own son.

Johnny could hear Peter Bowers's high-pitched voice through the chorus of objections. "What do you know, Johnny, you little spineless wimp. We should chop off your thumbs, boy! Black's cool."

"He's a liar!" Johnny shouted.

The room shut down. They seemed surprised that he was still up there, much less yelling at them.

Johnny forged ahead, as forcefully as he could. "The police are coming in the morning. I mean it; when they come, they'll put this all straight."

"You lie, boy," Black said in a low voice.

"If I'm wrong and they don't come, then string me up, for all I care. Chop off my thumbs, Peter. But I'm not wrong! You'll see. Thomas is coming. I promise you that."

Black looked amused.

Outrage broke out again.

"Silence!" Black shouted. Those standing took their seats.

Black eyed Johnny, still amused. He stepped toward the podium. Johnny stepped back. The man reached into his trench coat, calmly removed a book, and laid it on the pulpit as if it were a Bible.

But this was no Bible. It was a leather-bound book that reminded Johnny of the books that Samuel had described. A book from the monastery, the ones Billy was writing in.

Black rubbed his hands together slowly and lifted his eyes to the people. He seemed to be considering his next move. Johnny knew his. It was time to leave.

But he was momentarily fascinated by Black's disorientation. The news about Thomas had thrown Black for a loop. The man had a weak side after—

Black lifted his arm high and brought it down on the pulpit with a tremendous *crack*. The podium split in two. Black stood, trembling from head to foot. His right hand began to bleed.

"We will only be so tolerant of deceit!" Black said. "Continue down this road and you will end up like Billy."

A few scattered *amens* sounded to Johnny like the whispers of aimless ghosts.

Johnny ran for the door. He leapt off the platform, ran straight down the aisle over the carpet still smoldering from the lightning strike, smacked through the swinging doors, and staggered out into the howling wind. He doubled over there. Swirling dust filled his throat, and he coughed.

Exactly what had Black meant there at the end? Billy? He really didn't want to try to figure that out.

He believed that what Samuel told him was true, and he'd done what Samuel had asked. And that was that.

He believed. The rest did not.

Johnny headed into the wind to find a safe haven until morning.

CHAPTER TWENTY-SIX

PARADISE

Sunday morning

STANLEY YORDON sped down Highway 50 before sunrise Sunday morning filled with a sense of terrible unease. Not because he feared returning to Paradise—on the contrary, because he had *not* come back sooner. Four days ago the idea of staying in Denver for an extra day seemed inviting, a well-deserved break and, more importantly, some time away.

Time healed wounds, they said. He'd decided to give Paradise a little time. Time to come to their collective senses. Time for Marsuvees Black to move on.

But he tried repeatedly to raise someone in Paradise last night, and no one answered. For all he knew, they were all down at the church swaying to the tunes of Marsuvees Black.

Unable to sleep, he left Denver at two in the morning. It was now five a.m. The drive had given him the time to flesh out the sermon he intended to preach. No mercy this time. Not an ounce. Just the right mixture of authority and compassion, the thundering voice of reprimand, the gentle words of empathy. And in the end they would have to listen.

The air was still and quiet when he drove through Delta. It was blowing hard and hazy twenty miles later when he passed the sign that read *Paradise 3 Miles*.

Someone had erected a barricade across the turnoff to Paradise. A large orange sign leaned against it.

Road Damage. Road Closed Ahead.

Yordon came to a stop. Road damage?

An image of Black drawing that ridiculous two in the air flashed through his mind. He gunned the motor, steered around the barricade, and headed up the road.

No sign of road damage.

The sun was trying to rise, but weather smothered the mountains. Dark clouds socked in Paradise valley like a cork between the mountains. Mountain storms were notorious for coming up fast and furious. But this . . .

He frowned and drove on, cautiously. Thin wisps of sand whirled across the road through his beams. Quite a wind.

His thoughts returned to his meeting with Bishop Fraiser in Denver. The bishop was smiling at him, telling him he'd better start believing what he was teaching if he wanted to hold on to his congregation. And if there were any hidden sins in his heart, he'd best bring them into the light.

"What you do mean?" he asked, wary.

"Secrets, Stanley."

"We all have our secrets."

"Yes, we do. And some secrets are meant to be secrets, while others will eat away at your heart like a cancer. I've seen whole churches crumble over a single indiscretion that was swept under the rug. But the rug can only cover so much, Stanley."

He left the meeting assuring himself that the bishop had spoken in broad, general terms. He'd swept a hundred small indiscretions under the rug in his time, but nothing worthy of the glint in the bishop's eyes when he said "secrets." There was Sally, of course. There was a possibility that some fool said something out of turn about Sally. But that had been fourteen years ago.

Welcome to Paradise, Population . . .

The sign was missing. Wind?

Yordon turned the corner into Paradise and immediately pumped the brake. Blowing dust blasted by, nearly obscuring the small valley. Now *this* was a dust storm. That must be why they'd closed the road. Stanley couldn't recall a wind so heavily concentrated in the valley like this.

He dropped his eyes to the road's yellow lines to guide him in the early-morning light. The road leveled out and ran straight through the town without a bend. By the time Yordon passed the first outlying house, his orientation began to fail him. Following the yellow line made him dizzy.

The theater loomed on his right. He followed its outline. Looked different somehow. He couldn't see worth a darn, but he—

The car slammed into something. A joint-wrenching crash, shattering glass. His head snapped forward and hit the steering wheel. The fact that he'd been creeping along at under ten miles an hour saved him from any serious injury.

Yordon cursed, something he could only do alone in his car. He shoved his door open, climbed out, and staggered around to the hood. The Starlight sign lay smashed on the blacktop. His bumper had hit one of the support poles, buckling the chrome under the car. The pole must have ripped a hose from the radiator, because it whistled with the wind.

Yordon stared unbelieving at the ruined landmark. His eyes followed the poles back to where they had been chopped.

He swore again.

Past the poles, the theater's front wall had been stripped of its siding, slashed to ribbons. As far as he could see, which wasn't terribly far, the buildings had taken a beating. Telephone poles, shattered doors, branches, and an assortment of broken-beyond-recognition appliances littered the place.

He saw the silhouette of the church like a ghost in the wind and wondered about its condition. He turned toward it, squinting through the whipping sand. Leaves blasted by—brown fall leaves in the middle of summer. Yordon began to run.

"Hello?"

No use in this wind. The streets were vacant, but that wasn't surprising considering the storm.

It's more than a storm, Stanley. He fought a surge of panic.

A selfish little thought crossed his mind—conditions like these would undoubtedly keep a few farmers from attending the morning service. But a much bigger voice chased that possibility. *Not a soul, Stanley! Not a single soul will come to hear your pathetic sermon!*

For all he knew, they were all dead.

No, not possible.

To his right the black sky framed Claude's store—a store that should have a large blue sign along the length of the building three feet above the door.

One side of the large sign banged against the wall in the wind. Stubborn fragments of broken glass jutted from wooden window frames like frozen claws. The door was gone.

Yordon felt gooseflesh ripple up his arms. This was not the work of wind. Who could have done this? The telephone pole next to Claude's convenience store lay across the sidewalk. He stepped over it

Smither's Saloon was even worse off. The collapsed steps left a three-foot rise to the gaping door frame. The town's only bench had been reduced to matchsticks along the gravel walk.

Surely they wouldn't have trashed the church. Yordon was about to plunge ahead when he saw yellow light flicker in the bar's window.

Someone was inside at this hour?

He ran to the saloon, jumped onto the trashed landing, and shoved the dangling door aside. He stepped in and scanned the interior of Smither's Saloon.

A small fire at the center of the room spewed white smoke to the ceiling and for a moment Yordon thought the saloon was ablaze, but then he saw it was a campfire of sorts, fed by broken table legs that formed a teepee over the flames. The bar lay chopped to kindling; the broken glass of a hundred bottles covered the floor. Only one table remained standing. And around the table sat three chairs, sagging under the weight of three figures, sitting like ghosts by the fire.

Yordon stepped over the rubble. Two men and a boy—resembling Claude Bowers, Chris Ingles, and Claude's boy, Peter, respectively—all leaned on the table, clutching bottles of booze, looking at him through drooping eyes. A toppled can of beer fed a pool of liquid that glistened in the flames.

They saw him and then returned their focus on the spilt malt. Dirt matted their hair; ash streaked their faces; something had torn their clothing to shreds. Chris Ingles wore a sling on his right arm.

"Hi, Stanley," Chris said without looking at him.

At first Yordon couldn't find the voice to respond. *Hi, Stanley?* What was he supposed to say? *Oh, hi, Chris. Having a bad day are we? I see you have a nice fire going. Do you mind if I join you?*

What Chris needed was a good palm to the cheek. A thundering crash upside his right ear. *Wake up, boy! What do you think you're doing?*

But Claude was the leader here. Yordon could see it in his face, below all that crud. "Claude, what are you doing?"

The big Swede turned his head and stared at him. The flames' reflection danced in his glassy eyes. "Hi, Stan."

He looked back at the table. Peter glanced his way for a second, took a swig from the bottle in his hand, and turned back to the reflection of flames in the spilt beer.

Yordon walked up to the table and gave it a good shove. "What's wrong with you guys? Wake up, for crying out loud! You're going to burn this place down!"

The amber liquid spilled over their laps as the table tipped. Claude's eyes snapped wide, as if an electrode had just hit the muscle controlling his eyelids, and Yordon immediately knew that he might be in a spot of trouble.

Claude stared at the table, aghast. He stood abruptly, sending his chair flying across the room.

Yordon stepped back.

The others came to their feet as well, gawking in disbelief at the table. "Wha . . . what happened?" Chris stammered.

The stupidity of the question shoved Yordon into an offensive gear. *The best defense is sometimes a good offense. Sometimes, like when your opponent is a drooling fool wondering why his hands are on his arms.*

"What have you done to the town? Look at this place, you've trashed it!"

All three of their stares turned to him. "We didn't do this," Peter said.

"Then who did?"

"Black did it," Peter said. "*He* told us to do it."

Black? How was that possible? How could anyone turn men so quickly?

"He's just a traveling salesman," Yordon said. "He couldn't do this."

"He's a salesman and he's selling a lot." Claude grinned. "You think we care about your lousy church? You should go look at it now. I don't think you're gonna be preaching too much there anymore."

Claude's son snickered.

He could see it in his mind's eye—the pews hacked up like these tables, the carpet peeled back in long maroon strips, the cross blazing on the wall like at one of those KKK meetings.

Yordon launched himself at the three figures, and he knew with his first step that he was about to experience a great deal of pain.

Yordon never actually reached them. Claude's fist reached his forehead first, like a sledgehammer.

Wham!

He collapsed, belly down on the table, his arms draping limply over the edges. Pain swelled through his head.

"He's on our table," Chris said from a great distance.

"What should we do with him?"

"Let's get rid of him," Claude said.

They pulled him from the table and hauled him like a sack of onions. They heaved him into a hole. He crumpled to the floor. A door slammed. A latch was locked.

They've thrown you into a grave.

His brain crawled through the haze.

You belong in a grave, buried with the rest of your indiscretions. Your secrets.

Yordon opened his eyes. A cool, damp breeze ran across his face. The smell of fresh dirt filled his nostrils, the kind of dirt found six feet under. But the space around him wasn't the two-by-seven of a casket, it was more like ten-by-ten. A sliver of light penetrated some boards above him.

They had dropped him in the saloon's root cellar.

He laid his head on the earthen floor and closed his eyes against a throbbing headache. *Dear God, what have I done?*

CHAPTER TWENTY-SEVEN

THE MONASTERY
Sunday morning

BILLY OPENED the ink jar, dabbed the quill into the liquid, and sent his mind to Paradise. Except for the torch that popped and licked at the ancient walls, only his breathing sounded in the chamber. The quill hovered a centimeter above the blank page. Perspiration beaded his forehead and he brought his left wrist across his brow.

The idea of his sweat falling to the page seemed profane, which in turn struck him as ridiculous, considering where he was. He'd written a thousand stories above, where he was taught to write, encouraged to write. But down here, the writing was different. In fact, it was the writing that drew him now more than the worms. The monk was right, the writing attracted them all.

He focused on a minute droplet of red ink glistening on the pen's very tip. He lowered the tip to the page, watching the gap between it and the paper close. His breathing came to a ragged halt.

He swallowed and pressed down. The pen made contact with the paper, and Billy's world seemed to erupt with light, like a strobe in a pitch-dark cell. A tone hummed through his mind.

Hmmmmmm.

As if the pen had struck a tuning fork in his skull.

A window in his mind blew open. He grinned at the thought of the preacher sitting in the root cellar. *Now how do you like your Paradise? What do you think of your little church now?*

The red words on the page before him glistened, and he blew across the paper to speed their drying. He dipped the quill in the ink jar again.

Easy, bringing the preacher to his knees on the cellar floor, cold and damp, shivering in the darkness.

It had been the monk's idea to write a story about Paradise. And why not? He had heard a little of the nearby town, and what he didn't know, the monk told him. Details of the setting, names of characters. A basic plot that suggested a kind of story Billy had never explored before.

A story of evil, loosed.

The story was like nothing he'd ever written, and Billy figured it was because of the worm salve. When he wrote, he actually felt like he was in the story with real characters who had minds of their own, like all really good stories, only much better.

How many times had he written something, paused, realized that the character didn't want to do it that way, written again and again until finally he got it right and the character did things his way?

Or was it the character's way?

This was the most realistic story he could ever imagine.

Billy laid the tip to the paper.

What do you want, Stanley?

I want what I had.

And what did you have, Stan, that you don't have now?

Warmth. A bed. Light.

More, Stan. What do you really want?

Power.

Grace and hope, Stan. How about grace and hope?

Yes, grace and hope.

But Black brought you grace and hope and you rejected him, deep down there in your heart where no one knew.

Maybe I shouldn't have.

Well, if you stand up right now and cry like a baby and beat your head on the wall until it's bloody, I'll give you some power.

Billy chuckled. He brought his free hand to his neck and scratched.

He could fully imagine Stan's situation at this very moment. He could smell the musty dirt and see the darkness. He was inside Stan the man's mind. Of course he was, Stan was his character.

But right now, Stan didn't want to stand up and hit his head against the wall. He was considering it, but this wasn't where the character wanted to go.

Billy wrote again.

Then instead lay there and sulk, you stuffed-up fool.

I am in a very bad way. I'll lay here for a while.

Good enough. Time to move on to another character.

"Darcy?"

The girl beside him didn't turn from her writing. Billy rubbed his fingers into his shirt. The annoying infections were chronic, a rash of systemic boils. He'd tried bandages, but they wouldn't stick to his oily skin. Washing the area only seemed to keep the flesh clean for an hour. Only the worms' ointment held the sores at bay. And then only as long as he managed to avoid scratching, which proved almost impossible.

The other students suffered the same already, in less than a day. The disease overtook them much faster. This as much as the writing would keep them in the dungeons where they could access a ready supply of the ointment.

They ventured upstairs to the dining hall for short raiding trips only, before returning to the great library the monk had shown Billy. There they hunkered down under Paul's supervision. At least his version of supervision, which was really a kind of chaos.

"You've already ruined the tables," Billy observed after Paul and the others occupied the great library for only a few hours.

"We don't like the tables," Paul answered. "They're too wet and slimy."

"They're wet and slimy because you've spread that worm stuff all over them."

"Yes, well, we don't like them anymore."

Billy gave up. "Just don't let any of the others come to my hall. Keep them here."

"Sure. How many worms do you think you have in that tunnel?"

"I don't know. What difference does it make?"

"We have 338 in our hall alone," Paul said. "But I think they all want to be here. With us. What do you think?"

"I think you're wasting your time thinking about these stupid worms instead of writing our story!"

He left Paul standing in the hall just outside the library. That was last night. It was the last time he'd seen him.

Billy looked around the study. Apart from sludge stains all over the carpet and sofa, his study had survived the brats. Now only he and Darcy used the study.

Darcy grunted and brought her fingernails to her neck. Billy watched, revolted, as she scratched a wide swath of skin away, oblivious to any pain or blood. She resumed her writing, smiling. She smeared a large streak of blood along the margin of her page without noticing. She was writing some of the women. Women could be quite engrossing.

Billy closed his eyes and thought about Stanley again. *Stan the man. You should have run, Stan the man. Now you're in the can without a plan.* He bent over the desk and began to write again, this time in more developed prose.

He wrote for an hour, lost in the valley below, his senses dulled to everything but the story that he brought to life in his mind. And then he took a short walk through the hall to stretch.

His mind drifted back to the debate that he'd won so easily. Seemed like a week ago. Technically, if he remembered right, he could now do whatever he wanted upstairs. Funny thing, though, he didn't care about what happened upstairs anymore. As long as they left him alone to write down here, the monkeys upstairs could do whatever they wanted.

Billy padded lightly on the cold stone, warm and dazed. An image of Paul smiling at the entrance of the larger library popped into his mind. *Do you know how many worms you have?*

Billy shoved his hand into his pocket. It was slightly mushy but for the most part empty. Restocking worm gel would be a good idea. He held his torch to the wall and dipped his hand into a thick layer of the ointment.

Billy was stuffing his pockets when it occurred to him that there were no worms within the circle of light cast by his flame. He turned and walked along the wall, expecting a slug to appear in the light. But none did.

Gone?

Billy began to run. Where were they? They couldn't have just *left*! Slug slime still crisscrossed the walls, but it would eventually run out. Maybe even dry up, leaving nothing but crusty trails. He and Darcy needed the worms. He ran a full hundred meters beyond the study, but the walls were vacant.

Near panic now, Billy sprinted for the study. He had to get Darcy! Maybe they should find buckets and fill them with what ointment still clung to the walls. Store it in a cool damp corner, hidden from the others. Yes, they should do at least that. Maybe barricade their tunnel to keep the others out altogether.

Then he and Darcy could write in peace surrounded by buckets of worm gel. Finish their story. But then how would they get out to eat? The moment they left, the others would break in. Better to barricade them in *their* stinking tunnel!

When Billy raced through the entrance to the study, his torch slammed into the arch and flew from his hand in a shower of sparks.

"Darcy!" He retreated quickly to snatch up his torch then jumped back into the study and faced a glassy-eyed Darcy, pen still cocked in her right hand.

"The worms are gone!"

She was overdosed on writing. He leaned forward and yelled again. "You hear me? The worms are gone!"

She blinked and set her pen down. "Worms?"

"Come on, snap out of it. Yes, worms." He snaked his hand through the air in a slithering motion. "The worms on the walls are gone."

She stood, snatched the other torch from the wall, and ran past Billy into the tunnel. He turned and followed, leaving the study dark behind him. Darcy waved her torch about the cavern and followed the orange splash of light with her head.

"Gone?" she asked in a thin voice. "You sure?"

"You see them? They look gone to me."

"You check up that way?" She motioned toward the black hole Billy had just searched.

"Yes."

"Come on!" Darcy ran the opposite way, toward the main entrance, and Billy ran right on her heels. The slapping of their feet echoed down the tunnel. Their flames whooshed over their heads.

Darcy pulled up just before the tunnel ended, and Billy had to swerve to avoid her. His foot hooked under the tail of a massive worm and he found himself diving headlong.

Three distinct thoughts crashed through his mind as his body flew through the air. The first was one of self-preservation, *Heavens, I hope I don't break my neck. Maybe I should curl up and roll when I land.*

In that instant the second thought materialized. The worm had recoiled when his foot struck its soft flesh. It had compressed like an accordion and raised its head into the air. Maybe it would strike at him like a cobra while he lay on the floor with a broken neck.

But the third thought superseded even this danger. His flame washed across the tunnel and Billy thought, *Jiminy Cricket, there's a boy dragging that worm!*

Billy landed with a terrible grunt and rolled to his feet. A boy did indeed stand at the worm's opposite end, gripping a rope tied around it. Paul! Paul was dragging one of *their* worms from *their* tunnel! "What are you doing?" Billy demanded. But he knew what worm-boy was doing. Worm-boy was stealing one of their worms.

"Uh, nothing." Paul stepped backward, tugging at the rope. The worm slid easily on its smooth belly.

"What do you mean *nothing*?" Darcy snapped. "That doesn't look like nothing to me. Looks to me like you're dragging a worm. One of *our* worms."

Paul stopped his tugging and stared at them as though he were having difficulty placing their faces. After a moment he resumed his haul of the giant worm. Billy glanced at the ground and saw dozens of long mucus streaks running along the floor. This wasn't the first worm dragged down the corridor recently.

"Wake up, boy! You hear Darcy? What in heaven's name are you doing, dragging our worms out of our tunnel?"

Paul leaned into the rope, ignoring Billy's charge. He trudged down the hall like an ox pulling a heavy sled.

Billy dove for the worm's tail end. His fingers slipped through a thin layer of mucus and dug into the soft body flesh.

The worm slithered on, probably completely unaware of the failed assault. Billy fell to his rear with a grunt. Paul tugged the worm, their last one maybe, through the tunnel's gaping mouth and around the bend toward his own hall.

"Come on," Darcy said, pulling Billy to his feet. "That fool has no right to steal our worms."

Billy felt the throbbing pain of his disturbed boils aching to the bone and grimaced. "You'd think he has enough of his own."

He shoved a hand into his hip pocket, withdrew a palm full of worm salve, and slapped it along the forearm hit hardest by the first fall. "Man, this hurts!"

"Don't worry, Billy. We'll get our worms back. Sooner than he might think too, assuming he still has the ability to think. You see his eyes? That boy's lost it. He's out there in worm land."

"Come on," Billy said. "Let's find some ropes. No way we can haul those slugs without ropes."

"Yeah."

Twenty minutes later Billy and Darcy slipped into the far tunnel, laden with ropes they'd found in the study. They'd formed a plan of sorts, though it amounted to no more than sneak-in-and-steal-our-worms-back. And if any kid gets in the way, smack them on the neck where their sores hurt most.

They each held a torch and tiptoed along the corridor, hugging the right wall. Darcy watched their rear for any scoundrels who might be returning from the upper levels, and Billy took point, scanning the tunnel's face for their first worm.

But when the first worm didn't appear, Billy began to wonder if this tunnel had been cleared as well. Where had that sicko put the worms if not here, in his own tunnel? Of course, there were four other tunnels between them.

The entrance to the big library flickered in the torchlight and Billy drew up. So soon? And not one worm. Not one student, either. They were probably swinging from the chandeliers, ripping the paneling from the walls, and feasting on worm flesh.

He motioned Darcy forward and crept to the doors. With a deep breath he shoved through the doors and stepped into the library's outer hall. Nothing yet—that was good. He felt Darcy's hand on his hip, and he moved down the hall toward the balcony entrance. He reached it, pried the narrow door open, and peered down into the main library.

The flames of twenty torches burned along the walls, filling the room with dancing yellow light. From his position he couldn't see the tables below, but the library's eerie silence struck him as odd.

"Are they in there?" Darcy whispered.

"I can't tell. I don't hear anything." Billy eased out onto the balcony and crawled to the railing on all fours. He waited for Darcy to slide in beside him and then edged his head over the three-foot wall that bordered the upper level.

The first thought that rushed through his mind was that Paul's band of brats were dead. All of them, dead! Slumped on the floor, surrounded by a thick carpet of worms, twisting slowly on the carpet at their feet.

Billy caught his breath. Dead? No, they couldn't be dead! Writing, maybe. Writing in Paul's swimming pool of worms.

"What?" Darcy whispered. "What is it?" She raised her head above the railing.

"Good night! He's brought the worms *here!*" Darcy said, dropping back beside him. He nodded, thinking that his heart was pounding with enough force to be heard from below. His vision grew fuzzy, and he blinked to clear it.

He snaked his head back up and peered down. They'd returned the tables to the floor. Most, if not all, of Paul's students leaned over the circular tables, writing in books, seemingly unconscious of the thick blanket of slugs at their feet.

Paul's lost it. Completely. At least they're writing. How in the world had Paul managed to get the worms down there? More importantly, how would he and Darcy ever get them out?

The door latch behind them opened and Billy flinched. A boy appeared on the balcony, pulling and tugging at a slug, and Billy realized that Paul was just now arriving with their worm. How had they passed him? He must have taken another route, through one of the other tunnels.

He watched with amazement as the boy hauled the creature first to and then over the balcony railing without paying them any mind. The slug slithered over the handrail, writhing in protest, and then fell to the floor fifteen feet below. It landed with a mighty *thump*.

When Billy looked back up at the balcony, Paul was gone. There was no way they could get any of these worms. They would just have to find another supply—possibly in the other tunnels or farther in their own hall.

"Let's get out of here," he whispered and crawled for the door. He squeezed through and led Darcy from the library.

"You see that?" he asked as soon as they cleared the main doors.

"He's really flipped his lid, hasn't he?"

"Completely. At least he has them all writing. We'll find some others."

She nodded. "Yeah."

It took them half an hour to find another batch of worms deep in their own tunnel and drag them near the study. A few minutes later, Billy and Darcy were writing again.

"Billy?" Darcy said after her first few strokes.

"Hmm."

"You ever get the feeling that this story is, I don't know, maybe more than just a story?"

Actually he had. "Why'd you say that?"

"These tunnels. The worms. So many blank books. I know we're all writing these subplots that don't have a lot of meaning by themselves, but they *feel* like they have meaning. Like they're really happening."

"Yeah, well, I hope it is real. In fact, it is real."

"Really? Why?"

"I can't tell the difference, can you? When I'm writing, it's real to me. Real, period—that's what makes it so. That's why I like it. And I can tell you something, the main plot has more than a little meaning. I'm doing some damage." He grinned. "I mean, we're gonna chew them up and spit them out."

"Who?"

"Whoever doesn't follow us. Whoever rejects our version of hope and grace. Whoever Black wants to, that's who."

"And because they're the same as the overseers and Samuel and all those pukes upstairs who don't get it," Darcy snapped. He was surprised at her tone.

Billy nodded. "Yeah."

A moment passed with nothing to say. Then Billy and Darcy leaned over their books and began to write.

CHAPTER TWENTY-EIGHT

PARADISE

Sunday morning

JOHNNY AWOKE late Sunday morning—nearly noon by his alarm clock. Not surprising considering he'd stayed awake 'til three expecting Claude Bowers to beat down his door.

He glanced at the window, half-expecting a grinning face. It took him a few long seconds, squinting his eyes at the blinds to realize that something had changed. For the first time in five days, the sun's rays replaced the perpetual dusk framed in his window.

He jumped off his bed, bounded across the room, and yanked the blinds open. A white sky blinded him. In that one blast of light, the fear fell from his heart like loosed shackles and he could hardly stifle a cry of delight.

Samuel!

Johnny grabbed his three-day-old T-shirt from the bedpost and pulled it over his head with trembling arms. The town had changed.

How much, though?

"Mom?"

He jumped into his jeans, pulled on his shoes, and ran into the hall. "Mom!"

No response. He opened her door. She lay unmoving under the sheets.

"Mom?"

Dead to the world. Still, the sky had changed. That was a start.

Johnny hurried through the living room and out onto the porch. Several clouds still dotted the sky, but they weren't nearly as dark as before. And the wind was only a gentle breeze.

Johnny walked into the street and looked at Paradise with wide eyes. He saw something like the aftermath of a tornado that had touched down, ripped up the town, then vanished. Rows of miniature sand dunes, each about a foot tall, ran like ribbons over Main Street.

He looked south. The business section had been trashed. The Starlight Theater's sign had toppled to the street.

Then Johnny saw the man standing in the middle of the road next to the theater. He straddled a mound of sand, hands on his hips, surveying the damage from the other end of town.

He first thought it was Black, and a streak of terror hit him like lightning. But the man wore a blue uniform, not a black trench coat.

Samuel's cop.

Johnny scanned the town, looking for any other signs of life. Only the cop, standing on the same line that Marsuvees Black himself had first followed into town.

Johnny headed for the uniformed man, praying under his breath that this was Thomas.

This was a fictional character, he knew that, but looking at him now, Johnny had a hard time accepting it. He didn't look fictional. The only thing odd about him was that he didn't seem to notice Johnny.

Johnny stopped twenty feet from him. Still no sign of recognition. The lawman wore mirrored sunglasses. His hair was short and his face was bronzed by the sun.

The cop's legs were spread wide and his hands rested on the butts of two large pistols in hip holsters. His head moved slowly from left to right as he studied the town. Reminded Johnny of that movie *The Terminator*. Samuel had said something about a gunslinger, but the man looked more like a regular cop.

Was this guy really flesh and blood?

"Closer, son."

Johnny's pulse spiked. He hesitated, then walked up to the man. The cop extended his right hand. "Name's Thomas."

He knew it. Johnny stared into the mirrored glasses, at a loss. This wasn't a real man. He was standing in front of Samuel's gunslinger.

"I don't bite," Thomas said. "Not you anyway." He grinned briefly; then his face went stern again. Was that Samuel talking through him?

Johnny took the hand. Felt like regular flesh and blood. "I'm Johnny."

Thomas released his hand and smiled wide. For a moment he looked like someone different altogether. Same flesh and same clothes, but his face . . .

"Isn't this cool?" Thomas said. "I mean who'd have thought this would actually work?" He snapped his fingers and moved his arms and body in a little jive jig. "Cool, baby. Way cool!"

Johnny stepped back, images of the terminator gone.

Thomas caught himself and cleared his throat. He looked at Johnny for a moment, then returned his hands to his hips and straddled the road again.

"Sorry about that. This is all new to me. I have to stay in character. I'm a gunslinger, son. A bona fide blue-suited gunslinger, and don't you forget that." He looked down at Johnny. "You won't tell anybody about that, will you?"

"About what?"

"The, you know . . ." Thomas removed a hand from his hip and twirled it in a tight circle. "The little dance thing. It doesn't fit my image."

Johnny grinned. This was more Samuel's doing than Thomas's. Had to be.

"Not a word," he said.

"Appreciate it. You want to see some of my moves?"

He wanted to dance again?

Thomas's hands blurred. Then they were cocked on either side of his head and there was a gun in each one. "Pretty fast, huh?" The guns began to spin. His arms moved in steady symmetrical patterns, more like a kung fu master than any gunslinger that Johnny had seen. Jet Li with guns. Thomas snapped the guns back into position on either side of his head.

"Wow."

"That's nothing, son."

"So . . . can you do anything you want?"

"Like what?"

"I don't know. Fly?"

"I'm a gunslinger, not a bird. And even if I could fly, it wouldn't be any good to us."

Thomas returned the guns to his holsters. "Now, let's get down to business. Looks like you've had some trouble here. Mind telling me what happened?"

"Did . . . didn't Samuel tell you?"

"Samuel? Never mind anyone named Samuel right now. Just tell me everything."

Johnny led the cop behind the old theater and told him everything, starting with Black walking into town and ending with the meeting last night. Everything except his trip to the monastery. He assumed that Samuel wanted to keep Thomas focused on Paradise, although for all practical purposes, Thomas was Samuel, wasn't he?

Then again, maybe not. This was new territory. Maybe fictional characters could develop a mind of their own.

Thomas listened to every word patiently, intently, giving no sign that he doubted a single detail. He just nodded as if he understood precisely what had happened here in Paradise because he had faced a dozen identical scenarios in his time.

Every now and then he drew his guns and spun them like batons. To keep fresh, he said.

When Johnny finished, the cop took a deep breath and removed his glasses and twirled them. "You're braver than most kids. Gotta hand it to you."

Thomas placed a hand on his shoulder and squeezed gently. "Don't worry, we're going to clean this mess up. Black may have a few tricks, but then so do I."

"Yeah, about that. How does the *we* part work?"

"You just leave that to me. It may be we, but we follow me, *comprende*?"

"*Comprende*."

"Now . . ." The cop withdrew one gun, snapped the safety off, and cocked it up by his right ear. "Where do you suppose we might find these scoundrels?"

Johnny walked to the corner and looked up the street. "I'd start with the saloon. Either there or in the church. But they might still be sleeping in their houses too. A lot of people are sleeping a lot around here."

Thomas nodded at Smither's Saloon. "Saloon?"

"Smither's Saloon."

"Follow me."

THE SALOON'S exterior was trashed nearly beyond recognition. Of three steps that led to the landing, only the top one remained. Johnny stopped ten yards in front of it.

The streets were still bare. This surprised Johnny; he thought that people would start coming out of their homes when they saw the change in the weather.

Then again, Billy had a lot of help now. No telling how much damage they'd inflicted last night. The key now was to keep Thomas's identity hidden from Black. He had to think Thomas was a regular cop, not a fictional something that Samuel had pulled into the mix. If Billy and Black fought fire with fire, that could get nasty.

Thomas took his sunglasses off and stowed them in his pocket. His hazel eyes flashed with mischief.

"When you said that flying wouldn't help us," Johnny said, "it was because what matters here is what people think, right? You have to change their hearts and minds, not just throw them all in jail."

"That's right, son. But a little butt-kicking never hurt anyone."

"But you don't want to be too obvious, right? Black's out there somewhere. We don't want the wrong idea to make it back up the mountain."

He figured talking in code would be acceptable, although there was no one to hear them anyway.

"Unfortunately, yes." Thomas cocked his head and studied the door. "Do you think it would be too obvious if I kicked the door in?"

"Not really. Cops do that all the time in the movies."

Thomas held Johnny in his gaze for a second, then winked. "Goody."

Then he took three long steps, launched himself effortlessly into the air, planted one foot on the top step, and flew for the door.

He hit it with both feet extended. *Crash!* The door popped off its hinges and disappeared into the darkness with Thomas aboard.

Johnny glanced around the town. Not exactly your typical kicking-down-the-door thing, not even in the movies. He hoped Black wasn't watching.

He wouldn't mind getting his hands on one of those books. Course, it might not work for him. He probably didn't have the simple kind of belief that Samuel or the other kids in the monastery had.

Johnny jumped up and peered through the open doorway. Thomas stood on top of the door, like a surfer on his board, gun drawn. It took a second for his eyes to adjust to the dim light, and when they did, he gasped.

The saloon had been gutted by fire. Blackened wood smoldered around the perimeter. The tables, the pool table, the bar—every bit of it lay in ashes, and Johnny wondered why the frame hadn't gone up as well.

"Wow."

They both turned their heads to the sound of a muffled cry somewhere down low.

"You hear that?" Johnny whispered.

"This place have a basement?"

"There's a root cellar."

"Show me."

Johnny picked his way across the room toward the storage room. Heat rose from the charred floor, although he now saw that someone had doused it with water—probably what saved the building.

A blackened lock with a Master logo hung stubbornly on the blistered root-cellar door. "Here it is." Johnny stepped aside.

"Call out to them," Thomas said.

"Just call out?"

"Don't tell them I'm here. Just try to get a response so we know who we're dealing with."

Pretty smart. "Anybody in there?"

"Down here! Help me!" a muffled voice cried. Johnny could swear he'd heard that voice a thousand times.

Thomas cocked an eyebrow.

"I'm not sure," Johnny said.

"Try again."

He did. This time he knew the voice. Knew it because he *had* heard it a thousand times. Stanley Yordon was back in town.

"It's . . . I'm pretty sure it's the preacher."

"Black?"

"No, Father Yordon. He must have come back last night."

Thomas twirled his gun. Caught it snug. He shot without aiming.

The gun boomed and bucked in his hand. Johnny flinched.

When he looked back, the Master lock was gone. It lay twisted and broken on the floor near the back door.

Thomas raised his foot and nudged the burnt door. It creaked inward.

Stanley Yordon bolted from the dark pit. His foot caught on a burnt two-by-four, and he sprawled across the floor with a loud grunt.

Yordon pushed himself up and attempted to brush himself off. Soot streaked the man's face. And his hand . . .

Yordon followed Johnny's stare to his right hand. A single splinter the size of a ball-point ink refill ran out from under his index fingernail.

The man's hand began to tremble and he grabbed it to hold it still. "Oh, dear God!"

Thomas reached out and placed a comforting arm on Yordon's shoulder. "Tell you what, Father." He took Yordon's hand in his own. "I'm going to have to"—before the trembling man knew what was happening, the cop yanked the stick—"pull this out."

Yordon stared at his hand in shock. Then he did a strange thing for someone as uptight and highbrow as he tried to make himself out to be. He rested his head on the cop's shoulder and began to cry in earnest. For a full minute he sobbed into the officer's uniform, and Thomas just patted his back, like a father comforting a baby. No soothing words, thank goodness. That would definitely be out of character.

As soon as Johnny had completed the thought, Thomas said, "That's it, Stanley, just let it all out."

He looked at Johnny and raised a brow.

Johnny shook his head. *No, Thomas, not cool.*

Yordon quieted. He backed away from Thomas, cleared his throat, and lifted his head. "Sorry." He straightened his shirt. "Sorry, I don't know what came over me."

"You want to tell us who threw you in the cellar?" Thomas asked.

"Claude," he answered. "Claude Bowers, his son, Peter, and Chris Ingles."

"They're the ones who gutted the theater," Johnny said.

"Okay. What say we go around this town and round up some crazies," Thomas said with a wink. "It's time to show them who's boss."

Johnny grinned. He was feeling like a kid again.

AFTER SENDING Stanley Yordon home to collect himself, Thomas demanded his partner—that would be Johnny—lead him to the Bowerses' residence.

Claude's door was open, but the top floor was empty. Thomas headed for the basement with Johnny cautiously behind. The cop descended the stairs in silence, peering around the corner. A grin nudged his lips. He stepped into the basement, withdrawing both guns. Legs spread, guns cocked, Thomas faced the dim light beyond.

Johnny eased down the steps and craned his neck around the corner for a view.

Claude, Chris, Peter, and seven or eight other crazies were packed into the stuffy basement. They slouched like strung-out vampires, heads propped up, eyes drooping or closed. If they noticed the cop in the doorway, they didn't show it.

"Rise and shine!" Thomas yelled. "Morning is here."

Like a turtle watching a passing seagull, Claude Bowers turned his head toward the sound. His glassy, bloodshot eyes were only half-open.

The thought processing slowly in that thick head must have registered the sum of the matter, because his eyelids snapped open and he sat up straight.

"Hi, Claude," Thomas said.

The big man's upper lip lifted in a snarl. The others rustled around him, like bats waking from their slumber.

Thomas leveled his revolver at Claude's head. Then he brought it back to his ear quickly, paused, and leveled it again. He repeated this twice. Why, Johnny had no idea.

"Get up, Claude. Drop the bottle and put your hands on your head." Thomas leveled his second gun. "The rest of you too. Hands on your heads."

Most rose slowly to their feet. Two remained slumped in their chairs.

Claude eyed the gun without moving. Johnny watched his chest rise and fall. The man's upper lip glistened with sweat and twitched periodically, as if his circuits might be shorting.

And he wasn't putting his hands on his head. On the contrary, Johnny thought he might throw himself at Thomas and beat him to a pulp. He was twice the cop's size.

Thomas motioned to the two crazies who hadn't responded. "Rise and shine. Up."

Chris kicked his boot into the men's sides. "Get up you lazy vomit bags." A faint smile crossed his lips as the two men groaned. He didn't seem bothered by Thomas's interruption at all. Too wasted to realize what was happening, maybe.

A grunt from the left signaled Claude's charge. He moved quickly for a man his size.

Thomas didn't move. He'd offered half of his back to the Swede by turning to the two men who now struggled to their feet. Johnny watched the scene unfold with a knot in his throat.

Claude thundered forward, a runaway train.

Thomas still didn't seem to notice.

At the last possible instant, just before Claude's lowered head reached Thomas's, the cop dropped to a crouch and threw one leg forward for balance. He lifted his shoulders as Claude's knees struck him, then stood and sent the Swede catapulting headlong over him.

Claude struck the wall like a battering ram. The Swede dropped on the carpet, unconscious. Maybe dead.

Thomas waved his gun at the others, still ignoring Claude. "The first man who lowers his hands gets a bullet in the knee. You all hear that? I want you to nod if you understand me. No need getting your knee blown off just because you're too wasted to hear me."

They all nodded except for the two who'd just stood. "You two understand? You drop your hands and I'll blow your kneecaps off. Nod if you understand."

They nodded.

"Okay, let's all take a little trip together."

Thomas reached down, withdrew a smaller pistol from his boot, and handed it to Johnny. "Stand at the top of the stairs. If any of these men makes a move on me, you pull that trigger. Can you do that?"

Johnny took the revolver carefully, feeling the cold stainless steel in his hands. He'd shot a gun plenty of times, but not like this. Did Thomas really expect him to kill someone? Samuel would never go for that.

"You mean kill them?"

"If you have to."

Samuel would never suggest he kill anyone. Which must mean that Thomas, although inspired and directed by Samuel, could work on his own as well. Did Samuel know this?

Johnny looked at Claude. "What about him?"

Claude's face was turned to one side and his lips were smashed up into his cheeks. Thomas knelt and raised one of Claude's eyelids. He slapped Claude's cheek. The man groaned and moved his arms and legs, then lay still.

"Wake up, Claude," Thomas said. "Get your lard-self off the ground."

The big Swede struggled to his knees, then stood unsteadily.

"Let's go. Up the stairs. Hands high."

Johnny scrambled up the stairwell.

The sun was out, the wind was down, and they were locking up the bad guys. It was going to be a good day.

One by one they plodded past the cop and climbed the stairs. It took five minutes to march them single file to the church, where Thomas ushered them into the kitchen. He and Johnny removed the knives and other sharp instruments from the drawers and backed to the door.

"Try not to kill each other in here. And get some sleep." Thomas locked the door.

"So you think that'll hold them?"

"It's a steel door, it'll hold them," Thomas said.

"Now what?"

"More. We need more."

CHAPTER TWENTY-NINE

THE MONASTERY
Sunday afternoon

SAMUEL SKIPPED down the hall, mouth spread in an open smile, taking in so much air with each breath that he thought he might choke on it. It had been a good day.

He had to tell Christine and Tyler, who were waiting in the library. Everything was going to be okay now. He had written Thomas into Paradise, and he was sure that Paradise held the key to break the power that now gripped the other students' minds. Billy didn't seem to know what to do about Thomas, and Marsuvees Black was evidently frightened off by the presence of a real cop. This had to mean that neither was wise to the fact that Thomas was fictional.

Samuel had shown his father the pages he wrote, and his father walked to the cupboard with a fresh excitement. He pulled out a tall flask, lifted it triumphantly into the air.

"A toast!"

"A bit premature, isn't it?" Andrew said.

"Every good thing is worthy of celebration," his father said, pouring the liquid into crystal glasses. He winked at Samuel.

It had been a good day indeed.

Samuel rounded the corner into the library, heard sudden cries of rage, and stopped.

Billy! Two thoughts collided: *I must help Billy! Thank goodness he's here.* And *Billy! Oh no, not Billy!*

The monastery's main library was appropriately named *The Field of Books*. Scores of bookcases were arranged in a natural setting, complete with a grassy lawn, trees, and flower gardens. High above, a domed ceiling allowed light to flood the lawn.

Samuel walked around the peripheral bookcases and saw seven or eight students by the tall oak tree arguing among themselves. He quickly scanned the library—Christine and Tyler weren't here.

Billy and Darcy yelled and waved accusing arms at a group of six children who stood with slumped shoulders. Only Billy's red hair and scratchy voice identified him clearly. Large red and blue blotches covered the boy's puffy face. His bare arms were lumpy with sores. The disease was so advanced!

Samuel was overcome by an urge to run down the hill and throw his arms around the boy. *Come back, Billy,* he would say. *It's okay, we love you, Billy.*

He leaned against the bookcase as grief swept over him. Tears slipped down his cheeks despite his best effort to hold them back.

He took a deep breath, sniffed, wiped his sleeve across his eyes, and pushed off the bookcase. Well, Thomas had cleaned up Paradise. Now Samuel would clean up Billy.

He was halfway to them when Billy saw him and stopped his arguing midsentence, right arm still outstretched toward one of the boys.

Don't run, Billy. Please don't run.

Billy did not run, maybe could not run. If the sores didn't hamper his movement, the shock at seeing Samuel must have, because he didn't even find the presence of mind to drop his arm.

The others faced Samuel, one by one. Their faces were as disfigured by boils as Billy's. They'd smeared that gel over their entire bodies, including hair and clothes. Darcy stood by Billy's side staring at Samuel, hands on hips.

He came within ten feet of the group and stopped. An odor that reminded him of sewer water wafted through the air, and he shortened his breathing to keep from blanching in front of them.

"Hey, Billy."

The redhead dropped his arm and narrowed his eyes but didn't respond.

"What are you doing here?" Darcy asked.

Samuel wondered if she had assumed leadership of the group. "I live here, remember, Darcy?" He paused. "You guys getting enough to eat?"

It sounded dumb really, pretending nutrition was a matter of concern considering their present condition. Asking whether they had taken a bath lately might be more appropriate. "We have plenty to eat in the cafeteria, you know."

"Shut up, Samuel!" Darcy snapped. "Billy won the debate, not you."

Billy just stood there, lost.

"How about you, Billy? Is there anything I can get for you?" Sure it sounded ridiculous, but he meant it. "Those sores look like they hurt. Maybe we should get you some medical help. I'm sure we have some medicine in the infirmary that would help."

"Shut up, Samuel!" Darcy said again. "Just shut up!"

Billy finally broke his stare and glanced at Darcy. "Yeah, shut up, Samuel."

Samuel nodded and felt pity rising in his throat again. "We miss you, Billy," he said. "I miss you. I wish you would just come back before anything really bad happens."

"Anything really bad?" Billy said. "And what's really bad, Samuel?"

"Lots of things. You don't look so good. The whole project is being threatened. Paradise is having some problems."

"Paradise is having some problems," Darcy mocked, wagging her head. "What do you know about Paradise anyway?"

He shouldn't have brought it up. "Then let's talk about you. You look like you're in a lot of pain."

"Who said anything about pain?" Billy asked. "We have everything we need, and if you were smart you would quit bugging us here and have a look yourself."

"What kind of salve is that, Billy?"

Darcy answered again. "None of your business. This is our worm paste, and it's none of your stinking business what it is, you understand? So quit bugging us!"

"Worm paste? Does it help the pain?"

"No, we're just wearing the stinking stuff 'cause we can't find our coats. Of course it does! So just quit bugging us." The eloquent, polished Darcy he once knew so well had regressed. She was speaking like a seven-year-old brat. But at least she was talking.

"It comes from worms?" Samuel asked.

"It comes from the worms," a young boy said to Samuel's left.

The boy's eyes were nearly swollen shut. Samuel didn't even recognize the student.

"What's your name?"

The boy glanced at Billy and answered. "Bob," he said.

Bob? This was Bob? "Do your sores hurt, Bob?"

"Yes."

"And the salve helps the pain?"

"Yes."

"Do you like the pain, Bob?"

"No."

"Shut up, Samuel," Darcy said.

"Did you have pain like this before you went into the tunnels, Bob?"

The boy didn't answer.

A single, soft sob broke the silence. Samuel spotted the thin girl behind Darcy.

"Shut up, Shannon," Darcy said, but her voice was less demanding.

The young girl tilted her face into her hands and started to cry softly.

Samuel glanced at Billy and saw the boy staring at Shannon with tender eyes. And then another child on Shannon's left began to cry.

Billy lowered his eyes and nudged the grass with his shoe. So, the boy's heart still pumped red blood and swelled with real emotions.

A gentle hand on his shoulder startled Samuel. He turned to find Christine and Tyler standing there, smiling. Samuel acknowledged them with a nod and faced Billy again.

Billy was horribly deformed, bleeding, and covered in a disgusting salve. But Samuel saw a lost, lonely orphan, confused and dejected, mortally wounded and desperately wanting love. Emotion swelled in his chest. He felt his legs moving under him, carrying him to his old friend. He knew it was crazy, but he couldn't stop himself. And to make matters worse, he began to cry.

He reached Billy, completely not caring about the smell and the sores and the salve, and he encircled the boy's body with his arms and held him gently.

Billy froze.

"I'm sorry, Billy," Samuel said. "I'm so sorry."

Christine and Tyler walked behind Billy and gently laid their hands on him. They stood in silence for several seconds.

And then the beautiful, awkward moment ended, and Samuel dropped his arms. Billy stood still for a moment, his head bowed. He nudged the grass with his toe again.

Then he turned and walked away. Darcy hurried to catch up. As a unit the others followed.

Samuel tried to wipe the tears from his eyes, but he couldn't because of the salve on his hands and arms.

"Boy, do they need a bath," Christine said, sniffing her hand.

"And now I suppose we do too," Samuel said. "As soon as possible. I think this stuff messes with the mind."

Samuel watched the students exit the library. A few short days ago they would have been laughing at someone's joke, or talking in urgent tones about a theory raised in class.

But they'd chosen Billy's path. A path to freedom, they claimed, to the discovery of their true selves—to the creator in all of them. Well, they had discovered something all right, but it resembled slavery more than freedom.

"How's Paradise?" Christine asked.

"Good," Samuel said with a sigh. "Paradise is good."

CHAPTER THIRTY

PARADISE

Sunday night

BY THE end of the day Thomas had two dozen troublemakers in custody, including Steve Smither, who had evidently taken to putting the neighbors' pets out of their misery.

Thomas focused exclusively on those that Johnny considered dangerous. There was no way to round up the whole town, and no reason to do so. The plan was to eliminate Black's front guard before confronting him directly the next time he showed up. If there was a next time. If they were lucky, Thomas had already scared him off.

Good plan.

Only one, the owner of the feedlot, Burt Larson, put up any real fight. But Thomas put him on his back quicker than a heartbeat when the rabble-rouser went for a gun under the counter.

By nightfall they had all the instigators secured.

All but Marsuvees Black.

There was no sign of Black anywhere in Paradise. If any of the others had the slightest clue as to his whereabouts, they weren't saying. A search of the business district turned up nothing but empty buildings. Thomas inspected each of the ringleaders' homes and each time came away empty-handed. Marsuvees Black was simply nowhere to be found.

The only real challenge surfaced late that afternoon, after Thomas and Johnny returned to the church. Stanley Yordon, preacher-turned-jailer, met them at the top of the stairs.

"I'm not an expert on the law," he said, "but doesn't someone have to press charges for you to legally hold these prisoners?"

"Press charges? After what they've done, no."

"Well, actually, that could be a problem." Yordon led them into his office and turned around. "I can't seem to find anyone to press charges."

"Like I said, Reverend. No need."

Yordon continued as if he hadn't heard Thomas. "*I* could press charges, but I'm not sure I *should*. Most of the townsfolk are still behind Black." He shook his head. "God knows I'm not. But I have a certain responsibility to keep my people's confidence. I can't just turn against them. What would that do to their faith in me?"

"They kidnapped you," Johnny said. "They destroyed your church."

"They also paid for that church. And when this is over, I'll need their loyalty. I think you'll have to find someone else to press charges. And I hope you do, but I'm afraid I face a conflict of interest here."

"We don't need to press charges," Thomas said. "Is it just me, or am I repeating myself here?"

"All I'm saying is that I don't want to be associated with what you've done here. It wasn't my idea. I've only been doing what you've made me do. And I find it strange that there aren't more policemen here. I'd feel a lot better if there was a stronger law-enforcement presence to take the heat off me, if you catch my meaning."

Thomas pulled out a chair and sat down. "Fine, Stanley. With the phones out, I can't get help here tonight, but we'll bring the cavalry in at first light."

"What about your cruiser? Can't you call on your radio?"

The cop looked at Johnny. "No."

"Why can't you go for help?"

Thomas shifted in the seat. "You check the vehicles lately? Someone went to a lot of trouble putting everything with wheels out of commission. The distributor cap has been smashed on every car in town. Including yours, Stanley."

They'd discovered this universal damage several hours earlier. It had been Billy's doing—had to be. He could write one sentence in his book and the damage would be done. Samuel could fix them all just as easily, now that he knew about it, but Johnny didn't think he wanted to. That, just like bringing real cops into Paradise, could prove disastrous if Billy got smart to it.

"What about your car?" Yordon asked.

Thomas shook his head. "That won't work."

"So you'll spend the night?" Yordon asked.

"If you don't mind. I'd like to keep an eye on the prisoners."

"Sure," Yordon said, but Johnny could swear he detected a hint of reluctance in the man's voice.

Yordon lifted a hand to his lips and wiped the sweat gathered on his upper lip. "Where *is* your car?" he asked, training his eyes on the cop's face.

"I came on foot," the officer replied as though it were not only obvious but common in these parts.

"You say that as if you always walk around the mountains without wheels. What exactly brought you to Paradise?"

"I received a call," the cop said.

"How could you receive a call? The phones have been out for a while. Cell phones are even out."

The tone in Yordon's voice had just changed from inquisitive to demanding, and Johnny felt a bead of sweat pop from his forehead.

"My call didn't come over the phone, Stanley."

"Is that right? Don't tell me God told you to come."

Thomas just looked at the reverend. He was in a corner. Even if he wanted to lie, he would be hard-pressed for an explanation.

Yordon arched a brow. "Did God tell you it was two miles?" He drew the number two in the air.

"What does it matter?" Johnny asked. "He saved this town, didn't he?"

"No, Johnny, I want to hear this out. Sounds an awful lot like Black to me. What was that Black said? *God told me to bring grace and hope to Paradise?* Something like that if my memory serves me. You peddling grace and hope too?"

"You think Thomas is anything like Black? He's nothing like him."

"Doesn't it strike you as odd, Johnny, that our police officer here came into town on foot, just like Black, claims to hear from God, just like Black, even talks a bit like Black. And the only person we haven't rounded up today *is* Black. Don't you find that just a little strange?"

Johnny blinked. "What're you saying? That Thomas is Black?"

"Did I say that?" Yordon still didn't move his eyes, but now he wore a small grin. "Just stated the facts. You draw your own conclusion. Maybe we shouldn't be so hasty."

Was that possible? Actually, Johnny didn't have proof that Samuel had written Thomas into Paradise. What if something had happened to Samuel, and this was another scheme by Billy, like the story about the hallucinogenic sludge? Maybe he'd found out what was up and written Thomas himself.

"I'm not Black," Thomas said. "I'm the law. I'm the law come to set Paradise straight. Help her see the error of her ways. Consider these my commandments." He slipped one of his six-guns from the holster and spun the chamber. "And these bullets my precepts. And if these aren't enough, there's an awful lot more where they come from. Enough firepower to make your head spin clean off. I suggest you pay them some respect, Stanley."

Yordon stood and walked from the room, leaving Johnny and Thomas in the guest chairs without a host.

Thomas turned to Johnny and winked. "You okay?"

"I think so."

"Too obvious?"

"He's wrong, right?"

Thomas stared into his eyes for a long moment. "Believe, Johnny. Trust me, I am as un-Black as they come. Okay?"

"Okay."

"That's good." He sighed, then stood and ruffled Johnny's hair. "Come on, son. Let's get this place locked down for the evening. We have a big day ahead of us tomorrow."

STANLEY YORDON slept in his house, alone. More alone than he'd felt in a long time. He'd lost his stomach for the shepherding game for the time being. He had lost his flock and with it his power.

Now he had these voices about grace and hope—Black's grace and hope—droning relentlessly in his mind. To make matters worse, his sheep had been reduced to blithering idiots who didn't know how to blink much less think. There was nothing worse than a fixed stare, and this insipid bunch had perfected it.

When he finally drifted off, his head filled with the voices. *Time for church, Stan! Wake up, Stan the man. Suck up some grace-juice, Stan.*

Was he really hearing that?

Wake up! Wake, wake, wake!

Yordon's eyes sprang open. He jerked his head toward the door. Marsuvees Black stood tall, alive and in the flesh, not five feet from him.

"Am I your cowboy, Stan? I rather like that name. Endearing I think." Black's voice rasped as if he had a cold. He smelled musty—like a stale, damp dishrag.

Yordon scrambled off the bed. "How . . . how did you get in here?"

"You have a door, don't you, Stan? Everybody has a door. There's always a way in."

"But it was locked."

"Don't be a fool. Your door has never been locked."

"What are you talking about? I swear I locked it just last night."

"Stanley, Stanley. You're babbling about things that are meaningless. Powerless words. It is a bad habit with you. What does it matter how I came in? The fact is, I'm in."

Yordon felt the wall behind him. "So what do you want with me?"

Black wagged a finger. "Wrong question, Stan. I want nothing with a pitiful soul like you. I'm here because *I* can do something for *you.*"

Yordon swallowed. Black's thin black hair snaked past his thick neck. He still wore that blasted hat. What did he have to hide up there, a hole? The wind howled past the window behind Yordon—a storm rode on the air again.

"What can you do for me?" he asked.

"I can give you what you want, that's what."

"What?"

"What, what, what? Power! You want power. I've got it. I want to give it to you."

"Power?"

"What's the matter? You can't speak more than one word at a time now?" Black raised his hand in the air and brought them together in a booming clap. "Power!"

Yordon jumped. "You take me for an idiot? Stop patronizing me."

"Now that's more like it," Black said. "Show some spine. You're going to need it."

"Why?"

"You've always wanted to have power over people, Stanley. It's why you went to seminary in the first place. You weren't about to be a lowly butcher like your father, now were you? No, the idea of a hundred or so lost sheep licking at your hands was far more appealing. And in a small town like Paradise even the pagans respect you, don't they?"

Black clasped his hands behind his back and spread his legs. "But we have a problem in Paradise, Yordon. A very bad problem. The people no longer like you. You are powerless. Let's face it, the only power a preacher really possesses over any flock is bound up with their minds."

Black walked to the desk. He picked up a picture of Yordon standing out-side the church during his first week. A large sign that hung over the front doors read, *Welcome to Paradise, Father. We Love You.*

"And you know why they don't respect you. No? Then let's not waste time guessing—I'll tell you. They stopped respecting you the first year you were here, when you had your little fling with Sally Drake after she and Johnny came to town. You do remember that, don't you? You impregnated her, and then you forced her to put the boy up for adoption when she refused to terminate the pregnancy. Couldn't have a scandal in the town of Paradise, now could we?"

"How in the world do you know—"

"Shut up, Stan, I haven't finished. They would have forgiven you then; they always do. But your true indiscretion was sweeping the whole thing under the rug. You like secrets, Stan? You turned your back on your son, and on your lover, and on the commandments for which you stand, all to protect your little secret. And guess what? It worked. The town made it their secret. They pretended that you had the right to do what you did. Why? Because they are no better than you."

Yordon wasn't sure whether he was more terrified or outraged. It was that snake, Paula. Who else would make such a big deal out of something so small, so long ago?

"They played your game, Stanley, but they also lost their respect for you. Every time you stand up there and talk eloquently about the Word of God, half of this town is rolling their eyes and the other half is dead asleep. Not a single one of them believes a single word you have to say. Am I close?"

"How dare you accuse me!" Yordon's anger washed away his fear.

"I can give them back to you, Stanley," Black said, moving to the window. "I'll do one better than give them back to you. I'll make you the talk of the town. Their guardian angel. More power than you ever thought possible, right here over your own flock. When I'm through, they'll do anything for you. Anything."

The words ran into his mind like a hot steel rod.

He knew that, didn't he? And Stanley also knew that if Black could turn Claude into a blubbering fool, he could just as easily turn the man into an adoring fool.

"What about Sally? She's never stopped bad-mouthing me."

Black faced him. "I can make Sally suck your toes, my friend."

"What do I have to do?"

Black smiled thinly. "Give me Thomas."

Figured. One weirdo wanted the other. If Thomas really was the cop he professed, maybe he could prove it now. A confrontation between the lawman and the healer.

A burning sensation stung behind his ears, and Yordon wondered if the flames of hell had ignited there at the base of his brain. He stared at Black, knowing that with that stare he was saying yes.

"Why don't you just do it yourself? You seem to have the power."

"Much to my dismay, Thomas has more power over someone like me than he does over you. Amazing but true. That's half of it. The other half is that I want you to do it, my friend. I want to give you your power back."

"And what makes you think that I can give you Thomas?"

"He's here to protect you from me, not kill you. He's asleep at the moment. If he wakes up while you're in there doing your dastardly deed, I'll get his attention and make things easier for you, but you have to deal with him. Follow?"

"How do you know so much about our town? My affair with Sally was over a decade ago."

"Let's just say that I've been in a lot of people's minds lately. Think of it as one of my tricks."

Yordon didn't trust the man, but his risk was minimal. If Black didn't come through, he could just abort. As for the promise of returning his respect and power . . .

"Okay."

Black turned away. "You're a wise fool, Stanley. A very wise fool."

CHAPTER THIRTY-ONE

THE MONASTERY
Sunday night

EVEN IN Billy's distorted mind, the wholesale transformation of the students in the library tunnel was surprising. The epidemic of boils had become a kind of accelerated leprosy. If not for the worm salve, most of the children would probably be incapacitated. As it was, when slabs of skin tore loose from scratching, they replaced it with the worm gel.

"Worm gel is better than skin anyway," Paul kept saying.

Paul wandered the halls, all six of them, coaxing or dragging worms to the large library. In a show of reluctant good faith, he agreed to haul one worm to Billy's study for every five he hauled to the larger library. Billy had forced his authority with the agreement and reminded Paul of its terms each time he came huffing and puffing into the study, a slug in tow.

Most of the children devoted themselves to writing without complaint. Any grievances invariably centered on either the itching skin disease or the lack of dry writing spots. The itching came with an easy solution: "Get off your lazy butt and get your own gel!" The same advice could be heard given at least a dozen times each hour in precisely those terms. Another dozen in other terms.

But the gel itself gave rise to the second complaint. The more gel the children slapped around, the more of it landed on their books, which wouldn't be such a problem if it didn't cause the pages to stick together and the ink to smear. With so many children writing in the library, the dry nooks and crannies soon became gooey nooks and crannies.

Both Billy and Darcy noticed that everyone seemed happier when they ingested greater volumes of the gel. Together with the help of Paul, they agreed on the dungeon's first law:

To write in the lower levels, one is required to ingest six helpings of gel each day. And by helpings we mean two hands, cupped together, full. And by each day we mean every twenty-four-hour period, just in case there's any confusion.

They called it their first rule of writing. All of the children agreed that it was a good rule. It made things smooth. It helped them write. It kept them out of trouble.

Billy made his way back from the meeting in the sixth tunnel by himself, leaving Darcy to work out some details with Paul. The memory of his little encounter with Samuel earlier today made him sick. The business with Paul's worms and the new rule of writing distracted him for a few hours, but now the thought of Samuel lodged in his mind like a stubborn tick.

He started to jog. His teeth clacked together with every footfall, like cymbals punctuating the pounding of his heart. His muscles burned, and for a brief moment he wondered if some creatures, like ants maybe, were chewing on them. Maybe the boils housed little animals that fed on the worm ointment and burrowed.

He veered to the nearest wall, swiped his hand along a trail of gel, and slapped the salve on his stinging arms.

The fact was, he could hardly even remember what had happened upstairs, but he knew this: that last thing Samuel had done—that touching thing—that ridiculous display of feeling, that wasn't good. Bogus. Bogus, bogus, bogus! And he had stood there like a cornstalk, like a rebuked child afraid to move. Only he hadn't been rebuked by Samuel. Only touched and held. Man, that was disgusting!

You wanna die, boy? A voice rose above the melee in his mind. *You wanna die?*

Yeah, I wanna die. What's it to ya?

The salve wasn't working so well just now. He grunted and attacked his left forearm with an open claw, wincing as a slab of skin stuck to his fingernails.

No, fool! You can't die yet.

No? What's it to ya?

There's a story to write, boy. A story about grace and hope in Paradise. You know about grace and hope, don't you?

The thought of writing awakened Billy's desire. He saw the study looming ahead in the darkness, glowing. Darcy must have forgotten to take her torch.

The outline of a dozen large worms pulsed in the shadows. He stumbled into the study.

The monk stood in the torchlight.

The monk. He'd almost forgotten about the monk and his black mask. This cloak-and-dagger routine no longer impressed Billy. What did the man care if anyone knew who he was?

Billy cleared his throat. "What are you doing here?"

"I've come to clarify a few things for you."

"Be my guest, clarify."

"I'll start with the book you're writing in. They're blank history books discovered by Thomas Hunter. You do remember Thomas Hunter and the Raison Strain."

"He saved the world. Who wouldn't know about him?"

"In these books the word becomes flesh. Literally. Whatever is written in them actually happens. It becomes fact. History, thus the books of history."

Billy nodded. "And?" He knew the man expected him to be stunned by this revelation, but he relished sounding informed. Besides, it hardly surprised him. *Good. I hope you're right.*

"Have you noticed that the characters seem to have a mind of their own?"

"'Course I have."

"You can't force them, but your influence over them is powerful. Your words are flesh in their minds. Thanks to you, the little town has been coming apart at the seams."

"Good. I've only started." The monk's revelation made everything clear. At least as clear as Billy's foggy mind would allow.

Billy could see the man's eyes glistening in the torchlight through the two slits cut in the ceramic mask.

"Do you know about Thomas?"

"You just told me."

"The other Thomas."

"The cop," Billy said. "Yes, I'm working on that problem."

"Do you know he's not a real cop?"

"What do you mean? Of course he's real."

"He's written by Samuel."

It was the first stunning thing the man had said in days.

"Samuel? He's . . . he's writing into Paradise?"

"He's been writing for four days. If the people weren't so predisposed to listen to you, they'd be walking around in robes of white."

"And Thomas, that stupid kung-fu cop—"

"—has changed the balance of power. Aside from Johnny, he's the only real enemy you have down there. You handled Johnny stupidly by showing him Black's true character in the beginning. Now he's a problem. I suggest you handle Thomas with more skill."

"I couldn't resist giving him a scare. And I've handled myself just fine since then, so have some respect." Billy paused, irritated. "I can kill him, right? I mean, I can kill Thomas. If he's not real, then Black won't get into any trouble if the real law shows up."

The monk didn't answer. He clasped his hands behind his back and paced. "Did the students in the library touch the mucus?"

"Touch it? They're covered in it."

"I mean Samuel and his friends, when they touched you in the upper library."

"Yes."

"Well then. It's worth a try."

"The salve will turn them?" Billy asked.

"Soften them."

Billy couldn't imagine Tyler or Christine or Samuel entering the tunnels, salve or no salve. "There's no way they'll agree."

"No? Do they have greater resolve than you?"

"Of course not. They're just slower."

"Well then, it's time you brought them up to speed."

"What about the story?"

"The story is the point. Christine, Tyler, and Samuel are writing into Paradise too. Remove their influence and you'll be free to write your heart's desire. Your writing is far more concentrated than the others', something I'm still trying to understand. They're writing what you've told them to write, but half of it is conflicting mush that does nothing to achieve our primary objective. Yours and Darcy's is more focused and to the point. It's better to eliminate the opposition above and focus your own writing than to devote time to the others down here."

"What about the cop?" Billy asked.

"Go after Samuel and his friends, then write. And when you write, you can be as obvious as you want. You've already let the thread about the gel die—that's good, there's no need to pretend that a little hallucinogenic gel caused the people to see things. Your writing has seduced them already. It's time to go for their throats." He paused.

"I have some specific statements that I want you to write into your book. I'm working on the wording now. We've just begun, my friend. What I have in mind for this world will blow your mind."

He walked to the gate.

"And what about you? Why won't you show me your face?"

The monk turned back. He stared at Billy for a long time, then he casually raised his hand and lifted the mask off his face.

Billy blinked. How was this possible?

"How did you . . ."

"I didn't, Billy. You did."

IN THE wake of the monk's visit, Billy applied himself to his task with a new urgency.

He and Darcy found Christine and Tyler less than an hour later, walking from the dining room. They probably visited the cafeteria three times a day, like they all used to.

"Let me do the talking," he mumbled to Darcy.

"Yeah."

Christine and Tyler stopped talking and slowed when they were still twenty yards off.

"Hey, Billy," Christine said. She was trying to sound natural, but Billy heard the tightness in her throat, as if she had just swallowed a mouse in that dining room of theirs.

"Hey."

The pair stopped ten feet away. "You okay?" Christine asked.

Am I okay? Well now, that's ridiculous. Do I look okay? Of course I'm okay. Of course not.

"I beat you handily in the debate. Did I strike you as not being okay?"

She nodded. "Yes, you did. It was good to see you earlier."

Oh, quit the mushy stuff, like you're the one to be big here.

"Where's Samuel?"

"He's sleeping."

Honestly, Billy was more relieved than disappointed. "We have a problem," he said. "Down below."

Christine tilted her head in interest and waited for him to continue. He shifted on his feet, wishing he were in his study writing instead of up here playing tiddlywinks with Christine.

"We've had, umm . . . an accident. Shannon's sick and can't get out."

He held his breath for a moment and then forced himself to breathe, trying to think how a person would really act in his supposed predicament. Problem was, he didn't really care if Shannon or David or anybody was really sick, and he was having difficulty remembering how it felt to care.

"Shannon is sick? In the forbidden levels?" A spark of concern lit Christine's eyes.

"In the lower levels. They're no longer forbidden, thanks to you."

Christine didn't bat an eye. "Take her to the infirmary, Billy. It's still open."

"That's just it. We're all kind of weak." Christine would never buy this stupid little story. Even now she was probably on the verge of throwing her head back in laughter.

"You're all sick?" If she doubted his story, her face didn't betray her.

"No. We just have a lot to do down there and we don't get much sleep."

Since when did being tired preclude someone from taking a sick friend to the infirmary? He tried to strengthen his reasoning.

"We do things that take a lot of energy, so we could sleep for days, but we never do because there's just too much to do." He fidgeted with his fingers. "I mean, in a matter of speaking. Kind of like being tired only it feels like you're sick a little."

Billy was quite sure he'd just blown the whole thing, mumbling like a fool.

"Okay, take us to the entrance. But bring Shannon out to us there," Christine said.

Tyler stared at her. "We can't go down there!"

"We're not going *in*. We're just showing a little decency here."

"But it's forbidden! No one ever said we can't go down there unless Shannon is sick and needs a lift. They just said don't go down."

"Technically it's not forbidden, although I get your point, it is for us. But Shannon has never been sick down there, has she? How would you like to be Shannon?"

"I don't see why three or four of them can't carry her to the infirmary. She can't weigh more than seventy-five pounds. They climbed up the stairs to get here, didn't they? They can't be that weak."

"They *are* going to carry her, Tyler. To the entrance. Right, Billy? We'll just help her from there. I don't see how that really violates the spirit of any rule."

Billy watched the whole exchange with fascination. Students in the process of justifying.

"How bad is she?" Tyler asked.

It took a second for Billy to realize the question was directed to him. "Shannon? Yes, well . . . not really. She's okay but not for long. In fact she could die at any time. You never really know with sickness."

"Okay, let's go then," Christine said.

Billy did not move. A small voice objected somewhere inside of him. That was too easy, it said. He blinked and realized they were waiting for him. He trudged toward the staircase at the end of the hall.

It took them five minutes to get to the main floor. Both Tyler and Christine followed diligently. One more flight of stairs into the dungeon. From here the steps were stone, and they absorbed the sound of Billy's steps as he plodded down them.

Then they approached the charred black doors, closed like two tombstones, wavering in the torch's shadows. Billy remembered how his heart had pounded when he first saw the doors. Did Christine feel that now? If the doors didn't get to her, one look inside and she would fold. They all did.

He walked to the center of the room and turned around. Christine and Tyler entered with bulging eyes and parted lips, and if he wasn't mistaken, their apparent wavering resulted from weak knees, not the shifting flames.

He had his answer.

Billy glanced at Darcy, walked to the doors, and shoved them open inward. Darcy walked in ahead of him and he followed without looking back. No matter, he would see them soon enough.

The doors closed behind him, and he forgot about Christine and Tyler in favor of the writing ahead of him, down that hall to the right, where Paradise and Thomas and Claude and Steve waited.

"Come on," he said to Darcy, and together they jogged into the mountain.

CHAPTER THIRTY-TWO

PARADISE
Monday

FOR THE second day in a row, Johnny awoke with a start and bolted up in bed. For the second day in a row, he knew something had changed, but he couldn't place it.

Then he remembered Thomas.

It was barely light. He scrambled out of bed and shuffled through his drawers for a new shirt. Found one with a faded red Indy car and pulled it out. He started to shut the drawer, then remembered his socks and bent for the first pair his hand felt.

His mother's words rang in his head: *Every morning, Johnny, you hear? That doesn't mean every other morning or every week—you change your socks and underwear every morning!*

Behind him, the glass clattered and his mind posed a simple question. *Why is the glass rattling, Johnny?*

Because of the wind, of course.

Wind?

Johnny spun to the window. The wooden sill framed a nearly leafless forest, bowing to the east, backlit by a dark, overcast sky.

Did Thomas know? He had to get to the church! Unless Black stood in the street between his house and the church with his head raised to the sky, laughing. Johnny shuddered and yanked the shirt over his head.

He tore down the hall and shoved his head into his mother's bedroom. Empty.

Johnny ran through the living room and threw open the front door. The street was also empty. Wind blew in angry gusts, whipping sand around the buildings and batting at the few leaves that clung stubbornly to spindly branches. Above Paradise, the sky lay flat and black, a lid clamped over the valley. Worse than he'd seen it.

Johnny swallowed his dread and ran for the church, shielding his eyes from the wind with his hand.

An obscure thought floated lazily through his mind—a memory of walking along the beach in Florida, feeling the sand squish between his toes and giving way when he pushed hard. He realized he'd forgotten to put the socks on.

Johnny reached the railing, climbed the steps as fast as he could, ignoring a pain in his right leg. He pushed the doors open and stepped into the church, breathing hard.

He ran through the sanctuary toward the stairs that led into the basement.

Still no sign of anybody.

The stairway descended into darkness, and he wondered briefly if the town was still asleep. It couldn't be much past eight, and the way folks slept around here . . .

But the cop would be awake. As far as he knew, fictional characters didn't even sleep. Unless Samuel slept . . .

Maybe Thomas was down in the basement making coffee, waiting for him—for Johnny, his partner—to show up so they could go flush out Black and hang him.

Johnny crept down the stairs, scarcely making a sound. He landed safely on the basement floor and poked his head around the corner.

The room looked like a black cavern. He let his eyes adjust to darkness. Slowly, familiar forms took shape: the support posts rising to the ceiling every ten feet, a Nerf basketball hoop mounted on the far wall, the white door leading to Paula's office.

The kitchen door stood in the shadows across the room. Johnny imagined a dozen pairs of eyes glowing behind the door like trapped owls. He focused on a faint white smudge that appeared in the middle of the door. It looked like someone had hung a plate there. Maybe Thomas, so that if it moved it would bang. Smart. But it wasn't really hanging, was it? No, it was sitting. On a counter.

And then Johnny knew he wasn't looking at the kitchen door at all. He was staring *into* the kitchen itself, through a wide-open door, at the far counter where a plate leaned against the wall.

The kitchen was empty!

He spun, half-expecting to see Claude on the stairs, glaring down at him. But the stairs were empty too.

He tore up the steps, terrified.

He wanted to scream out. To shout out the cop's name. "Thomas! Thomas, they're gone! Thomaaaaass!" But Thomas was gone too. Maybe being chased by crazies; maybe chasing crazies.

Or maybe he'd already moved them. Maybe other cops had come with a paddy wagon and taken them all to Junction.

Johnny made the snap decision to run out the back, just in case they were waiting for him in the street. He tore past Father Yordon's open office and struck out for the door, gulping at the air like he had just thrust his head through the waves after being submerged for a full minute.

The door pulled open in his hand, and the black sky filled its frame. Johnny leapt through and found himself face to face with a scene that made the image of Black walking into town seem toasty warm by comparison.

The church's back lawn ran seventy-five feet before meeting the forest. Wooden picnic tables sat along the fence, leaving most of the lawn open for children to play. A large oak tree spread its thick arms over a jungle gym to Johnny's right. The congregation had a running debate over the tree. Half wanted to lop the encroaching oak to the ground so they wouldn't have to constantly repair the damage inflicted to the roof; half wanted to preserve the oak for its shade and beauty.

But none of that mattered right now. Right now Johnny's eyes fell on the crazies who stood on the grass where the children normally played.

They stood like a mob of looters caught red-handed, thirty or forty of them, with their hands hanging by their sides.

A dozen miniature sunflower windmills mounted to the fence posts spun madly in the wind. The door behind Johnny slammed shut, but he barely heard it. He stood frozen on the small porch, his arms and feet spread in a defensive crouch.

Claude Bowers and his little gang stood atop the picnic tables. They might have been gathered for a class photo, all wielding hammers and axes and other heavy objects.

A larger group bunched closer to the building. Johnny recognized Katie Bowers, her long strawberry hair flying back from her head. Nancy stood on the edge like a big piggy bank. No one spoke. Only a few even turned their heads toward Johnny. The rest stared past him to his right, where the huge oak reached for the sky.

All of this he saw in a second.

Then Johnny followed their eyes.

Thomas's body hung from a hemp rope wrapped crudely around his neck and tossed over a wide branch above the jungle gym. The body jerked spastically, as though it had dropped just moments before.

The body had been stripped naked except for a white T-shirt, white boxer briefs, and white socks. They'd cut him up with a machete or maybe an ax. His lower lip sagged, swollen to three times its natural size. His eyes were gone, leaving round red sockets staring into the wind.

They'd tied his hands behind his back and hog-tied them to his ankles, so he appeared to be kneeling in the air.

Johnny's chest froze up. His only movement came from his knees—they shook violently.

Steve Smither stood below the spinning body, looking up at Thomas like a third grader beaming at his first-place science project. His hands were bloody.

They were all killers here, but Steve had wrapped the rope around the neck and yanked. And Black had been there breathing in his ear the whole time.

Johnny's heart and lungs still weren't working right, but he turned around and clambered for the door. By some miracle it swung in and he lurched forward. His head felt like a sounding gong, mounted on his shoulders, vibrating. A taunting voice warbled back there somewhere.

Wanna trip like I do? Wanna trip? Wanna wanna trip?

From deep in his gut, fury rose into his chest. He stumbled down the hall and then began to run. By the time Johnny reached the front doors, he was sprinting. A thousand voices were screaming in his head, but he couldn't make them out anymore. He crashed through the doors and tumbled down the concrete steps.

The first sob broke from his throat there, while he was sprawled on the sidewalk at the foot of the church.

Then Johnny Drake leapt to his feet and fled Paradise.

CHAPTER THIRTY-THREE

THE MONASTERY
Monday

SAMUEL'S PLAN had failed.

Johnny had no clue how the offenders got out of the locked kitchen, or how they managed to overpower Thomas, but they had. That was all that mattered.

Johnny tore up the mountain, cutting his bare feet and scraping his knuckles. He'd believed. At least yesterday he'd believed. Today he wasn't sure about much except that he didn't have too many alternatives left. Even if he could find a way to Delta, he couldn't risk bringing more people into Billy's line of sight. And he couldn't try to outwit Black's next move. After Johnny's performance at the meeting Saturday night, he probably *was* Black's next move.

Fleeing to the monastery was his only choice. Samuel would be there, waiting for him. Maybe he could get his hands on one of those books. Maybe he could give himself some powers.

Johnny reached the large canyon quickly. He raced around the boulder and faced the cliff where the monastery hid.

"Samuel!"

His voice echoed, then drifted off.

"Samuel!"

Nothing. Johnny called the name repeatedly for the next ten minutes without a response. He took a few more minutes to gather himself. Then he walked to the outer door, twisted the rusted handle, and pushed the door open.

The monastery reached for the cliff top. Anything powerful enough to put this huge, ancient monastery here surely had the power to kill Black.

"Samuel?"

He couldn't just stand here forever. For all he knew, Samuel had gone into the tunnels himself. Or been killed.

The awful possibilities mushroomed in his mind. Why else wasn't Samuel coming out? Thomas had been killed because something terrible happened to Samuel. Billy had done something.

Believe, Johnny. Believe.

He strode to the front doors, turned the handle, and walked right in. The massive foyer was empty except for the paintings and doors and table. His heart echoed in his ears.

"And what about the basement?"

Samuel had hesitated. "Off the main hall to the left. A long series of stairs take you down. Not a place anyone in their right mind would want to go."

Johnny located the main hall before he could tell himself any different. The hall was wide, carved from stone and paved with bricks. Indirect sunlight filtered from high above.

Off the main hall to the left.

"Hello?"

Johnny jumped back. A boy stood by a door down the hall, looking at him. His skin was bleeding, and he'd smeared some kind of ointment all over his body. He looked worse than the crazies in Paradise.

"Hello?" the boy said again. "Who are you?"

"Johnny."

"Have you seen Paul?"

"No."

The boy looked back the way he'd come. "One of the worms died."

Johnny knew he was looking at one of the students who'd entered the lower tunnels. The worm salve had done this to him.

"Have you seen Samuel?" Johnny asked.

"No. I think he's with Billy. Do you know where Paul is?"

"I haven't seen him." The boy wasn't lucid. "How do I find Billy?"

"He's in the first tunnel. The one on the right."

Then the boy walked by him, headed off to find Paul.

The boy hadn't tried to kill him. That was promising. Johnny ran for the door and stepped into the darkness beyond.

Now what? He couldn't go down without light. He was about to turn back to search for a light of some kind, when it struck him that the darkness seemed to thin farther down. Maybe just because his eyes were adjusting to the dark.

He put a hand on the rough wall and descended several steps. Then several more. The stairway curved to his left. And, yes, a yellow light filtered up from below.

Johnny went down on his tiptoes. The light came from a torch in a small room outside a large black door.

The door to hell.

He stared at the door and realized that he was making a terrible mistake. Running from Claude on familiar territory was one thing. Knocking down the gates of hell to take on Black was another. He glanced back at the stairs.

If it was true—if Samuel was with Billy—then as far as Johnny knew, he might be the only thing standing between Billy and Paradise. He wasn't at all confident that anything he wrote in a book would happen. He wasn't even sure he could find a book. Or survive Billy. Or survive Samuel, if he'd been lured down.

Johnny's hands trembled, but he forced them to grip the torch, pull it free, and push on the black door. It swung open.

He stepped into an inner room that smelled like a sewer. The walls glistened with a thin coating of the worm gel. The room branched into several tunnels. Johnny veered into the one on his far right.

He stared down the long dark passage. Thick pipes ran along . . .

One of the pipes began to move. He stood rooted in place for a long minute, breathing hard. Worms!

But he couldn't go back. Not now.

"Samuel!"

His voice echoed down the hall.

"Samuel! It's Johnny."

There was water dripping somewhere. His head felt odd—dizzy. A bit numbed.

"Billy!"

No one responded. He took a few steps and stopped again. The slugs throbbed in his torchlight. What was he thinking? He should find Samuel's father first.

"Come on back," a faint voice called.

Billy? It didn't sound like Samuel.

Johnny hesitated, then switched the torch to his left hand, gave the worm a wide berth, and walked down the hall.

He saw light and headed for it, jogging now.

On the right, a gate dawned. Past the gate, a room with a desk and some bookcases. In the room a boy with red hair sat at the desk. Next to the boy sat a girl. Both had pens in their hands. Both were covered with sores and bleeding skin.

Both stared at him absently.

"Well?" the boy asked. No threats. Not yet.

Johnny stepped into the room, barely breathing even though his lungs strained.

"You're Billy?"

"Yeah."

Just that. Just *yeah*. Now what?

"Is . . . is Samuel here?"

"No."

"You're destroying Paradise," Johnny said. "Do you know that?"

The girl next to him answered. "Take a hike, Johnny."

They were just kids—Samuel had told him that—but somehow he'd half-expected monsters. They looked more lost than mean.

"Who are you?" he asked the girl.

"That's Darcy," Billy said. "And like she said, take a hike."

The books they were writing in looked old, fragile. He could see the out-line of Billy's writing. Hard to believe it had done so much damage. But he knew a few things about this writing. That it could be resisted, for example. He'd done it a hundred times in the last few days. And whatever smell was trying to make his head spin down here could probably be resisted as well. Johnny set his jaw.

Billy laid his pen down. A grin tugged at his lips. "So tell me, Johnny? How does it feel to be the lone holdout? We'll get you soon enough. You can't hold out forever. Samuel can only do so much. He's put all his eggs into one little fool, and if I'm not mistaken, the little fool has just wandered into the forbidden dungeons. Have you tried our slime yet? Tastes pretty good."

"It's not too late to stop," Johnny said. "You just killed someone. Do you know what they do to murderers?"

"Steve killed him," Billy said. "Not me. And obviously you're a little short on the uptake. Thomas was no more a real person than Black is."

Black?

"What do you mean, Black? He's a teacher from the monastery."

"Sure he is. The one up here is anyway. The monk told me to write a character named Marsuvees Black who would have a little fun with Paradise, so I did. I wrote him just like the real Marsuvees Black. But the real Marsuvees Black is still here. I saw him yesterday. He never left the mountain."

"You're saying that the man I saw walk into town is just like Thomas?"

"Well, not just like Thomas. Personally I think he's way more interesting."

"Thomas was a bore," Darcy said.

"You see?" Billy said. "I was the first one to write a character into Paradise, and unless I'm mistaken, he's kicked some major Thomas butt."

"Forgive me, boys, but this is boring me to tears," Darcy said. "Johnny, please, please, please take a hike. You can talk till you're blue in the face. While you're at it, give us a hug or something. Show a little love. Samuel tried that. It won't work. We're busy, and you rudely interrupted. Now, take a hike."

Their minds were scrambled. Duped. Doped. No different from the people in Paradise. Deceived to the core.

He looked at the shelves packed with black leather-bound books. An idea dropped into his mind.

"Maybe you're right," he said, edging up to the desk. They looked up at him in a stupor. Several pens lay beside Darcy.

"If I joined you now, would you let me share this office with you?"

"Who said anything about joining us?" Darcy said.

"I just did. What would I have to do?"

"Eat the worm gel," Billy said. "But nobody except me and Darcy write in here."

"When this story of Paradise is over, what will you do?" he said, putting his torch in the receptacle by the boar head.

"Over?" They clearly hadn't thought that far.

"Will you go after another town? Where will it end?" Johnny moved closer to the desk. If he reached out his hand, he could touch it.

"Who says it ever ends?"

"Well, maybe I just have a point that you should listen to," Johnny said. He pointed at the gate. "When you see that gate, what does it make you think of?"

They both turned and looked.

Johnny picked up one of the pens, reached over to Darcy's book, and wrote as fast as he could, speaking to cover the scratch of the pen on paper.

"If you look hard enough, you can see someone's face, can't you?"

Johnny was given great powers to destroy Billy . . .

He scratched out *Billy*.

. . . anyone who stood in the way of truth.

"What are you doing?" Darcy shrieked, jumping up. She slapped his hand. The pen drew a long scratch on the page and flew across the room.

"He tricked us! He wrote in my book!"

Billy was on his feet, eyes round. "What did he write?"

She read aloud. "*Johnny was given great powers to destroy anyone who stood in the way of truth.* He wrote your name but scratched it out."

Johnny clenched his eyes and tried to think things that might bring out a great power. But his mind was blank.

"Give me that!" Billy said. He grabbed a pen and scrawled words below what Johnny had written.

"There. *Billy was given great powers like Johnny, only to destroy whoever he wants.*"

Darcy pulled the book away and spoke as she wrote. "*And so was Darcy.*"

She slammed the pen down. "You thought we were so stupid? Go ahead, destroy us with your great power."

But Johnny had no great power.

"The books don't work like that, you idiot," Billy said, face flushed. "I'll give you exactly one minute to get out of here, or I'm going to make every last one of the students switch to write one character and one character only. Three guesses who that might be."

"You can't turn me that—"

"Not you. Sally."

"My . . . my mom?"

Billy nodded, grinning now. "She'll join the cop before nightfall, I can promise you that. The clock's ticking, boy. Forty-five seconds."

"You can't do that!" Johnny felt smothered. "She has nothing to do with this!"

"She has everything to do with this. Forty."

"I'd start running," Darcy said. "Save Mama."

"Thirty-five."

Johnny grabbed his torch and bolted. "Leave her out of this. Promise me—"

"Thirty. It's a long climb up those stairs, boy."

JOHNNY RAN. Down the tunnel, through the black door. He took the stairs two at a time, challenged by a spinning head. Into the hall. He made it, he was sure he'd made it.

But knowing Billy . . . How would the boy *know* he'd made it?

"Johnny?"

Johnny spun. Samuel stood by the entrance to the atrium, staring at him.

Johnny hurried away from the door, past Samuel, into the light. He was trembling, a jumbled ball of confusion.

"You've . . . you've been down there!" Samuel said. "You have to wash that smell before—"

"Marsuvees Black is Billy's character," Johnny said.

Samuel blinked. "Black? He's not the real one?"

"As real or not real as Thomas."

"You're sure? How—"

"I was down there, Samuel." Johnny wasn't sure why, but he was yelling. Not that he didn't like Samuel. On the contrary, he was desperate for Samuel to save them.

"I saw Billy. He told me that the teacher you know is the one who convinced Billy to write Black into Paradise."

"Then Marsuvees is still in the dungeons! The real one. And it means that Billy knows he can bring characters to life. He must have known about Thomas!"

"And what's to keep Billy from writing a hundred Blacks into Paradise?"

Samuel recovered from his shock and glanced around the atrium. For a moment Johnny thought the boy might burst into tears.

Samuel ran to Johnny and threw his arms around him. "I'm so sorry, Johnny! I was with my father after we found out what happened to Thomas. Then I knew you were coming, but I couldn't make sense of . . . The lower levels must have cut me off. And you're right, Paradise is in terrible trouble. It's hopeless!"

Johnny felt awkward standing there with Samuel's arms around him. Samuel's surreal blend of innocence and intelligence unnerved him.

"What are you going to do?"

Samuel pulled back. He was trying to be brave, but he couldn't hide a frantic light in his eyes.

"I don't know. I think my father is terrified. It's not only the dungeons, it's the town. This was never supposed to happen!"

"You don't have any ideas?"

"It's falling apart. It's all unraveling. I'm the only one left; the rest of the students are below. The overseers . . ." Samuel lowered his head into his hands.

"Have you thought about using the books to give yourself power?"

"I have the books. What more power do I need? It's hopeless!"

"No, I mean give *yourself* the power to deal with Black. You're the person who believes. You could move mountains, couldn't you?"

Samuel looked at him.

"Then you could go down yourself," Johnny said. "With that power."

"Down where?"

"To Paradise."

SAMUEL RAN all the way to the top floor. He'd washed Johnny off at the well and then sent him back to Paradise to scope things out in hiding. His father was meeting with desperate teachers. He would join them, but not until he was sure.

Ever since Thomas's death, which had awakened him at four in the morning, he'd racked his brain to understand his failure and the remaining alternatives. He'd pieced most of it together, but Johnny had given him the key.

Samuel slipped into his father's study and crossed to the desk. Behind it stood a bookshelf. On the top shelf, David had placed the original Book of History that Christopher and Samuel had written in.

He stood on his father's chair and pulled the black volume down. Set it on the desk. Opened the cover. His father kept a sheaf of loose-leaf paper in the front. It was a journal of sorts, documenting his experience with the book.

He turned to the book's first page. An entry about Thomas Hunter stared up at him. Next page.

Christopher's childish handwriting. Several entries. One about a desk and one about a cat and a dozen others that looked like experimental entries testing the book's limitations.

Next page. The entry about the books going into hiding.

Another page. Here. Two entries in his own, though much younger, handwriting.

The first entry limited the books to the residents of the monastery and clarified the way the books must lead to love. . . . *which is written by any person not currently residing in the monastery at this time, and/or which does not lead to the discovery of love will be powerless. This rule is irrevocable.*

The second entry. He read it quickly.

Samuel settled into his father's chair. He reread the entry. Again. And he knew he'd found the key.

Samuel returned the volume to its place on the upper shelf. He set the chair as he'd found it and left the office.

He could hear Raul's voice at the conference-room door when he laid his hand on the doorknob. He paused and listened, calming his nerves.

"You have to call the authorities, David. The project has failed! Samuel could write ten Thomases into Paradise without a guarantee that Black wouldn't string up every single one of them. It's over!"

"We're beyond the authorities," his father said. "How do you suppose they'll deal with Marsuvees Black? He's beyond the reach of ordinary mortals!"

"Then what?"

"We have to trust the books."

"There's no one left to write in the books! The rest of the children have fallen."

"There is *Samuel* to write in the books!" his father's voice boomed. They were desperate—all of them. Even his father. Especially his father.

Samuel pushed the door open and stepped into the room. Seven of the overseers were gathered around his father. All turned to look at him when the door opened.

He shut the door and faced them. "Marsuvees Black is in the dungeons," he said.

"He's left Paradise?" Andrew asked.

"He never left the monastery. At least not for long. The one in Paradise is Billy's creation, inspired by the real Marsuvees Black."

Raul struck the table with his fist. "I knew it! Billy would never have gone below without being lured down by that monster!"

"You're sure about this, Samuel?" his father asked.

"I'm sure."

"Then we have to stop him!" Raul said. "That could be the key!"

"It's the students who are writing, not Marsuvees," David said. "I'm not sure stopping him a week ago would have helped. Billy made his own choice. He's the one who holds the power."

Raul stood and paced behind his chair. "What was the man thinking? What does he stand to gain by doing this?"

"That should be obvious," Andrew answered. "He found David's journal and learned about the history books' power. God only knows how long he walked these halls with that knowledge before deciding to use the books.

But to do so he needed the children. I argued six months ago that he should be replaced. As I recall, Raul, you stood with David in suggesting that the students were old enough to consider a few alternative ways of thinking."

"Marsuvees never suggested open rebellion!" Raul said. "The children had to start drawing lines for themselves— better here than out there!" He threw his hand toward the window.

"Enough," David said. "This gets us nowhere. We'll deal with Marsuvees later. The students are our concern now. And Paradise."

"But knowing that Marsuvees has been complicit may help us to determine their objective," Raul said. "Where does Billy hope to take this story of his?"

Andrew shook his head slowly. "Can you imagine the power someone like Marsuvees Black would have if he could control the books?"

"You can't control the books," Raul said. "It's the children you have to control. Where's Billy taking this story?"

"I don't think Billy knows," Samuel said, moving to his father's end of the table. "Marsuvees may, but Billy and the others are writing for the thrill of it. If you had any idea how it feels . . ." He looked at them, wondering if they could understand. "The power to do what you want is nearly irresistible," he said. "Pure free will, with the power to back it up. It's like a drug."

Several of them nodded.

"Then you're saying that Billy writes just because he can," Andrew said. "Literally. He has no ambition except to write until the desire for it begins to burn him. If that's the case, his passions will be insatiable. He'll go from destroying things to killing things. People. And when he's done with Paradise, he'll move on. To what town? Or what country? We must stop him!"

Mark Anthony spoke. "As I see it, there is no way to stop him."

No one argued this time, not even David.

"I have a plan."

They all looked at Samuel.

"We have to get to Billy, or you're right, he won't stop. The key to Paradise is Billy. Are we agreed to that?"

"Go on," David said.

"The key to Paradise is Billy, but the key to Billy is Paradise. Or more precisely, the key to Billy is defeating him in Paradise. The only way to change Billy may be from within the story itself. That's why I sent Thomas, but

Thomas failed because his power was limited to skills given to him by me. You're right, for every character that I write into Paradise, Billy can just write another character with the power to outwit or overpower my character."

They watched him.

"But what if I could write another kind of character who has more power than any character Billy can ever write?"

"What do you mean?" Raul said. "You already tried that with Thomas."

Samuel placed his hands on the back of a chair. "Thomas was fictional. A fictional character is once removed. I doubt he can act or feel on his own. But I think I can write a character who has the power to love and to affect love."

"What kind of character?" his father asked.

"Me," Samuel said. "I can write myself into Paradise, and I can give myself a power that not even Billy can overcome."

They stared at him.

David stood. "You?"

Samuel exchanged a long look with his father. "A character based completely on me. A character that is a perfect representation of me in every way."

"I still don't see how that is so different from Thomas," Andrew said.

"Samuel will be a character that will do exactly what I would do, equipped with my feelings because I know myself and am myself," Samuel said. "But he will also be more than me, because I'll give him a special power to blow Black back into the hole he came from." He paused. "A superhero."

"Do we know what happens if such a character is hurt?"

"What do you mean?"

"Could it backfire?" Andrew clarified. "If Marsuvees Black were killed in Paradise, would the real Marsuvees die here?"

Samuel hadn't thought about that. It didn't matter. He looked at his father, who was now staring at him with round eyes.

"We must trust the books, Father. You said it yourself. This story *will* lead to the discovery of love. If I can't affect Paradise this way . . . I'm not sure there *is* another way."

"You realize you're the last student with the power to write love," Raul said. "It is critical that nothing happen to you."

Nausea stirred Samuel's stomach.

"Nothing will."

CHAPTER THIRTY-FOUR

PARADISE

Monday

JOHNNY REVIEWED the simple plan he and Samuel hatched before he left the monastery. Johnny would go to Paradise, take complete stock of the situation, and wait for the Samuel that Samuel would write behind the old theater.

Showdown at noon.

That was it. Johnny wanted more, but Samuel couldn't or didn't want to give him more. Johnny also wanted to wait for Samuel so they could go down together, but as Samuel pointed out, someone needed to make sure that Sally's life wasn't in danger.

Johnny would be the eyes on the ground. Again.

He reached the overlook and pulled up, panting. The sky was dark, very dark. Black was definitely back.

He looked down into Paradise. The first thing he saw was the smoke, boiling to the sky. Not at an angle, whipped by wind, but straight up. That meant no wind. But this wasn't necessarily a good thing. It was more likely a condition that Billy needed to move his story forward.

His eyes followed the smoke down to a huge ring of fire on the ground, twice as wide as Main Street. It took Johnny a second to make out people through the cloud of smoke, but they were present, maybe half the town, standing around in no particular pattern, watching the fire.

Johnny dropped to one knee to give his right leg a rest. He didn't know what they were doing but one thing was clear—Billy's story was changing. Today was a day of firsts. First time for no wind while Black was in town, assuming Black still was in town. First time any of them had gathered outside around a ring of fire. First time they'd killed a man.

Johnny looked past the smoke toward the church. He could see the oak behind. No body. They'd taken the cop down.

A figure ran toward the fire. Too hard to see who. Johnny watched him cross the line of flame, take something from . . .

He saw the black-clad man in the middle of the ring for the first time. Marsuvees Black.

He handed a blazing torch to the runner, who then sprinted to the south. Toward the old theater. Smoke rose from the building twenty seconds later. They were torching the town?

Johnny stood to his feet. Was Samuel catching this?

The old Starlight Theater began to burn quickly. Flames licked at the roof and spread down the east wall. Johnny watched in wonder as the wood blazed with orange flames that rose three times the height of the building.

This was it. They were reducing Paradise to ashes. What was he supposed to do now? He couldn't just go down there and throw water on the fire.

Something on the theater's roof caught his eyes. It was something wrapped up, strapped to the top. Something the size of a body. Something like Thomas.

This was their funeral pyre!

Marsuvees Black was burning the cop's body and doing it with enough overkill to permanently impress the town. *Mess with me and I'll burn you bad. Real bad. Real, real bad.*

In that case, they probably wouldn't burn the rest of the town. Indiscriminate burning would be too simpleminded for Billy. Then again, in his doped-up state, simpleminded might be just his ticket.

Johnny thought about turning around and running back up the mountain, but the only way he could really help Samuel was to stay here and take stock, as planned. It would be awhile before he could meet Samuel at the theater.

Johnny sat down, pulled his knees to his chest, and watched the Starlight burn.

Black was the first to leave, about twenty minutes later. He walked straight to the church, flung open the door, and entered. The people began to disperse then, in small groups, headed back to their homes or to various buildings to do only God knew what.

In the end only one small group remained. Had to be Claude and company. They hauled a car into the middle of Black's ring of fire, which had now smoldered to the cast of the still-blazing theater. One of them threw something—a homemade bomb?—at the car. It burst into flames to the delight of several smaller figures in the group. Fred, Peter, Roland, and another kid.

Ten minutes later, they all left.

Johnny finally stood. He couldn't tell the time by the black sky, but if he figured things right—an hour up at daybreak, an hour at the monastery, a half hour to this point, another hour here—it was about midmorning. Samuel would come in two hours. Johnny gave himself a full sixty minutes to reach the town—no need to rush.

He could hear the dying flames crackling when he was still a good fifty yards this side of the meadow behind the old theater.

Then he was there, at the tree line, staring at the charred and burning remains of what used to be the old theater. No sign of anyone.

He hurried around the south edge of town, toward the alley that led to his house. Still no one. And still no wind. The trees were stripped bare of leaves, and the sand was still piled against the buildings. But something felt different.

Johnny stopped fifty feet from the convenience store. It was the sky. The sky wasn't as dark as it had been when he left the overlook.

Samuel?

Johnny felt a burst of courage and headed up the alley, watching left and right like a hawk.

Still not a soul.

He was supposed to be taking stock. There was nothing to take stock of. At least no people. Thank God.

Someone yelled somewhere, and Johnny dove behind someone's house. But it was distant, he quickly realized. Coming from inside a house where an argument had broken out. Maybe from the saloon. He hurried on.

Johnny entered his house from the back, listened for a moment, and sighed with relief. Not that he was safe here, but the familiar hall with its familiar silence was at least a good sign.

He checked his mother's room and found it empty. He donned the socks he'd left behind and found his shoes. Put them on.

Now what? The church? Not a chance. Black was in there.

Johnny stood in the hall for a full five minutes, trying to think things through, but he really didn't know what he could do short of running out into the street and yelling for Black to come and get him.

His vision blurred. The wall moved.

Billy.

Johnny pressed his palms against his temples and focused on an image of Samuel. The wall became still. Someone, maybe Billy himself, was sitting in that damp dungeon below the monastery, trying to break into his mind. He didn't know how it worked, but he knew enough for it to terrify him.

At least he knew how to fight the images that . . .

The house moved under his feet. That was it, he had to get out. Johnny ran down the hall. The walls bent in, the door buckled. He plunged ahead anyway, slammed through the door and out into the alley.

The ground was shaking out here. Not a slight tremor, but a violent vibration that blurred his feet. He cried out in terror, turned south and sprinted.

Whether by Samuel's doing or his own he didn't know, but the world returned to normal after he'd taken three or four steps. Either way, he had to get out of Paradise. He'd seen all he could afford to see.

Johnny reached the tree line south of town and pulled up behind a large aspen, out of the town's sight. He lifted his hands to his face and leaned against the trunk. The ground might not be shaking anymore, but his fingers were.

Johnny eased his seat to the base of the tree. He would wait for Samuel here.

CHAPTER THIRTY-FIVE

PARADISE

Monday afternoon

"JOHNNY."

Samuel's voice cut through the still air, and Johnny jerked upright.

"Samuel?"

"Here." The boy walked from the trees. He was dressed in the same cotton shorts and white button-down shirt he'd worn both times Johnny had seen him. The only difference was his shoes, which were now brown walking boots. He seemed a bit frail, but in every way Johnny could imagine he looked exactly like Samuel.

Johnny scrambled to his feet. "Thank God! Thank God you came."

"Of course I came." Samuel flashed a mischievous grin. "Did you have any doubts?"

He even talked like Samuel. As far as Johnny was concerned, this was Samuel.

Johnny glanced back in the direction of the town. "Did you see?"

"I saw."

"You saw. And you're not worried?"

Samuel winked. "I have a plan, remember? It was your idea."

"Not really. What now?"

"Now we do some damage. To Black, that is."

"Exactly. But how?"

"Do you doubt me?"

Johnny wasn't sure what he doubted or didn't doubt. A week ago he spent most of his time trying to figure out how to spend another lazy summer day.

Now he spent every minute trying to figure out how to survive the chaos. He trusted Samuel, sure. But he'd trusted him with Thomas too.

"They burned Thomas," Johnny said.

"I saw that."

Johnny looked at the boy's arms and hands. "So, what did you do?"

Samuel held out his hands, palms up, and studied them. "You mean what powers do I have in these hands?"

"Did it work?"

"I guess we'll find out."

"So, what are they?"

"Well, it's pretty powerful stuff, I guarantee you that. Would you like to see me throw a few fireballs?"

The idea that fire could actually come out of those white hands was incredible. He reached out and touched Samuel's palms. "You can do that? Sure."

"Actually no, I can't." Samuel lowered his arms. "It'll take a lot more than a few fireballs to deal with Black. Trust me, Johnny, the power I've written into these hands will terrify even Black. Now"—Samuel walked past him—"shall we go give it a try?"

"Hold on."

Samuel walked toward the town as if he hadn't heard Johnny. He was actually going in to confront Black now? It was all moving too fast. They should take a few hours, maybe the night, to plot a careful plan of attack.

"You're just going to walk in there? Hold up!"

Samuel turned back. "Repeat after me, Johnny. *I believe.* Say that with me. *I believe.*"

"I do believe. And I believed with Thomas, but—"

"No, Johnny, you believed in a lawman named Thomas. Now I'm asking you to believe in me."

Was there a difference?

"There's a difference," Samuel said.

"Okay then. I believe."

Samuel smiled. "Shout it."

"Now? They'll hear! We can't just waltz in there like this!"

"That's the point. I want them to know you're with me. Scream it out, Johnny. The louder the better."

Johnny glanced past Samuel at the buildings just visible on the other side of the trees. The sound might not carry too far out here in the woods.

"I have a better idea," Samuel said. He turned and walked toward the town again. "Come on, this way."

Johnny hurried to catch him. "What idea?"

"Stay close, Johnny. This way." Samuel picked up his pace. He walked right out into the open and crossed the clearing, headed for Main Street.

Johnny followed quickly, thinking that Samuel had a point about staying close. At least nobody was in the streets. He scanned the buildings. Saloon was clear, convenience store looked deserted, the church . . .

Johnny stopped. Marsuvees Black stood outside the church, leaning against the back corner, watching them.

"Samuel?"

"Keep walking, Johnny."

"He's right—"

"I see him. Keep walking. You're with me. Remember that. You're with me."

Johnny kept walking. The next time he looked up, he saw that Black was smiling.

They walked out into the middle of Main Street, to the center of the smoldering ring of fire, up next to the car that was still sending up black smoke from its tires.

Samuel stopped. "Here, Johnny. Shout it out for the whole town to hear. *I believe.*"

He was committed now. Surprisingly, Johnny wanted to shout it out. Not in defiance, but in self-defense. He prayed that whatever power Samuel had written into himself was more than what Black could throw at them. This was their last hope.

He had no choice but to align himself with that hope.

He gripped his hands into fists. "I believe!" he yelled. "I believe!"

Fire crackled behind them. Samuel stared at Marsuvees Black, who now stood with his feet planted wide, hands on hips.

Billy's character began to chuckle. He grinned wickedly and walked to his left, keeping his eyes on them. The black-clad monk mounted the church steps. Stretched his neck back and around at unnatural angles as if loosening up. Then disappeared through the doors.

"Come on," Samuel said. "This way." He headed for the church.

Watching Samuel strut straight for the gates of hell, Johnny wasn't sure how much he *wanted* to believe anymore.

"Samuel—"

"Stay close, Johnny."

Then again, he wasn't in a position not to believe. He followed, heart in his throat once again.

THE CHURCH had been nearly gutted by fire. Johnny stared over Samuel's shoulder, through the open inner doors, past the pews, to the stage.

To Marsuvees Black, with his hands flat on the charred pulpit, grinning back at them.

Two nights ago Johnny stood on that very stage, confronting Black in front of the whole town. But that was before. Before the church had been burned. Before they'd torched the theater. Before Thomas had been cut open and hung from the tree.

Before Johnny really understood what Billy could do.

Black tilted his head down and stared up from under the rim of his hat. "Welcome to my home, Samuel," he said.

Samuel walked in and stopped just behind the last pew. Johnny kept the boy between him and Black.

"Do you like what I've done to the place?" Black asked.

"If you ask me, it lacks imagination," Samuel said. "I'm more interested in you. First time I've actually seen someone who's stepped out of a book."

"Then pay close attention, my little friend. Your last creation was a bit of a disappointment. But he bled, I'll give you that. Thomas did bleed."

"I'll be sure not to disappoint you again."

"Do you bleed, Samuel?" Black asked, grin still fixed.

Samuel hesitated. Not good.

"Why don't you find out?" he finally said.

"I intend to. But we really should give this town a little show, don't you think?"

"What's wrong with now?"

"They've waited so long that we have to draw it out. Bring the climax to a slow boil. It's what they want, you know. They want blood."

"Now, Marsuvees. Take my blood now."

"I would love to, but—"

"Now!"

Johnny started. He fought a terrible urge to run for his life.

"Say it again, Samuel. Say it to me."

"You're reluctant to show me your power, then?"

Black spread his arms wide and faced the ceiling. "Oh, how I love the sound of begging. Show me your power, Marsuvees. Please show me."

Samuel clasped his hands behind his back. "That's what I thought. You're thinking that I'm trying to goad you, and you know that the man who gives into goading is the weaker one. But you're wrong. I just want to see if you're half as frightening as my friend Johnny here says you are. All I see now is the copy of a failed monk who's found some fancy black clothes."

Black lowered his head. His grin had softened. "Perhaps I should be the one testing your power."

"Perhaps."

"Then show me what you have. Prove yourself. Show me that you are more than a stupid, reckless little boy."

"No," Samuel said.

"No?"

"Not now. Three days have passed since the debate," Samuel said. "I challenge you to a new debate, at nightfall in two hours, in front of the people of this town. This time they, not the students, will be the judge. Win the debate and I am gone. Lose the debate and you are gone."

Black blinked. "You'll have to take that up with Billy."

"You take it up with Billy. You're his creation. I will debate Billy through you. It's my right to demand a debate, the only difference is that you are my opponent and the people are my judge. Don't tell me you're weaker than Billy."

Black came around the podium. "A two-thirds majority—the same as the monastery?"

"Yes."

"I accept," Black said.

"Then I bind you to the terms."

"Bind all you like. I own their hearts."

Samuel was silent for a moment. "You are in their hearts." He slowly lifted his hand, palm out.

Black's eyes widened. He took a step back. Without any further warning, the man in black began to tremble from head to foot. Johnny had never seen a look that resembled the terror that masked his face.

How could that be?

As quickly as the fear swept over Black, it left him. He began to laugh, as if delighted by the horror he'd just experienced.

Samuel stared him down for a long moment, turned, and walked straight for Johnny, who ducked in front of him and exited the sanctuary first, just in case Black had any parting . . . things to throw their way.

The door closed behind them. Johnny whirled to Samuel. "What was that?"

"The beginning of the end, I would say."

"But what did you do to him?"

Samuel stepped past the outer door and looked out at the smoldering remains of the old theater, a hundred yards south.

"I showed Black himself," he said. "Think of me as the human mirror." He winked and walked down the steps. "Seems as though evil loves evil."

"That's it? You're just going to debate him? What about the town?"

"Don't worry, Johnny, I haven't begun to show my power. We're going to save this town, you can count on that."

CHAPTER THIRTY-SIX

THE MONASTERY
Monday night

RAUL BALANCED the round silver platter in his right hand and carefully lifted the white lace that covered the delicacies he'd arranged for David. He selected the foods himself from a short list of favorites he kept for special occasions. A delicious crab bisque, sliced Hungarian cheese on crackers, and a small pound cake stuffed with vanilla pudding. He arranged them neatly around a tall glass of passion-fruit juice.

David had retired to his bedroom after Samuel left the conference room several hours earlier. Frankly the food seemed like an empty gesture, but Raul knew that the director hadn't eaten since learning this morning that Thomas had died. For that matter, neither had Raul.

He rapped on the tall cherrywood door twice.

"Come in." The voice sounded strained.

Raul stepped into David's chambers and spoke before looking up. "I've brought you food, sir. Some of your favorites, I think." He shut the door and faced the room. "Andrew prepared this crab . . ."

David's bed lay stripped of its sheets, which were strewn to one side of the mattress. One of the pillows leaked goose feathers, which littered the maroon carpet like large snowflakes. A toppled chair lay beside a tray of untouched food Raul had delivered the previous evening. So even last night, when Thomas had taken the town, David was more worried than any of them knew.

David leaned against a window that overlooked the valley, one hand on the sill, the other cocked on his hip. His hair looked like a mop, his face was gaunt and unshaven.

"Sir?" What could he say to this?

"Yes, Raul. What is it?"

"I've brought food."

"So you have said. Put it down."

David stretched his neck as if fighting off a wrenching headache. His eyes remained closed.

"You haven't even touched the other."

"Yes. Please take it, Raul. Take it all. I appreciate the thought, but I'm not hungry."

Raul noted that a drape had been pulled loose.

"How do you expect me to eat while . . ." He trailed off.

"Truly, I can't imagine your anxiousness." Raul set the tray on the bed. "But isn't this our only hope? You seemed quite confident. It's the safest way, all things considered."

David paced in front of the window. "Don't get me wrong, I care for the town, but when it comes to my son, I think of them as butchers."

"There's nothing concrete to suggest that any harm will come to your son. Besides, Samuel's a strong boy. I'm sure he's doing well."

"And what do we really know?" David demanded. "Only what we can see from the overlook. Anything could happen in any one of those buildings without our knowledge."

Samuel had received his father's reluctant yet firm commitment during the meeting not to send anyone else to the town. It was too dangerous not only for them, but for the town itself. They couldn't risk setting Billy off. "Trust the books, Father. And trust me," Samuel had said.

"Trust the books," Raul said. "Isn't that—"

"This from you, who insisted we shut the project down?"

"I was wrong! Anyway, we're beyond that now. We're committed to this course. At this point no matter what happens we can't interfere. There's too much at stake."

David sighed. "I'm afraid, Raul. For the first time I'm really afraid. What if this fails?"

"Then we're in serious trouble."

"We can't lock them in the dungeon; we can't force the books away from them. God only knows what they've written to protect themselves. We can't just kill them all."

"We still have Samuel."

"And what can Samuel do? If this fails . . ."

David turned back to the window and lowered his head. Raul waited a full minute before breaking the silence.

"Sir?"

But David had slipped into his own world and refused to be interrupted. He stood there, his head hung, leaning on the window overlooking Paradise far below.

Raul finally took the old food tray, replaced it with the fresh one, and slipped into the hall.

God help them all.

MARSUVEES BLACK barged through the lower library doors, his black robe flowing behind him like trailing bat wings.

"Are they all here?" he demanded.

Billy stood by Darcy and Paul, just inside, his hands folded behind his back. "Yes," he replied.

The overseer stormed past them and disappeared through the side door leading to the balcony. Billy nodded at the others and followed. He had never seen the man so agitated.

Samuel was up to something, that much he'd discovered when Black had barged into his small study, cursing the worms on the floor.

"Get these slugs out of here! Remove them immediately, you fools!"

At first Billy had thought it was Black, yelling in his ear from Paradise. But then he turned and saw the gaunt overseer.

"Marsuvees?"

"What are you doing down here? Sleeping? For heaven's sake, boy! Don't you know what's going on?"

Darcy came awake beside him and lifted her head. "Marsuvees Black? You look just like what I imagined."

"Wonderful. Are you as dense as Billy?"

"What do you mean?"

"What do you mean? If you would quit eating so much of that sludge, maybe your minds would be able to see beyond your own stinking noses!"

"It was *your* idea that we eat so much sludge," Billy said.

"I didn't say to drug yourselves into a stupor! Your whole story's falling apart around your ears and you don't even see it!"

"Of course I see—"

"Wake up, boy!" Black yelled. "Samuel's undoing your story!"

"No, he's not. I have things under control."

"You do not! I want every single child in the main library in twenty minutes. You have them there, you understand? Everyone!"

That was twenty minutes ago.

Billy edged up to the balcony railing beside Black. The children were all in the library, slouched over the tables below, some asleep with their faces buried in their books, a few still writing. Black scanned the room and evaluated the scene like a general might measure his troops before a battle. Billy counted them quickly. Thirty-two . . . thirty-three? Oh, right. He, Darcy, and Paul. That made thirty-six.

"Wake up!" Black screamed.

Billy jumped, but the writers below hardly noticed. They turned slowly toward the voice. Billy could almost see their minds crawling from the slumber of deep fantasy where words became flesh.

"Wake up!" This time a few jerked up. The rest lifted their faces toward the balcony.

"Look at you, all slobbering over your own puny stories." Now thirty-three sets of eyes focused in on him like bats.

"What are you writing? I'll tell you what you're writing. You're writing meaningless, disjointed pap!"

He stabbed a finger toward the far wall. "They should have been dead by now! Dead! But does even one of you know what is really happening in our lovely town of Paradise?"

No one provided an answer.

"No! You don't. And do you know *how* I know you don't know? Because if you did know, you would stop it. But you aren't stopping it. You're too busy pacifying your own pathetic fantasies with your individual characters."

What could the man possibly be ranting about? They had been writing nonstop. How could he come in here and accuse them of this nonsense? The monk had lost his lid.

"Does anybody know where Samuel is?"

"He's writing," Billy said. "We know that. He's written a character based on himself to debate—"

"He's in Paradise!" Black said, without looking Billy's way.

"The real Samuel?"

"The real Samuel is in Paradise."

Billy blinked. Samuel in Paradise?

"He's in *your* town, waltzing around as if he owns the place!"

"Physically?" Billy asked.

"Physically, your leader wants to know." Black turned and leaned toward Billy. "Yes, physically!" Spittle flew from his mouth.

Marsuvees turned back to the children, who sat up now, paralyzed by his outrage.

"Now, I want you to write into the minds of Paradise like you've never written before, you hear me? I won't permit a single child to leave this library until we have our way with him."

The statement hung in the air like the reverberation of a gong. "No one will move. For any reason. You don't eat, you don't sleep, you don't talk, you don't even breathe more than absolutely necessary. I want every last cell in your measly, mindless brains to narrow on Paradise. You hear me?"

No one moved. "Well, don't just sit there. Give me a nod or something!"

Like a room full of little pistons, their heads bobbed.

Billy felt Black's eyes on him. "What, me? You don't expect *me* to write here, do you?" Impossible! He could never write with these slobs!

"Have I been speaking to the wall? What does *no one* mean to you? No one but the first fool who fell?"

Black looked back at the statues below. "And I want six of you"—he motioned to a table of six to his left—"you there will do. I want you to write, two each into Paula, Sally, and that cursed preacher."

"But, sir," a small boy said, "what would you have us write into them?"

"Have you learned nothing?" Black asked with a quiet, quivering voice. He began to yell. "Write deception! Write wickedness! Write hate! Write murder! Write death! Just write, you blithering idiot!"

Black spun from the railing and stormed from the balcony. The door to the library slammed and the outer tunnel filled with a horrendous scream that bent the children over their books.

"What do we do?" Darcy asked.

"We write," Billy said.

CHAPTER THIRTY-SEVEN

PARADISE

Monday night

THE TOWN of Paradise waited in eerie silence. A red sunset, the first in a week, glowed on the horizon. A string of citizens shuffled soundlessly into the church.

"If there's trouble," Johnny said, "if things don't go like you want, if we get separated or anything—not that I'm saying we will—but if anything happens, we could meet in the forest behind the theater where we met earlier."

Samuel looked at him without answering.

"I'm just saying if, you know? Just in case," Johnny said.

"And if that doesn't work, we can meet at the monastery."

"That's even better. They'll never find us there." Johnny looked up as the last of them straggled into the church. "We should try to get a jump on Black, don't you think?"

Samuel stepped from under the tree north of Main Street. "Follow me." He walked toward the church.

Johnny followed Samuel down the street and up the front steps. He paused in the entryway, expecting Samuel to give him a word of encouragement before walking into the crowded sanctuary—it seemed like a good thing.

But the boy didn't even look back. He walked straight inside and pushed the inner doors wide, like he was shoving saloon doors open for a six-gun showdown.

Johnny hurried to catch Samuel, fixing his eyes on the boy's heels as they touched the carpet. No one moved as they walked by, at least not that he could see from the corner of his eyes.

He imagined Steve sitting on the far side, bloodied as he had been the last time Johnny had tried to talk sense into them. Of course, Johnny didn't have Samuel's power. Claude and his gang would be sitting like zombies, clutching bottles, eyelids drooping.

Samuel stepped up onto the stage and approached the pulpit. Johnny followed him, walked halfway to the podium, and stopped. He raised his head and scanned the room, careful not to look into anyone's eyes.

Claude and gang sat in the first row, gripping bottles as he'd imagined. Crud and dried blood matted most of those present. Some wore it on their hands, as if the blood had come from another body; others below their nostrils, where they'd ignored a bleeding nose; some bore long, scabbed gashes. The blowing dust had stuck to the mess and hardened, so their skin looked like it was peeling. They sat in the pews, arms limp or crossed.

Steve Smither sat on the far left, grinning wickedly. Father Yordon avoided Johnny's eyes. Paula wore a loose halter top. Her hair was twisted like a nest of snakes, and her eyes were glazed over. He couldn't see his mother.

Then he did, near the back, dress torn and dirtied, face puffy. He could hardly recognize her! Johnny felt a tremor shake his bones.

Samuel cleared his throat. "Hello. My name is Samuel, and I've come here tonight to debate Marsuvees Black. You'll decide who wins. Okay?"

No response from the zombies.

"Black isn't here yet, but I'm sure he'll show himself soon enough. It will be a debate of few words, because most of you aren't hearing too well anymore. But you'll be presented with a clear choice and you'll have to decide. Do you understand?"

Still no reaction.

"Without love, everything falls apart," Samuel said. Something had changed in his voice. "Love is what I offer you today."

The words seemed to flow from Samuel's mouth like red-hot lava, smothering the auditorium, including Johnny, who could barely breathe from the sudden tightness in his chest. This was more like it. Samuel would have them wrapped up before Black even arrived.

"Have you forgotten what true love is?" Samuel choked up. He swallowed, and Johnny wanted to cry.

"No." Steve Smither stood, grinning.

"No, no, we do remember."

Four hundred crazies shifted their gazes to the man.

Steve walked toward the stage, hands clasped behind his back. "He's right, you know. We've been deceived. We're a brood of vipers. We're sick with the stench of death. Just like the boy says."

Samuel hadn't said that.

Steve spread his arms and faced the crowd as if he were the preacher now. "This little stranger here who came out of nowhere is right. We are deceived. All of us, blithering fools wrapped in a web of deceit that's strangling us to death."

Steve stepped onto the platform. Johnny took a step backward. The man's eyes were glassy and bloodshot. Samuel stood by the pulpit quietly, eyes fixed on Steve.

"We're all sick, disgusting perverts. Spineless, puny pukes."

Steve crossed toward Samuel, who stood still, expressionless. No relief, no joy, no anger, nothing but sadness. And that small chin tilting up to Steve—those soft lips, those long lashes unblinking.

Do it, Samuel! Tell him! Tell them all. Tell them you come from a monastery and you have enough power to flatten them with a single word! Tell them, Samuel. Tell them now!

Samuel didn't move.

"And what do vipers do, Samuel? Hmm? You're quite an intelligent little runt; you surely know what vipers do, don't you?" He still grinned and then added in a low raspy voice, "You little puke."

Johnny's knees began to tremble. This wasn't the way Steve normally talked, not even close. Someone was talking through him. Billy or Black. Johnny glanced at the crowd. Some of them sat up a little straighter, he thought, but their faces remained blank.

The grin vanished from Steve's face as if someone had cut the strings that lifted it. "Vipers bite, Samuel. You come down into our town and try to mess with our story and see what you get? You get bit, 'cause our worms are snakes too. Did you know that?"

"This is your idea of a debate, Billy?" Samuel said.

"That's right, I am Billy. And if this isn't a debate, what is? We're all down here in the dungeons and you're up there. What does that tell you? It tells you that you're dead meat."

Samuel had expected to confront Black. Why had Billy chosen Steve? "You know the consequences of evil?" Samuel said.

"Love!" Steve cried, spreading his arms. "I think it all leads to—"

Steve gasped and went white. He stared at Samuel in shock. Slowly his face twisted, first with anguish and then with horror. He threw his arms to his face, doubled over, and screamed bloody murder.

The crowd didn't react. Neither did Samuel at first, he let Steve scream and scream. And then he spoke softly, so that only he and Steve could hear.

"Steve, meet Billy. Billy, meet yourself."

Think of me as the human mirror, Samuel had said. He'd just shown Steve and Billy their own souls.

And then he released the man.

Steve's screaming stopped while he was still bent over. For a moment Steve remained frozen, staring at Samuel from a half crouch. Then his eyes flashed. He stood up slowly. His lips curled back, and his whole body began to vibrate.

Johnny couldn't move.

Steve's face flushed and the veins stood out on his neck. His jaws snapped wide in a shriek that nearly brought Johnny to his knees. Beyond Steve a dozen crazies rose to their feet. Steve was screaming words, Johnny realized. "It was my choice! I deserved that much. *My* choice!"

The man paused to catch his breath and then flung out his arm. "Take him! Take him, take him, take him!"

Mumbles and grunts swept through the crowd. A bunch of them climbed over their pews and started for the stage.

Johnny couldn't move his feet. Steve kept screaming, "Take him, take him, take *them*!"

Take *them*?

Samuel calmly lifted one hand to the dissenters who rushed the platform. "Back," he said.

The power of the word hit the auditorium like a thunderclap. Four hundred people staggered back. If they were seated, their heads bent back as if struck by a gale-force wind. If they were standing, or climbing over a pew, or walking for the stage, they were thrown backward into their pews or on their seats.

Steve had stopped his screaming.

"I love you, Billy. Do you still know that?"

Steve fell to his knees, face drooping in anguish. "I'm sorry, I . . ."

Silence.

Steve's lips twisted to a snarl. He jumped to his feet.

"I hate you! I hate you, Samuel, you sick little puke." He flung his arm out. "Take them! Take him!"

Claude was on one knee, staring like a fool.

A single, unmistakable voice cut across the room. "Stevieeeeeee . . ."

Black stood at the back, head tilted down, blue eyes flashing.

Every head turned.

"Why are you just standing there, Steve? Hmm? I've been so good to you and now you turn on me? Am I wretched or vile? I should slit your gut and let you bleed dry."

Steve stared, eyes wide with confusion. "I didn't say—"

"Do you like our debate, Samuel? I think it's time for the people to vote." Black walked down the aisle, fixated on Samuel. Johnny turned to Samuel in a panic. For the first time he saw fear on the boy's face. Sweat was leaking down his temple and his eyes were wide.

Just two hours ago he'd thrown off Black's attacks easily. Had something changed?

Marsuvees Black stepped up on the stage. "So, you think that throwing around a little love will do the trick, do you? I'll admit, it's a tad fascinating, but ultimately boring."

He jerked his head to face the people.

"Thing is, I have the same power. Do you mind if I show you, Samuel? I'd like to show you my power." He walked to the far edge of the stage, eyes on the congregation. "I think the people would like a little show."

Black cocked his head back like a Pez dispenser. His neck doubled back, nearly at a right angle to his shoulders. For a moment he gave them a side profile of the stunning pose.

Then his whole body turned, upper torso first, followed by hips and legs, like a robot. Black's round dark mouth faced them like a gaping cannon.

The air blurred with a white streak. Straight from Black's open jaw. Then two, then ten, then two dozen white streaks, flying in formation toward Samuel.

Before they had crossed half the pews, the white objects converged into a cohesive unit. Formed a set of razor-sharp teeth. They were too long and too sharp and too white to be Black's teeth, but from the corner of his eye Johnny saw that Black's mouth was bleeding onto his shirt, and he knew that they *were* his teeth.

The jaw came to an abrupt halt two inches from Samuel's nose. It snapped at the air once, paused, then again. *Clack*, pause, *clack*.

The teeth retreated in another sudden flash and snapped back into Black's jaw. He leveled his head.

"And?" Samuel said. "The point is?"

It struck Johnny that this wasn't Black and Samuel as much as it was Billy and Samuel. Two kids, dueling.

The smirk on Black's face faded. He opened his mouth wide, thrust his head forward, and roared at Samuel. His lips stretched as wide as his head and his teeth flashed like a piranha's.

Three things came from Black's throat. A crackling roar that shook the whole building, a heat wave that blasted Samuel, and a black vapor.

The force of the roar bounced off an invisible shield that enveloped Samuel and rushed past Johnny. He could see it because of the black vapor, like a jet stream in a wind tunnel, and he could feel the heat. Without the shield, a person would probably be burned to a crisp, Johnny thought, cringing behind the boy. Samuel was protecting him.

The roar lasted at least ten seconds. And then Black's mouth clamped shut.

For a moment Billy's character stared at Samuel, amazed that he hadn't dislodged a hair, much less damaged him.

Slowly Samuel lifted his right hand, palm out. Something came from that hand. Johnny couldn't see it, but Black could.

His face twisted into an unholy mess of distorted features. For a moment Johnny thought that his face was melting. His lower jaw came loose from its joints and ran a slow circle. Black began to shake so badly that Johnny thought he might come apart.

Instead, he began to laugh.

He grabbed at his face and pulled at his flesh and shrieked with laughter, delighted with himself.

He was seeing himself. Evil loved evil, like Samuel had said.

Black cocked his head back at a right angle, twisted it to face the church, and let his laughter echo over the auditorium.

As one the people began to scream. Their faces contorted in fear. They pulled at their hair, and their eyes rolled back into their heads.

Then they lunged at each other and began tearing at each other's faces.

Samuel faced the people and held both hands out like a mime pushing a wall. "No," he said.

A barely visible shock wave emanated from him. It rippled through the air and through the people, starting at the first pew and picking up speed as it spread to the very back. As the wave struck them, it cut off their screams. They gasped and were thrown back more forcefully than the first time.

They collapsed, groaning and sobbing.

Even though Johnny wasn't in the wave's path, he felt its effect. A warm force cut through his muscles like an electric current that charged him with love and desire for more love. He staggered back and dropped to one knee. Tears flooded his eyes, and he knew that Samuel would win this contest.

Wailing and sorrow and love swallowed the church.

Black recovered and glared at Samuel in a rage.

Samuel lowered his arms and everything changed. Instantly. The power that had come from Samuel vanished.

Claude struggled to his feet, dazed and confused. Then others, like the resurrected dead.

"The choice is theirs," Samuel said.

For an endless moment no one else moved.

Steve stood on the stage, lost to the world. Claude's face settled and he breathed heavily through his nostrils. Chris and Peter waited behind him, blinking and waiting. Katie looked like a rag doll.

A slow smile formed on Black's face. "The choice is theirs," he said. Then he thrust his hand out toward Samuel. "Take him!" he said.

Still no one moved.

Black stretched his mouth wide, like a snake preparing to swallow a goat, and roared again. Again the building's foundations shook.

But this time Samuel didn't stop it. His body shielded Johnny from most of the shock, but the air around him seemed to shake.

Claude was ten feet from the stage when Black's blast hit him. He grunted and rushed forward, eager to reach Samuel now. At least fifty rushed the stage.

Samuel did not resist. He was either caught off guard or had something planned for the last moment.

Black's roar didn't ease up. His thundering mouth gaped, as long and wide as his face.

Claude leaped onto the platform.

"Samuel!" Johnny didn't wait for a reply. He whirled from the podium and ran.

He's just standing there. This isn't possible!

From the corner of his eye, he saw Samuel collapse under Claude's huge body. He disappeared under a sea of flesh.

A handful of crazies were scrambling over the pews to intercept Johnny.

Fists pounded flesh behind him as he dove for the entrance below the red *Baptismal* sign. He reached the brass knob and yanked the door open.

You're leaving Samuel. You can't leave Samuel!

He turned his head back, just enough to stare into the twisted face of Chris Ingles, just strides away. Johnny bolted.

He slammed through the rear door, stumbled out to the back porch, and took a hard left, over the steps. The dark lawn met his feet hard. He rolled over the grass and spun back just in time to see a large object fill his vision. It smashed into his head and knocked him on his back.

He twisted to one side, fighting for breath, but they stood over him now like grim reapers. Then Johnny was screaming. Long vowels that hurt his throat. His mind could barely form thoughts, much less words.

Hands grabbed at his arms and legs and yanked him roughly from the ground. A big hand pounded down on his forehead, and he heard his screams taper off. Another fist hit his head, and his world began to fade.

It hurts, he thought.

And then he didn't think anything for a while.

A little later or much later—he didn't know which—he opened his eyes and it was dark. The musty smell of dishrags filled his nose. He managed to turn on his back. Slowly, like the coming of the tide, he thought some things.

He thought he was alive. He must be alive because his head was throbbing with pain. He thought he shouldn't be alive—he wasn't even sure he wanted to be alive. He thought he might be in the root cellar below Smither's Saloon.

He thought Samuel was . . .

Actually, he didn't know what Samuel was. Maybe Samuel had opened his mouth at the end there and knocked them all over. Maybe Samuel was dead.

Johnny closed his eyes and wished he were dead.

CHAPTER THIRTY-EIGHT

THE MONASTERY
Monday night

BILLY DIPPED his quill into the inkwell, trying to gauge the emotions that ran through him. A drop of sweat fell from his forehead and marked the page by his thumb.

How would he describe this story? Enthralling, exhilarating to be sure. But there was more. The pen clinked against the glass jar of red ink as he withdrew his hand. An unsteady hand did not suit writing. He swallowed to wet his parched throat.

He'd been writing in the balcony for hours, barely aware of time, forgetting the fact that Black had driven him from his study. He'd lost himself in the singular objective of pushing this story to the ending for which it begged. The shaking in his hand had started when he heard Samuel's voice, like an echo in his skull.

"I love you, Billy."

His first instinct had been to search the balcony for the voice. *Samuel has escaped! He's left Paradise and come here to turn me over to David!*

But the voice hadn't spoken from the balcony. It echoed like a church bell in his mind.

He'd stared back at the writing book, hands trembling. The story was speaking back to him now, as if he were actually there in Paradise, not just whispering suggestions to his characters, but participating with them.

The writing no longer focused on Paradise. Samuel had changed that. The boy was trying to destroy the power *behind* Paradise. He had reached past the people in the church down there and was trying to quiet *him!*

But Billy had no intention of being quieted. Paradise was his. His town, his story. No one would throw him out. Not even Samuel and his precious father. *Especially* not Samuel and his father.

And the boy had the audacity to say, *I love you, Billy,* right there, out loud, as if *that* would gain him favor.

Wake up, boy! Things don't revolve around the four rules down here. We make our own rules, and they're not rules of love. *I love you*—please! Love was for stories.

Of course, this was a story. Everything was really a story, penned or thought or acted out at some time by someone.

Billy brought his trembling fingers to the paper. He could do so much on this page! This was the power of storytelling, that he could tell whatever story he chose.

A stray thought hit him. Thomas Hunter found the books in a place called the Black Forest. Billy impulsively wrote a sentence in the bottom margin, as much to break the tension as for any other purpose.

Then the man named Thomas found himself in the Black Forest, where he fell and hit his head and lost his memory.

Ha. He wondered what *that* would do.

Another drop of sweat plopped onto the page. Billy brushed it aside with his little finger and continued writing into Paradise. The tension of the story immediately gripped him again.

Now let us see about your powers, Samuel. What move will you make now in this chess match of ours?

Samuel had given up too early.

The red lines ran jagged from his quivering hand. A nervous hand doesn't suit good writing, Billy thought again, and then lost himself in the story. His story.

CHAPTER THIRTY-NINE

PARADISE
Monday night

FOR THE seventh time in a week, Marsuvees Black stepped out of the trees to meet Marsuvees Black, the character that Billy had written into existence based on him. The black trench coat and Stetson hat, the boots and belt were figments of Billy's imagination, taken from costumes he'd seen in one of the dungeon rooms, but otherwise Black looked exactly like Marsuvees. In so many ways, he was him.

In so many ways, he wasn't him.

It was odd how the progression of evil worked. It always went from bad to worse, no matter how much mind he'd ever applied to the matter. And in the progression was a line which, if crossed, offered no retreat. He reached that line seven years ago, while he still worked in Vegas, but he'd turned and run into the desert for solitude and repentance.

This time he'd crossed the line. Now there was no turning back, any fool could see that. The strange thing was, he really didn't have any ambition to rule the world or wipe out the country or even Las Vegas, that beautiful den of iniquity that spoiled his soul to start with.

He'd joined Project Showdown because of its fantastic promise to test good against evil in the most unusual way. David Abraham had essentially created an incubator for good in these children, believing that if properly protected, good would prevail.

His whole life had been a raging battle between good and evil, and as far as he could see, evil, not good, always ended up on top. The pig always returned to its sty; dogs always lapped up their vomit.

But then he'd found the blank books and discovered the inscription that destined them for the purposes of love. After three months of careful deliberation, Marsuvees could not ignore his one and only conclusion: the books had been found by him, as by David, because he was *meant* to use them.

And how? To test good versus evil, naturally. To test the rule of good and evil that had waged eternal war in his own heart. If by their own irrevocable rule the books would lead to the discovery of love, then he would force their hands, so to speak.

He embraced evil with abandon, knowing that in the end he was really embracing love. Isn't that what the rule meant? If by his embrace of evil he could produce love, didn't that make evil itself a kind of good?

Yes! And a good thing too, because in these last two weeks he'd been once again reminded how much he loved evil. How delicious each terrible, wonderful, delightful act really was.

Why did evil always feel so good? Because evil was in fact a kind of love. True or not, he swam in the hope that it was more true than all the nonsense thrown his way over the past forty years.

Marsuvees stared at his fictional counterpart, who stood on the edge of the greenbelt staring at the now-deserted church across town. The charred remains of the old theater smoldered in the waning light off to their left. Marsuvees wasn't sure what Black had done to Samuel after the meeting, but he knew what had to be done now.

He walked toward Black. In all honesty, if his gamble paid off and evil did turn out to be a kind of good, then he was obligated to flex the muscle of evil as much as possible, wasn't he? And he would have no problem doing so.

In the meantime, there was only one thing that stood in his way.

"So you came after all," Black said without turning to him.

"Was there ever a doubt?" Marsuvees said.

"I never needed you," Black said. "I have this under control."

Amazing how perfectly Billy had formed the character. Black had developed his own idiosyncrasies in the last week, but most of him came from Billy. Or more accurately, from Billy's understanding of the monk named Marsuvees Black. Him. The boy was perceptive, rendering him with surprising accuracy—the mischievous grins, the arching eyebrows, the curvature of his fingers, even his accent.

"Didn't need me? You are me," Marsuvees said.

"You mean my flesh?" Black jerked his head around and flashed a searing smile. He lifted his arm, bit deeply, and pulled a chunk of flesh from his hand like a wolf might pull the flesh from a fresh deer kill. He spit the hunk of meat at Marsuvees.

"Have a bite."

Marsuvees sidestepped the flying flesh. The child in Billy had become part of Black. At this very moment, he wasn't sure if Billy had suggested to Black that he bite his own arm, or if Black had done it on his own.

He stepped up beside the character and stared ahead. Dusk was coming fast. By morning this would all be finished.

"You're sure you can do this?" Marsuvees said.

"You're insulting me?" Black asked.

"No, I just want to know. We have a lot riding on it."

"We? I think you're assuming too much."

"Without me, you have nothing. I've made sure of that. Only I have the knowledge required to take this further. And tonight I will extend my own power by having Billy write several far-reaching statements into the books."

Black pulled a book from his pocket and lifted it up. "You mean the books like this one?"

He had one of the blank books?

Black grunted, replaced the book in his pocket, and faced the town.

Marsuvees would take care of the book later. The last thing he needed was this monstrosity running around with a book in his possession.

"When we're finished here, we'll hand the monks in the monastery the same fate and start over," Marsuvees said. "Only this time it won't be a small town sitting conveniently at the bottom of the mountain."

"It's been a real drag working with you," Black said. Billy talking. "I have to be honest, although I had some respect for you in the beginning, I've come to hate you. Maybe it was the mask you insisted on wearing. Maybe it's the fact that you look like . . ." Black faced him, eyeball to eyeball, not a foot away. "Black."

"Just remember who the real flesh is around here," Marsuvees said.

"I'm not sure I like real flesh." There was a glint in his eyes. If Marsuvees didn't know Billy's dependence on him better, he might suspect a foolish streak of murder in there.

Black sniffed. "Do I smell like that?"

"You smell like the sewer that you came . . ."

Black's right hand shot forward. Marsuvees felt the intense pressure before he felt the pain. He looked down, stunned.

Billy's character had thrust his hand through his midsection. The man's black-sleeved arm was buried up to the elbow in Marsuvees' gut.

Pain overtook him like a tsunami. He felt his body start to fold over the arm and it occurred to him that Black had shoved his hand right through his spine. It had to be broken.

Billy had knifed him with Black's arm! Or Black had done it on his own. Marsuvees tried to speak, but his facial nerves were paralyzed, and his head felt like it might explode. He could hear a loud thumping and then splashing. Blood, from the exit wound.

Black jerked his arm free.

Marsuvees buckled. He heard a chuckle.

Then his world went black.

CHAPTER FORTY

THE MONASTERY
Tuesday morning

GASPING FOR breath from the climb, Raul banged on David's door and then barged in without waiting for a response.

The rising sunlight burst through the window across the room. David lay on the bed, raising to his elbows, eyes wide and lost. Raul's banging had obviously aroused him from deep slumber.

"I beg your pardon, sir, but I have news."

David swung his legs to the floor. "News? Well, tell me."

Raul hesitated. How could he say—

"Tell me!"

"I'm afraid it's not so—"

"Just tell me, man!"

Raul paused, terrified to speak. "Samuel has been taken. Or should I say the character that Samuel has written has been taken."

"Taken? What do you mean, *taken?*"

"They have him. I . . . I don't know how. I can't seem to find Samuel in the—"

"Have they hurt him?" David stood.

Raul stepped back. "They used force. They had to restrain him."

David's face washed white with shock. "My . . . my boy would never resist them!" He swallowed. "Did . . . did they hurt him?"

"Pardon me for saying, but he wasn't—"

"He's my son! Samuel didn't write a character. It's him down there!"

Raul stared at the director, aghast. Samuel himself had gone down? "How could . . ."

"It was the only way! He had to go himself. Have they hurt him?" David demanded.

David's erratic behavior earlier now made perfect sense. Raul wanted to fall down and beg David to end this madness, to save his son, to yank Billy from his tunnels and punish him so that he would never forget. But he knew they were past all that.

So, instead he nodded. Once.

For a moment David stood like stone. His face flushed and he began to quiver. His eyes glassed with tears that dripped straight down his cheeks and to the floor.

Then the father threw his hands to his face and wailed. "Oh, my son! Dear Father, have mercy on my son!"

He stepped across the room, blind to his steps, smothering his face with large hands. "No, no, no!"

Raul could hardly bear the sight.

"Jesus, our blessed Savior, have mercy. My son! How could they hurt you? How . . ."

He whirled to Raul, who jerked in fright. David's face twisted into a furious snarl.

"If they hurt a single hair on his body, I'll kill them!" he roared. "You hear me, man? I'll kill them all!"

Raul settled to one knee, waiting for David to collect himself.

David looked through the open door, hesitated, and then bolted past Raul into the outer hall.

"David! You can't . . ."

He leaped to his feet and ran after David. *He's going down there! He's going down to Paradise to rescue Samuel!* He'd seen the look in those inflamed eyes—that desperate love of a father willing to cast his own head on the block for the sake of his son.

But if Samuel couldn't stop them, neither could David. For the first time since Raul had learned the truth about the books, he knew they had to trust their power or suffer even more harm. He was suddenly certain that if David ran into Paradise, they would kill him along with his son.

The tail of David's nightshirt disappeared into the stairwell.

"David!"

Raul flew down the stairs in threes, hand on the rail to keep from tumbling headlong into the stone walls. David was taking the stairs even faster. The slapping of his bare feet echoed up to Raul. Only once did he see David, and then only his heel.

When Raul burst into the atrium, the large doors were already swinging closed.

"David!"

Raul ran for the doors, yanked them open, and sprinted into the canyon. His sandals slipped in the soft sand as he rounded the first corner. The canyon gaped, a dry riverbed littered with large stones. Now a full fifty yards ahead David sprinted, his arms and legs pumping like a world-class athlete.

Surely he didn't intend to run all the way down to Paradise. But wouldn't Raul do the same? What kind of good sense could overcome blind passion for a son?

On the other hand, if David was right about the books, interfering with them might be the undoing of them all! In trying to save his son, David might condemn him.

Raul ran hard, panting through burning lungs, praying that David would come to his senses. There had to be a way, but it wouldn't be up to a man like David, who had no power. Samuel was a strong boy. He had more power than the lot of them. Including Black. Samuel would find a way.

Raul lost sight of David at the canyon's mouth. If David stopped, it would be at the overlook.

Falling more than running, Raul stumbled down to the overlook. He burst from the brush fifteen minutes later and doubled over, gasping. David knelt at the ledge, silhouetted against the overcast sky. The town of Paradise lay like charred sugar cubes two miles beyond him.

"Sir."

Raul approached carefully. David faced the town and rocked back and forth on his knees, wind whipping at his thin cotton shirt. His body shook with sobs, Raul now saw.

A lump rose into his throat. He knelt beside David and placed a gentle hand on his back. "I'm sorry," he said, feeling the words inadequate. Possibly even insensitive. But he said them anyway, over and over.

"I'm sorry, I'm sorry."

CHAPTER FORTY-ONE

PARADISE
Tuesday morning

JOHNNY AWOKE with the smell of onions and earth in his nostrils. At first he thought his mother had let him sleep late and was out in the kitchen preparing dinner, but then the image of four hundred crazies sitting in church pews filled his mind, and he jerked his head off the cellar's dirt floor.

His temples throbbed and he groaned. He rolled on his back and tried to focus on his dark surroundings. He'd put potatoes in the cellar for Steve on occasion—on the wood shelves lining the walls. Their roots grew like long white tentacles.

"Pretty smart, eh?" Steve had said once when Johnny pointed them out. "They only grow toward the light. Like snakes trying to escape." He'd chuckled and Johnny decided then that he didn't like root cellars with hairy potatoes.

A distant sound drifted into the cellar, something like a whistle at a soccer match.

Johnny rolled toward the wall—the one made of wood with the crack near the top above ground level. He saw it now, tangled with a dozen roots reaching through. If he remembered right, the crazies had thrown him in here at night, but now daylight glowed through the small crack.

The whistle came again. But it sounded more human this time—a high-pitched shriek, the kind made by placing a thumb and a forefinger in your mouth. Johnny never could whistle that way. Who could possibly be whistling out there?

Samuel.

The boy's face filled his mind. That blond head and those blue eyes, smiling softly.

The whistle came again, a little sharper now. But it wasn't a whistle, was it? It didn't have that piercing, harsh quality. Had more of a throat . . .

Johnny caught his breath and snapped to a sitting position. A scream! It was a scream!

The sound reached his ears again, only this time with a word.

"Pleeeeeease!"

It was Samuel's voice. Johnny scrambled to his feet, ignoring the raging headache.

"Samuel?" The name echoed around him. What were they doing to him? "Samuel!"

He tore at the shelves, sweeping potatoes and onions onto the floor. He yanked the spud roots from the crack and pried his right eye to the thin opening.

A large tin garbage can blocked half his view on the right. The alley lay vacant on his left. Fifty yards ahead tall evergreens bent in the wind under a gray sky.

The morning air carried the sound to him again, and Johnny knew they were doing something to Samuel out on the front street. Something that made the small boy scream.

He beat against the boards on both sides of the crack. The planks were rotted nearly clean through.

Dirt drifted into his eyes. He brushed at it, and then in a fit of frustration he threw himself at the slit.

With a *crack* the rotted board caved out and hot wind blasted into the cellar. Johnny jumped back, surprised that he'd broken the board.

A sharp report chased by a shriek rode the wind. Johnny dove at the opening and pulled desperately at the rotting boards. They came away in clumps. He pulled four down and clambered though the opening into the alley.

He jerked his head each way. The alley was empty. He edged along the back wall to the south corner of the saloon, dropped to his knees, and crept between Smither's Saloon and the convenience store, trembling.

Five yards from the end, he eased down on his belly and snaked along the ground. Then Johnny poked his head around the corner and looked out to where the blacktop split the town of Paradise in two.

The whole town had gathered, right out there on the asphalt, kneeling in a large semicircle with their backs to Johnny. Claude Bowers and his son Peter were dressed in the same overalls they'd worn for a week. Paula was there, on the edge closest to Johnny. Crying. Katie knelt ten feet from Paula, glaring at her with contempt, draped in a weasel or bear or some other fur.

Father Yordon knelt on the far side, his head hung low, his hands folded like he was giving a blessing for the gathering. The rest of the people knelt into the wind, facing Steve. The only missing character in this gathering was Black. No sign of Billy's black-clad preacher.

Steve Smither stood in the center of the circle with arms spread. He had a whip in his right hand, and he was gloating at something on the pavement.

From his perspective hugging the dirt, Johnny couldn't see over their heads to see what Steve was looking at. Very slowly, with quivering muscles, Johnny pushed himself to his knees.

They'd stripped Samuel's shirt off. He knelt with his head bowed to the black pavement, facing away from Steve. His shoulders and arms were bleeding. Long streaks of red and blue on his back.

Johnny's vision swam.

Steve lunged forward with the whip. A black streak lashed through the air and cracked just above the boy's back. A thin red gash opened on Samuel's white skin, as if he were a painting and the artist had flipped a red brush over the canvas.

The boy jerked without screaming. Then settled back to his knees. His soft sobs reached Johnny's ears.

Johnny collapsed face down. He started to push himself up and immediately thought better of it. What if they saw him? Would they beat him like they were beating Samuel? Would they strip him and whip him?

Samuel's quiet cry rose into the wind. But not a scream like before. And no crack of the whip. Johnny lifted his head.

Samuel had struggled to his feet. The young boy stood with the wind at his back, his legs spread and slightly bent at the knees. He was calling out in a thin voice.

"Father . . ."

The words sliced into Johnny's heart like a razor.

"Father, please . . . please help me . . ."

Johnny glanced at the mountains. The lookout jutted from the rocky face like a gray shoe far above them. Beyond it . . .

"Father! Fatherrr! Please, Father! Save me!"

Samuel was wailing now.

The frail boy sucked at the air with a dreadful groaning sound and then shrieked again. "Don't let me die! Don't . . ." He was sobbing now, screaming between gasps. "Please, please, I'm just a boy . . ."

Tears streamed from Johnny's eyes. He began to groan softly, and he knew they might hear him, but he didn't care anymore. He wanted to die. A thought forced its way into his mind.

Why didn't Samuel run?

Samuel stood on the road at least five paces from Steve and the rest of them. The Starlight Theater's remains hid the path leading to the mountain behind. The boy had a way of escape. He had to know that he could reach the theater and lose himself in the hills before the mob caught him.

But Samuel did not run.

He stood there and begged the empty sky to save him. In long weeping wails he cried to the wind until Johnny thought his heart would burst.

The people knelt in their semicircle, unmoved. Steve still gloated, Yordon still bobbed his head. Only Paula wept—possibly for Samuel, possibly for herself.

"Whip him, Stevie," Katie said.

The whip flashed. Samuel fell. His body smacked onto the asphalt like a slab of meat. The fall took the wind from him and he twisted in agony. Then his soft groans carried to Johnny again.

"Father, please. Father, please!"

Anguish. Such anguish.

Johnny clenched his eyes and pushed himself back, keeping his belly low. He turned first to his right and then to his left, undecided where to go, only knowing that he had to get away.

Away from where the people watched the boy rolling before them with mild interest, like chicken farmers watching another rooster go under the ax. *Why do they flop like that, honey? Why? I don't know, they all do.*

Then Johnny staggered to his feet, covered his ears against Samuel's wails, and ran for the trees.

CHAPTER FORTY-TWO

THE MONASTERY
Tuesday morning

RAUL SAT on his haunches ten yards from the edge, rocking back and forth, a monk committed to a mantra. He'd watched David's endless pacing along the lookout for an hour. In the beginning he'd attempted several approaches of consolation.

"Samuel's a strong boy," he said, and David just wept harder, leaning against a lone tree whose roots had found purchase on the rock surface. "Trust God," he said. "He gave us these books. Trust the books, David. In the end, love will prevail." But David just whirled to him.

"He's my son! Every *moment* is the end!"

Raul had changed tactics then. Never mind that a wrong turn now could wreak havoc throughout the earth; the pain of this one moment seemed to supersede any such risk.

"Go down and save him, David! Together, we could."

"You don't understand," David groaned.

"You're his father, man! What else is there to understand? We'll burn the town to the ground!"

"I can't!" David's cry sounded guttural and horrid, and it struck Raul that he was tormenting the man with such absurd statements. If Thomas and Samuel couldn't stop Black, surely a troop of unarmed monks would only walk to their deaths.

But how could a father stand by while his son was brutalized? David would give his life for Samuel without a second thought. There was more here than Raul knew. More than this simple agreement they'd made to trust the books.

"Samuel!" David groaned loudly. "My son, my son, Samuel!" He tore at his hair with both hands and stepped up to the very edge, sobbing. For a terrifying moment, Raul thought he would leap from the cliff. But he just stood there, moaning in the wind for a long time.

"Please tell me that you know what you're doing, sir! Just tell me that there is a way out of this madness."

But David refused to respond. He hadn't spoken since. He only paced from the tree to a large boulder thirty feet away, bursting into tears so often that Raul wondered where the tears could possibly come from.

After an hour, just as a numbness settled in Raul's mind, the first wail reached them from Paradise, like an arrow shot from the valley below. They both jerked their heads toward the sound.

Raul caught his breath. Could it be a bird? Yes, it could . . .

The cry sounded again, and Raul began to tremble. The sound came from Paradise. From Samuel. Samuel was crying out in Paradise.

David threw himself to his knees and gripped his hair with both hands. His mouth stretched in anguish, but only small sounds broke through his swollen throat.

The next cry carried words, surprisingly clear on the morning air: "*Father! Fatherrr! Please, Father! Save me!*"

David fell apart then. He simply fell to his side and lay there on the ground, still clutching his head. The cries came again and again. But the father did nothing, *could* do nothing. He only wept, face twisted and body quaking.

Raul rocked, crying. He had never imagined such pain was possible, that any living soul could endure so much sorrow and manage to keep their organs from hemorrhaging.

For the first time in his memory, he wanted to die. He wanted everything to end.

CHAPTER FORTY-THREE

PARADISE

Tuesday

JOHNNY TORE into the hills without caring where he was going as long as it was away from the terrifying sounds in Paradise.

But he couldn't escape them. They drifted through the trees, and they filled his mind, pushing him faster and farther.

Maybe he should have gone home instead of running out here. Surely his mother wasn't part of this. He'd been so overcome by the horror on Main Street that he didn't look for her among the others.

Johnny pulled up, his breathing ragged. Something had changed. He looked around, lost. Tall pines leaned in the gusting wind. The sky seemed darker.

What had changed?

Samuel had stopped wailing.

Johnny whipped his head back to the town. Samuel wasn't crying—maybe they'd let him go. He turned back downhill.

Samuel's faint voice was calling to him. Or at least to his memory.

You and I, Johnny. We'll fix this town.

Johnny found his bearings and cut through the trees, toward Smither's Saloon. His mind played back Samuel's voice, soft and sweet.

In the end we will prevail, Johnny.

Prevail, Samuel? Where did you learn words like that? I've got news for you. We're not prevailing here.

He burst through the trees behind the saloon, slid to a stop, and listened carefully over the pounding of his heart. A muffled cry came from his right, in the direction of the church.

He hurried for the back of Katie's Nails and Tan and leaned against the back wall to catch his breath. Laughter drifted over the wind. Lead by Steve's, Johnny thought.

A *smack* and a *grunt*.

Chills broke over Johnny's skull. He eased around the building, slipped under the steps that led to Katie's side entrance, and pried his eyes through the gaps that faced the street.

The mob stood on the church's front lawn and crowded the steps. They had Samuel on the concrete porch in front of the double oak doors. His body sagged between Claude and Chris, who held him by an arm.

Johnny could see his blond head roll to one side, but the people blocked his view of Samuel's body. A man Johnny thought might be Dr. Malone reached out and slapped the boy somewhere on his body.

Johnny withdrew and slumped to his haunches against the wall. Another *thud*, another *grunt*. He buried his head between his knees and began to sob quietly.

He could hear the sounds when his ears weren't covered by his arms. More thudding blows, more helpless cries, and then mostly garbled shouting and laughter. A dozen times Johnny wanted to run, almost did run. But he couldn't move.

The air grew quiet for a while. Maybe now they were letting him go.

Johnny poked his head around the corner and peered through the gap again. He could see Samuel now, from head to foot.

They held Samuel up against the solid oak doors, with his arms spread and his head lolling on his chest. Johnny watched in horror as Roland strolled up casually and slugged Samuel in the stomach with his fist. Samuel grunted, and the boy turned around.

Johnny's friend walked to the circle's edge and stood next to a woman who stared ahead, face whitewashed and barely recognizable, but there, within five paces of Samuel's sagging body. The woman was Johnny's mother. Every muscle in Johnny's body froze at the sight. He knelt under the steps, eyes wide, heart slamming madly, unable to move. His mind insisted that he had to get away.

Mom?

Wanna trip, baby?

Steve Smither stepped into the circle, gripping one of his sharp stakes low like a spear. A grin split his jaw and he braced himself.

The rest of the mob stood perfectly still, expressionless. The wind whipped their hair to the south.

Steve lowered his head and stared at Samuel. Johnny tried to pull away then—he really did. But his muscles . . .

Samuel's eyes suddenly opened, bright and blue, and he stared past the crowd, directly at Johnny.

Steve Smither lunged forward and shoved his stake at the boy's side, up under his rib cage into his chest.

It sounded like a plunger. Samuel gasped and raised to his toes, face white with shock. Blood poured from the wound, over Steve's fists, and to the ground.

Then the boy screamed.

But this time Samuel's scream was different. A blinding white light rushed from his mouth. Johnny watched in amazement as the shaft of light blazed over the heads of the gathered killers. It cut down the middle of the town, over the charred remains of the car that Claude had burned, and smashed into Smither's Saloon.

The building imploded in a ball of dust. But no sound.

Only Samuel's scream, which wasn't stopping.

The beam of light sliced to the right, leveling buildings in the same puff of dust as it touched them. Katie's Nails and Tan vanished. All Right Convenience was vaporized. The old Starlight Theater, already a black skeleton, turned to white powder and settled flat.

In a matter of ten seconds, the whole southern half of the town was leveled.

And then the scream fell silent, and the beam of light disappeared.

Johnny spun his head back to the church.

Samuel slumped over the stake and was still.

He's dead.

A ball of fire exploded in Johnny's head and shot through his nerves in one blinding flash. He slumped to his right side, and his mind went blank.

CHAPTER FORTY-FOUR

THE MONASTERY
Tuesday

BILLY JERKED upright. A pain flashed through his chest, and he lifted his pen from the page, surprised. Did it come from the *killing* of Samuel or the *death* of Samuel?

He reached down to the floor, scooped some worm salve in his palm, and slapped it on his chest.

Of course, the killing and the death were one and the same, weren't they? No, not really. That was the problem—they carried different meanings. Meanings that now began to flash in Billy's mind.

The killing. Yes, the killing came from his pen as it bit angrily into white paper, inflaming sick hearts. *What did you think you were doing, coming to my town, Samuel? You wanna see what happens to stuck-up kids who try to ruin my fun? Wanna see what it feels like to trip? Wanna die? Huh? I'll show you, you puke!*

The whole thing went down perfectly, like a carefully choreographed dance deserving of thundering applause and satisfaction.

But the satisfaction wasn't flowing. Not even dribbling.

Samuel is dead.

Yes, I killed him. Billy began to shake.

The killing had been one thing, but there was the death. And it felt like the death of writing.

Billy lifted his head and peered over the railing at the library below. Thirty-four children sat upright, pens suspended over paper, looking about as if they had just awakened from a long dream. Not a single one continued to write.

Billy's eyes swung to his right, where Darcy stared at him with wide eyes. *The story has ended. We have written the end.*

Then another thought blasted through his mind. Maybe they hadn't ended the story. Maybe not at all.

Maybe *Samuel* had ended the story.

CHAPTER FORTY-FIVE

PARADISE
Tuesday

A LOUD *clink* sounded in his head. Someone had taken a nail and hammer to his skull.

Clink, clink, clink.

Come on, boy, wake up!

Clink, clink, clink.

Try his forehead, Doctor. Clink on his forehead. See if that wakes him.

It slowly occurred to Johnny that the sound wasn't in his head. It was on the wind, like they were building a railroad through Paradise. Trains were coming to Paradise. Maybe they would bring some help. Some more cops to hang on the trees.

Or maybe it was coming from the church. Wasn't there something bad going on at the church?

Johnny opened his eyes and peered through a gap at the bottom of the steps. The town was half gone. Reduced to lumps of dust and ash. Claude and his gang stood where the old theater used to be and kicked dust. But he didn't care about them anymore.

He turned his head to look at the church. The crowd had left. Only Steve remained. He had backed up and was staring at his handiwork.

Samuel was there, stapled to the solid-oak church doors. They had driven two metal stakes through his shoulders and into the wood. Wide trails of blood had flowed down his sides, pooled on the floor at his feet, and run over the concrete steps.

Johnny rolled over, clambered to his feet, and lumbered toward the alley. He gripped the rear corner of the building and vomited.

I think they killed him. Yes, they most definitely killed him.

Johnny wiped his mouth with the back of his hand, turned into the alley, and staggered into the forest.

WANNA TRIP, baby?

He'd tripped, all right. He'd tripped real good.

It was the only thought that passed through Steve's mind as he stared at the boy's dead body on the church door. Something wasn't right about what had happened here, he figured that much, but it was all he figured.

Was he upset? No, not really. The kid had it coming. He had tried to ruin a good thing, and that wasn't part of the plan. Steve wasn't sure what the plan was really, but this kid wasn't in it. Or maybe this was the plan, killing this boy.

He stared at the bloody stake in his right hand. A wave of nausea swept over him. Then passed.

"Quite something, isn't it?"

Steve turned to the voice. Black stood with his hands on his hips, all dressed up in black without a spot of dirt on him. His blue eyes were fixed on the church doors where the boy hung.

"Yeah," Steve said.

Black looked into his eyes and flashed a tempting smile. "Makes you want to do it all over again."

Steve felt his head nod once. "Yeah." There was some truth to that. He might not want to do it again right away, but a faint hint of desire pulled at his heart.

"Yeah," he said again.

"I'm free, baby," Black said, looking back at the boy. "I do believe that I'm free."

"Yeah," Steve said. This time he had no idea what Black was talking about.

"Do you know what we've done here, Steve? Hmm? Do you know how far we've come in seven short days?"

Steve couldn't really remember that far back. He looked at the saloon that he used to own. That whole part of town was gone, but he didn't mind. He had his stakes, didn't he?

Another wave of nausea hit his gut, then passed.

"Well, I've got good news, buddy boy. It's just the beginning."

"It is?"

"Do you know what we have to do now?"

Steve tried to think of an answer but couldn't. "No."

"We have to kill the rest."

"Really?"

"Yes, really. Every one of them. Starting with Johnny. We'll have to find him first. He gave us the slip. But we will, and when we do, we'll do it again."

Steve just stared at him. He didn't know what to think about that. But then maybe he did. If Black said that's what they had to do, then that was what they had to do.

"Yeah," he finally said.

Black chuckled and winked. "That's my boy. Take a break. Celebrate."

"Umm . . . when are we?"

"When are we what? Say it."

"Killing."

"That's better," Black said. "Six hours. We'll start the killing in six hours."
He lowered his arms, turned his back, and walked away.

He thrust an arm out toward the dead boy and spoke without looking back. "And get rid of that body. I don't want to see it again."

JOHNNY SAT on an outcropping of rocks just above Paradise and cried. Below him lay the remains of a town that only seven days ago had been his home. Now it was a graveyard.

He had never felt so desperate in his life. He either had to go to Delta or back to the monastery now. The monastery was closer, but with Samuel dead, he didn't know what waited up there. Billy might have killed them all. Delta was farther, and he would have to walk.

The fact that his mother was still down in Paradise prevented him from taking either option. He didn't know what to do, so he just hugged his legs to his chest and cried.

Then he lay down on his side, curled up in a ball, and tried to lose himself in a safe corner of his mind. If there was one left.

CHAPTER FORTY-SIX

THE MONASTERY
Tuesday afternoon

RAUL HEARD the rap on his door. It sounded like a woodpecker search-ing for entrance to his skull. He looked up from the chair in which he'd col-lapsed, exhausted. According to the clock on the wall it was three in the afternoon.

Samuel's wails came back to him. Unless it had all been a nightmare. No . . . no, it had actually happened. The world had come to an end. At least Samuel's world had come to an end. And David had been sentenced to a life of regret.

"Yes, one moment, please." He stood and took a deep breath, straighten-ing his shirt.

The books had failed. Which meant that the project had failed. And worse, much worse, Billy was still in the dungeons with the books at his fingertips. Somehow, no matter what the cost, the monks had to destroy the monastery and, if necessary, the children.

The overseers had met without David late morning and agreed. They would wait until morning, but then they would do whatever they could to wipe out what they'd created here.

The books were limited to the monastery and the children in the monastery. If they could destroy this place, they could remove the threat. That's where they would begin.

"Come."

The door opened and Andrew stood in the frame. "I'm sorry, Raul, but it's urgent. David insists we come immediately."

"David? Now?"

"Right away, in his study."

Andrew hurried away.

What could he possibly offer David now? No words would suffice; no gesture could comfort him in the wake of his son's death. In fact, their decision to destroy David's life work would surely make things worse.

Raul left his room and climbed the stairs, fighting off stark images that lingered. After the wails ceased, David lay on the stone slab overlooking Paradise for another hour, like a dead man. Twice Raul knelt over him to check his breathing. But David grunted him away.

Black clouds pressed low over the town below. The day was the darkest in Raul's memory, both physically and spiritually.

David finally pushed himself to his feet, looked about, dazed, and returned to the monastery.

Raul had followed him. David showed no further signs of remorse. He simply slogged his way up the mountain, up through the monastery, and to his chambers, where he closed the door.

And now David wished to see Andrew and him.

Raul followed Andrew into the study, closed the door, and faced David. Unlike David's bedroom, everything here was in perfect order, including David. Gone were the bedclothes. He wore his long stately black robe customary for formal visits. His hair was neatly groomed and the stubble had been shaved from his chin.

Had the man gone mad? Or was he simply suffering an utter denial of all that had just happened?

Andrew stood behind one of the guest chairs in front of David's desk.

"Good afternoon, sir." Raul dipped his head.

"Please, have a seat." He motioned to the chairs.

They sat.

David had withdrawn the first history book—the one he showed them three days earlier for the first time. Raul shifted his gaze from the book to David's eyes and found them locked on his.

"You're wondering if I've lost my mind. Perhaps I have. I lost my son Christopher. Then my wife. Now Samuel. I'm within my rights."

Raul glanced at Andrew.

"But I don't believe I have. I believe I have been drawn into the raw creative power of free will. I believe I have been tested and have proven myself worthy of that power."

"Samuel is dead," Raul said. It sounded crass, and he immediately regretted having said it. But it was also true.

"He is," David said. "And why is he dead? Because of the books. Because of the power behind the books. Because the evil in the children's minds was too strong for them to ignore and resist. But isn't that the course we expected of spoiled minds?"

"At some level," Andrew said. "But surely you didn't expect this. Even with the books, this was never the point."

"No, I didn't expect this. But I knew it was a possibility, even from the beginning."

"And yet you went through with it?"

"I didn't truly believe it could happen at first—"

"And when did you suspect?" Raul demanded, frustrated at David's dismissive tone.

The director put his hand on the book and stared at its cover. "I suspected several months ago, when Marsuvees Black found this book. I was nearly sure of it when Samuel insisted that he should go to Paradise."

"That was only yesterday," Andrew said. "Then why didn't you stop him from going?"

David struck the desk with an open palm. "Because it was the only way!"

He glared at Raul. "The project was failing! This reckless notion of mine to unleash the power of the books for good had gone amuck. You so eloquently pointed that out on a dozen occasions."

"Then why—"

"Do you have any idea what kind of monster we may have unleashed here?"

The man was confessing, Raul thought. He had insisted that only love would result, because no history could be written in the books unless it led ultimately to love. Now he would admit his mistake.

David took a calming breath. Beads of sweat rose on his forehead. "As you know, I had Samuel write a new rule into the books seven years ago limiting the book's power to only those in the monastery and reaffirming the requirement that they lead to the discovery of love."

"We know this," Andrew said.

"Assuming these rules you've written actually work," Raul said.

"I think the fact that this monastery exists, created by the books themselves, proves the books' power," David said. "I assume you don't dispute that much."

Raul couldn't. "No, not that much."

"Good. Then assume with me please, for my sake, that the rules do work. Assume that this will lead to the discovery of love. For me."

"Of course."

"Good. Then we believe that love will eventually win the day. But when? The fact of the matter is I saw no way to curb the amount of destruction the books would allow before love finally won the day."

"The rule you had Samuel write made the outcome certain, but not the path to that outcome," Andrew said.

"Exactly. I could foresee inadvertently unleashing terrible horrors on the world that might only turn to good far down the road. I couldn't risk that."

"Yet you did," Raul said.

David took a deep breath.

"You didn't? Then what . . ."

CHAPTER FORTY-SEVEN

PARADISE

Tuesday afternoon

THE AFTERNOON was dark. Darker than any Steve could remember. Then again, that could be his mind.

He walked out into the street and headed for the church. Black had said six hours. He didn't know if six hours had come and gone, but best he could figure, it was something like that.

He'd spent the hours making twelve new stakes. One for Katie, one for Yordon, one for Claude, and one for Paula maybe. Then the rest for some of the others, yet unnamed. He could hardly remember their names.

For Johnny he would use the same stake he'd used for the kid.

Maybe he could use all of these more than once.

He would need one for himself. Eventually it would come to that, wouldn't it? Sure, why not. Kill 'em all—that meant him too. Or maybe he could kill Black.

Not with a stake, he couldn't. Black ate stakes for breakfast.

Steve stopped beside the still-smoldering car in the middle of town. Speaking of his maker, where was Black? No sign of him anywhere he could see.

He'd pulled the boy's body off the church doors and hauled it outside of town limits, about a hundred yards west of the old theater. Dumped it in the dry creek bed there. He started to pile rocks on it, but gave up after a few minutes because his time would be better spent making those stakes.

Steve looked at the bloodstained stake in his hand. The red had dried to black. He looked around. Where was Black?

CHAPTER FORTY-EIGHT

THE MONASTERY

Tuesday afternoon

"I HAD Samuel write a *second* entry into the books," David said.

"Two entries? You made no mention—"

"You weren't ready for it. Now you are."

David turned the book on his desk and slid it toward them.

Raul and Andrew leaned forward. Samuel's familiar handwriting stared up at them. Raul scanned the entry at the top of the page. This was the one David had revealed earlier in the week, limiting the book's power to the children.

"I am as skeptical as both of you. I had to have my insurance."

There was a paragraph break, Raul saw. Then another sentence.

If a writer unleashes death on the path to love, the evil may be reversed by the display of a commensurate love fitting with the nature of these books. At that time, the writer who has unleashed death will no longer be able to write in these books. This rule is irrevocable.

Raul's head buzzed with the new revelation.

"Samuel *knew* this?"

"He was in my office, reading from this book just before announcing his intention to go to Paradise," David said. "He knew."

"You're saying that his death was . . ." Andrew sat back.

"There is no greater love than to lay down your life for a friend," David said. "It wasn't what I had in mind when I asked him to write it, but I now realize that what has happened is precisely within the nature of these books. Billy unleashed death, and Samuel gave his life willingly, my friends."

To think that Samuel had entered the town in full knowledge that his death might be the only way to turn the tide . . .

345

"Then the tide has been turned?" he asked, shifting forward in his chair. "And Billy's now powerless?"

"Billy should be." Tears moistened David's eyes now. He looked like he would burst out in tears all over again. But he fought back the emotion. "Has anything happened since Samuel's death?"

"Not that we know."

David frowned. "The story is over. Samuel ended it. I have nothing left but to trust the books given to us by God."

For the first time, Raul began to see through David's eyes. He'd sacrificed his own son for the sake of the town. For the children here. But there was something strange about David's demeanor. Regardless of any victory, David should be torn in two over his son's death.

With the thought came a question that lodged itself in Raul's mind and refused to go. How could any father this side of heaven give up his son, regardless of what good it might bring? What kind of man would do that?

"Forgive me, David, but you knew Samuel could die. How—"

"How could I send my son down to those butchers?" David's eyes flashed. He took a breath. "Because I am Samuel's only hope. His life rests in my hands."

"How can you say that? You *didn't* save him."

"The books could still bring him back."

"How? There's no one left to write in them. The books can no longer work for any of the children below, you said so yourself. The rule is irrevocable. The books are limited."

"To those in the monastery with the faith of a child," David said. "That doesn't mean only the children. If you or I were to have this kind of faith, then we could write in the books. Preventing Samuel from going would have completely undermined my own faith. I had to let him go to prove my own faith."

Raul stood abruptly. "It's why you had to let them kill him!" He saw the reasoning clearly. "It was the only way you could save both him *and* the other students!"

The hours of torment leading up to Samuel's death had new meaning now. David had known! He was in essence proving his faith in God by trusting the Word of the book. David had become Abraham, whose faith was tested by offering up his son, Isaac!

Only in this case, the son really had been killed.

Unless by proving his faith, David now had a power the children no longer had. The power to write in the books with power!

"Have you tried?" Raul demanded.

"No."

"What are you waiting for? Write!" He was forgetting his manners. "Forgive me, but you must write."

"I am waiting for the right moment. My whole world comes down to this moment, Raul. It can't be wasted in haste. Either I have been right, or I have been wrong. I'm not sure I want to face the moment of truth."

Raul pushed the history book toward David with a trembling hand. "The moment has arrived."

David stared at Andrew, then at Raul for a long moment. He winked. "So it has."

He hesitated a full ten seconds, then withdrew a quill from its receptacle and touched the tip to his tongue. "I believe, Raul, I really do. God help my unbelief."

He dipped the quill in a jar of ink and brought it to the page. For a while the pen hovered.

Then David withdrew it. What was he doing?

He sighed, and a tear fell from his cheek onto the page. "What if—"

"The books peer into the heart, David," Raul said. "You have given your heart in its entirety to this matter. It *will* work. If I had demonstrated even half the virtue that you have in these last days, I would rip the pen from your fingers and write it myself. Write!"

David nodded and gathered himself. He dipped the pen again for good measure, then lowered it to the page.

He wrote quickly. Several long sentences.

The scratching nearly drove Raul mad with anticipation. He couldn't see what David was writing and leaning closer for a look didn't seem appropriate, so he sat back down, lowered his head, and waited.

The sound stopped.

Raul looked up. David glanced at him, then blew on the page. He replaced the quill.

Closed the book.

David sat back, folded his hands, and stared at the book.

Raul wanted to ask him what he wrote, but this too seemed inappropriate.

But after watching David in silence for a full minute, he couldn't help himself.

"What did you write?"

David refused to remove his eyes from the book. His fingers trembled. "I wrote Samuel, my son, whom I love more than life itself, back to life."

Raul swallowed and exchanged a glance with Andrew. "What else?"

"I wrote the healing of Paradise and the full physical recovery of all our students."

Good. This was good. But there was more, he could see it in David's eyes. "And?"

"And then I wrote that all of the Books of History would vanish, never again to be found by any living soul. For any reason."

Raul's eyes fell to the book on the desk. There was no way to know if Samuel was walking around Paradise at this very moment. There was no way to know immediately if that the town would be healed of her wounds, or if the children would be restored.

But the books vanishing into hiding—such a vanishing would include this one.

It sat on the desk, a black lump of leather and paper, defiant.

Vanish! Be gone! Say to this mountain be thou removed and it shall be removed. Yet this small mountain either hadn't heard the teaching or wasn't listening. The book would not bow to David's will.

The plan had failed?

CHAPTER FORTY-NINE

PARADISE

Tuesday afternoon

THE SOUND of the man's boots crunching on the gravel from behind him was the first sign that Black had arrived.

Steve stifled a shiver of pleasure and fear and let Black come. He wanted to wait and not turn because he thought that showed some backbone, but his determination failed him. He turned.

Black strode with confidence, trench coat swirling around his polyester pants, hat pulled down low over his eyes. He wasn't looking at Steve, but at the far edge of town, in the direction of the dry creek where he'd dumped the kid.

Then he turned his head and glared at Steve with bloodshot eyes. "I told you to get *rid* of his body. Did I tell you to dump him on the edge of town for the first tourist to find? Did I tell you to roll a stone or two against him and call it good?"

Black stopped three feet from him, rolled his head so that his neck cracked, and then swung an open hand at Steve's face. His palm struck Steve's cheek with a loud smack that sent him reeling onto his rump. His head throbbed with pain.

"I . . . I . . ."

Black kicked his boot into Steve's gut. His whole body jerked off the ground, flew several feet, and landed hard.

He still had his stake in his right hand though.

"Stand up."

Steve struggled to his feet.

Black hit him again, this time with a fist to his left shoulder. It popped loudly and dangled at an odd angle, dislocated. Pain flared down Steve's arm. Why was Black doing this? Wasn't he his right-hand man?

"Do you think you'll still be able to kill without eyes, Steve?"

"My eyes?"

"I have a thing for eyes," Black said.

CHAPTER FIFTY

THE MONASTERY
Tuesday afternoon

THE SECONDS passed, one by agonizing one. And with each tick, Raul felt his heart sink. Deeper and deeper. He could hardly imagine the despondency ravaging David's heart now.

Andrew looked on in silence.

David suddenly slammed both fists on the desk, one on either side of the book. It bounced slightly, then rested still. Lifeless.

David's jaw was fixed and his eyes glassy. He stood and strode toward the window, face flushed. He wore his failure on his entire body.

He stifled a sob, then brought his fist to his mouth to control any outburst.

Raul rose and approached David. For the second time in this day he wondered if he wouldn't prefer death to the pain of such great sorrow.

"You have to be patient—"

"I am finished being patient!" David cried, spinning. "I have nothing left to give. I would rather die now than live without my son!"

"You would fall on your sword rather than lead us—"

David's eyes went wide. "What did you do with it?"

"Your sword. A figure of speech—"

"Not the sword, the book!" He was staring over Raul's shoulder.

Raul whirled.

The book was gone!

He glanced at the floor, thinking it might have fallen. "I . . . I didn't touch it," he stammered.

"It's gone!" Andrew cried.

They stood like three schoolchildren, transfixed by the sight of the empty desk.

"It's gone," David said.

Raul ran to the desk. Placed his hand on the spot where the book had laid. "It's gone. The book is—"

The door swung open to Raul's left. There in the door frame stood a boy. It was Billy.

He was covered in blood and sores, and the rotting gel of worms covered what was left of his flesh. He looked utterly lost.

The boy's arms hung limp, and in his right hand he held a pen.

Raul looked at the boy's face. Only then did he see that Billy was crying. Tears streamed down his cheeks.

His shoulders began to shake with sobs. The pen slipped from his fingers and fell to the floor.

CHAPTER FIFTY-ONE

PARADISE

Tuesday afternoon

MARSUVEES BLACK cocked two fingers like a rattler's fangs and gripped Steve's dislocated shoulder with his other hand, ready to take his eyes.

Oddly enough, Steve didn't wince. He felt the pain in his shoulder all right. He thought he might pass out from it. He heard the crunching of his bones. But he saw the bright lights in Black's eyes and knew the man was finding fascination and pleasure in this violence, and for some reason that made it all okay.

"I don't need you, Steve, any more than I needed the monk. I can use Claude or Chris. I can use Paula."

Nausea again. This time it didn't pass. It welled up through his chest and stung his eyes. He was going to throw up.

But he didn't. The feeling was worse than the pain in his shoulder. Tears filled his eyes. For the first time since Black had come into town, Steve wanted to die.

"I'll kill them all," Steve said. "I swear, I'll . . ."

His ears began to ring. Black jerked his head up and looked at the sky. Steve followed his stare.

At first he couldn't see that anything had happened. Then he squinted and he saw it. The sun was out. And the black clouds were moving.

Boiling, rolling, flying up and back and away, as if a huge vacuum cleaner was sucking them into deep space. Behind it all was blue sky.

And a brilliant afternoon sun.

Black still had his hand on Steve's shoulder. He twisted his head toward the entrance to town. Nothing there. What was happening?

It was hot. Hazy hot. Midafternoon-on-a-hot-summer-day hot. And so bright.

But nothing else.

Black's face beaded with sweat. Steve followed his gaze again. Nothing but shimmering heat above the flattened buildings. What was happening?

And then Steve saw a distortion in the haze. Something was moving toward them, walking down the middle of Main Street in the distance. A small figure obscured by the heat.

The boy?

Black's hand began to tremble on his shoulder. His arm twitched. Two fingers still raised to strike.

As for Steve, the nausea had passed. Beyond that he didn't know what to feel.

The boy walked toward the edge of town, arms loose at his sides, small and frail, hardly more than an apparition distorted by heat waves. He didn't have a shirt on, and his skin was covered in dried blood, but he was definitely alive. And looking right at them.

Then the child entered Paradise, and the buildings began to rise from the dust.

JOHNNY JUMPED to his feet and stared at the clearing sky. Something was happening! He'd watched Black walk up to Steve and slap him around, but now both of them were still.

Something was happening; he could feel it in the air. Not just the clouds, not just the sun, not just the sudden heat. Something bigger.

He scrambled to the edge of the rocks and strained for a better view. Black still hadn't moved. For a while nothing moved.

And then the old theater began to move.

Johnny crouched, disbelieving what his eyes were seeing. The old theater was rising from the ground, rebuilding itself layer by layer, quicker than he could keep track of, like one of those demolitions he'd seen on the television, only in reverse.

And not just the old theater, but all the buildings around it. Paradise was being rebuilt from the ground up.

Johnny blinked, then blinked again. The Starlight Theater, Smither's Saloon, Claude's convenience store, Katie's Nails and Tan. Houses. How could . . .

He saw the boy then, walking down the middle of Main Street. A snapshot of Marsuvees Black walking into town the same way seven days earlier filled his mind for a second, and then was gone.

This wasn't Black.

This was Samuel!

Johnny tore down the mountain.

STEVE COULDN'T process what was happening around him at first. Things were going backward, rising and flying and moving at impossible angles.

The town was rising from the ashes.

And the small boy was walking straight toward them, right past the buildings as if they weren't rising from the ground miraculously. His eyes were fixed on Steve.

Black cursed once under his breath. He dropped his hand from Steve's shoulder and cursed again, a long string of hushed, vile words punctuated by spittle. His tirade ended midsentence, and in a fit of fury he slugged Steve in the gut, hard enough to break some ribs. Steve gasped and doubled over.

From the corner of his eyes Steve watched as Black grabbed his own coat, spun once, and vanished into the folds of cloth.

Black's clothing collapsed to the ground over his boots. His broad-brimmed hat bounced once, rolled to one side, and came to rest three feet from the pile of clothes.

Steve couldn't breathe. Where had Black gone? What was happening?

But he knew. This boy was happening.

When he managed to stand straight again, he saw two things: he saw that the town was the way it had been a week ago, before any of this had happened, except the leaves were still gone from the trees and sand still dusted the streets. And he saw that the boy had stopped ten feet from him and was staring up at him with soft, round eyes.

He felt dizzy. Hadn't he killed this boy? There was no hole in his side where Steve stuck the stake, but there was caked blood all over. Black had told him to kill the boy and he had done it, done it good.

Others came out of their houses and stared at the town in awe.

Was this a test? Was this how he could keep Black from taking his eyes? Should he take the stake in his hand and kill Samuel again? Maybe that's what Black wanted him to do.

"Look at me, Steve," the boy said.

JOHNNY SPRINTED past the old theater, which now stood in mint condition, or at least in as mint condition as it had been seven days ago, which was pretty tattered but mint, sweet mint, to Johnny.

He ran right into town, briefly glancing at several dozen people who were staring at Samuel and Steve. Claude and Chris stood with Peter and Roland, immobilized by the sudden change. Paula stood on her porch, eyes fixed on Johnny as he ran.

What did I tell you? Huh, what did I tell you?

His eyes searched for his mother. She was standing between their house and the next, watching Samuel.

What did I tell you! Now this, this is the truth. Black was from the pit of hell, but God has sent us a hero. A superhero.

Johnny slid to a stop to the left and behind Samuel.

"Look at me, Steve," Samuel said.

Samuel was naked except for his shorts and shoes. Blood had dried on his body. But Johnny had to hold himself back from throwing his arms around Samuel's chest.

Steve looked at Samuel. His eyes widened and his lips softened. Samuel was showing him love, and Steve wasn't quite sure what to do with it.

What did I tell you all? What did I say? Johnny felt like his chest would explode.

Samuel looked at Johnny. The boy didn't smile; he didn't say anything; he just winked. Then he turned his gaze back to Steve.

The man stood dazed. His hands and clothes were streaked with blood, and he smelled like he'd rolled in a pile of compost. But the glassy look in his eyes faded away, and his mouth opened in dumb wonderment.

"Grace and hope are dead without love, Steve," Samuel said. Just those words. Johnny felt a lump rise into his throat.

"Love, Steve. Do you want me to love you?"

Steve's face wrinkled under the words. He dropped the stake in his right hand. "Yes?" It was more a question than an answer, but that was evidently fine by Samuel.

The air brightened with a white light. A strobe had gone off. A strobe from Samuel.

Johnny gasped and stepped back. White light smothered Steve's face. He threw his hands wide and began to wail.

The light spread out from Samuel in a growing circle. It hit Father Yordon, who'd come out on the church steps. The man staggered under its power. It hit a man who stood under the trees by the church, and the man put a hand on a trunk to steady himself.

Johnny began to cry. He couldn't help it. He just began to shake with sobs. *I believe. I believe.*

"You are loved, Steve," Samuel said.

"Oh, God!" Steve groaned. "Oh my God, what have I done?"

Johnny was going to burst. "I believe," he whispered.

"Louder, Johnny," Samuel said. "Say it louder."

Samuel was looking at Steve but speaking to Johnny. He felt unraveled, like a frayed hemp rope. Steve was trembling now, but so was Johnny.

"I believe," Johnny said as loud as his constricted throat would allow him. Then he screamed it at the top of his lungs. "I believe!"

The light hit him with a force that seared his mind, paralyzed his spine, and left him dazed and warm.

Johnny sat hard, dumbstruck. This was love.

Time seemed to slow. He might have been down for only a minute, lost to the world, but it felt like an hour.

The sound of sobbing pulled him back into Paradise. He lifted his head. Steve was on his knees, bawling like a baby. Samuel was holding his head, chin lifted to the sky. Tears streamed down his cheeks. His lips were moving, but Johnny couldn't make out the words.

The sound of wailing smothered him. From the corner of his eyes he saw Claude flat on his belly, shaking with sorrow. Paula was walking toward them, one hand outstretched, weeping.

Father Yordon lay in a ball on the church steps.

Johnny pushed himself to his feet and watched Samuel, straining to catch the boy's words. But he didn't need to strain because Samuel's words suddenly rang out clearly for all of them to hear.

"Father," he sobbed. He drew a breath. "Father, we have done it."

CHAPTER FIFTY-TWO

THE MONASTERY
Thursday

THE BOOKS were gone. All of them.

Two days had passed since Samuel's death. One and a half days since he'd awakened in the creek bed and walked into Paradise. He'd told the story a hundred times. How he'd been beaten and killed and then left to rot. How his father had brought him back to life and healed Paradise.

"I still can't believe it all happened," Johnny said, staring down at Paradise from the ledge. "How did it feel?" Billy and Darcy looked at Samuel.

The four children had come together for the first time since the story ended. Like the rest of the children in the monastery, Billy and Darcy were healed almost immediately and were eager to renew their acquaintance with the boy who had resisted their writings.

"How did what feel, the dying or the living?" Samuel asked.

Johnny hesitated, unsure he wanted an answer. "Either," he said.

Samuel shuddered. "The dying . . . I'm not sure I can describe how terrible it felt. But I kept telling myself that my father could save me. I had to believe that."

Darcy stared out at the blue sky. She wasn't the same girl Johnny had met in the dungeons. The whole experience seemed to have knocked the wind out of her.

"If you don't mind, can we talk about something more uplifting?" Billy asked. "Considering it was Darcy and I who were responsible."

"Were you?" Samuel asked. "They didn't have to listen to you. Johnny didn't."

Billy shrugged. "And I didn't have to listen to Black. But I did."

Thinking of Billy as his brother was a mighty strange thing. Half brother, actually. Johnny and Billy had different fathers, but they had both been born to Sally, his mother, and that was weird. Samuel's father had taken Billy in as the thirty-seventh orphan when he learned that Stanley Yordon was forcing Sally to put him up for adoption.

In a strange way, Billy's writing had been an act of unwitting vengeance on the town that abandoned him. Maybe it was this wrongdoing that made them so receptive to Billy's writing. Maybe not.

"Where is Black?" Johnny asked.

"You mean the real Black? Dead," Billy said. "My Black killed him."

"In a week the other teachers will be gone too," Samuel said.

"Your father's abandoning the monastery?"

"Burying it. The books are gone, and without the books, there is no project."

"What will you do?"

"My father's going back to Harvard. Andrew and Raul are setting up an orphanage in New Jersey for any of the kids who want to stay with them. Some want to go back to their home countries. You guys decide yet?"

Billy and Darcy shook their heads. Johnny felt sorry for them. All they knew was up in that monastery, about to be buried.

"Maybe you could live with me and my father," Samuel said.

"Maybe."

They sat in silence for a few minutes.

"The thing I can't get out of my mind is Black," Billy said. "The one I wrote."

"Yeah, Black," Darcy agreed.

"Anyone really know what happened to him?"

Samuel pulled the stalk of grass he'd been nibbling on from his mouth. "Hopefully he vanished with the books."

"Hopefully?"

"That's the thing—my dad isn't sure about Black. The books are gone, the monastery is being buried, the town is back to normal, even the people down there are getting back to normal life, right, Johnny?"

"I wouldn't call it normal. They spend a lot of time in the church. Hardly anyone wants to talk about Black, if that's what you mean."

"He's gotta be gone."

"Even if he isn't," Billy said, "I was the one pulling his strings, right? So without the books, he's powerless."

"He had a book," Johnny said. "I saw it on the church podium once."

"A blank book?" Billy asked. "You sure?"

"Looked exactly like the ones you wrote in."

"But it must have disappeared too," Samuel said. "Had to have. Right?"

"Right," Darcy said.

"Then Black's history," Samuel said.

"Probably," Darcy said.

"Probably," Billy agreed.

"And we're not," Johnny said.

They all looked at him. A slow smile formed on Billy's mouth. "Yeah, I guess that's the whole point, isn't it. Black's history and we're not."

"Thanks to Samuel," Darcy said.

"Thanks to Samuel," Billy said.

"Thanks to Samuel," Johnny said.

And then no one said anything for a while.

SAINT

PROLOGUE

OUR STORY began two thousand years in the future, because the Books of History came into our world from that future.

After they arrived, the Books of History lay in obscurity for many years until a Turkish dealer unwittingly sold the dusty old tomes to David Abraham, a tenured Harvard University professor and collector of antiquities. Upon discovering that the books contained the power to animate the choices of men by turning the written words of innocent children into living, breathing, flesh, he swore to preserve the books in a manner consistent with their nature.

Deep in a monastery hidden from all men near a Colorado mountain town called Paradise, Father Abraham and twelve monks gave their lives to raise thirty-six orphans, lovingly nurturing them and teaching them all things virtuous. One day these children would use the books for the good of all mankind.

And so was born Project Showdown.

But Billy, the brightest of the students, was lured into the dungeons below the monastery, where he found the Books of History. And there, surrounded by intoxicating power, the thirteen-year-old boy wrote into existence an embodiment of his deepest fears and fantasies. And he called his creation Marsuvees Black.

Fueled by the power of evil spun from Billy's own heart, Marsuvees Black became flesh and entered the small mountain town called Paradise. There, with Marsuvees Black, Billy wreaked terrible havoc and Paradise fell.

The correction of Billy's transgression came at a terrible price, but before everything could be set right again, Marsuvees Black escaped with a book, which he used to spawn more manifestations of evil like himself.

Since that day many years ago, Black's creations have lived among us in fleshly form, determined to learn how to make all men evil like Billy was evil.

But good also came out of Paradise when it fell. Three children used the Books of History to write a great power into themselves. Their names were Johnny, Billy, and Darcy.

For twelve years, thankful only that they had survived the failed project, they forgot about what they had written in the Books. But then, when it was least expected, the power began to reveal itself.

CHAPTER ONE

I SEE darkness. I'm lying spread-eagle on my back, ankles and wrists tied tightly to the bedposts so that I can't pull them free.

A woman is crying beside me. I've been kidnapped.

My name is Carl.

But there's more that I know about myself, fragments that don't quite make sense. Pieces of a puzzle forced into place. I know that I'm a quarter inch shy of six feet tall and that my physical conditioning has been stretched to its limits. I have a son whom I love more than my own life and a wife named . . . named Kelly, of course, Kelly. How could I hesitate on that one? I'm unconscious or asleep, yes, but how could I ever misplace my wife's name?

I was born in New York and joined the army when I was eighteen. Special Forces at age twenty, now twenty-five. My father left home when I was eight, and I took care of three younger sisters—Eve, Ashley, Pearl—and my mother, Betty Strople, who was always proud of me for being such a strong boy. When I was fourteen, Brad Stenko slapped my mother. I hit him over the head with a two-by-four and called the police. I remember his name because his intent to marry my mother terrified me. I remember things like that. Events and facts cemented into place by pain.

My wife's name is Kelly. See, I know that, I really do. And my son's name is Matthew. Matt. Matt and Kelly, right?

I'm a prisoner. A woman is crying beside me.

CARL SNAPPED his eyes wide open, stared into the white light above him, and closed his eyes again.

Opening his eyes had been a mistake that could have alerted anyone watching to his awakening. He scrambled for orientation. In that brief moment, eyes opened wide to the ceiling, his peripheral vision had seen the plain room. Smudged white walls. Natural light from a small window. A single fluorescent fixture above, a dirty mattress under him.

And the crying woman, strapped down beside him.

Otherwise the room appeared empty. If there was any immediate danger, he hadn't seen it. So it was safe to open his eyes.

Carl did, quickly confirmed his estimation of the room, then glanced down at a thick red nylon cord bound around each ankle and tied to two metal bedposts. Beside him, the woman was strapped down in similar manner.

His black dungarees had been shoved up to his knees. No shoes. The woman's left leg lay over his right and was strapped to the same post. Her legs had been cut and bruised, and the cord was tied tightly enough around her ankles to leave marks. She wore a pleated navy-blue skirt, torn at the hem, and a white blouse that looked as if it had been dragged through a field with her.

This was Kelly. He knew that, and he knew that he cared for Kelly deeply, but he was suddenly unsure why. He blinked, searching his memory for details, but his memory remained fractured. Perhaps his captors had used drugs.

The woman whose name was Kelly faced the ceiling, eyes closed.

Her tears left streaks down dirty cheeks and into short blond hair. Small nose, high cheekbones, a bloody nose. Several scratches on her forehead.

I'm strapped to a bed next to a woman named Kelly who's been brutalized. My name is Carl and I should feel panic, but I feel nothing.

The woman suddenly caught her breath, jerked her head to face him, and stared into his soul with wide blue eyes.

In the space of one breath, Carl's world changed. Like a heat wave vented from a sauna, emotion swept over him. A terrible wave of empathy laced with a bitterness he couldn't understand. But he understood that he cared for the woman behind these blue eyes very much.

And then, as quickly as the feeling had come, it fell away.

"Carl . . ." Her face twisted with anguish. Fresh tears flooded her eyes and ran down her left cheek.

"Kelly?"

She began to speak in a frantic whisper. "We have to get out of here! They're going to kill us." Her eyes darted toward the door. "We have to do something before he comes back. He's going to kill . . ." Her voice choked on tears.

Carl's mind refused to clear. He knew who she was, who he was, why he cared for her, but he couldn't readily access that knowledge. Worse, he didn't seem capable of emotion, not for more than a few seconds.

"Who . . . who are you?"

She blinked, as if she wasn't sure she'd heard him right. "What did they do to you?"

He didn't know. They'd hurt him, he knew that. Who were they? Who was she?

She spoke urgently through her tears. "I'm your wife! We were on vacation, at port in Istanbul when they took us. Three days ago. They . . . I think they took Matthew. Don't tell me you can't remember!"

Details that he'd rehearsed in his mind before waking flooded him.

He was with the army, Special Forces. His family had been taken by force from a market in Istanbul. Matthew was their son. Kelly was his wife.

Panicked, Carl jerked hard against the restraints. He was rewarded with a squealing metal bed frame, no more.

Another mistake. Whoever had the resources to kidnap them undoubtedly had the foresight to use the right restraints. He was reacting impulsively rather than with calculation. Carl closed his eyes and calmed himself. *Focus, you have to focus.*

"They brought you in here unconscious half an hour ago and gave you a shot." Her words came out in a rush. "I think . . . I'm pretty sure they want you to kill someone." Her fingers touched the palm of his hand above their heads. Clasped his wrist. "I'm afraid, Carl. I'm so afraid." Crying again.

"Please, Kelly. Slow down."

"Slow down? I've been tied to this bed for three days! I thought you were dead! They took our son!"

The room faded and then came back into focus. They stared at each other for a few silent seconds. There was something strange about her eyes. He was remembering scant details of their kidnapping, even fewer details of their life together, but her eyes were a window into a world that felt familiar and right.

They had Matthew. Rage began to swell, but he cut it off and was surprised to feel it wane. His training was kicking in. He'd been trained not to let feelings cloud his judgment. So then his not feeling was a good thing.

"I need you to tell me what you know."

"I've told you. We were on a cruise—"

"No, everything. Who we are, how we were taken. What's happened since we arrived. Everything."

"What did they do to you?"

"I'm okay. I just can't remember—"

"You're bleeding." She stared at the base of his head. "Your hair . . ."

He felt no pain, no wetness from blood. He lifted his head and twisted it for a look at the mattress under his hair. A fist-sized red blotch stained the cover.

The pain came then, a deep, throbbing ache at the base of his skull. He laid his head back down and stared at the ceiling. With only a little effort he disconnected himself from the pain.

"Tell me what you remember."

She blinked, breathed deliberately, as if she might forget to if she didn't concentrate. "You had a month off from your post in Kuwait and we decided to take a cruise to celebrate our seventh anniversary. Matthew was buying some crystallized ginger when a man grabbed him and went into an alley between the tents. You went after him. I saw someone hit you from behind with a metal pipe. Then a rag with some kind of chemical was clamped over my face and I passed out. Today's the first time I've seen you." She closed her eyes. "They tortured me, Carl."

Anger rose, but again he suppressed it. Not now. There would be time for anger later, if they survived.

His head seemed to be clearing. More than likely they'd kept him drugged for days, and whatever they'd put into his system half an hour ago was waking him up. That would explain his temporary memory loss.

"What nationality are they?"

"Hungarian, I think. The one named Dale is a sickening . . ." She stopped, but the look of hatred in her eyes spoke plenty.

Carl blocked scattered images of all the possible things Dale might have done to her. Again, that he was able to do this so easily surprised him. Was he so insensitive to his own wife?

No, he was brutally efficient. For her sake he had to be.

Their captors had left their mouths free—if he could find a way to reach their restraints . . .

The door swung open. A man with short-cropped blond hair stepped into the room. Medium height. Knifelike nose and chin. Fiercely eager blue eyes. Khaki cotton pants, black shirt, hairy arms. Dale.

Carl knew this man.

This was Dale Crompton. This was a man who'd spent some time in the dark spaces of Carl's mind, securing Carl's hatred. Kelly had said Hungarian, but she must have meant someone else, because Dale was an Englishman.

The man's right arm hung by his side, hand snugged around an Eastern Bloc Makarov 9mm pistol. The detail was brightly lit in Carl's mind while other details remained stubbornly shrouded by darkness. He knew his weapons.

Without any warning or fanfare, Dale rounded the foot of the bed, pressed the barrel of the Makarov against Kelly's right thigh, and pulled the trigger.

The gun bucked with a thunderclap. Kelly arched her back, screamed, and thrashed against her restraints, then dropped to the mattress in a faint.

Carl's mind passed the threshold of whatever training he'd received. His mind demanded he feel nothing, lie uncaring in the face of brutal manipulation, but his body had already begun its defense of his wife. He snarled and bolted up, oblivious to the pain in his wrists and ankles.

The movement proved useless. He might as well be a dog on a thick chain, jerked violently back at the end of a sprint for freedom.

He collapsed back onto the bed and gathered himself. Kelly lay still. A single glance told him that the bullet had expended its energy without passing through her leg, which meant it had struck the femur, probably shattering it.

"I hope I have your attention," Dale said. "Her leg will heal. A similar bullet to her head, on the other hand, will produce far more satisfying results. I'd love to kill her. And your son. What is his name? Matthew?"

Carl just stared at him. *Focus. Believe. You must believe in your ability to save them.*

"Pity to destroy such a beautiful woman," Dale said, walking to the window. "Just so you know, I argued to tie your son next to you and keep Kelly for other uses, but Kalman overruled me. He says the boy will be useful if you fail us the first time."

Englishman put the gun on the sill, unlatched the window, and pulled it up. Fresh breezes carried a lone bird's chirping into the room. *It's spring. I can smell fresh grass and spring flowers. I can smell fresh blood.*

Englishman faced him. "A simple and quite lethal device has been surgically implanted at the base of your hypothalamus gland. This explains the bleeding at the back of your head. Any attempt to remove this device will result in the release of chemicals that will destroy your brain within ten seconds. Your life is in our hands. Is this clear?"

The revelation struck Carl as perfectly natural. Exactly what he would have expected, knowing what he did, whatever that was.

"Yes."

"Good. Your mission is to kill a man and his wife currently housed in a heavily guarded hotel at the edge of the town directly to our south, three miles away. Joseph and Mary Fabin will be in their room on the third floor. Number 312. No one else is to be killed. Only the targets. You have two cartridges in the gun, only two. No head shots. We need their faces for television. Do you understand?"

A wave of dizziness swept through Carl. Aside from a slight tic in his right eye, he showed none of it. Beside him, Kelly moaned. How could he ignore his wife's suffering so easily?

Carl eyed the pistol on the sill. "I understand."

"We will watch you closely. If you make any contact with the authorities, your wife will die. If you step outside the mission parameters, she dies. If you haven't returned within sixty minutes, both she and your son will die. Do you understand?"

Carl spoke quickly to cover any fear in his eyes. "The name of the hotel?"

"The Andrassy," Dale said. He withdrew a knife from his waistband, walked over to Carl, and laid the sharp edge against the red nylon rope that tied Carl's right leg to the bed frame.

"I'm sure you would like to kill me," Dale said. "This is impossible, of course. But if you try, you, your wife, and your son will be dead within the minute."

"Who are the targets?"

"They are the two people who can save your wife and son by dying within the hour." The man cut through the bonds around Carl's ankles, then casually went to work on the rope at his wrists. "You'll find some shoes and clean clothes outside the window." With a faint *pop,* the last tie yielded to Englishman's blade.

Kelly whimpered, and Carl looked over to see that her eyes were open again. Face white, muted by horror and pain.

For a long moment, lying there freed beside the woman he loved, Carl allowed a terrible fury to roll through his mind. Despite Dale's claim, Carl knew that he stood at least an even chance of killing their captor.

He wanted to touch Kelly and to tell her that she would be okay. That he would save her and their son. He wanted to tear the heart out of the man who was now watching them with a dispassionate stare, like a robot assigned to a simple task.

He wanted to scream. He wanted to cry. He wanted to kill himself.

Instead, he lay still.

Kelly closed her eyes and started to sob again. He wished she would stop. He wanted to shout at her and demand that she stop this awful display of fear. Didn't she know that fear was now their greatest enemy?

"Fifty-eight minutes," Dale said. "It's quite a long run."

Carl slid his legs off the bed, stood, and walked to the window, thinking that he was a monster for being so callous, never mind that it was for her sake that he steeled himself.

I'm in a nightmare. He reached for the gun. But the Makarov's cold steel handle felt nothing like a dream. It felt like salvation.

"Carl?"

Kelly's voice shattered his reprieve. Carl was sure that he would spin where he stood, shoot Dale through the forehead, and take his chances with the implant or whatever other means they had of killing him and his family. The only way he knew to deal with such a compelling urge was to shut down his emotions entirely. He clenched his jaw and shoved the gun into his waistband.

"I love you, Carl."

He looked at her without seeing her, swallowed his terror. "It'll be okay," he said. "I'll be back."

He grabbed both sides of the window, thrust his head out to scan the grounds, withdrew, shoved his right leg through the opening, and rolled onto the grass outside. When he came to his feet, he was facing south. How did he know it was south? He just did.

He would go south and he would kill.

CHAPTER TWO

CARL FOUND the clothes in a small duffel bag behind a bush along the outside wall. He dressed quickly, pulled on a pair of cargo pants and black running shoes, and tied a red bandanna around his neck to hide the blood that had oozed from a cut at the base of his skull, roughly two inches behind his right ear. Odd to think that a single remote signal could take his life.

Odd, not terrifying. Not even odd, actually. Interesting. Familiar.

He snatched up the Makarov, shoved it behind his back, and set out at a fast jog. South.

He was in a small compound, ten buildings in a small valley surrounded by a deciduous forest. Three of the buildings were concrete; the rest appeared to be made of wood. Most had small windows, perhaps eighteen inches square. Tin roofs. No landscaping, just bare dirt and grass. To the west, a shooting range stretched into the trees farther than he could see, well over three thousand yards.

The day was hot, midafternoon. Quiet except for the chirping of a few birds and the rustle of a light breeze through the trees.

On stilts, a single observation post with narrow, rectangular windows towered over the trees. There were eyes behind those windows, watching him.

All of this he assimilated before realizing that he was taking in his surroundings in such a calculating, clinical manner. His wife lay on a bed with a shattered femur, his son was in some dark hole in one of these buildings, and Carl was running south, away from them in order to save them.

Three miles would take fifteen minutes at a healthy jog for the fittest man. Was he fit? He'd run a hundred yards and felt only slightly winded. He was fit. As part of Special Forces, he would be.

But why was he forced to rely on instinct and calculation instead of clear memory to determine even these simple facts?

He brought his mind back to the task at hand. What were the consequences of entering a hotel and murdering a man and his wife? Death for the man and his wife. Orphaned children. A prison sentence for the killer.

What were the consequences of allowing this man and his wife to live? Death for Kelly and Matthew.

He was in a black hole from which there was no escape. But blackness was familiar territory to him, wasn't it? A pang of sorrow stabbed him. There was something about blackness that made him want to cry.

Carl ran faster now, weaving through the trees, pushing back the emotions that flogged him, and doing so quite easily. When the blackness encroached, he focused on a single pinprick of light at the end of the tunnel, because only there, in the light, could he find the strength to hold the darkness at bay.

He had no way to know with any certainty when the hour he'd been given would expire, but time was now irrelevant. He possessed limits and he would push himself to those limits. Any distraction caused by worry or fear would only interfere with his success.

He crested a gentle hill outside the forest roughly fifteen minutes into the run. He pulled up behind a tree, panting. There was the town. Only one neighborhood in his line of sight contained multi-story buildings—the Andrassy would be there. After a quick scan of the country leading to the town, he angled for the buildings at a jog, slower now, senses keen.

His shirttail hid the gun at his waist, but nothing else about him would be so easily hidden once he encountered people. Was Kelly right? Were they really in Hungary? He didn't speak Hungarian but doubted he looked much different from any ordinary Hungarian. On the other hand, he was sweating from a hard run and his neck was wrapped in a bright bandanna—these facts wouldn't go unnoticed.

The hotel was heavily guarded, Englishman had said. How could Carl possibly race into a completely foreign town, barge into a well-guarded hotel, shoot two possible innocents, and expect any good to come of it?

Images of Kelly flooded his mind. She was strapped to the bed, right femur shattered, face stained with tears, praying desperately for him to save her. And Matthew . . .

He ran past farming lots that bordered the blacktop entering the town from his angle of approach; past people milking a cow, raking straw, riding a bicycle, kicking a soccer ball. He ignored them all and jogged.

How empty his mind was. How vacant. How hopeless. How disconnected from the details swimming around him, though he noticed everything.

He slowed to a fast walk when he reached the edge of town and searched for a hotel matching Englishman's description.

None. No hotel at all. And time was running low.

Carl flagged the rider of an old black Schwinn bicycle and spoke quickly when the older man's blue eyes fixed on him. "Andrassy Hotel?"

The man put his feet down to balance himself, looked Carl over once, and then pointed toward the west, spouting something in Hungarian.

Carl nodded and ran west. On each side of the asphalt ribbon, people stopped to watch him. Clearly, he looked like more than a commoner out for an afternoon jog. But unless they represented an immediate threat, he would ignore them. For the moment they were only curious.

Assault has three allies: speed, surprise, and power. Carl didn't have the power to overwhelm more than a few guards. Speed and surprise, on the other hand, could work for him, assuming he was unexpected.

The Andrassy was a square four-story building constructed out of red brick. A Hungarian flag flapped lazily on a pole jutting out from the wall above large revolving doors. Two long black Mercedes waited in the circular drive—possibly part of the guard.

Carl veered toward the back of the hotel. A large garbage bin smelled of rotting vegetables. The kitchen was nearby.

He bounded over three metal steps and tried a gray metal door. Unlocked. He pushed it open, stepped into a dim hallway, and pulled the door shut behind him.

He followed the sound of clattering dishes down the cluttered hall and through a doorway ten paces ahead on his right. He grabbed an apron from a laundry bin against the wall and wiped the sweat from his face. He slipped into the apron. Barely there long enough to answer a casual glance from a passing employee.

It was all about speed now.

If he was right, there would be a service elevator nearby. If he was right, there would be guards posted outside the third-floor room that held the targets. If he was right, he had roughly ten minutes to kill and run.

Carl took deep breaths, calming his heart and lungs. The soft *ding* of an elevator bell confirmed his first guess.

Kill and run. Somewhere deep in the black places of his mind, a voice objected, echoing faintly, but his mind refused to focus on that voice. His mind was on the killings because the killings would save his wife and son.

There were two ways to the third floor. The first required stealth—assuming a server's identity on a mission to deliver room service, perhaps. He dismissed this idea because it was predictable, thus undermining his greatest allies, speed and surprise.

The second approach was far bolder and therefore less predictable.

Carl breathed deeply through his nostrils and closed his eyes. He'd been here before, hadn't he? He couldn't remember where or why, but he was in familiar territory.

Unless the guards were exceptional, they would hesitate before shooting an unarmed man who approached them.

There were towels in the laundry basket. Carl quickly pulled off his shoes, socks, apron, bandanna, and shirt, pushing them behind the laundry bin. With a flip of his fingers, he unsnapped his cargo pants, let them fall around his ankles, and tied the pistol to his thigh using the bandanna. He pulled his pants back up and rolled up the legs to just below his knees.

Bare feet, bare legs, bare chest, bare back—no sign of a weapon, even to a trained eye.

Satisfied, he draped a large white towel over his head and around his neck so that it covered the blood at the back of his neck and fell over his chest on either side. A man who'd just come from a swim or a shower. Unusual to be found walking through a hotel, particularly one that didn't have a pool, which he suspected to be the case here, but not so unusual as to cause alarm. He had taken a shower upstairs, come down on a quick errand, and was headed back to his room.

Carl grabbed the towel on each side, strolled down the hall, and walked into the open, whistling a nondescript tune.

LASZLO KALMAN drummed his thin fingers on the table, a habit that annoyed Agotha more than she cared to admit. His uncut nails made a clicking sound like a rat running across a wooden floor. They were all firmly in this man's grasp: she as much as his killers.

Agotha loved and hated him. Kalman could not be defined easily, only because he refused to explain himself. But then, evil rarely did explain itself.

Still, she could not ignore her attraction to the raw power that accompanied Kalman's exceptional lust for death. He feared nothing except his own creations, killers who could slay a man with as little feeling as he himself possessed.

Of all his understudies, Englishman was the one he feared most, although soon enough Carl might surpass even Englishman, a fact that wasn't lost on anyone. It was this tenuous nature of the game that brought Kalman satisfaction, not the millions of Euros this X Group of his was paid for its assassins' skills.

"How much time?" Kalman asked.

Agotha glanced at the wall clock behind them. "Thirty-five minutes. Perhaps I should call Englishman."

"He knows the price of failure."

"And if he does fail? We've come so far."

Agotha rarely got involved in any of the operations directly. Her place was here, in the compound's hospital. But now they were on the verge of something that even she struggled to understand.

"Englishman won't fail," Laszlo said.

"I was speaking of Carl."

Laszlo hesitated. "That's your department. I don't care either way."

Agotha bit her lower lip. To fail now would be a terrible setback. The shooting of two people was all that stood in the way. Correction: the shooting of two people by this one man who had been meticulously selected and trained was all that stood in the way.

"There's something different about Carl," she said.

Kalman looked at her without emotion. Without comment.

He returned his gaze to the monitor and resumed clicking his finger-nails on the wood.

CHAPTER THREE

CARL STROLLED toward the service elevator in bare feet, hoping that his wet bangs looked like the work of a shower rather than a hard run. In the event he raised an alarm prematurely, he would resort to force.

He'd timed his approach by the elevator's bell, but by the time he caught sight of it, the door was already closing. Empty or not, he didn't know.

At least a dozen people were staring his way from the main lobby on the right. Casual stares, curious stares. For the moment.

Carl stopped his whistling and ran for the door—a man hurrying to catch an elevator. The towel slipped off his neck and fell to the ground. He reached the elevator call button, gave it a quick hit with his palm, and reached back for the towel as the door slid open.

The car was empty. Good.

He stepped in, pushed the button for the fourth floor, and resumed his whistling. The door slid closed, and he shut his eyes to calm his nerves.

Who are you, Carl?

He didn't know precisely who he was, did he? He knew his name. Scattered details of a dark past. He knew that Kelly was his wife and that Matthew was his son, and he knew that he would give his life for them if he needed to.

But why was his past so foggy? Who were his captors? Why had they chosen him to do their killing? Whatever they'd done to his head was more profound than a mere drug-induced effect.

He grunted and shoved the questions aside.

Do you believe?

"I believe," he said softly.

What do you believe?

"I believe that I will kill these two to save my wife and son."

Belief. Something about belief mattered greatly.

The elevator bell clanged.

He stepped onto the fourth floor, reached back into the elevator, pushed the button for the third floor, and was running toward the stairwell at the end of the hall before the elevator doors closed.

Despite the absence of specific memories, he seemed to be able to access whatever information he needed for this killing business from a vast pool of knowledge without a second thought. For example, the basic fact that going to a target's floor by elevator was unwise on two counts: First, because all eyes watching the elevator call numbers above the doors on any floor would know where it stopped. Second, because the elevator's arrival was almost always preceded by a bell, which would naturally warn any posted guard.

Better to take the stairs or the elevator to a different floor. Carl had chosen the elevator because that's what would be expected of a nutty tourist who'd gone down to the lobby for a candy bar or something after a shower.

These kinds of techniques didn't require any thought on his part. His training in the Special Forces had clearly become instinctive.

Carl ran down the stairs, pulled up by the third-floor access door, and waited for the sound of the elevator bell, heart pounding. This was it.

Kill and run. *What am I doing?*

The bell sounded. He pushed the door open and stepped into the third-floor hall.

Two guards dressed in dark suits stood across the hall, twenty yards down. Neither sported a weapon. Their heads were turned away from him, toward the elevator.

He hurried toward them, covered half the distance before the closest guard turned his way.

Carl cried out in pain, doubled over, and grabbed his right foot. Without hesitation, he inserted his thumb between his second and third toes and dug his nail into the skin with enough force to draw blood.

He pulled his hand away, red with a streak of blood.

The guard demanded something of him in Hungarian.

Carl ignored him. Examined his foot, feigning shock. Muttered loudly.

Another question, this one from the second guard.

He gave them a quizzical look. Both had their eyes on his foot. He hobbled toward them. "Sorry. Sorry, I just . . ."

Carl was three paces from them when one of the guards reached under his jacket. Carl took two fast strides, smashed his left palm under the closest guard's chin while stepping past him. The second guard had pulled a pistol clear of his coat when Carl's right fist slammed into the man's gun hand. Using his momentum, Carl propelled his head into the guard's chin.

No one else dies, Englishman had said.

The first guard slumped, unconscious, hopefully not dead. The second stood dazed. Carl grabbed a fistful of hair and jerked the man's head into his rising knee.

The man grunted and dropped like a sack of coal. Carl broke his fall with his right leg. The tussle may have been heard inside, but he couldn't change that now.

One of the two should have a key card to gain access to the room if needed. He quickly searched both men, found the card in the second guard's jacket.

Hall still clear.

No need for the Makarov tied to his leg. Carl retrieved both of the guards' guns, shoved one behind his back and checked the other for a chambered cartridge, slipped the key card into its slot, and twisted the knob when a green light indicated he'd successfully unlocked the door.

He stepped into the room, gun extended.

THE ABSENCE of a bed indicated that the room Joseph and Mary Fabin had rented was a suite. He'd been prepared to shoot from the threshold if necessary—time was running short and there was a chance the guards would regain consciousness soon.

He stepped into the room, gun still leading.

That distant voice in his head was asking him questions—such as whether he should reconsider shooting two people in cold blood, challenging how he could do this without considerable turmoil. He shut the voice down.

Two doors led out of the room, one on each side. Voices from the one on the left. He broke toward the left, turned the door handle slowly, and then crashed through with enough force to bury the doorknob in the wall plaster.

A black-haired Caucasian with gray bangs and sideburns sat across a table from a lanky woman with straight blond hair rolled into a bun. They looked at him, not surprised. He hesitated, thrown off by their calm demeanor. Carl knew the look of a man about to die. This wasn't it.

"Hello, Peter," the man said.

No head shots. Carl leveled the gun at the man who'd spoken. "Joseph and Mary Fabin?"

"Yes," the woman said. "Please lower the weapon, Peter."

American accent. No fear, only calm resolve. The man and woman had been expecting him. And they both called him Peter, not Carl. On their own, neither of these facts would have kept Carl from squeezing the trigger. Together, they presented an obstacle that distracted him from the light at the end of his tunnel, from killing and running and saving his wife and his son.

Joseph Fabin stood. "They told you your name was Carl Strople, am I correct?"

One hour. Kelly's and Matthew's lives hung in the balance, and he was standing here contemplating nonsense from an American who should be dead by now.

Carl didn't answer.

"But your name isn't Carl. It's Peter Marker. You were an independent contractor for the CIA before you went missing two years ago. It seems that you have more stored up in that mind of yours than the agency is willing to surrender."

Carl doubted he had more than twenty minutes left.

"Remove your jacket," he said to Joseph.

Fabin's eyes narrowed barely, but after thinking his situation through, he peeled off his jacket.

"I have something I think you should hear," Joseph said. He reached into his jacket, which now lay over his right arm. "May I?"

Carl hesitated.

Joseph pulled out a small black tape recorder, tossed the jacket on the couch to his right, and pressed the Play button. A woman's voice spoke through a light static.

"Peter, it's Kelly. I'm begging you, please come home to us. Matthew cries at night . . ." Her voice trailed off, then came back stronger. "I don't care what they've done to you, you hear? I need you, Matthew needs you. Please, I'm begging you. I'm making this recording for a Mr. Joseph Fabin with the CIA. Please come home with him, Peter. If you can hear me, please."

Fabin turned the tape off. "Do you recognize her voice?"

The room faded for a brief moment, then sprang back into focus. Was it Kelly? He couldn't tell. Impossible! Kelly had been bound by his side today! He'd seen her eyes and known the truth.

"It's your wife," Mary said. "I talked to her this morning by phone in Brussels, where you were stationed. Two years is a long time. Longer than I would wait for a missing husband. She obviously loves you. Our orders are to take you home."

"I saw my wife less than an hour ago," Carl said.

"Whoever you saw an hour ago wasn't Kelly. Impossible, my friend. Kelly is in Brussels."

"How did you know I would be coming here? If you're with the CIA, why the guard outside?"

Joseph studied him for several seconds, then sighed and sat back down. "Have a seat, Peter." He indicated a third chair.

Confusion swarmed Carl, but he refused to let the light at the end of the tunnel wink out. His palms had gone sweaty and his tongue was dry and his heart was pounding, but he forced his mind to the point.

The hour was expiring. Even if he left now, he would have trouble returning to the compound in time.

"Fine, stand. But lower the weapon. Really, Peter."

Send the bullet. Send it now.

"We've been closing in on a highly specialized underground operation known only as the X Group, which was founded by a man named Laszlo Kalman," the man said. "They have been known to kidnap government operatives, agents, even military regulars who fit a certain profile, strip their minds of memories and identities, and then retrain them as assassins. You were sighted six days ago after a two-year absence, which explains the tape recording."

Carl hit a wall. He knew he was faced with a decision that couldn't wait more than a few seconds. Either the woman who'd been strapped down beside him had been lying and wasn't his wife, or the man before him was lying.

"We know everything, Peter. We know you were sent to kill us, and we let you come because we know something that neither you nor Kalman could possibly—"

Carl shot the man in the chest.

Joseph Fabin grunted and grabbed at a red hole in his shirt. Carl swiveled the gun to the woman. His slug knocked her clean off her chair, like a mule kick to the gut. They both hit the ground at the same time, only because the man's fall had been stalled by his chair.

The sound of his gunshots lingered, chased by a high-pitched whine in his ears.

He didn't know who Joseph and Mary Fabin were, but he knew they were lying. Not because they'd slipped up, but because he knew that the woman who'd looked into his soul while they were strapped to a bed back at the compound was the woman he loved.

He'd come to save Kelly and Matthew, and their lives depended on his ability to kill these two and return within the hour. Carl hurried to the couch, slipped into Joseph Fabin's jacket, and headed out.

The killing had been a strangely emotionless affair. That was the last analytical thought that Carl allowed himself before running from the room. He stopped long enough outside the door to return the guards' guns and pull the Makarov from his thigh.

No sign that anyone had heard the shots. He sprinted to the stairs and descended quickly, shoving the Makarov into the waistband at his back.

Carl exited the stairwell and walked directly toward the kitchen, nodding once to a maid who watched him casually. Still no pursuit.

Shoes. He needed his shoes for the run. He snatched them from behind the laundry bin and stepped out into the sunshine.

A thin layer of sweat coated his body, and the base of his skull throbbed with pain. These he could deal with easily enough. But he required more than mental strength to reach the compound in time to save Kelly.

He shrugged out of the jacket and donned his shoes. For a moment he felt panic edge into his nerves. He wasn't going to make it, was he? *And what if the man I just killed was speaking the truth?* The thought fueled his panic, but just as he had done a dozen times in the last hour, he shut the emotion out.

When Carl stood from tying his shoes, his hands were shaking. He could actually see them quivering in the afternoon light, as if connected to a circuit that had been thrown. The sight didn't correlate with his thin reality. There was more, so much more to what was happening to him than this mission revealed. Somewhere deep below his consciousness, the voice protested.

Carl clenched his hands to still the tremor, turned north, and ran toward the light at the end of the tunnel.

HE DIDN'T know how long he'd been running. Every nerve, every muscle, every brain wave was focused on reaching that light as fast as humanly possible.

He tapped reservoirs of strength that exceeded reasonable ability. Deep in the blackness of his own mind, he found a place of power. He knew because he'd been there before.

The realization gave him some warmth. Hope. Whoever he was, Kelly would help him understand. He'd looked into her eyes and seen love. And Matthew . . .

The thought of his son filled him with an unexpected burst of love and energy. He whispered Matthew's name as he ran.

To his surprise, the emotion grew until he thought he might cry. He was still running, but his focus had been shattered and his vision blurred. Allowing himself to feel this kind of love for his son was intoxicating—like a drug equally pleasing and destructive.

He caught himself, steeled his mind against the destructive power of the emotion, and refocused on the tunnel.

The compound looked vacated when Carl crested the hill that hid it. But it wasn't. The buildings were all there, hiding their secrets, like Jonestown in the jungles of Guyana.

He sprinted toward the building that had held Kelly. The window he'd climbed from an hour ago was still open, as if it, too, had been abandoned. He reached it and pulled up, panting hard.

The bed was there, red nylon cords cut and dangling from the metal frame. Kelly was not.

Carl dove through the window, smashing his knee in the process. He landed on the floor.

"Kelly?"

Only his hard breathing answered him. He was too late!

The tremble returned to his hands and spread to his whole body. For the briefest of moments, he felt shame, not for failing Kelly, but for being overcome. He staggered to his feet and let a new emotion crowd his mind. Anger. Rage.

"Kelly! Where is my wife?"

He was wheezing. Standing with fists tight, wheezing like a . . .

Sssss . . .

Carl spun to his right. A translucent vapor hissed from a small hole in the wall. They were gassing him. He knew this because he'd been gassed before. And he also knew that it was too late to run from it. He would pass out in less than five seconds, no matter what he did, or where he went.

Kelly is alive.

It was his last thought before he fell.

CHAPTER FOUR

"CARL?"

The sound of her distant voice came to him like an angel.

"Carl."

His mind began to clear. How many times had he awakened with the sound of an angel in his ear? This time Kelly was here, which meant that . . .

Kelly?

Carl opened his eyes. He was on a hospital bed with the bright round lamps above him and the large humming machines on each side. But he wasn't restrained.

He sat up.

"Hello, Carl."

He turned to the voice and saw a familiar man. Tall, thin, dark hair that was graying on the sides. Bushy eyebrows. Did he know this man? Yes. This was Kalman. Laszlo Kalman.

Beside him stood the doctor. Agotha Balogh. She wore a white smock over a blue dress and held a cup of tea, which she now set down on the counter.

"Hello, Carl."

Carl looked to his right. Kelly leaned against the counter, arms crossed, smiling. There was no sign of any injury on her leg where he'd seen Englishman shoot her. She wore black dungarees, much like his own. A brown cotton turtleneck.

"Welcome home," she said.

His first impulse was relief. Sweet, sweet relief. Enough to make him feel weak. His wife was safe.

But why no wound?

"Kelly?"

"Yes. Kelly." Her eyes flashed blue like the sea. She stepped away from the counter. "You did well. I'm very proud of you."

Carl stared at her leg. It supported her without any sign of weakness. *How . . . ?*

He looked into her eyes, suddenly terrified by confusion. "Is Matthew—"

"You have no son," Kalman said. "Kelly is not your wife."

Familiar voices screamed through his mind, but he couldn't make out what they were saying. He'd been here before, but he didn't know where *here* was.

Had he killed two people in the Andrassy Hotel, or was that all part of an elaborate dream? He lifted his hand to the back of his head and felt the small cut at the base of his skull. Real. He wiggled his toes and felt the small pain of the wound between them. Real.

Kelly stepped closer and stopped five feet from him, still looking into his eyes with pride. Still smiling.

"The drugs are still in your system, but they'll wear off. You did very well this time, Carl. I knew you could do it."

Did he love this woman? Or was that a deception?

Agotha spoke with a distinct Hungarian accent. "Your name is Carl Strople. Do you remember?"

He hesitated. "Yes."

"You've been in training here for nearly a year. The mission you just completed was your tenth of twelve before we put you into the field. Do you remember?"

Now that she'd said it, he did. Not the missions specifically, but the fact that he had been here a long time. Training. His mind was still on Kelly. What did she mean to him? What had he done for her?

He couldn't think clearly enough to ask, much less answer, the questions.

"We call you Saint," Agotha said.

The name ignited a light in Carl's mind. He blinked. Saint. He'd been covertly recruited for Black Ops and given his life to the most brutal kind of training any man or woman could endure. He was here because he belonged here. To the X Group.

"You remember?"

"I remember."

"Good," Agotha said. "The mission you just executed was an important test of your skills. You must forgive us for deceiving you, but it was necessary to test your progress. Naturally, Englishman didn't actually shoot Kelly in her leg. It was only made to look like he did. The two people you shot at the Andrassy wore vests with pockets of red dye. The woman suffered a broken rib, but otherwise they are quite alive."

Carl stared at her, stupefied. *No head shots. No one else may be killed.* The whole mission was a setup.

"You performed exceptionally well," Agotha said. "We are proud of you."

"Thank you." He lowered his eyes and rubbed his fingers, trying to fill in a thousand blanks. But he couldn't. "Why can't I remember?"

Agotha nodded once, slowly, as if she had expected this question. "Our training is invasive. We train the mind as much as we train the body. You knew this when you agreed to the Group's terms. It was what you wanted. And you have proven that our techniques produce results. And rewards. You are important to your country, Carl."

"Which country?"

"The United States."

Kalman seemed satisfied to study Carl with a dark stare. There was something about him that struck Carl as obscene. But in a good way, perhaps.

Carl held Kalman's gaze for a long time, trying to understand his confusion. But he was trained not to trust his feelings, wasn't he? He was, in fact, trained to *control* his feelings by shutting them down entirely.

He didn't know how he felt about Laszlo Kalman.

Or Kelly, for that matter.

"The implant is real?" he asked Agotha.

"Yes. You've had it for many months. It is our way of tracking you."

"Or terminating you," Kalman said.

So Englishman had spoken the truth on that count. Carl avoided Kelly's eyes. For some reason she alone was able to penetrate his emotional guard.

Agotha frowned at Kalman. "We made a small incision this morning to create the impression that it was recently inserted."

"I'm being trained as an assassin," he said.

"You already are one. But you're much more than just an assassin. Only seven of more than a hundred recruits have ever finished all twelve training missions and entered the field."

"The rest?"

"Are dead," Kalman said.

Carl remembered that now. He was quite sure he'd asked these same questions dozens of times.

"As you will be if you fail."

"You kill your own recruits?"

"Only when they fail. We all die."

Maybe this was why he found Kalman obscene. But he didn't think so—deep down he understood what the dark man said.

"You'll spend two days in regression before your next training exercise," Kalman said. He walked toward the door. "Take him to his quarters." The director of the X Group left him with Agotha and Kelly, whose eyes he still avoided.

Agotha put her hand on his shoulder. She seemed enthralled by him, a scientist examining her prize specimen.

"I knew you could do it," she said. "One day you may be stronger than Englishman."

Agotha glanced at Kelly, then walked out of the room.

"You're upset with me," Kelly said.

"Am I?"

"Yes, you are."

Carl looked at her. "I'm confused. I'm not quite sure who I am. Or, for that matter, who you are."

"Then I'll tell you who we are."

She stepped up to him and reached out her hand. He took it only because she offered it in such a way that suggested she'd done so many times before.

Kelly led him from the room into a long, familiar concrete hall, offering no explanation of who either of them was.

His thoughts returned to the outburst of love he'd felt when he heard his son's name. Matthew. Even now the name pulled at his heart. How could that be, if it was only a name?

"I don't have a son named Matthew."

"No. But we helped you believe that you did for the sake of this test. You acted under that pretense and you did precisely as you should have done. I'm very pleased."

They walked through a door at the hall's end, onto a cement landing, then down five concrete steps that led to browned grass. She waited until they were twenty yards away from the building before speaking again.

"We have recording devices in all the buildings. I wanted to speak to you without being heard. I'm sorry for the confusion, Carl. I really am. Every time they do this to you, you forget that you can trust me."

How could he answer that? She'd lied to him; he could never trust her. And yet he knew already that he not only wanted to trust her but would.

"What I did was horrible," she continued. "I laid next to you and convinced you that I was your wife. That we had a child. Terrible, yes, but I did it for you." Her grip on his hand momentarily tightened. "You have to succeed, Carl. My greatest gift to you today was convincing you beyond any shadow of a doubt that you loved me and would do anything for me, including shooting two people who offered you a plausible alternate truth. If you failed to show complete loyalty to the set of facts you were fed, you would be dead now, and I couldn't live with that."

She looked at the forest, jaw clenched.

Carl's confusion lifted like a fog before the sun. He'd been here before, too, which only made sense. He was undoubtedly practiced at stepping out of the fog when presented with the right information.

In that moment, Carl heard the sincerity in her voice and knew that Kelly had done precisely what she said she'd done. She'd saved his life. There was a bond between them, which explained the emotions he'd allowed himself when he looked into her eyes as they laid tied to the bed.

"I'm sorry," he said. "It's just . . ." He didn't know what to say.

"Confusing," Kelly said for him. "Their invasive techniques are designed to strip you of your identity and reshape you. They spent three days force-feeding you the fabricated memories prior to this last test. Now they've taken those memories from you with a simple injection. They've trained your mind to respond to their manipulation. But there are some things they can't take from you. Trusting me is one of them. Remember that, Carl. Please remember that."

"I will." He swallowed, unsure how he felt about anything, including the woman who led him across the browned field toward the bunkhouse.

Familiar. The bunkhouse made his stomach turn, but such an emotional reaction was unreliable. "Tell me who I am."

"You're Carl Strople. Also known as Saint. Your memory has been stripped and reconstructed many times, and each time it becomes more difficult for you to remember who you really are. I won't bore you with the science behind it, but it's based on the relationship between memory and emotion that every human experiences. Here, a normal lifelong process is compacted into days, weeks, and months."

"But *who* am I?"

"You were in the United States Army, Special Forces, when you were recruited for this assignment. You've never been married and have no children. When you first came to the X Group, a man named Charles was your handler. He was terminated and they gave you to me."

"Why are you here?" he asked.

Kelly hesitated, then answered in a distant voice. "Because I survived the training just like you."

"Then you're what they made you?"

Another break. "I suppose. I won't be deployed in the field. I'm here to help you make it in the field."

"This is all an elaborate extension of the Special Forces? Why in Hungary?"

As soon as he'd asked the question, the answer came to him from his own memory. He answered himself.

"Black Ops. No one in the United States government has officially approved of these operations."

"You're remembering. Good. And you'll quickly remember that Englishman is the most dangerous person in this compound, perhaps more than Kalman. You won't see much of him, but he's stronger than you. Be careful around him. Play by the rules and I'll make sure you survive."

"I can't remember who my father is," he said.

She didn't answer.

"Or my mother."

Still no answer.

They walked up to the bunkhouse. It was made of concrete blocks with a single door. This was his home. The darkness inside, under the first floor, was bittersweet to him. He remembered. Once bitter, now sweet.

Kelly walked up to the door and pulled it open. "Do you remember your specialties?"

Carl followed her into an empty building with a concrete floor. A stairwell descended to their right. Kelly walked toward it.

He stopped and stared at the concrete steps. "I can walk into a dark tunnel," he said. "Nothing will hurt me."

She reached the rail and turned back. Their eyes met. "Yes, you have a strong mind. Stronger than you think. Are you coming?"

He stepped after her, focusing anew. Shutting down his uncertainties. Once bitter, now sweet. He had to remember that it was now sweet, or he might be tempted to think it was still bitter.

"What else?" she asked, walking down the steps.

Carl followed. "I can kill with almost anything. But I am first a sniper."

"Not just a sniper. You can handle a rifle like no one in recorded history. Do you remember?"

Her voice echoed in the narrow cement stairwell. She unlocked a metal door at the base and pushed it open. It was cool down here. Damp but not wet. The musty smell of undisturbed earth filled his nostrils. He walked through the door into a long tunnel lit by a single caged incandescent bulb.

"It's okay," she said, reaching back for him. "I've been here too."

He took her hand and walked beside her, deeper into the tunnel.

His fingers began to tremble, so he squeezed her hand tighter. She let him walk without speaking now. This journey to the pit was always a quiet one. Bittersweet, but sweet now. Lingering ghosts that had once been memories tried to haunt him, but he refused to succumb to their power.

They walked past two gray metal doors, one on the left and one on the right. The door on their right led to the training room, which featured a large sensory-deprivation tank that they'd used many times in his early training. When they lowered him into the warm salted water with headgear that masked his sight and hearing, he floated weightless without sensory perception, left only to the dark spaces of his mind. Terrible, beautiful, comforting, lost. But in the end he always found himself.

The other room had a small kitchen, a refrigerator, a shower, and a hard bunk without a mattress. When he wasn't in the pit, he slept and ate here.

The hall took a sharp right turn, then descended one more flight of stairs into the pit. They called it the pit, but it was really just a small, square concrete room with black walls. A single metal chair was bolted to the floor in the center of the room. There was a small metal door to an access tunnel at the back of the cell, but it was always locked. No other features.

No lights.

He paused at the open door, then stepped in, walked to the chair, and turned around.

Kelly stood by the door, staring at him. If he wasn't mistaken, she looked sad. She didn't like his being here. Why not? It was what he needed to succeed. And it wasn't nearly as bad as the hospital bed or the electricity.

They controlled the temperature of the room by heating or cooling the floor. He was forced to spend most of his time in the chair with his feet off the floor. The only way to survive the extended periods of time was to sleep sitting in extreme temperatures, something he could do only with considerable focus.

They monitored his vital signs with remote sensors.

"How long will I be here?"

"Two days."

He slipped off his shoes. Tossed them to the floor by her feet. She picked them up by the laces and tossed them onto the steps behind her.

"And then more training?" he asked.

"Yes. I want you to forget everything that happened at the Andrassy."

He nodded. They stared at each other for a few seconds.

"Be strong, Carl. You have to make it. We're almost done. I'm so proud of you. You know that, don't you?"

"Yes."

"They'll try to break you this last month. Promise me you won't break."

"I won't break."

"I think that you'll change the world. They have something very special in mind for you. All of this will soon make sense."

"It already does," he said. "Why are you helping me?"

Kelly walked into the room, put her right hand on his chest, and kissed him gently on the lips. "Maybe this will help you remember," she said.

Then she walked out and shut the door behind her. An electronically triggered bolt slammed into place. Familiar silence settled. He couldn't hear her ascending the stairs.

Carl stood with one hand on the chair, staring at the blackness. It made no difference in here whether he had his eyes open or closed. The darkness was like a pool of black ink.

He stood without moving for a long time, at least an hour. The questions that had plagued him up in the light no longer mattered. He'd spent countless hours asking those questions and never received answers, only frayed emotions, which he could not afford.

The only way to survive for Kelly was to shut down.

The floor began to cool, and he knew it would soon be covered in ice. He climbed onto the chair and sat cross-legged.

It was time to enter the safe tunnel in his mind.

CHAPTER FIVE

THE PRESIDENT of the United States walked along the long book-case in his office at Camp David and ran a finger along the leather-bound titles. How many presidents before him had added volumes to this collection? It contained the expected law books, history books, countless classics. But it was the eclectic mix of fiction that intrigued him most.

Stephen King. Which president had taken the time to read Stephen King? Or had *The Stand* simply been placed on the book-shelf unread? Dean Koontz, John Grisham, James Patterson. A book called *This Present Darkness* by Frank Peretti. He had heard the name.

Behind him, Secretary of State Calvin Bromley cleared his throat. "I think it's a mistake to underestimate the polls, Mr. President. The country isn't where it was ten years ago."

"Robert, Calvin. My name is Robert Stenton. If I've learned any-thing from my son, it's that even presidents have to be real." He faced the two men seated in the overstuffed leather chairs flanking the cof-fee table. "I feel more like a real person when my friends use my given name in private."

"And when will you feel the realness of being the leader of the free world?" David Abraham asked, stroking his white beard.

The president frowned, then cracked a grin. "Give me time. I've only been at this for a year." He walked to the couch and sighed. "I know the polls are leaning toward the Iranian defense minister's proposal to disarm Israel, but I can't ignore the fact that it goes against every bit of good sense I've ever had."

"Mr. Feroz's proposal makes some strategic sense," Bromley said. "I'm not counseling you to throw in the towel, but more than a few nations are backing this initiative. I think the American people see what the rest of the world is seeing—a plausible scenario for real peace in the region. And you are the people's president."

Robert looked at the secretary of state. Calvin Bromley, graduate of Harvard, two years his elder, but they'd known each other through the track-and-field program. The large Scandinavian man's blond hair was now graying, and he'd put on a good fifty pounds in the last thirty years, but his clear blue eyes glinted with the same determination that had served him so well throughout his career.

All three were Harvard men. David Abraham, retired professor of history and psychology who'd taught three of Stenton's undergraduate classes, now served as a confidant, a kind of spiritual adviser. The professor had experienced a spiritual renaissance later in life and had reconnected with Robert when Robert was the governor of Arizona.

The seventy-year-old mentor sat stoically, one leg crossed over the other. David had called this meeting. The weekend had originally been scheduled as a time to unwind, but when David suggested that the secretary of state come as well, Robert dismissed the hope of rest altogether.

"You're right, Calvin, I am the people's president. The minute I put my leg over the Harley and thundered down the highway to that infamous rally in Ohio, I became the people's candidate. I don't intend to ignore them. But that doesn't mean I'm always going to agree."

"I'm only suggesting you reconsider your judgment."

"I reconsider my judgment every day of the week," the president said. "I spend half my nights wondering if I'm making the right decisions."

"Forcing Israel to disarm in exchange for the mutual disarmament of all her neighbors, assuming it all could be reasonably executed and verified, would go a long way in reducing the risk of a major conflict in the region."

"Assuming it could be executed and verified," Robert said. "And enforced. That's a significant assumption, isn't it?"

"Both the French and the Germans will aid us in enforcing the Iranian initiative, should it be approved."

"The initiative isn't officially Iranian."

"No, but it's been proposed by their minister of defense, and they are backing him. The United States is now the *only* Western nation openly opposing the plan."

"And how many Middle Eastern countries are paying lip service with no intention to disarm?"

"If they don't disarm, Israel doesn't disarm." Bromley shrugged. "The execution could stall and fade into oblivion like every other treaty signed in the Middle East. But by backing the plan, we gain considerable political capital."

The president closed his eyes and rubbed the back of his neck. There was some good logic behind the plan. Each Middle Eastern country would be allowed an army large enough to carry out regional defensive operations only. No air forces, no nuclear programs, no mechanized armies.

The United Nations would establish a full-scale nuclear defense in the region under the strict obligation to deal immediately and forcefully with any threats.

It was a bold, audacious, improbable plan that made sense only on paper. But his staff had analyzed it for nine months now, and the fact remained, it did indeed make sense on paper. The Iranian minister of defense, Assim Feroz, might be a crook to the bone, but he certainly wasn't short on intelligence.

All of Europe and Asia had provisionally endorsed the plan.

Israel had rejected the plan outright, but that only played into the hands of her enemies.

"Our alternative is to dissent along with Israel, further degrading our good standing with Europe and Asia," Bromley said.

"The Israelis will never agree."

"If we back the UN force, they may have to."

Still no comment from David Abraham. The man was biding his time. He sat in his black tweed suit, legs still crossed, one hand still rubbing his beard.

"The initiative will come to a head at the United Nations Middle Eastern summit next month," Bromley said.

David Abraham spoke quietly, but his voice was thick. "This is unacceptable. If you agree to the terms of this initiative, pain and suffering will haunt the world forever."

They stared at him in silence. David had never really concerned himself with policy—why the strong reaction now? What had prompted him to suggest the meeting in the first place? Robert gave him space.

"I'm not sure I understand," Bromley said.

"Without an army, Israel is powerless against an enemy sworn to her destruction. I don't profess to be an adviser of world politics, but I am a historian. A simple glance down the corridors of time will reveal the foolishness of any disarmament on this scale. You can forcibly disarm a country, but you can't disarm the heart. The hatred of Israel's enemies will find its own way."

"Which is why the United Nations—"

"You assume the United Nations will always have Israel's interests in mind." David lowered his hand from his beard and drilled Bromley with a stare. "Don't forget that the United Nations is made up of Israel's enemies as well as friends."

"I think the secretary's suggesting that we play ball without intending to follow through," the president said.

"Assuming that's possible. You agree one day, and the next day you are bound by your word. You must not do this, Robert. As your adviser on spiritual matters, I cannot overemphasize my strenuous objection to agreeing to this initiative."

David was now out of character. He was known to give strong opinions at times, but always with a smile and a nod. Robert couldn't recall ever seeing the man so agitated.

"You see this as a spiritual matter?" the secretary asked.

David settled back in his chair. "Isn't everything? At the risk of sounding arrogant, let me suggest that I know of things in this matter that would make no sense to either of you." He shifted his gaze to Robert. "Words can become reality, Robert. And when those words are evil, someone had better be fighting the good fight, or the world could very well be swallowed up by evil."

The president felt his heart pause. *Project Showdown.*

There was far more here than David was saying openly. The secretary's presence was now a liability.

"Could you give us a minute, Calvin?"

Bromley glanced at David, then stood. "No problem."

"Dinner's in an hour. Join us?"

"Of course, Mr. President."

"Robert."

"Right." He left without another word.

Robert and David sat in silence for a few seconds. Robert wasn't sure how to draw out his mentor. When he'd invited David to serve as his spiritual adviser, the professor's first response had been that he couldn't, not until he told the president everything.

It was then, nearly a year ago now, that David had sat down with Robert in the Oval Office and told him about Project Showdown. The story spun by this man on that day had sounded like something out of the Old Testament, a series of fantastic events of mythical proportion. Such an account made it seem as if Joshua were a real man who really had knocked over the walls of Jericho with a blast of horns. As if John's Revelation were a real possibility, in literal terms.

David had insisted that Robert know the full extent of Project Showdown, because he wasn't sure that the president of the United States would want someone with such a résumé to serve as his spiritual adviser.

At first, Robert wasn't sure either. He commissioned a private study to determine if the events described by David Abraham could possibly have happened as the man claimed. The man he'd put in charge was a proud agnostic with the FBI named Christian Larkin.

One month after receiving the assignment, Larkin had walked into Robert's office a changed man. The only copy of his report, simply titled *Showdown*, was now in Robert's closet at the White House residence.

Larkin had analyzed satellite images of Colorado, which showed some spectacular anomalies if you knew what to look for. He had conducted hundreds of interviews, analyzed the material from many of the buildings, and explored the canyon in question with ultrasonic equipment.

In the end, there was no room for doubt. Evil had indeed visited the small town of Paradise, Colorado, in a most stunning fashion twelve years earlier. What started out as a covert experiment to study the noble savage in a controlled environment had spun horribly out of control. The shocking events of Project Showdown required three hundred pages.

Robert had called David Abraham within an hour of reading Christian Larkin's full report and insisted that he fill the role of his personal spiritual adviser.

He looked at David, who was watching him, calm now.

"Okay. Tell me what's on your mind."

"I have," David said.

"You know what I mean, Father. I'm not making the connection here."

"I'm not a priest," David said. "But I appreciate your confidence in me. Can you look past the simple ways of man?"

Meaning what? Robert wasn't a man of subtleties—he never liked it when David employed them to make his points. "Don't tell me this decision I'm about to make has anything to do with what happened twelve years ago."

"Maybe yes, maybe no. But I have a feeling. I haven't had a feeling like this for twelve years. I can tell you that this Iranian defense minister, this Assim Feroz, is not where he is by accident. He will be the destruction of Israel if you allow him."

David stood and walked across the room, staring at the books. He'd always been a great lover of books. He collected them, tens of thousands of them. Some said that his was the most valuable private collection of books in the world.

"There is an evil stirring, Robert," David said behind him. "I realize you would prefer some evidence, but nothing I can tell you would satisfy your demand for plain facts. I came here to tell you and the secretary that you must not, under any circumstances, yield to Feroz."

"What do you suggest I do?"

"I suggest you pray, Robert. You do still pray, don't you? For your son?"

"More than you know."

"Then pray more. And know that Assim Feroz is your enemy." He turned and faced the president. "Have you ever heard of a man named Laszlo Kalman?"

"Doesn't ring a bell, no."

"The X Group, then?"

Robert frowned and shook his head. "No. Should I?"

"Yes, I think you should. But not from me. You should talk to the CIA."

"What does this have to do with the initiative?"

David hesitated. "I believe they're connected. I can't prove it any more than I can prove any of this has anything to do with Project Showdown, but I have a very strong feeling, Robert. A feeling I haven't had in twelve years."

"So you said."

A soft knock interrupted them. He knew that knock—two raps. It was his son, Jamie, who had carte blanche permission to join him in any unclassified meeting he wished during these last few months of his life. The doctors had given him two, but they all knew he would outlast any doctor's prognosis. He had lived eighteen years with a very mild case of Down's syndrome complicated by a congenital thyroid dysfunction that was supposed to have killed him before he turned four. Other than being short for his age, he showed no physical clue of his illness, unusual for those with Down's.

His mind was a different matter. Although Jamie was eighteen, he had the mind of a twelve-year-old.

There was nothing that Robert and Wendy, his wife, loved more about their son.

"It's Jamie," he said.

David nodded once. Smiled. He had his own affection for children, didn't he? *It's why he and Jamie have struck up such a friendship,* Robert thought.

"Come in."

The door swung open. A short boy, blond and sweet, stared at them with wide brown eyes. "Can I come in?"

"Of course. I've been expecting you."

Jamie walked in and shut the door. His one love in life was politics. He lived and breathed the business of government, which in his simple world primarily meant scanning the news channels, listening to a good three hours of talk radio each day, and sitting in on whatever meeting his father would allow him to. It didn't matter that half of it flew over his head; Jamie had a way with politics. His outlook on life gave him a unique insight into the public psyche. If Robert wanted to know how the American public felt about a certain initiative, nine times out of ten Jamie's perspective would tell him.

In ways his staff would never truly appreciate, Robert credited Jamie for his ascent from Arizona governor to president. At his son's suggestion, he'd revamped his entire campaign during the primaries, bought himself a Harley, and become the people's man from Arizona. And that was only the beginning. His wife, Wendy, had once teased him that he'd won the presidency by thinking like a twelve-year-old.

The very least he could do for his son was to allow him unfettered access to a political life that most could only dream about. He took Jamie anywhere and everywhere that he could.

Jamie looked sheepishly from his father back to David. "Heavy discussion?"

"David thinks that Assim Feroz isn't who he says he is," Robert said. "What do you think?"

"I think Feroz is a bad goat," the boy said. "I think he's lying and won't disarm anyone but Israel."

"Really?" Robert lifted a brow and smiled. "What brings you to this conclusion?"

Jamie shrugged. "I don't believe him."

David put his arm around Jamie and faced the president. "Listen to your son, Robert. For the sake of his generation, listen to Jamie."

CHAPTER SIX

DEEP IN the darkness beyond the black tunnel, a terrible enemy had gathered and was waging war against the light.

The light was a tiny pinprick at the end of the tunnel, and Carl's mind and soul were fixated on that light. Two days or maybe ten days ago—he'd lost his sense of time completely—that light had been the murder of two people in the Andrassy Hotel. But he'd extinguished that light, as Kelly had asked him to. He'd learned long ago that if he didn't obliterate certain memories, Agotha would, and he didn't favor her methods.

Now the light at the end of his tunnel was survival.

He'd learned how to ignore the darkness and focus on the light by disciplined repetition. His ability to control his mind and by extension his body was his greatest strength.

In fact, his mind, not a gun or a knife, was his greatest weapon, and his handlers had helped him learn how to wield his mind in a way that few could.

The enemy changed shape regularly. Right now it was an intense heat that threatened to suck the moisture out of his body and leave him so dehydrated that his organs might stop functioning. But if he forced his mind to accept the impression that it was cool in the room rather than hot, he could maintain his energy for an extended period of time.

He sat cross-legged on the metal chair, willing his flesh in contact with the chair to stay cool, sitting perfectly still so the rest of his skin would not be unexpectedly scalded.

He'd slowed his heart rate to fifty beats per minute to compensate for the heat in the same way that he increased his heart rate to compensate for extreme cold. He did not eat or drink or pass any waste. These were the easiest functions to control. More difficult were his emotions, which seemed predisposed to rise up in offense at such treatment. In the worst conditions, he resorted to turning his emotions to Kelly. To her blue eyes, which were pools of kindness and love. The only such pools he knew.

All of this information registered as part of his subconscious, like a program that ran in the background. The light at the end of his tunnel remained at the center of his attention. Carl was so used to the torturous conditions of his pit that he no longer thought of them as torment. They were simply the path to the light.

Agotha had asked him recently whether he thought he could ever step outside the mental tunnel. "If your tunnel protects you from threats, could you not deal with those threats offensively rather than merely defensively?" she'd asked.

"I *am* offensive," Carl replied. "My aim is to survive."

"Yes, and you achieve that aim very well. But have you ever tried to deal with the threats more directly?"

"I'm not sure what you mean."

"You ward off the heat by controlling your mind and changing the way your body reacts to it. Have you ever tried to change the heat itself?"

Was she suggesting he try to lower the room's temperature? It was absurd, and he politely told her as much.

"Is it? What if I were to tell you that it's been done?"

"How? When?"

"In many documented cases studied by science. The pH balance of water, for example, can be significantly raised or lowered strictly through focused thought. This was first published by William Tiller, PhD, in a book titled *Conscious Acts of Creation*. There have been dozens of studies by quantum physicists since. None of this fits well with the older understanding of Newtonian physics based on sub-atomic particles, but it makes sense in accepted quantum theory, in which waves of energy, not particles, form the foundation of the world we know. It is possible, Carl, to affect these waves. They are connected to your mind."

"I can push an object with my hand and make it move," he said. "I can't do that with a wave from my mind."

"Because you don't think of the wave as an object." She walked to the chalkboard and drew a dime-sized circle. "Imagine that this is an atom, one of the smallest particles we know, yes?"

He could remember this now that she said it. "Yes."

She drew an arrow to the end of the board. "If an atom were enlarged to the size of a dime, the space between it and the next closest atom would be ten miles in every direction. There are a countless number of atoms that make up your hand, correct?"

"Yes."

"But in reality, most of your hand is this empty space *between* the atoms." She tossed the chalk into its tray. "This space, which was once thought of as a true vacuum, is actually a sea of energy. This is the zero-point field, most evident at a temperature of absolute zero. But it rages with energy at all times. Does this make sense?"

"This is all proven?"

"Yes. Finding ways to predictably influence this field is where theory takes over."

The light in Agotha's eyes was infectious. She smiled. "Do you know how much energy the empty space between atoms holds?"

"No."

"A single cubic yard of this so-called empty space, this sea of raw energy known as the zero-point field, holds enough energy to boil away all of the earth's oceans."

Hard to comprehend, much less believe.

"I want you to begin thinking of ways to step past your safe walls into this sea of energy. Imagine that your mind is connected to other objects through the zero-point field, just like islands are connected to each other by the sea. Can you do that?"

The thought of going beyond the black tunnel of safety unnerved him.

"If you were to stand on your island—your mind—and send out a large wave toward another distant mountain in the sea, could you destroy that mountain? Or at least move it?"

"I suppose you could."

"With an idea the size of a mustard seed, you could move a mountain," she said. "It's all a matter of perspective. When you first tried to see the light at the end of your tunnel, what did you see?"

"I closed my eyes and saw nothing but blackness."

"And what did you feel?"

He hesitated. For some reason the memory of failure had never been stripped away. The first time they'd inserted a needle through his shoulder, he screamed until he passed out.

"Pain," he said.

"But you found a way to construct the tunnel by pushing through the blackness to the light."

"Yes."

"Maybe you should try to punch a hole in the side of the tunnel and push back the sea of heat. Change the heat, rather than just protect yourself from it. It's theoretically possible."

The discussion with Agotha had been a few days ago, perhaps a week, perhaps a year. No, it was recent, very recent. Now in the safety of his tunnel, seated on the metal chair in the very hot/cold place, Carl decided that he would try again. He'd managed to take part of his mind off the light without the tunnel collapsing around him only three or four times, but each time, finding a way beyond the black tunnel's walls had proven too difficult.

It wasn't easy to take even a fraction of his focus off the light. The light was his survival, his comfort, his life. He'd become very good at giving it his complete attention.

Splitting the mind's eye was not unlike moving his physical eyes independent of each other, something he'd learned with great difficulty as a sniper. He moved now with caution, first allowing the tunnel wall on his right to come into his field of vision while never breaking contact with the light far ahead. He gradually began to isolate features on the tunnel wall.

The process was slow but fascinating. The tunnel protected him from the heat beyond. So far so good. He lingered there for an hour or ten, growing comfortable with his divided focus.

What if he could form a second tunnel to punch through the first tunnel?

The thought took him by surprise. The light faded, and for a moment he thought the tunnel had collapsed. But it remained straight and true, and the distant pinpoint of light came back into sharp focus.

He considered this new thought. Maybe a *second* tunnel of focus could break through the walls he'd constructed.

KELLY LARINE sat at a round metal table in the main laboratory, watching the monitor as the lines of numbers ran by. Carl's vitals had held rock steady since he'd gone deep, nearly three days ago now. In terms of controlling his emotions, he was better than Englishman, who, although the more accomplished killer, seemed to have less control over his mind, which could in time make him the lesser of the two.

Then again, Englishman had appeared on the scene a full month after Carl and was already well ahead of him. He had come to them practically ready-made, which only eroded her own trust of the man. On occasion she couldn't escape the vague notion that he was far more than who he said he was. More than even Kalman or Agotha knew. A puppet master who was simply playing games here while he waited for his true purpose to reveal itself.

Laszlo Kalman fears the man, she thought.

There were never more than three assassins in the X Group at any one time. Sometimes up to a dozen were in training, but in operation, only three. At the moment only two: Dale Crompton, known as Englishman; and Jenine, the dark-skinned, soft-spoken feline from the Ukraine. Neither of them had the same control over their emotions as Carl, but both more than compensated with skill and determination.

All three had full control of their vitals and had developed nearly inhuman thresholds for pain, although how Englishman and the Ukrainian managed so well without mastery over emotion was still a bit of a mystery to Kelly.

On the other hand, maybe their achievements weren't really that much of a mystery. The training methods perfected by Agotha were all founded on a guiding principle that had yet to fail: the appropriation of identity. The assassins thought they were surrendering their memories, but Agotha wasn't concerned with erasing memory as much as erasing identity.

Identity was the linchpin.

Commandeering a person's identity allowed Agotha to manipulate the memories associated with who a person was and what he had done without compromising his knowledge of how things worked. How to operate a car, for example, or brush teeth, or kill a man in the most effective way depending on the circumstance.

Agotha Balogh wore the same yellow dress she so often wore, always half-covered by a white lab apron. At the moment she was calibrating the powerful spinning magnets that she used in conjunction with powerful drugs to rewrite the identities. The machine was a common MRI machine, the kind found at any decent hospital, but its magnets had been adjusted to Agotha's specifications. The drugs she'd been testing for the last decade, however, were evidently nothing so common.

Everything about the X Group was extraordinary, from the operatives they'd managed to sequester away in the hills of Hungary, to their incredible success rate, to the highly controversial techniques they used to train, to the personalities at the helm. Kalman. Agotha. And now she could add her name to that list. Kelly.

"No change?" Agotha asked.

It was a rhetorical question, to add some noise to the room. "None," Kelly said. They returned to silence.

Kalman. Kelly knew little more than what Agotha had told her about his background. He'd killed his first man when he was eight. The dead bodies in his wake could not be counted, Agotha had said. Somewhere along the line he'd become convinced that the mind was man's most powerful weapon, not a gun. His interest in manipulating the mind had started when he met Agotha at the University of Newcastle in the UK.

"What is this?"

Kelly looked at Agotha, who was staring at the monitor. She glanced back at Carl's vitals.

"What's what?"

"His heart rate," Agotha said.

Kelly saw the numbers blinking on the screen. Saint's heart rate had risen from roughly fifty beats per minute to ninety. They stared, caught off guard by the sudden change.

"How long?" Agotha asked. "Were you watching?"

"It was fifty less than five minutes ago. It's been fifty since I came in half an hour ago. Did you check the logs from the last twenty-four hours?"

"Yes. He's been static for more than forty-eight hours. Something's happened." Agotha hurried over to the computer and punched up his record. "Less than a minute ago. The rest of the indicators are steady."

Carl's pulse steadied at ninety-one beats per minute. Kelly watched for thirty seconds. The rate changed again.

"It's dropping."

"So it is."

"What do you think caused that?" Kelly asked.

Agotha watched as Carl's heart rate fell to sixty, then hold steady.

"We're not dealing with the known here," Agotha said. "It's amazing enough that Carl can alter his vitals as easily as he does."

"A simple break in concentration could be enough to cause this."

"True, but he's not given to simple breaks. I would guess that it was emotionally induced. Controlling the receptor cells' ability to receive peptides in response to various stimuli is practically unheard of. Carl is the first candidate we've had who's demonstrated a capability to do this."

The chemical reactions of emotions were one of Agotha's primary areas of research. Because emotions were in essence chemical reactions in the brain, science had long accepted the fact that it was possible to manipulate the chemicals and therefore the emotions. A number of drugs on the market did this. But for a person to exercise control over his brain's chemicals was a different matter.

"You know that he's progressed in other areas," Agotha said.

"Such as?"

"His marksmanship. You know that he's matched the limits of ballistics accuracy out to two thousand yards. He placed ten consecutive rounds within a twelve-inch grouping at one and a half miles. According to all conventional knowledge, Saint can't possibly improve. The bullet would require its own guidance system to do any better."

Kelly knew of his latest scores—she'd overseen the testing herself. Her involvement with him was primarily to manipulate, and she was playing her role well, building his trust, earning his love so that her power over him would be unchallenged. His only weakness was her, and it was a weakness by design.

But lying awake late at night, she wasn't sure that all of her emotions were as calculated as they had once been. She couldn't tell Agotha, of course, but what if Carl was now becoming her greatest weakness?

Impossible. But if it became true, Kalman would eliminate her.

"Why doesn't Kalman trust Saint?" Kelly asked.

"Who said any such thing?"

"No one. I see it in his eyes. And he's called up another ten recruits."

At present, Carl was the only recruit. They had been confident enough in him to stall the solicitation of more, but Kalman had put out an order for ten new candidates to be filled within sixty days. Only one in ten would survive the first three months of training. The rest were killed and their bodies incinerated. Clearly, Kalman was thinking that either Carl, Dale, or Jenine would need replacing soon.

Agotha nodded absently. "A man like Carl presents certain risks. Frankly, his relationship with you could become a concern. Has he asked about his father since the last treatment?"

Kelly blinked. "It was your plan that we bond. And yes, he said he couldn't remember who his father was."

"Yes, my plan, but I'm not sure the bond is strong enough. If his bond with you is ever compromised, he may become obsessive about knowing his origin, this father figure of his."

"You want me to strengthen his bond with me?"

"I didn't say that. If the bond is too strong and something happens to you, we may lose him. It's a tenuous balance."

"With Carl as my guardian, it's unlikely anything will happen to me. Right?"

"Regardless. With Saint going on his first mission in two weeks, we need a new recruit."

"Two weeks? So soon? You have the mission?"

Agotha turned back to the monitor. "We've had it for a long—"

She froze, eyes on the monitor.

Kelly scanned the stats. "What?" For the second time in ten minutes, something about Carl's situation had changed. This time it had nothing to do with his vitals.

"Did you change the room temperature?" Kelly asked.

"No. It should read 150. You did nothing?"

"Nothing."

The temperature was now 140.

"It must be a malfunction," Kelly said. "It's happened—"

"The control hasn't moved. How could it be a malfunction?"

The same system that regulated the temperature in Carl's pit fed a small closet that was measured by separate sensors. In this control, the temperature was still 150 degrees.

"Then the thermometer has malfunctioned?" But she knew three separate meters measured temperature, and a quick glance at the computer told her that all three were down to 138.

Agotha grabbed the phone, called Kalman, and then promptly hung up.

"It's going back up," Kelly said.

They watched as the temperature rose and finally settled at 150.

"How's that possible?"

"By the same physics that allow a monk to change the pH balance in water through meditation," Agotha said excitedly. "By affecting the zero-point field. Let me know if it changes again." Agotha changed screens, ran a quick diagnostic test for any system anomalies, then walked to the printer and watched her report print on continuous-feed paper. The printer stopped and she ripped the paper off the spool.

"Changes?" she demanded.

"Still 150."

The door behind them opened, and Kalman stepped in. He approached them, expressionless.

Agotha handed him the report. He glanced up and down, then eyed her. "What is it?"

"The graph showing room temperature."

"So you changed the temperature."

"We didn't change it." The fire in Agotha's eyes betrayed her passion. She was a scientist, not easily excitable, but at the moment, no matter how she tried to hide her feelings, she looked as if she might explode.

He glanced at the chart again. Studied it in silence. His eyes lifted, but he did not lower the paper. "You're suggesting that he did this?"

"Do you have another idea?"

He obviously didn't.

"When is he scheduled to come out?" Kalman asked.

"He has an afternoon drill with the others," Kelly said.

Kalman set the report on the table. "Bring him out now."

Agotha had talked often about the quantum physics behind the brain's ability to affect its surroundings, but Kelly had never seen evidence of it. Focusing the mind, stripping memory, shutting out pain, seizing control of typically involuntary bodily functions, controlling emotions—mastery over these was unusual but had been demonstrated for years among the greatest warriors and spiritual masters.

The notion that Carl had actually managed to control the temperature in his pit by affecting the zero-point field was altogether earth-shattering. It may have been proven that the empty space between atoms was filled with large amounts of energy, but she wasn't sure she was ready to believe that Carl could affect this field.

"Put him on the range," Kalman said. "Let's see what he can do."

"He'll need a few hours to normalize and eat."

"He shoots before he normalizes."

"Every man has his limits."

"We've broken his limits many times."

"The drill he faces this afternoon will test his shooting in an optimum setting before stretching him to his limits," Kelly said. "I suggest we wait as planned."

Kalman looked at her, and the darkness in his eyes made Kelly regret her suggestion. But he didn't object.

He simply turned and left the room.

CHAPTER SEVEN

THE ENGLISHMAN watched the man cross the compound with his typical nonchalant amble. Tall and well toned, with shortcropped hair and a small nose that made him look boyish. He had become ruthless as required, but his soft eyes contradicted his stature.

I am lost, I am found—Carl was trapped between the two without the slightest clue as to how lost and found he would truly be before it was all over. Lost to himself, found to the darkness that waited below hell.

Englishman wanted to grin and spit at the same time. It was all growing a bit tedious, but he'd known from the moment he walked into this terrible camp that he would grow bored before the fun began.

Soon. Maybe he could change his name from Englishman to Soon. *Soon* rhymed with *noon*, as in Daniel Boone.

There was no way he could adequately describe the depths of his hatred for the man who was stealing the show with all of his move-this-move-that emotional control nonsense. Englishman could and would drop Daniel Boone the moment he felt good and ready.

Which would be soon.

He took a deep breath and shifted his eyes toward the pretty girl. Kelly. She was playing her part well enough, but he wasn't sure she could toe the line. Her emotions could get in the way, despite all her training. Did she know the true stakes? He wasn't sure. Either way, he wouldn't trust her. He'd come here to make sure Carl did what was expected of him, or kill him if he didn't, and Englishman was hoping it would be the latter, because he hated Carl more than he thought humanly possible.

If they only knew why he was here, what lay in store for them, how he would do it all . . . My, my.

Hallelujah, amen, you are dismissed.

NEARLY FIVE hours had passed since Kelly liberated Carl from his pit. She'd hooked him up to an IV and pumped enough glucose and electrolytes into his system to wake the dead. He'd been in his pit for two days, she told him. A meaningless bit of trivia.

He ate a light, balanced meal, then showered, shaved, and dressed in his usual training clothes per her instructions. A short run brought him fully back to the present, the physical world outside the tunnel.

Kelly had asked him to meet her and the others at the southern shooting range precisely at three for a drill. He wandered the compound for half an hour, then made his way south, past the hospital, which doubled as the administration building; past the barracks; past a small mess hall that they rarely used and a weight room that they frequently used.

He supposed that he spent an average of three days every week in the pit, but he rarely recalled anything about them. In the beginning his training was filled with the pain required to break him. Needles and electricity and drugs. They still used electricity, but once he'd learned to control his body, his training had turned more to his mind.

The mental training sessions, like the kind he endured in the pit,

were now hardly more than a good, hard run. So long as he successfully blocked the pain. But today was different. At some point, he'd
tried to split his focus and succeeded. Then he tried to break through
the wall in his tunnel and, to his surprise, again succeeded. In fact, if he
wasn't mistaken, he had pushed back the heat crowding his safe place.

He wondered if Agotha had noticed anything in her detailed charts.
Kelly hadn't said a word of it, but if he wasn't mistaken, the light in
her eyes was brighter. Regardless of what caused this, he was glad for
her. She was pleased with him, which made him happy.

Where do I come from?

The stray thought surprised him. He briefly wondered who his
father was, then put the question away. There was no answer to it, he
remembered.

They were waiting by the sandbags when Carl made his way down
the slope to the shooting range. The vegetation had been cleared four
thousand yards to the south—he could see the trees bordering the
encroaching forest but no detail from this distance.

There was something ominous about those trees, he remembered
now. Oh yes. The compound didn't need a fence to keep them in,
because if any of them stepped beyond the trees, their implants would
send a debilitating electrical charge into their brains. He'd tried it on
two occasions with disastrous effects, but he couldn't remember anything beyond that.

At least a dozen assorted personnel drifted in and out of contact
with him in any given week, guards and scientists and the like. He
knew a few by name, but most existed like ghosts in his mind,
beyond the scope of his immediate concern, which was survival and
success.

Two of these personnel stood fifty yards to each side of the sandbags now. Carl focused on the three people who were in the scope of
his immediate concern. Kelly, Englishman, and Jenine.

The recruits were not allowed to talk to one another except as required by their training. As far as he remembered, he'd never spoken to either Englishman or Jenine without Kelly present.

Jenine. The sight of her standing in black slacks and brown pullover, facing the south with her arms crossed, evoked nothing but curiosity in him. Did she have a pit? Jenine looked at him without expression. Her hair was black, shoulder-length, framing a face with fine features browned by the sun. The Ukrainian, as they called her, was always quiet and hard to read. She could smile softly and slit your throat before you realized that her smile had left her face.

Carl wasn't sure if he liked her or not.

Englishman. From twenty yards he looked angry, but this was nothing new. The man often looked angry, as if he resented being in Carl's company. This wasn't a weakness necessarily. He compensated for his lack of emotional control in other ways. There was something profoundly unusual about the sandy-haired man who stared at him over crossed arms, wasn't there? Whereas Carl could shut out distractions and focus on his intentions, Englishman seemed to join the distraction and use it to his advantage. He didn't strike Carl as a man who needed to be taught anything by either Kalman or Agotha. Kelly said that the exercises kept Englishman's skills sharp. One day, when Carl was truly skilled, maybe he would learn to do what Englishman did.

"Hello, Carl." Kelly smiled. "You look refreshed."

"Thank you. I feel good."

Not a word from the other two. Though often pitted against one another, they rarely trained together with a common objective. By the looks of the three sandbags set thirty yards apart, the X Group was going to be shooting downrange. *That will change before the end of the training exercise,* Carl thought. Beside each shooting post lay a crate. He had no idea what these were for.

Kelly faced all three of them. "The reactive targets are set at twelve hundred yards. You will each use the M40A3 with a 150-grain boat tail bullet today. All three rifles have been sighted in at four hundred yards."

She walked to the left, eyeing Jenine. "You will expend ten rounds on the reactive targets. Consider it a warm-up. Beyond the yellow reactive targets are the static targets. Do not shoot these targets. Dale, take the far left; Jenine, center; Carl, on the right. Take your places, find the targets, and fire at will."

Carl turned to his right and walked to his sandbag. He'd shot more rounds on this field than he could count, much less remember. What he could remember with surprising detail were the technical specifications of the rifles, handguns, and cartridges that he'd spent so many hours with.

The rifle leaned against a small fiberglass rack by the sandbags. It wasn't just any M40A3, he saw. It was his. He'd sighted it in at four hundred yards himself; he could remember that clearly now.

Warmth spread through his chest. He wanted to run for the weapon, to pick it up gingerly and examine it to be sure they hadn't scratched it or hurt it in any way. His heart began to pound, and he stopped, surprised by his strong emotional reaction to the weapon.

A hand touched his elbow. "It's okay," Kelly said softly. "Pick it up." She looked at him sheepishly, as if she'd given him the very gift he'd been waiting for so long. And she had, he realized.

Kelly winked. "Go on, it's yours."

Carl walked to the rifle, hesitated only a moment, then picked it up and turned it in his hands. So familiar. Yet so new. The sniper rifle fired a .308 round through its free-floating twenty-four-inch barrel. Internal five-round magazine, six including the one chambered.

He ran his hand over the well-worn fiberglass stock and noticed that his fingers were trembling. He had to seize control, but these feelings were so comforting that he allowed them to linger.

Did he always feel this way when he picked up his rifle? Did the others feel this way?

He lifted his eyes and saw that Kelly was watching him with interest. Maybe some understanding.

He knew that the rifle he held was nothing more than a tool formed with precision, but then, so was a woman's hand. Or an eye. It was what he could do with this rifle that fascinated him.

"Thank you," he said.

"You're welcome. Shoot well today."

"I will."

She walked back toward the others.

Carl picked up a box of .308 rounds and set his emotions aside. Shooting well, as she put it, was like the beating of his own heart. Both could be controlled, both gave him life, both could be performed without much conscious thought.

He dropped to one knee and set the box of cartridges on top of the sandbag. A quick examination satisfied him that the mechanisms of the rifle were in perfect working order. He pressed five rounds into the magazine, disengaged the bolt, slid a cartridge into the barrel, seated the bolt, and took a deep breath.

He was eager—too eager. After the jumble/void of the last day/week, he felt fully alive, kneeling here, staring downrange. A slight, steady breeze, five miles per hour, he estimated, from the east. Temperature, seventy Fahrenheit. Low humidity.

It was a perfect day for killing.

Carl unfolded the bipod and lay down behind the rifle. Scope cover off. The thin thread that hung from the barrel to indicate wind barely moved. He drew the weapon back into his shoulder and glassed the field.

Three rubber cubes—yellow, blue, and red, each five inches square—sat on the ground. The yellow was his. When hit, the cube would bounce, thus its identification as a reactive target.

Carl snugged the weapon and swung the Leopold's familiar crosshairs over the target. He knew the charts for dozens of rounds intimately. The 150-grain boat tail bullet had a muzzle velocity of twenty-nine hundred feet per second. It would take the projectile just under half a second to reach twelve hundred feet. In that time the bullet would fall 22.7 inches and slow to nineteen hundred feet per second.

But his target was thirty-six hundred feet away. Twelve football fields. In that time the bullet would slow below one thousand feet per second and fall more than five feet.

If he placed the crosshairs directly on a target that was four hundred yards out, he would hit it precisely as aimed. But at this distance, he had to place the crosshairs more than five feet above the target.

He steadied his aim, lowered his heart rate, released the air in his lungs, and focused on a spot roughly five feet above and slightly to the left of the yellow cube.

A round went off to his left. Englishman. The red target leaped. All of this was peripheral to Carl. He slowly increased the tension in his trigger finger.

His rifle jerked in his arms. It took the bullet almost two seconds to reach the yellow cube. When it did, the cube bounced high, rolled to the left, and came to a rest.

Carl ejected the spent shell and chambered a second cartridge.

A breeze cooled his neck. A musty odor from the dust under his chin and the gun oil mixed with the sharp smells of burned gunpowder. His body hugged the earth. He was a killer. His preferred instrument was the rifle, and his weapon was his mind.

Carl shot the second round, waited for the target to bounce, reloaded quickly, and reacquired the yellow cube.

He was a man who loved and hated only if and when it facilitated his objective to kill. To kill he had to survive. Survive and kill, this was his purpose.

He sent a third round speeding down the range.

"Do you know what happened today?" Kelly asked behind him and to his right.

He held the scope over the target until it settled for a fourth shot. "No," he said.

"In the pit, do you know what you did?"

Carl considered the question, trusting his instincts on the fourth shot. She was talking about the heat. Rifle cracks filled the air in rapid succession. Three cubes bounced downrange, like three puppets on strings.

"No."

"Did you try to lower the temperature in your pit?"

"Yes."

She lay down beside him, glassing the field with binoculars. "You succeeded, Carl."

So. His mind was connected to his immediate environment through this quantum field that Agotha had told him about.

He shot the target for the fifth time. Successfully. Chambered his last round.

"Do you see the white target on the right farther down range?"

He moved his scope. "Yes."

"It's over three thousand feet. Can you hit this target for me?"

She knew he could—he'd done so many times in a row. Carl answered anyway. "Yes."

"But by the time the bullet reaches that distance, its parabolic rotation will be nearly ten inches in diameter. You can't control the bullet's wobbling to place it where you want in that ten-inch circle."

"Correct."

"But if you can lower the heat in your pit, can you affect the flight path of a bullet?"

Carl eased off the scope and looked at her. Was she serious?

"I want you to shoot your next five shots at the static target. Shoot for the center."

"I was in a different place when I lowered the heat."

"Go there now."

"I was in the pit for three days. My mind was focused. And I don't know what I did. I created a second tunnel, but beyond that I don't really know what happened."

"You can't create a second tunnel now?"

He didn't know. Even if he could, he had no idea how to affect the flight path of a bullet leaving the end of his barrel at twenty-nine hundred feet per second.

"Please, they insist."

He would try, of course. He would do whatever they wanted. He would do it for Kelly, but he was quite sure he would fail.

And what were the consequences of failing this time?

"They don't care if you succeed or fail; they only want you to try."

Carl nodded.

The 150-grain bullet would fall much farther over two thousand feet. And the target looked much smaller, barely more than a white speck in the distance.

He spent a full minute bringing his focus into alignment and entering his tunnel. The light at the end was the target. It was here, on the range, that he'd first thought of consciousness as a tunnel.

The air had become still; there were no shots from the others. There was a path between where he lay and the white target. He walked that path, feeling the wind, the humidity, and the trajectory that the bullet would take, arching over the field to fall precisely into the porous white electronic board.

He lowered his heart rate so that he would have enough time to shoot between beats. Made his muscles like rubber so there would be no movement conducted through his bones into his shoulder, or forearms, or trigger finger.

It was time to send the bullet. He knew that he would hit the target if he shot now.

But they wanted more.

Carl tried to form a second tunnel as he had in the pit. But no matter how he focused his mind, it refused to form. *Why?*

Maybe he didn't need a second tunnel. Maybe he could just focus on the bullet and force it to fly straight.

He brought all of his mind to the bullet. For a moment everything around him simply stopped. His breathing, his heart, the air itself seemed to pause.

Carl sent the bullet.

He couldn't see the impact on a static target at this distance, but through her scope, Kelly could.

"Again," she said.

"Did I hit it?"

"Again," she repeated.

Carl reloaded and repeated the same shot five times to her urging.

"Did I hit it?"

She lowered her binoculars. "You did fine, Carl. I'm very proud of you."

Kelly handed him the binoculars and walked toward the others, who were watching patiently.

"We're going to play a game," she said loudly enough for all of them to hear. Carl lifted the binoculars and quickly studied the target.

He'd hit it, he saw, but in a scattered pattern, with no more accuracy than any other time. The marks winked out as the target electronically cleared itself. He lowered the binoculars. Kelly had reset the target with the remote in her hand. She offered him a small smile and continued.

"Each of you will lie down in a crate with your weapon. The crates have been treated with a chemical that agitates hornets. You have a six-inch opening in the front panel through which to shoot at the reactive twelve-hundred-yard targets. Once you are ready, three dozen black hornets will be funneled into each of your crates. Their stings will adversely affect your muscles. The first to place five rounds into the target will win this contest. Do you understand?"

None of them responded.

"Good. The winner will be freed and given a knife. The next one to succeed will be armed with a handgun and will hunt the winner until one of you is either killed or incapacitated. The third will be left in the crate for an additional five minutes and then taken to the infirmary."

Carl dropped the binoculars on a sandbag and picked up his rifle.

CHAPTER EIGHT

ROBERT STENTON ruffled Jamie's short blond hair and hugged him tight with one arm. "You're smarter than most of the senators in Washington, buddy. That's why I insist you hang around."

Jamie smiled sheepishly, then pulled away.

They were in the Oval Office, where the secretary of commerce had just briefed the president on the progress of a White House initiative to increase import tariffs. Jamie had sat on the couch and fidgeted through most of the meeting. He'd had a bad night, the first in a week. The pain in his stomach hadn't settled until he finally vomited at three in the morning.

"Can I go?" he asked.

"Sure." *He's not himself,* Robert thought. "You sure you're okay?"

His son shrugged. "I'm tired is all."

"Okay, go get some rest. Mom will get you something to eat."

"'Kay."

Candace poked her head in the door. "Your next appointment is here, Mr. President."

"Send him in."

Jamie turned back. "Who's that?"

"Classified, buddy."

"'Kay."

Jamie passed a thick, short, dark-haired man at the door and was gone.

"Sir?"

"Come in, Frank. Have a seat."

"Yes, sir."

It was clear that Frank Meyers wasn't accustomed to visits to the White House, particularly not the Oval Office. The few times Robert had met with the CIA had always been with the director, Ed Carter. This time Carter wasn't even aware of a meeting.

"Drink?"

"No, sir."

Robert seated himself on the sofa facing the director of special operations. "What do you know about the X Group?"

Frank Meyers blinked. Clearly he hadn't expected the question.

Robert grinned. "No sense beating around the bush. I realize that most of what you do is classified and rarely discussed with us political types, but it's a direct question and I want a direct answer."

Meyers cleared his throat and clasped his hands together. "The X Group. I'm not sure I know precisely what they are. Or precisely—"

"I don't need you to be precise. Just tell me what you know. If you don't know, then give me the word on the street."

"Well, I'm not sure there is a word on the street. Very few are even aware of their existence."

"But you are."

"Don't misunderstand me; I'll tell you everything I know. It's just that this group is an unusual animal. We aren't sure where they're located or which hits they carry out, but—"

"So they are assassins."

"Yes, sir."

"Ordered by?"

18

"They have no apparent political or ideological interests. Strictly guns for hire. Mercenaries. They're run by a man named Laszlo Kalman. Hungarian descent. From what we know, they use cutting-edge psychiatric science to train their people. Phase-three memory wipes, torture, extreme forms of psychological manipulation. But they get results."

"Phase-three memory wipes?"

"There are three levels of memory manipulation. The first pertains to specific memories, dates, occurrences—the kind that comes with age. The subject forgets what has happened. The second involves time-space disorientation. Not knowing who you are or where you are. The third and most invasive is forgetting that you *should* know who you are or where you are. The Chinese proved fifty years ago that even otherwise healthy men can be effectively reduced to a phase-three memory wipe in less than forty days. The assassins employed by the X Group are first reduced to shells of their former identities and then trained as extremely loyal and lethal killers."

"So this group has been used?"

"By us?"

Robert lifted an eyebrow. "That would be illegal, right?"

"Under most circumstances, yes."

"Most?"

"I have to say, sir, I'm not sure—"

"I know that both the military and the CIA have been known to take out a bad guy now and then."

"The rules change under declared war."

"So we declare war on drug lords and take out a cartel in Colombia. Just give it to me straight. To your knowledge, has the CIA ever employed the X Group to carry out an assassination?"

"That's not the way it works. We hire people who hire lawyers who have clients protected by their attorney-client privilege who have other clients who hire assassins. Follow?"

Robert grinned. "I'll take that as a yes."

"Some of our offshore interests have contracted the X Group. The fact of the matter is there's no organization as isolated and as sure to give us the desired results. Some people say they've never failed in the ten years they've been on the market."

"I wasn't aware the market was so well organized."

"On the contrary, the black market requires more organization than the open market to avoid authorities."

So the X Group peddled assassinations on the black market. David Abraham not only knew about them but thought they were somehow linked to Assim Feroz.

Robert stood and walked behind the couch. "Who do they typically target?"

"At five million dollars a hit, the targets are pretty far up the food chain. High-level executives. You heard about the death of Sung Yishita, president of the Bank of Japan? It was reported as an accident, but it wasn't. His throat was cut two minutes after a high-level speech in Tokyo."

"Government officials would make natural targets," Robert said. "Heads of state."

"Yes. Which is why we have established an agreement with them to reject any contract on a United States federal government official."

The revelation surprised him. It was tantamount to paying off terrorists. At the same time, it gave him some comfort. He hated to ask how much they paid.

"Sounds like the agency's in pretty deep with them," Robert said.

"In this regard it's unavoidable."

Robert walked to his desk, wondering how far he really wanted to go with this.

"You have any reason to believe there might be any connection between Assim Feroz and the X Group?" he asked, facing the man.

Like most politicians, he'd learned to judge people by how they reacted to questions. Being asked this run of questions by the president of the United States was usually disarming even for someone as practiced as the director of special operations. Meyers showed no visible sign of surprise, but his answer was too long in coming. He stared at the president, mute.

Robert pushed. "I have reason to believe that there is a connection. I want to know whether there's any plan on or off the books to deal with Feroz using the X Group."

A pause. "There's been some discussion. Only that, I'm afraid I simply can't say more."

"You can't possibly think that killing Feroz would resolve the dilemma we're facing with the Iranian initiative."

"No."

"It would only fuel their fires."

"I agree. But killing a man isn't the only way to remove him from the scene."

"What, you wound him? Give him a disease that turns him into a vegetable? Poison him?"

"They've all been done, but no." Frank Meyers averted his eyes. "With all due respect, I really don't know of any operational plan involving the X Group. I've already said way more—"

"Remember which office you're in, Mr. Meyers."

A direct stare. "That's my point."

Robert knew he'd pushed the topic to its limits. He already knew more than he wanted to know.

"You're right. I'm sorry, I don't mean to compromise your position. But I assure you that the last thing we need is to make the Iranian defense minister a martyr."

"Absolutely, I agree."

But there was still a plan. What then? It would make no sense for anyone to attempt to kill Feroz or him. Or, for that matter, the Israeli prime minister.

"Does Director Carter know about this 'discussion' with the Group?"

Another slight pause. "I believe he's aware of some things."

Then a formal plan existed. A plan that was being considered at the highest level. And his spiritual adviser seemed terrified by this business. Which part of it, David himself probably couldn't explain. The man operated on spiritual discernment as much as on facts. Evil was lurking.

Then again, David Abraham had come face-to-face with evil and lived to tell of it. The president of the United States had Gandalf the White as a spiritual adviser.

Robert regarded the director of special operations steadily. "You know that I've decided to oppose the Iranian initiative at the UN summit in two weeks?"

"Yes, sir."

"Please tell whoever you need to that I want no agency involvement in this. Are we clear? If I have to, I'll talk to the director, but the last thing we need is some kind of cover-up in a matter as critical as this."

"Understood, sir."

"Thank you, Frank."

CHAPTER NINE

CARL LAY on his belly in the narrow crate, rifle extended, ready, with the barrel an inch from a small wooden door he assumed would be opened when it was time to shoot. A strong medicinal scent made it hard to breathe.

The implications of his predicament were clear. He was expected to win. Neither Jenine nor Englishman could place five rounds in a target at two thousand yards as quickly as he could.

And if he won, one of the others would hunt him. He would have less hornet venom in his system, but the hunter would have a gun. He wasn't sure which he preferred, to be the hunter filled with poison, or the hunted with far less poison. They both sounded like a kind of death. The thoughts crashed through his mind as he tried to focus.

A gate opened behind him, and a faint, then loud, buzzing swarmed in his ears. Closing his eyes would compromise his accuracy now and his sight later. He wondered briefly if a hornet could sting someone in the eyeballs.

He searched for his tunnel, ignoring the soft bump of frantic hornets along his legs, then up his back. He shut down methodically, easing into the safe place of darkness.

A hornet buzzed past his right ear and slammed into the crate in front of him. For a moment it came into focus. A large black insect with gangly legs and appendages sticking out in every direction. It ricocheted off the wood and struck his right cheek.

The gate slid open in front of him. He peered through his scope at the tiny white target. The hornets were slamming into his shoulder blades now, buzzing loudly around his head.

A sharp pain cut into his neck, and he gasped. This pain had sliced past the wall of protection he'd erected. How?

Panic crowded his mind. He'd felt fear before, and he knew how to shut it down. It had to go first, before he could shut down his nerves. He couldn't hope to hit the target until he'd rid himself of pain.

The buzzing became a roar. Carl reluctantly took his eyes off the target and closed his eyes. He felt another bite, this one on the small of his back.

He disassociated his mind from the pain and let himself fall into a soft black pillow. There he formed his tunnel from the blackness.

Another sting on his shoulder, but this one hurt less. The poison would affect him more than the pain now.

Slowly the sound faded.

Slowly the pain eased.

Then he was in.

He snapped his eyes open and peered through the scope, no longer noticing the blur of insects streaking by. He didn't even know where they were biting him now, only that they were.

Carl found the target as he would on any other day, adjusted for the same range and wind factors he had earlier, and walked the trajectory the bullet would take. Then he squeezed his trigger finger and sent the bullet away.

The report crashed against his ears in the enclosed space, but he took strength from it. His rifle was his savior, speaking to him with undeniable power.

He chambered another round and sent it down the same path. Kissing cousins.

Bullets were his dear friends, following his every instruction until they had wasted all of their energy in his service. There was no loyalty greater than a bullet's, speeding to a certain and willing death.

The sensation of hornets stinging him felt like popcorn popping on his skin. A dull ache spread beyond the tunnel.

Carl didn't know how long it took him to fire the five rounds; he only knew that he was finished. And that the crate's lid had been pulled off.

He clambered to his feet and handed Kelly his rifle. Pain flared through his body. Kelly was yelling something at the guards. "Two pills only. Handgun, remember."

She placed a knife in Carl's right hand, two pills in his left. "These won't help the pain, but they'll minimize the swelling and keep you alive. I will go with you."

He shoved the pills into his mouth and stumbled forward, glancing back at the other two crates. The buzzing inside would cover any sound he made now, but it wouldn't take either assassin long to find his tracks.

He cleared his head, turned to the north, and ran into the compound with Kelly close behind.

THE SUN would be down in three or four hours. *Nothing matters more than survival.* This one thought hung before Carl, calling him forward. A buzz lingered in his mind, not from the hornets, but from their venom.

He understood less of the world than he once had, but some things he understood better, and one of them was survival.

The other was killing.

Kelly ran lightly on her feet beside him, trusting him completely. At one time she would have offered him advice, but those days were behind them. He could now survive by instinct.

"Do you have the key to my pit?" Carl asked.

"Yes. Do you think—"

"To the door in the wall behind my chair?"

Hesitation. "Yes."

The guns were still booming behind them. Carl veered west and ran for his bunkhouse.

"Carl, are you sure—"

"We have to get in before they're out. Faster."

They sprinted the last hundred yards, then flew up the steps and into the concrete barracks. The air was suddenly quiet. One of them, likely Englishman, had completed the task.

Carl spun back to be sure they'd left no marks on the cement steps. None. He closed the door.

"Into the pit," he whispered. They descended the stairs on the fly.

Kelly didn't need her key for the pit; it was open. But the small door at the back was secured tightly with a dead bolt, which he assumed could be operated from either side of the door.

"Where's the key?"

She pulled out a small ring of keys from her pocket. "I hope you know what you're doing."

"I do."

He pulled the door open, revealing a dark earthen tunnel reinforced with wooden beams. He stepped in and pulled her in behind him.

"Do you know where this leads?" she asked.

"No. Lock the door."

"There's no light. The door on the other end is locked."

"Hurry, please. Lock it."

Kelly pushed the door shut, fumbled for the lock, and engaged the dead bolt.

"Is there anything in this tunnel?" he asked.

"No. It's for emergency evacuation. Leads to the hospital."

"It's a direct path? Straight?"

"Yes."

Carl turned and walked into the darkness.

"I can't see a thing. Where are you going? There's nowhere to go."

He reached back for her, felt her stomach, then her hand. Together they walked into the inky blackness. "Tell me when you think we've reached the halfway point."

She stopped him in twenty seconds. "Here." He knew that they were nowhere close to halfway, but he decided it was far enough, so he stopped. Released her hand.

Silence engulfed them. He listened for any sound of pursuit but expected none. Even if Englishman or Jenine stumbled into his pit, neither had a key to the tunnel. There was no way they could verify his presence here.

"Now what?" Kelly whispered after a minute.

A tension in her voice betrayed her insecurity. She'd been through training similar to his own, but he didn't know how far they'd pushed her. And she hadn't been in a pit since his coming. Perhaps that explained her fear of it.

"Now we wait," he said. "Please don't talk."

Carl squatted. And waited. Home.

"HOW LONG are we going to stay in here?" Kelly whispered.

They'd only been in the tunnel for an hour.

"Until I've rested and have the advantage," he said aloud, thankful for the dirt walls that absorbed the sound of their voices.

He could hear Kelly moving toward him. Only now had she realized that he'd moved away from her during the last hour so that he could hear above her breathing. It occurred to him that he was her protector here. In the tunnel, he was the master and she was the student. It made him proud.

Do you believe?

The soft voice echoed through his mind. Believe in what? In the Group, of course. His belief in everything he'd learned here was the fabric of his survival. He'd actually lowered the temperature in his cell! Imagine that.

"Why did you move away from me?" Kelly asked, closer now.

"I wanted to be able to hear," he said, standing.

"And?"

"They entered my pit, walked around, and then left."

"This is like your mental tunnel," she said.

"Yes."

Her hand felt for him, touched his chest, his neck, and then drew back.

"How are the bites?"

He hadn't given them much thought, but he felt his neck now. "Gone mostly."

For a long while they stood in silence.

"When do you think you will have the advantage?" she asked.

He shrugged in the darkness. "A day."

"A day? That long?"

"Patience is always—"

"I know about patience. I taught you that, remember? But how will a day help you?"

"Do you want to leave now?"

"I'm only the observer. I stay with you."

"Maybe it'll be less than a day," he said.

He really was in complete control, not only of her safety, but in some ways of how she felt. Kelly settled to the ground, and he joined her.

For several hours neither of them spoke. Carl was doing what he did best. He didn't know what Kelly was doing.

"Do you mind if I touch you?" she finally asked. "As much as I hate to admit it, the darkness is a bit disorienting."

"Okay," he said.

She felt for his knee, then found his hand. "Okay?"

"Okay."

They held hands in the dark for a while.

"Do you know what's so special about you?"

He didn't answer.

"Your innocence. You're like a child in some ways."

A child? He wasn't sure what to think about that.

"But there's a man inside, waiting to be set free," she said. "I'm very proud of you."

Her statement confused him, so he still said nothing.

"Do you remember Nevada?" she asked.

"Yes."

"I've always wanted to go to the desert. It's so vast. Uncaring of the rest of the world. It's just there, no matter what else happens. Golden sands and towering rocks. Coyotes that roam the land, free. When this is all over, I think I'd like to go to the desert in Nevada."

"When what is over?" he asked.

She didn't answer for a while. "It's just a fantasy," she said. "Something stuck in my head. I can imagine you and I walking into the desert like this, hand in hand, away from all of this. Do you ever think about leaving?"

"To the desert?"

"Not necessarily. Just leaving this place."

"I can't leave."

"I know, but if you could. If you didn't have the implant, would you go?"

"I don't know. It's not so bad here."

"I once lived in the desert," Kelly said. "In Ethiopia when I was ten. I was born in Israel and sold on the black market. To an Afghan warlord who loved me for my fair skin and hated me because I wouldn't do what he wanted. I escaped into the desert when I was fifteen and ended up in Hungary, where I met Agotha. I studied under her, you know."

Another long stretch of comfortable silence filled the tunnel.

"You're scheduled to go on your first mission in two weeks if you succeed in your training," Kelly said.

"I will succeed."

She didn't immediately agree, and he wondered why.

"I've always succeeded."

"The final test will be very difficult. If you fail, Kalman will kill you, assuming the challenge hasn't killed you already. Kalman doesn't want anyone to succeed—it's his way of making sure only the best enter the field."

She tightened her grip on his hand. "But I want you to succeed."

"I always succeed," he said again.

"If you do, you'll be leaving this place."

"But with you. And then we'll return."

"Yes, with me. Always with me."

"Will I always be in training?"

"Is there any other way to stay sharp?"

"Do you enjoy hurting me?" he asked.

Carl had no clue where the question had come from. He was talking without really thinking. Half of his mind was still in the darkness, focused on the current objective, listening for any sound of approach. The other half was asking this odd question.

She wasn't answering him.

"I know that your hurting me leads to strength," he said, ashamed that he'd asked. "You're helping me be strong. I'm thankful for that."

Kelly removed her hand from his. He'd hurt her feelings! She was upset with him. He wanted to shut his emotions down now, but he wondered if he really should. There was a strange life in this terrible empathy that had suddenly overtaken him. He wanted to comfort her heart. He was her protector, every part of her, which meant he could only protect her emotions with his own.

It was the first time he'd thought of his role this way. But he felt powerless to do anything, so he just sat in the darkness and let himself feel uncomfortable.

Kelly started to cry. The sound was very soft, a sniffing followed by a nearly silent sob.

Carl reached his hand into the darkness. When he found her, he realized that she'd rolled over to her side and had curled up in a ball. She lay on the tunnel's dirt floor, sobbing softly.

But why? Didn't she know that he loved her? Maybe she didn't.

Carl rested his hand on her hip, frozen by awkwardness. He couldn't remember her ever being so hurt. It reminded him of a time, long ago, when he lay sobbing on his cell floor, overcome by his training. They'd cut him and inserted needles into him and placed electrodes on different parts of his body and forced him to look into light for long hours and then left him alone in his pit for two days. These things had made him want to die, and he cried like Kelly was crying now.

It made him want to cry again.

Carl laid his head on her hip. Before he could stop himself, he was crying with her. He didn't know why.

She cried harder then, which made him feel an even deeper sorrow. A flood of anguish gushed from the darkest place of his soul, and he couldn't stop himself. He began to shake with sobs.

It must have lasted for a full five minutes. Strange and terrifying minutes.

Kelly sat up and wrapped her arms around him. She cried into his neck. "I'm sorry, Carl. I don't want to hurt you. I hate myself for hurting you. I just . . ." Her voice was choked off by sobs.

Carl sat back against the tunnel wall like an emptying sandbag, still unable to stop the flow of unidentified grief. He loved Kelly. He loved her so very much. The pain she was feeling was his fault. How could he have done this to the only person who cared about him?

They held each other for a very long time until their crying finally subsided. Then stopped. Then they sat in silence.

And Carl began to forget the way he'd felt. Englishman was out there somewhere, waiting.

"IT'S TIME," Carl said.

They'd been in the black tunnel for almost a day, he guessed. Exhausted by his time in the pit leading up to this day, he'd fallen asleep and rested for ten hours. Kelly had slept through the night as well, although they couldn't tell day or night down here.

They didn't speak of their emotional outburst, but Kelly kissed him on the lips and assured him that it wasn't his fault. She loved him very much. They'd left it at that, much to his relief.

"Can you open the door that leads to the hospital?"

"You don't want to exit through the hospital."

"My opponent, likely Englishman, is either there or waiting upstairs in my barracks."

"How do you know?"

"He'll know by now that we hid close, beyond the reach of the GPS monitors, which he's likely examined. The monitors are in the hospital. My guess is that he's there, waiting for me to show my signature, or above, waiting for me to show my body. I'll show myself in the barracks, and if he's not there, I'll backtrack through here and come around behind him."

"If Englishman isn't in the hospital?"

"Then I'll hunt him. Either way I have to go on the offensive."

She considered this for a moment, then agreed. "I'll exit through the hospital and leave the door unlocked."

Carl started to leave, but she held his arm. "No matter what happens here, Carl, remember that I love you."

"I will."

She reached up in the dark and kissed him on the cheek. "Remember."

Carl waited until she opened the door at the far end before walking toward his pit. He hurried up the stairs, found the barracks empty, and waited by the window, eyes on the hospital a hundred yards away. From his vantage he would see anyone who attempted to leave the building.

Five minutes passed. Then ten. Still no sign. If he was right, there should have been a sign by now. He had to change his course of action now, before—

The door to the hospital flew open. Kelly ran out. Still no sign of Englishman. Was there a problem? Maybe something had happened after they'd gone into hiding. Why was she sprinting toward his bunker?

He retreated to the stairwell so that his field of vision covered both the hall below and the door. If Dale came either way, he could make an escape under cover.

Kelly pulled up to the door and threw it open. "He's not there!"

She was telling him this? Ordinarily she would only observe, never report. She'd unlocked the door for him only at his suggestion, not hers. The games were always between the recruits, never the handlers.

Yet she was telling him that Dale wasn't at the hospital.

And then he knew for himself that Englishman wasn't at the hospital, because he stepped up behind Kelly.

Carl dropped into the stairwell. He landed on the fifth step and saw then that Englishman didn't have the gun trained on him.

He'd shoved it into Kelly's temple and was pushing her into the bunkhouse.

"You go, she dies," Englishman said.

Carl's first thought was that this maneuver had been planned by both of them. Why else would Englishman have waited for Kelly to arrive before stepping out? The coordination was too tight.

Englishman smiled and jerked Kelly's head back by her hair. "She's right. I'm not in the hospital because I'm here, and I'm here because I knew within the hour yesterday that *you* were here, in your pathetic little pit. I've been waiting too. I didn't expect such eager assistance from your lover. In the middle of the room, or she gets a bullet."

"He's lying!" Kelly cried. "What do you think you're going to do, shoot me? Agotha will kill you with the flip of a switch in a matter of seconds."

"I didn't hear anyone say that I couldn't use you to get to him. I have more than forty bites on my body, and they all tell me I should kill Saint. Why not the woman who loves Saint as well? We all know she's nothing more than a mouthpiece for Kalman. I doubt he'd miss her that much."

To Carl he said, "Get up here, wonder boy."

Something was wrong, drastically wrong, but Carl couldn't identify it. Surely Kelly had no role in Englishman's appearance. She seemed genuinely frantic. Never mind that; she would never betray him!

He came out of the stairwell in two long steps.

"Knife on the floor," Englishman said, pressing the gun into Kelly's cheek.

Carl backed toward the middle of the room.

"Knife on the floor!"

He raced through alternatives. In the moment Englishman removed his gun from Kelly's head to adjust his aim, Carl could and would throw the knife. Englishman knew this. A quick flip of Carl's wrist, and Englishman would have a knife buried in his eye.

Carl could throw the knife now, while the gun was pointed at Kelly's temple, but a simple spasm from Englishman and she would die.

There were several other alternatives, but the only ones in which both he and Kelly lived depended on Englishman. Would he really hurt Kelly? The man would kill him, Carl was sure of that, but killing a handler was another matter.

Unless there was more to it.

There was a way for Kelly, Carl saw. She might be able to get them out of this situation. But would she? If he dropped his knife now, he would be completely dependent on her to move at the right time, or Englishman would likely kill him.

Their eyes met, but he saw no encouragement in Kelly, only fear

"Now I count, and her shoulder goes first," Englishman said. "Please don't make this difficult on yourself. Just drop the knife."

Carl opened his fingers and let the knife clatter to the floor.

Englishman smiled. He licked Kelly's ear. "Had to throw in some cliché, you know."

Cliché? Something to be expected.

"Now it's time for me to shove her to the side. That's the way it always goes. The villain shoves the princess to one side, thus making a convenient opening for the prince to kill the villain without hurting the princess."

His words seemed out of place. But that was exactly what Englishman wanted. Carl had been here before.

Englishman shoved Kelly to his left. "No interference, princess. I haven't hurt you, remember that. I simply used you the way Carl used you to escape. No penalties."

He was right. She wouldn't interfere. She couldn't, not without facing consequences from Kalman. The training protocols were inflexible.

Kelly glared at Englishman but stayed where she was.

The man leveled his gun at Carl. "You do know that I've been given permission to kill you. *Incapacitate* or *kill* were the words used, I believe."

Carl said nothing.

"The fact that you stand there like a piece of wood makes me think

I should just get it over with. On the other hand, a bullet through the leg would be a little more interesting, wouldn't it?"

For a long moment he stared at Carl. Then he tilted the gun down and aimed at Carl's thigh.

The room rocked with a thunderclap.

But it wasn't Dale's gun. It was Kelly's. She had a gun in her right fist, pointed at Englishman, who was looking at a bloodied hand. His gun had flown across the room.

"No," Kelly said. "It doesn't end like this. Carl had you beat."

The man lowered his hand and let it bleed on the floor. His face was white, but he showed no other outward sign of pain.

Kelly walked over to Englishman and slammed her gun into his temple. He dropped, unconscious.

She's broken the rules. She's saved me but only by breaking the rules at terrible risk to herself.

"No one hears about this," Kelly said in a low voice. She stared at him with shining eyes. "Not a word, you hear, Carl? Remove this from your memory. Remember only if you ever doubt my loyalty to you."

"Why did you do this?"

"He was going to shoot you through the leg. I love you."

"My leg would have healed."

"Not in time for your mission. As far as Kalman's concerned, you shot Dale."

"What will Englishman say?"

"What I tell him to. Agotha's waiting for you."

Carl stepped past them, but he paused at the door and turned back. Kelly's blue eyes searched his soul.

He would die for her.

CHAPTER TEN

DAVID ABRAHAM paced Air Force One's conference room, stroking his beard. Robert had never seen the man so bothered. Gone was that stoic confidence that came with his seasoned spiritual father persona. Gone was the calm and collected demeanor of wisdom. The man before Robert and CIA Director Ed Carter looked downright tormented.

"Please, David, sit. You're making me nervous."

"And you should be nervous. *I'm* nervous."

"I can see that. But I don't think I understand why. Nothing you've said sounds as ominous as you're suggesting."

Robert had invited David to ride along for the sake of this conversation with the director, but he was beginning to think that it was a mistake.

Carter clearly wasn't comfortable speaking frankly with David in the room, and David hadn't clarified his concern regarding Assim Feroz in any way that made sense, perhaps because Carter was still present.

"Sit, David, I insist."

David pulled out a chair and sat. "Forgive me, Robert. I simply don't have the kind of details that would justify my concern to anyone other than myself. I can only say what my son saw."

"In this"—the president waved his right hand through the air—"this foggy vision Samuel had nearly a year ago."

"Yes, it was quite some time ago, and yes, what he saw was admittedly rather general. But he's not given to visions. It's the first one he's ever had, I think. But what he saw is now knocking on our door."

"None of this strikes you as a bit . . . absurd? It was just a vision—"

"Not *just*. No more than you're *just* the president."

"I wasn't in this vision of his, right? I don't understand the concern." It couldn't possibly be a sound idea to base a policy or decision on a vision, even if it came from a source like David, even if it contained alarming details about the X Group that no ordinary person could have possibly stumbled upon.

"Assim Feroz will destroy whoever crosses his path," David said. "You're now in his path, so yes, you were in the vision, if only by association."

"Either way, the summit is sponsored by the United Nations. There'll be no lack of security."

David Abraham took a deep breath and nodded, but his eyes were heavy with concern. *He isn't telling us everything,* Robert thought.

He faced Carter. "Well, Ed, now you know how the president of the United States makes decisions that change history." He winked at David. "Sorry about that. I couldn't resist."

David was too involved to find humor in his comment.

Robert leaned back, sighed, and regarded the director. Ed Carter was well over two hundred pounds and had a double chin that looked exaggerated below his small round spectacles.

"So would you mind telling us this plan involving the X Group, Ed?" Robert asked. He'd already told Ed Carter about his earlier conversation with the head of special operations, but this would be the first confirmation David would hear that any such plan was afoot.

David gave them both an alarmed look.

"Don't worry, I think we're past secrets here," Robert said. "We all know about this little assassination club. According to Samuel's vision, the X Group is connected to one of my greatest enemies. I think that qualifies me to hear everything and anything, don't you?"

Carter looked as if he was still trying to figure out whether to take the whole business of this vision seriously. But then, so was Robert.

Carter cleared his throat. "Well, some ideas have been thrown around. I'm not sure you'd approve—"

"Just give it to me straight. We'll go from there."

"Okay." Carter spread both hands. "No plans at this point, actually. I think you'll see why."

"Please. Just tell me."

Carter frowned. "What if, and I really do mean *what if*, Assim Feroz were eliminated? His death could fatally undermine his initiative."

"First of all, any such plan would be highly illegal and morally reprehensible. Second, he'd become a martyr. His death would probably energize support for his plan."

"Unless Feroz was eliminated because he was attacking innocents. As a terrorist."

"Terrorist? I don't follow."

"What if Feroz was killed while attempting to assassinate one of his enemies?"

"Such as?"

"Such as you, sir."

Robert wasn't sure he'd heard correctly. He coughed once. "You can't just tell the world that such and such a leader was planning on killing me and so we took him out. We're not at war."

"Assassinations are provoked by policy rather than war. In this case, we're talking about a policy that would threaten the national security of our ally Israel. I'm not suggesting or defending this course of action; I'm merely explaining the rationale." He put his palms on the table. "As for the world believing, you're right. The assassination attempt would have to be real. If it was, and we could produce definitive evidence linking Mr. Feroz to the attack, we would win world sympathy by taking him down."

"You're actually suggesting that we stage an assassination attempt on me and blame it on Feroz? And then kill him?"

"That was the idea, sir. Not the plan, mind you. There are some problems, of course, but it does have some merit if you consider—"

"No. It would never work. And even if it did, it breaks more international laws than . . . Forget the laws—it's murder."

"As are all assassinations. Maybe you could declare war on Iran to cover our moral quandaries and send a hundred thousand men and women to their graves instead. Forgive the sarcasm. My point is, assassinations save lives. Kill one drug lord, save the hundred men he will kill. Kill one tyrant, save a hundred thousand of his subjects. In the case of Feroz, I'm not sure I follow Dr. Abraham's reasoning, but I think we all agree that this man's life will cost the world dearly."

"Tell me straight, Carter. You've been with the agency for what, fifteen years? Does every president hear this assassination speech?"

"Yes. And are made aware of its merits. What was the human cost of removing Hitler or Saddam Hussein by war rather—"

"Point made," Robert said. "But Feroz isn't Saddam or Hitler."

"Not today, no. Maybe David has some thoughts on this."

They both looked at David Abraham, who regarded them with an ashen face. He pushed his chair back. "Forgive me, gentlemen. I'm afraid I must excuse myself from this discussion. I would say you're both right, but I'm not in a position to inform your final decision. Do you mind, Robert?"

He'd never known David to refuse a good philosophical debate. Clearly the man was plagued by more than he'd revealed. And just as clearly he wasn't going to divulge any more.

"Feel free to use my quarters to get some rest if you need it."

"Thank you, but I think I'll be fine. Please, continue." David left the room and closed the door behind him.

Robert turned to Carter. "What happens to the people involved in the assassinations, or fake assassinations as the case may be?"

"They would probably need to be eliminated."

"So more innocents die."

"Soldiers, guns for hire, not innocents."

"And this is where the X Group comes in," Robert said. "You're planning on hiring the X Group to take out Feroz as a matter of foiling his nonexistent assassination attempt on me."

"It's a thought. You would need to agree, of course."

"Exactly when were you planning on discussing this with me?"

"I believe I have a meeting scheduled with you this Friday."

Robert pushed back his chair. "Cancel it, The answer is no. I don't care what rationale you throw my way, I won't be involved in this. If you can find a way to turn Feroz into a bumbling idiot who makes a fool of himself at the summit, I'm all ears. But I don't play politics with bullets."

"Of course, sir. It was just an option."

"An option you were ready to recommend."

"Not without your endorsement. Consider it a nonstarter."

CHAPTER ELEVEN

BECAUSE KELLY had told him that he was going to be tested and then, if he succeeded, go into the field in two weeks, Carl kept track of the days for the first time in months.

After speaking with Agotha for a long time, he went into the pit again, to fight the cold this time. And he was able to nudge the cold back each time, but not much. He could add a few degrees to the room's temperature. Maybe five, once ten, she told him. This was like someone changing the pH balance of water through meditation, she insisted, something that had been proven possible.

She was trying to help him believe, but he already did believe, so he mostly just listened. Agotha was sure that he could do more, but he couldn't.

On three different occasions, they brought him to the hospital for additional training, as they had for many months. They asked him to lie on a metal bed with his head inside the large white magnetic resonance imaging machine, put drugs into his veins, clipped electrodes to his toes and fingers, and then asked him to repeat what he knew for long periods of time. If he got the answers wrong, they turned dials and sent sharp shafts of electricity through his body.

He couldn't turn off the pain easily when they did this, because he had to focus on the right answers. In the early days, he'd passed out nearly every time. Now he rarely gave them a wrong answer. His memory was very good.

When he wasn't in the hospital or in the pit, he was with Kelly, practicing. He would often be put into a room with several objects and a fixed amount of time to create a weapon. Next to focus, improvisation was the assassin's greatest asset. He'd learned to make weapons out of almost anything that was small enough to wield:

A sharp knife that could be held and used like any blade made from an aluminum soda can in under ten seconds.

A stiletto made from a coat hanger in even less time.

A bomb with enough power to gut a man at three paces made out of chemicals available in most bathrooms.

These tasks came easily. Kelly told him that both Jenine and Dale could do the tasks as easily. In fact, they were better than he in many disciplines, particularly Englishman, who had more natural strength and speed. But Carl had the better mind, she told him. And the mind is an assassin's greatest weapon.

Whenever they were pitted against each other, Englishman always held the edge. In hand-to-hand, in knife wielding, in strategic field exercises that challenged both reaction time and decision making, Englishman was better. The only clear edge that Carl had was his ability to control his emotions and his bodily functions, which in turn made him the better sniper.

If all three were compared head-to-head in all disciplines, their rank would fall thus: Englishman, Saint, and then the Ukrainian, but not by much.

Agotha was eager for him to shoot straighter at a long range. Each day that he wasn't in the pit, he sent hundreds of bullets toward the static target at two thousand yards.

Each day he landed more than three hundred of them in the twelve-inch circle. There was always the bad bullet that strayed because of poor construction. Carl didn't let the few wayward bother him. The rest were reliable. In the field, he would inspect each round before using it to be sure it met his standards, but on the range he didn't bother.

For some reason Kelly didn't tell him whether he was actually able to make the bullet defy its physical ballistic limits and fly straighter. There was no way for him to know, even by looking at the target. Just because a bullet landed in the bull's-eye didn't mean he'd made it go there. At two thousand yards, the bullet was wobbling in a ten-inch circle and could land anywhere in the target.

But a computer was tracking his every shot to see if he was beating the odds. He didn't think he was. They would be shouting about it if he was.

In all of Carl's training, a single word called to him, like a father urging him forward. Through his tunnel.

Believe. Just believe, Carl, and you will find the light at the end of the tunnel.

When Kelly came for him in his pit on the tenth day, he knew by the fear in her eyes that the day for his final test had arrived. He'd survived the last two—the hornets, and before that the Andrassy Hotel. Today he would face the ultimate measure of his skill.

"Shower, eat, and report to the hospital," she said.

They stood on the floor of his pit, looking at each other. Carl had always thought he'd be proud on this day, but the darkness in her eyes ruined his confidence.

"You're coming with me?" he asked.

"No, not this time, Carl."

"Do you know what they'll ask me to do?"

"They wouldn't tell me. They insist that I remain here."

"In my pit? Why?"

"Not down here, necessarily. Just in your bunker. They said it wouldn't be long."

Carl put his hand on the metal chair, unsure he wanted to leave her here and cross the field to the hospital alone.

Kelly moved closer to him, eyes fixed on his. "You can do this, Carl. I know you can. You will succeed. You always have."

She took his hand and kissed him on the cheek. "You'll succeed for me. There's nothing you can't do for me. Promise me."

"I promise."

"Kiss me, Carl."

He leaned forward and kissed her lips. The warmth of her mouth seemed to swallow him. They lingered, hot, wet, sharing the same space deep in his mind where everything was safe.

"Go to them," she finally said, smiling softly. "Keep my face and my smile with you."

"I love you," he said.

"I love you too."

THE HOSPITAL had three floors including the basement. Carl had never been to the basement or the third floor, both of which were off-limits. The main floor had four smaller examination rooms and the main laboratory, where Agotha administered her drugs and electric shock treatments that helped her subjects forget and remember.

Carl felt well rested and full of energy. He'd eaten twenty carrots, half a bag of jerky, and a chocolate bar to give him the energy he might need for the test. Then he'd showered and dressed in black fatigues and a brown nylon pullover. The shoes he wore were also black, made of canvas with rubber soles. Agotha was in the laboratory when he entered it.

"Hello, Carl."

"Hello."

"Thank you for coming."

"Kelly told me to come."

She studied him with eyes that seemed to move too quickly. Concern. "Kalman is waiting downstairs. Please follow me."

They walked down the hall to a staircase that descended into the basement. Agotha opened the metal door that led into the lower floor, and a strong medicinal odor stung his nose. Three large picture windows lined a long white cinderblock hall. Each looked into a room.

Agotha opened the door into the first room and waited for him to enter. Carl walked past her and studied the room.

Kalman sat in a brown leather chair with wooden arms, smoking a cigar, watching him. Next to him was a large metal chair with buckled straps on the arm and leg rests. A round leather bowl was suspended above the chair, and from this headpiece extended several large electrical cords.

It was an electric chair.

Three guards stood to the left of the electric chair.

"Hello, Carl."

Carl stared at the chair, at a loss. He'd been told that to fail meant execution, but he'd always imagined a bullet to the brain. The chair didn't make him afraid—he had no intention of failing.

"Today you will either become the third assassin, or you will die," Kalman said. "I've decided that I will electrocute you when you fail. I think you have some considerable strength and should put on a good show, but not even a bull could withstand the electricity that will boil your blood when you fail us today. Do you understand this?"

"Yes."

Kalman shifted the cigar from one side of his mouth to the other, then stood. He ran a finger over the leather headpiece, removing dust, which he smelled and then wiped on his pants.

"If you execute your mission successfully, you won't have to face the chair, but I don't expect it. Tell me, what is your primary objective?"

"To survive."

"To survive why?"

"So that I can execute my mission."

"Good. Your first assassination was to be in five days, but I've decided to make it today. Today you will find and kill your handler. If you fail, I will kill you."

"My handler . . ." Carl wasn't sure he'd heard correctly. He had to be sure that he had the right target.

"Kelly Larine," Kalman said. "The one who has ordered you around for ten months She knows too much and is too valuable to you. It's good to cleanse the system now and then. You know where she is?"

"Yes."

"You have one hour to kill her and bring her body to the hospital." Kalman pulled out a stopwatch and thumbed the knob on top.

Carl could not focus. He knew his mission, but he wasn't sure how to execute it.

"You may kill her however you wish," Agotha said.

"You may go," Kalman said.

"Thank you, sir." Carl dipped his head and ran down the hall. Up the stairs, out into the sunshine.

"LEAVE US," Agotha ordered.

The three guards left the room. The only thing more reliable than the assassins they sent into the field was one of their personnel. They were paid significant sums of money for their cooperation and threatened with significant consequence for any failure. Mostly thugs, but not stupid ones.

The door swung shut. "I want to voice my final objection to this," Agotha said. "Both are too valuable."

"She cares for him too much."

"Which only ensures that she will keep him safe. She knows that if he ever betrays us, we'll kill him with the implant. You're stripping away everything I've worked for!"

Kalman did not reply. He knew what he was taking from her and took pleasure from it. This was his twisted way.

"You think she's weak?" she demanded. "What would you know about a woman's weakness for a man? And this is no ordinary man whose life you're toying with. His shooting scores have improved all week. He's manipulating the field, for heaven's sake! You would kill a man like that?"

"Then perhaps he's too dangerous."

"Not if you leave his loyalty to me. We've led him to believe that she's his savior. Our manipulation has been extensive and effective. Last week he gave up a knife to save her in a test I designed for Kelly. He's dangerous, but not to us, not as long as we have his loyalty. But today you may compromise that."

"One of them has to go. I don't care which."

"Are you listening to me? Their emotional bond is a good thing. I'll leave the killing to you, but you will leave the manipulation to me."

Kalman drilled her with a dark stare.

"He's been carefully programmed both to survive and to love Kelly," she said. "This scenario presents no solutions for him. We are fighting ourselves with this mad game of yours."

"Then we will kill both of them."

"And accomplish what?"

Kalman rose, impatient. "If he is what you say he is, then let him prove it, and he will live according to the terms."

"He's a gold mine."

"You favor this one too much. We both know that Englishman is the better man. It takes more than good marksmanship to make a good assassin."

Agotha walked to the door and pulled it open. "Englishman could kill Saint easily enough now, but in a year or two?"

"If he survives today, we'll give him his year or two. If he dies, he wasn't meant to live."

CHAPTER TWELVE

CARL WALKED toward the bunker on legs filled with lead. His head swam in dizzy circles. He couldn't seem to make sense of the mission that lay ahead of him, much less form a tunnel of security from which to execute it.

So he just walked. He didn't feel the urgency to run. He didn't feel the need to use stealth. He just walked.

Birds chirped from the nearby forest. He wondered if Englishman had been faced with a challenge similar to this one. Or Jenine. They had both passed their final tests and been deployed. Soon he would join them.

But without Kelly?

Kelly was his life as much as the blood that coursed through his veins. Killing her was the same as killing himself. He couldn't kill himself. So he just walked.

But he had to kill her. If draining his blood was the only way to complete his mission, he would drain his blood.

Why would he agree to kill Kelly? Why did he long for an assassin's life? The answers, clear on some days, eluded him now. But he knew with more certainty than he knew anything else that his role in this operation was far more important than the dilemma immediately before him. His failure to execute the task would end badly for everyone, including Kelly.

If killing Kelly was the only way to become the assassin he was meant to be, he simply had to kill her, no matter how much he cared for her. She herself would insist.

The truth of the notion suddenly struck him as insane.

She was standing in the corner when he entered the bunkhouse. "You're finished?" She hurried over to him. "What's going on?"

Carl closed the door, heard it clank shut, surprised by how loud it sounded. He looked into her wide blue eyes and knew then that he couldn't kill her—not here in the light where he could see her eyes.

When he spoke he could barely hear his own voice. "Can we go to my pit?"

"Sure. What is it? Are you finished?"

"Maybe we should go to my pit," he said.

Her eyes searched his, concerned. "Sure, Carl."

He let her lead. They descended the stairs, walked down the long hall with its single caged incandescent light, down the concrete steps that led to his pit.

Kelly paused at the entrance, then entered the dark room lit only by the open doorway. She turned around by his chair and waited for him to follow her in.

But even here, in the safest place he knew, Carl felt powerless to kill her. He needed to go deeper.

"Do you have the key to the tunnel?"

She glanced at the locked door behind her. "Yes."

"Could we go inside?"

"Tell me what's happening, Carl. You're scaring me."

"I will tell you. But we have to go inside the tunnel where it's dark."

She found the key on a ring that she withdrew from her pocket, opened the door, and stepped aside to let him pass first.

He walked into the inky blackness a full fifty yards before stopping and turning back. She'd left the door open, but only a pale beam of gray followed them in. She reached for his arm and stared into his face. He couldn't see her eyes.

"I've never seen you like this. Whatever it is, you can do it, Carl. I believe in you. You have to believe in yourself."

"My final test is to kill you."

They were surrounded by silence and darkness, and ordinarily Carl would have found comfort in both. But he could feel the heat drain from her fingers around his arm, and the sensation terrified him.

"They want you to kill me?" she asked.

"If I don't kill you, they will kill me," he said.

They stood still for a full minute. *When she has the solution, she will give it to me*, he thought. But he knew that there was no solution. He would have to choose between killing her or being killed. If it was Agotha or Kalman or anyone else, the choice would be simple.

But his need for Kelly was as great as his need for his own life.

She placed her free hand on his chest. "How long did they give you?"

"One hour."

Kelly lowered both hands and swore in a whisper. "You can't let them kill you!"

She might as well have screamed the words, because in his mind they were deafening.

Her voice trembled. "You know very well that I'm expendable. What am I, just a slave girl that came to Agotha off the streets of Budapest—"

"Did you really shoot Englishman?"

He still couldn't see her eyes. "No. We used special effects to make it look like I shot him. The test was ordered by Agotha to test your loyalty to me."

"And is this a test too?"

"No! Kalman will kill you with pleasure. No doubt, we've destroyed your mind, I'm so sorry, but you have to listen to me. This is it—you have no choice. You have to kill me. It will be my penance."

"But you said yourself, you only deceived me to save me. It's why you hurt me. And when you did hurt me, you hurt yourself, not just me. We're linked, see? If I kill you, I'll be killing myself. I can't do that."

She looked at him without speaking. Then she lowered her head so that her forehead rested against his shoulder. "Dear Lord, what have I done?"

"I'll go to the hospital and see what they do."

"No."

"I've survived electrical currents running through—"

"No!" She slammed her fist against his chest. "No, no, no! You will not let them kill you!"

Then what? What could he do? She loved him; he believed it now. Whatever lingering doubts he'd had were denied. He could not kill her. He would not.

Either way, he would die. But there was a way for her to live.

Carl broke away from her and began to pace. "Time is running out." He still had forty-five minutes, but it seemed like only a second. "I have to do something. I can't . . ."

Desperation was an enemy he'd beat long ago. But this time there was no light at the end of this tunnel. It was black to the bottom, no solution, no objective that could be achieved in this place where he no longer knew who he was.

"It's the end this time, Carl," Kelly said softly. "There's no way out. No tunnel that will lead both of us to safety. I won't let you go to your death. Use the drugs on me. They're the kindest."

Something moved in Carl's mind. Something Kelly had said. He stopped pacing and peered into the darkness. "What did you say?"

"Drugs. They're—"

"No! You said there's no tunnel."

"Is there?"

He began to pace again as the idea blossomed.

Carl grabbed her arm and ran past her, jerking her after him. "Is the tank full?"

"The isolation tank? Yes, why?"

"I have to go in. We have to hurry!"

She ran behind to stay up with him. "What about the mission?"

"I can't kill you."

CHAPTER THIRTEEN

HIS PLAN was simple, but it made no sense, and Kelly told him that a dozen times before he lowered himself into the huge cast-iron ball they called the isolation tank.

It contained warm, salted water, heated to 98.6 degrees. In this water the body felt nothing. Carl would wear a modified deep-sea diving mask that effectively cut off all sensory input to the ears, the eyes, the mouth, and the nose, leaving him completely sense-free.

The isolation tank provided the simplest, easiest, and quickest way for most subjects to enter stasis. They rarely used it anymore because Carl had advanced beyond the need for such an unwieldy tool, but with it he could move most quickly, and time was now an issue.

He was going deep, he said. Very deep. Deep enough so that he would remain in partial stasis for some time after he came out.

As agreed, Kelly left him in the tank for thirty minutes before pulling him out, dripping wet. Despite an almost uncontrollable urge to ask him how successful his trip had been, she worked quietly. She dried his body and dressed him in a dry pair of pants. She did all with the ring of insanity in her ears. In many ways she felt as if she were performing last rites on an animal to be sacrificed in a sick ritual.

He had no more than ten minutes to complete his mission when he followed her back into the tunnel, shirtless and shoeless.

Kelly led him toward the hospital, groping through the darkness with her free hand. She could hear his breathing, a full fifteen seconds between each breath, and she knew that he was still deep in the safety of his world.

She, on the other hand, was in a world of more peril than she could remember ever experiencing. She could no longer deny the fact that she felt deeply for him. She was meant to earn his love, and she had, but in the process, he had found a way to earn something from her. It made everything she was doing feel like a betrayal.

Leading him in silence now, she couldn't hold back quiet tears.

He was going to die. She had tried to tell him as much, but he was adamant. Even angry. Now any attempt on her part to change his mind would only compromise his concentration.

She unlocked the door at the end of the tunnel and led him up the stairs into the hospital basement, still vacated of personnel. The door to the execution chamber was open. His breathing now came once every twelve seconds. He was normalizing!

Moving as fast as she could, Kelly strapped him in as Kalman had shown her several months earlier when he was in an especially cheerful mood. Each contact had to be coated with gel to ensure conductivity. Normally they would shave the head, but there was no time. She attached the electrodes to his forehead and to the back of his neck.

THE PLACE was as black as any Carl could remember.

He had formed his tunnel within seconds of entering the tank. He knew that he had a limited amount of time, but time ceased in here, so he didn't think of himself as in a race against the clock.

He was here to protect the tunnel. A terrible force would come to destroy it, he knew. An enemy far greater than any he'd ever faced.

He would have to do something new. He couldn't rely on the wall to protect him.

This time he would have to go outside the wall in a new tunnel, as he had recently, but with far more focus. His one advantage was that he knew how the attack would come. The force would come through his hands and skull.

If he could lower the heat in a room; if the pH balance of water could be altered so easily; if the faithful could walk into the fiery furnace and not be burned by flames or walk on water without drowning, then his mission wasn't impossible.

It had been done before.

Carl swam outside the tunnel, sending wave after wave of the sea to his extremities, to the place where the enemy would attack. It was all in his mind, of course, but the mind was his greatest weapon.

He remembered being led down the underground tunnel and being strapped into the chair, but these were noises and sensations of another world.

Then voices. Urgent. Arguing, perhaps. Excited, perhaps.

He smiled. Did they know that he was outside the tunnel? Agotha would be proud!

The voices ceased, and he knew that the attack was going to come.

And then it did, in a red-hot wave that took his breath away and flooded his eyes with blinding light.

"TEN, ELEVEN . . ." Agotha stared at the jerking body through the picture window. There was no way he could possibly survive!

Inside Kalman continued his count. "Thirteen, fourteen, fifteen." He nodded at the operator inside. "As agreed."

A loud clank signaled the break. The hall lights brightened, then one sputtered and winked out. Kalman stood beside the chair, wearing a look of fascination. At times like these Agotha hated him.

She pulled the door open and stopped short. The smell of burned hair was strong. He was surely dead. If not physically, then mentally. A vegetable. They'd found no record of a man surviving fifteen seconds at this voltage, the only reason Kalman had agreed to the terms.

"Carl?"

He was slumped against his straps, headpiece firmly in place.

"IL's dead," Kalman said on her left.

The hall door crashed open, and Kelly pulled up by the large window. She rushed into the room and brushed past Agotha, not caring that her face was still wet with tears.

"Carl? Carl, please tell me you can hear me." She frantically unbuckled the leather mask and flung it from his head. She ripped the blindfold off his face. Then she went to work on the attachments on his arms and legs, practically tearing them free.

Agotha blinked. Carl's cheeks and lips were dry, not wet from tears or saliva. *Surely his eyes would be gone,* she thought. *Surely his—*

His left hand twitched. Residual current.

"Carl?" Kelly's voice was filled with desperation. She had deeper feelings for the man than even Agotha had guessed.

"He's not breathing!" Kelly cried. She dropped her head against his chest and listened for a heartbeat. But if he wasn't breathing now, a full minute since they'd turned off the electricity, he was dead.

As if in response to her thought, Carl's left hand lifted an inch from the armrest. Stopped. Then it twisted, and his forearm slowly rose.

Agotha was no longer breathing. Carl, on the other hand, had to be! Kelly had seen none of it, not yet.

Carl's hand rose slowly and touched the back of Kelly's head. Her whole body froze.

Carl smiled. "Hello, Kelly."

His eyes snapped open.

Kelly began to cry.

Behind Agotha, Kalman grunted.

"I OWE you my life," Kelly said.

"And I owe you mine." It was true. Without his love for her, Carl didn't think he'd have survived the last ten months, assuming that was truly how long he'd been in training.

They sat at a round table for four in his bunker kitchen, eating nuts and jerky.

"You know what this means, don't you?" she asked.

Carl put a peanut in his mouth and bit into it around a big grin. Honestly, he couldn't remember feeling this happy, so he let the feeling ride. "That I'll go into the field."

"Yes. Agotha is thrilled. If you were her pet project before, you're her golden calf now."

"And Kalman?"

She shrugged. "Kalman is Kalman. He lives for killing."

"Like a good father," Carl said. "Sets the rules and makes sure they're kept."

She gave him a strange look. Picked up a piece of jerky and tore off a strip. "You're not angry at him?"

"That would be impractical. He's only doing what he thinks is best. Can any of us argue with the results?"

She nodded. "What else can you do?"

"What do you mean?"

"If you can protect your body against the currents of an electric chair, shouldn't you be able to do more?"

"Anyone can ignore heat. I just do it better than most. That doesn't mean I can fly."

She laughed at that, and he joined her. The pleasure in her blue eyes, the soft curve of her neck, the shine in her wavy hair—he found her stunning. And he'd saved her, hadn't he? He had saved the one he loved.

"I have your mission, Carl," she said, flashing a mischievous grin.

"You do?"

"I do." But she didn't offer it.

"When?"

"In five days."

"Where?"

"New York City. They say it's a wonderful place. I can hardly wait."

"Who is it?"

"An Iranian leader named Assim Feroz."

Carl slapped the table with his palm. "Finally," he said and snatched up his glass for a toast. "To Assim Feroz. May he accept the bullet I send him with grace." Even as he said it, he wondered if such eagerness was appropriate. Was he really so excited to kill?

Kelly lifted her glass and clinked it against his. "To Assim Feroz."

CHAPTER FOURTEEN

THE UNITED Nations Middle Eastern summit attracted a large number of protesters, as expected, but the media kept most of their coverage focused on the conflict brewing inside the UN rather than on the street. *Viewers can look only so long on a nineteen-year-old woman with stringy hair waving a banner that reads "Stenton Kills Babies,"* David Abraham thought, flipping through channels.

In his way of thinking, such slander should have to defend itself with logic. Even minimal logic. No panel of jurors in the country would convict Robert Stenton of killing fleas, much less babies. And yet too frequently, highly educated journalists reported such accusations as serious charges worthy of attention.

He should have gone to New York, even though he could not stop whatever might happen. Now all he could do was pray that God would save those who needed saving and let the rest find their own way.

He sat on the couch in his Connecticut home and switched to FOX News. The president was holding a press conference. David turned the volume up.

President Stenton was saying, ". . . that I strongly objected to forcing Israel into a corner where her national defense rests in the hands of a foreign government, which is what the United Nations would be doing in this situation. As I see it, the Feroz initiative threatens Israel's sovereignty."

Steven Ace of NBC asked, "Sir, the United States is now the only country that opposes the plan. Does that fact pose any problem for you?"

Stenton replied, "Uniting world opinion always poses problems. Clearly we have a ways to go. But when it comes to standing up for an ally that's facing potential extermination, I think those problems are worth grappling with, don't you?"

"I have a follow-up, if that's okay," Ace said.

"Go ahead, Steve," Stenton replied.

"I understand that there's growing support in Congress for the initiative. Are there any plans for a congressional vote on the matter?"

"No," Stenton said, excusing himself with a nod. "Thank you, that will be all." With that, the most powerful man in the world stepped away from the flashing lights and walked through a blue curtain behind the podium.

David grinned. *That's it, Robert. No mincing words.*

Then again, they both knew that the president was indeed being strong-armed to reconsider by members from both sides of the aisle. Robert had told David two days earlier that the price he was paying for his immovability was turning out to be much higher than he'd expected. There was talk on Capitol Hill of shelving his domestic agenda altogether.

World opinion boiled down to what each government thought of the United Nation's charter. In this new role suggested by Feroz, the United Nations would become the strongest government in the Middle East. Why the leaders of Europe and Asia didn't feel threatened by this was beyond David.

Unless, of course, they saw Israel as their enemy as well.

David sighed and switched to another news channel. Protester coverage.

Another channel. Commentary on the president's brief conference.

Another channel. ABC was interviewing none other than Assim Feroz outside the Waldorf-Astoria, where the UN was hosting several major social events for the dignitaries.

David sat back, crossed his legs, and pressed the DVR record button. The Iranian was tall and gaunt with eyelids that hung lower than most. Fair skin and dark hair, clearly of Persian descent. That the Iranian minister of defense had worked his way into the spotlight with this transparent initiative disgusted David.

Feroz was answering the questions with a polite smile.

"Naturally, it's unacceptable. But we believe that the United States will soon see the wisdom of stopping the ongoing bloodshed in the Middle East through this peace initiative. You cannot turn your back on suffering for too long."

"What will you do if the United States vetoes the initiative at the summit?" the ABC anchor asked.

A crowd of security personnel and reporters was gathered around the defense minister. A limousine door gaped open behind him, apparently waiting on him.

"We will not rest until we have peace. How can one man stand against so many?" Feroz answered. "Now the whole world will unite and bring peace where there has been no peace for centuries."

"Thank you, Mr. Feroz."

"Thank you," he replied.

David saw the reporter, Mary Sanders, for the first time as the camera faced her. "There you have it . . ."

David muted the television. Another journalist in a black sports coat faced the camera, then abruptly turned his back and walked away. The man was familiar to David, but then, so were the faces of a hundred reporters.

Stenton had a fight on his hands. The summit was clearly doing him no favors. David had expected nothing else.

But there was something out of place about that reporter in the sports coat. Strange how the memory worked. Déjà vu?

David started to change the channel. Instead, he pressed the rewind button on the DVR. The reporter's face came and went.

Forward, slow motion this time. David paused the picture as the man turned. He stared for five full seconds before recognition struck.

"No . . ."

It was him!

David stood, studied the profile on the screen. Could he be mistaken? His heart was pounding at twice its normal pace.

He was at the interview with Assim Feroz. There, in New York!

Still gripping the remote control in his left hand, David ran around the couch and snatched up the phone. He dropped the remote on the desk. Dialed the president's number with a shaky finger.

"Dear Lord, help us . . ."

"Brian Macteary."

"Brian—Brian, it's David. I must speak to the president."

"David? David Abraham?"

"Yes. Please tell him it's important."

"I'm sorry, he's unavailable. Is there something I can help you with?"

"No, I have to speak with him. It's very important."

"I'm under strict orders not to interrupt them. He's just gone into a short meeting with the British prime minister. I can pass him a message when he comes out. Shouldn't be more than fifteen minutes."

David quickly considered his options and settled on the only course that presented itself with any clarity.

"It's very important that you tell him something in the strictest of confidence. Tell him that I have reason to believe that there will be an attempt made on the life of Assim Feroz. The security is tight, I'm sure."

"I've never seen more security." Brian paused. "You're saying that someone may be trying to kill the Iranian defense minister?"

"Yes."

"Nothing more? How—"

"Never mind how I know—tell him! I'm taking the first flight I can into New York. Tell him that."

"I should pass this through the Secret Service."

"No! Please, just tell the president and let him decide how to proceed."

"I'm obligated—"

"No, Brian. This isn't a formal threat. Just the president. Promise me!"

The president's press secretary was hesitant. "I'll tell him," he finally said.

CHAPTER FIFTEEN

CARL HAD never been as happy as he was now, walking the streets of New York with Kelly.

He'd been in many exercises that felt like true assignments at the time, but walking down Park Avenue toward the Waldorf-Astoria with such a show of security as far as the eye could see swept away any lingering suspicions, however small, that this, too, was simply an exercise.

He really was here to kill Assim Feroz. And that was good. Better than he'd dreamed. He told himself so on many occasions.

Kelly had taken care of a number of details that facilitated his mission, but in the end, it would be his finger on the trigger, sending the bullet on a trajectory determined solely by him. It would make them both proud. And he wanted to be proud, he'd decided. This was now an emotion that he embraced whenever it presented itself.

As with any assassination, it wasn't only the opportunity to kill but the opportunity to kill and then escape to one day kill again that drove the preparations leading up to this day. Prior to leaving Hungary, Carl had spent dozens of hours with Kelly, viewing video footage provided by the X Group and planning the hit. They had a good plan.

He made his way toward a security line at Park Avenue and Fifty-second Street, two full city blocks from the Waldorf. He wore a foreign press badge that identified him as Armin Tesler, Ukraine, KYYTP Television. Beside him, Kelly was identified by a similar badge as Ionna Petriv. *We play our roles flawlessly,* he thought.

But not as flawlessly as all the others who had delivered them to Park Avenue as two Ukrainian reporters. This feat had required substantial support from Kalman and his host of contacts, none of whom Carl knew or cared to know.

They'd left Hungary by train three days ago, bound for the Ukraine, where their current covers—complete with passports, history, and press identification papers—had been previously arranged. Their fingerprints had even been registered with the CIA and Secret Service. Kelly told him that these kinds of details had been handled long in advance through an extensive identity-requisition program that Kalman had fine-tuned over the years.

From Kiev, they'd flown through London into New York, arriving two days earlier.

First order of business: establishment of an operations center out of a hotel in Manhattan. This task required renting three separate rooms in their assumed names. Two were dummy rooms, in which they'd hidden miniature video cameras that sent signals to the third room, in which they would actually sleep and operate. In one of these dummy rooms, #202 in the Peking Grand Hotel, they'd left several spent rifle cartridges and a red message painted on the wall: "Death to America, Praise Be to Allah." They'd made the room appear lived in and demanded that housekeeping not disturb them. Strategically planted clues would lead investigators to this room and slow down the post-assassination investigation. The delay would buy them time to chart an alternate escape if their planned route was cut off.

Another dummy room, #301 in the Chinatown Best Western, was reserved in the event that they needed to switch operational centers.

They'd bagged several weapons and hidden them in the toilet tank. Otherwise the room was left undisturbed.

The hotel they selected as their actual operations center was a seedy place in Chinatown called the New York Dragon.

Second order of business: weapons. There was only one weapon Carl needed for the actual operation: a rifle. Anything else he might need, he could fabricate out of materials at hand.

Kelly had obtained the rifle he would use from a contact in New Jersey. An M40A3, nearly identical to the one Carl preferred in Hungary, sighted in at four hundred yards, with a Leopold Vari-X 4x12 scope, three-inch eye relief, and nonglare lens. The rifle had been modified for quick disassembly. It fit neatly into a soft-sided tripod bag normally used for a camera.

The host of assassin's tools common to the trade was useless in this setting. No vest, no night-vision equipment, no knives, nothing that smelled or looked anything remotely like something an assassin would wear. In this kill, Carl would simply be a shooter who pulled off a shot that only a couple of living souls could pull off.

Third order of business: reconnaissance of both the kill zones and the general area of operations. They'd spent the better part of the previous day walking the streets of midtown Manhattan, riding the subway from Central Park to Chinatown and taking taxis to a dozen destinations both in Manhattan and the two kill zones.

Fourth order of business: rehearsal of execution. Essentially a walk-through of the actual assassination. Carl had developed two alternate plans: one for a dinner of dignitaries at the Waldorf, which Assim Feroz was expected to attend; and one for a press conference scheduled at Central Park the following day, which Feroz would also participate in.

Each zone had been identified by Kalman—how, Carl didn't care. His task had been to find a place from which to shoot and escape during a narrow window of opportunity. He'd scouted both zones on foot in the dead of night, and then again the following day while the streets were crowded with cars and pedestrians. One shot would be made from a hotel room. The second, if required, would be made from a garbage bin.

Fifth order of business: performance of their roles, which they were doing now. Part of the X Group's training had involved role-playing, not simply on a conscious level, but deep down where belief was formed. Because he'd frequently been manipulated into assuming a particular identity, Carl now found that willfully playing a Ukrainian correspondent came easily.

He took a deep breath and regarded the bustle of the crowd around him. He judged each face that passed into his field of vision to determine if any threat might hide behind the eyes.

"We should go into the hotel," he said softly.

Kelly cast him a natural glance. "It wasn't planned."

"Then we should change the plan. We have time."

She didn't respond. Any changes were his prerogative—she trusted him. Her trust made him proud.

A line of police cars and construction barriers cut off the street ahead. Carl walked toward the security check.

The guard eyed him with a steely stare, and Carl smiled gently. "Busy day," he said, shifting to a nondescript European accent. With the blending of cultures in Europe, nearly any would do.

"Yes, it is. Can I see your identification?"

Carl unclipped his badge and handed it to the man. They were using a scanner that matched the thumbprint on the card to the thumbprint of the person carrying it. The information was relayed to a central processing station, where the authorities monitored the comings and goings of authorized cardholders.

The guard held out a small scanner, and Carl pressed his thumb on the glass surface. A soft *blip* sounded. After a few moments, the man nodded.

"Thank you, Mr. Tesler."

It took only a minute for Kelly to pass in the same manner. Then they were in the outer security barrier. They would have to watch what they said here. Randomly placed recording devices monitored conversation. According to CNN, not all in the press were thrilled with the new security measure. Evidently they wanted to keep their comments private.

They'd passed through the second security checkpoint and were approaching the entrance to the Astoria when Assim Feroz stopped out with a small entourage and was swarmed by journalists.

Carl felt his pulse spike. Beside him, Kelly stiffened slightly—he felt it more than saw it.

It was the first time they'd seen the target in the flesh. Tall, gaunt, dark-haired, Iranian. This was the life that Carl would end, because that's what he did.

For a brief moment Carl wondered why they wanted him dead. *Who* wanted him dead? *What* had this man done to invite the bullet? And *why* was he agreeing to kill this man?

The last question came out of the blue, uninvited and unwelcome. The answer was obvious, of course—he wasn't so much agreeing to kill this man as he was agreeing to be himself. He was a killer. He was a man who knew nothing except killing. He could no more not kill than a heart could arbitrarily not beat. If he hadn't always been a killer, he was one now. And he'd been one for as long as he could properly remember.

His exposure to this noisy, confusing city was interfering with his focus. He blinked and shut out the thought.

"Closer," he said, angling for the man who was now taking questions from an ABC correspondent. Kelly followed, pulling out a notebook.

Carl slipped between a heavyset reporter and a woman in a purple blouse, eyes fixed on the man. They were behind and to the right of

the Iranian defense minister and the camera that captured the interview.

It took little effort to work his way to the front of the other journalists who were yielding space to ABC for the moment. Carl stopped
ten feet from Feroz.

This was his prey. From his right, the scent of a flowery perfume.
From his left, the smell of the asphalt and pollution and cooking
meat. Feroz himself had practically doused himself in a spicy cologne
laced with nutmeg.

Carl stepped from the circle, eyes fixed on the man's dark hair and
gently working jaw. Assim's jaw was sharp and pitted, from acne,
perhaps. His voice was low and gravelly. His dark, purposeful eyes
cut through the crowd.

". . . not rest until we have peace. How can one man stand against
so many? Now the whole world will unite and bring peace where
there has been no peace for centuries."

An interesting voice. Carl wouldn't risk detection, despite the strong
urge to pass closer to this man in his perfectly tailored suit.

Carl turned back and eyed Kelly. She stared at him, emotionless.
He started to face Feroz again, saw that the camera was panning, and
thought better of being caught in a full shot in the proximity of the
target. Their appearances and identities would be changed immediately after the assassination, but his instinct warned him off.

A thin sheen of sweat covered Kelly's face. She wasn't comfortable
with his admittedly unorthodox approach in this surveillance mission. They'd come to walk the perimeter, not enter the hotel. They
hadn't expected to see the target, let alone make such a bold approach
in the event that they did.

Carl guided her toward the Waldorf's revolving entry doors.

"I hope you know what you're doing," she said.

"I wanted to know who he is."

She didn't respond.

I want to know him so that I can know myself. I am a killer. Who and how I kill define me.

They waited in line fifteen minutes before security would allow them to enter the hotel. It seemed that only a limited number of people were allowed inside at any given time. They walked up marble steps and entered a large atrium with towering pillars. Exotic floral arrangements that stood twice the height of a man blossomed in huge urns every seven paces.

Carl stopped below the arches that opened to the lobby and allowed the room to soak in. Magnificent. The old walls and ceiling were inspiring.

He scanned the room, detected no threat, and walked out to the center. Being taped by the hotel security cameras was actually to his benefit. The typical assassin would never be so bold. He faced the ceiling, where he knew the cameras hid, and examined the intricate designs etched into the wood.

Here was a building with a history. Unlike him.

Carl turned, refreshed by a sense of destiny. He was going to find himself here, in New York. The ceiling seemed to be staring down at him like a proud father. Rotating to his right like a camera on a wire. And in the center, him, staring up, lost to the world.

Are you my mother?

A hand touched his elbow. "We should go."

Carl lowered his head. She was right. They'd come inside to see the reception hall on the tenth floor, where Assim Feroz would die this very night.

But a single sign made that impossible. A white placard etched in black calligraphy that read "No Press Above Lobby Floor." Two guards stood at each elevator and beside the stairwell to enforce the restriction.

Carl walked toward an archway that led to specialty shops, the first of which he could see at the hall's end. "Should we go shopping?"

Kelly walked abreast and talked quietly. "Are you feeling all right?"

"What do you mean?" he asked. There were fewer people back here. "I'm feeling what I choose to feel."

"You seem a bit erratic."

"Because I'm making erratic choices. If it's any comfort, I can assure you that every one of these guards has been trained to pick out the calm, cool behavior of a potential assassin. It's better to play the part of an awed foreign correspondent, don't you think?"

"It just feels . . . odd. The way you're acting."

"I don't feel odd. This building fascinates me."

"And that's not odd? When was the last time you were fascinated by anything?"

Carl gave her a shallow grin. "I'm fascinated by you."

Her face went red, and try as she might, she couldn't hide a grin. It was the first time he'd ever seen her so embarrassed, and strangely enough it thrilled him.

They walked by a shop window displaying gold and silver jewelry, something that held no fascination for him at the moment. The next store looked as if it sold dolls and stuffed animals. Toys. More fascinating.

"We should get back to the hotel," Kelly said.

"I agree."

A tall, dark-skinned man in a black suit stepped from the toy shop and faced them, eyes skittering along the hall. Secret Service.

A boy half Carl's height walked out after him, holding his purchase: a pair of compact binoculars. Polaroid XLVs—Carl knew of them. From where he couldn't remember, but he knew the binoculars. Perhaps he'd owned a pair himself when he was younger.

The boy turned blue eyes toward Carl and stopped. For a moment they exchanged stares.

"You're from the Ukraine?" he asked in a small but confident voice.

Carl wasn't sure how to respond. He should acknowledge the guess, but something about this boy struck a reverberating chord deep inside him.

"Yes," Kelly said.

"That's good. I hope you support our president's position on Israel."

Had he seen this boy before? No, he didn't think so. As far as he knew, he hadn't really known any boys before. At least none he could remember.

The sound of feet clacking down the hall reached him. *Seven, maybe eight pair,* he thought absently.

The Secret Service agent stepped around the boy, shielding him from Carl and Kelly. "Your father's coming, Jamie."

Jamie.

They came around the corner, five agents and a lean, blond-headed man whom Carl immediately recognized as the president of the United States, Robert Stenton.

The boy was his son. Jamie.

The boy's guard put a hand on his shoulder and eased him forward, toward his father, who beamed at the sight of his son.

"What did you get?" the president asked, stopping twenty yards away.

Jamie hurried to his father and held up the binoculars.

Secret Service agents circled father and son like hens gathering chicks. Carl and Kelly had been scanned by every one of them, including the two responsible for the president's back.

Robert Stenton took the binoculars and held them up. "Fantastic!" He peered through them, past Carl, down the hall. "Perfect choice," the president said.

Then he put his arm around his son's shoulders and walked back the way he'd come. The entourage disappeared around the corner, trailed by Jamie's dark-skinned agent, who turned and cast one last look at them before following.

Carl stared after them, mesmerized by the interaction between father and son. What was it about them that confused him?

He smiled at the guard, dipped his head, and turned around. "We should go," he said.

"Yes. We should."

CHAPTER SIXTEEN

ROBERT STENTON glanced at David Abraham, who was watching him like a hawk. For the first time the president was beginning to understand his mentor's distress. Accepting Samuel's vision might require any ordinary person to jump through mind-blowing mental hoops, but there was a resounding ring of authenticity to everything David had just said.

One of his aides handed him a phone. "Ed Carter is on the line for you, Mr. President."

Robert took the cell phone. "Thank you." He walked to the window overlooking Manhattan and spoke softly to the director of the Central Intelligence Agency.

"Thank you for stepping out of your meeting, Ed."

"Of course, sir."

"I have a very simple question, Ed, and I want a simple answer. Is there an agency plan to deal with Assim Feroz? And when I say plan, I mean of any sort, technically sanctioned or not."

That question caught him off guard, Robert thought. Carter hesitated, then spoke plainly. "Not to my knowledge, no. We discussed this—"

"I know what we discussed. Now I'm being sure. I assume the bulletin that went out an hour ago was brought to your attention?"

"Yes."

"Does the subject match anything you have?"

"We're still running the comparison against our database, but nothing on the list of priors matches. If this guy's an assassin, he's never been spotted."

"Regardless, we have reason to believe there may be a threat to the Iranian defense minister's life. Do you know how badly this could go if he were killed on American soil during this summit?"

"I couldn't agree more. Wrong place, wrong time."

"There is no right place or right time. I thought I made that clear."

"A figure of speech. The security surrounding the minister's schedule would be difficult to penetrate."

"Unless there was an inside operation," Robert said. "But you're telling me that there isn't."

"That's correct. None whatsoever."

"If anything happens to Assim Feroz while he's in our country, you'll answer, Ed. I assume you understand that."

"I don't think we have a problem, sir."

"Please make sure of it."

He hung up and faced David. "I don't know what else we can do at this point."

"Nothing. You have to prevent him from killing Feroz, but you can't pick him up. Not yet."

"So you've said." David's explanation had taken a full fifteen minutes, laying out details that explained far more than Samuel's vision. What David revealed was tantamount to conspiracy. Their discussion still made his head hurt.

It was no wonder David Abraham had been wringing his hands for the last month.

"Are you absolutely sure the person you saw was him?"

"Yes," David said. "I could never mistake that face, trust me."

The president took a deep breath and set the cell phone on the lamp stand. "I have to be honest, David. I'm having a hard time buying into all of this. It's a stretch."

"It's only a stretch for a mind that hasn't been where mine's been."

"Well, if you're right about all of this, you've taken immeasurable risks and overstepped your place. I'm not sure how I feel about that."

"Let's pray I made the right decision, then," David said. "I'm sure you understand why I've said nothing about this before now."

"That doesn't make it right."

"Only time will tell. You can decide then whether to burn me at the stake or build a statue of me."

CHAPTER SEVENTEEN

MANHATTAN OFFERED a dozen possible sites from which Carl could kill Assim Feroz while he dined on the Waldorf-Astoria's tenth floor, but after only short consideration, he'd agreed that shooting from a hotel room would best facilitate the objective. There were numerous advantages to the protection offered by a room, chief among them silence and isolation. The room would absorb much of the sound, critical because a sound suppressor would affect the bullet's path and therefore would not be used.

There were as many disadvantages, perhaps the greatest being that most hotel rooms weren't conveniently positioned to offer a shot into the Waldorf. As far as Carl could see, there were only seven possible rooms, four of which were aligned vertically in the hotel in which he now prepared himself.

Seven hotel rooms, seven different shots, seven escape routes. But of these seven, only one was available—the one he now occupied. Regardless, it was an excellent choice. An obvious choice. Obvious because it was far *too* obvious to be taken seriously by even well-trained security personnel.

Carl sat cross-legged on the bed, staring at the round oak table next to the window. His rifle rested on its bipod, pointed at the pulled curtain less than a foot beyond the muzzle. He would wait until the three-minute mark to pull the curtain and prepare the window for the shot.

He kept his eyes on the rifle and his mind in his tunnel.

Strange and wonderful and frightening emotions swam in the blackness beyond the pinprick of light that was his mission, but he held them all at bay easily enough. He didn't have to control fear, because there was none. He hadn't expected any. Instead, there was excitement, an emotion that could easily affect his pulse and by extension his accuracy.

And there was some empathy, an emotion he'd expected even less than fear. He was about to send a bullet toward a man who had done nothing to harm him. Kelly had told him what a danger this man was to the world, but none of her words mattered. Carl was simply a killer who would kill whomever she told him to kill. He needed no other motivation to please her.

Yet now, just a few minutes from doing precisely that, he was aware of this strange empathy lingering beyond his tunnel. He dismissed it and kept his mind on the light ahead.

Carl stared at the barrel of his rifle, allowing peripheral elements to stream into his vision without distraction. A four-inch LED monitor on the table captured the high-bandwidth video images transmitted from a small camera he'd positioned under the room's front door, peering into the hall. In the event his location was compromised, he would see any approach in enough time to make a quick exit into the adjoining room.

The room was warm. He'd turned off the air conditioner when he first entered in order to equalize the pressure between this room and the air outside. A part of him wished he could turn the heat up to better simulate his pit when it was hot.

He missed his pit.

But he'd left the safe world of that pit to fulfill his purpose. As soon as he'd reached the light at the end of this tunnel, he would be allowed to return to Hungary.

The light. That circle of white now beckoned him. Excitement tried to enter his tunnel again, but he deflected it without conscious thought and stared at the light.

He would kill the Iranian defense minister while the man ate his dinner on the tenth floor of the Waldorf, and he would do it with a bullet that came from the tenth floor of the Crowne Plaza on Broadway, roughly twelve hundred yards away. It would be a two-shot kill.

His first bullet would leave the hotel room Kelly had reserved for him, cross over one of the busiest streets in Manhattan, and travel down Forty-ninth Street for five blocks before crashing into a thick window. The bullet's soft, hollow point would allow the projectile to spread at first impact and blow the window inward.

His second bullet would follow on the heels of the first, free to fly unobstructed through the broken window, through an open doorway, and into a second room, where Assim Feroz would be seated.

The second shot had to be fired within two seconds of the first so that it would reach the target before the sound created by the exploding window elicited any reaction.

The strings that Kalman had pulled to give Carl a line of sight into the kill zone could have been pulled only by very influential people. Being sure that Feroz was seated at one of three tables facing the doors, for example. Making sure the doors were open. The drapes pulled. But none of that concerned Carl.

His task was to place the bullet in the target's chest at 9:45 p.m.

Kelly's soft voice spoke through his radio headset. "Four minutes." The frequency was scrambled on both ends, allowing them untraceable communication.

"Four minutes," he repeated.

He didn't need a spotter at this range, so Kelly coordinated the mission from the Dragon in Chinatown. Her contact inside the Waldorf had two tasks. The first was to raise the blinds on the window. The second was to make sure the double doors that led into the dining room were opened at 9:45 p.m., a far more difficult task in this security-rich environment than in any other. The server was being paid $100,000 in U.S. currency, a good payday, Kelly said.

A thousand men could hit a target at twelve hundred yards. But very few could shoot a bullet into a window, chamber a second cartridge even as the glass fell, acquire a target seated next to twenty other dignitaries through a narrow doorway, and place a bullet in the target's chest in the space of two seconds.

This was the light at the end of Carl's tunnel.

"Three minutes."

Two minutes and fifty-nine seconds by the clock on the table.

"Three minutes," he repeated.

Carl waited a beat. He unfolded his legs and stood. The only emotion that now threatened him was excitement, and he blocked it out forcefully.

He stepped up to the window, pulled the heavy curtains a foot to each side. A sea of lights filled his view. Times Square was two blocks south, Central Park a half mile north. A hundred feet below him, heavy traffic ran along Broadway, refusing to sleep just as the brochure Carl had studied claimed.

Two minutes and thirty-five seconds.

He lifted a black cutting tool from the table, pressed five suction cups against the glass, and ran the glass cutter's diamond bit in a two-inch circle. Three full turns and a gentle tug. The glass popped softly.

He set the glass cutout on the table and lowered the bit so that it rested on the window's outer pane.

A soft gust of air blew through the two-inch opening as he pulled the second circle of glass free. No wind in Manhattan, as forecasted. Wind had been Carl's greatest concern during the planning, but no more.

One minute and thirty-two seconds.

He eased into the chair, took the rifle gently in his hands, leaned over the table, and aligned the barrel with the hole. The weapon's smooth, cool barrel and familiar trigger brought him comfort, and he accepted it.

He peered through the light-gathering scope, quickly found the corner window that he would punch through in just over one minute, and let the air seep from his lungs.

The hot gases blown forward by the .308 cartridge would create both sound and light. The first would be absorbed in part by the room, baffled by the glass, and then muffled by the heavy traffic below. The fire would be dimmed by the flash suppressor affixed to the end of his barrel. Unless someone was peering directly at this window, the shots would likely go unnoticed.

He would escape easily enough either way.

"One minute."

"One minute," he repeated.

A stray thought penetrated his consciousness. *Is this just another test?*

And then another thought. *It doesn't matter.*

Carl let his mind go where it now begged to go, into the scope. Into the tunnel. Through the dark passage toward that light. He walked his bullet's trajectory as he had a thousand times before.

"Thirty seconds." Kelly's voice sounded distant.

As agreed, he did not reply now, but he wanted to. He wanted to say, "I'm in, Kelly. I'm going to kill Assim Feroz for you."

Carl went deeper. His breathing slowed. His heart slogged through a gentle beat. Absolute peace. If called upon to do so, he thought he might be able to walk the bullet into a quarter at two thousand yards.

Yes, he could do that, couldn't he?

"Abort."

The shade was up, but the window was still dark. At any moment the doors would swing open and reveal the dining . . .

"Carl, do you hear me? Abort the current shot. There's been a change. There's a new target."

Only now did her first word penetrate his dark place. *Abort.*

No. No, he couldn't have heard it correctly.

I'm inside, Kelly. I will kill Assim Feroz for you. Please let me do this one thing for you. For us.

"Carl, acknowledge! You can't kill Assim Feroz. Do you hear me?"

The urgency in her voice made his vision swim for a brief moment.

"Acknowledged," he said.

"There is a new target. Acknowledge."

He could hear his breathing now, not a good thing. "Acknowledged."

"Your new target is the president of the United States, Robert Stenton. Acknowledge."

Light suddenly filled the open window five blocks away. He could see through the window, through the open doorway into the dining room now. Several dozen men and women, most in dark suits, seated at round tables.

Assim Feroz sat on the right, precisely where he'd been told to sit. But this wasn't the man Carl would kill. There was another. He hadn't known the president would be in the room. Where was this new target of his?

"Acknowledge, Carl."

"Where is he?" Carl asked.

"Third from the right at the long head table."

Carl eased his aim up and over. Third from the right. The president's torso filled the scope. Dark suit—too far for any other details. This is where he would send his bullet.

"Do you have him?"

"Yes."

He raised the crosshairs above the man's head, allowing for the drop of the bullet.

"Take the shot," Kelly said.

The president leaned to Carl's right. He was listening to the boy who sat on his left. This was his son, the one who'd purchased binoculars from the toy shop on the main floor.

Do I know this boy?

Jamie. *Do I know Jamie?*

Jamie looked as if he was laughing with his father.

The image froze in Carl's mind. He stared at father and son, mesmerized by the strange and wonderful display of affection.

"Take the shot, Carl."

His tunnel wavered, and he knew he couldn't take the shot without reacquiring perfect peace. The first shot would be easy; it was the second that concerned him. Under no circumstances could he jeopardize the mission by compromising the second shot. Any failed attempt would result in the target's immediate evacuation.

Carl dismissed the unique tension that had come from seeing father and son together. His body obeyed him.

He would take the shot now.

Why had they changed targets? Had they changed their minds? No. They'd known all along that the president was the target.

Then why hadn't they told him earlier?

Because they are afraid I won't kill the president of the United States. It was the only answer that made any sense.

"What's going on, Carl? Do you have a shot?"

Fear spread through Carl's body. Something about the father and son shut his muscles down. An instinctive impulse that screamed out of his dark past.

He would take the shot now. He had a clear shot. Less than an ounce of pressure and the president would be dead.

But this wasn't just the president of the United States. This was the boy's father. How could he possibly kill Jamie's father?

"Listen to me, Carl." Kelly's voice came gently, calming his confusion. "Whatever's going through your mind right now, let it go and send your bullets. For me. For us. They won't allow us to live if you fail."

She was right. He had to shoot.

"My heart is pounding, Kelly," he said. The realization that his tunnel was breaking down only made the matter worse. "I don't know if I have the shot."

She didn't respond.

"Kelly?"

Silence in his headset.

Now the fear that he'd hurt Kelly joined his confusion and sent a visible tremble through his fingers.

I'm breaking down!

For the first time in many months, Carl began to panic.

"Kelly!"

"Shh. Shh . . ." Her voice fell over him, milky soft.

"What's happening to me, Kelly?"

"It's okay, Carl."

But it wasn't okay, he knew that. The doors had been open for more than a minute already—at any moment the lapse in security would be identified and the opportunity for his shot would be closed.

Who is your father, Carl? You can't shoot this father.

A figure stepped into the doorway, peered out, then crossed to the window and pulled the shade closed.

Carl closed his eyes.

"They've pulled the shade," he said.

There was no response.

A terrible remorse swallowed him. He held his rifle tightly, feeling the familiar surfaces on his cheek and shoulder and in his hands. This gave him some comfort. He could have taken the shot. He could have killed the president for Kelly.

You can't shoot this father.

"Come home, Carl."

Her voice was like an angel's to him, calling him from the valley of death.

"Repair the glass, scrub the room, and come home. I'm here for you."

CHAPTER EIGHTEEN

THE NEW York Dragon was located a block west of the East River, where the small boat that would depart Manhattan Island waited in hiding. The authorities would undoubtedly shut down both bridges and tunnels as soon as they learned of any assassination attempt, thereby trapping all suspects on the island.

A withdrawal under cover of darkness was preferable, but the point was now moot. There was no need for a withdrawal.

Kelly watched Carl pace over the worn brown carpet. He'd returned at eleven, one hour earlier, after gluing the circles of glass back into the window, wiping down all surfaces, and packing his tools into the golf bag.

She felt ambivalent about his failure. A part of her ached with him. He was struggling to control his emotions, which threw him into a terrible funk. Confusion raced through his eyes. Her own feelings for him had grown far deeper than she had expected over the last month. Not only could she feel his pain; she found herself wanting to lighten it.

But she now suspected that she was *supposed* to feel this way. Her own feelings were part of the design. Surely they knew she would come to respect, perhaps even love Carl.

"Do you mind if I tell you what I think happened?" she asked.

Carl slid into the metal chair at the table and formed a teepee over the bridge of his nose, eyes lost on the wall.

"I think you've progressed exactly how Agotha expected you would. She told me that you'd fail the first attempt. She told me that you were meant to."

His eyes darted toward her. "That makes no sense."

"Neither did any of your training at first. But look at you now."

"Why was the target switched? They want me to kill the president—"

"Does that matter to you? Or does it matter more that you trust me? You've always believed in me, and nothing's changed now."

"I failed now."

She took a deep breath and told him what she'd been waiting to say. "You failed by design, to strengthen your resolve."

He didn't look her way.

Kelly walked over to the table and sat down across from him. "Listen to me, Carl. Look into my eyes."

His round brown eyes turned to her.

"I'm about to tell you something that might confuse you, but I want you to resist that confusion. For my sake. It's very important that you trust me now, like you've never trusted me before."

"I've always trusted you."

"I know you have. But you have to dig even deeper. Can you do that?"

"I love you," he said.

"I know you do. And I love you. We trust each other, even when the worst happens."

Kelly reached across the table's Formica top and offered him her hand. He took it.

"Do you remember your last treatment in the hospital?"

He thought for a moment. "No."

"No. You always put them behind you, don't you? But you were treated with drugs and shock therapy on the hospital bed the day before we left Hungary. During that treatment, you were led to believe that you could never take the life of Robert Stenton because he's the father of Jamie, a son. You, too, want—need—to be a son. That's why you hesitated. Only because Agotha wanted you to hesitate."

"Why?"

"Because this is your first real mission for the X Group. You may not think you can differentiate between real missions and the training, but your subconscious mind can. It's important that you understand that even in the field, you will feel only what Agotha wants you to feel."

"She wanted me to feel confusion."

"Yes."

"But I still failed."

"Yes, you did. But the next time you feel any hesitation or confusion, you'll remember that those feelings can't be trusted. You didn't really have any feelings for the son or the father, did you? The feelings were planted by Agotha."

A light grew in his eyes.

"The next time you feel anything in the field, you'll know. Even the feelings that break through aren't to be trusted. You'll know that they are simply tests from Agotha and you'll have the strength to set them aside."

"I'm not sure I understand. I don't want or need a father?"

"No. Why would you? You're twenty-five years old."

He grunted, then frowned at his own failure to recognize this.

"Agotha's methods are strange, but only because they are so advanced. I think you hold a special place in her heart. For all practical purposes, *she's* your mother. You can trust her with your life."

He grunted again. Shook his head and grinned sheepishly. "So it was all planned. I haven't failed, then."

Kelly stood and walked behind him. She placed her hands on his neck and messaged lightly. "Not really, no. You're as strong as ever. Even stronger."

She bent over and spoke gently behind his right ear. "How do you feel?"

"Foolish."

"Can you set this feeling aside?"

"Yes."

"Then please do it. How can the man I love feel foolish if he knows that I love him?"

Carl turned his head and looked into her eyes.

"If you're foolish, is your love for me also foolish?" she asked.

"No."

"Then you're not a fool."

"No."

She leaned around him and kissed him on the lips. "I didn't think so," she breathed. Carl's breathing thickened.

The idea that I can generate this response from him is without question the most satisfying part of loving him, she thought. And she did love him.

She was meant to.

Kelly straightened, unable to hide the coy smile on her face. She returned to her chair and sat slowly. "The president is scheduled to speak from the same stage that Assim Feroz will use tomorrow. One hour earlier."

"Then I should get into position," Carl said, standing. He walked to the window, pulled back the curtain, evidently saw nothing of interest, and turned to face her.

"If you fail tomorrow, they will kill us both," Kelly said. "You know that, right?"

"Why would I fail?"

"You won't. The only reason they haven't triggered the implant yet is because they expected you to fail. If you want proof that all of this is by design, there's your proof. You're still alive."

He nodded. "Then I'll kill the president of the United States tomorrow as planned."

"And then we can go home."

Carl pulled back the curtain again. "I like it here," he said. "The city is a good place to hide."

"So is the desert," Kelly said. "Nevada isn't so far from here. When all this is over, maybe we can go to the desert where no one will bother us."

"When what is over?"

"A figure of speech. We both know this will end only if we fail."

"I won't let that happen," Carl said. "I will never let them hurt you."

CHAPTER NINETEEN

THE GARBAGE trucks picked up trash along Avenue of the Americas every two days. Today was not one of those days.

Night still darkened Manhattan when Carl pushed the steel manhole cover off its seating. Unlike the first hit from the hotel, this one required far more direct coordination between Kelly and him.

Carl slid the heavy steel lid aside. He lit the portable acetylene torch, adjusted the flame until it was a bright blue, and began his cut into the bottom of the large garbage bin that Kelly had rolled over the hole.

The sound of wheels peeling along the street on his left muted the soft crackle of cutting steel. Kelly had pulled the bin into the alley and taped a rubber skirt around the bottom before pushing it into place. She was now playing the role of a janitor from the adjacent towers on Thirty-eighth Street, loading the bin with spent rags and rearranging the garbage already inside to make his entry possible.

It took Carl less than a minute to cut the two-foot hole and remove the hot steel plate from the bottom of the bin.

It took him a full three minutes to push his equipment through the hole and climb in after it, only because even with Kelly's efforts, he was forced to make room by shoving the bags around.

Once in the bin, he reached down to the sidewalk, slid the cover back into place, and rapped on the side of the bin.

Within seconds, the metal box was rolling. Twenty feet before it came to rest at the corner of the alley as planned, he heard the rubber skirt pull free. For several minutes Carl waited in the darkness.

The half-filled container smelled like spoiled milk, but he'd expected worse. He placed his feet against the wall he expected to work through and crammed the garbage to his rear.

Kelly's voice spoke quietly into his headset. "You copy?"

"Copy."

"You're clear."

Carl lit the torch and cut a seven-inch hole from the sidewall, leaving a half-inch section connected at the top. Using a screwdriver, he pried the lid that he'd cut in and up. The alley gaped in darkness, empty.

Satisfied, he pushed the metal plate back down into place.

"Ready," he said.

"Copy."

Thirty seconds later he heard a scraping sound around the hole he'd cut. She was filling the crack with putty and spraying it green.

"All clear," she finally said. "You're good?"

"Good."

"Still clear."

Kelly would watch the box from a dozen surveillance vantages, some of which they'd already selected, others she would find as the day passed.

Carl pushed the torch under the garbage behind him and extracted his rifle from the golf bag. He rested the gun on the metal floor, careful not to jar the scope. There was only one way to position himself for the shot—on his belly with his legs bent up and his rifle inside his elbow, resting on its bipod. He maneuvered slowly, shoving and rearranging bags as he moved. The hole he'd cut in the floor of the bin clipped his left forearm—unavoidable. He would have to reposition himself just before shooting. Once in place, he pulled the bags of rags over his head, shaping a clearing around the scope as he did so.

He snugged the weapon to his shoulder and peered into blackness. Kelly would move the bin into position and open the hole he'd cut for his shot thirty seconds before the kill.

Once again, the level of information that the X Group had secured to facilitate this opportunity was beyond his ability to comprehend. Feroz would be standing on the stage they'd erected just inside Central Park South, on Avenue of the Americas. He knew now that it would be the president of the United States, not Assim Feroz, but nothing else about the kill had changed.

The street would be closed to both pedestrian through-traffic and cars at Thirty-eighth Street three hours prior to the press conference. The unprecedented security measures would require an enormous effort on the part of the NYPD. But any security envelope could be penetrated by the right person.

In this case, Carl was that person.

Their effort might remove most conceivable threats to those who took the stage, but it would also clear a corridor down Avenue of the Americas for an improbable shot. Perhaps impossible.

To all but him.

"I'm in position," he said.

"It's 4:36 a.m.," Kelly said. "You have just over ten hours before the press conference. I'll check in every hour unless we have a problem."

He would have preferred to set up closer to the target, but there were no garbage bins suitably located for both the shot and the escape. His shot would be just under two thousand yards. As long as the weather cooperated and he was able to acquire the target, he would have a good shot.

"You're okay?"

"I'm fine."

It was now time to wait.

OUTSIDE, CARS roared by and pedestrians rode a wave of indistinct voices, but in the pitch-black container, Carl lay facedown on a cushion of darkness, shut off from everything except the hourly sound of Kelly's gentle voice.

They didn't talk. She called him on the hour and asked for acknowledgment, which he offered and then retreated into his darkness. He was in his pit, right here on Avenue of the Americas. Truth be told, he was more comfortable in this place than he'd been anywhere since leaving the compound. *In the future, I'll shoot from the darkness whenever I have the opportunity,* he thought. Maybe always.

The pressure on his elbows and hip bones, the cramping of his muscles, and the stuffy heat reassured him that very few could withstand such discomfort. He alone could satisfy Kelly with success, because to him the pain wasn't pain at all—he'd shut it down. How many men could do that?

Even though he couldn't yet see the target, he walked an imaginary path from the garbage bin to Robert Stenton. He'd selected a 150-gram full-metal jacket for the task, preferring the increased accuracy it offered over a bullet that would flatten upon impact, even though the latter would increase the likelihood of a kill should the bullet miss the chest.

He had no intention of missing the target's chest.

The father was about to die.

Could he kill Jamie's father? Of course he could.

The sound of traffic ceased at noon, when they closed the street fifty yards behind him.

"One o'clock," Kelly said. "We're on schedule."

"One o'clock."

Time drifted by. Twice someone opened the bin, threw some garbage in, then let the lid clang noisily back in place, oblivious to his body hiding below the bags.

At times like this, deep in stasis, he felt as though he might actually be hallucinating. The darkness seemed to touch him as if it were matter.

Agotha had once told him that he drew all of his power from his own mind, that a person who finds silence and solitude boring is a person who is himself boring, empty of anything worth consideration. "These empty shells require outside stimulation to keep them from blowing away in a gentle breeze," she'd said.

"Two," Kelly said.

Carl grunted.

In one hour he would send the bullet into the father's chest.

Less than a week ago he'd been strapped into an electric chair and survived an onslaught of electricity. How? By going very deep and affecting the zero-point field that connected him to the objects around him. It was nothing more than mind over matter. Not so different from embracing the dark or slowing his heart rate.

With belief as small as a mustard seed, you can move mountains— a famous teacher had said that. But what if Agotha was wrong about the source of his power? What if he'd tapped into something far greater than the dark musings of quantum theory?

Whatever it was, it had worked. Could work. Would work. More important, his success pleased both Agotha and Kalman. And even more than either of these, it pleased Kelly.

Carl wasn't even aware of the last hour. It was simply there one minute and gone the next.

"Five minutes."

He methodically reached up and flipped a small switch on the side of his scope. Battery-powered light filled the glass. Without it, his vision would be distorted by the flood of light when Kelly opened the metal flap. He let his pupils adjust.

"We have a go. The target has just taken the stage. I'm coming in."
No need to answer.

The bin swayed once and then began to clatter along the rough
concrete. He was like a battleship being maneuvered to bring its guns
to bear.

Kelly's boot kicked the metal circle, forcing it inward a few inches.
He reached forward and bent it all the way up. Now Carl had a clear
view of the street and, thanks to the blockade behind him, the distant park.

"Clear?"

"Clear," he said.

Avenue of the Americas fell and rose between this point and the
park, but on balance it dropped about ten feet on its way to the stage.
He would have to compensate accordingly.

Carl peered through the scope, down the street, all the way to the
park, a mile and a half away. The bullet would fly a second and a half
and drop nearly eight feet before striking the target.

And now Carl could see that target.

The last time he'd seen this view was two days earlier, when he
dropped to one knee while picking up a dropped pen to study this
line. Then, he'd had to visualize the street vacant of cars and pedestrians. Now a dozen obstacles rose between him and the president—
street lamps, light posts, a few tree branches at the end—but the
target's torso was in plain view. His bullet would pass under a branch
that cut the target off at the neck and enter his chest for a kill. There
were no obstacles between his barrel and the father. He studied the
man's chest.

"It's your call, Carl. Take your shot."

Again, he felt no need to respond.

His pulse slowed. His breathing stalled. He was home.

A man in a blue suit stood to the target's left. Secret Service. An
older man in a tweed blazer sat behind the president.

I know this man.

He stared, transfixed by the older man. Aside from the man's beard and general features, he couldn't make out fine details, but he was suddenly and forcefully certain that he knew this man. It was the way he sat with arms folded. The way his head sat on his shoulders. The way he crossed his legs.

Carl blinked, stunned. His heart thumped, ruining his aim, forcing him to reacquire the stillness the bullet would need as it sped down the barrel.

But he knew this man! As a father. The man was his father?

You can't kill the father.

Carl stilled his body. Raised the barrel ever so slightly. Found the light.

But there was more than light in his mind. There was a voice, and it was screaming bloody murder, raging through his concentration.

You cannot kill the father!

Carl began to panic.

KELLY WATCHED the president through powerful binoculars from her perch half a block behind the garbage bin in which Carl lay, wondering why he hadn't taken the shot.

She'd wheeled the green steel box onto the sidewalk and left it directly above the manhole as planned. Carl would make the shot, drop into the service tunnel, discard the weapon, and run one block south, where he would exit through a manhole in an alley and then meet her at the Dragon.

As they'd suspected, the NYPD was too busy rerouting traffic and dealing with mobs of pedestrians behind the barricades to care about a single garbage bin half a block up the street. A handful of workers from nearby office buildings still loitered on Avenue of the Americas, occasionally passing near the bin. Although through-traffic had been cut off, these people were allowed. The streets of New York were accustomed to change. The presence of a garbage bin ten feet from its normal resting place attracted no attention.

So far, so good.

According to the media, the summit had accomplished little or nothing—neither side budged. The president was already into his speech, presumably pitching his final position to the media.

Take the shot, Carl. Now, take the shot!

Most of the expanding gases responsible for the noise of Carl's shot would be baffled by the bin's metal wall, but the few dozen pedestrians within a hundred yards would hear the sound clearly enough. Still, it would take them many seconds to isolate the sound's source and react. By then, Carl would be gone.

This was the plan.

But she wasn't sure that Carl was following the plan.

The president had been talking for several minutes now, and still no shot. She knew he had a clear line for the simple reason that he hadn't said otherwise.

"We are clear." She spoke deliberately but very softly. "It's time, my dear."

No shot.

It was this business about his father. She cursed under her breath. *Please, Carl, please shoot.*

What if this was a profound weakness in Agotha's training? *What if Carl simply cannot bring himself to fire upon a father figure because he, like me, really does need—*

A muffled explosion stopped her thought short—the sound of a car backfiring. But today it wasn't a car.

Carl had fired!

Her hands trembled, momentarily distorting the image on the platform a mile and a half away. The bullet would travel for two seconds before—

Robert Stenton grabbed his chest. He sat hard, then dropped back.

For a brief second there was no movement. Then the stage blurred into a picture of confusion as Secret Service swarmed the prone body.

Kelly jerked the binoculars from her eyes. Two dozen people were scattered down the street. Some had stopped what they were doing and were looking around for the source of the sound. Others had probably concluded that a taxi had backfired. None were paying any special attention to the green garbage bin. By now Carl would have already shoved the green metal flap back into place.

She lowered her eyes to the gap between the bin and the sidewalk just in time to see Carl drop through. Then he was gone.

Saint had just killed the president of the United States.

CHAPTER TWENTY

CARL PUSHED his rifle through the manhole, heard it splash below. To abuse a weapon so intentionally struck him as profane, but this was the plan. His plan.

He swung his feet into the hole, dropped down to the fifth rung, and pulled the manhole cover back into place. Dim light filtered through a thin gap around the heavy metal plate. He descended the ladder quickly.

Who had he shot? What had he done? *Father*—the word refused to stop pounding through his skull.

Father, father, father. Father!

A foot of dirty water ran down the passage, soaking his canvas boots. He felt for the rifle, found it, and ran south along the walkway on the east side of the tunnel.

The bullet had followed a perfect trajectory, he knew that. What he didn't know was whether he'd succeeded. Or who the old man was. His need to know smothered his judgment.

He had to escape, and he would. But he also had to know what had happened. Why he'd believed with such certainty that he was peering through the scope at his father!

He threw the rifle into a deep alcove two hundred yards south as planned and ran on. They would find the rifle without a serial number and without prints.

Heart pounding like a sledge, Carl reached his exit ladder and climbed from a manhole in the alley two blocks south of the barricades. His radio should work now.

"Are you there?"

Kelly was breathing hard when she responded. "I'm here. You did well, Carl."

He turned up the alley and ran eastward.

"I'll meet you as planned," he said.

"Hurry."

Carl ripped the headset from his ears and threw the device into a garbage can at Thirty-seventh Street and Fifth Avenue. They'd blockaded Fifth as well, but the traffic would be flowing freely on Third.

Bellevue Hospital was located on First. Although South New York Hospital was technically closer to Central Park, they would take the president down Avenue of the Americas to Bellevue, he'd been told.

He wasn't sure why he hadn't told Kelly of his impulsive change in plan, but the five-block side trip would hold him up for only ten minutes and wouldn't compromise their exit, which wasn't planned until nightfall anyway.

He had to go to Bellevue Hospital because he had to know.

A host of sirens wailed through the streets. If the bullet hadn't killed the president outright, toxic shock soon would. They would waste no time speeding to the trauma unit.

But Carl was much closer to Bellevue than they were.

He sprinted down Thirty-seventh, ignoring the casual gazes of pedestrians, clearly clueless about the events behind him. The city exploded back to life at Third Avenue, but no one in this part of town had heard the news that the president had just been shot twenty-two blocks north. They still sold their magazines and walked briskly to their meetings and hailed their cabs.

Carl ignored the red lights and tore across the street, ignoring a long horn blast from a motorist. The chorus of sirens reached him above the street noise. The ambulance and its police escort were behind him on Avenue of the Americas, screaming toward him.

What are you doing, Carl? You think you're going to find your father? Every step is a step closer to death.

Left on First Avenue. He could see that they'd already closed the Midtown Tunnel in an attempt to cut off escape routes. Confusion was backing up. News was spreading.

Carl reached Bellevue Hospital on First and Thirty-fourth ahead of the piercing sirens. He stepped into an alley opposite the emergency ramp as the first police swept around the corner, sped past the alley, and squealed to a stop one block north. Another car joined the first. Two others peeled south to cut off any approach from Twenty-third Street.

The ambulance slowed to take the corner, then accelerated toward the emergency ramp, directly across from Carl.

He eased back into the shadows, panting from his run. But he couldn't stay here; there was no direct view of the ramp.

He glanced behind, saw that the alley was clear all the way to Second Avenue, shoved his hands into his pockets, and headed directly for the ramp, head down.

Why are you risking exposure, Carl?

I'm not. I'm simply a curious bystander, oblivious to the contents of that ambulance.

You'll be seen.

I've already been seen at a dozen events. My face is undoubtedly on film. Faces can be changed.

You haven't mapped this escape route. If they grow suspicious, you'll be running blind.

I do well running blind.

Do you think the old man is your father?

He couldn't answer the question.

Then Carl was behind a waist-high retaining wall, staring down a slight incline at the red ambulance. The doors flew open. A paramedic spilled out and was quickly joined by six medical staff who'd been waiting.

The gurney slid out. The man he'd come face-to-face with yesterday in the Waldorf lay on his back with a green oxygen mask over his face. A silver pole with a bag of fluid was affixed to the gurney.

But it was the blood that held Carl's attention. The sheets draped over his chest were red with blood. This had been his bullet's doing.

The old man in tweed stepped from the back of the ambulance, and Carl's heart skipped a beat. *Father.* Surely this couldn't be his father!

The man hurried beside the gurney as they wheeled it to the open doors. He seemed to be praying.

The distant features that had transfixed his mind as he settled for the shot now confronted him in full color at less than fifty paces.

He did know this man!

He didn't know who he was, or how he knew him, or even how well he knew him, but he did know him.

As a father.

Carl stared, wide-eyed. His father? Or his spiritual father?

They call me Saint.

A STRANGE calm had stilled David Abraham's heart the moment Robert dropped to the stage floor. He knew then that one of two things had happened.

Which meant that he'd been right all along.

Or dreadfully wrong.

He was second to reach the president, just behind an agent who ran between Robert and the audience to intercept a second shot.

But one look at the president, and there was no doubt that a second shot would not be needed. Robert Stenton lay on his back, eyes closed, red blood spreading from a small tear in his white shirt.

David's inexplicable peace quickly changed to an urgency. Perhaps some panic. The president of the United States had been assassinated, right here in front of a hundred cameras. And he had played a role!

He began to pray, loudly and fervently, pausing every few seconds to demand they work on him faster, load him faster, get to the hospital faster.

Now they had arrived at the hospital, and the singular calm returned to him. He prayed as he hurried to stay by Robert's side. Disbelief gripped the staff as they rushed him in. A doctor spoke urgently, issuing orders, but David wasn't listening. His own prayers crowded his mind.

Not until he'd crossed the threshold did he notice a lone figure in his peripheral vision, watching them from behind. He turned his head.

David froze. Dear Lord, it was *him*!

They exchanged a long stare.

Someone touched his elbow. "Sir—"

"I'll be right in."

David turned and walked toward the man, who still stood with his hands in his pockets, mesmerized by the scene. He stopped less than ten feet from the man, separated from him by a waist-high barrier.

David found his voice. "Do you know who I am?"

The man searched his face, eyes blank.

"Do you know what's happening?"

"Are you my father?"

The sound of his voice—he would never mistake that voice!

"No. My name is David Abraham. Do you know who I am?"

No response.

"I know who you are," David said.

The air was thick between them.

"Who am I?" the man asked.

David glanced back and satisfied himself that they could not be overheard. A part of him demanded that he call security. Unless he was wrong about everything up to this point, he was facing the man who'd assassinated the president of the United States.

But if he wasn't wrong, calling out for help would be the worst thing he could do.

He jerked his head back to the man. "You're more than I can tell you here. Did you kill the president?"

"Was that the president?"

"Yes. He was shot. Did you do the shooting?"

"No."

As far as David could see, the denial wasn't a lie. But that meant nothing; he couldn't see into the mind.

"Do you know my father?" the man asked.

"No, I don't."

The man hesitated a moment, then turned to his right and began to walk away.

"They've lied to you," David said. "It's all a lie."

The man stopped and turned back.

He knew it! David pushed forward while he had the advantage. "Tell me where I can find you. I'll send a boy to talk to you. He's my son. No one else, you have my word."

The man stood still, considering. Then he pulled his hand out of his pocket and dropped something on the ground. Without a word or a glance, he jogged across the street and into the alley.

David hoisted his leg over the short wall and struggled over. It was a matchbook, he could see that now. He ran to the matches and picked them up.

Peking Grand Hotel. Chinatown.

Hands trembling, lips mumbling in prayer, David pulled out his cell phone and made the call.

CHAPTER TWENTY-ONE

CARL UNLOCKED the hotel room door, stepped in, and eased the door closed.

"Thank goodness you made it! Is everything okay? You're late."

He felt lost but refused to show it. "I'm here, aren't I?"

A wide smile split Kelly's face. She hurried over to him, threw her arms around his neck, and kissed him on the lips.

Her enthusiasm washed over him, and the desperation that had plagued him for the last hour faded.

"We did it, Carl." She kissed him again, and this time he kissed her back. It was a great moment, wasn't it? They'd completed their first mission together. Kelly had never been so happy when he'd successfully executed an exercise, but now, in the field, her joy was practically spilling over.

It was a very good day to be alive.

Carl suddenly wanted to see their work. "Is it on the news?"

"Are you kidding? They've been playing it nonstop. A perfect hit, Carl. Agotha will be so proud."

"I don't care about Agotha," he said. He clarified his statement when she raised her brow. "Not like I care for you."

"She's your mother," Kelly said. "I'm your lover."

He winked at her. Imagine that, he actually winked at her. He wasn't used to being so forward with her, preferring instead to let her take the lead. She was, after all, his handler as well.

But he was emboldened by his tremendous success. "One day we should get married," he said.

Her eyes lit up. "And run off to Nevada?"

"Why not? We're lovers. Isn't that what lovers do? Run off?"

They stared at each other.

"You want to see it?" Kelly plopped down on the bed and faced the television.

Carl sat next to her and watched the muted images. A reporter was speaking below a large graphic that read "President Stenton Shot." At the bottom was a disclaimer that the images were graphic.

He stared as the footage of his kill played in slow motion. It looked surreal. The president talking, pointing to someone in the crowd. A sudden tug at his shirt, his mouth caught open in a gasp, clutching a growing red spot on his chest. He dropped to his seat hard, then toppled back and lay still.

Kelly was biting her fingernail when Carl looked at her for approval. "Amazing," she said.

He shrugged. "Just a day on the range."

But there was more to it, wasn't there? Far more. He was playing her game now, as he always had, but if she knew he'd spoken to someone at the hospital, she wouldn't be so happy.

Carl knew he faced a predicament that could end his life. He had to tell her. She would help him figure it out—she always had. But he couldn't bring himself to ruin her happiness.

"What's wrong?" Kelly asked.

He looked at her. "Hmm? Nothing."

"You're sweating."

"Am I?" He drew his fingers across a moist forehead.

"What's wrong?"

Here it was, then. He couldn't lie to her. Never. Yet he'd just lied, hadn't he? He felt nauseated. He'd felt this way before, many times. When he lied to Agotha while on the hospital bed. When he'd mistaken the truth about who he was and answered incorrectly. In that moment before they turned up the electrical current to help him understand the truth, he'd often felt nauseated.

"What is it?" Worry laced Kelly's voice.

"Our lives might be in danger," he said.

Kelly stood up. "They know?"

"No, not from them. From Kalman."

She looked at the television. "But you've executed the hit perfectly."

Carl blurted the truth as he knew he must. "I talked to him, Kelly! I went to the hospital and talked to the old man. He said his name was David Abraham."

"What old man? What on earth are you talking about?"

Carl pointed at the television, which was replaying the scene.

"Him. The old man behind the target. I recognized him. I felt as though I had to be sure . . ."

"Sure about what? The hit? We can verify through the media! You . . . You're saying you went to the hospital?"

"They took him into the emergency room. The man was there. He said he knew who I—"

"You *talked* to him?"

"I told him I didn't shoot the president."

"He actually asked you that?" Kelly stared at him, face white, eyes round. She was angry. Or shocked. Both. At moments like this Carl felt nothing like the hero who could kill any man he wished. He felt more like a child.

Kelly walked to the laptops that showed the views of the dummy rooms, slammed them closed.

"What are you doing?"

"We're getting out of here! You've been identified. It's only a matter of time before the old man matches you to file footage taken over the last few days. They'll have your face on every television in the world by tonight."

"He gave me his word that he wouldn't do that. He's sending his son."

Kelly faced him, aghast. "Here?"

"No. To the Peking."

"How could you do this? You've just killed the president of the United States! Do you think some old man loyal to the president will let you walk away because you told him you didn't kill the leader of the free world?"

Carl fought the nausea sweeping through his stomach. He'd never seen her so distraught. He'd made a terrible mistake, he knew that now. They would terminate him as soon as they discovered it.

And Kelly with him.

He stood and paced in front of the television. "I'm sorry, Kelly. I don't know why I did it. He *knew* me!"

"And I know you," she said quietly.

"Then tell me what to do."

She studied him. She loved him—he could see it in her eyes. Even when he made such a terrible mistake as this, she loved him.

Kelly closed her eyes, trying to think. "Okay. Forget what happened. Right now we have to survive." Her eyes drilled his. "You tell me, what will increase our likelihood of survival now?"

He'd already thought this through. Perhaps, if the cards fell in his favor, he could undo the damage before Kalman discovered the truth. "Even if the man sends his son to the Peking, they have no idea where we are. Our exit window is still four hours away. We should watch the room. If the boy arrives, we may be able to use him. We may also choose to ignore him."

"How will we know if the boy arrives?"

"Before coming here I went by the Peking and opened the door for him." Carl pointed at the computers she'd closed. "We'll see him enter the room."

"We could never trust him. It's likely a trap."

"He could have alerted the police at the hospital, but he didn't. If the son comes, it won't be a trap."

She considered his logic. "We have no way of knowing he's really the man's son. I don't understand why we would need the boy in any case."

"We may need him to kill the president."

"The president's dead!"

"No, I don't think he is."

DAVID ABRAHAM walked briskly down the corridor, following the signs to radiology. Dr. Tom Davis was the chief radiologist. He would be the first to know what the X-rays showed.

They were working on Robert Stenton with an urgency that called for the immediate dismissal of all well-wishers, regardless of their political clout. Two Secret Service staff were posted outside the private room, and the hall was lined with staff, but not even his closest advisers knew the president's condition. All they knew was that he'd arrived at the hospital with a very weak pulse.

It wasn't great news. Many victims of gunshot wounds managed to hang on to life for an hour, even two, before expiring. In the case of such a prominent figure, no word on his condition would be given until it was certain.

The only thing the world knew at this point was that the president of the United States had been shot in the chest.

But David had to know more. He pushed open the door to the main radiology reception room. A dozen patients waited their turn.

The door twenty yards down the hall marked Authorized Personnel

Only would lead into the same department. David hurried to the door and walked through.

"May I help you?"

He faced a nurse who'd stopped in the hall on his right. "Yes, I must see Dr. Tom Davis immediately. Can you tell me where—"

"Dr. Davis is tied up. Have you checked in at reception?"

"I don't think you understand. I'm with the president. It's a matter of life and death."

She wasn't impressed. "You'll have to—"

"Now!" He started to walk. "Another minute and he could be dead. Now!"

She hurried after him. "Sir, they specifically—"

"I'm President Stenton's spiritual adviser, for heaven's sake. I don't have time for this!"

She hesitated only a beat. "Third office on the left. He's in his reading room."

David reached the door and put his hand on the knob. "This room?"

"Yes."

"Thank you."

He stepped into a dimly lit room with four large monitors on one wall and a large vertical light surface on the opposite wall. The man he presumed to be Dr. Tom Davis stood in front of a row of large flat-screen monitors, reading a dozen X-rays. He didn't seem to notice David's entry.

"You're Dr. Davis?"

No response. The man was clearly focused.

David approached, scanning the backlit negatives. "My name is David Abraham. I'm the president's spiritual adviser. Are these his X-rays?"

"CAT scans. I've already sent the digital images down to surgery," the radiologist said without looking over. "Interesting."

"What do you see?" David asked.

Now the radiologist looked at him. "Spiritual adviser, huh?"

"That's correct. I must know if you've found any anomalies."

"Not that I can see."

"Nothing?"

"Nothing."

"Show me nothing."

The radiologist picked up a telescoping pointer, stretched it out, and tapped the image in front of him. "The bullet entered here, between the seventh and eighth lateral ribs. No break. If you want to consider that an anomaly, be my guest."

"That's unusual?"

"It happens sometimes. Depends on the entry angle."

He rested the point on a dark spot just below what looked to David like the president's heart. "Missed the heart and the lungs by a hair. We have some minor bleeding here, but I would guess it's from the surface wound. You could also call that an anomaly, I suppose."

"That's not unusual?"

"It happens. But yes, it's unusual."

He tapped a third image. "The bullet exited here, between the fifth and sixth vertebrae."

"No breaks in the spinal column?"

"No."

"So that, too, is unusual?"

Dr. Tom Davis put his hands on his hips and stared at the three images he'd just pointed out. "None of these is particularly unusual. Put them all together, and I would say you have an impossibility."

David's pulse strengthened. "Meaning what?"

"Meaning that I've never seen anything like it. The bullet entered his torso in one of the only places it could have to miss all the internal organs and exit without so much as breaking a bone. Normally I'd expect to see the bullet break up and tear things to shreds. Most exit wounds leave holes large enough to put your fist through."

The radiologist faced him with a grin. "This is no anomaly, my friend. If I were a man of faith, I'd call this a miracle."

He knew it! David could hardly contain himself. Waves of relief washed over his body.

"And what injuries did he sustain?"

"You'll have to take that up with the surgeon. By what I can see, I'd say he sustained two flesh wounds. No internal bleeding. Nothing but a couple of minor cuts to his chest and back."

"Then why surgery?"

"For starters, they just got these pictures. They'll sew him up. His greatest danger was from toxic shock, but they got to him pretty quickly. If I were a betting man, I'd say the president will be up and out of bed in two or three days."

"And this isn't an anomaly?" David cried.

"I once read the X-rays of a skydiver whose chute failed to open. He sustained one broken finger and bruises. Unusual, yes; anomaly, no."

David hardly heard him. He whirled toward the door. "I have to talk to him."

"He's in surgery."

David exited the reading room and suppressed a temptation to run. He hadn't felt so full of life in twelve years. There was no telling how Robert would react to this turn of events, but David would tell him everything. Today. As soon as he woke up.

Project Showdown was breathing still.

CHAPTER TWENTY-TWO

HE WASN'T sure, he said. His mind had entered a strange place, and he didn't know what had happened, because he really, really didn't want his bullet to kill the president. But he would now make it right. He would; he swore he would.

Kelly's worst fears were realized half an hour later when an NBC reporter giving a live report on location at Central Park was cut off by the anchor.

"... was here on this platform, where a forensic team is still looking for the bullet that—"

"I'm sorry to interrupt, Susan, but we have a live update on the president's condition. Reuters is reporting that the president of the United States has survived the assassination attempt that took place an hour and a half ago. I repeat, it appears that the president has survived the attempt on his life. The report goes on to say that the bullet resulted in flesh wounds only."

Kelly stared at the screen, disbelieving. "How's that possible?"

Kelly muted the television and sat on the bed, stunned. Kalman would receive the news soon enough, if he hadn't already. It would be the end.

Behind her, Carl remained silent.

"Do you know what this means?" she asked.

"That I've failed," he said. "But I can fix it."

She stood with her back to him. "Agotha will know."

"She'll know what?"

"That your failure was intentional."

"*I* don't even know that!"

Kelly could feel her world collapsing around her. So much training, so many hard nights—in one moment, gone. Both she and Carl were now expendable.

Was this also part of the plan? She sometimes found it difficult to determine what was real and what was part of the game.

She looked at Carl, who was still staring at the silent news broadcast. "You affected the bullet's trajectory the same way you have been for the last two weeks."

He refused to look at her.

"Today you placed the bullet precisely where it had to travel to knock him down without killing him. We taught you more about the anatomy of the kill zones in the human body than most medical students ever learn. Now you've used that information to save your target. And by doing so, you've signed our death warrants."

"We don't know that," he said. "If it was intentional, I would remember."

"Then what do you remember?"

"That I didn't want the president to die. I thought that the old man behind him might be my father. Or that the president himself might be. I was confused and knew that Agotha had probably put these ideas in my head to test me. As you said."

"But you couldn't overcome the confusion?"

"I thought I had."

She sighed and closed her eyes. "It doesn't matter. Kalman will assume that you've countermanded his order to kill. He will never accept such a failure."

Her cell phone chirped.

"That will be him." Kelly picked up the phone. "Yes."

Kalman's distant, gravelly voice spoke into her ear. "I see he missed."

"Yes. We're working on a third attempt."

The phone hissed.

"Carl's leading the son of the president's adviser—"

"I don't want the details," Kalman said. "Englishman is standing by. You have until midnight. If I haven't received confirmation by then, your man must be eliminated." He paused. "I want you to do it personally. I'll give you two hours following any such failure on his part. If you don't follow through, I'll trigger the implant and hold you responsible. Are we clear?"

She hesitated. "Of course."

The line clicked off.

Kelly kept her back to Carl and gathered her wits. He couldn't see her face flushed.

"If the boy shows, can you do what you've suggested?" she asked, setting the phone down slowly.

He'd formulated a simple plan for a third attempt, but she had her doubts about his willingness to finish the job. If he didn't, she would.

"Why wouldn't I?"

Carl's mind is so fried that he can hardly hold a conviction for an hour, she thought.

"You've failed to finish the job twice now, both times because you associated the target with a father figure. None of this will change."

"But I know why now," Carl said. "Agotha put the desire in me."

"That knowledge didn't help you execute the hit today."

He didn't respond to her obvious point. It didn't matter. Her psychological manipulation had failed to affect him as she'd hoped. Perhaps the truth would work better.

"I have a confession to make," she said. "I lied to you yesterday. Agotha didn't plant the thoughts of your father. I needed you to feel strong about today's attempt, so I gave you a plausible reason for your failure. It seems that this father business is coming from your own mind on its own terms."

Carl looked lost. Stunned.

"Maybe it's my fault you feel so conflicted. I was trying to help you."

"And I would have done the same for you," he said. "It must have been horrible to have to lie. Yet you did it to protect me. Thank you."

She couldn't bear this manipulation. What had they done to him? The mental stripping was one thing in the compound, but here in the middle of New York, it seemed inhumane.

"Can you do it?"

"Send the boy back with a message for the president?"

"Unwittingly armed with a toxic canister," she finished. "It would kill everyone in the room."

"Of course I can do it. It's what I've been trained to do."

"You were also trained to put a bullet in a target's heart, yet you willfully missed."

"I don't remember willfully—"

"There he is!"

The laptop showed a short boy standing inside their room at the Peking, looking around.

Carl walked up to the desk, studied the image for a few moments, then slammed the laptop closed.

"Let's go," he said and strode toward the door.

THE PEKING Grand Hotel was a five-minute walk. With any luck the boy would find Carl's note instructing him to wait ten minutes.

They walked quickly, silently.

He was less sure of what he was doing now than at any time in his memory. His response to the confusion was to retreat. There were many times when survival depended on retreat. It was how he defeated the heat in his pit. The hornets on the shooting range. The hospital bed under Agotha's care. There was always a safe place in his mind somewhere. He just had to find it.

At this moment, that safe place was probably execution without thought. They had until midnight to undo the mess he'd made. Poison was the preferred weapon of many assassins, and tonight Carl would remember why.

If his plan failed, he would be left with only one alternative. He would find a few more-familiar weapons and go after the president in the hospital. His chances of survival were minimal, but he would be dead at midnight anyway. If he was going to die, he would die fighting for Kelly's survival. He owed her his life.

They entered the Peking through a rear door that required a plastic key card to open. Second floor. First door on the right, room 202.

The small device that Kelly carried in her purse consisted of a remote triggering device and a small canister of colorless, odorless hydrogen cyanide gas, potent enough to kill any living creature in a ten-by-ten room within five minutes. The boy's mission would be a simple one: in the president's hospital room, he would call a given telephone number and then verbally relay a message intended only for the president. In this way, they could reasonably believe that the boy was talking to the president, not a third party.

There would be no message, of course. As soon as the boy confirmed the president's presence, they would trigger the canister hidden on the boy's person with a certain degree of confidence that both were in the same room. A similar method using explosives rather than gas had been used successfully among drug cartels in South America. Certainly not infallible, but with nothing to lose, Carl was willing to assume the odds before he attempted anything more direct.

The door was still cracked open. He entered the room, followed by Kelly.

It was empty. David Abraham's son had left?

"Hello, Johnny."

Carl turned to face a blond-headed boy standing in the bathroom doorway. He looked to be thirteen or fourteen. A sheepish smile curved below bright blue eyes.

"My name is Samuel," the boy said. "You don't remember me, do you?"

"Should I?"

Carl had no intention of remembering anything. Memory only brought confusion and contributed to his failure.

"They've stripped you of your identity," Samuel said. "You really don't know who you are anymore. Amazing. We knew . . ." His eyes shifted to Kelly, then returned to Carl. He carried himself with surprising confidence for such a small boy.

"We knew you couldn't do it. The truth runs too deep in you, Johnny. We always knew that you could only go so far."

A ringing bothered Carl's ears. "Why do you keep calling me Johnny?"

"Johnny Drake. That's your real name. You were a chaplain in the army when the X Group took you. You were on leave in Egypt."

"A chaplain?"

"You're mistaken," Kelly said. "You're confusing him with someone else."

"Don't let my appearance deceive you," Samuel said. "I'm much older than I look. And I can prove all of this if you give me the chance."

The ringing in Carl's ears had become a soft roar. He'd been a chaplain who was now called Saint? How would the boy know? Why would the boy lie?

He tried to think of himself as Johnny. The name sounded odd.

"Do you mind excusing us for a moment?" Kelly asked Samuel.

"Now?"

"Yes. Could you step outside? Just for a moment."

"Okay."

The boy stepped out into the hall, and Kelly closed the door behind him. She returned, motioning silence.

"Do you know this boy?" she whispered.

"I don't remember."

"It's Kalman. I can smell it on him."

"I don't understand. How could Kalman know—"

"The old man knew you. Who's to say that he's not with Kalman?"

Carl's mind spun. He'd faced and accepted more confusion in the last twenty-four hours than he'd allowed himself in many months. The nausea he'd felt earlier made a comeback.

"It's like Kalman to put redundancies in place to deal with the possibility that you will fail to assassinate the president. Why not the old man and the boy?"

"Why two people instead of just one? And why would he use a boy?"

"What better way to gain your trust and lead us to a place where Englishman can kill us both? The one thing that Kalman fears more than anything else is his own assassins." She took a deep breath. "I've seen this before, in Indonesia once. If I'm right, the boy will suggest you go somewhere."

"I don't understand why—"

"Then trust me! I lied to you once, but I won't lie to you again. Kalman knows your weakness for a father figure and he's exploiting it."

"Kalman doesn't need the boy. He could kill me with the implant."

She nodded and paced. "True. But I don't like it. Kalman is a suspicious snake. This would be like him. I think the boy is lying!"

"What are you suggesting?" he asked.

"That we walk away from this boy. We can't believe his lies, and we can't use him the way we planned. If he's connected to Kalman, there'll be a trap waiting for us."

Carl nodded. It made sense in a twisted way. He'd never considered betraying Kalman, but at the moment he was desperate for any sense at all. He accepted her truth and felt his nausea ease.

"Then we'll dismiss him and I'll go after the president on my own."

"It's the only way we can prove ourselves to Kalman without risking being caught in a trap," she said.

Kelly let the boy back into the room.

"You don't trust me, do you?" the boy said. "I came because my father and I know what you did, Johnny. You shot a bullet through the president's chest in a way that wouldn't kill him. They found the garbage bin that you shot from. Hitting a man at two thousand yards is very difficult. Sending a bullet through a precise point at that distance is impossible. Yet you did it."

The boy knew all of this? Carl glanced at Kelly. She was as confused as he.

Samuel continued. "You may think there's some kind of scientific explanation for your abilities, but the truth is not so simple. Your real power is much greater than anything you've seen. In fact, you were more powerful before they took you. By messing with your mind, they messed with your power."

"How do you know this?" Kelly demanded.

"Because I've been watching Johnny ever since he left Paradise."

A strobe ignited in the back of Carl's mind. Paradise. It was familiar. Terribly familiar. But he couldn't place it.

"Do you remember?" Samuel asked. "I'm here because I want you to go to Paradise, Johnny. Your mother still lives there. Her name is Sally, and she's been sick about your disappearance."

Samuel's words fell into his mind like bright flashes along a line of lost history. *Sally. Paradise. Colorado. Chaplain.*

Johnny.

Johnny.

My name is Johnny.

But he couldn't remember any of it!

"If I were Kalman, I would tell you to say all these things," Kelly said. "Be careful, Carl."

"His name is Johnny," the boy said. "Not Carl."

"And why are you speaking as if you know more than any boy should?" Kelly demanded.

"Because I am no ordinary boy," Samuel said. "And now I have to go."

He turned and walked to the door. "Remember, Johnny," he said, turning back. "Go to Paradise. It'll all become clear in Paradise. Project Showdown still lives."

And then the boy was gone.

CHAPTER TWENTY-THREE

THE PRESIDENT wants to see you."

"Thank you."

David Abraham brushed past the nurse and hurried toward the guards posted outside Robert's room. The president had been out of surgery for forty-five minutes, and David knew that the local anesthetics hadn't dimmed his mind in the least. If he knew what David had for him, he'd have told the nurse to let him through sooner.

He dipped his head at the guards, one of whom opened the door for him. "Thank you."

"David!" The president grinned from his hospital bed as David crossed the room.

"Miracles never cease," Robert said.

"Clearly. How are you feeling?"

"Sore but otherwise surprisingly well. They're using local anesthetic at my request, but I'm not sure how well it's working."

"Your mind's clear, then. That's good. Your prognosis?"

"I'll be up in two days, they say."

David glanced at two aides who sat by the window. "I need to speak to you privately."

"Give us a moment."

David waited for the aides to leave before he spoke again.

"Do they have any leads?"

"You're asking if I told anyone about this man you recognized?"

"Yes."

"I've only been conscious for an hour, half of that time on a table with bright lights overhead. The game's changed, I'm sure you understand that. Someone just put a bullet through me. An attempt was made on the life of the president of the United States—this is far bigger than either of us."

David knew that what he had to say wouldn't be easy. Knew that Robert might very well reject it. Most sane men would.

"Robert, please. What I am about to tell you may offend you at the deepest level. God knows that I am culpable in matters you know nothing about, and I'm willing to suffer any fitting consequences when this is all over. But I'm begging you to open your mind."

The president studied him for a moment, then looked at the ceiling. "God willing, this *is* over. Whoever's behind this will be dealt with in a manner expected by both the office and the nation."

"Of course. But you're wrong—it's not over. In some ways it's just beginning."

"I'm a reasonable man, David. But you've caught me in a down moment. Please don't patronize me."

"Down but not dead. That's the point, isn't it? Why are you down but not dead? You know the details of the shooting?"

"I was shot. The bullet missed my internal organs. Evidently somebody up there still wants me around."

"You were shot from a garbage bin at over two thousand yards. There are only a handful of shooters in the world who could accomplish such a feat. Do you know what a bullet's trajectory looks like after it's traveled a mile and a half?"

"I didn't realize you were so interested in shooting."

"I've become interested as of late. I'm sure that the FBI will get around to filling you in on this, but let me put it in layman's terms. When a bullet leaves a barrel, it's spinning. That spinning motion eventually forces the bullet to move off its axis and rotate in circles. They call it parabolic rotation."

David moved his finger through the air like a corkscrew.

"At two thousand yards, the diameter of the bullet's parabolic rotation is about a foot. There's no way the shooter can know which part of the rotation the bullet will be in when it strikes a body, only that if it's perfectly aimed, it will strike somewhere in a twelve-inch circle. Did you know this?"

"No. Go on."

"Since the bullet is moving in a circular pattern, it will enter the body at a slight angle and tear the flesh in that direction. Like a corkscrew. Lateral tear."

"Okay, so what's the point?"

"The point is that I've seen the images of your wound. The path of the bullet was perfectly straight. It entered and exited your body in a perfectly straight line. And that straight line happened to be through one of the only paths a bullet could travel without causing significant injury."

"Like I said, a miracle."

"The lack of damage was intentional, Robert!"

"That's impossible."

"Of course it is. Which is why you have to listen to me."

David had pushed Robert to the edges of his reasoning many times, and he knew the look of a man being stretched. Robert was being stretched.

The president sighed. "I'm listening."

David stood and walked to the end of the bed, dragging his hand on the bed rail. "You're alive because the shooter is a man named Johnny Drake. Do you recognize the name?"

"That's the name of the man you recognized in the footage of Assim Feroz?"

"Yes."

"Then he's in custody? You thought he was after Feroz!"

"No, he's not in custody. And I was wrong about Feroz being the target. In hindsight, I realize I should have known. Samuel didn't know *who* would be killed, only that a very powerful man would be assassinated, resulting in Israel's disarmament and downfall. Either way, this doesn't change the fact that the killer made an impossible shot. I believe that the only man alive who could do this is named Johnny Drake."

"This has to do with Project Showdown."

"Johnny was one of the children in Paradise, yes."

Robert closed his eyes, brought both hands to his forehead, and swept his hair back, sighing. "David . . ."

"I'm not finished. Please, you know about Project Showdown. You of all people should consider what I'm telling you. Without reservation!"

"I thought the children were all placed in homes with strict confidence so that they couldn't be tracked."

"They were, all but a few who were special cases."

"It's one thing to believe that dragons once existed. It's another to actually go hunting for one because someone believes they still exist!"

"You won't have that problem long, my friend. You'll believe soon enough. I have a feeling that you're going to meet more than a dragon before this is over."

"It *is* over!"

"Not until you die, if you go after the only man who can save you. Johnny Drake *must* be allowed to follow the path he is on. No charges, no media leaks, not a word."

He'd said it. Prematurely, perhaps. Not as part of a carefully constructed argument that had the president eating out of his hand, but there it was.

"I should let the man who tried to kill me walk? Please, David, you're—"

"You're alive because Johnny Drake wants you alive. If he wanted you dead, believe me, you would be dead. He's capable of far more than even he knows. Take him out of the equation, and another man will shoot you. That man will shoot to kill. You will die."

"This . . ." Robert stalled. "You're making an assassin out to be some kind of hero."

"Call him what you like. He's the only thing standing between you and death."

"Based on a vision—"

"Based on what I know!"

A knock sounded. One of the guards opened the door. "Is everything okay?"

"Unless you hear a scream, assume I'm fine," the president said.

The man bowed out.

"Forgive me for raising my voice, but I can't overemphasize my conviction on this matter. I'll explain everything when we have more time, but for your sake I'm begging you to do everything in your power to thwart any investigation that leads to Johnny as the shooter."

Robert closed his eyes again. He wondered if David knew what kind of stress he had just put Robert under.

"What else are you not telling me, David?"

"Only what makes no difference to you."

"You're right, you are culpable. What makes you think Johnny has this supposed power?"

"Besides what he just pulled off? Read the report again. We didn't pick up on it until three years ago, but it makes sense. He has . . . a gift."

He couldn't read the president's reaction to this.

"And what made you so sure he wouldn't kill me?"

"I thought he was after Feroz, and I *wasn't* sure Johnny wouldn't

kill him. As for killing you, it's not in his nature. Again, read the
report and you'll understand far more than I can convince you of.
We are dealing with matters that reside between the head and the
heart, Robert. I had faith in Johnny. Enough to put the world on his
shoulders."

"Including my life?"

"Samuel's vision saved your life. If we hadn't intervened, you would
be dead right now. I would expect some gratitude when this finally
sinks in."

"Intervened? How did you know Johnny was with the X Group?"

David took a deep breath. He bit his lip and answered slowly, with
a tremble in his voice.

"Because we put him there."

The president kept his eyes locked on David for a long moment.
"My, my, you have been busy."

"For your sake. For the sake of Israel."

"Based on a *vision*."

"Based on Project Showdown, which gave me the faith to believe
in this vision."

"And would you happen to know who ordered my assassination?"

"No. The X Group has no political agenda."

"If you had to guess?"

David hesitated. "Assim Feroz. Impossible to prove. It's not over,
Robert. The X Group will not accept failure."

"And neither will I."

"I don't think you can neutralize them. Certainly not in the time
we have. How long did it take to deal with Al Qaeda? From what I
understand, the X Group is far more organized."

"Then what?"

"Keep a heavy guard. Make sure everyone around you is armed to
the teeth. And pray that I'm still right about Johnny."

CHAPTER TWENTY-FOUR

JOHNNY.

The more Carl allowed the name to reside in his mind, the more disoriented he felt.

He and Kelly had walked back to their hotel room in a dizzy silence. She'd fashioned her own theory as to how and why the old man David and his son, Samuel, would make such outrageous claims, and she convinced him to follow a logical course based on that theory. But he knew her own confidence was shaken.

He also knew that he would follow whatever direction she gave him, but he couldn't dislodge a terrible suspicion that something was wrong.

Kelly left him sitting at the table and went for a list of weapons that he needed for his final mission against the president. Using Samuel was no longer an option. He would have to do this himself. She did her best to assure him that everything would be okay. That they were only doing what they were both destined to do. That the only truth was the truth he knew when he looked into her eyes.

Carl believed her. She was Kelly. She was the only person who truly loved him. He would die for Kelly.

But would *Johnny* die for her?

Would Johnny believe her?

Would Johnny kill the president of the United States?

Then there was Samuel, a boy of maybe thirteen who talked and acted like someone twice that age. An apparition from Johnny's past, or another lie sent from Agotha to challenge Carl. Or an associate of Kelly's like Englishman, playing some deep psychological game that would ultimately manipulate him into a position of yet deeper loyalty.

His body began to sweat thirty minutes after Kelly left. He tried to stop it by retreating into the safe blackness of his mind, but his face continued to flush with heat.

Frightened by his inability to control the emotions or his response, he hurried into the bathroom, stripped off his clothing, and took a cold shower. The water felt like heaven on his body, and for a few minutes he successfully put Samuel out of his mind.

Satisfied, he dried and donned the black pants and shirt he would wear tonight. He didn't have to form a plan as much as select one from several dozen already waiting on the edge of his consciousness, then modify it to meet the current situation. The fact that he didn't know the hospital's layout limited him. He would have to make adjustments during the operation.

Johnny. Your mother's name is Sally. She is waiting for you in a town called Paradise. My name is Samuel. I'm not an ordinary boy.

The sweat returned five minutes after he'd dressed. Buckets of it, soaking his shirt in less than a minute.

He quickly stripped and jumped back in the shower. This time the cold made him shiver. First sweat, now shivers—he was losing his self-control!

Carl stepped from the shower and attempted to forcefully towel away the gooseflesh. But he wasn't successful. He stared at his reflection in a full-length mirror affixed to the inside of the bathroom door. Pale from the months in darkness. Lean, ribbed with muscle, marked by dozens of scars on his shoulders, hips, and feet—Agotha's little gifts to him. But it was the way his skin prickled with a thousand goose bumps that fascinated him now. More accurately, the fact that he wasn't able to make them go away.

He should ask Kelly to give him a treatment! Maybe she carried some of the drugs with her. She could strap him to the bed and use the electricity from the wall outlet to encourage his mind to react as it was trained.

No, no, what was he thinking? He had to complete the mission tonight, before midnight! And it was always Agotha, not Kelly, who administered his lessons—he doubted Kelly would want to shock him.

"Who are you?" he asked the shaking image in the mirror.

He answered himself. "My name is Carl."

"And who is Carl?"

"Carl is Johnny."

The thin sheen of sweat glistened on his skin. Somewhere deep in his mind, where he erected walls of blackness and formed friendly tunnels that led him to the light, his understanding of truth seemed to have shut down.

Carl who was Johnny began to panic, and this time he couldn't stop himself. He stood before the long mirror, shaking and sweating and panicking.

He had to get to the bed! Lying down would allow him to relax and focus. He stumbled to the bed, still shaking, and lay down on his back. The white ceiling dissolved into a sea of lights that made him dizzy.

Why was his body doing this? Why was he afraid? He was afraid because he was shaking, and he was shaking because he was afraid, because he couldn't stop sweating.

He heard the door open and close, but he couldn't seem to do anything about it. He couldn't stop shaking.

"Carl?"

"Kelly . . ."

"Carl!" She dropped her bag and rushed over to him. "Carl, it's okay. Shh, shh, shh. You're shaking!"

She placed her hands on his chest and face. "You're burning up! What's happening? Please, you're scaring me."

"Kelly . . ." He couldn't seem to say any more past his violent shakes.

"Shh, shh, shh . . . I'm here now. I'm home. It's okay. I'm so sorry."

"I'm afraid," he managed.

Kelly lowered her head to his chest and began to cry. "Johnny," she whispered.

Johnny?

"Please, Johnny. I'm so sorry, I'm so sorry. Please stop."

He closed his eyes and let his mind fall back into blackness. He suddenly didn't feel anything. No hot, no cold, not even Kelly on his chest.

She was calling him by his name. His real name. In a moment of stunning clarity, he knew what was happening. Kelly was loving him as she'd never loved him before. She was speaking a deep and personal truth. Something he himself didn't even know.

Her soft whisper, calling him Johnny, cut to his soul in a way that no kiss ever had. He was swallowed by a profound sense of intimacy that he'd never imagined could exist between two people.

Carl stopped shaking. He opened his eyes. Kelly was weeping. In that moment he knew that she'd wept with him in the tunnel because she was torn by this terrible secret.

The secret that he was Johnny.

She carried the burden for him because she loved him. He put his hand on her head and stared at the white ceiling, moved by her great love. And by this revelation that he really was Johnny Drake, not Carl Strople. They stayed that way for a long time.

It was Kelly who broke the spell, long after she'd stopped sniffing, long after her breathing settled. She lifted her head from his chest, searched his eyes, then retrieved his clothes from the bathroom and set them on the end of the bed. Carl sat up slowly.

"Dress," she said, walking to the window. She pulled back the drapes and stared out at the darkness.

He dressed, numb and directionless.

"Your name is Johnny Drake," she said, crossing her arms. "You were a chaplain with the United States Army. They took you by force when you were on leave in Cairo. That's the way the X Group works."

"Then . . . Then the boy was right?"

"Yes. I'm sorry, I panicked. I didn't know what to do. I'm so sorry. I lied to you."

"My name is Johnny," he said.

"Yes."

"Johnny Drake."

"Yes, yes. I'm so sorry. I—"

"I'm from Colorado?"

"I don't know." She turned around and looked at him with cried-out eyes. "I don't know about the rest. Please, please, I beg you to forgive me."

Carl felt as if he was going to burst into tears. But he wasn't Carl, was he? He was Johnny.

"You have to leave me, Carl. I don't care what they do to me, you have to run."

"I could never leave you. I have to finish this or they'll kill you!"

"No, listen to me. It's not too late for you to reclaim your life. We can never be together again, not after what I've done. You have to—"

"No!" Rage welled up in his chest. This is why she'd been so quiet while she lay on his chest. She'd been convincing herself that she had to leave him, although she loved him desperately. "You can never leave me! I need you."

"You think you do, but you don't." She walked to him, keeping her eyes locked onto his. "Please, Carl, you're an innocent child, don't you see? Agotha's turned you into an innocent child and then abused you. And I've been her accomplice. You even talk like a child!"

"Tell me one thing. Do you love me?"

Her eyes pooled with tears. "Yes."

"You're sure?"

"Yes. At first it was one of Agotha's games. But it's become much more. I love you very much."

"Then don't hurt me more by leaving me. I don't know who I am. If I'm a child, you can't leave me alone!"

His words rang in the small room, silencing with their truth. There were only two things that Carl knew about himself. The first was that his name was Johnny. The second was that apart from names and places, he was totally and terribly lost.

His identity had been stripped.

"I'm lost," he said. "And without you, I'm hopelessly lost."

"I've *tortured* you!"

"And now you will help me heal. I'll do what they've asked me to do. With your help, we can play their game and find a way to beat them."

Kelly paced between Carl and the bathroom door, staring intently at the floor. Then at him.

"You can't finish this mission. You may not understand why now, because your moral compass has been dashed, but you can't."

"They'll kill me with the implant."

"Unless . . ."

"Unless what?"

She was anxious now. "Unless you can block the implant. Long enough for it to be removed."

"I couldn't even stop myself from shaking. How can I block—"

"That's why Kalman is so nervous about you! You survived the electric chair, why not the implant? It's designed to detonate if tampered with in any way, but what if you could shut it off just long enough for a surgeon to remove it?"

"Because the tunnel is gone!"

"Then I'll help you find it again."

"Electric shock?"

"No, not that way!" She grabbed his hand and kissed it, then held it against her cheek. "Never that way again, I promise."

Carl considered her words. What choice did he have? He could either kill the president or take his chances with the implant. She was right, there was no real choice. He would have to set his mind on shutting out the implant long enough for a surgeon, assuming there was one, to take the implant out, assuming such an operation could be done without damaging his brain.

"They'll still come after us," Kelly said.

"And without me, you don't have a chance."

Her eyes searched his, side to side. He felt a moment of deep empathy with her. She would pay such a price to love him.

What if all of this is just part of the game?

Carl dismissed the absurd thought. See, he could still control his mind. He'd just done it.

He leaned forward and kissed her. "I will die for you, my love."

"No, you won't. If you die, then I die. They'll never quit. It's forever, Carl. Do you understand that? If we do this, we'll be on the run together for the rest of our lives."

"Maybe we can find some life before we die."

"Maybe."

"Then we should go to Paradise."

Kelly grabbed the bag of weapons off her bed. "Not until we take care of the implant. We have six hours. There's a doctor outside the city that we've used before. The implant sits behind the brain, set to trigger if exposed." She glanced at him. "You'll have to remain conscious so you can block—"

"Kalman will trigger the device before then."

"Not if we leave now. We still have some time."

"Does this doctor have a pit?"

She looked surprised that he'd asked the question. It was a ridiculous question, of course. He didn't know why it came out.

"This is New York. There will be no pits in New York. Ever."

"Okay. I'll find another way to block the pain. And the implant."

"You'll have to find a way to block the tracking device for a few hours, or he'll know we've left the city. Can you do that?"

"I can try. Do we have a choice?"

Kelly shook her head and closed her eyes. "I can't believe we're doing this. Even if we get rid of the implant, Kalman will send Englishman after us."

"I've beat him before."

Her eyes opened. "Not in real life, you haven't " There was a strange darkness in her eyes that bothered him. "Not when he pulls out the stops. We'll have to find a hole to live in."

"I love the dark," he said.

"And I hate it."

They quickly packed two duffel bags, one for weapons and one for the rest. This was their collective material wealth, this and $87,000 in U.S. currency remaining from the $250,000 Kelly had brought with her.

Kelly scanned the room after they'd wiped it down. "One last question before we leave. Should I call you Carl or Johnny?"

He thought for a moment.

"Carl," he said. "I don't know who Johnny is."

CHAPTER TWENTY-FIVE

HE IS called Englishman. He's not the Englishman, of course. Neither is he Dale Crompton. He doesn't really know who he is anymore, so he is who he wants to be, which is far more and far less than any Englishman.

The man taps his thumb on the leather steering wheel in the Buick he took from a nameless parking lot this morning. The radio is on. He dislikes the song's lyrics, but the beat fills him with energy.

Pain is in the game,
And the game is in the name

The singer has no idea what pain is. If Englishman had enough time, he might find the singer's home and rearrange his view of pain.

The name is Slayer
If you really want to know
He hunts in the dark and kills in the light

Any man who can sing such words without knowing their meaning deserves to be hunted down. Still, the beat is good and Englishman hums with the guitars, unbothered by his butchering of the tune.

He's not Englishman. He's Jude Law. He's Robert De Niro. He's Hannibal Lecter. He's whoever he wants to be . . .

The one called Englishman cracked his neck and cleared his mind. His drive to tell the story perfectly dogged him like those irritating hornets. And by *perfectly* he meant in a way that kept them forever in the dark where they belonged.

The story had to be more personal. First person. He started again.

I am called Englishman. I'm not the Englishman, of course. Neither am I Dale Crompton. I don't know who I am, so I am who I want to be, which is far more and far less than any Englishman. An Englishman has a history; I do not. An Englishman is weak; I am not.

I look like Jude Law. I smile like Robert De Niro. I laugh like Hannibal Lecter. Dust to dust, ashes to ashes. Hallelujah, amen, you are dismissed.

Englishman nodded and repeated the words that had become a kind of mantra to him. He'd touched the hand of the gas station attendant fifteen minutes earlier when he'd stopped to fill his tank. Did the girl have any idea whose hand she was touching? No.

Did she know how many throats he'd cut? No.

Did she even suspect that he hated women? No.

Did she want to kiss him? Yes.

Did she love him more than she loved Jude Law? Yes.

Did she realize how much he liked corn nuts? No.

Would he return and kill her for wanting to kiss him? He didn't know. Probably not—he wouldn't have much idle time in the next few days.

Englishman paused. He understood the plan, but he'd never liked it much. Yes, he embraced the idea in the very beginning, but that was before he understood that he had the power to find a better plan. Like telling a better story.

Playing the part of Englishman had grown stale and tired. The killings had become boring. How many ways could you kill a person anyway?

There would come a time when he would walk into Kalman's hospital and take off his head with a machete. Better yet, shave him bald and fry him in that electric chair of his.

Johnny had picked up some skills, but he was still weak. The showdown ahead made Englishman's skin crawl with anticipation.

I look like Jude Law and I'm . . . He didn't bother finishing the thought because he drew a blank.

It didn't matter; he was close to the target now. He would kill the doctor as Kalman had ordered, and then, with any luck at all, the true game—the one he'd waited so patiently for—would begin.

He'd been watching Johnny's progress since he and the woman, whom he hated only slightly less than Johnny, set foot in New York. They'd gone off the reservation last night, leaving the hotel room spotless. Even so, Englishman knew their ultimate destination and in fact had anticipated that Johnny would do what he was now doing.

Englishman knew not only where they were heading but *how* they would get there, based on the last few tracking signals emitted by the implant before it had stopped transmitting.

He exited the freeway, backtracked a mile on the frontage road, cut west for half a mile, and pulled into a long gravel driveway. Horses grazed in a fenced green pasture on his right. He'd killed a horse once. The experience had left him cold. They were dumb animals. Household pets offered only slightly more fascination.

Dr. Henry Humphries was a veterinarian. Englishman had never needed his veterinary services, but the good doctor had once sewn part of the Ukrainian's finger back on.

"I am not Englishman today," he said, parking by the large barn.

"Today I am simply . . ." He considered several choices. "*Un*man. I'm Unman."

He put the Buick in park, interlaced his fingers, and cracked his knuckles loudly. This was a cliché, of course. But he loved cliché because it had become so vogue to hate cliché. In truth, those who cringed at the use of cliché were their own cliché.

He stepped from the car and scanned the barn. His favorite movie was *Kill Bill*. Despite his general hatred of women, he liked Black Mamba because she fought like a man. And she wore yellow leather, which appealed to him for no reason that he could understand, no matter how much he thought about it.

Unman. Unman walked up to the door and wiped his black canvas shoes on a mat that read "All Animals Welcome, Whites Use Front Entrance."

For a moment Unman wished he was black. Maybe he was. He tried the door, turned the knob, and walked in without announcing himself.

Fireweed Mexican tile floor. White walls in need of a fresh coat. Clean at first glance but dirty under the skin, like most people. The place smelled of manure.

Manure and Johnny.

A man in a brown tweed jacket stood to the right of a workbench that held a large metal tub, something you might wash an animal in. Behind him, a dozen stalls housed a couple of horses, some pigs, and a lamb of all things. A fluffy white lamb.

The lamb bleated.

"May I help you?"

Unman took his eyes off the sheep and faced the man. White, fat, and old. Not fat-fat, but a good fifty pounds of blubber on his gut. Unman imagined the man without a shirt because he had both the time and the imagination to do so. Evidently sewing up animals didn't burn the calories as much as, say, kickboxing or jumping on a trampoline, either one of which would do the doctor good.

The man wore gray polyester pants and an untucked yellow shirt. He held a syringe in his right hand. If he was expecting any female company, he wasn't concerned with impressing them. Maybe Unman liked this doctor.

"What's your name?" Unman asked.

"I'm sorry, was I expecting you?" The man showed only slight fear. He filled the syringe from a vial and laid both on the table.

"I'm Unman. I'm looking for a man and a woman who stopped here last night. Good-looking fellow, about so tall, and a hot woman who tends to boss him around. The man had a small device buried in his skull that evidently didn't go off as it was designed to. We think someone here took it out, thereby sealing his own fate. So I guess I'm not really looking for the man who's all that, or the woman who bosses him around, but the doctor who helped them escape. Need to clean things up, if you know what I mean."

Surprisingly, the man still showed minimal fear. Interesting. Maybe Unman should drop the clever-meant-to-be-terrifying cliché and be more sinister. But that failed to interest him, so he continued.

"If you are that doctor, I'll need the implant. Then I'll have to kill you so that you don't tell anyone else about it. If you're not the doctor I'm looking for, then I'll have to kill you for knowing that I'm looking for a doctor to kill. So who are you, the doctor who needs killing, or the innocent bystander who needs killing?"

Now more fear showed on the man's face. Clichés and all.

"They were here," the doctor said.

"And the implant?"

The man produced a small box from under the bench in front of him and held it out.

Unman walked forward. He knew what would happen now. Any man who showed only a little fear when presented with the prospect of his own death had a plan. The doctor obviously thought he could survive this meeting.

The clichés weren't working as well as Unman had hoped. He wanted to get this over with and make the call.

He stopped twenty feet from the man. "Throw it here," he said.

The doctor made as if to throw the device with his left hand, but Unman didn't care about the implant. Syringe man was right-handed, and his right hand was under the bench top, holding something— probably a gun—that filled the doctor with confidence.

Unman could have waited for the man's hopeless attempt to distract him by throwing the implant.

He could have waited for the man's gun to clear the counter.

He could have even waited for the gun to go off. All of these would have been consistent with a tough villain defying death with elegance. Cliché.

But the time for cliché was gone, so Unman pulled a gun from his right hip and shot the doctor through his nose.

The man dropped like an elevator car, smacked the bottom of his jaw on the bench, bounced back with a few shattered teeth to go with his broken nose, and fell heavily to the ground.

In all likelihood, the doctor hadn't even seen Unman draw.

He walked to the window and pulled out his cell phone. Dialed the number. Two of the horses were looking at the barn, alerted by the gunshot. He wondered who would take care of the doctor's horses now.

"Yes?"

"The doctor is dead. I have the implant."

He could hear Kalman's breathing in the silence.

"Kill Saint first," Kalman said. "Then complete the contract."

"Thank you." Unman closed the phone.

Englishman hated Kalman, but he hated Johnny more. In fact, he'd been born to hate Johnny. Kalman didn't know this, Agotha didn't know, but Englishman knew. And now he was finally in a position to do something about that hate.

"Game on, Johnny," he said. Was that cliché?

CHAPTER TWENTY-SIX

PARADISE WAS nestled in the Colorado mountains off the beaten path, several miles from the main road that passed through Delta.

The trees in Colorado were different from any Carl had ever seen. Tall evergreens that pointed to the sky mixed with deciduous trees similar to the ones that surrounded the compound in Hungary. The terrain was severe and sharp, with cliffs and huge outcroppings of rocks.

The Rocky Mountains. Carl watched from the car with fascination. It was familiar to him only because the boy had suggested it should be. Or did he remember?

They'd flown into Denver as Elmer and Jane Austring, knowing full well that Kalman could trace the false identities he himself had provided. But it would take even someone as powerful as Kalman at least a day to track them down. By then, they'd be gone. As soon as they'd visited Paradise, they would assume new identities and move on.

A taxi had taken them from Denver International Airport to a used car dealer off Interstate 70, where Kelly had paid $8,000 for the old blue Ford truck she now drove. They'd exchanged license plates with another vehicle in Vail, and then with yet another in Grand Junction.

None of this would prevent Kalman from tracking them, but it would
hold off the authorities in the event that Carl had been fingered as a
suspect in the president's shooting.

News of the assassination attempt was everywhere. Shouting from
all of the newspapers in the airport, all of the television monitors in
the waiting areas, every station on the radio.

Carl was amazed by the reach of his one bullet. No one knew what
to do with the information that the assassin's bullet had caused so
little damage. The White House had released no specifics—a good
thing, Kelly said. Any trained ballistics expert would know that the
shot had been impossible. Better that the public didn't know.

"Why?" he'd asked.

She just shrugged her shoulders. "It's our secret."

He nodded. "Paradise, three miles," he said, reading a sign ahead
on their right.

She took the turnoff and angled the truck up a narrow paved road.
Within half a mile they were driving down a winding strip of blacktop. The edge fell sharply on the right into a deep valley. A metal
guardrail provided a measure of security.

This was the road to Paradise. It could have been the road to Mexico
as far as Carl knew. None of it was more familiar than a suggestion.

"I like the mountains," Kelly said.

"They're nice," Carl said.

"Wait until you see the desert."

They both knew that if the boy had been right and Paradise was
Carl's home, Kalman would know as well. Regardless of what happened here, they had to be gone by the end of the day.

They would go to the desert in Nevada.

Kelly glanced at him. "Do you recognize anything?"

"No."

"Maybe when you see the town."

"Maybe."

The road descended, took a sharp turn, and fed into a valley. One moment they were watching trees rush by; the next they were looking down at a town.

Carl wasn't sure if it was Paradise at first. Then they passed a sign that said it was. *Welcome to Paradise, Colorado, Population 450.*

He began to sweat.

"This is it," Kelly said. "Do you recognize anything?"

A large building with a five-foot sign that read "Paradise Community Center" loomed ahead on the right. Beyond it, a grocery store with gas pumps out front. Houses on the left, running up to a tall church with a pointed steeple.

"Can you pull over?"

"Here?"

"Yes, pull over."

He didn't recognize anything, but his heart was hammering and he thought that might be a good sign.

Kelly pulled the pickup truck onto a dusty shoulder a hundred feet from the community center. "Do you recognize it?"

Carl stared ahead, searching his memory. This building had once been something else. A burned-down pile of rubble. Or a theater. Or maybe his mind was just making things up.

"Carl?"

"I . . . I don't know." He climbed out and faced the town. Something had happened here, he could sense it if not remember it. His body was reacting even if his mind wasn't. Kelly joined him, exchanging looks between him and the town.

"Why can't I remember?" he asked.

"Agotha's no amateur. Only the strongest minds can endure her methods. She told me she'd never seen a mind as strong as yours. She was determined to either break you or kill you."

She looked up at the cliffs to their right. "She broke you," she said softly. "She tore your identity down until it was nothing, and then she rebuilt it, many times over. Your mind is still strong, stronger than before, but now its walls are built around the wrong identity."

"Then it'll have to be broken again," Carl said.

She didn't answer.

"I don't know if I want to be broken again."

"I understand. But if you reclaim your true identity, you'll have fewer scars. You have a strong mind, Carl. A very, very strong mind."

Carl started forward along the road's dusty shoulder. Kelly followed. He spread his hands, palms facedown by his sides. A slight breeze passed through his fingers. He could smell the dust rising from his feet. The hot afternoon sun cut through the cool mountain air. He felt as if he was walking into a dream on legs of soggy cardboard and a body cut from paper.

The street was deserted. A bench . . .

Carl stopped and stared at the empty bench on a boardwalk in front of a rustic building called Smither's Barbecue.

"What is it?"

"Does that bench look familiar to you?"

She stopped beside him. "I've never been here—why would it?"

His breathing thickened. For a moment he thought he might start to shake and sweat like he had in the hotel room. A tingle lit through his fingertips.

He stepped out onto pavement and angled for the middle of the road. He wasn't sure why he wanted to walk down this road—maybe it gave him a better view—but he picked up his pace and crossed to the yellow dotted lines that split the blacktop in two.

The tingle spread from his fingertips into his bones. He pushed his feet over the dashes, striding with purpose. But in his mind it was all happening in slow motion. He was staring at the bench and marching into a mesmerizing dream without the slightest idea of where it would take him.

But he'd been here before.

"Carl?"

He veered to his right and angled for the bench. He fought an urge to run up to the bench and tear it from the ground.

His breathing came hard, pulling at air that refused to fill his lungs.

Something was wrong with the bench. He hated this bench. This bench was—

"Carl!"

He stopped.

"What's wrong?"

It was just a wooden bench. Sitting on the boardwalk, ten feet away now. He looked up at the restaurant behind the bench. Smither's Barbecue. Beside it the grocery store with the gas pumps. All Right Convenience. The large building behind and to his right. Paradise Community Center.

Carl slowly turned and studied the rest of the town. A dozen small businesses on the right side of the street. A hair salon, a flower shop, an automotive shop . . . others. Houses.

Houses were on the opposite side. A large lawn ran up to the church.

"I don't think I've ever been here," he said.

"Why were you running for the bench?"

"I don't know. Why was I shaking in the hotel room? Why did I believe that you were my wife? Why did I climb into a crate full of hornets? Why did I put myself in an electric chair to die?"

Kelly shifted her eyes. He'd hurt her feelings.

"I'm not complaining," he said. "I just don't know anything anymore. I used to know who I was. Now I don't. I wish we'd never gone to New York."

"Johnny?" A voice was calling his name.

Kelly's eyes darted over his shoulder. He turned and faced a medium-built man with dark hair who stood in the restaurant's open doorway. The man's eyes widened with a smile.

"Johnny Drake. Well I'll be . . ." He twisted his head and yelled through the door. "Paula, get yourself out here and see who's come back."

The man marched down the steps and across the boardwalk and was nearly upon him before it occurred to Carl that showing his ignorance would raise unwanted questions. He smiled.

"Give me a hug, boy!" The man took Carl's hand and wrapped his arm around his back, pulling him close. "Good to see you, Johnny." The man slapped his back.

Carl didn't know what to say.

"And who's your friend?"

"This is Kelly."

The man extended his hand. "Hello, Kelly. I'm Steve. Welcome to Paradise. Pun intended, always intended, although I can guarantee we don't always live up to the name."

A woman in a blue dress ran down the steps toward him. "Johnny? Johnny Drake, my goodness! We heard you were missing!"

Carl assumed she was the woman Steve called Paula. Their excitement in seeing him was infectious. He felt his face flush with an odd mixture of embarrassment and comfort.

They liked him.

Paula gave him a hug and kissed his cheek. "Are you okay?"

She smelled like a flower—a familiar and warming scent. He must find out what perfume she was wearing.

"Johnny?"

"Yes?"

"Are . . . Are you okay?"

"Yes. I'm fine. Just a little . . ."

"He's on pain medication," Kelly said, offering her hand. "Nothing serious. I'm Kelly."

"Hello, Kelly. You're . . ." Paula glanced between them. "You're not . . ."

"No, no." Kelly laughed. "Just good friends."

"Well, I must say, Johnny, you know how to pick beautiful friends."

"Thank you," Kelly said.

Steve patted him on the back again. "Well then, come in and have a drink. On the house, of course. It's not every day we get a hero coming home."

"Actually . . ." Kelly caught Carl's eyes.

"Actually, I would like to go home," Carl said.

"Of course you would," Paula said. "Does Sally know you're here?"

"Sally? No. Has she moved?"

"From town? Goodness, no. She really doesn't know? She's going to faint! You go on. Don't let us keep you. How long will you be in town?"

"Just a day," Kelly said.

"Only a day? Then promise me you'll stop by and fill us in. The others'll be thrilled to see you. Does anyone else know?"

"No."

"Most of them are at the fair in Delta, but they'll be back by night. We'll do something. Right, Steve? We could have a barbecue."

"Absolutely."

"Okay."

"Perfect. I haven't seen Sally today, but that doesn't mean much. We don't see her much these days. She's kept to herself lately. She might have gone to Delta, but she might be home. You go on, don't mind us."

"Okay."

Steve and Paula, presumably the proprietors of Smither's Barbecue, stared at Carl, clearly expecting him to go home.

"What perfume are you wearing?" Carl asked.

Paula seemed slightly taken aback, but she smiled. "You like it?"

"Yes."

"It's called Lavender Lace. Sally gave it to me for my birthday."

It was his mother's perfume!

"Can you tell me which house she lives in?"

Steve and Paula looked at each other, clearly baffled.

"You don't remember?" Steve asked. "You sure you're okay?"

"I'm sorry, it's just this . . . I get bad headaches . . . I'm trying out a new pain medication, and it's making me . . ." He searched for the word.

"Loopy," Kelly said.

"Loopy," Carl said.

"Well, loopy or not, it's good to have you home, Chaplain." Steve pointed down the street. "Third house on the right. The white one."

Carl turned and started to walk.

Kelly thanked Steve and Paula—*Something I should have done myself,* Carl thought—and caught up to him.

"Hold on, Carl. Please."

"What is it?"

She grabbed his arm and pulled him back. "Just stop for a second. I realize this is important to you, but we have to be careful. You can't be so obvious. We'll be followed here. Kalman will stop at nothing to squeeze these people for information if he suspects that you've told them anything that could implicate him. We were here—that's all. Nothing more."

"Obvious? Why am I obvious?"

"For starters, you *are* acting loopy. This is nothing like the calculating killer you were trained to be. *I* don't even know who you are anymore. I'm just asking you to be careful."

"I was a chaplain," Carl said. "Did I have faith?"

Kelly studied his eyes for a few moments. Her features softened, and she offered a consoling smile, touching his cheek with her thumb. "I'm sure you did. I'm sorry. Just try to be . . . normal."

"I'm not normal—Agotha saw to that. I want to be normal. You know that's all I want. But I don't even know if my true self *is* normal."

He glanced back down the street and saw that Steve and Paula were at the door of their restaurant, watching them. Kelly had a point—Kalman could cause them some trouble.

"I can be normal for them, as normal as I can bring myself to be. But with my mother . . ."

With his mother he didn't know what. He probably wouldn't even recognize her.

Kelly took his hand in hers and turned him back toward his mother's house.

"Come on," she said. "Your mother is waiting."

ENGLISHMAN WALKED the B concourse in Denver International Airport, wondering what it would be like to be the thin rail of a man who hurried just ahead of him. The man was late for a flight, judging by his periodic watch-check. Was he going home to his wife and children?

Was he flying to Boston for a meeting with powerful bankers the next morning?

Was he eager to catch a plane that would deliver him to his mistress in Dallas?

Was he going to die of leukemia in twenty years or get hit by a car in two days, or did he already have a terminal disease and not know it?

Why did this man even want to live? Didn't he know that it would all end soon enough anyway? Didn't he know that a billion people with two legs and two arms, full of vim and vigor just like him, had lived and died and were now just memories in a few people's minds? Assuming they were lucky—most didn't even survive as memories. They were simply gone.

The simple, terrible tragedy of life's story was that it all ended on the last page. It didn't matter what clichés or wonderful descriptions or clever words people used to tell their stories; the greatest certainty any person had was that it would be over in about four hundred pages or eighty years, depending on how you looked at it. *Hallelujah, amen, you are dismissed.*

Of course, there were those who believed in the afterlife. Englishman hated those people. Not because he thought that they were right, but because he knew that if by some small chance they were right, he would not be joining them in their new journey of bliss.

Englishman lost interest in the skinny man and entered the moving sidewalk, letting his eyes rove over the concourse.

Hundreds of people hurried to and fro or sat at the gates waiting for their planes. Tall ones, short ones, skinny ones, lots of fat ones, blond ones, brown ones, black ones, young ones, old ones. Meat, thousands and thousands of meat packages. And every one of them thought they were that one package that actually mattered.

Englishman could easily kill any one of them at this very moment and walk away to tell how their particular story ended.

This meant he actually had *control* over their stories. He could write the last chapter of their lives. The end. *Hallelujah, amen, you are dismissed.*

He could actually end a few dozen stories right now, at this moment, before the authorities managed to stop him.

Not catch him, mind you. Stop him.

Englishman wasn't proud of his ability to control others by writing their final chapter. He was simply fascinated by it. The killing itself had long ago become rather tedious, but the power he possessed to end them made his mind buzz.

He crossed his arms, spread his legs, cocked his head all the way back, and closed his eyes.

No doubt dozens of people were staring at him at this moment, wondering why in the world the famous actor named Jude Law was passing through the Denver airport without an armed guard, drawing so much attention to himself by striking such a presumptuous pose.

Small minds.

Paradise, Colorado, was a five-hour drive from the airport. Six counting the slight detour to collect the weapons stashed at the safe house they'd prepared in Grand Junction. If his intel had informed him that the lovebirds had caught on to his very good plan, he would have flown to Grand Junction and driven from there. But the pair was clueless, so he had plenty of time. And Englishman preferred to drive. It offered more flexibility and was safer.

Without looking, Englishman knew precisely where the moving sidewalk ended. He stepped onto the carpet and took five full steps before opening his eyes.

Johnny Drake's story was coming to an end.

CHAPTER TWENTY-SEVEN

CARL STOOD at the white house's front door, staring through the screen at the small, octagonal crystalline window that revealed a fragmented image of the inside.

Fragmented like him.

"Go ahead," Kelly said softly.

He lifted his hand, rapped on the screen door's metal frame, then stepped back.

Hello, Sally.

Hello, Johnny.

Are you my mother?

No one came to the door.

"Maybe she's not home," Kelly said.

Carl was about to knock again when the latch rattled. The knob turned. The door swung in.

A woman stood behind the screen door. "Sorry for the wait, I was—"

She froze, eyes round. Carl's heart pounded. He didn't recognize her, but it could be because the screen impaired his view. She was his mother, had to be his mother, would be his mother. Somehow everything was going to be okay now.

"Johnny?" She lifted a hand to her mouth. "Johnny!"

He was Johnny and this was Sally. His mother.

"Hello, Mother."

She flung the screen door open and rushed to him, throwing her arms around his neck. He staggered back a step and instinctively put his arms around her torso.

"Johnny, oh, Johnny! You're alive! I was so worried."

She kissed him on his cheek, then squeezed him tight and buried her face in his neck.

Carl, who knew he was Johnny, held her gently as she wept.

Are you my mother?

Surprisingly, he didn't remember her as he'd expected to. She was wearing a different perfume—roses. She was beautiful and her tears were real and her eyes were a light brown, like his, but he couldn't remember. He stood still, suddenly frightened.

Sally stepped back, took his face in both hands, and studied his features. "Look at you. You haven't changed a bit." Her eyes darted over his shoulders. "You've leaned out. Are you okay?"

"Yes."

He could see the questions flooding her mind. One of them was probably why he wasn't doing the things sons were supposed to do in reunions like this, whatever those were. Jumping up and down or whooping and hollering with joy? He could manage a handshake, no more than a cold handshake.

Carl stepped forward and hugged Sally rather awkwardly. "It's good to be home," he said.

She patted him on the back. "Come in, come in. Who's your friend?"

"This is Kelly. She's the woman that I'm in love with."

Kelly looked surprised, then quickly blushed.

"My, we are full of surprises," Sally said, smiling warmly. "Please, come in."

They walked into the house. Brown carpet. Tan leather couch and love seat. Kitchen with yellow daisies on the wallpaper. A counter divided the kitchen from the eating area. The hall ran past three doors on its way to the back entrance. This was the house he'd grown up in?

He stared hard, intent on remembering. If he'd spent eighteen years in this house, the memories would be here, in the darkness some- where. They had to be. Just there, beyond the black veil.

It occurred to Carl that he was in darkness. He'd entered his tun- nel. At the end of the tunnel he saw a light. That light was what, his identity? His childhood?

Sally was saying something about cookies, but Carl's mind was now running, running down the tunnel toward the light. He could hear his feet slapping on the wood floor. Hear his breathing, heavy in his pursuit.

The light seemed to be moving away from him. The farther and faster he ran, the farther the light moved.

His mother was calling his name.

Johnny?

Sally was crying out for him to rescue her. Rescue him, trapped in this tunnel.

Johnny!

"Where are you?" he cried.

KELLY WAS standing by the sofa table with Sally when Carl bolted down the hall. He ran to the first door and threw it open.

Sally watched him go, dumbstruck. "Johnny?"

"Where are you?" he cried.

"Johnny?"

"Where are you?"

He spun from the room, took a sharp right, and slid to a stop by the next door. Opened it. Stared. Slammed it shut.

"Where are you?"

Confusion laced Sally's voice. "Johnny!"

Carl stumbled toward the last door, shrouded by shadows. He banged through and disappeared.

"What's wrong?" The blood had suddenly left Sally's face. "What's he doing?"

"I think he's looking for himself," Kelly said.

"That's his room. What's . . . ? Is he okay?"

How could she explain the horrors that had brought Carl to this place? "No. No, he's not okay, but I think he will be."

No sound came from the bedroom.

"What's he doing?" Sally asked again.

Carl suddenly appeared in the doorway to his bedroom and stared at them. He looked as though he might have seen an apparition intent on torturing his soul.

"Mom?"

"Johnny . . ." Sally's voice was twisted with anguish.

Carl walked down the hall, eyes fixed on Sally. Something had changed. His eyes were large and streaming tears. The sight brought a painful knot to Kelly's throat. How could she ever forgive herself for what she'd done to this man?

And yet, she was meant to walk this path with him. She'd known this would happen. Now that it really was happening, she wondered how she could have allowed herself to fall in love with him.

Johnny rushed toward them, blubbering like an open tap.

"Mom. I'm so scared." The rest of his words were garbled by a gushing sob. He ran into Sally's arms and hugged her with desperation.

Kelly began to cry.

Mother and son were both blurting things now, but their words were stepping on one another, so she couldn't make them out. Then she heard Carl say, "I'm sorry, I'm so sorry, I'm so sorry, please forgive me." He was blaming himself for what Kelly had done.

Kelly turned from them, walked into the living room, and eased herself down into the love seat. This was her doing.

Every switch thrown by Agotha as she stood silently by.

Every needle that had pierced his flesh.

Every drug that had weakened his resolve.

Every treachery, every betrayal, every moment of loneliness that he'd endured out of misplaced love for her.

"No, no, no," the mother kept crying. "It's not your fault. You didn't do anything. Please, Johnny. Please, I love you. I love you."

"I put you through so much pain," Carl cried. "I can't live with myself."

"No, no, no. Stop it, you can't talk like that. Whatever they did, it's okay now. You're home, Johnny. I'm here for you."

Kelly covered her face with her hands, put her head back on the cushion behind her, and joined them in their sorrow.

"JOHNNY," CARL said. "I want you to call me Johnny now."

"Okay." Kelly offered him a small smile. "Johnny."

Something in Carl had broken. He was now Johnny even though he still felt like Carl.

He'd caught up to the light in his tunnel, passed through it, and stepped into a new world in which Sally was his mother. The room he'd run into was the room he'd grown up in, he could remember that with perfect clarity. This was his house. They'd spent an hour in the house, and he'd viewed each room a dozen times, desperately mining his memory for more, more.

He still couldn't remember any details of what had happened during his childhood without being told, but when Sally told him, he did remember, however vaguely.

Did it matter? He'd found his mother. He was whatever she was.

Johnny stood up from the couch, walked over to where his mother was seated, and bent over and hugged her again. Then he returned to the couch, sat down, and swallowed a terrible knot in his windpipe.

"You've become very emotional," Kelly said.

He couldn't seem to stop the gushing.

"I'm still having a hard time believing all of this," Sally said. "A year ago you were a chaplain in the army, stationed in Kuwait. Now you're . . ."

Her voice trailed off. They hadn't told her about his mission or the extent of his training. Only generalities that suggested why he was so different from the way she remembered him. She deserved that much. The rest would come in time. Johnny was afraid she might take Kelly's head off if she knew the whole truth.

"I'm not an assassin," Johnny said. "I haven't killed anyone. I was only trained as an assassin."

"What about your faith? You were a man of great faith—surely that hasn't just disappeared."

"I don't know. I just learned who I was last night. I can't. My mind's still spinning."

"How can the United States government make someone forget their own mother? It's inhuman!"

"I remember you," Johnny said, fighting emotion again. "I do remember you." Although he wasn't really sure he did. Perhaps he was forming a fact in his mind now rather than actually recalling her face.

"The training was extensive," Kelly said. "And these people in Black Ops have developed ways of erasing a soldier's identity, not only his memories. Johnny's mind is much stronger than most, which makes his recovery even more difficult. Did Carl show any unusual . . . abilities when he was younger?"

"Johnny," Johnny said. "Please call me Johnny."

"Sorry. Johnny."

Sally looked at him inquisitively. "Not that I can remember. Do you remember Project Showdown?"

Samuel had mentioned the name. *Project Showdown still lives.* But Johnny drew a blank. "No."

"You can't remember anything about it?"

"No, why? What's Project Showdown?"

"Wow. Well, I don't know where to begin, really."

The phone rang shrilly. Sally ignored it.

"Do you remember the monastery up in the canyon?"

"No. I remember you and this house and what you've told me, that's all."

The answering machine kicked on after five rings. Sally's voice. "You've reached the Drakes. Please leave a message."

Drakes. Not Sally Drake, but the *Drakes,* as in more than one. She'd never given up on her son. It made Johnny want to hug her again.

"This is David Abraham. It's critical that I reach you, Ms. Drake. Please call me immediately on my . . ."

Johnny didn't wait for the rest. This was the old man from the hospital. Samuel's father. He went for the phone and snatched it from the cradle as David repeated his number.

"Hello, this is Johnny."

A pounding of machinery in the background filled a long pause.

"So you *have* gone home," the voice said.

Johnny looked at Sally and Kelly. "Yes."

"Thank goodness. How much do you remember?"

"I only remember who my mother is."

"They'll be coming for you. If *I* can find you, they'll find you."

"Yes, I know."

"How many people besides your mother have you talked to?"

"Just Steve and Paula. The Smithers."

"Good. Can you trust me?"

"Do I have a choice?" He *wanted* to trust the man. "I think so, yes."

"Then I want you to meet me in the canyon above Paradise. Do you remember it?"

"No."

"Sally can tell you how to reach it, but come alone. It's where all of this started. And it's critical that you leave no evidence of your visit. Sally has to leave town with Steve and Paula. Immediately. I obviously don't have to explain—"

"She's leaving in an hour," Johnny said. "We've already explained enough of the situation to persuade her to leave."

"Good. Meet me at the mouth to the canyon."

"Kelly will come with me. She's my . . . She's with me."

"Can she be trusted?"

"Without reservation."

"She's from the X Group."

Johnny turned to face the kitchen sink. "She loves me."

"I'm sure that you think she does. I don't know—"

"She's with me," Johnny said.

"Fine. Meet me in one hour. You'll have to leave soon."

"Where are you?"

"In a helicopter, headed your way. One hour, Johnny. You'll want to hear what I have to say, I can promise you."

THE AFTERNOON light was fading as Dale Crompton steered the rental car through the mountain pass on Interstate 70. The problem with labels like Englishman was that they tended to pigeonhole you, and he refused to be pigeonholed. Those strong of mind could be the Unman or Englishman or Dale Crompton or Robert De Niro, whichever suited them.

This afternoon he was Dale.

The car he drove was a Dodge Ram pickup, a powerful vehicle that would take him to Paradise quickly. He'd rented a sedan at the airport, driven to another rental location in Englewood, parked it in a nearby lot, and then rented the Dodge under an alias.

Renting the truck in Englewood had taken longer than expected because the clerk was belligerent in his feeble attempt to impress Dale.

The clerk's name was Lawrence. Twice Dale's size and as dull as a lump of charcoal. He expected Dale to pay him respect for those qualities. Dale drove away fighting a terrible urge to return and teach Lawrence a few lessons about life and death.

Dust to dust, ashes to ashes.

He was tempted to light this particular lump of coal on fire, thereby reducing him to ashes. Instead, he drove on, up the mountain, after more enticing prey. *Hallelujah, amen, you are dismissed.*

Dale removed his right hand from the steering wheel and formed a C above the cup holder between the seats. The Styrofoam cup in the holder began to vibrate below his hand.

Time after time he'd held back his power while they continued to strip Johnny of his identity.

The cup stopped shaking and rose an inch.

There had been days of reprieve, of course. Assignments to kill in which he'd shown his victims more than a bullet. But on balance, the whole experience had tried his patience to the snapping point.

He glanced at the cup. It flew vertically and stopped in his hand.

The question he had to settle in the next three or four hours was a simple one: Should he kill the mother now or use her as leverage if Johnny managed to surprise him?

For that matter, should he kill Sally first or Kelly first?

They both had five letters.

They both ended in *lly.*

They were both two syllables.

They were both dear, dear, dear to Johnny, Johnny, Johnny.

One had given birth to Johnny, which was an offense worthy of death in and of itself.

The other had humiliated Englishman a hundred times, which would earn her a place in the hall of wide eyes and open mouths on sticks.

He lifted the cup to his lips and drank the scalding coffee.

Which would it be? Maybe both. Yes. Why not both?

CHAPTER TWENTY-EIGHT

DO YOU see anything?" Kelly asked, adjusting the small duffel bag on her shoulder. They'd hidden the other bag with their papers, the money, and two pistols behind the seats and brought two handguns, the knives, and their personal effects with them.

Johnny studied the rocks ahead. "It's a canyon."

"I can see that. He's not here."

"He said at the mouth of the canyon. This has to be it."

"Maybe this is the wrong canyon."

"My mother was specific."

Johnny stared up at the towering cliffs on each side. Night was coming fast. Already the canyon was encased in deep shadows. The encroaching darkness was comforting.

"I think I've been here before," he said. "It's like a tunnel."

"You remember being here, or does it just remind you of where you've been?"

"No . . . No, I think I've actually been here." Johnny headed into the canyon.

"This is the mouth. We should wait—"

"I've been here!" He began to run. "It's coming back! I've been up here before."

She ran after him. "Johnny!"

Johnny spun around and skipped backward. He flung his arms wide and yelled at the tops of the cliffs. "I've been here! I've been here, Kelly. I can remember it now. I remember."

Kelly grinned despite herself. "That's good, Johnny." Her eyes scanned the sheer stone walls on each side. "Meanwhile, our truck's down in the town. Englishman's probably sifting through it right now. We should have left."

"We *are* gone. How will he know about this place?"

"I don't trust him."

"Then trust me! I've been here, and there's no way he knows about this place."

"Johnny!" The voice echoed softly through the canyon behind him.

Johnny spun. There, thirty yards up the canyon, stood the old man from the hospital. David Abraham.

"That's him," Johnny said under his breath. "Do you recognize him?"

"He was on the stage at the president's press conference."

They walked up to David. When they stopped twenty feet from him, he approached them, wearing a mischievous grin.

"The helicopter dropped me off twenty minutes ago. They'll spend the night on top of the cliff."

"And us?" Kelly asked.

David's eyes shifted to her. "Kelly, I presume."

"This is Kelly Larine," Johnny said.

David let his gaze linger on Kelly for several long seconds. "Welcome to ground zero, Kelly Larine. As for us, we will be spending the night around the corner. Come."

David turned on his heels and angled toward a massive boulder on their left. Johnny followed with Kelly hurrying to catch them. The wall behind the towering boulder split to reveal a second, smaller canyon.

"I've been here," Johnny said, picking up his pace.

The older man's chuckle bounced eerily off the cliffs.

Johnny grinned. He'd been here. He was so eager to embrace the memories triggering the distinct déjà vu that he began to sprint. Past David, around the boulder, up to the mouth of the smaller canyon, where he slid to a halt.

The smaller canyon ran thirty meters in and then stopped abruptly at a rock slide that rose sharply to the top of the cliffs. A small log cabin had been built on the sand at the base.

This was wrong. He didn't know why or what, but something was wrong with the scene. The déjà vu popped like a soap bubble meeting a needle.

"What happened?" Johnny asked.

"So then you do remember," David said. "The monastery that used to be here. Project Showdown."

"No. Samuel and my mother both mentioned Project Showdown. I . . . I know that I've been here, just like I know I lived in Paradise and that my mother is Sally. The rest . . ."

"The rest will come," David said. "Shall we?"

They walked to the log cabin in silence. Inside, an oil lamp burned on a crude wooden table flanked by two benches. There were no stairs leading to the loft over the kitchen, only a rather unstable ladder made of twine-bound branches. One bed upstairs. Two beds in a bedroom along the back wall. That was it.

"Outhouse is behind," David said. "It's not the Waldorf, but it allows me to get away and reflect on Project Showdown whenever I am tempted to doubt. If you ever find yourself in that same place, doubting, you may come here. In fact, I strongly recommend it. Please, have a seat."

Kelly and Johnny sat on one side of the table facing David, who still wore his mischievous grin.

"Your mother and the Smithers left Paradise?" David asked.

"She said she'd make the arrangements. They'll spend the next two days in Delta."

An image of the young boy who'd confronted them in New York filled Johnny's mind. Samuel was a younger version of his father. Staring at the older man now, Johnny was sure he did know them both as they claimed. Samuel had been his friend.

But that was impossible.

"How could I have known Samuel?" Johnny asked. "He's still a boy."

"Is he?" David looked at Kelly. "What I say tonight must stay with you. No one can know. Not a soul. I don't think anyone would believe you, but that's not the point. What I tell you tonight is sacred. I don't mind saying that I'm nervous about your hearing this, Kelly."

"Then maybe you shouldn't tell me. I've done my share of damage already."

"She has to hear," Johnny said. "Without her I'm lost. What sense does it make to love someone you can't trust? If I'm ever going to be normal again, it will be with Kelly's help."

"As you insist. But I don't think you'll ever be normal, Johnny."

Then I'd rather die. He kept the thought to himself and watched David's kind eyes. There was a mystery hidden there that Johnny had to uncover.

"You shot the president?" David asked.

Johnny hesitated. "Yes."

"He saved the president," Kelly said. "If not for Johnny, Englishman would have been given the assignment, and the president would be dead."

"I know. And so does the president. He's given us a window while he decides what to do. It won't be easy convincing the authorities that the president's shooter was actually his savior." David drummed his fingers on the table. "My, my, where to begin."

"Who am I?" Johnny asked. "Start with that."

"You're Sally's son. You grew up in Paradise—"

"Not my history. Who I am."

"You're someone who knows how to ask the right questions. That's a start."

David cleared his throat and continued when faced by silence. "To know who you are, you have to believe some things you may not want to believe. How do you think you managed to affect the bullet's flight path?"

Johnny thought about his training. Lowering the heat in his pit. The electric chair. He glanced at Kelly.

"By affecting the zero-point field," she said. "The quantum theory behind observable telekinetics. Are you familiar with quantum theory?"

"Quite. I was fascinated with the theory years ago. There's some merit to zero-point-field research, more than most realize, but I can guarantee you that Johnny's power doesn't originate in his mind."

"Then where?"

David took a deep breath. He drummed his fingers again. "Do you believe in the supernatural, Johnny?"

DALE CROMPTON parked the truck behind the large theater and strode down the yellow dashes of the lone paved street in Paradise, Colorado, imagining the showdown that once occurred here.

The town was empty, as far as he could see. He stopped in the middle of the road and studied the buildings in the waning light. It had all started here. Fitting that it would also end here. Even more fitting that it would end because of him.

A screen door slammed to his right. He turned slowly and saw her standing on the porch of a white house. Johnny's Sally. *Hello, Mommy.*

For a moment they just looked at each other. No surprise from either him or her. The stuff of a perfect plan. *May all ye who don't kiss my feet rot in hell. Amen.*

She stepped off the porch and made her way to the car parked on the street.

Dale broke his stare and strode for the bar.

"SUPERNATURAL?" JOHNNY said. "I don't know what I believe. I used to, I think. I was a chaplain, but I can't remember my faith. Do I still have a faith?"

"Your faith has clearly remembered you," David said. "Your power comes from your faith. At least partially."

"You're saying his power is supernatural," Kelly said.

"Regardless of what we believe or want to believe, there is evidence of a great power that supersedes anything explained by our current understanding of science. Yes, the supernatural. How is it possible for one man to see events that will happen hundreds or thousands of years after his death?"

Johnny had never heard of such a thing. Actually, he was sure he had, but he didn't remember.

"I don't know."

"It's a gift. Words that one day come to life. Do you think something like this is possible?"

"I don't see how, but obviously I should. So I'll say yes."

"Even agnostics can't deny the writings of Nostradamus and certain prophets whose words have come to life. Saint John. Trust me for now, the ability to know the future, however misunderstood by science, is not *unknown* by science."

"Fine. I'll take your word for it."

"Good. Because there's hardly a leap between knowing the future and changing the present. Do you remember a man named Samson? He was a prophet—a judge, actually, but like a prophet—in Israel thousands of years ago."

"Samson?"

"How was it possible for a man named Samson to kill thousands of Philistines with the jawbone of an ass? Or level a massive stone building with one hard push? You think it was a fable?"

Johnny blinked. There was something here that he could remember. Comic books with superheroes that he read when he was younger. Samson was a superhero.

"Supernatural," he said.

David grinned. "I won't give you all the specifics of Project Showdown yet—they would overwhelm you. All in good time. But let me tell you what you need to understand your power."

He sat back in his chair. "Twelve years ago a confrontation between good and evil of biblical proportions visited this valley. Many things happened that week. It was then that a student named Billy found, among other things, some books in the dungeons beneath the monastery. Ancient books that demonstrate the power of the word and free will."

None of this rang a bell with Johnny. David saw his blank look and moved on without elaborating.

"Never mind. You don't need to know any of this to understand. But these books that Billy found held a power that few have been fortunate enough to witness firsthand. I mentioned Samson's strength. But there are accounts of hundreds of these sorts of things, manifestations of superhuman power that changed the course of history."

David drew a deep breath. "In the case of these books, certain things written in them would actually happen. Like the scrolls in John's revelation. Do you follow?"

Johnny put his elbows on the table. He didn't know what to think about any of this. None of it was harder to believe than a prophecy, he supposed, and he'd agreed to believe the possibility of at least that much.

"Books that create truth," Johnny said. "Things that happen because they're written."

"Correct. At any rate, an event occurred that week that was so inconsequential at the time that we hardly noticed it. Evidently you and two other children each made entries into the books and then promptly forgot about those entries. I don't blame you. There was no evidence at the time that your entries had any significance or would come true."

"What entries?"

"'Johnny was given great powers to destroy anyone who stood in the way of truth.' Those were your exact words."

"That's it?"

David smiled and cocked an eyebrow. "Pretty broad statement, isn't it?"

"What happened to the books?"

"Let's just say that as far as we know, they went missing forever. It wasn't until you earned your first Purple Heart in Iraq that I took any notice. You were a chaplain and braved impossible odds to save a colonel stranded at a post. The rest of your company had been killed. Yet you, a noncombatant, went back. You evidently faced a barrage of gunfire without being hit. I talked to the colonel myself. He described a scene that he himself had difficulty believing. But he was alive. You had to have done what he saw you do. Samuel began to watch you then."

"Samuel, who is just a boy."

"No, no, not just a boy. He was part of Project Showdown as well. He was the only survivor immediately affected. Since that week twelve years ago, my son hasn't aged a day."

Johnny wanted to say something to express his doubt, but he couldn't think of anything. He looked at Kelly, who was studying the old man skeptically.

"You saw him. I can prove a hundred ways over that he's lived for twenty-five years. If you need any proof that what I've said about Project Showdown is true, Samuel is your proof."

"And you're saying that I gained certain capabilities as a result of writing in these books," Johnny said.

"Yes, you were given certain supernatural gifts. Not unlike Samson. Samuel watched you closely and recorded a dozen instances where you used them. He approached you about your gifts when he noticed they were growing stronger. Evidently you weren't certain of your gifts even then. But you were a man of incredible faith, a profound believer who was willing to give his life for the defense of truth. Truth, Johnny. Ever since Project Showdown, you've been consumed with the truth."

And now I don't possess an ounce of truth. It's been stripped from me. I don't even know if what I'm being told is the truth.

"Then Samuel had his dream," David said. "He saw into the future."

He said it as though this new bit of information was the anchor that would awaken Johnny's understanding. It did nothing of the kind.

"He saw the assassination of a world leader, which we now know was the president, and he saw the resulting destruction of Israel. The killer came from the X Group. Samuel had never heard of the X Group, naturally. You can imagine his surprise to discover that there actually *was* such a group that did indeed undertake assassinations. It took him months to get to the bottom of it, or as near to the bottom as one can get with the X Group. He hatched the plan then."

"Hatched what plan?"

"The plan to get you into the X Group. They are connected to certain parts of the Central Intelligence Agency that sometimes gave assistance to the X Group. Samuel saw to it that the CIA suggested your recruitment. With your record, you were the perfect candidate."

Johnny stared at the kind eyes that watched him. He had been kidnapped and destroyed *because* of this man and his son, Samuel?

"Please, you have to know that neither of us had any understanding of how destructive their techniques were at the time," David said.

Johnny wanted to feel anger, but he felt nothing.

"We didn't know about the torture," David said. "Or the invasive identity manipulation."

"Why didn't you tell me?" Johnny demanded. "How could Samuel do this and call himself my friend?"

"No, never! When Samuel told you of his vision and the X Group, you insisted that you should do exactly as he suggested. You said it was the least you could do after what he did for you. You were a man of deep faith. In your mind, infiltrating the enemy's camp was the only right thing to do."

"I don't remember any of this! You make me sound like some kind of crazy superhero!"

"Superhero? Aren't we all? Isn't that what all men, women, and children of faith are? Isn't that what Project Showdown was all about? We, the ostracized few, given power to aid the very society that fears us? You just happen to have an extra portion, thanks to the books. You're this world's Samson, Johnny."

"I don't know what you're talking about."

"And I don't believe you," Kelly said. "What kind of person would actually think he could infiltrate the X Group without being killed?"

"A boy who once faced the vilest evil and walked away. A boy who survived Project Showdown: Johnny. And a person who would give his life for Johnny at a moment's notice: my son, Samuel." The tremble in David's voice vibrated along Johnny's nerves. "And I don't mind adding," the older man continued, calmer now, "they were right. The president's alive today because of what Samuel and Johnny did."

"You don't know that," Johnny said. "Assim Feroz ordered the hit on the president. Kalman won't back off just because I failed. For all we know the president will be dead in an hour."

"You're sure it was Feroz who ordered the hit?"

Johnny looked at Kelly, who nodded. "Yes. There's no way to prove it, but that was my understanding."

"If the world knew, Feroz might call off any second attempt. If he was implicated in any way, it would destroy his initiative to disarm Israel."

"No. He would deny it," Kelly said. "And he'd make the United States look foolish for suggesting it."

"It would be his word against ours, surely—"

"Your own CIA would probably also deny it," Kelly interrupted. "They're in bed with Kalman. You've put us in an impossible situation! Our lives, your life, Sally's life, the president's life, and who knows how many others'—they're all in Kalman's line of sight. Clearly you don't understand how ruthless he is."

"I've seen worse, believe me. Perhaps he should be dealt with directly."

"Kill Kalman?" Kelly said. "This isn't a simple matter. He's no longer in Hungary. Any sign of trouble and Kalman would move immediately. Even if I could find them, they would know I'd compromised them and take the necessary precautions."

"They've moved my pit?" Johnny asked, surprised.

"They've abandoned the camp, at least temporarily."

He wanted to ask when he and Kelly might go back, but he immediately felt foolish for even thinking such a thing. He was done with them. Wasn't he? Of course he was!

"How would Kalman suspect that he was in danger?" David asked.

Kelly shook her head. "He's tied in with all of them. Interpol, CIA, NSA, the Russians, the Chinese, the French—they all need him. They all want him. He has many, many guarantees. If he dies, every country that's ever used him will be exposed, and they know it."

"There has to be a way."

"If I supposedly once had power from these books," Johnny said, "isn't it possible that others also have a power from them?"

"Yes. Two others. But we've been watching them. The rest were confidentially integrated back into society for their own protection."

"How do you know it's only two? What if someone else used the books? Someone evil?"

"No." David motioned emphatically with his hand. "We'd have seen it by now."

For a few moments they each were lost in thought. Johnny tried to remember a conversation with a boy named Samuel about being recruited by the X Group, but he didn't have the slightest recollection of talking, much less agreeing. What kind of man would agree to such a thing?

A man of virtue. But he didn't feel like a man of virtue.

A man of great faith. But he didn't have any faith.

A man who was unique and powerful. But he didn't want to be either unique or powerful.

A man who was still expected to do great things. But Johnny was overwhelmed by a desire to be normal. Hadn't he paid enough of a price these last ten months? Hadn't he done what he and Samuel had agreed to do by saving the president?

He stood and crossed the room, suddenly angry. He couldn't remember the last time he'd been truly angry. It was the emotion he'd first learned to shut down in order to survive Agotha. But now, learning who he was or had been, he embraced the sentiment—enough of it to raise his pulse a few beats.

"Why are you telling me this?" He knew the answer, but he asked anyway and then answered himself. "What do you expect me to do, protect the president? I don't even know how to protect myself anymore. The skills I had were dependent on my singular focus." He shoved a finger against his head. "On my mind! Now I'm full of doubts. I probably couldn't hit a barrel at a hundred yards now."

"No one's suggesting that you need your skills to protect the president," David said.

"Then what?"

David interlaced his fingers and put both elbows on the table. "I don't know. I'm not the one with the power."

"I *have* no power! How can I convince you of that? Should we test it? Strap me to a bed, electrocute me, see if I can withstand the heat?"

They both stared at him.

"Do you want to place me in a box full of hornets, see if I can survive their stings? Shove a needle through my shoulder, see if I can withstand the pain?"

David's face was white.

"Has it ever occurred to you that I've only been able to do a few things beyond what's considered natural even after intense training and focus? Now that you've undermined my faith by introducing all of this nonsense that only a child could possibly accept, I'm a shadow of myself."

"Only by choice," David said.

"I don't want to be this person you're describing! I don't want to be Johnny if Johnny is anyone but Sally's son. I'm Carl! Everything else is foreign to me. I've tried, believe me—I've racked my mind trying to be someone else, but I'm not. I'm Carl, and Carl loves two things: Kelly and his pit."

Kelly stared at him. It occurred to Johnny that his anger could be justifiably directed at her. If he continued down this path, she would be faced with more pain than she could bear, and in front of David. He didn't want to do that to her.

Johnny let his anger dissipate. His outburst wasn't satisfying anyway. He wasn't sure he even understood it. Why *wouldn't* he want to be the person David described? Because he wanted to be normal. Just himself, as he knew himself to be.

Carl.

He could still control his emotions to some extent, which was good. Maybe he still had some of the other skills he'd come to this country with. Maybe he was still a good sniper. A good assassin. He hoped so. Their survival might depend on it.

He returned to his seat. "I hate to disappoint you, but I'm not the one with power either. I can't do anything more than nudge a bullet to follow a path ingrained in my head. And don't tell me I haven't tried hard enough. If there's one thing Agotha taught me well, it's how to try. I tried in ways most can't or won't, and I have the scars to prove it."

Kelly put her hand on his arm. Johnny closed his eyes and swallowed. He wanted to throw himself at her and beg her to hold him. To comfort him. But he could no more break down again than he could stand and run around the cabin naked.

They sat in silence, sifting through these agonies.

Kelly finally broke the silence. "Can you tell us more about Project Showdown?"

David stared at her. It took awhile for him to respond. "Why don't we eat something? I brought some steaks. Then I'll tell you about Project Showdown. I trust you're not given to nightmares."

CHAPTER TWENTY-NINE

IT WAS midnight. The orange light that flickered in the cabin's windows had winked out an hour ago. Englishman—now clearly cognizant of how boring the name Dale really was after trying it on for a few hours—had seated himself cross-legged on a boulder fifty feet from the shack two hours earlier and watched in silence, listening to the soft murmur of voices inside.

All three had come out once to use the outhouse behind the cabin, but none of them had seen him staring at them from the shadows beyond the ring of light cast by their lamps inside.

The canyon rested in perfect peace under a half-moon's pale gaze. A pebble clicked on his right, dislodged by a lizard or a small rodent that scampered away. Then peace again.

He could hear the silence. Feel its stillness. Smell its crisp purity.

The town of Paradise was a disappointment. Nightlife was evidently something these mountain folk didn't regard with much interest. Obviously they'd given up their affinity for grace juice.

He'd considered making a bit of a ruckus in the town before going up the mountain but decided that now was not a good time to leave a trail. There was nothing the hapless mountain folk could offer him that he didn't already have anyway.

He had bigger plans. Johnny.

They were in a test of wills, a contest of choices, and thus far Englishman had made the superior choices. In all likelihood, Johnny was only now even learning that he had a choice.

The fast-approaching end to this game seemed rushed after nearly a year of patience. A shame that he wouldn't need to use his trump card after all. Part of Englishman didn't want to end it so quickly. Perhaps he should extend the game. The decision momentarily paralyzed him.

Being human wasn't always the easiest way to make a living. He let the angst fade.

Englishman stretched out his left hand, shoulder-high, and opened his palm, eyes still fixed on the dark cabin. Something whistled softly through the night. A stone slightly smaller than his fist smacked into his open palm.

He had half a mind to take this rock back to Hungary and bury it in Agotha's throat. *Are we impressed with lowering the temperature and nudging bullets, Agotha?*

He tossed the stone into the air. Instead of falling back with gravity, it reached its apex two feet above his hand and was summarily snatched away by the night behind him. He heard it strike the distant canyon wall to his rear, hardly more than a *tick*.

He stretched his arms and shoulders by crossing them in front of his chest, then reached for his feet. Two hours without moving had left him stiff. He put his hands on his hips and swung his body around at the waist, cracking his back with the motion.

The black leather coat over his shirt fell long, roughly a foot below his belt. He pulled both sides back and hooked them behind two holstered pistols like a gunslinger.

Black canvas shoes. Black nylon pants that stretched easily if his maneuvers required them to. The only part of him that wasn't camouflaged by the night was his sandy-blond Jude Law hair.

He hopped off the rock and landed on the sand with a soft *thump*. Careless, but with odds like this he hardly needed to creep up on them like a mouse. Still, he walked soundlessly toward the door, hands ready.

He withdrew one of the guns from his hip, a Colt Model 1911 .45 caliber. Jacketed hollow-point 230-grain bullets with enough kick to knock a man across the room. Single-action, recoil-driven semiautomatic with a magazine of 10 +1. Custom blue-steel barrel. Englishman's pistol of choice.

He stepped up to the door, took a deep breath, cocked the gun by his ear, and tried the door. Unlocked.

Here it was, then.

Dale twisted the knob and pushed the door open, leveling the gun as he did so. His eyes were fully accustomed to the dark, so before the door had completed its full swing, he'd taken in the table, the kitchen, the loft above the kitchen, and the bedroom door on the back wall.

Still not a sound.

Moving fast, he slid to the loft ladder, hopped up onto the fifth rung, and scanned the sleeping area. Bed with rumpled blankets. No body.

No body.

He spun and dropped, catlike. The wood floor creaked. All three must be behind the bedroom door, sleeping soundlessly.

Moving more on instinct than with calculation, Dale flew across the room, shoved the door open, and trained his weapon on an empty bed.

Empty bed.

Empty room.

Empty cabin.

"Don't move."

The voice, which he immediately recognized as Johnny's, came from behind.

"Drop the guns. All of them."

He could have leveled the man then and there, without even turning. But he did have a couple of challenges if he made a move now.

His first challenge was that any one of Johnny's bullets would kill him as quickly as any other man's. The less-skilled man would undoubtedly get off a shot before falling from Englishman's attack, and at this range, he wouldn't miss Englishman's head.

His second challenge was that he didn't know where the others were. They'd obviously been more alert than he guessed. Kelly might not be Johnny, but with a gun at close range, she could kill just as easily.

Englishman turned slowly, gun hand raised.

He'd turned three-quarters of the way around when Johnny shot him in his leg. "I said drop the gun. The next one goes through a bone."

Englishman felt the pain spread through his thigh. Flesh wound, right thigh, hardly more than a crease. Still, he dropped the Colt.

"The other guns as well. And the knives."

No sign of Kelly or the old man. Englishman searched the darkness for any clue of the woman. Nothing. If Kelly hid nearby, she was silent.

"Now," Johnny said.

Englishman complied. The other Colt from his hip. The two 9mm's at his back. Two knives from his calves. He'd misjudged Johnny, but if the chaplain knew the extent of Englishman's skills, he'd have shot him while he had the chance. Instead, Johnny thought he had the upper hand and intended to question him. Or use him.

Englishman let a shallow grin cross his mouth. Johnny still didn't know the truth.

He spread his empty hands. "Satisfied?"

The man who loved the dark stared at him in the pale moonlight. "Hello, Englishman. You walk too loudly. I'm surprised you found us as quickly as you did."

"It won't be your last surprise," Englishman said. "Why don't you kill me?"

"I'm going to. How did you know about this place?"

"Kalman knows many things."

"He's ordered you to kill the president?"

"We never fail, you know that."

"Yet you failed now. It seems that Kalman forgot to tell you about the trap door in the bedroom. Only a fool would build a cabin at the end of this particular box canyon without an escape route. David Abraham is no fool."

So Kelly and the old man had escaped through some sort of hatch in the bedroom floor. They were probably on top of the cliffs already. This meant that there was no gun trained on him, other than Johnny's.

"You should have gone with them," he said.

"After you tell me what I need to know. Where is Jenine?"

Englishman grew impatient. One of the knives on the floor began to float. It lifted three inches from the ground and slid horizontally above the wood floor.

Johnny glanced down, eyes registering surprise.

The knife sprang shoulder-high and sliced toward Johnny in silence. Englishman was prepared to dodge a shot from Johnny's gun, but it never came. Johnny was immobilized by indecision. Or he'd already concluded that shooting would guarantee his death, even if he did hit Englishman.

"I know other tricks as well. I suggest you drop the gun."

Johnny studied the blade at his neck, then lifted his eyes. They exchanged a long stare.

Englishman winked.

Johnny slowly lowered his gun. "You're affecting the zero-point field?"

"Drop the gun."

Johnny's pistol fell from his fingers and clattered on the floor.

"Actually, it's nothing so scientific as the zero-point field or any of Agotha's theories. I'm surprised that you, of all people, don't know that."

"Who are you?"

"I'm Dale Crompton. I'm Englishman. I am the personification of man's worst fears. I am Jude—"

A creak behind Englishman stopped him cold. He dropped to one knee and felt the sting on his cheek a thousandth of a second after he heard the crash of gunfire from the room behind him.

Kelly had returned for her lover. Her bullet smashed through the window as it exited the cabin.

He palmed a 9mm from the floor where he'd dropped it and was twisted halfway around when her second shot split the night. He rolled to one side of the door and brought his gun up for a clean shot.

From his peripheral vision he saw a blur.

Johnny was coming for him.

Englishman's momentary lapse in concentration had let the knife fall from Johnny's neck. Now he was forced to consider both Johnny and Kelly. But this wasn't a problem for Englishman. As long as he had direct sensory input from each of them, he could . . .

The window behind Johnny crashed.

In that split second, Englishman knew what had happened. Johnny wasn't coming for him. He had thrown himself backward through the window.

Englishman was already in the process of shooting a bullet into Kelly's head when this realization hit him. And with the realization came another: Johnny had just gained the upper hand. Evidently he knew enough about how these powers worked to know that Englishman needed a line of sight or sound to affect any object. He was removing himself from that line of sight.

So Englishman would simply kill the woman now and go after Johnny.

Unless going after Johnny proved more difficult than he'd estimated, in which case having the girl alive might prove useful.

All of this crossed his mind before Johnny crashed to the ground outside the window. Kelly was screaming something as her third bullet whipped through the bedroom doorway.

The Englishman reached around the door frame and shot the pistol from her hand.

She cried out and snatched her hand close to her chest.

"Stay!" he snapped.

"You want *me*, not him!"

Englishman jumped to his feet and bounded for the door. He could hear stones tumbling outside as Johnny climbed the rock slide behind the cabin, but the sounds were scattered. The thought of Johnny escaping him now mucked up his instincts.

Kelly was reaching for the gun behind him. Furious, he jabbed his finger back at her. "Stay!"

The gun by her hand flew through the air as if it were on a string. He accepted it with his open fist, stepped into the night air, and fired wildly at the mound of boulders behind the cabin.

He fired seven shots in rapid succession. But he knew as he pulled the trigger that he couldn't direct the bullets with so much confusion at hand. His bullets smacked into rocks, unguided.

Englishman cried out in rage. The man was escaping. He could kill the girl and go after him, but Johnny undoubtedly had another gun strapped somewhere to his body. Johnny didn't have Englishman's power, but his aim was astonishingly accurate. And he loved the dark even more than Englishman. Johnny could sit in silence at the top of the cliff and pick him off at his leisure.

Englishman threw one of his guns on the ground and walked back into the cabin, calming himself. Johnny knew Englishman wouldn't kill Kelly now. A hostage was too valuable given the circumstances. And Johnny made the judgment quickly. Much more quickly than Englishman expected.

He stared at Kelly, who was evidently still stunned by the flying-gun trick.

"Get up," he said.

"What are you going to do?"

"We're leaving for a place better suited to our objective. If Johnny doesn't follow, I'm going to kill you."

"He'll never do that."

"He'll die for you. Or do you think he was just pulling your leg?"

"He'll know you're just using me."

"It doesn't matter. He's foolish enough to love you; he'll be foolish enough to die for you."

The sound of a helicopter winding up on the cliff cut through the night. He cursed himself for not taking the time to scout it out and disable it earlier.

Englishman eyed Kelly, who had gathered herself and was scowling. He allowed himself a smile. The woman he'd allowed to toy with him for so many months was beautiful; he could never deny that much. And wearing her anger, she was downright fascinating. Little did she know how much she cared for him.

But Englishman knew. Deep down where the black and the white traded blows, Kelly was desperate for him.

He lifted his pistol toward her, thumbed the release, and let the spent clip clatter to the floor. "Round one, Johnny."

Englishman slammed a fresh clip into the gun, chambered a round, and let go of the handle. The pistol hung in the air unmoving, aimed at Kelly. He stepped away from the obedient weapon.

"Stay," he said. "If she tries to run, shoot her in the leg."

Englishman looked at Kelly, who had traded her scowl for a look of amazement. Some fear. Respect and admiration. She was smitten by him. It was a pity he hated her; they would have made a good pair.

So why was he making such a display about showing her his power? Was he trying to impress her? They both knew there was no need for him to release the gun. It would shoot just as well in his fist.

He was toying with her, rubbing her hopelessness in her face.

Or maybe he was trying to win her respect because he didn't hate her as much as he thought he did.

Englishman grunted, stepped forward, and snatched the weapon out of the air, his bad mood at having lost Johnny now fouler because of this minor indiscretion.

He pointed the gun at the door. "Go."

"Where?"

"After Johnny."

"Where is Johnny going?"

Englishman hesitated, deciding whether to demonstrate his flawless logic in determining Johnny's next steps, which he had indeed calculated in the last sixty seconds while unwisely indulging in this gun-floating trick. He owed her no explanation. But he gave her a short one anyway, perhaps to impress her once again. He chastised himself even as he spoke.

"He's going to prove his love for you."

JOHNNY RAN down the mountain, propelled by his need to save. To liberate. To kill.

With each plunging step through the underbrush, his decision to put so much distance between him and the woman he loved haunted him. He had to force his legs forward, down, over logs, through the branches grabbing at his legs.

But his instinct told him that his decision was a good one. Perhaps the only way to save Kelly. If Englishman guessed his course and prevented him from succeeding, on the other hand, this flight away from Kelly could prove disastrous.

The helicopter had wound up and left with David. He'd protested Johnny's insistence that he leave immediately, but a short discussion had persuaded him. If Kalman had sent Englishman after them, it would be for Johnny and Kelly, not David. The last thing they could risk was making the helicopter a target, which it would become if Johnny and Kelly were in it. Shooting a helicopter out of the air would be an easy task for Englishman.

More than this, Johnny wasn't interested in fleeing. He and Kelly knew they would have to deal with this threat directly.

He'd come instantly and fully awake at the sound of a distant rock hitting the cliff. Not rolling down with a series of clicks as others had done through the night, but striking a far rock wall with some force.

Unnatural. Then he'd heard the soft thump of two feet landing on sand and knew that Englishman was outside.

Now, Johnny broke from the brush onto a wide ledge that over-looked the sleeping, moonlit town below.

He'd been here. He'd seen something significant from this very ledge. The events that David had described hours earlier flooded his mind. He'd seen part of them from this vantage point. The only thing that was more difficult to believe than this story of David's was that Johnny had some power hidden in his bones today because of it.

But the details of his past weren't germane to his mission today. They would tell him who he'd once been, not who he was now. They wouldn't save Kelly or him. They would not kill Englishman.

Englishman, who evidently wasn't the same man Johnny had always known him to be.

Johnny turned onto the path on his right and continued his descent at a fast run. A shiver passed down his spine. He'd seen Englishman's knife lift from the floor as if manipulated by a magnetic field. Seen it floating toward him, picking up speed, flashing through the night.

His instinct told him to block the weapon before it reached his neck. His mind told him not to. It understood something that wasn't apparent to his instincts.

It understood that if Englishman could do this, he could easily kill Johnny at any time. Could kill Johnny at his leisure. If Johnny tried to stop the knife, he would only injure himself. Perhaps lose his fingers or a hand.

His mind buzzed with the implication of Englishman's power. Either Englishman had perfected control of the zero-point field, or he possessed a power far beyond any Agotha knew about. Or David Abraham, for that matter, because David had said that only two others possessed such power, and both were being watched.

Johnny had affected the flight of a bullet with supreme focus, but Englishman had done far more. Any direct conflict with the man would end disastrously.

He ran with a growing fear. What he was about to attempt was nothing short of impossible. Yet he saw no other way.

His fear gave way to anger as he approached Paradise. The town was in deep sleep when he ran past the Paradise Community Center, toward the blue truck. A dog barked at him from a front yard. He sprinted past, eager to get out of this hole from his past.

The keys were still in the wheel well where they'd left them. The money behind the seats. Blowing a breath of relief, he slid behind the wheel, fired the truck, peeled through a U-turn, and roared out of the valley.

Miles flew by in a confusing haze. The tunnel in his mind obediently formed, leading to the familiar light. Success depended on reaching the target before it was removed from his scope of operation. If he was too late, the mission would present him with significant new challenges that would set him back days.

He had money. He had a set of papers that identified him as Saul Matheson. And he had the skills of an assassin—the fact that he could so easily form his tunnel now under duress assured him of this much.

Johnny drove north, through Delta, toward Grand Junction, slipping deeper and deeper into his tunnel, energized by a growing anger that surprisingly didn't compromise his focus. In fact, this new fury boiling in him seemed to make the light brighter.

He reached the airport north of Grand Junction as the sun edged above the mesas. The guns he left in the truck; the rest he took.

The only seat available on the 6:49 flight to Denver was a first-class seat identical in every way to the rest of the seats on the nineteen-seat United Express turboprop. The first-class seat on the Boeing 757 to New York was more comfortable, but comfort wasn't a thing he could easily judge. In his mind, the pit was still his safest and by extension his most comfortable place.

He didn't belong in the pit. Not now.

Now he belonged behind a gun, preparing to send a bullet into a target's brain to save the one woman besides his mother whom he loved.

He would kill anyone to save her. Anyone or everyone.

The decision satisfied a deep yearning in his psyche to justify the hours of torment during which Johnny had become Carl. The training would be redeemed—it would now help him save the woman he loved.

He was really Carl, he decided. He would be Carl and he would do what Carl would do.

He would force Dale's hand by killing the man he'd crossed the oceans to kill.

CHAPTER THIRTY

CARL AND Kelly had selected the Best Western in Chinatown as one of their two dummy rooms. The authorities may have traced him to the Peking Grand Hotel, where he met Samuel, but there was little chance that anyone had found the room they rented for a week at the Best Western.

If they had, Carl doubted they'd found the small stash of weapons in the toilet tank. He was right.

Carl pulled out the bag, ripped open the plastic, and spilled two 9mm handguns, two extra clips, two sheathed knives, and one cell phone onto the bed. He shoved both guns into his belt behind him, dropped the clips into the pocket of his jacket, and strapped one knife to each of his ankles.

Grabbing the cell phone, he strode from the room, hurried down the stairs, and caught a yellow cab at the curb.

"Bellevue Hospital," he said.

"Bellevue, First Street," the cabby repeated, punching his meter, which immediately began its count from $4.20.

"Please."

The car pulled into traffic. The late-afternoon sun was setting

behind them as they angled northeast on Houston. Carl had never
put much thought into whether a target deserved to be killed, at least
not in his time of training with the X Group. But now he did, and
he'd come to the conclusion en route to New York that this target
deserved to die, no matter what the world thought of him.

This man deserved to die to save Kelly.

This man deserved to die because Johnny had sworn to kill him.

This man deserved to die because Carl had been trained to kill him.

KELLY WAS tempted to cry out to one of the security guards as they
exited La Guardia Airport, but she knew the impulse was a bad one.
Not only were they all on the wrong side of justice, but they were playing a game that no security guard or policeman would understand.

Englishman had driven her north to Grand Junction, where he'd
found the blue truck parked at the airport. He grunted in satisfaction
and then booked them on the 7:50 flight through Denver to New
York.

Kelly had asked him questions on the drive from Paradise, but
Englishman refused to respond. She wasn't sure if he was sulking or
simply playing his cards close. Afterward, they didn't exchange a
single word all the way to New York. He had her in a virtual prison.
One wrong move and he would kill her with as little effort as it took
him to cough.

Who was the man? Certainly not the same assassin she'd ordered
around in Hungary. But he *was* the same man, which could only
mean that he had been playing her the whole time. Did Agotha or
Kalman know that he had these incredible powers?

No, she didn't think so. Agotha wouldn't have shown so much
interest in Carl's small feats if she knew that next door there was a
man who could float a gun around the room.

If she hadn't seen Englishman float the gun with her own eyes, she would still think the old man had spun a piece of pure fiction with his tale of magical books. She'd often thought of the Bible as precisely such a fictional book of fables.

But now she'd seen the impossible, and she was quite sure there was such a thing as supernatural power after all. On any other day, the revelation would have thrilled her to the bone.

Instead, it left her flat. Of course this power existed. She'd known it all along, somewhere beyond her immediate consciousness.

None of it mattered anymore. The man she'd fallen in love with was going to die. And if he was going to die, she was also going to die.

Englishman hailed a cab and held the door for her without meeting her eyes. She could swear he was sulking.

"UN Headquarters," he told the driver.

The cab pulled out, braked hard to avoid colliding with a sedan, then surged into the flow of cars.

"Why are we going to the United Nations?" she asked.

Englishman spoke to her for the first time since leaving Colorado. "To kill Johnny."

EVERYTHING IN Carl's mind was black except for that light at the end of his tunnel. The light of his plan, the light of Kelly's freedom.

"Could you pull over here?" Carl asked, motioning to a side street.

"Not Bellevue?" The man's eyes searched the rearview mirror.

"Pull over here."

The cab pulled over.

"Is this your cab?"

"Yes. I lease name and sign from company."

"I need to borrow it. Two hours, ten thousand dollars. Does that sound fair?"

The man looked back and waved a hand. "No, it is illegal. I cannot—"

"Fifteen thousand, then." This time Carl pushed three banded stacks of hundred-dollar bills through the hole in the Plexiglas shield that separated them. "You can buy a new car if I damage this one."

The driver gawked at him, either thrilled by such an extravagant offer or terrified by it.

"No questions. If you'd rather, I'll make the same offer to the next cab. I don't have much time."

"How will I get car—"

"Parked in front of Bellevue Hospital in two hours. Yes or no?"

The man hesitated only a second before taking the money and flipping through it. He cast a long, furtive glance back, then tapped his watch. "Seven o'clock, Bellevue Hospital?"

"Yes."

The man climbed out and looked around nervously as Johnny rounded the cab and slid behind the wheel.

He drove the car north, past Bellevue, past Thirty-fourth, past Forty-second, and parked near the UN Headquarters on the corner of First and Forty-sixth.

Most meetings on the original summit schedule had been disrupted by his attempt on the president's life, but according to the CNN report that Carl had seen in the Denver airport, the meeting now under way in the UN Building wasn't one of them.

Under any other circumstance, he would have set up with a rifle and taken a shot from a safe distance. But with Englishman undoubtedly in pursuit, he didn't have time for such luxury.

Carl waited in the cab patiently, staring with fixed eyes at the doors through which the target would exit, acutely aware of details that his training had taught him to absorb.

The man fifty yards up the street who ambled slowly with a bottle in one hand and a stick in the other, poking through each garbage receptacle he passed.

The child across the street who'd stopped with his mother to gaze at the UN entrance.

A bird on the street lamp twenty meters north, cocking its eyes at him.

The security guards stationed by the front door, who had cast frequent glances his way before crossing the street and accepting his explanation that he was waiting for an aide, whom he named from a memorized list.

Each limousine and cab that approached and passed, which he examined like a machine searching for defective eggs at a poultry factory.

Most of this occurred outside of Carl's direct focus. Only one objective mattered to him now, and that objective received most of his attention.

Carl sat with both hands on the steering wheel, drilling the doors with an unbroken stare, sweating with cold fury now. He didn't want to sweat, but he wanted to feel, so he let his body react normally to the anger that filled the black walls of his tunnel.

Only when a tremble overtook his fingers did Carl rein in his rage. Within seconds his fingers stilled, and within five minutes the sweat on his skin had dried.

Then the doors opened and a dozen dark-suited guards and dignitaries spilled from the UN Headquarters.

It was time.

CHAPTER THIRTY-ONE

ENGLISHMAN HAD a choice.

He always had a choice. Choice, choice, choice, that was his middle name. But he knew what he would choose.

At the moment his choices were as follows: One, kill Kelly now, as she rode muted in the backseat of the cab, and then kill the cabby and take the car on his own. Two, kill Kelly and let the cabby live. Three, kill only the cabby and take the car with Kelly beside him. Four, kill neither Kelly nor the cabby and let the cabby do the driving under the persuasion of his gun.

This was only one set of choices. There were others, any of which would affect the desired end result. Which was what?

Which was to destroy Johnny. Not simply kill him, mind you. Destroy him.

Englishman had been sent to the X Group for the explicit purpose of bringing Johnny to his knees and then, when he was ruined beyond recognition, when he was a shell of the man he once was, destroying him. In the end, Johnny would die in humiliation, but only after he'd been brought to a place where he could appreciate the true horror of his own demise.

Only after he learned to hate.

Then and only then would Johnny's undoing satisfy their collective hate for Samuel and the others who managed to survive Project Showdown. Samuel may have once survived that creep Black's assault, thereby rendering himself untouchable, but his heart wouldn't survive Johnny's demise, not after what they'd been through twelve years earlier.

The turn of events at the cabin hadn't been planned, but even that played to Englishman's favor. Johnny was learning to hate in a way that he'd never hated, and that was the point. He would eventually hate himself. And then the end would come.

If Englishman could use his trump card now, Johnny's hand would be forced. But he couldn't, not yet.

"Pull over," Englishman said.

The cabby grunted something in another language and pulled to the curb. Englishman had made his choice and was happy with it. Reaching under his coat, he quickly affixed a silencer to the barrel of his pistol.

Kelly watched him. "What are you doing?"

The moment the cab came to a stop, he climbed out, hurried around to the driver's window, and shot the man through the temple. But he stopped the bullet in the man's brain so that it wouldn't make a mess.

The man slumped over so that his head lay across the bench seat. Englishman stuck his head through the window and winked at Kelly.

"Get up front, please."

She didn't obey at first, and he thought about changing his choice. If she became a problem, he'd find another way.

She evidently had figured as much and now came to her senses. "He's up there," she said.

"There's room for three."

Englishman climbed in, shoving the man out of the way. Kelly opened the front door, studied the dead body. A man dressed in a blue business suit approached the car, apparently dumbstruck. Englishman shot the man in the chest. This time he didn't bother stopping the bullet. A little distraction here, a block from the UN, might come in handy.

He jerked the driver upright to give Kelly more room. "Please, hurry."

Kelly obliged.

There was yelling on the curb when he pulled back into traffic, but nothing was so shocking in this city to generate immediate and forceful action. Another of Englishman's favorite movies was *The Terminator*. At the moment he felt a little like Arnold Schwarzenegger must have felt pretending to be a ruthless, emotionless killer from the future.

Unlike the Terminator, Englishman was real. And Englishman had emotions, and right now he was both happy and excited.

The UN Building loomed ahead on his right.

"You'll never get away with being so careless," Kelly said. Her tone reminded him of her cocky superiority back in Hungary. "They'll come down on us like the plague."

"I would think that would please you." A long line of black limousines waited patiently for their respective dignitaries. They'd arrived in time, then. Good.

"We are all implicated in this," she said, pushing the dead driver's head off her shoulder. The man slumped forward and struck the dash with his face. It was a good position.

Everything was working out. Good car, good timing, good hostage, good dead driver.

"Maybe we should work together," she said. "Last I remember, we were on the same team. If you insist on killing me later, fine, but don't get us all killed before our time."

"You don't have the slightest clue what you're talking about. Please be quiet."

Englishman scanned the street, much in the same way he remembered Arnold scanning the street in *The Terminator*. If she knew the full extent of his power, she wouldn't question his choices. She certainly wouldn't be trying this pathetic attempt to gain his confidence. Surely she realized that he knew how much she cared for Johnny. Love had been in her every glance in Hungary, and it lit her eyes even now.

Kelly was madly in love with Johnny. End of story. End of story soon enough anyway.

"I may not be—"

The dead driver's hand flew up and backhanded her across the face with a loud *smack*.

Then Englishman did it again, this time as she watched fully aware of what was happening. The dead man's arm lifted, stopped six inches from her cheek, and then patted her face gently.

"Please be quiet," Englishman said and let the arm drop.

She obeyed him.

The mission was going well. Very well.

And then suddenly the mission wasn't going so well, because suddenly the doors to the UN Building flew open and dignitaries began to pour out and Englishman hadn't yet spotted Johnny.

He searched the streets quickly. Dozens of cars of all colors, mostly black limousines and yellow cabs—Johnny could be in any one of them. Pedestrians of all stripes—Johnny could be masquerading as a businessman or a dignitary or a security guard for that matter. His time had been limited, but a killer as resourceful as Johnny could have adopted any one of dozens of personas.

Kelly was searching as well, and Englishman kept her in his peripheral vision, watching for her recognition. Love was a strange and horrible beast, binding in mysterious ways.

Englishman slowed the car, ignoring horns behind him. Another cab drove by on his right and cut in front of him, horn blaring. Englishman wreaked havoc on the other car's engine with a burst of frustration. He couldn't isolate the specific damage without being able to directly determine the engine's layout through line of sight or sound, but he could send disruption to the general vicinity.

The car's front grille began to boil white smoke. Radiator. Englishman pulled around the car, through the clouds of steam.

A dozen cookie-cutter agents had exited the building during his brief distraction. The target stepped into the sun. Still no sign of Johnny. Had he misjudged the man? Was it possible that Johnny was still in Paradise, plotting to recover Kelly through other means?

Unlikely.

A taxi pulled away from the curb and roared away from the scene without a fare. Odd, but not singularly odd in a place where a thousand cabs went a thousand places known only to the driver and the fare. Englishman dismissed the sight.

The target was getting in a large black limousine.

Still no sign of Johnny.

A train of black cars, two in advance of the target's vehicle and two behind, pulled into traffic just ahead.

Still no sign of Johnny.

Englishman searched frantically now. Pedestrians, security, black-and-whites, government officials, cameramen, news crews—the street in front of the UN Building was now a scene of mass confusion. Behind them sirens wailed—presumably headed for the man Englishman had shot a couple of blocks back.

He hesitated, expecting the assassin's approach at any moment.

Still no sign of Johnny.

Englishman cursed and floored the accelerator just as the target's limousine disappeared around Fiftieth Street, a quarter of a mile ahead.

CARL'S THOROUGH reconnaissance of these streets before his first attempt on the president's life gave him the knowledge he now needed.

He knew the target was headed for the airport. Which meant his entourage would probably turn on Fiftieth if they passed Forty-eighth, which they had. But to be sure, Carl waited at the alley two blocks west of the turn until they actually made it. If they continued past Fiftieth, he would have to circle north and catch them . . .

The first black car in the train pulled into the intersection and signaled. They were coming down Fiftieth Street.

Carl slammed the car into drive and sped down the alley, away from Fiftieth Street. He skidded to a stop fifty yards short of where the alley met Forty-ninth, exited the still-running cab, and ran to the trunk, stripping off his black shirt and ripping it in two as he did so.

He stuffed one half of the shirt into the cracks around the license plate, effectively covering it. The second half he looped around the sign on the roof that identified the cab as #651.

Then he doubled back toward Fiftieth at a full sprint. If someone stole the car in the few minutes it would take him to execute this leg of the mission, he would have to find another. It was a chance he was willing to take.

Both of his guns found their way into his hands as he ran. Closing on Fiftieth. Fifty yards. Twenty-five. He was going to make it. The first car drove by. Close, very close.

Carl ran into Fiftieth at a full sprint as the second of the two lead cars passed the alley. He came to an abrupt stop in the middle of the street, turned toward the fast-approaching armored car hosting the target, lifted the gun in his right hand, and fired a shot directly at the driver.

What Carl knew about bulletproof windshields proved true: most could indeed stop a bullet, but few could stop three if all three struck precisely the same spot on the glass. Virtually impossible unless Carl was the one pulling the trigger.

He sent the three bullets in rapid succession, confident.

The third bullet pierced the glass and struck the driver in the throat.

Carl shifted his aim and fired three more rounds into the passenger's side, where a guard was frantically groping for his gun. Once again the third bullet ended his attempt when it entered his throat.

Carl dropped the half-spent clip and slammed a fresh one home as he ran toward the car, which had swerved to a stop. There were no more guards in the car—Carl had watched them enter in his rearview mirror. But the passengers in the entourage were enough to concern him.

They'd pulled up short, thrown open the doors. Carl stood beside the target's car, panting. He raised a gun in each hand, one aimed at the lead cars, one pointed at the rear cars. A man rose from behind the passenger door of the first rear car, and Carl shot him through his right shoulder. A second gunman stood from the closest lead car and received a bullet alongside his cheek.

This would make them hesitate long enough.

Carl turned his attention to the target's car. Side windows were typically thicker than windshields and required five perfectly placed rounds, which Carl placed low and to the right, over the door lock. He reached in through the hole he'd created, unlocked the door, pulled the driver onto the asphalt, and slid into his seat as the first bullet from the guards snapped through the air where he'd stood.

But he was now in an armored car, safe from their bullets. A thick pane of reinforced glass separated him from the man in the rear seat. Carl paid him no mind.

He jerked the stick into reverse and surged back ten yards before reversing the direction of the car and roaring forward.

No shots. They wouldn't risk shooting into a car that held the man they were sworn to protect.

Carl sideswiped both lead cars as he passed, only to slow their pursuit. The light at Third Avenue was red when he cut across oncoming traffic to a chorus of horns.

He called 911 on the cell phone and gave the operator instructions that would lead an ambulance to the badly bleeding guard in the passenger seat within minutes. He'd hoped that neither would be mortally wounded—had he done that? The guard on his right was still breathing. Why had he shot the man through the muscle on the right side of his throat rather than taken him out with a head shot?

Because he'd come to kill the man behind him, not his guards.

Carl cut back onto Forty-ninth Street before the pursuit entered the road behind him. He braked hard, popped the lock on all four doors, jumped out, and threw the rear door open, gun extended.

"Out!"

Assim Feroz had a small pistol in his right hand, but he wasn't sure whether to use it. Carl slapped it out of his fist.

"Quickly!"

He grabbed the man by his collar and jerked him through the doorway into the street. Pedestrians scrambled for cover; a woman in a lime-green dress with pink and yellow stripes began to shriek.

Carl shoved the Iranian defense minister toward the alley.

"You have no right—"

"Run!"

Feroz ran.

"Into the alley."

His yellow cab waited, nose toward them.

"In the front seat."

The man Carl had come to America to kill scrambled into the car, followed by Carl.

"One word and I put a bullet in your leg."

Five seconds later they raced away from the parked limousine. He turned right two blocks up and pulled over long enough to remove his torn shirt from the cab's sign and license plate.

The Iranian was shaking with fury when Carl reentered the car. "I demand—"

Carl slammed his door and shot Feroz in his leg at the same moment, so that the two sounded as one.

"Ahhhh!" Feroz grabbed his leg.

"I said no talking."

JOHNNY WAS in the yellow cab that had just turned west one block ahead. A piece of black cloth flapped from the sign on its roof; this was how Englishman knew.

He'd followed the Iranian motorcade onto Fiftieth Street and came upon four of them, backing up traffic just as the fifth limousine screamed around the corner.

By the time Englishman blasted his way through the corner, Carl had already traded the black car for another. It was Englishman's quick eye that caught the flapping black cloth.

But then the yellow cab disappeared around another corner. He swore and floored the gas pedal. All he needed was one moment of clear sight, and he could reach out and touch Johnny.

He wiped the sweat leaking into his eyes with his palm. Beside him, Kelly was saying something about slowing down, but his mind was dangerously removed from her. He noted this and adjusted. She wasn't Johnny, but she knew how to kill.

"I'm going to end this now," he muttered.

"He's going to kill Feroz," Kelly said. "He's going to fulfill his original order from Kalman and his oath to serve his country."

"You're forgetting that I have you," Englishman said. "If Feroz dies, then you die—the fool must know that."

Kelly ignored him. "He's going to undermine Kalman by killing the party who ordered the hit."

Englishman had figured this much out in Paradise, but hearing her say it sent a shaft of fear through his mind. He hated Kalman, but he was under the strictest order to protect the integrity of the X Group at all costs.

Englishman could choose to follow or reject the order. Although he'd fantasized many times about killing Kalman, he knew that he never would. It would be like cutting off his own arm.

"No," she suddenly blurted. "He's going to . . . He's . . ." Kelly stopped.

But she didn't need to say it. They both knew what Johnny was planning to do.

Englishman took the car to seventy miles per hour.

CARL WAS just entering the next turn when the cab began to shake violently.

Assim Feroz cried out and gripped the dashboard.

It wasn't the kind of shake he would expect from mechanical difficulties but the kind that might come from an earthquake.

At first Carl thought it was just that, an earthquake. But a quick glance in the rearview mirror showed him a yellow cab racing around traffic, bouncing up over the sidewalk and back on the street.

Englishman.

Englishman was making his car shake.

Carl gunned the car through the turn, felt the back end buck at least a foot off the ground and then settle. They were out of Englishman's line of sight.

Carl now had only one objective: to reach Bellevue Hospital in one piece and hope the cabdriver who owned this car was waiting as agreed.

He saw an opening in traffic and cut left, across the oncoming lanes, into an alley that headed east toward the hospital. He didn't know how long Englishman needed to wreak havoc with his car—more than a passing moment judging by the fact that he hadn't already stopped them. Carl didn't intend to give him even a moment. Second Avenue fast approached at the end of the alley, dead ahead. He would cut right and then—

The car began to shake again, more violently this time, bouncing as much as shaking. Feroz shouted something unintelligible about Allah. Englishman's yellow cab filled the narrow alley a hundred and fifty yards to their rear.

Panic began a ferocious assault on Carl's mind, but he cut it short. Fifty yards to the turn.

He angled for a row of tin garbage cans on their right and blasted through them at high speed. *Chunk, chunk, chunk, chunk.* The large cans bounced high and tumbled over the car, spewing refuse as they flipped through the air.

Twenty yards.

Carl glanced into the mirror. What he saw nearly made him miss the turn onto Second. The garbage cans were now flying off at right angles, smashing into the alley walls. Not only the ones he'd hit but others farther back, filling the air with paper and plastic and large stuffed bags.

Then they were on Second, squealing through a right turn, side-swiping a green sedan, narrowly missing a large bus. He was in the oncoming lanes, diving into a sea of headlights blazing in the failing light.

But Carl had stored the layout of these streets in his mind with precision. Rather than swerve back into the right lanes, he shot toward another alley on the far side of the street. Bounced over the curb. Cut into the narrow passageway, scraping the right mirror off against the far wall.

Metal screeched. Sparks flew. Assim Feroz cowered, head between his knees.

First Avenue was now in sight. And half a block south, Bellevue Hospital. They had made it.

Carl slammed his foot on the brake pedal and brought the car to an abrupt halt.

THE GARBAGE cans were flying, and Johnny's car was bouncing, and Englishman was happy.

He grunted, amused by his own power. Nothing short of amazing. And Kelly was impressed, he could sense it, see her mouth gaping with wonder in his peripheral vision. He hadn't shown her the half of it.

He impulsively sent the rest of the cans in the alley flying, like rockets shot from canisters. They slammed into the walls and streaked up, free from gravity for a moment.

It was a mistake.

He'd removed his attention from Johnny for only a moment, but that moment had allowed him to exit the alley and disappear.

Something smashed ahead. Johnny had hit a car.

Run, Johnny, run. Like a bat out of hell, because hell is coming sooner than you think. Even if you escape me, hell is coming. You will be destroyed.

In the end you will be your own undoing.

You can't escape you.

Englishman exited the alley, braking so as not to pile into whatever Johnny had hit. Traffic had stopped, allowing him plain view of what had happened even in the fading light. He could see the rubber marks that chronicled the car's trajectory. Across the street. Into an alley.

Johnny was undoubtedly still in the alley. And the path to the alley was clear.

Englishman roared across the lanes and angled into the alley. It would be over now. He wouldn't be so careless this—

They collided with a large steel garbage bin that promptly tipped over and stopped the car cold. Englishman's head smashed into the steering wheel. Beside him, Kelly crashed into the dashboard with her elbows.

It took him a moment to collect himself. The car had stalled. But neither the car stalling nor the large steel bin that had stopped the car concerned him. In the confusion Johnny's car had exited the alley without his seeing which way it had turned. This annoyed him.

Sirens wailed from several directions, racing to the string of disruptions Johnny had left in his wake.

Englishman grunted and shoved the garbage bin out of his way with a thought. He started the car, sent the steel container flying vertically, and drove under it. The bin crashed back down on the cab's roof and tumbled off the trunk behind him.

You think you've made an escape, Johnny. You're wrong.

CARL BROUGHT the cab to a screeching stop in front of a stunned cabby. Assim Feroz had taken off his jacket as instructed while Carl rolled the garbage bin to block the alley behind them. He'd known the maneuver would only waylay Englishman momentarily, but he also knew there was no other way to block his line of sight before they exited the alley.

Carl snatched the jacket from Feroz. "Straight to the parking lot behind the building. One move I don't like and I'll shoot your hand off." He shrugged into the jacket.

The Iranian defense minister was white with fear. "My leg . . ."

"Your leg isn't broken. Swallow the pain and run." Carl shoved his door open.

The cabby rounded his cab, frantically eyeing the damage. "What have you done to my car?"

Carl pressed one gun to the cabby's gut while training the other on Feroz. Not lost on the Iranian. "If you want to live, you'll drive this car south one block and leave it parked on the side of the road. Get in."

"What? What is—"

"Now! Now, now, now! Before I change my mind and kill you."

The driver piled into the car.

"Get out in one block, before the bomb blows." Carl slammed the door shut and the car jerked forward.

"Run," Carl ordered the Iranian.

The man hobbled toward a sidewalk that led to the parking lot behind the hospital. Englishman would exit the alley at any moment, and when he did they had to be out of his line of sight.

If they could manage that much, Carl would save Kelly. If he could not reach the corner in time, both he and Kelly would die.

Under no circumstances would Carl allow Kelly to die.

CHAPTER THIRTY-TWO

THEY ROARED from the alley onto First Avenue. Englishman searched frantically for the yellow car among a dozen yellow cars strung up and down the street, a half mile in each direction. And then he saw it, a full block south, pulling to the side of the road.

Only the fact that the car was stopping convinced Englishman to hold back his full fury. What was Johnny doing? Surely he realized that he was in danger. Unless he knew that by stopping he would make Englishman hesitate.

"David Abraham knows that Feroz ordered the hit on the president," Kelly said, eyes on the car as it pulled over. "That means the president also knows by now."

"I'm quite sure I told you to keep your mouth sealed," Englishman said.

"Fine, but if you refuse to consider what I have to say, you'll have to answer to Kalman."

Englishman guided the car toward the yellow cab. "What makes you think I care about Kalman? You think I don't know what Johnny's up to? You think waiting until now to give me advice isn't an obvious ploy to distract—"

Englishman stopped. A man had tumbled out of the car. Even from this distance he could see that it was neither Johnny nor Assim Feroz. Who, then?

He quickly reaffirmed the cab's identification. Black cloth tied around the number. The side was badly torn and the mirror was missing. This was Johnny's cab. Unless . . .

Englishman slammed on the brakes. Tires squealed and the car behind them tapped their rear bumper. But Englishman didn't care. His eyes and mind were on the yellow cab a hundred yards up the street. The car that Johnny had managed to ditch. The car that another man had taken for a short drive before ditching it himself.

Why?

His secure phone chirped. Horns blared. Englishman searched for any sign of Johnny or Feroz. Nothing.

The volume on his phone rose one level as he'd programmed it to do if left unanswered after three rings. He smiled. But he didn't feel happy. Waves of heat spread over his skull and down his back. Still he smiled. He had to respect the simple victory that his enemy was about to take.

Englishman took a deep breath, pulled out his phone, and answered without removing his eyes from the cab. "Yes?"

"Carl has Feroz." Kalman's voice crackled in his ear. "He will kill the fool unless you let the woman go. I have no doubt he means what he says."

"Yes."

Englishman had decided in Paradise that Johnny would return to New York to take Assim Feroz hostage in exchange for Kelly. It's what Englishman would have done, because assuming it could be done, the plan was nearly fail-safe.

"If Feroz dies, our credibility will be crippled. We can't kill the people who hire us!"

"I know."

"Then let her go."

"He'll kill Feroz anyway."

"I'll take the risk. Let her go and drive south past Houston Street. Give her your phone. Carl will contact her when he's convinced she isn't being followed. When you've done this, I want you to complete the hit on the president."

"He'll kill Feroz anyway. It's what I would do."

Englishman was tempted to tell Kalman about his trump card. Instead, he closed the phone. There was no way to flush out Johnny now, and no way to estimate where he might have run off to. North, east, west, south? On foot? In another car?

"Look at the car, Kelly."

She followed his gaze and looked at the vacant yellow cab. Cars were now squealing around him, blasting him with their pathetic horns. Some drivers even had the gall to gesture, as if that would offend him.

"If you ever find Johnny, the real Johnny, tell him about me. The real me."

The yellow cab bucked as if a bomb had been detonated beneath it. The car rose ten, twenty feet into the air, turned lazily in a complete flip, then began its descent.

The ascent was silent, because the power that had lifted the car came from him, not a bang beneath. But the landing was thunderous. The cab landed on its roof with a mighty crash.

Cars and pedestrians spread from the vicinity like ripples on a pond. They no doubt thought that aliens had just commenced an attack on New York City.

"You may go," Englishman said, handing her his phone. "Tell Johnny that his end is in himself, his real self. But I still plan on facilitating."

CARL SNAPPED the phone shut and sagged against the wall. Kelly was coming to him. Englishman was gone, at least for the time being.

They waited at the base of a deserted concrete loading ramp behind the hospital. Half an hour had passed since his call to Kalman, and darkness had settled over the grounds.

Feroz sat on the ground staring up at him. His slicked hair flopped over his sweaty, hawkish face. This was the man who had gone to such lengths to kill the president. He'd paid an insane amount of money to hire the X Group, because he trusted only the very best to handle the murder.

But Carl had been sent to kill Feroz, not the president. Yes, it was a bluff, but he no longer would accept bluffs. They'd bluffed him for ten months, and this was their last.

Carl had also once been a member of the United States Army, sworn to serve the commander in chief. So then, his obligation was clear. He had used Feroz to save the woman he loved. He must now kill the man who had hired him to kill the president. He must kill Feroz.

"You have what you want. Release me." The man's face was scowling and dark, as if he thought he was in charge.

"You hired me to kill the president," Carl said.

No answer. Good. Any other answer would have been foolish considering the circumstances.

"But they told me I was to kill you."

The man spit to one side.

"I have also taken an oath to protect the president. Since your life is a threat to his, I have an obligation to kill you."

Carl could hear the sound of running feet, presumably Kelly's. She was coming to him. He lifted his gun and placed it against his prisoner's skull. He would wait until he was sure she was safe.

"You are nothing but a hired killer," the man said. "Do you know who I am?"

"You are a dead man."

"Johnny?"

Kelly stopped at the top of the ramp, panting.

"Are you safe?" he called.

She hurried down the ramp. "I doubled back. There's no way he could have followed. Thank heaven, Johnny. I thought—"

"My name is Carl" he said and pulled the trigger.

The 9mm bucked in his hand. The target's head snapped back, struck the concrete wall behind him, and then fell to one side. The gun's report echoed in the small concrete depression. Assim Feroz stared ahead through black, vacuous eyes. Dead.

Carl lowered his gun.

Who am I?

He began to tremble, suddenly terrified. Kelly was standing halfway down the ramp, staring at him, taken aback by his execution of Assim Feroz, perhaps. He didn't care. He would do anything to save her. But now that she was safe, he was terrified to be with her. To be seen by her.

But more than this, to endanger her life. Englishman would hunt Carl before he hunted Kelly. He had no choice but to leave Kelly for her own safety, at least until he made sense of the madness of these past three days.

"Johnny?"

Why was she calling him Johnny? He'd always been Carl to her. He didn't want to be Johnny any more than he wanted to be Carl.

He forced himself to look up at her. She was safe. Safe and deserving of more than he could ever offer her.

Feeling like a fool, he ran up the ramp past her.

"What are you doing?"

He stopped at the top long enough to throw out a useless, pitiful word. "Sorry." Then he added just as pitifully, "Stay away from me. Englishman will come for me. Save yourself."

And then Carl, who was Johnny, who wanted to be neither Carl nor Johnny, ran into the night.

CHAPTER THIRTY-THREE

WHAT I'M telling you is that my son and I were right," David Abraham said. "And Johnny penetrated the X Group in full cooperation. He insisted we set him up."

"How can you be sure that it was Johnny Drake who tore up New York and killed Feroz?" Stenton demanded.

"His marks are all over it. You've heard the reports? They found no explosives on the car that blew up." David paced at the foot of the president's bed. "It's him! He's learning who he is!"

"Unless it was this other assassin, Englishman."

The name gave David pause. Englishman was a mystery. If it turned out that he rather than Johnny had flipped the cab, then they were all in a hopeless mess. He would leave it up to Samuel to sort it out.

"Perhaps. The point is, you owe your life and your presidency to Johnny. You must issue a statement that evidence implicating Feroz in your assassination attempt has surfaced, prompting a successful preemptive strike by our people."

"Johnny's not our people. He's a chaplain who—"

"A chaplain in our army!"

Stenton eyed David. "What evidence do we have that Feroz was behind this?"

"The sworn affidavits of Johnny Drake and a high-level operative from the X Group named Kelly Larine. They gave these statements to me verbally, but we can get them in writing if . . ."

"If?"

"They survive. I doubt this is over. The X Group has never failed to make good on a contract. Feroz has paid for your death—it doesn't matter that he's now dead. If you implicate the Iranian minister of defense with even a shred of evidence, two things will happen. The first is that his support for the initiative to disarm the Middle East will evaporate. A major victory. For this alone I would think you'd want the evidence needed to implicate him, particularly knowing it's true."

"And second?"

"The X Group will pull out all the stops to silence those who expose a paying client."

"Meaning they will come after me hard."

This much David had already accepted.

"And you're hoping Johnny can stop this so-called Englishman," the president said.

"He may be your best hope."

"Assuming that Johnny, not Englishman, has this supernatural power."

"Yes. Assuming that."

"I'm not sure which is harder, being caught in the wake of this Project Showdown, or believing it even exists."

"Clearly, being caught in its wake."

"Don't you ever doubt?"

This silenced him. They both knew he did on occasion. Anything unnatural was not naturally believed. Faith, in essence, was unnatural.

"On occasion," David said. "This isn't one of those occasions."

Stenton looked as though he'd aged ten years in the last two days. Perhaps he had.

"I want a sworn statement from you. I'll pass all of this by Ed Carter as soon as you leave. If the director is in agreement, we'll hold a press conference in the morning explaining how Feroz's own hired guns took him out to keep him from ever fingering them. There'll be plenty of international fallout, but I think you're right. When the dust settles, it'll go our way. If, and I do mean if, you're right about all of this, your Johnny may have just saved Israel."

"Which was undoubtedly why Samuel received the vision he did."

"Doesn't mean this Johnny is innocent. I've been given the green light to be discharged tomorrow. I think I'll move it up."

"Where will you be going?"

"To my ranch in Arizona. I think disappearing for a few days is in order considering all that's happened." He caught David's concerned surprise. "Don't worry, my ranch is armed to the teeth."

THE DIRECTOR of the Central Intelligence Agency, Ed Carter, now faced an impossible decision. He had thought betrayal would get easier with time.

It didn't.

What he and a small group of well-informed U.S. leaders were doing wasn't a true betrayal in that they weren't betraying their nation. Only their president, and only for altruistic reasons grounded in sound moral principles. The large sums of money flowing through their hands were enough to grease the wheels, but hardly motivation for assassination. So he'd told himself a thousand times.

There was good reason why virtually every nation in the world supported the Iranian initiative to disarm the Middle East. After more than a thousand years of bloody conflict, it was time to bring the region under control. The Iranian initiative had a better than average chance of doing just that.

The only person who stood in the way was Robert Stenton. One gunslinging president who had no right to subvert the will of the world or, for that matter, the will of the United States. They all knew that on balance the American people supported the Iranian initiative. If, as Stenton had repeatedly warned, Israel was ultimately destroyed by her neighbors, well then, the world would go on with one less brewing conflict.

As he saw it, disarming the region and putting a United Nations peace force in place was far less risky than allowing ideologically driven conflicts to fester.

His role was strictly to provide intelligence. Schedules, names, weaknesses in security. None of it traceable to him. With Assim Feroz now dead, Stenton would fan the shocked world into flame and kill the initiative. The agency couldn't contradict the evidence that Feroz was behind the attempt on the president's life without themselves appearing complicit.

The only way out of this mess was to continue as planned. Deal with the president. There would be a dozen Assim Ferozes willing to carry his torch in the absence of opposition.

Ed pushed his wire-rimmed glasses up on his nose and picked up the satellite phone. He called an attorney in Brussels. From there he was passed through no fewer than six filters before finally reaching Kalman within fifteen minutes. An amazing network the Russians had established, superior in every way to their own.

The phone clicked twice. "Yes?"

"The operative has fixed the customer. The other will be going home immediately. His withdrawal papers will be handled through normal New York channels."

Translation: *Johnny killed Feroz. The president will be going to his ranch in Arizona. Details of his location and the planned security measures will be left in the same subway tunnel used last time.*

"Yes, sir."

Ed Carter, trembling, set the phone down.

It was now out of his hands.

CHAPTER THIRTY-FOUR

CARL DECIDED to do the thing expected of him.

Children did what was expected of them, and he felt more like a child now than he had since last entering his pit. But that wasn't entirely true, because when he'd last entered the pit's familiar darkness, he felt warm and secure. Now he felt cold and afraid.

But he returned to Paradise anyway.

He caught a red-eye out of New York to Dallas and then an early-morning flight to Denver and on to Grand Junction. He was going back to Colorado because the blue pickup truck was there. He was going back to Paradise because the cabin was there, hidden up in the canyon where no one waited.

He struggled with the decision to find Sally again, but in the end realized that he couldn't go back to his mother because he wasn't sure that he was her son anymore. How many times had he been led down a path of "truth" only to discover that it was simply part of a grand scheme to convince him of a lie? More times than he could remember.

All he wanted was to be a son and a lover. Sally's boy and Kelly's lover. But by being Johnny he could be neither—not really, not if it meant that Sally and Kelly would be hounded by hell. If Johnny could be a normal person and an ordinary lover, then he would like to be Johnny. But Johnny wasn't ordinary and Carl hated him for it.

The problem was, Johnny hated Carl even more. For this reason alone, Carl decided that he would call himself Johnny, the lesser of two evils.

In the end he was just a lost boy who didn't belong.

In the end he was rejected by both worlds.

In the end he was numb, flying and driving and walking up the mountain in a haze, choking on the lump that had lodged itself so firmly in his throat that he was sure it would never leave.

He was regressing. He was becoming a boy. The only problem was that he didn't *know* that boy, and he didn't want to know the boy who had become Carl.

Johnny stopped on the ledge high above Paradise, trying to recall some of the fun boyhood memories that must reside somewhere in his mind. Running down Main Street chasing a girl with pigtails. Lazing behind the community center on a hot summer day, bragging about impossible feats.

Nothing came. There was only his blue truck parked behind the community center. No memories, no friends, no sign of Sally.

Johnny hated another thing about himself. He hated this sentimentality that riddled him with weakness. Carl would detest such a show of self-degradation. Carl did.

Johnny impulsively gripped his hands into fists and screamed at the valley. He closed his eyes, leaned into the cry, and shredded the still air with a blood-boiling cry until his lungs were exhausted.

Then he opened his eyes and listened.

There was no answer. No reaction at all. No one ran out into the streets of Paradise to attend to the call for help. Wind passed softly through the trees around him. Birds chirped nearby. A lizard scuttled through the underbrush on his right, undeterred by the boy's wail.

He was alone. No one cared.

He hated himself.

The tears broke through his protective shell when he stepped back on the path that led up to the canyon. If Kelly saw him now, eyes leaking, she might suggest a treatment from Agotha for his own benefit.

The suggestion sent a shiver through his arms. It was Agotha who'd hurt him, never Kelly. Kelly only protected him. She was as much a victim as he had been.

And neither of them was really a victim, because both had been made strong by the training. Carl was perhaps the best sniper who had ever walked the face of the earth! You couldn't get much better than that. As for Kelly, Agotha had saved her from a lonely and abusive childhood.

Kelly. She was another reason he was going back to the cabin, wasn't she? He knew that Kelly could find him here.

He walked into the canyon, bearing an ache in his heart that hurt worse than any needle he'd received through the shoulder. If Agotha could find a way to inflict this kind of pain on her subjects, she would strip them in less time than it took with electroshock or sensory depravation. Physical pain was a faint shadow of this pain in his mind.

Then Johnny was there, standing on the rocky sand, facing the cabin at the end of the short canyon that had once hidden Project Showdown.

He felt nothing but utter loneliness.

He wanted Kelly to come and hold him.

He wanted to die.

Johnny sat on the sand, failing to find the energy required to walk into the cabin. There was no reason to approach the cabin. No reason to leave the cabin.

He lay on his side, pulled his knees into his chest, and continued to cry.

SAMUEL HEARD the soft sobbing and ran to the cabin's window. He'd come?

His childhood friend lay on the ground twenty-five yards from the porch, rolled into a fetal position.

Samuel sat hard on the bench facing the window. Both he and Johnny had known that Johnny would pay a significant price for going under, but he'd never suspected the terrible lengths that the X Group would go to unmake his friend.

Johnny was only a shadow of the child he'd once been. And no one knew as well as Samuel that being a child was what it was all about.

Unless you become like a child . . . Unless you become like a child, you can't do much of anything good in this world.

But at what cost? What was the cost of following the path into this kingdom where power flowed beyond the comprehension of most?

Samuel stared at his friend, unable to hold back his own tears. Not only because he empathized with the pain Johnny felt as he lay in a heap, but because Samuel knew that the price had not yet been fully paid.

Johnny was desperate for the end, but he was only at the beginning.

Samuel's father had made the right call when he'd guessed that Johnny would return to the cabin. They both knew that if anyone could reach Johnny now, it would be Samuel, but even he wasn't sure Johnny could be reached by anyone.

Samuel's mind flashed back to that day in Paradise a dozen years ago when they'd first met. When heaven had collided with hell. Neither he nor Johnny had been normal since that day.

They were both outcasts. Unless Johnny embraced his alienation and stepped willingly into the role, he would fade into powerless obscurity—so it was with all of the faithful.

It took Samuel ten minutes to compose himself and wipe the evidence of tears from his face. Then he took a deep breath, stepped up to the door, and went out to meet Johnny.

THERE WERE only two places Kelly thought Johnny might go.

The pit in Hungary.

The cabin in Colorado.

The pit would be the more difficult destination. So she went to Colorado.

If there was a way to flog herself and thereby accept punishment for what she'd done to him, she would gladly accept each blow. If she could find a way to repay him, no matter how ludicrous or how great the cost, she would do so. Betrayal was a terrible, terrible thing.

She had betrayed Johnny by making him someone he wasn't. By stripping his identity and forcing another one upon him. By pretending to love him only to win his allegiance.

She'd never expected to fall for him. It cost her dearly, but not a fraction of what she was willing to pay to win his trust one more time, this time as the Kelly who truly loved him.

She wept openly on the plane, leaning against the window to hide her face from the other passengers but not caring if they stared, which they did. It was another lesson she was learning: when this much sorrow ravaged the heart, the mind shut down any respect for etiquette.

Assim Feroz was dead. That was good.

The president was alive. That was good.

Englishman was not only alive, but brimming with a power that Kelly had only dreamed about. This was bad.

But Kelly didn't care, because there was another power at work within them all, and this power was intent on destroying the only man she'd ever loved, with or without Englishman's help.

Back in the Egyptian desert, she'd been abandoned and abused before escaping. She remembered how it had felt to be rejected and alone, without a mother, a father, or a true sense of belonging. Humans went to great lengths to belong. To fit in. Agotha had taught her this, and together they'd leveraged the tendency against Carl, luring him to belong to them. To her.

They'd done the job well. Too well.

If they survived this ordeal, Kelly would take him to the desert, where they could heal together. To Nevada, where no one knew them. To the place she had always intended to take him.

If they survived. And if they died, she wanted to die in his arms no matter how melodramatic that sounded. They were all a page ripped from the story of life anyway. All humans were, whether they realized it or not.

Dear Johnny . . . Dear Johnny, what have I done to you?

THE FACT that Johnny had outwitted him turned all of Englishman's happiness into bitter anger. It didn't matter that he was the Terminator or that in the end the Terminator always won. This setback was humiliating.

There was still hope. More than hope, certainty. Even when Johnny won, he was really losing. But this didn't make Englishman feel any better. He would first kill the president, not because he had been ordered to do so, but because by killing Robert Stenton he would undo what Johnny had done in saving the man's life.

Then he would find Johnny, and he would reduce him to a desperate, blubbering fool.

And then, when Johnny was only a shell of himself, he would choose to kill him. That wasn't the original plan, but the original plan was now obsolete.

This new plan made Englishman happy. Not as happy as he'd once been, plotting and planning all these months, but still happy. He still had the trump card, and this, too, made him happy. But Johnny was turning out to be a more worthy adversary than he'd originally calculated.

He'd retrieved the information on Stenton's ranch and would soon board an airplane bound first for Denver and then Grand Junction, where he would collect all he needed from the safe house. He would then head for Arizona, where he would be free to level whatever paltry security they threw his way and take the man's life at his leisure. The Terminator would undoubtedly kill the whole family—father, mother, and son. So would Rambo if pressed.

So would Englishman.

He didn't need the information Kalman had provided, only the destination. But he had it nonetheless. Better not to be overconfident, considering a single stray bullet could end his life as easily as the president's.

Englishman began to whistle in the backseat of the cab that was taking him to the airport. But his whistle sounded hollow. In all honesty, none of these mental gymnastics were bringing him happiness. His identification with the Terminator and Rambo wasn't helping. He couldn't remember such a profound lack of happiness.

He stopped whistling.

When he met Johnny again, he would make sure that Johnny never whistled again. Ever.

CHAPTER THIRTY-FIVE

"HELLO, JOHNNY."

Johnny opened his eyes.

"I remember the first time we met here," Samuel said.

Johnny pushed himself up on his elbow. The blond boy stood ten feet away, smiling at him. He was here? Johnny blinked. The image was still there. Samuel was here. He climbed to his feet, embarrassed to have been caught in such a vulnerable state.

"You remember?" Samuel repeated.

"No."

"You will. Give it time. My father tells me that you remember your mother."

"Some."

"Then the rest will come too."

Johnny felt dazed. Trapped in a hopeless depression. "I'm not sure I care anymore."

Samuel clasped his hands behind his back and paced. He stood under five feet, a short boy. His eyes were blue, like his father's, and his skin fair. He wore tan shorts that ended just above knobby knees. His beige socks were scrunched down around the lips of brown leather hiking boots. It was amazing to think that he was the same age as Johnny. But was that really true?

Even though Johnny no longer cared to remember his childhood, he couldn't deny the strong sense that he'd known Samuel before New York.

"My father told you about Project Showdown," Samuel said.

Was that a question? "Yes."

"And about our meeting to discuss the vision I had. Your insistence to enter the X Group."

"Yes."

"That the X Group robbed you of your faith, like the world does in a much slower way with the rest of the faithful. That you became Carl, the one who lost his faith. So now you must become Johnny again."

Had David Abraham said that?

"Do you know what I did in New York?" Johnny asked.

"You saved the president and then killed his enemy."

So they'd found the body. Not that it mattered.

"Do you know if Kelly's safe?" he asked.

"I don't know."

Johnny nodded and turned to face the cliff. Samuel was undoubtedly here to talk more nonsense about Project Showdown, but Johnny only wanted to be alone. Or with Kelly. For all he knew she was dead. The terrible sadness he'd felt earlier returned.

"You haven't finished the task, Johnny. You know that, don't you?"

He looked at the boy. At the man who looked like a boy. Samuel drilled him with soft, kind eyes. Did he like Samuel? Johnny did. Maybe even Carl did. But the person trapped between Johnny and Carl felt too lost to care about a man who looked like a boy and claimed to be his best friend.

"You haven't become what you're meant to become," Samuel said.

Johnny wasn't sure he'd heard right. "What I've done isn't enough for you?" He knew he was giving in to self-pity, but he felt justified.

He couldn't imagine a man, woman, or child who'd been put through as much as he had been put through in these last few months.

"Enough? No. I know that sounds harsh, but you're not the only one to walk this path."

What on earth did the boy think he was saying?

"Unless you become who you were meant to be, untold harm will come to an untold number of people. You are chosen, Johnny. I would be more gentle if we weren't so short on time, but you may be the only one who can stop the X Group from killing the president."

"Me? You have the wrong person. I don't stand a chance against Englishman!"

Samuel blinked and stilled. "You've foiled him twice now. What do you mean?"

"Twice? You mean here and in New York. I was lucky that Kelly came back here, and I just managed to stay out of his line of sight as I fled him in New York. I wouldn't characterize either as foiling him. The next time he'll kill me."

Samuel stopped pacing and dropped his arms. "You . . . You're saying that Englishman has power?"

"You don't know?"

"My father assumed the reports were about you."

"Your father was wrong. I don't know who Englishman is, but he can maneuver physical objects with his mind. Knives and guns. Cars. I have no doubt he could walk up to this cabin and level it with a hard look. Me, on the other hand, I can change the temperature. Maybe the gift will come in handy when I find myself standing among the flames of hell."

Samuel's face had lightened a shade. Two shades. For a long moment he stood stock-still, staring at Johnny without so much as breathing, it seemed.

"You're sure . . ."

"Do you think I would have fled his initial assault if I thought there was any way to take him? The only way to keep Kelly alive was to force Englishman into using her as a hostage."

"That means . . ." Samuel had come upon a revelation of great weight. "Then he must be either a fictitious character or someone else who was given power by the books."

"Fictitious character? He's real, I can swear that much."

"Real, yes, yes, of course. But written from the books, not born of this earth."

"A demon?"

"Or a human given power by the books like you were."

"I don't have power! Why is it so difficult for you and your father to understand that? It isn't there!"

"I think it is. But I also think you're so lost that you no longer can truly imagine it. Belief begins with the imagination, you know. The day a faith loses imagination is the day it dies."

"I have no idea what you're talking about."

"Of course you do. You never read *Spider-Man*? Accepting your true identity means understanding that you are a stranger to this world. A freak, ostracized by the very people you want to help."

The words struck a chord. At least the bit about being a freak. But the idea of his being someone who had a unique power to dispatch evil seemed absurd. Even if it wasn't a fantasy, he honestly didn't know who he was or had been or wanted to be. He was trapped.

"I see it every day," Samuel said.

"Sure," he said. "There are thousands of superheroes running around this planet, struggling to find their magic."

"Not like you, no. Unless I'm mistaken, there are only two others, not counting Englishman. But the path you're on is essentially identical to the path all men, women, and children of faith finds themselves on. To be or not to be, that is the question, as they say."

Johnny honestly didn't know what the boy was saying. Samuel elaborated.

"Once born into childlike faith, brimming with belief, typical people begin to lose their faith. Society mocks them. Their friends smirk. They come to change the world, but over time the world changes them. Soon they forget who they were; they forget the faith they once had. Then one day someone tells them the truth, but they don't want to go back, because they're comfortable in their new skin. Being a stranger in this world is never easy. Look at me, I should know. Don't feel sorry for yourself, Johnny."

"Have you been in my pit? No? Have you been strapped to my hospital bed? No? Then you have no right to tell me anything, including how to feel."

"Actually, I do. I've been through worse. But I admit I'm being a bit direct. We are running out of time. And if you're right about Englishman, we may already be out of time."

"I don't want to be—"

"Stop it!" Samuel yelled at him. "Stop it!" His face was red, and a single vein throbbed on his temple. "This isn't about you anymore!"

Johnny was dumbstruck. His heart pounded and his face felt hot, but more than either of these, his heart felt sick.

Samuel just stared, his face slowly losing its bright red hue.

The sickness in Johnny's heart slowly rose to his throat. He was no longer sure whether the emotions that swallowed him were self-pity or profound anguish at his own pathetic excuses for not stepping into the role he was destined to take.

A tear leaked from his right eye.

"I'm sorry, Johnny. I'm truly sorry for what you've been through."

Johnny closed his eyes and fought the waves of remorse that crashed through his heart. He lifted a hand and rested it against his forehead, as if to hold back the pain in his head or to hide from it. He accomplished neither.

A cool hand touched his hand by his side. Samuel was standing next to him now, looking up at him with tears rimming his eyes. In that moment Samuel who was a man was only a boy. Johnny remembered this. He remembered Samuel this way.

"Will you trust me?" Samuel asked.

"Yes," Johnny said without thinking. Then he asked a very stupid question. "Will it save Kelly?"

Samuel smiled. "You see, you're still a child. Yes, I think it will. And it just might save you."

Johnny nodded.

"You should know that if you walk where I'm going to ask you to walk, there will be a price."

"I'll be strange. Ostracized by society. Rejected."

"Yes, that too. But more. I don't know specifics, but it'll affect you physically. Like me. I stopped growing."

Johnny considered the implications. "You're saying that I'll never be normal. That I'll be rejected by normal people. That I was chosen to be an outcast. And that if I manage to embrace this childlike faith of yours, I'll wear my abnormality in some debilitating way?"

"Yes. But you'll have the power to change the world."

"A freak with a magic stick."

"No magic. But a freak, probably. At least in the minds of most. In fact, the being-a-freak part will probably precede the power part."

"Will I be able to defeat Englishman?"

"Maybe. Maybe you've been chosen to die to rid the world of him. The rules are different in the supernatural reality."

Johnny nodded. "All of this assuming I can become like a child and believe like I once supposedly did."

"Yes. Will you?"

"I'll try."

Samuel let go of his hand and stepped back. "Okay. That's good. That's real good."

Johnny felt stupid, but he didn't know what he could do other than offer Samuel a stupid grin.

"Wow, that was easy," Samuel said, smiling.

"Not as easy as you think. Now what?"

"Now what?"

"What do I do?"

"You believe," Samuel said.

"Believe what?"

"Believe what you believed as a child. All of it."

"What if I don't?" Johnny asked.

"Well, do you?"

"What?"

"Believe. Do you believe?"

"It depends on what I'm believing."

They stared at each other, caught in their circular questions.

"I think I believe," Johnny said. "How will I know?"

Samuel stepped back. "Try it. Do what you do in your pit."

Johnny nodded and closed his eyes, focusing his mind to form a tunnel. The long, dark space formed easily enough, but he didn't know what to form as the objective.

He looked at Samuel. "What am I trying to do?"

"I think your gift involves affecting the physical world. Like the temperature. Or bullets. Stones. Anything physical. Probably not the free will of people, though. I'm guessing inanimate objects."

"Samson," Johnny said.

Samuel grinned. "Samson. But I like Saint better."

This time Johnny turned to his right and rested his eyes on a stone on the sand ten yards away.

He was able to enter the tunnel again.

He was able to step outside the tunnel and see the rock on the sand.

He was able to imagine the rock lifting off the ground and flying toward him, and he was quite sure that it was doing just that.

For a long time he watched the stone fly to him and around him.

His pulse surged. Maybe everything Samuel had said was true after all. Maybe he really did have a supernatural gift as written in the book twelve years ago. Maybe he could do what Englishman did.

Johnny opened his eyes.

The stone lay on the ground, ten yards away, unmoved.

He stared at it, stunned. "It . . . It didn't move."

No response from Samuel.

"I saw it move in my mind." He spun to the boy. "I gave it everything! You're wrong. I can't—"

"You're not believing," Samuel said. "You're focusing but not believing. This isn't some random force that you can tap into because Yoda says so." Samuel gripped his hand into a fist. "Believe, Johnny. Believe!"

Unless you become like a child . . .

The midday sun blazed high above them. A hawk screeched as it flew in a lazy circle above the cliffs. Here on the bare ground stood two boys trying to enter a kingdom in a different realm, beyond the rocks and cliffs and sand, beyond the hawk that called to them.

"Say it, Johnny."

"Say what?"

"Say you believe. Out loud. Shout it."

"I believe?"

"Don't mumble it like a question! Shout it out so that the whole world can hear it. You did it once; do it again."

Johnny imagined himself standing in a busy city square, Times Square, shouting out his belief for all the wayward to hear. It was a terrifying thought. Why? Because he didn't believe? Or because he was ashamed to believe?

Because he didn't want to be a freak. He wanted to be normal, accepted. His desire to be accepted was stronger than his belief.

Samuel walked toward him, drilling him with a stare. "Say it. There's no one here to hear you except me."

"I believe," Johnny said.

"Louder. Shout it."

He hesitated.

"What's the matter, Johnny? You're enslaved by the same pathetic weakness that holds the agnostic in chains? Hmm? It's not that you don't have the capacity to accept the truth. You don't *want* to accept it, and you hide behind your own logic and intelligence while the truth marches by. Step out and join it, for goodness' sake! Shout it out in full step! *I believe!*"

Samuel shouted the last two words, startling Johnny.

He impulsively matched the cry. "I believe!"

A mischievous smirk tugged at Samuel's mouth. "I believe!" he cried.

"I believe!" Johnny cried.

"I believe!" Samuel screamed, at the top of his lungs now.

"I believe!" Johnny screamed.

Samuel thrust his hand toward the stone. "Now move it."

Johnny faced the stone and brought the full weight of his belief to bear on the small fist-sized piece of rock, confident that it would rise and fly. He focused, he willed, he clenched his teeth. When nothing happened, he closed his eyes and entered the dark place, focusing until the rock was zipping around in his mind's eye.

When he looked again, the stone lay still.

For several long seconds Johnny stood in stunned silence. Then he closed his mouth, walked to a large boulder on his right, and sat down on top of it.

His utter foolishness swallowed him.

"We'll try again in ten minutes," Samuel said. "Time is running out."

"Then time *has* run out," Johnny said. "I'm not who you think I am."

"We'll try again in ten minutes," Samuel said.

CHAPTER THIRTY-SIX

ROBERT STENTON sat on the porch's bench swing, gazing out at the twin rows of tall pines that bordered the long paved driveway leading up to the ranch house. He'd built the place when he was the governor of Arizona. Here, the stress of the presidency was a distant reality. At least for a few hours.

Here, he was just Robert. Bob. Wealthy and savvy many would say, but just Bob, the rancher, a political outsider who'd upended Arizona's electoral traditions and taken the governorship by storm. The fact that he'd done the same in Washington never ceased to make him shake his head just to be sure it was all real.

It was. As real as the high-desert wind blowing hot through the trees that were scattered around the ranch.

A pile of huge boulders sat to the right of the house. At Jamie's suggestion, they'd hauled in the rocks to form a cave that reached nearly a hundred feet into the pile, then reinforced the boulders with a steel mesh to prevent them from slipping.

This was Jamie's Bat Cave. It said so on the wood sign at the entrance.

A tall electric fence that Robert had agreed to put up at the insistence of the Secret Service stood back three hundred yards and circled the house, the riding stables, and all of the outbuildings. Three hundred yards beyond this was another fence loaded with the most advanced surveillance technology available. Nothing within a thousand yards of the ranch house went unidentified.

Their lines of defense ended in a natural boundary three miles away. A long mound of massive boulders cut across the valley, offering both position and cover for more than a hundred men. Beyond the boulders, a ten-foot concrete wall nearly two thousand yards long connected the cliffs on either side.

The gentle hills behind the ranch house hid the fact that the property was technically in a box canyon. Six observation posts covered every square inch of the ranch from their positions on top of the hills. The Stenton ranch was as well protected as any piece of real estate in the United States.

David Abraham had come with them, but as was his normal practice when invited, he stayed out of the way, letting them "be a family," as he put it.

The screen door behind Robert slammed. Jamie walked out in bare feet, trailed by Wendy, who held two tall glasses of iced tea.

"Drink, Commander?"

"Commander?" Robert reached for the condensation-beaded glass.

"Jamie was just informing me of the difference between a good commander in chief and a bad one. We both agreed that you're a good one."

Jamie lowered himself gingerly to his seat on the swing beside Robert. He wasn't as strong as he'd been even last week, and his skin seemed paler, but it was hard to tell with his ghost-white complexion.

"With potential to become the best," Jamie said.

Robert smiled and smoothed his son's hair. Pulled him close. "I'll try not to disappoint."

Wendy sat down on his right. This was the Stenton family, three abreast, sitting on their front porch grappling with the latest of many challenges they'd faced over the years.

Although the struggles facing them now promised to be more intense than most. A sniper had just put a bullet through Robert's chest. Jamie was dying. Wendy was about to lose a son and feared for her husband's life.

"How's your chest?" Wendy asked.

Robert touched the bandage under his shirt. "Not bad considering a bullet passed through it three days ago. The painkillers help."

"You're sure this is the best place for us?" she asked. Her eyes always smiled, even when she was sad or afraid. An amazing thing, her eyes. At times Robert was sure he'd married Wendy for the mystery behind her eyes alone. They were certainly what prompted his interest in the beginning. No woman could have such a radiant face and not be as kind as she looked. So far she'd proven him right.

"No one knows we're here—that's a start," he said. "Sam's holding a press conference." He glanced at his watch. "Correction: just held a press conference, during which he made it clear without actually saying it that we are in the White House."

"Wouldn't take a rocket scientist to track us down."

"Blake told me that we have over a hundred National Guardsmen directed by a unit from the Special Forces," Jamie said. "And that's on top of the Secret Service. Do you know they have aerial reconnaissance on us at this very moment? Two unmanned Predator drones. Nobody gets within a hundred miles of here without us knowing."

Robert winked at his wife. "Yeah, Wendy. Quit your worrying. We're armed to the gills."

JOHNNY DID try again, half a dozen times, to no avail. One time the rock moved, possibly—Johnny couldn't be sure. Otherwise he experienced nothing except growing frustration and unbelief. If not for the image of Englishman, doing his tricks, gunning for them all, Johnny would have given up after the first attempt.

The afternoon wore on. Samuel didn't press too hard after the first failure, just enough to persuade Johnny to try again. And again, six times.

They talked about the past—about good times, about bad times. Slowly, like a cold honey pouring out, the memories began to come back. Unless they were simply new memories being informed by the details that Samuel fed him. *No, it was more,* Johnny thought. The more they talked, the more he recalled specific unrelated events.

"You do realize that when you find your power, more will be required from you," Samuel said after a particularly long pause. He was unrelenting. "I don't want you to walk into this blindly. You won't be able to come head-to-head with someone like Englishman and expect to defeat him with a bigger rock."

Johnny dismissed the notion with a quick word. "Sure."

Even though the superhero-making had been decidedly derailed, Johnny took some comfort in his friend, whom he evidently once loved like a brother. It was still amazing that such a wise, mature person could be embodied in such a young body.

Several times he took Samuel's hand and felt his young skin, awed by the appearance. If the power Samuel spoke of had done this, perhaps he could believe. Encouraged, he would agree to try his hand at stone-moving again.

Not even a budge.

With the setting of the sun, Johnny felt his own mood sink. Then fall. Then crash to pieces on the ground.

He was lost. He wasn't Carl, and he was proving that he wasn't Johnny either, not any longer. He couldn't be what he was meant to be because he'd become someone else over time. Recapturing his true childlike faith was impossible because a different life had beat it out of him.

Johnny excused himself from the cabin when it was night. He walked into the darkness, comforted by it. But then he remembered that he would never go back to the pit. The pit had been a lie.

Still, he liked the darkness.

Johnny lay down on the large boulder at the small canyon's entrance, stared at the stars, and let himself feel completely hopeless.

BY THE time Englishman reached Denver, his blood was very nearly boiling. And he still had another flight. The fact that a few thunderstorms had caused such delays could only be explained by the spineless nature of people who thought they were wiser than they were for shutting down the system to avoid a few bumps in the air.

He hated airports.

He hated the people who worked in airports.

He hated most of all gate agents who clicked away incessantly on hidden keyboards, rarely raising their eyes, summoning people, informing whomever they wished of whatever they wished, all of it bad. Gate agents were powerless power mongers.

Englishman sat in a hard plastic seat staring at the dark-haired, dark-skinned, dark-hearted, dark stain of a gate agent whose head jerked ever so slightly with her every keystroke. She'd told him twice already to have a seat and wait for his name to be called.

He had no intention of waiting in his seat for his name to be called. The plane was at the gate and they were boarding the first-class passengers and she was still ignoring him. This devil in the blue dress fastened by eight brass buttons that ran from her skinny brown neck to her knees was thinking of him even now, consumed by thoughts that immobilized her—all very flattering on any other day, but today he hated this devil.

He knew a thing or two about devils.

He also knew as an absolute matter of fact that unless the story was about a man stuck in an airport terminal or an airplane—such as *The Terminal* or *Airport*—movie stars never sat for two hours waiting for a devil in disguise to let them on the plane. In reality, most movies skipped the airport scene altogether, because everyone knew that it was no more interesting or eventful than pulling on your socks or underwear after rising each morning. For the most part these details were inconsequential.

And yet this woman trying so sincerely to hide her passion for Englishman by avoiding his stare was making his boarding of the plane consequential.

Englishman stood and approached the podium, further angered by her refusal to confess her interest in him with even a casual glance.

He put both palms on the podium. "Pardon me, mademoiselle, but I'm growing tired of this silly act of yours."

She looked up at him, feigning surprise. It took a serious amount of self-control on Englishman's part not to strike her on the cheek. He couldn't use his power to make her slap herself or gouge her eyes out or begin screaming like a bloody lunatic, but he could do a few other things that would ruin her day.

"I want to board the aircraft now. Please give me whatever documentation I need to do so at this time."

"Excuse me?" She was growing red. This pleased Englishman.

"Are my words too big for you? Let me restate. Please. Seat. Me. Now."

For a moment she seemed too stunned to speak. Unfortunately for her, she overcame her shyness.

"If you don't have a seat immediately, I'll have to call security. Please sit and wait like everyone else. The flight is overbooked. Next time I suggest you avoid flying standby."

She had no intention of putting him on, Englishman realized. He wasn't going to his destination on this plane. And if he wasn't, no one was.

"I must tell you something, mademoiselle. You are an ugly and pathetic woman. And you're upsetting me."

For an unbearable moment, Englishman forced himself into submission, ignoring the impulse to punch her in the face. Instead, he wreaked havoc with her keyboard, popping the keys out like popping corn so that they sprang loose and flew up to hit her on her chest and chin. He simultaneously fried the monitor so that smoke rose in a thin coil.

The agent jumped back and let out a startled cry.

Not trusting himself to stop there with her, he turned his back on the devil in the blue dress and walked to the window. The jet was parked just outside, taking on the last few bags from handlers who plopped them on a long conveyor belt that fed into the fuselage's belly.

Englishman made all the suitcases he could see fly from the belt with enough force to send them tumbling and skidding on the tarmac for a hundred feet.

He popped the tires on the plane as well. Then he sent one particularly heavy-looking bag flying into the engine with such force that he was sure it did some serious damage. The ground crew scrambled for cover like rats.

Satisfied, Englishman walked toward the sign that pointed to the rental cars. It was a good night for a drive anyway.

CHAPTER THIRTY-SEVEN

JOHNNY SLEPT on the sand outside the cabin, uncaring, unwanting, unmade. He dreamed of nothing. Just the black tunnel without a light at the end. Somewhere in the fog of nothingness, he realized that he had finally and firmly been reduced to nothing more than a blind mole. His light had been extinguished.

He slept in blackness. It was his only reprieve.

A voice called to him from the dark. "Johnny?"

I'm not Johnny.

"Johnny." Something was shaking him. "Johnny."

Kelly was calling him. His pulse spiked. He wanted to be held by Kelly. He wanted to be comforted and loved and made alive by her love.

Do you love me, Kelly?

Yes, Johnny.

Do you mean that? Do you really, really love me?

Yes, I do mean that. I love you, Johnny.

Then will you hold my head in your lap and brush my hair from my forehead and smile down at me? Will you breathe your undying love into my mouth and swear to love no other man the way you love me?

Yes.

Kelly was crying.

Do you love me, Johnny?

Yes! I love you more than life!

Are you sure?

It's the only thing I'm sure of.

Will you kiss my cheek and my neck and hold me tenderly? Will you kiss my lips and breathe on my neck and tell me that I belong to you?

Yes.

Johnny opened his eyes. Someone was lying beside him on the canyon floor under the stars, crying softly.

Kelly was here?

He sat up, startled. "Kelly?"

She lay on her back, and her right hand covered her eyes. She was torn by sorrow or relief or another emotion so gripping that she felt unable to respond to him.

"How . . . How did you find me? Are you okay?"

No response.

"You shouldn't have come."

She still didn't answer. There was nothing else to say, so he laid his head beside her shoulder. He was glad she'd come, but his guilt at having endangered her life and reduced her to this wasted soul on the sand was too much.

Was this a dream?

No. He could feel her hand touch his head now. Stroke his hair.

She shifted to her side and whispered, "I love you, Johnny."

"Do you really, really love me?"

"I really, really love you."

"Then will you hold my head in your lap and brush my hair from my forehead and smile down at me? Will you kiss my lips and breathe on my neck and tell me that I belong to you?"

Johnny said it all before he realized that he was actually saying it out loud.

"As long as I live," she said.

They lay in silence a long time without speaking. What was there to say? Kelly was safe. As far as Johnny was concerned, she was all he had, and she was no small thing. He didn't know himself, but he knew Kelly and that was enough for now.

"How did you find me?" he finally asked.

Where else would he go? She knew him, she said. She told him about her cross-country flight. She'd rented a car in Denver after missing a flight because of thunderstorms.

"Englishman is out there," she said.

"He's going to kill the president," Johnny said. "No one can stop him."

"You don't have his power?"

Her bringing the subject up bothered him. He pushed himself to his seat and stared back at the cabin. To his surprise, Samuel was seated on a chair beside the front door, watching them.

"Englishman told me to tell you that your end is in yourself. That you'll hate yourself."

"And if you ever see him again, you can tell him that I already do."

"I think I know what he meant," Kelly said. "You don't feel loved. Your mind is too preoccupied with your own worthlessness to accept love."

"I know that you love me. How can you say that I can't accept love?"

"Why do you need to ask me, then?"

"To know, to really know."

"Exactly. Because you're unsure."

"I wanted to hear you say it."

"Why? To reassure yourself, which is the same as asking to know. You can't believe that I love you because you're absolutely certain that you're unlovable."

Johnny blinked in the moon's dim light. She did indeed know him better than he knew himself.

"Maybe you're right. But I don't see what that has to do with my not having Englishman's power."

"That's not what I care about," Kelly said. "Englishman can go rot in hell as far as I'm concerned. But I want the man I love to know how much I love him. I know now that unless you can believe you're loved, you'll ruin yourself, just as Englishman said."

"You don't want Englishman's power," Samuel said. He stood less than ten feet away. "Trust me, you want nothing that Englishman has. But I think Kelly's right, and I think love might be the key that unlocks your power, Johnny."

Kelly sat up and stared at the boy with Johnny. Samuel could take the slightest suggestion and turn it into a ray of hope; it was his nature to do so. *But this is a last desperate attempt,* Johnny thought. What did love have to do with power?

And then he thought about Samuel's own story.

"What do you mean?"

"I don't think you know how to love," Samuel said. "I don't mean to hurt you, but I've been racking my brain trying to think of the problem, trying to understand why you can't seem to believe the way you once did, and I think Kelly's right—it's love. Your inability to accept love, yes, but as a result, your inability to love."

Was that true?

"Not that I blame you, Johnny, but I don't think you really care about anyone other than yourself. You've had to focus almost exclusively on yourself in order to survive. As a result, you don't care about having the power to fight evil unless it threatens something you care deeply for, which no longer includes you because you don't even love yourself anymore. Make sense?"

"No. Yes."

Samuel rounded them, bright-eyed despite the darkness. "That has to be it. You can't believe because you are too preoccupied with yourself, which is the opposite of love. You have to learn to love so you can believe. You have to become selfless to fill the shoes you are meant to fill."

"Now I can add the inability to love to my list of failures?" Johnny said. "Splendid."

"You have to learn tonight," Samuel added.

"I think you're being just a bit unfair, don't you?" Kelly asked.

"Unfair? No. Direct, yes. We don't have time to be less direct."

"Your being direct will only push him away. Is this the way your father taught you how to love?"

No! She doesn't know what she is saying, Johnny thought. She couldn't understand how cutting and terrible her words were. Samuel watched her like a wise man looking on with patience.

Maybe Samuel was right. What did Johnny really know of love? What could a man learn about love while strapped to a hospital bed as those who claimed to love him shot electricity through his bones?

Love. He didn't remember everything about Project Showdown, but he was now remembering enough and had certainly been told enough to know that in the end it was all about love. About the discovery of love, no matter how terrifying the path might be.

"Love," Johnny said. He pushed himself to his feet, inspired by the notion that Samuel had hit upon something.

"Love," Samuel repeated. "Do you believe?"

"That would mean I don't really love Kelly at all. I need her comfort and I need someone to comfort so that I feel useful, but that's not true love. I don't love her at all."

Samuel's eyes flitted to Kelly.

"No, I do love her," Johnny said. "I do love you. And even if I don't, I want to more than anything, because you're the world to me. But what if Samuel's right and I'm really loving you for my own sake? That's not real love, right?"

"Do any of us really love?" she demanded. "This kind of talk can only conclude that there *is* no love in the world!"

"But there is love in this world," Samuel said. "I see it every day. Johnny's just had it beaten out of him."

"By me," Kelly said.

"No!" Johnny cried. "You were only doing what you thought was best for me. What else is a girl who's been sold into slavery as a child supposed to think?" He waved his hand angrily through the air. "Forget it. I love you. And if I don't, then I choose to love you now, from this moment forward."

"Love," Samuel said. "It's always about love."

"Love," Johnny repeated. There was something very familiar about this exchange. "Will you love me?" he asked Kelly, not wanting her to feel isolated.

"I do love you," she said.

"Samuel's right—this may be our only way of surviving Englishman. Englishman said I'd hate myself, so maybe I should learn to love myself."

"But then aren't you loving for your own sake again? So that you can survive Englishman?"

"No," Johnny said after a long pause. "I choose to love for your sake. To save you from Englishman."

"Tonight," Samuel said.

"Is love something you can just turn on with a switch?" Johnny asked.

"Yes, I think so. It can be. It has to be. Is knowledge a switch? Knowledge can turn the world on with a single throw of the switch." Samuel put his hands behind his back and circled to their right. "Do you have the power?"

Johnny stared off into the night, focusing on a pile of stones fifty feet away. Not one of them stirred. After a minute he gave up.

"Evidently not."

"Then forget about the power," Samuel said, turning back to the cabin. "Focus instead on love. True love. Selfless love in your heart."

"How?"

"Love Kelly, of course."

CHAPTER THIRTY-EIGHT

THE NIGHT was failing in the high desert, giving way to a pale early-morning sky in the east. He'd driven from Denver to the safe house in Grand Junction, collected all he needed, and then broke every possible speed limit on his way to Arizona.

Twice the highway patrol had tried to pull him over. Twice he popped their tires and melted their radios. He was such a major stud.

It was cool outside, but the black asphalt still held some heat after baking in the sun for twelve hours the previous day. Englishman drove with the Honda Accord's windows down, left arm stuck out so that he could feel both the heat from below and the cool from above. Opposites.

Life was about opposites. Hot and cold, mostly hot. Hate and love, mostly hate. Fiction and flesh, mostly fiction.

That was him, anyway. Made by the monk, Marsuvees Black— quite literally made. Englishman had been given one objective in life: He was to watch Johnny Drake. If this person named Johnny ever began to manifest any unusual powers, Englishman was to destroy Johnny.

There were more like Englishman, created to wreak havoc at the appropriate time. Barsidious White, who'd played games with unsuspecting travelers in abandoned houses, for example. A killer with interesting dimensions, to say the least. Black had failed in Paradise; White had failed in Alabama. Englishman would not fail. And neither, for that matter, would the others. Learning, always learning and growing smarter.

Englishman had wandered aimlessly for years, prowling like a lion, until the day when Johnny had indeed manifested an unusual power. Just as predicted.

Englishman killed Dale Crompton and made himself exactly like the man. He liked Dale Crompton's body very much. Not only had it been conveniently located in the same camp with Johnny, but Crompton's body was quite a magnificent specimen of lean and finely sculpted flesh. He would keep it if everything worked out.

Whenever a car pulled up behind him, Englishman slowed, then cut into the left lane when they attempted to pass. After several attempts he let them pass, blasting their horns. He did this because it gave him power over them without so much as moving a finger or throwing a thought. He wrought misery by merely sharing the same space with these motorists.

He turned onto a gravel road and headed north, farther north. If they were worth half the salt paid for them, the security forces who had dug in to save the president had already spotted his car pulling off the highway. It was the only road that led to the ranch forty miles ahead.

Forty miles till showdown.

Englishman was happy.

CHAPTER THIRTY-NINE

SAMUEL AWOKE to the sound of screaming.

He jerked up and listened. Silence. The door to the bedroom flew open and Kelly stumbled out. "What was that?"

Then it came again, a fuller sound now.

"Johnny!"

Samuel rolled from the mat and dropped out of the loft, bothering to touch only one rung as he did. Johnny must have awakened early and gone out by himself. Samuel yanked the door open and was through before thinking to let Kelly out first. Never mind, she was on his heels.

Dawn had broken. The small canyon was empty, no sign of Johnny.

His scream came again, echoing through the outer canyon, a furious howl that screeched with such intensity that Samuel felt momentarily frozen by fear for Johnny's life.

He ran barefoot over the sand, ignoring the rocks that dug into the soles of his feet.

Kelly kept up. "Samuel? What's—"

"I don't know."

Again the piercing scream. He still couldn't make it out.

He tore around the huge boulder on the west side of the canyon's mouth and pulled up sharply. Kelly clipped his shoulder and slid to a stop.

There, not thirty meters away, knelt Johnny, tearstained face raised to the sky, eyes clenched, arms spread wide, hands squeezed into fists, screaming.

Samuel gasped. The canyon was a hundred yards wide here, like a dry riverbed littered with hundreds of rocks that ran its length to the edge of the mountain.

But the boulders were not on the sand.

They were floating twenty meters above Johnny's head.

A thousand boulders, at least, all at the exact same height, moving very slowly toward the canyon mouth, as if defying gravity were a regular morning exercise.

Johnny screamed his belief.

Samuel's heart crashed.

Kelly grabbed Samuel's arm.

Johnny had found his power. Did he even know? And if not, would the canyon rain boulders if he became distracted?

The floating rocks above them looked like an asteroid belt that floated lazily, undirected except by a general force that came from Johnny.

Samuel wanted to shout out with glee. He wanted to jump up and down and pump his fist into the air, crying victory.

"Say nothing," he whispered.

He said it between Johnny's screams. But the sound of his whisper had been too loud. Johnny lowered his head and opened his eyes.

The boulders did not fall.

Samuel exchanged a long stare with his friend. He still didn't know?

"You've found your power?" Samuel asked.

Johnny slowly lowered his arms. "No. I don't care about the power. I just want to be Johnny again."

Samuel took a step toward him. "Then do you at least understand love now?"

"Yes, I think I do." Johnny's eyes darted to Kelly. When he spoke again, his voice was choked with emotion. "I really think I do. Forgive me for not truly loving you before. Forgive me, please."

Kelly was still speechless. Her eyes lifted to the sky above him, but Johnny did not notice.

"I feel . . . myself." Johnny staggered to his feet. "Real again." A grin tugged at his mouth.

"Johnny," Samuel said. Without raising his arm, he lifted one finger toward the sky. "What's that?"

Johnny looked up. Saw the floating boulders, a particularly large one directly above him. He shrieked and dove to safety, tumbling in the sand.

The rocks still did not fall.

"Whoa! What?" Johnny slowly stood and craned his neck to take in the belt of rocks above him. "What's happening?"

"I don't know," Samuel said. "You're making them float."

"Me? Are you sure?"

"It's not me."

"Englishman?" Kelly asked.

Samuel scanned the cliffs. He didn't think it was Englishman.

They watched the rocks, soaking in the abnormality of it all.

One of the rocks above Johnny jerked. He looked at Samuel, eyes wide.

"Try again."

Johnny looked up at the same rock. It hung still for a moment. Without warning it flew into the canyon with blinding speed, like a UFO accelerating from zero to sixty in a single, undefined moment. The rock streaked for the end wall, a projectile fired from Johnny's mind. It slammed into the cliff and shattered, bringing a shower of smaller boulders tumbling down.

Johnny and Samuel spoke at the same time. "Wow!"

"Wow," Kelly said.

Johnny raised both hands and moved them toward the canyon mouth. The flotilla moved with his suggestion.

"Wow."

He moved his arms back the other way, like a conductor instructing a symphony.

The boulders stopped on a dime and reversed their direction, flying toward the end of the canyon now.

Johnny whooped with enthusiasm and swept his arms toward the sky beyond the canyon, above Paradise, as if he were sending a fighter jet off an aircraft carrier. *Go get 'em, boys!*

The boulders streamed east, increased their speed, and then disappeared into the horizon.

Johnny stared after them, stunned. "When will they stop?"

It was Kelly who asked the question on all of their minds. "What if they fall? On Paradise?"

Johnny frantically flung his arms to the sky and motioned the rocks back, like the ground crew might wave a jetliner into the gate, only with twice the animation.

The tiny specks reappeared in the dawn sky. "They're coming back," Johnny cried, motioning with even more vigor.

The small spots became larger spots, and from Samuel's angle the boulders looked as if they were headed directly for Johnny at an unstoppable speed. He instinctively crouched.

Johnny stopped motioning and threw himself to the ground as the flood of rocks zoomed silently into the canyon. A thousand boulders blasted twenty yards over their heads. The flyby took less than a second, followed by a huge wake of air that nearly blew Samuel over.

The squadron of rocks slammed into the far wall with enough force to shake the ground. Half the cliff caved with a thunderous roar. Dust boiled to the sky.

They stared at the destruction in awe. This time all three spoke at once.

"Wow!"

This is it, then, Samuel thought. *This is why I chose Johnny and why Johnny agreed to enter the X Group.* And yet he knew that it would take more than this to overpower Englishman.

"That's it," Samuel said. "Time to go."

"Did I really do that?" Johnny asked, staring at the rising dust. "Go where?"

"The president is at his ranch in Arizona, an hour by helicopter."

"You have a helicopter?"

"How do you think I got here? Top of the cliffs. The crew are running around like rats at the moment, trying to figure out what caused the ground to shake, but their orders are explicit."

"Don't . . . Don't you think I should practice or something?"

"Englishman has a full day on us," Kelly said. "The president's probably already dead."

"He's with my father, safe for the moment. But we have to leave now," Samuel said.

"You can't be serious!" Kelly said. "You can't just throw him to the wolves without proper planning!"

"We'll plan on the way."

Samuel turned and strode toward the cabin with resolution.

"Hold on."

He glanced back, saw that Johnny wasn't following him, and turned around. "We're not going to make it if we don't go now, Johnny."

"You said I couldn't defeat Englishman with a few boulders anyway. Do I have any other powers?"

The question caught Samuel off guard.

"To be honest, I doubt moving stones around is your gift. This is probably just a byproduct. I don't know. You'll have to figure that out as you go."

Johnny measured him for a long moment, then turned his head to face a two-story boulder that rested at the base of the cliff.

"Do you believe, Samuel?"

Before Samuel could respond, the boulder rose soundlessly from the ground. It slowly floated toward Samuel and came to a rest two feet over his head.

Do you believe, Samuel? Truth be told, he was unnerved. Perhaps terrified. It wasn't every day his faith was tested by a boulder weighing several hundred thousand tons.

He reached up and felt the reddish sandstone surface with both hands. A vibration hummed through his palms, down his arms, and along his spine and shot to his heels. There was enough power here to level a city. Amazing.

"I do," he finally said.

Johnny smiled and winked. "Just checking to make sure I still have the power," he said. "I think Samson would be a bit jealous."

The boulder floated to the other side of the canyon and settled quietly on the ground.

"Let's rock," Johnny said, striding forward. "No pun intended."

It was then that Samuel first noticed his eyes. They seemed gray instead of brown. Or was it the light? If Samuel hadn't been expecting some kind of change, he probably wouldn't have noticed. Apparently Kelly hadn't. She would soon enough.

Samuel turned and led them toward the cabin. "The truth will set you free, Johnny," he said, staring forward. "Show them the truth."

CHAPTER FORTY

THE GUARDS waited for him at the gate. He could see their tiny figures moving in the dawn light. Naturally, they'd been alerted to the sedan that had exited the freeway and made its way toward them. They would need to turn the lost tourist around.

Englishman could execute this bit of fun in an unlimited number of ways. He'd considered the possibilities on the long night-drive from Phoenix. But almost all of those ways failed to interest him.

The only way to execute this mission without boring himself to tears was to go right up their throat with a few fireworks to announce his arrival.

He would have to save Dale Crompton's body from all of the heavy metal they would hurl at him. He couldn't dodge bullets, but he had other skills.

"Dust to dust, ashes to ashes," he whispered. And then aloud but with a low voice, "Hallelujah, amen, you are dismissed. Every last hell-bound one of you."

Englishman stopped the car a hundred yards from the gate. With the high walls running both ways to the cliffs on each side, he would have to go straight through the entrance. Four armed men now stood before the gate, patiently waiting their turn to die. He would reward their patience by letting them go first.

He pried his eyes skyward, wondering if the drones were armed. A projectile in the back from a low-flying Predator would be most unwelcome. He'd have to keep moving and watch the skies. This could be slightly more challenging than he'd anticipated.

Now *that* was interesting.

One of the guards was waving at him. Stupid fool was motioning him forward. *Do you want me to come? Is that what you want, Jack Black?*

A Bradley fighting vehicle was parked on the right, and a tank was parked on the left. He saw now that their guns were manned and aimed at him. According to the docket that he'd breezed through on the flight from New York, the real threat would come from the second line of defense a mile up the road where the troops were dug in.

Englishman gunned the motor, but he kept it in neutral. Sweat tickled both temples. His heart was pounding like tumbling boulders. Now that he was here, staring down so many guns, he wondered if he'd been a little overzealous in choosing this particular approach.

A tremor ran through his fingers.

The sensation was so foreign to him that he found it impossible not to remove his eyes from the gate to look at his hand. Trembling with eager, joyous anticipation. And with fear.

Opposites. Love and hate. Good and evil. It was a good day for a showdown.

Englishman took a deep breath, blinked the sweat from his eyes, dropped the gearshift into drive, put both hands on the steering wheel, and slammed the accelerator to the floor.

The tires spun on the gravel road, caught some traction, and propelled the black Honda Accord forward.

JOHNNY PUT both feet on the helicopter's skid and readied himself to jump as soon as the pilot gave him the signal. They approached a guard post on a hill behind the main ranch buildings, the largest of six similarly equipped hills.

Something was wrong with his eyes, but he wasn't sure what. Even now, looking down at the passing ground, he thought his vision was somewhat impaired. The stones and bending weeds were slightly out of focus.

Kelly had been a nervous wreck since their departure.

It was his eyes, she finally told him. His eyes were gray and she found it disturbing.

Gray?

Riding the side of the helicopter twenty feet in the air, Johnny was struck by the other changes in himself. He wasn't the same person he'd been even three days ago. The thought of jumping from this height wouldn't have bothered him in the least, but now even looking down put butterflies in his gut.

The helicopter swept in low and flared to a hover a few feet above the rocky earth.

"Go!"

Kelly placed a hand on his shoulder. He turned around and saw that she was crying. She gazed at his face, then quickly averted her eyes.

Something was clearly wrong with his eyes. He should find out what, but the prospect of throwing himself into battle with Englishman dominated his concern.

Kelly wrapped both arms around him and spoke into his ear. "I'm afraid, Johnny."

He smoothed her hair, at a loss for words. He didn't even know what he was supposed to do up here on the hill. They'd developed no real plan other than for Johnny to do something if Englishman showed up.

Samuel held a pair of sunglasses out to him, the mirrored kind that pilots wore. "Wear these."

He didn't know why Samuel thought he should wear them, but maybe they would help his eyesight. Maybe it was the sunlight that distorted his vision. He took the glasses and put them on.

Was he going blind?

"The truth, Johnny. Show them truth." Samuel nodded, as if this should mean something to him. "The truth will set us all free."

Johnny returned the nod.

Kelly released him and he jumped from the skid, landed on a patch of hard sand, and ran toward the four soldiers who waited in the outpost. The helicopter blades lifted the bird up, then toward the ranch house with a blast of hot air.

The ten-by-ten post was built of half walls and sandbags that gave the soldiers inside a 360-degree view of the valley. Four large machine guns were mounted to cover all four sides. Johnny ducked his head under the eaves and faced a Special Forces lieutenant and three guardsmen.

The lieutenant eyed him. "Pardon my ignorance, but remind me what it is you're supposed to do here?"

Good question.

"We don't have a place for you to sit."

Johnny stuck out his hand. "I'm Johnny. They want me to watch over . . . things."

The commander took his hand without enthusiasm. "Watch what, the weeds grow?"

The radio under one of the grinning guardsmen squawked. "We have a situation at the front gate. Black sedan's headed our way at high speed. Unresponsive. Do we shoot?"

A crackle of static.

"Blow his tires out."

"Copy. Disabling veh—"

The radio went abruptly silent.

The guard manning the radio keyed the transmitter to no avail. "What was that?"

"I don't know."

But Johnny knew, and the knowledge immobilized him. Englishman had come. So soon?

He looked past the gun on his right to the ranch below, where the helicopter was just now landing safely. The horizon offered only a gray morning sky above distant cliffs. Or were his eyes making the sky gray? He removed the sunglasses, but the sky was no less gray, so he replaced them.

He was going blind, wasn't he?

"What happened?" one of the guardsmen asked.

The lieutenant hesitated, scanning the forward perimeter. "We may have some trouble." He jabbed a finger at Johnny. "Sit."

Instead, Johnny walked out of the post.

One of them yelled something at him—his heart was pounding so loud that he couldn't hear the words. He walked twenty paces and faced the south. No sign of Englishman. That was something to be thankful for. But he knew his gratitude would be short-lived.

A chorus of frantic calls barked over the radio in the post. The lieutenant leaned out of the post and shouted angrily at him, barking orders about getting his butt back inside, punctuated with obscenities.

Johnny faced the man and floated a dozen sandbags from the ground. He held them suspended in front of the man.

"Holy—"

All four soldiers stepped back, silenced and slack-jawed.

Johnny let the bags fall. "Please," he said, pausing to catch his breath over the panic that was gripping him. "Let me do my job."

ENGLISHMAN WAITED until he was absolutely sure they were about to fire before making his first move.

It was a thought more than a move, but it did move some things. Three things to be precise. The guardhouse, the Bradley fighting vehicle, and the tank. He moved them up and out of the way. Fifty very quick feet straight up. The underground electrical wires that fed the guardhouse separated in a spray of sparks as the shack flew up before coming to a sudden stop next to the tank and the Bradley high above the gate.

The guards lucky enough to be left on the ground seemed disturbed by the sudden skyward display. Englishman made their guns hot, instantly hot enough to fry their hands.

He couldn't hear their cries because the car was roaring and the windows were down, but he could see their faces. They dropped the guns.

Johnny wouldn't have. Even in Hungary he would have controlled his reaction to the heat long enough to get off at least one shot, and one shot from Johnny was enough to kill even Englishman's flesh-and-blood body.

"Ha!" He couldn't resist the cry of delight. In the space of five seconds he'd neutralized the front gate.

Englishman slammed his foot on the brake pedal, and the sedan skidded sideways before coming to a dusty stop. The sharpshooters would be climbing out of their holes at any moment. Guns from the sky would begin blazing. Missiles even. They would unleash all hell without the foggiest idea of what hell really was.

He stared up at the floating guardhouse and saw that someone had thrown open a window and was bringing out a rifle. On each side, the hatches to the tank and the Bradley were flopping open, and crew members were poking their heads out.

Englishman let the guardhouse, the tank, and the Bradley fighting vehicle fall to the ground together.

The earth shook. Amazingly, the tank bounced a good five feet

before slamming to rest on broken tracks. Its suspension had survived
the fall, which was certainly more than could be said for those inside.
The Bradley's undercarriage shattered upon landing. And the guardhouse became a pile of kindling. *Dust to dust, ashes to ashes. You are*
dismissed.

Englishman floored the Accord, smashed through the gates, and
then sent a hundred boulders flying toward the ranch house.

The Englishman cometh.

CHAPTER FORTY-ONE

WHAT JOHNNY first mistook for a bird flying through the sky grew as it hurtled toward them and became boulders. They flew in an arc like debris lobbed from a catapult and crashed into the ground several hundred yards from the ranch house.

One of the guards voiced his shock. "What the . . . ? Did you . . . ?"

Johnny did the only thing he knew to do in that moment. He pictured the boulders flying back.

They flew. Iike missiles propelled from a silent canon, in precisely the same trajectory in which they'd come. So, then, he'd just announced himself to the Englishman.

A strong voice cut through the radio chatter. "The gates are down! I repeat, the gates are down and we have an intruder. Black sedan coming in like a bat out of hell. Blasted through the front guard, tank and all. Get the drones over here and take him out!"

Johnny watched in horror as a line of boulders that formed a perimeter suddenly rose and streaked into the sky.

Johnny quickly envisioned the rocks flying back, but they came on, faster now. He couldn't affect the flight of objects in Englishman's control?

The rocks gathered into six groupings, turned sharply in differing directions, and blasted toward the hills. They were going for the out-posts, including the one twenty feet from where Johnny now stood.

Before he fully knew what was happening, the rocks slammed into the hill on his left, driving the outpost and everything inside it below the ground. The earth shook.

Dust rose.

Johnny remained rooted to the ground. Men lay crushed and broken under tons of rock where only a moment ago the four-sided post had topped the hill. Not only here, but at the other five outposts as well.

He jerked his head back to the valley. If Englishman wielded this much power, he could easily crush the ranch house.

Johnny ripped his legs free and sprinted down the hill toward the house. He didn't know why he was running; he was only running.

"WE HAVE to get you out now, sir!" Bruce Wyatt was the president's most trusted Secret Service agent. He grabbed Robert's arm. "The chopper's ready."

"What's that noise?" Robert demanded.

David Abraham ran from the window, motioning to the first family, Samuel, and Kelly. "No, you can't leave. He'll destroy the helicopter as soon as it takes off. You have a shelter?"

"The basement."

"In the basement! Now!" David spun to the other three Secret Servicemen who stood with sidearms drawn. "Everyone! The house is going to be hit. Let's go!"

"Hit? By what?" Robert asked.

He still couldn't wrap his mind around what David's son, Samuel, had suggested to him moments earlier. The notion that two men with supernatural powers were duking it out in his front yard wasn't making it through his reality grid.

Elijah had fought the prophets of Baal—an event recorded by an ancient writer. Samson had pushed over some pillars, another story written down by another ancient writer. Johnny had saved his life by affecting the flight of a bullet, an event that was recorded by an X-ray. But here in the backyard of the president's ranch, stories of soaring rocks and flying tanks were in an entirely different category.

They were real. Happening now.

This stuff wasn't supposed to be real. Not unless you were David Abraham and had broken into the supernatural plane with Project Showdown.

Robert repeated his question. "Hit by what?"

"Boulders," Samuel said.

JOHNNY! JOHNNY was here! Englishman nearly drove off the road in his exuberance.

He had intended to use his power to accelerate the Honda Accord to a speed far beyond its limits. He would have blasted through the narrow gap in the defenses like an unstoppable roadrunner from hell. *Beep-beep*.

Then the rocks had come flying back and Englishman did not laugh. Laughing at a time like this would be far too cliché. If it was just the president waiting to die, he might have allowed himself a cliché or two. But now that Johnny had inserted himself into the mix and demonstrated that he knew a thing or two about rock-flinging, Englishman would avoid cliché.

He increased the Honda's speed. They would be able to see the lone, small Honda Accord leading the charge now, assuming they had the presence of mind to take their eyes off the big show in the sky to realize that *he* was the big show.

The air was crystal clear this morning. With the dust behind him, he could see all the way to the large grouping of trees and scattered boulders that presumably surrounded the ranch house.

If Johnny had a rifle, he might be able to take out Englishman now.

The thought sent a chill down his back.

Am I ready to die?

No.

Was Johnny ready to die?

Yes.

Do I want to kill Johnny?

Yes.

Have I destroyed Johnny?

Yes.

Then why was Johnny throwing rocks back at him?

Because Johnny didn't know about Englishman's trump card.

He blinked. Still, it was a good question that hadn't presented itself until now. Johnny had some power, more power than yesterday, enough power to throw boulders around.

Wasn't it understood from the beginning that Johnny might find the power before he was utterly destroyed?

"Yes."

And he has found the power. So now you have to kill him. Crush him, defeat him, pulverize him, decimate him, ruin him, shred him, chew him up and spit him out. Minus the cliché.

"Dust to dust, ashes to ashes, hallelujah, amen, you are permanently dismissed."

Englishman hated Johnny. He despised him in the worst way, so much that in that moment, he realized not having Johnny to hate might be *his* end.

If Johnny dies, I might die.

The thought made him sweat again. Heavily.

JOHNNY GOT halfway down the hill toward the ranch house before he saw the car blazing a dusty trail toward the ranch house with an armada of boulders flying above it.

Englishman.

His mind flipped through options as if they were playing cards fanned by a thumb.

Stop the boulders. No.

Stop the car. He tried. It was being controlled by Englishman. No.

Divert the boulders. Again, under Englishman's control. No.

Stand in the way of the boulders. No, that couldn't possibly be a good idea.

No, no, no. Nothing could be done to the boulders.

But to the car . .

Johnny scanned the valley floor for a large rock, found one, lifted it a hundred feet into the air, and then sent it flying toward the car.

Fast. Faster than he could see. A streak of granite packing enough striking power to bury the car a hundred feet under the ground.

Englishman was still too far away for Johnny to make out any detail, but he did see a few things.

He saw the car skidding to a stop. He saw a boulder leave those over the car, streak toward the rock he'd sent, and slam into it in midair. He saw a hundred fragments rain down around the car.

Johnny immediately returned the favor. He lifted a hundred boulders sitting idly on the hillside and flung them toward the boulders in the sky. The valley filled with the sound of otherworldly bowling balls crashing down into pins as his rocks slammed into those over Englishman, filling the air with billowing clouds of dust.

His heart skipped a beat.

Silence seemed to echo.

He'd done it? Johnny's heart pounded, a heavy, thick bass drum in a hollow chest. He'd really done it?

"Johnny!"

His named drifted over the valley floor, barely reaching him. Englishman was where? On the mound of dirt? He couldn't see too clearly.

With alarm Johnny realized that the sky was darker now, definitely darker than it had been just minutes earlier.

He really was going blind?

Show them the truth, Samuel had said. *The truth will set us all free.*

The truth had turned Samson blind.

Englishman cried his name again. "Johnny!"

The cliffs at the entrance began to crumble. He saw the car then, emerging from behind several tall boulders.

Johnny ran. Down the hill. Like Elijah racing the rains, down, down, stretching each leg in front of the other, afraid to look up. Knowing that Samuel had been right. He couldn't win this battle with a few boulders or a ton of boulders. A single large chunk of granite from the sky would destroy the ranch house—there was no way Johnny could protect them forever.

He had to get to Englishman before Englishman got to them.

Johnny cut to his right, hoping that he could intercept the car, but even as he ran, he knew Englishman would beat him to the ranch house.

He passed a small wooden outbuilding at the base of the hill— perhaps a tool shack, but he couldn't tell because with each step the world seemed to darken. He could hardly see the distant tumbling cliffs now, but he could tell that they were floating in large broken chunks. Englishman was gathering an armada. This time it would float. Their end was clearly in sight.

Or not so clearly.

Johnny ran faster, on the level valley floor now, terrified as much by his failing sight as by the coming catastrophe. He could make out forms, but they seemed shrouded in dusk. A faint glimmer followed the edges of most things. The rocks, the trees on his right, the speeding car angling in from his left.

The faint glimmer of light that surrounded the objects seemed to have intensified. But the world that held the objects was most definitely darker.

Maybe every time he used his power, he lost some of his eyesight.

Was it the sunglasses? He lifted them as he sprinted and was rewarded with a blast of air that stung his eyes. The light on the edges of this dark world was bright enough to hurt his eyes.

He lowered the glasses back onto his nose.

Englishman raced on, his jagged armada flying above him. Johnny was halfway to the ranch house when he acted more out of panic than with any real plan.

He gathered several hundred boulders from the hills and sent them directly toward Englishman's floating rocks.

Light glimmered and crackled on the surface of the flying debris. The large rocks he'd hurled collided with the massive chunks of stone that Englishman had gathered for his assault.

The valley filled with the sound of a thousand detonations and the boulders rained to the ground. It was nothing more than a distraction; he was only providing Englishman with more rocks to fling.

They were locked in an impossible duel. But Englishman was not slowing, not swerving, not dissuaded from his task in the least. It was almost as if he'd seen not Johnny's power but Johnny himself. He had to get the man's attention and distract him from his mission.

"Englishman!"

The car sped on, filling the air with dust from its wheels.

"Englishman!"

As if on cue, the car suddenly slowed, then rolled to a stop a hundred yards from the house.

Why didn't he just take out the house? *Because, Johnny, you, not the president, are his target. He knows you are all that stands between him and far more than just the president.*

The sky to his right blossomed with an exploding ball of light. Johnny ducked. Samuel had mentioned drones. Englishman had just taken one out. As if in answer, a second explosion rocked the dusty sky.

When he looked ahead again, he saw that Englishman was out of the car, standing with hands on hips, waiting for him in brimming light, like a gunslinger with one last cowpoke to kill before he called it good.

Johnny slowed to a walk, then stopped, thirty yards from the man.

Englishman grinned. "Hello, Johnny."

CHAPTER FORTY-TWO

ENGLISHMAN STRODE to within ten paces of Johnny, ready to preempt his slightest move. But Johnny neither moved nor made anything around them move.

The kid was wearing dark reflective glasses. Odd. No, not odd. Cliché. Still, the sight of those black, shiny glasses unnerved Englishman.

He put both hands on his hips, planted his feet in the sand, and faced the boy he'd waited so patiently to crush.

A rock came screaming out of the north toward him. Did Johnny think he could accomplish anything with a stray stone? He lifted a large boulder near the hills and flung it at the incoming projectile. The two collided with a loud pop a hundred yards out. Dust hung in the air as a hundred shattered fragments fell harmlessly to the ground.

"It will take more than a few boulders," Englishman said.

He saw his reflection in Johnny's silver glasses, and the sight amused him. *Two of me, one of you.* A fitting symbol. Did the boy actually think he had a chance against Englishman? Surely Johnny didn't think he could get the upper hand with some stone-throwing.

Another boulder came hurtling in, from the south this time.

Englishman destroyed it with another while it was still small in the sky. He grunted with disappointment.

The pain came out of nowhere. A sharp jab that sliced through his right shoulder. He knew immediately that Johnny had tricked him by drawing his attention to the boulder in the sky while bringing a much smaller stone in from behind.

Englishman did the same to Johnny even as he dropped his body flat.

Johnny gasped and staggered forward.

But one was not enough. Englishman lifted a hundred small stones into the air behind Johnny and poised them to strike.

"Behind you, Johnny."

Johnny glanced behind. Saw the stones. Swung back around.

"Behind you, Englishman."

He didn't have to look to know that Johnny had already placed as many stones in the air behind him, but he did anyway. He was right. More than a thousand, maybe ten thousand. Englishman rose to his feet.

"There is no way to deflect a thousand stones," Johnny said. "You can kill me, but know that before I die, I'll do the same and you'll die as well."

"And you should know that I've taken similar precautions. You will deeply regret any real attempt to kill me."

"How so?" Johnny asked.

"Because although you think you returned to Paradise and hugged your mother and learned the truth about who you are in the canyon above, nothing could be further from the truth." Englishman was happy to finally offer up these nuggets of information. He could hardly stand the pleasure of it all. "Aren't we clever? Two hounds of hell trading tricks."

"I'm no hound of hell," Johnny said. "I did hug my mother. I do know who I am. The truth *is* with me."

"Is that why you're trembling?"

"I'm trembling because I finally figured out who you are."

"Is that so? And who am I?"

"Who am I?" Johnny asked.

"You're an innocent fool."

"And you may not have his face or his hands, but you are the one born of hell and determined to drag the rest down with you."

Englishman wanted to destroy Johnny now by stripping the boy's faith from his underbelly, he really did, but the talk felt satisfying after so much secrecy.

Johnny circled slowly to the left, and Englishman kept the stones at his back. He walked to his left and knew that Johnny returned the favor. They were two circling vultures, each guarded by a flotilla of stones to keep things even.

"Do you believe, Johnny? I mean really, really believe?"

"How could I not with all of these flying rocks?"

"I'm not talking about the power that moves the rocks. Do you really believe that this power comes from some benevolent God in the sky? Because if you do, you're sadly mistaken."

"What do you mean?"

A soft, comfortable warmth filled Englishman's veins. The time had come to tell Johnny the truth.

DAVID ABRAHAM studied the images on the large flat-screen, frozen by what his eyes had witnessed. The pictures were being relayed from a C140 reconnaissance platform that was circling the ranch at twenty thousand feet, but they were amazingly clear.

A squadron of F-15s was on its way from Nellis Air Force Base in southern Nevada, because the compound's defenses were quite literally crushed. Even the two drones. Only what remained of the interior guard remained, and none of them were volunteering to go stand in the way of the massive bowling balls that had crisscrossed the valley.

Robert Stenton stood by his side, watching the picture, face white. "They've isolated the target on their radar," he said quietly. "This— I don't have any words for this."

"You won't need any words for this. As far as the rest of the world is concerned, this isn't happening."

"How's it even possible?"

"Do you know how small those huge boulders look from the vantage of a Boeing 747 flying overhead? Like specks of sand. Imagine how small they look from the moon. Now Mars. Now the other side of the solar system."

"Meaning what?"

"Meaning what you're seeing today is nothing more than ants' play from a thirty-thousand-foot vantage point."

One of the Secret Servicemen flung the door wide. "Sir, the fighters have a lock on the target. Waiting your order."

"No," David said.

He faced the screen again. Both Johnny and Englishman were in clear view, circling each other and surrounded by a cloud of levitating stones.

"Even if you could isolate one of them, what makes you think Englishman will just stand by while a missile streaks in to obliterate him? He'll more likely send it back on its own heat trail. I'd tell the planes to stay out of visual and keep their fingers away from any triggers for the time being."

"Then what?" Stenton demanded. "For that matter, what are *they* doing?"

"I think they're getting down to the truth of the matter," David said. He headed for the door. "I'm going out there."

"David—"

"I'm going. The rest of you stay here."

CHAPTER FORTY-THREE

IF THE power came from a benevolent God, wouldn't he hand out more of it so that mortals could rid the world of nasty men like me?" Englishman asked.

Johnny was remembering now. Dogma embraced during his tenure as a chaplain flooded his mind. "Because I'm an exception, just like Samson was an exception. And for the record, I am going to rid the world of you."

Englishman didn't speak for a long time. The world was a charcoal gray, highlighted by bright edges. It was clear to Johnny that his coming out to meet Englishman without a plan would end badly. He was facing off like the local sheriff while thinking about how to make it back into the hills in one piece. At least he was stalling the attack on the ranch house. In this way he was fulfilling his mission.

In every other way he was lost. And going blind.

Englishman's shoulders suddenly relaxed. He crossed his arms. Johnny heard a smile in his voice. "Well, well, well. You've gone and done it. Congratulations, Carl. Your training is complete. You've done well—far better than we had hoped." Englishman walked toward him.

"Stop."

He lowered his arms, totally relaxed now. "I realize you may be confused about this. I was too. But it's over. You've just completed your final test. We've reintegrated you into your own history, most of which is true."

"What do you mean, *integrated*? That's a lie. I'm Johnny."

"You are. And you were a chaplain as well. And you did volunteer for X Group. And now you are Saint. All of it's true. The continuing story of Project Showdown, on the other hand, is a fabrication. It's Agotha's version of a crutch. Like religion. We gave you a reason to believe that you could move mountains and rocks. You were hitting a wall in Hungary, so we set this up for you. But like any human's journey of faith, you eventually learn that it's all a bunch of made-up stories. The real power to change life and float rocks comes from something much less fantastic than faith."

Englishman spread both hands, indicating the valley. "This, my friend, is *you*, not God. It's all you and me. I'm the only other person who's succeeded in manipulating the zero-point field."

"I don't believe you." Johnny was feeling nauseated. The world was black, like his pit, and maybe that was good. Maybe he did belong in the blackness of a pit, only surviving to kill.

"I denied it too," Englishman said. "I stood right here and screamed my bloody head off. It took me a week before I could move another rock, and only then when I finally realized that I had done it with my own power, not with some power from the sky."

Englishman tapped his head. "It's up here, Carl. A simple matter of quantum physics. The zero-point field. And believe me, you've done well. Statistically, fewer than one in ten million humans have the mental strength to pull off what you have, and only then with considerable training. Gurus and such."

Johnny stared at Englishman, stunned by the possibility, however thin, that he was hearing the truth. But even then, he knew it had to be a trick. It had to be! He'd lost himself in their lies once, a hundred times. He couldn't accept them this time.

"You're wrong. I've finally discovered who I am, and it begins with Project Showdown. Now you have the gall to think I'd just throw it all out for the same lies Agotha fed me for a year? What do you take me for?"

"Please, Johnny. If you insist, we can resort to drug therapy."

"Kelly knows the truth. This is crazy!"

"Kelly is the same person today that she was a month ago! A woman willing to betray you for your own sake. She does love you, but she's under no delusion that this exercise is anything more than a very carefully executed hoax to help you believe in yourself. Believe, for crying out loud! Believe, but believe in yourself, not some faceless god!"

"I *can't* believe in myself."

"You can. As of this moment, you can. You're finally understanding who you really are. You are Johnny. You love Kelly and Kelly loves you. You did not kill the president because we didn't want you to. You did kill Feroz because you were meant to. You were put into the most inhumane pressure cooker of a test to draw out your strength, and it has succeeded. Everything else is a sham! Everything! Even your mother. It wasn't Sally you met. She was one of ours."

The claim blindsided Johnny. "That's impossible. I . . . I felt her love."

"You felt what we wanted you to feel," Englishman said. "The woman you wept over in Paradise was not your mother. We stashed Mommy away in a safe house the day after you bolted from New York. It was all a lie to bring you to the point you've finally come to." Englishman nodded at the floating stones. "And it was well worth it, don't you think?"

Johnny's head swam in confusion. He simply couldn't accept that Sally wasn't his mother. Reuniting with her was the beginning of his awakening. If she was a lie, then the rest was a sham.

Or was it? He refused to let down his guard. The woman he'd embraced in Paradise *was* his mother!

"Samuel," he said. "David Abraham . . ."

"Unwitting accomplices we used because of their connection to you. It was all a setup, beginning with Samuel's vision, which was nothing more than a simple case of strong suggestion in a drug-induced state, followed up by numerous uncanny confirmations. It was *our* vision, and we made sure it came to pass. Does Samuel have any powers? I don't think so. He's a thirteen-year-old boy who knows only what we've wanted him to know."

This was incredible. "What about his age?"

"So he has a growth issue connected to Project Showdown. So what? That doesn't change the fact that we pulled his strings all along."

"David Abraham?"

"Fed off of Samuel's vision."

"The president. You're saying that even—"

"No. You shot him, remember? But it wasn't your bullet that struck the president. It was mine, and I was much closer. I have the power to affect a bullet's path. I did. Your bullet went where our scope told it to go, far over his head. Not that you couldn't have pulled off the hit, but we didn't want a dead president on our hands. At some point we will retrace every last detail and explain it for you. Trust me, it all fits like a glove."

Johnny's worlds were colliding. Did Englishman know about his eyesight? Was that also part of the deception?

There was a sound of hard rain behind Englishman. Johnny's stones, falling to the sand. He didn't mean for them to fall; they just did.

He had supposedly passed the greatest test of all time and felt only desperation. Neither the anger nor the righteousness he would expect to feel at this moment.

"You," Johnny said. "You don't fit."

Englishman smiled. "I fit perfectly. I'm the only person on the globe who has the power you have. I know your pain. Unless a seed falls to the ground and dies, it can't bear fruit, isn't that the truth? We've been destroyed so that we can live, and frankly I hate that. But there it is."

"Why?" Johnny asked. "Why did you do this to me?"

"Look around. You just moved a mountain! You tested off the charts on your military entrance exams and were noticed. Then followed for three years before it was determined that you'd make a good candidate. Now you've proven them right. And to prove it to me, there's one last thing I need you to do."

"What?"

"Kill the president."

Outrage flooded Johnny, then ebbed. He swallowed. "I thought you didn't want him dead."

"Not until after you'd killed Feroz. With Feroz and the president out of the way, the Iranian initiative can move forward without the threat of two idealists duking it out."

"No." He clenched his fists. The stones behind Englishman sprang back into the air. Courage filled his chest. Englishman was lying.

"I don't believe you. You're here to kill me. Samuel and David have told me the truth. Sally is my mother. You're taking me for a fool!"

Englishman took a long time in answering. "Then you are a fool, Carl. And in this business, all fools die. You decide today: either you believe me when I say you were deceived in Paradise, or you believe them that I'm lying. One way you kill the president and live, the other you die."

"I found the truth in Paradise. I embraced my mother."

For a moment Englishman just stared at him. A loud wrench of tearing metal split the air. Thirty yards behind Englishman, the trunk hatch on the Honda Accord flew to the sky.

A large object tumbled from the trunk and rolled toward them. As if manipulated by unseen hands, it was jerked upright not fifteen yards off. Johnny saw then that it was a body.

A woman. With long hair and wide eyes, bound with rope and silenced with gray duct tape. His heart hammered.

"One wrong move and she dies," Englishman said. "Is this the woman you embraced in Paradise? No, I don't think so. Say hello to Mommy."

The tape ripped from her face. She screamed, terrified. "Johnny?"

This was not the woman he'd embraced in Paradise. Johnny began to tremble from the bottom of his feet to the base of his head.

"Johnny," the woman whimpered.

The sound of her voice haunted him. *Are you my mother?*

"Mother?"

"Johnny, what have they done to you?"

He knew then that this woman was his mother. And he felt powerless to move.

"The woman you found in Paradise was an operative. A rather brilliant operative, as you can attest. We orchestrated it all, Johnny."

"Let her go," he said. Emotion choked him. "Just let her go!"

"You are like me, Johnny. You're a pretender who doesn't believe in what he's pretending anymore. You're a child of illusion who's been fed dogma and doctrine as a form of manipulation."

Johnny had been here before, on the barely surviving end of a hundred less-distorting games. What was one more?

"Will you?" Englishman asked.

The question echoed through Johnny's skull. *Will you?* He tried to focus on Englishman and was struck again by the darkness. Maybe his blindness was psychosomatic and would soon end.

"How?" he heard himself asking.

"Just walk in and kill him. You're their hero. They won't question your return, particularly if I've given a show of surrender."

From the beginning this had been their intention. To break him as he'd never been broken before and to kill both Feroz and the president at the same time. This was the mission he'd been so carefully trained for.

He exhaled slowly to calm himself. The familiar resolve that had been his friend in so many tests lapped at his mind. There was comfort there, in the dark tunnel where he was safe by himself.

"Johnny!" David Abraham stepped out from behind a large boulder and marched straight toward them. "Don't listen to his lies, Johnny."

"The old fool has come out to die." Englishman rolled his eyes.

"Is she my mother?" Johnny asked.

David stopped twenty yards from them and glanced at Sally. "I thought you met her in Paradise."

David knew Sally from before. And this was her. "Not her," Johnny said.

David's eyes widened slightly.

"Game over, old man," Englishman said. "We have all firmly in hand. Your presence is no longer required."

"Samuel told me about your eyes, Johnny," David said. "They show the truth. The truth will set you—"

Before David could finish, a hole blew through his shirt. He gasped and stared at a growing stain of red blood over his left breast pocket. Englishman had sent a pebble through the old man.

Johnny spun back to Englishman as David Abraham fell to the ground.

"One wrong move and she dies too," Englishman said.

"Stop it!" Johnny screamed. It sounded silly, but he felt so overwhelmed that nothing else came to mind. So he yelled it again. "Just stop it!"

"Only you can stop it. Kill the president, Johnny."

David's last words still rang in his ears. His eyes. There was something about his eyes . . .

His mother stood shaking, hands tied tightly behind her. She was crying now, begging him to do something. He saw her more in shades of light and shadows than in full color, but oddly enough, this way of seeing didn't compromise his ability to understand exactly what he was looking at.

"Trust David, Johnny," she said. "Use your eyes."

THIS MATTER of the eyes again, Englishman thought. He didn't care for the black stare. He preferred looking a man in the eyes before killing him.

Oh yes, he was indeed going to kill Johnny. As soon as Johnny killed the president. That was the deal, the new deal, the deal he should have made long ago.

Johnny looked at him dumbly—those shiny, silver-coated glasses made him look like an alien. They bothered Englishman immensely.

"My eyes?"

"Enough with the eyes crap, Johnny," Englishman said. "Either you kill the president, or I do the lot of you. This is growing old."

"I think something might be wrong with my eyes," Johnny said. "I thought I was going blind. But it's stopped now."

Blind? He wasn't sure why the idea of blindness sent a shaft of fear through his chest, but he knew about opposites. He knew that when darkness encroached, the light was often just over the horizon.

"I see glimmers of light on the edge of everything. Otherwise it's dark," Johnny said.

"Enough!"

"David told me to show you the truth." Johnny reached up and lifted the sunglasses from his face. "Do you know what he meant?"

Englishman's nerves stretched to the snapping point when he saw Johnny's eyes. Behind him, the mother gasped. Johnny didn't have eyes in the common understanding of the word. No blue or brown or green irises with black dots dead-center.

Instead, where his eyes should have been were two white orbs. If they didn't actually seem to glow, Englishman would have thought they were Johnny's eyes turned back into his head.

But these were solid white, like fluorescent cue balls.

"What's wrong?" Johnny asked.

He didn't know. Johnny really didn't know.

Englishman spoke the simple truth. "Your eyes are white."

And then they weren't white. They were black and monstrous and flowing with blood. Not just any blackness or any monstrosity or any blood, but Englishman's.

He was staring directly into himself.

Into hell.

Behind him, the mother screamed.

JOHNNY KNEW that something had changed the moment he removed his sunglasses. One look at Englishman, gawking at him, and Johnny knew that whatever had preceded this point, Englishman was now seeing the truth, and whatever that was, it stunned him.

"What's wrong?" he asked.

"Your eyes are white," Englishman said.

This, too, was the truth, spoken plainly. Englishman was only being truthful, and he, Johnny, was responsible for the man's truthfulness. And the truth was that his eyes had become white.

But what if there was more truth to be shown?

Realization dawned on Johnny so suddenly that he blinked. Then blinked again. Blindness was his price. He could give up his eyesight—for what?

He drilled the man with a hard stare, willing the layers of truth to be laid bare.

Englishman's mouth flew wide, and his eyes filled with terror. He began to suck in air and shove it out like a pump that had lost its prime.

The stones suspended all around them hailed to the ground. He was dumbstruck. The confidence and strength he'd felt in the canyon above Paradise flooded his mind, quickened his breathing, and hammered through his chest. Sally had dropped to her knees and shielded her eyes with both hands.

Johnny bore down on Englishman again, baring layers of truth that he himself could not see.

Englishman began to shake violently from head to foot. His torso vibrated as if it had been crammed into a blender, and his head jerked from side to side, slowly at first, then gaining speed until it shook back and forth like a spring-loaded punching bag, fast enough to obscure his features, all except his black mouth, gaping obscenely wide.

Johnny took a step forward, gripped his fists tight, and leaned into whatever power flowed from his eyes. His muscles were stretched tight, and he was still breathing hard.

"I believe," he said. "I believe, Englishman. I am not the lie. You are the lie!"

A piercing wail came from the man's throat. Not animal. Not human. More insect. Englishman was seeing the truth about himself, and he didn't like what he saw.

Johnny began to scream. An openmouthed, wordless scream of rage and remorse and terror and love and belief all wrapped around a single chord that he leveled at the lie with enough force to hurt his throat.

Englishman's entire body became a screeching blur of agony. The thing's terrible insectlike shrieks rose in pitch until they overpowered Johnny's cry. The desert air was cut to ribbons with this earsplitting shriek of anguish.

The blur that was Englishman suddenly became an empty shirt and trousers that hung in the air.

Johnny's scream caught in his throat.

Silence.

Then the *whoosh* of falling clothes, which plopped lightly on the ground between two shoes. A thin tendril of smoke rose from the shirt's collar. Englishman occupied space with his unfathomable contortions one second, and became empty air with a twist of smoke the next.

Johnny took a step back, legs like spaghetti, heart hammering. He turned to face David Abraham's fallen form, the dark stain of blood discoloring the desert sand, and if his world weren't so twisted, so fractured, he might have thrown up. Instead, he swallowed hard and faced his mother, who wept through her fingers.

Somehow he managed to replace his glasses, but his legs were giving out. He sank to his knees, dumbstruck and spent. The world spun around him.

With a failing conscious effort, he released the cords that held his mother. Sensed more than saw her rushing toward him. Felt her arms crash around him. Heard her sobs of relief.

Someone was wailing, high-pitched. Samuel, tearing at them from the ranch house.

Then Johnny's world went black.

CHAPTER FORTY-FOUR

JOHNNY AND Kelly stood hand in hand, staring at the town of Paradise from the overlook high above. Sally stood beside them, arms crossed, sober.

Johnny had spent a week hidden away here with Kelly and Sally, discovering himself—his new self, his old self. His mother, his old friends, his place of birth, and his place of new birth.

He'd spent half that time in tears. Tears of sadness, tears of gladness, tears of relief and shame and love.

Samuel's world had imploded with the death of his father. He'd fallen on his body and wept for an hour before allowing them to pull him away. They buried David Abraham four days ago, and the funeral had been a terrible mix of good and bad for Samuel.

Good because the president had given his father a burial of highest honor, which his father deserved.

Bad because in his speech, the president vowed to bring all involved in the assassination attempts and the death of his beloved friend to justice. This, Samuel learned in short order, included Johnny.

He'd attempted to kill the president of the United States of America.

Still faint from sorrow, Samuel had rushed back to Paradise and convinced Johnny to disappear. In good time, he would turn himself in. In good time.

Not now.

The threat from Kalman still loomed. The X Group had reportedly gone deep, but they would rear their heads again—these kind always did. Samuel wondered if Johnny wouldn't quietly put an end to them in the next week or so. He certainly had the means to do it.

The press still had no idea about what had happened this last year. They probably never would know. What they did know for certain was straightforward:

The president was alive.

His would-be assassins were a man named Dale Crompton, better known as Englishman, now dead, and Johnny Drake, now missing.

Assim Feroz, who had masterminded the president's assassination attempt, was now also dead, killed by his own hired guns.

Robert Stenton vetoed the Iranian initiative, and no other world leader had yet come forward to resurrect it.

Samuel approached them and studied the peaceful town. "Have you decided?"

"We are going to the desert," Johnny said. "To Nevada."

"Nevada. Plenty of desert."

"Plenty of desert," Johnny said. "Have you heard any news about the president's son?"

"His condition continues to deteriorate."

Johnny frowned but offered no comment. He maintained that it was Jamie who'd first broken through his shell and got him thinking about a father figure, which David ended up being.

"Any change in your eyes?" Sally asked, placing her hand on his shoulder.

Johnny turned his head south so that he faced neither of them, then lifted his glasses for a moment before lowering them back into place.

"No."

"I don't think it will ever change," Samuel said.

Johnny remained silent. Samuel had been right, Johnny's true gift was in his eyes, not in any ability to float boulders. That evidently had been something that came while his eyes were changing from brown to white and then left. He hadn't been able to budge a pebble much less a boulder since.

He wore the mirrored glasses for their sakes as much as his own. He could see well enough, but not the way the rest of them did. No color. Only black and white. With definition and acute depth perception formed by a thin crackle of white light that outlined everything, he said.

Samuel had looked into the whites of his eyes only once and then very briefly. Johnny wasn't sure how it would affect his and Kelly's relationship. She'd seen enough on the helicopter, when his eyes were just starting to go milky, to swear off ever looking into his eyes again.

In some ways Johnny was like Samson, whose gift had come at a great price. Johnny's greatest gift was his revealing sight. Imagine what he could do in a session of Congress with those eyes.

"I think the other powers could return," Samuel said, speaking of his other power.

"I'm not sure I want it to."

"Then it won't."

Kelly reached up and kissed Johnny lightly on his cheek. "I love you the way you are."

He placed his arm around her and kissed her forehead. "And I love you the way you are."

They returned their gazes to the valley.

"Really what you've experienced is the same journey that many are confronted with in our agnostic world," Samuel said.

"There are others like me?"

"In some ways all people of faith are like you. You once had great faith but the world methodically stripped it out of you, granted in your case rather brutally, courtesy of the X group. But we all face similar pressures to forget the simple truth of who we are. Particularly the truths that don't jive with what we see around us. As time wears us down we can forget who we once were."

"And recovering that faith can be . . . difficult," Johnny said.

"To say the least."

Johnny nodded and exhaled slowly. "Are you ready, Kelly?"

"I am," she replied.

Johnny had recovered his faith, but he was still unsure about his role. For now he was a brooding hero trying to stay alive long enough to come to terms with who he was.

"So this is it," Sally mused. "There really is no alternative?"

"The authorities will be in Paradise by nightfall. This is it. I either turn myself in or buy some time. Would you rather I stay?"

"No," Sally said. "Run. But promise me you'll come back."

"I promise."

Johnny wasn't sure what to think about the other two who'd written in the same book that had given Johnny such power. Or if there were still other characters like Englishman lurking, created by the monk Marsuvees Black before his demise.

Samuel extended a hand to Johnny. "Take care, my friend. Try not to get lost in that desert."

"I think I've been lost enough for one lifetime." He clasped Samuel's fingers and smiled.

Samuel stepped forward and hugged Johnny, who returned the hug with strong arms. "Be careful."

"I'll see you again, Samuel. I just need some time."

"You know I'll have to tell them that you went into the desert."

"I know. Keep your nose clean. I have a feeling I'll be needing your help again."

Samuel pulled back, kissed Kelly's hand, and let them go. Johnny kissed Sally. Tears brimmed in her eyes.

"I love you, Mother."

"I love you, Johnny."

Kelly and Johnny walked away, hand in hand.

"Saint."

Johnny turned back. "Saint?"

"Remember what I said about your power," Samuel said. "The giver of the gift doesn't take it back so easily."

Johnny stared at him as if unsure of what he meant. Then he smiled, turned back down the mountain, and stepped onto the path.

"Remember that, Saint."

"I will," Johnny said without turning. "I will."

SINNER

I

WORDS OF PERSUASION

The apostle who saw the Light with his own two eyes said this:

*I came to you in weakness
and fear, and with much trembling.*

*My message was not with wise
and persuasive words,
but with
power.*

First-century letter written by
Paul to those in Corinth

PROLOGUE

OUR STORY began two thousand years in the future, because the Books of History came into our world from that future.

After they arrived, the Books of History lay in obscurity for many years until a Turkish dealer unwittingly sold the dusty old tomes to David Abraham, a tenured Harvard University professor and collector of antiquities. Upon discovering that the books contained the power to animate the choices of men by turning the written words of innocent children into living, breathing flesh, he swore to preserve the books in a manner consistent with their nature.

Deep in a monastery hidden from all men near a Colorado mountain town called Paradise, Father Abraham and twelve monks vowed their lives to raise thirty-seven orphans, lovingly nurturing them and teaching them all things virtuous. One day these children would use the books for the good of all mankind.

And so was born Project Showdown.

But Billy, the brightest of the students, was lured into the dungeons below the monastery, where he found the Books of History. And there, surrounded by intoxicating power, the thirteen-year-old boy wrote into existence an embodiment of his deepest fears and fantasies. And he called his creation Marsuvees Black.

Fueled by the power of evil spun from Billy's own heart, Marsuvees Black became flesh and entered the small mountain town called Paradise. There, with Marsuvees Black, Billy wreaked terrible havoc and Paradise fell.

The correction of Billy's transgression came at a terrible price, but before everything could be set right again, Marsuvees Black escaped with a book, which he used to spawn more manifestations of evil like himself.

Since that day many years ago, Black's creations have lived among us in fleshly form, determined to learn how to make all men evil as Billy was evil.

But good also came out of Paradise when it fell. Three children used the Books of History to write a great power into themselves. Their names were Johnny, Billy, and Darcy.

For twelve years, thankful only that they had survived the failed project, they forgot about what they had written in the books. But then, unknown to Billy or Darcy, the power revealed itself to Johnny, the Saint, in stunning fashion.

Now Johnny waits in the desert for his time to come, because he knows that Marsuvees Black has not been sleeping. Because he knows that the time is near.

In fact, that time has come.

CHAPTER ZERO

MARSUVEES BLACK reread the words penned on the yellow sheet of paper, intrigued by the knowledge they contained. He felt exposed, almost naked against this sheet of pulp that had come his way.

August 21, 2033

Dear Johnny,

If you're reading this letter, then my attempt to help you has failed and I've gone to meet my Maker. You are likely in hiding, so I can only hope that this letter finds you. Either way, I feel compelled to explain so that you might know my own convictions in the matter that faces us. I will be brief.

None of what's happened to you has been by accident, Johnny. I've always known this, but never with as much clarity as now, after being approached by a woman named Karas, who spoke of the Books of History with more understanding than I can express here. Not even my son, Samuel, knows what I now believe to be the whole truth.

Where to start . . . ?

The world is rushing to the brink of an abyss destined to swallow it whole. Conflict among the United States, Israel, and Iran is escalating at a frightening pace. Europe's repressing our economy. Famine is overrunning Russia, China's rattling its sabers, South America is battling the clobbering disease—all terrible issues, and I could go on.

But these challenges pale in comparison to the damage that pervasive agnosticism will cause us. The disparaging of ultimate truth is a disease worse by far than the Raison Strain.

Listen to me carefully, Johnny. I now believe that all of this was foreseen. That the Books of History came into our world for this day.

As you know, the world changed thirteen years ago when Project Showdown was shut down. I, and a dozen trusted priests, sequestered thirty-six orphans in the monastery in an attempt to raise children who were pure in heart, worthy of the ancient books hidden in the dungeons beneath the monastery. The Books of History, which came to us from another reality, contained the power to make words flesh. Whatever was written on their blank pages became real. If the world only knew what was happening!

Billy used the books to write raw evil into existence in the form of Marsuvees Black, a living, breathing man who now walks this earth, personifying Lucifer himself. He (and I cringe at calling Black anything so humane as a "he") was defeated once, but he hasn't rested since that day. There are others like him, you know that by now. At least four, maybe many more, written by Black himself from several pages he managed to escape with. I believe he's used up the pages, but he's set into motion something that he believes will undo his defeat. Something far more ominous than killers who come to steal and destroy in the dead of night. An insidious evil that walks by day, shaking our hands and offering a comforting smile before ripping our hearts out.

Billy may have repented, but his childish indiscretions will plague the world yet, as much as Adam's indiscretion has plagued the world since the Fall.

Yet all of this was foreseen! In fact, I am convinced that all of these events may have been allowed as part of a larger plan. The Books of History may have spawned raw evil in the form of Black, but those same books also exposed truth. And with that truth, your gifting. Your power!

And Billy's power. And Darcy's power. (Though they may not know of it yet.)

Do you hear me, son? The West teeters on the brink of disbelief and at the same time is infested with the very object of their disbelief. With incarnate evil! Black and the other walking dead.

But there are three who stand in his way. Johnny, Billy, Darcy.

Black is determined to obtain all the books. If he does, God help us all. Even if he fails, he escaped Paradise with a few pages and has wreaked enough havoc to plunge the world into darkness. I am convinced that only the three of you can stop him.

Find Billy. Find Darcy. Stop Black.

And pray, Johnny. Pray for your own soul. Pray for the soul of our world.

David Abraham

Marsuvees frowned. *Yes, pray, Johnny. Pray for your pathetic, wretched soul.*

He crushed the letter in his gloved hand, shoved it into the bucket of gasoline by his side, and ignited the thing with a lighter he'd withdrawn from his pocket after the first reading. Flames whooshed high, enveloping his hand along with the paper.

He could have lit the fire another way, of course, but he'd learned a number of things from his experimentation in the last decade or so. How to blend in. Be human. Humans didn't start fires by snapping their fingers.

He'd learned that subtlety could be a far more effective weapon than some of the more blatant methods they'd tried.

Black dropped the flaming page to the earth and flicked his wrist to extinguish the flame roaring about his hand. He ground the smoldering ash into the dirt with a black, silver-tipped boot and inhaled long through his nostrils.

So, the old man had known a thing or two before dying, enough to unnerve a less informed man than Black. He already knew Johnny and company were the only living souls who stood a chance of slowing him down.

But he was taking care of that. Had taken care of that.

Marsuvees spit into the black ash at his feet. Johnny's receipt of this letter would have changed nothing. It was too late for change now.

And in the end there was faith, hope, and love.

No. In the end there was Johnny, Billy, and Darcy. And the greatest of these was . . .

. . . as clueless as a brick.

CHAPTER ONE

Day One

WEDNESDAY, DAY six of a seven-day jury trial in Atlantic City, New Jersey, May 13, 2034. A thick blanket of smog hung over the city, locking in early summer's heat—ninety-five degrees at 10:05 a.m. and on its way to the forecasted one hundred and five mark, thanks to thirty years of rising global temperatures.

Billy hooked his finger over the tie knot at his collar and tugged it loose, thinking the halls of the courthouse felt like a sauna. What now? City Hall was shutting down its air-conditioning system to appease its guilt over mismanaging energy costs for the last ten years? The casinos suffered no such guilt. The air conditioners in the New Yorker would be blasting cool air, comforting those willing to make donations at its slot machines.

Billy shifted his eyes from the stares of two well-dressed attorneys passing by and headed for the large double doors that opened to Courtroom 1. His stomach turned and he had to force himself to stride on, chin held level. But there was no hiding his disheveled hair, the wrinkles in his white shirt, the hint of red in his eyes from lack of sleep. The three twelve-ounce cans of Rockstar he'd slammed for breakfast a half hour ago were just now kicking in.

He'd won his share of poker hands in the past five years—had a real streak going there last year. But at the moment he was sinking. Free-falling. Screaming in like a kamikaze pilot. Ground zero was in that courtroom and it was coming up fast. It would all end today.

The district attorney's murder case against Anthony Sacks was open and shut. Billy Rediger knew as much because he'd spent six days defending the scumbag with nothing but fast talk and pseudolitigation just to keep the jury from convicting by default.

During pretrial discovery, Billy had seen that any concrete defense was out of the question. The prosecution had an extensive amount of evidence, had subpoenaed numerous character witnesses, and retained a pair of expert witnesses to elaborate on the physical evidence. By the end of exhibition, the jury was laughing up its collective sleeve at Sacks's plea of not guilty. By the time the third witness took the stand, the jury had lost all presumption of innocence, and that was two days ago.

If left to themselves at this point, the jurors would reach a conviction in less time than it took them to reach the deliberation room. All that remained now was cross-examination and closing arguments.

Billy knew more than the court, but not much. And the jury was catching up to the facts:

Sacks was a known midlevel boss in Atlantic City's organized crime world, headed by Ricardo Muness.

Sacks ran the lower-side gambling rackets and had a long history of enforcing loans with extreme prejudice. The kind that left debtors either dead in a landfill or shopping for prosthetic limbs.

Sacks had allegedly murdered a local imam, Mohammed Ilah, for interfering with the gambling trade by speaking out against it to the Muslim community and threatening to expose Sacks personally.

The most relevant fact? Criminal defense attorney Billy Rediger, who owed just over $300,000 to Sacks, had been coerced into his defense by Ricardo Muness, the most notorious crime personality from the boardwalks to the turnpike.

It all made perfect sense to the crime boss. Sacks had loaned Billy far more than Billy could repay. Now both were in the toilet.

Solution: Billy would defend Sacks in his upcoming murder trial. If Billy got Sacks off, he would be absolved of his debt. If not, he would be relieved of his arms.

Sacks had complained bitterly. Billy might be a clever defense attorney, but at twenty-six he was only three years out of law school and already washed up, hamstrung by his addiction to gambling.

Now Sacks's life was in the hands of the man he'd unwisely extended credit to. Poetic justice, Muness had said, boots propped up on his large maple desk, grinning plastic.

A chiseled relief over the courtroom door said it all: *Permissum Justicia Exsisto Servo*, Let Justice Be Served.

Billy took a deep breath, shifted his briefcase from one sweaty palm to the other, nodded at the security guard who was watching him with one eyebrow cocked, and pushed the heavy oak door inward.

A hush fell over the packed room; every head turned, every eye focused. He was a few minutes late to his own funeral; wasn't a man allowed that much? By their reaction, *he* might as well have been on trial.

You are, Billy. You are.

The Honorable Mary Brighton was already seated behind the bench, gavel in hand, as if she *had* just, or *was* just about to issue a ruling. The prosecutor, a thin man with a long nose and sharp cheekbones, stood on the right looking smug, if looking smug was possible for a face fashioned from an ax.

"Forgive me, Your Honor." Billy dipped his head and walked briskly forward. The gallery seated one hundred, and every seat was filled. Media, well-wishers from both sides, and entertainment seekers who followed this sort of thing for a living.

"You are late, Counselor," the judge snapped. "Again."

"I am, and I regret it deeply. From the bottom of my soul. Unavoidable, I'm afraid. I called your office. Did you get my message? I was, shall we say, held up. It won't happen again."

She eyed him with the same gleam that had lit her eyes over the last six days. The Honorable Mary Brighton was known as a hard judge, but Billy thought she might have a soft spot for him. At the very least she found his methods interesting. Not that any of that mattered in this case.

"No, it won't," she said. "I expect we'll wrap up arguments today."

"Yes. I understand, Your Honor." He slipped behind the defendant's table on the left and dipped his head once more.

"This is the last of my leniency with your tardiness, Counselor. I will find you in contempt if it happens again, and I suggest you take me seriously."

"Of course. My sincere apologies, Your Honor."

Anthony Sacks sat to his left, sweating like a pig, true to form. The Greek weighed a good three hundred pounds at six feet tall and was dressed in a black pinstripe suit that failed to hide any of his bulk. He glared past bushy black brows.

"You're late!" he whispered.

"I know." Billy opened the latches to his briefcase, withdrew the Sacks file, a legal pad and pen, then eased into his seat.

"This is ridiculous!"

"I concur," Billy whispered.

"Don't screw this up."

"No, Tony, I won't screw this up."

But Billy wasn't sure he wouldn't screw *this* up. Muness had tossed them a last-minute witness . . . last night. A man who was deposed to testify in court that the victim, Imam Mohammed Ilah, had been murdered by an extremist from his own mosque. Despite the court's rigid adherence to the rules of discovery, Her Honor could allow the defense to produce the witness on the grounds that the witness was inherently material to the case, the testimony was to be given in court rather than in deposition, and the witness had volunteered to undergo vigorous cross-examination. A lucky break. A defense attorney's gift, all things considered.

But the man would be a liar. Had to be a plant. Muness couldn't produce an honest witness any more than he could join the Mormon Tabernacle Choir. His testimony would be perjury, and Billy knew it as well as he knew he still had two arms. Producing a fraudulent witness would get Billy disbarred, and he would do time for subornation of perjury. A legal term from prelaw filtered into the front of his mind: *the miscarriage of justice . . .*

And here it was, right in front of him. The miscarriage of justice.

The judge cleared her throat. "Would you like your breakfast served first, Counselor? Or are you ready to call your next witness?"

Billy stood. "Yes. No, no breakfast, Your Honor. Defense calls Musa bin Salman."

The DA was on his feet. "Objection, Your Honor. The prosecution doesn't have a Musa bin Salman listed. The defense cannot produce a witness without our knowledge unless . . ." The prosecutor, Dean Coulter, looked genuinely surprised, but trailed off. An associate attorney from his team was rifling through some papers.

"Counsel, approach the bench. *Now.*"

Billy got there first. "I sent it over last night, Your Honor. The witness is material to the case, is willing to testify before the court—"

"Please tell me you're not just posturing, Counselor," the judge said. "I am not going to take another deposition, and if you're stalling for time . . ."

"Of course he is," Coulter whispered. "Your Honor—nobody calls a material witness in the eleventh hour. We have subpoenaed every possible witness of every kind, and he just *now* finds a shake-and-bake testimony?"

"No, Your Honor. I can promise a court testimony without deposition. I believe Mr. Bin Salman is materially relevant to this trial. The prosecution is perfectly free to cross-examine him." He looked sideways at the DA, swallowed, then continued. "Discovery shouldn't preclude a material witness."

The judge nodded. "I'll allow the witness."

"His testimony will be inadmissible," the DA said. "This is unprecedented."

"Take your seats, Counsel. Both of you. Now."

Billy held his head level out, but his heart fell into his stomach. He took his seat next to Sacks and pretended to scribble some notes. He had gone out on a limb with his law license in hand, and he would most likely cnd the week with neither limb nor hand.

Miscarriage of justice was an understatement.

The door opened and the bailiff escorted a gray-suited man with a beard and slicked black hair to the stand.

"Please state your name for the record." He did. Musa put his hand on a copy of the United States Constitution. "Do you swear to tell the truth, the whole truth, and nothing but the truth?"

"I do."

"Please be seated."

"Your witness," Her Honor said.

Billy strolled to the podium and sized up the man on the stand for the first time. Clean-cut. Intelligent looking. A kind face, if a bit sharp. One of the millions of foreigners who'd taken up residence in this country and saved it from bankruptcy when the government's trade policies had softened a dozen years ago.

The country's socioreligious complexion had steadily changed since. So-called religious tolerance had made by far the largest gains in the West; the number of Muslims had grown to match the number of Christians. None of this mattered to Billy, but it might make for some fireworks during cross-examination, if the DA would take any bait.

"Thank you for joining us, Mr. Bin Salman. Can you tell the court what you do for a living?"

"I'm a student at the new Center for Islamic Studies."

"I see. So you are a religious man?"

"Yes."

Amazing how those words brought a deeper silence to the courtroom. Everyone was aware of religious people, saw them all the time, talked to them at work, watched sporting events with them. But for one to actually discuss a religious affiliation was frowned upon in the name of tolerance. The new cultural taboo.

"And what is your religion?"

"Islam. I am a Muslim."

The DA stood. "Objection. I don't see what a man's personal faith has to do with his testimony."

"Understood." Judge Brighton turned. "Exactly what is your point, Counselor?"

"Defense wishes to establish the relevance of the witness to alternate motives for murdering an Islamic cleric, Your Honor," Billy said. He didn't wait for her to overrule the objection and got back into question ing. Momentum was often the most critical element of persuasive litigation. He turned to the witness. "Have you ever met my client, Anthony Sacks, before today?"

"No."

"What about the victim, Imam Mohammed Ilah?" Billy hefted an enlarged photograph of the victim.

"Yes. I knew him."

"When did you meet him?"

"I met with him frequently, both as a student and at the mosque. We knew each other by name."

Billy knew where all of this was headed, of course. It made him cringe, but he pushed on, shoving aside his own objections. He shoved a hand into his pocket and slowly crossed to the jury box, eyeing each member in turn.

"How would you describe your relationship with the imam?"

"We were friends."

Alice Springs, third juror from the left, second row, doubted the witness. Billy had a knack for reading people, whether in a poker game or in a courtroom.

Billy kept his eyes on Alice. "So there was no . . . disparity between your beliefs and his teaching?"

"No."

"You both believed in tolerance?"

"Yes."

A breath from Alice signaled her acceptance of this fact, at least for the moment.

Billy put his other hand into his front pocket and faced the witness. "Musa bin Salman, do you find my client distasteful?"

Silence.

"Just be truthful. That's why we're here, to get to the truth. Do you find Anthony Sacks as disgusting a human being as I do?"

"Objection, leading the witness . . ."

Billy held up a hand. "Quite right, let me be more clear. Ignoring the fact that I think my client is a piece of human waste and should probably fry for a thousand offenses, none of which I am privy to, what is your opinion of him?"

"Your Honor, I must protest this line of argument. The witness just stated that he's never met the defendant."

"Clarification of motive, Your Honor," Billy said.

"Answer the question."

Musa looked at Sacks. "I've heard that he's a distasteful man."

"So you have no motivation to try to protect him?"

"As I said, he is a distasteful man."

"Just answer the question," Billy pushed. "Do you have any reason to protect the defendant, Anthony Sacks?"

"No."

"Good." He strolled in front of the jury, watching their eyes. Truth was always in the eyes. Not windows to the souls. Windows to a person's thoughts. At the moment, most of them were a bit lost. That would change now.

"And do you believe that Anthony Sacks murdered Mohammed Ilah as the state has accused?"

"No."

"No? You're a religious man who finds the accused distasteful, and you're presumably outraged by the murder of your friend, the imam. Yet you wouldn't want the murder pinned on this monstrous—my defendant? Why?"

"Because he didn't kill the imam."

The courtroom stilled.

"You're sure about this?"

"Yes."

"Can you tell the court why you are so sure?"

"Because I know who did kill Imam Mohammed Ilah."

The room erupted in protests and gasps, all quickly brought to an end by the judge's gavel.

"Order! Counselor, I hope you know how thin the ice beneath your feet is. I will not hear tertiary allegations—"

"He has material knowledge, Your Honor," Billy said.

"The first hint that this is a red herring and I'll have you thrown from my courtroom."

"I understand."

"Continue."

Billy pulled his hands from his pockets and walked back to the podium. He looked into the man's brown eyes. "Will you please tell the court how you came into this knowledge."

You're going to lose your arms.

The man hadn't said it, of course. Billy was thinking this himself, because although he had within his grasp the tools to free his client and save his arms, he wasn't sure he could wield those tools, knowing what he did.

Knowing that the witness was lying through his teeth, even now.

". . . the extremists last Thursday night. Seven of them."

"And what did they say?"

"That tolerance was the greatest evil in the West. That any Muslim who was afraid to stand up for the truth and convert the West was no Muslim at all, but a pretender who is worthy of death."

"Go on."

That Muness has won this case, not you. Therefore he will expect payment in full from you.

"That the imam Mohammed Ilah, in his stand for tolerance toward

Christianity and others' disbelief in God, is a stench in God's nostrils. For this reason they killed him."

Billy heard it all like a distant recording, exactly what he'd expected. And there was more to come, enough to cast doubt in any reasonable juror's mind.

But his mind was on none of it. His mind was distracted by what he was seeing in the witness's brown eyes. On what they'd said to him.

Muness has won this case, not you. Therefore he will expect payment in full from you.

Intuition was one thing, but this . . .

He stared at Salman, unable to take his eyes off the man's face. There was more there. Whispering to him. *Both arms. The punishment for stealing.*

"Counselor?"

Billy snapped out of his lapse. "Sorry." He stepped from behind the podium and regarded the judge. "I have no intention of bringing evidence that will incriminate another party, Your Honor . . ."

A thin hum erupted at the base of his skull, like a miniature buzz saw or a tiny Cox engine firing away at a million revolutions per minute. *Buzzzzzzzzzzzzzzzz.*

The faint sound spread up through his head, tingling his ears as it passed. He could feel it on his skin, inside his skin, in his brain, in his eyes. Like a thousand gnats had been let in and were exploring their new home.

His eyes stared into the judge's. *Look at you, boy. Such a bright mind being wasted.*

". . . ummm . . ." he said. Had he just heard her say that? "But I do need to finish up . . ."

Billy had lost his train of thought. He wasn't sure what he was trying to say, so he just stopped.

"This whole line of questioning is outrageous!" the DA was protesting. "I object. Vigorously."

"Noted. Let's move on. Counselor?"

But Billy was staring at the witness and hearing that voice in the back of his mind again. *Just ask it, you fool. I will say it all as agreed.*

The hum in his mind faded to a distant distraction.

Ask, ask, ask!

It occurred to Billy then, staring in Musa bin Salman's eyes, that he really was picking up the man's thoughts. Hearing them, so to speak. And as stunning as this revelation was, another one was as disturbing. Namely, what the voice behind those eyes was telling him.

He was going to lose both arms. Even if he did get the Sacks of garbage off the hook. In fact, as *soon* as he got the Sacks of garbage off.

"No more questions," he said, turning, legs numb. "Your witness."

The courtroom seemed to stop breathing. He'd led them up to the edge of an acquittal and then stepped back.

A point that wasn't lost on Anthony Sacks. "What?"

Billy glanced at the man. A string of profanity flooded his mind. The contents of Tony's mind. Billy's fingertips tingled. His lungs were working harder than they should to keep his blood supplied with oxygen. The room was feeling like a sauna again.

He hurried to his table, reached for the bottle of water, and sat hard. Then he was drinking and the prosecutor was crossing to the witness, and Billy was sure that they were all staring at him.

He had just lost his mind.

CHAPTER TWO

Wednesday

THE DAY the world changed for Darcy Lange of Lewiston, Pennsylvania, was like any other day at the Hyundai assembly plant except for one bothersome detail. Today she would suffer through yet one more annual review, her seventh to be exact, return to her workstation overlooking twenty of the assembly robots, and go home a dollar or so an hour richer than when she started the day.

Honestly, she couldn't care less about the annual raise and would have gladly forgone the money if doing so meant she didn't have to endure the tedious review.

Nevertheless, here she sat, facing the slob who spilled out of his white shirt and the flat-chested rail who peered at Darcy over pencil-thin spectacles. Robert Hamblin and Ethil Ridge. Her managers, although they did nothing of the sort. She had run her station perfectly fine for the last five years without so much as a weekly nod from these two or the four sets of managers who'd preceded them.

Darcy liked it that way.

"So, you've done well," Robert said. His dark hair was shaved on either side of his head, a military cut that hardened his square face. Darcy could never quite get used to the way his upper lip came to a slight point at the center, under a sharp nose. She caught herself wondering if the vertical trough that ran between his pointed lip and his nose wasn't there by evolution's design. A facial drain for mucus were it to leak from either nostril.

"You've done your tasks as ordered," Ethil said.

Well said, Pinocchio.

Robert frowned and set the ream of production reports on the desk. He clasped his hands together, elbows bridging the papers.

"The company is changing, Ms. Lange. Progress eventually catches up to all of us. Unfortunately, today it's caught up to you as well."

They both held her in their stares, expecting a response. So she gave them one. "And?"

"And . . . we've decided that your lack of forward progression is an indication of a poor attitude. A tendency toward reclusiveness that demonstrates passivity to coworkers."

Darcy knew what he was trying to say, but the slight wag of his head as he leveled each word was enough to drive a needle into her skull. She had to clench her jaw to keep from objecting.

"Meaning?"

"Meaning," said Ethil, "that the company's needs have changed. We no longer merely need proficient workers in positions such as yours. We need employees who are both proficient and exude an enthusiasm for the workplace."

Robert took the ball. "Research tells Hyundai that the degree of enthusiasm in the workplace directly influences proficiency and turnover."

"Enthusiasm," Darcy repeated.

"Enthusiasm," Ethil said.

"You're saying you want me to punch the start button with more gusto, then," Darcy said. "Maybe use my whole fist instead of one measly finger, for example."

Robert's bottom lip twitched.

"You want me to lean forward while I watch the robots. It's not enough to make sure every weld looks right. I must make sure with a banana grin plastered on my face, is that it? Okay, sure, I get it. I'll do that. Is that all?"

"Actually, no. This is exactly the kind of misplaced enthusiasm we're talking about."

"So now you're saying I *do* have enthusiasm, but not about the right things? Things like the green buttons on high-efficiency automated assembly machines?"

"Please, Darcy. You're not making this easy."

"I wasn't aware I was supposed to make this easy for you."

"I think he meant easy for you," Ethil said. "Your hostility proves your lack of enthusiasm. Wouldn't you at least agree to that?"

Darcy sat back and crossed her legs. She wore jeans and a light sweater, as she often did. The plant was an icebox, comfortable for most maybe, but freezing for those without layers of fat to keep them warm. At the moment, however, she was sweating.

She crossed her arms, decided that her posture might come off as hostile, and set her hands on her lap. She couldn't deny that they had her pegged. Everyone knew that Darcy would just as soon be left alone to her task, keeping a watchful eye on the robotic arms as they flipped and turned and welded the automobiles on the assembly line. She'd take music or an audiobook over another person in her glass booth any day.

"I'm comfortable with myself," she said.

"Well, that's not good enough anymore," Ethil said. "You're not the nineteen-year-old girl we hired to work on the line seven years ago. You sit above the floor for the whole floor to see. We need leaders to lead by example. I'm afraid we need a change."

It wasn't until Ethil smugly uttered the last word that Darcy believed they were actually setting her up to be fired. The realization froze her solid.

She'd never even been reprimanded. Never a day late. Only three operating errors at her station in five years. She had the best record on a high-efficiency automated assembly machine in the company.

And they were going to dismiss her?

A buzz burst from the base of her neck and swarmed her mind. For a brief moment she wondered if she was suffering a stroke or something. But then she wrote off the swelling hum in her head to a panic attack. It had been awhile, but she'd had a few since her release from the monastery when she was thirteen.

"I can lead by example," she snapped. "Why sit? I'll stand up in my glass booth, pounding buttons like a drummer in a marching band. Is that what you need? Anything for the company."

"What did I tell you? Hopeless," Ethil muttered, turning away.

"No, Darcy, I'm afraid that won't do. We're going to replace you at the controls. This isn't a demotion per se. You'll still get the same wage, but we think you'd fit in better on the line among the others."

The buzz in her head grew angry. The very idea of being put back on the line was enough to send her packing immediately. She'd fought hard for the relative isolation provided by the control booth, for good reason.

"You might as well fire me," Darcy snapped, staring directly into the man's eyes.

Robert blinked. Sat back, eyes narrowed. He exchanged a glance with Ethil.

"No, no, that's not what this is about," Ethil said. "Don't think for a moment that you'll be able to run off to an attorney and file a claim for unlawful termination."

"Actually . . ." Robert looked slightly confused. "She might have a point."

Darcy felt her self-control slipping. "This is ridiculous!" she cried, leaning forward. "You have no right to demote me, and don't think that's not exactly what this is. I don't care what you say!"

She pointed at the wall to her right without removing her eyes from them. "Nobody is better suited for the control booth than I am! *Nobody!*

I like it, it likes me. We do a near perfect job together. You're idiots to think anyone would do better just because they walk around grinning like a monkey!"

Robert's jaw parted slightly. He looked like she'd slapped him in the face. Ethil stared, eyes round. Neither looked like they could quite believe she'd been so frank.

"I dare you." Darcy stood, trembling. "Tell me here and now that you have someone who could do a better job."

Neither spoke.

"You can't! Because you don't, isn't that right?"

"That's right," Robert said.

"You bet your fat—"

Darcy stopped. He'd agreed? She continued with slightly less force.

"—wallet that's right."

"Yes, you are right about that," Ethil said.

"You would be *crazy* to fire me."

"We would," Robert said. "And we didn't say we were going to fire you. In fact, we specifically said we *weren't* going to fire you."

"Or demote me. It's the same thing."

Ethil shook her head. "You're not listening to us. We aren't demoting you, we specifically—"

"I know you said that, but I'm telling you it's the same to me. You can't put me back on the line!" She walked to her right and spun back. "The line and I aren't friends. Do you hear me? You can't do that to me."

Robert looked at Ethil. For a moment Darcy thought he was actually reconsidering. But it wasn't Robert who changed the tone.

"She's right," Ethil said, walking behind Robert, eyes shifting to Darcy. "We can't put her on the line. It would be tantamount to firing her. The lawyers would have a field day."

A barely perceptible nod from Robert. "They would."

She had no intention of hiring a lawyer, but if the threat helped her position, let them tremble in their boots.

"I can't believe you actually threatened to do this to me," she snapped. "If you had any sense at all, you'd be offering me a raise rather than tearing down your most productive operator. Excellence needs to be rewarded, not chastised."

"She does have a point," Robert said. "And we were considering that."

"We were." Ethil took her seat, folded one leg over the other, and looked into Darcy's eyes. "How much?"

"Excuse me?"

"How much of a raise do you think you deserve?"

Darcy felt her blood rush through her face with renewed anger. They were mocking her. Maybe an attorney wouldn't be such a bad idea after all.

"You guys don't know how to quit, do you?" she snapped. "I'm worth twice what you pay me!"

"Double?" Robert said. "That's a lot of money for an automated assembly machine operator."

"And that's another thing. Titles don't mean squat. Call me whatever you want, but don't try to cover up an unlawful termination by throwing around titles. Let me do the job I do well and leave it at that."

The room went quiet. Both of them looked at her as if she'd lost her mind.

"A new title," Robert said. "Makes sense."

"She's earned it, after all."

"Assembly machines supervisor. Joseph mentioned the idea once."

Ethil frowned. "I think it could work."

"And we passed her by at the five-year mark. She's due."

They fell silent.

Darcy wasn't sure what was happening or why, but it occurred to her that they weren't mocking her as she'd assumed. They had actually seen some sense in her comments.

"You're serious?"

Ethil forced a grin. "Should we be?"

"Yes. Of course you should be."

The grin softened. "There you are, then."

"Congratulations," Robert said. "We've just doubled your salary and given you a new title. Assembly machines supervisor."

CHAPTER THREE

BILLY REDIGER knew a few things with particular clarity as he sat and focused on the papers spread across the defendant's table.

He'd just committed an unpardonable sin by walking away from a defense that undoubtedly would have improved his client's fate.

He'd done so because he'd also come into certain and disturbing information about his own fate, namely that he was about to lose both arms for failing to come through on his own, with or without this witness, whom Muness so conveniently dropped in his lap at the last moment.

And he'd come into such disturbing information by . . .

This was where everything became a bit trickier. Unnerving. Troubling on its own face, wholly apart from the prospect of amputation.

He'd gained it by hearing, as clear as day, the thoughts of Musa bin Salman, who seemed to have no doubts as to the accuracy of said information.

Furthermore, Billy had heard the judge's thoughts. *Such a bright mind being wasted.*

The prosecutor had risen and was subjecting the witness to a brutal cross-examination that all but associated the man with maggots worming though week-old garbage. But Billy wasn't listening.

He was busy avoiding his client's glare. And plotting his next move, which would directly involve said client.

Tony's hot breath filled his ear. "You get your useless butt back up there and ask what you were told to ask. I go down for this and you'll spend the rest of your life in a wheelchair. You hear me?"

Billy looked in the man's eyes and heard it all, again, this time with more detail than he needed. A flood of thoughts rushed him, some abstract, some very clear. Like the one involving chainsaws and machetes and his legs.

"I do." He shifted his sight from the man and the thoughts were silenced.

The sounds of the courtroom faded completely, this time because Billy's consciousness was thoroughly focused on the phenomenon afflicting him.

So it was real? He was actually hearing the thoughts of whomever he made eye contact with? An image of the monastery he'd grown up in flashed through his mind. Was it possible?

Marsuvees Black.

Sweat seeped from his pores. He shut the name out of his thoughts and opened his eyes.

"So what you're telling us," the prosecutor was saying, "is that you didn't actually see any of this with your own eyes."

"No, but—"

"That however compelled you were by what you *think* you heard, all you really know is hearsay. Isn't that right? Sir?"

The prosecutor was leading the witness while arguing his case. There were several clear objections Billy could have voiced and had upheld by the judge, but a new thought was drowning out the usefulness of continuing with Musa bin Salman.

"No. That is not what I said."

"Thank you, no further questions."

Dean Coulter took a seat, picked up a pen, and began tapping his notepad, eyes dead ahead. He'd stemmed the tide for the moment, but Billy could blow it all open easily enough with a redirect.

The judge looked at Billy. *I don't know what trick you think you're pulling, but honestly, I can't wait to hear this one.*

"Counselor?" she said

Billy remained seated. "No further questions."

Anthony Sacks clambered to his feet. "I object!"

"Sit down!" the judge snapped.

The defendant glared from the judge to Billy, then slowly sat.

"One more outburst like that and I'll have you removed. There's a reason why we have order in a court, Mr. Sacks. Your counsel speaks for your defense. Unless you have an entire legal firm in your back pocket, don't sabotage your own case."

The man muttered a curse under his breath.

"The witness is excused."

Musa stood, having been refused his chance to spill the lies he was either being forced or paid to tell. Billy wondered how long the man had to live. Muness would be fuming already.

"Any more witnesses?"

Billy leaned over to Sacks. "You go along with me here or you spend the rest of your natural life in prison. *Capisce?*"

Without waiting for a response, he stood and stepped behind the podium, knowing that what he was about to do would change his life forever. But as he saw it, he had no good alternatives.

He pushed his sweating hands into his pockets. "Your Honor, I would like to call the defendant, Anthony Sacks, to the stand to testify on his own behalf."

The barely audible gasp behind him betrayed his client's surprise. Billy turned, drilled him with a stare, and winked.

All he got from the man was a mental flood of obscenities, so he cut it off by glancing at the jury. Their thoughts came to him quickly and with amazing clarity as he scanned their eyes.

He's trying to sabotage his own client?

What if the towel-head was on to something?

Flat out guilty, doesn't matter what anybody says at this point.

I'm going to ask Nancy for her hand in marriage and she's going to agree. Just because her friends have put the fear of God in her doesn't mean she's stopped loving me.

Reddish-brown hair, green eyes, the cutest face . . . Gasp, he's looking at me! Man, he's sexy.

That last thought from Candice, juror number nine, a forty-nine-year-old banker who'd gone out of her way to tell him that she tended bar at the New Yorker on weekends for extra money.

"I'll allow the witness," Judge Brighton said. "Mr. Sacks, you have been called. Please take the stand."

Sacks did, trying his best to put on a good face, but it was red and hid none of his agitation. He stated his name and was sworn in.

"Proceed."

Billy lifted his eyes to the jury and fired off his first question to Sacks. "Anthony Sacks, I want you to state clearly for the court your true beliefs in this case. Are you guilty of murder as charged, or are you innocent?"

A quick look at the man settled the matter for Billy. *I cut the rat's throat, and you know that, you fool.*

"Innocent. Totally, completely innocent."

But Billy was more interested in the jury's reaction.

Guilty.

Guilty.

This guy was born guilty.

Only three had any doubts at all, that Billy could tell. So, as of now he had only one objective. He left the podium and casually approached the witness stand, hands still in his pockets.

"Innocent," he said, careful to prevent his eyes from making contact with anyone for the moment. "Mr. Sacks, do you consider yourself an upstanding citizen?"

"Yes."

But the man was fuming inside, spewing filth.

"A family man?"

"Of course."

"Of course," Billy repeated. "Do you find this charge of murder offensive?"

"Deeply."

"How many daughters do you have?"

"Three."

"And sons?"

Anthony hesitated. "None."

"None? Did you ever want a son?"

"Yes. My . . . we lost one at childbirth."

"I'm sorry."

Billy ran through the questions staring at the man's forehead rather than his eyes.

"What do you know, the monster's got a soft spot in his heart for the son he always wanted."

The prosecutor stood. "Objection, Your Honor. This grandstanding is a transparent attempt to illicit sympathy. It has no bearing on the facts of the case."

"I'm establishing character as allowed," Billy said, withdrawing his hands from his pockets.

The judge dipped her head. "Don't belabor character that has no relation to the charges. Insults constitute contempt, Counselor. I suggest you weigh your words. Continue."

"Thank you." To the accused, looking at the wall over the man's shoulder: "I'm going to run down a series of questions, and I want you to answer them as quickly and as frankly as you can, okay?"

"Okay."

"What is your age?"

"Forty-nine."

"What is your height?"

"Six foot."

"How much do you weigh?"

"Two hundred ten."

"Good. Are you on a diet?"

"Depends who you ask."

"I'm asking you."

"Then no. I always eat healthy."

"You never indulge?"

"Not lately, no."

Billy glanced at him. Evidently Sacks considered Double Stuf Oreo cookies healthy, because they were filling his mind at the moment.

"Waist size?"

"Forty-two."

"Shoe size?"

"Fourteen."

Another plea from the prosecution. "Please, Your Honor."

"Hurry it up, Counselor," the judge warned.

"Do you ever cheat on your wife, Anthony?"

"No."

Billy didn't bother looking.

"Cheat on your taxes?"

"No."

"Never? Not even a little bit? Fail to report that tip money you receive at the tables now and then?"

"Never."

Wrong answer, Billy thought. The man had just thrown out his credibility.

"Good." Billy looked at his client. "Tell the court how much money you reported on your return last year. Roughly."

Sacks looked at the judge.

"Answer the question."

"A hundred ninety thousand."

"And that was all the income that passed through your hands from all sources? No more cash?"

Now the numbers started to come, streaming into Billy's mind as if fired from a machine gun.

Seven million, cash, gambling only.

Twenty-nine million if you count the trades.

The gravy though, only two million five.

What the heck is he doing?

"Cash? Less cash actually. That was my total income."

"Have you ever had the opportunity to steal, Mr. Sacks?"

He stared the man down and let the answers flow.

I make my living stealing. If they only knew how much I skimmed . . .

"Sure."

"And have you ever stolen from your employer?"

Of course. Everyone steals.

Billy pushed on before the man could answer. "Let me rephrase the question. How much did you steal from your employer?"

Which time? Half a mil. What are you doing? The man's right cheek twitched.

Billy rescued him. "I realize this line of questioning seems strange. I mean, I'm your attorney, right? I have no business even bringing up the possibility that you might steal money from your employer. But I do because I know what you know, Mr. Sacks. That you wouldn't dare steal from your employer. Isn't that right?"

"Objection, leading the witness."

None of what Billy was saying could mean anything, and that was part of the point. He had to get Sacks off his center quickly, before the judge stepped in.

Billy held up his hand to accept the objection. "My point is, Mr. Sacks is a family man who has his daughters' well-being on his mind. Even if he did steal a dime here or a dime there, he wouldn't dare confess it here, in court, any more than he would tell us where he put that dime. Or if he still had that dime." He paused. "Or how to get to that dime. The account numbers . . ." Another pause. "The PIN numbers . . ."

Billy let the numbers flow into his mind.

". . . all of it buried in his mind. It'll go with him to his grave."

"Counselor! " Now the judge was beyond herself. "Approach the bench."

"I'm coming in for a landing, Your Honor. I promise, I have a point. Please don't stop this midstream."

Billy took the courtroom's absolute silence as an invitation to proceed, and he did so quickly, spinning to the jury.

"My point is this: every one of you on the jury has stolen at some point in your lives. Cheated your employer, misreported to the IRS, lied to your husband—"

"Objection! The jury is not on trial here. Your Honor?" the DA squealed, face red.

Billy continued. The jurists looked at him, and he threw their answers back at them without using names.

"A hundred dollars from the teacher's lunch fund, fifty thousand in charity donations you never made, your secretary, Barbara, Pete, Joe, Susan. Those tips are income, all twenty thousand of them. Those SAT scores that got you into Harvard . . ."

Their eyes widened ever so slightly as he named their sins.

"If you've done that and yet refuse to confess, can you really blame my client for doing the same as you?"

"Counselor, this is *enough!*" The judge slammed her gavel down.

Time for an exit. His argument was convoluted. Butchered. Meaningless. But he didn't care. Nothing mattered except for the numbers that already ran circles in his head.

Anthony Sacks's numbers were his only means of salvation now.

Billy raised his voice and made his final impassioned plea. "Just because a man is a liar and a cheat doesn't mean he's a murderer. You may not like

Anthony Sacks any more than I do, but don't hold his lying against him—you're as guilty as he."

He faced the courtroom and spread his hands. "We all are. No more questions."

CHAPTER FOUR

THERE WAS a God after all, Darcy thought, pouring boiling water over a mint tea bag. Then she immediately pushed the thought from her mind.

At the very least it was a good day to be alive. She dropped in two cubes of sugar, stirred the tea with a teaspoon, and stepped lightly across the tile floor toward the living room, warming her hands with the steaming porcelain cup.

Eight p.m. She could either watch the latest episode of *The Thirty*, which she recorded weekly, or settle for a bit of Net surfing before curling up in bed with the latest Frakes novel, *Birthright*, which had to be the best of the vampire series so far.

Thinking of the book, she stopped halfway to the love seat in the middle of her living room. Maybe she should just skip the Net and head to bed. Nothing was worse than reading too late and falling asleep two or three pages into a novel. It had taken her a month to read a novel in fits and starts last year—some vampire-romance book that wasn't very interesting, but that was beside the point. She vowed never to read in such short spurts again.

No, she would surf first and see if anyone had left her any messages while she was at it. She eased into the large leather seat and tapped the built-in controller on the right arm. A five-foot screen on the wall brightened.

Loading . . .

Her mind tripped back to the review at the plant. She still wasn't entirely sure what had happened. The world was running scared from lawsuits, and her employers had seen her aggressive reaction as a sure sign of her intent.

Had they really doubled her salary? Or had she misunderstood that part? Either way, she hardly cared as long as they left her alone, which they were. For now.

She had a near perfect job.

She had her sweet mint tea.

She had the Net.

It was indeed good to be alive.

Truth be told, she couldn't remember ever feeling so content as she did now. It had taken years of hard work and hundreds of hours of counseling, but she was finally coming to grips with her demons. So to speak.

She'd repressed large chunks of her memory in an effort to survive a tortured past in a monastery, her therapist had concluded. Dissociative amnesia resulting from traumatic events. This was why she'd withdrawn from normal living in favor of the protected environment she'd built for herself.

Billy.

A smile tempted her lips. She did remember her first love. More of a crush, maybe.

The screen waited, homepage loaded. Square windows into her customized on-demand world displayed slots for *Entertainment, News, Friends, Services,* and *Other.*

She quickly checked to see if any messages had come from Susan, a Net friend whom she'd met only once in person but a thousand times on the screen. The only person other than her therapist who knew everything about Darcy. No messages.

The only noteworthy news was a story about a lynching in Kansas City, the third such lynching in three states. Race related. You'd think the world would have learned by now that race had nothing to do with anything. She had no patience for such stories.

No need to order groceries. She spun through the menus, running through a mental checklist of loose ends and options. This screen was her world in a box. A nice, easy world that accommodated her love of vampires and heroes and saber-toothed villains capped in black. Fictional bad guys, mythical monsters. *Safe* fantasy.

Finding nothing that drew her attention, Darcy got stuck on a half-hour comedy show that she found only vaguely humorous, *Three's Company*, a new show that made fun of one Hindu, one Muslim, and one Christian who shared an apartment in Manhattan.

She found anything religious unsettling; anything to do with priests deeply disturbing. But the writers of this show leveled some of the most audacious religious slurs imaginable with a humorous boldness that she found at times irresistible, if a bit embarrassing. Particularly when it came to Christians, or, as the show sometimes characterized them using the most offensive of all religious slurs, *blood*—

Darcy cut the thought short. However wounded she might be over her own run-in with the church, she wouldn't stoop to such bigoted name-calling. Society at large had turned against Christianity with a vengeance over the past decade, and for good reason, Darcy thought. But poking fun at those who still embraced the faith was mean-spirited.

She changed the feed and began to surf. News? No, not news. Reality game shows? She didn't have enough patience to watch others make a spectacle of themselves tonight. She should just head to bed with the Frakes novel.

She rotated into the Discovery feed. Tonight's documentary examined events that led to the two assassination attempts on President Robert Stenton last year—the second of which succeeded. Numerous theories were still argued, but the one that dominated suggested that Stenton had been hit by Muslim extremists in retaliation for the Iranian prime minister's death—while on U.S. soil.

If there was a silver lining to the upheaval last year, it was the West's final awaking to the volatility of religion, or more rightly, faith. The last twenty years were replete with examples of violence carried out in the name of God or Allah or whatever the fundamental extremists worshipped with their raging hearts and bloody swords.

Tolerance had become the watchword of the day. A modest but important bit of progress in world history. Or at least American history. It was a step in the right direction, to be sure, but only a step. What the world needed was a thousand more steps in the same direction.

Darcy sipped her tea and lingered on the feed. The commentator switched to an interview with an expert on the subject. The peace in Darcy's small, protected bubble was shattered with a single image.

A priest in a black robe.

She set her cup down, felt it tip as she scrambled for the controls. Hot tea burned her thumb, but her mind was more interested in changing channels.

Not until she'd successfully done so did she manage a curse. That was it; she was done with the screen tonight.

She cleaned up the mess with a towel, went through what she called her retiring ritual—pink flannel pajamas, face wash, face cream, tall glass of iced water, covers back, book in hand—and slipped between her sheets with a sigh.

That night Darcy read two chapters of *Birthright* before setting the book on the nightstand, turning the lights off, and snuggling three pillows tight against her body as her mind drifted into the land of flying black beasts seducing young maidens with promises of immortality and power.

She was asleep before she had time to wonder if she would fall asleep quickly.

The sounds began at one that morning. At first in her dreams, a

steady thumping knocked about the edges of the tale she was construct-
ing deep in REM sleep.

Knock, knock, knock.

An innocent construction of a healthy imagination.

I'm a-knockin', knockin', knockin' at your back door, baby.

She felt herself smile at the sound of that voice. She knew it, of course.
It was Billy.

*Wanna take a look, Darcy? Just one look, one taste, one tiny spike in their
minds. Wanna trip, baby?*

I don't know, should I, Billy?

One look, baby. Only one.

Thunk, thunk, thunk.

Darcy's eyes snapped open. The clock read 1:23 in bold red letters.
She'd had a nightmare. They came and went every few months, not like
they used to.

She flipped her pillow over so the cool side would rest against her
cheek. Wouldn't really call them nightmares anymore. Just recurring
dreams. They hardly bothered—

Thunk. Thunk. Thunk.

Darcy gasped and pushed herself up. Had she actually *heard* that?

Rat-a-tat-tat. Thunk, thunk.

Her heart slammed into her throat. Someone was beating on the house.
The front door?

Thunk, thunk . . . crash.

Darcy threw the sheets off and slid her feet to the floor. Someone
or something was beating on the front door. She lived in a small two-
bedroom house surrounded by three acres just outside of Lewiston. She'd
chosen the place because it was affordable and private. Animals were
known to come in now and then, but this sounded too . . . regular . . .

Bang, bang, bang, bang, bang!

The sound was now loud enough to wake the dead. Like a hammer.

She jumped from the bed and whirled, looking for . . . unsure of what to look for. A weapon, but she had no gun. A knife.

Slow down, Darcy. It's a deer or a raccoon. Just go out and take a look.

Thunk, thunk, thunk.

The sound had shifted. Darcy reached a trembling hand for the bedroom doorknob, turned it slowly, and eased the door open.

She crouched and hurried into the dark living room on the balls of her feet, eyes peeled and pointed toward the front door.

Bang.

Just one, but it was loud and it was most definitely the sound of something hitting the front door. Right there, not ten feet from where Darcy stood in the dark. Then another one.

Bang!

Move, move, go, go. Go where? She stood fixed to the floor with fear. Should she call out? What? *Hey you? What do you want?* No.

Should she call the police? Yes. Yes, the police. And tell them what? The thoughts crashing through her mind were chased off by another loud *bang.*

There was a window that looked out onto the front door from the breakfast nook on her left. Without allowing herself any more delay, Darcy crept to the window, carefully spread two of the blinds, and peered out into the night.

There was a large man at her door dressed in a black trench coat. He held a hammer the length of his arm and was sealing her in with planks and long nails through the door. *Thunk, thunk.*

Had sealed her doorway.

The man stood back, lowered the huge hammer. Slowly, as if it were controlled by small electric motors, his head turned and looked in her direction.

Darcy's blood turned to ice.

CHAPTER FIVE

NOT EVERYONE knew where in Atlantic City Ricardo Muness could be found, but Billy did. He knew because he'd been in the office at the back of the Lady Luck Hotel and Casino twice before. Once with Anthony Sacks, making a desperate and successful plea to double his credit from $150,000, and again three months later to be told that he would be defending that same scumbag, Anthony Sacks, who had vouched for his credit worthiness.

Tonight he went alone, knowing that his chances of leaving the Lady Luck with all four limbs intact were smaller than a blind throw of the dice at the craps table.

He hadn't changed his shirt or the black slacks since leaving the courtroom. Personal hygiene, dress, food—none of these rated high on his list of priorities today.

Survival went straight to the top spot. Self-preservation was the only thing on his mind, gnawing the edges of his brain into frayed pasta.

He walked down a dingy hall behind the casino, ducked into a stairwell, and descended to the underground level.

After a series of motions and objections thrown about by his own client and the prosecution, the judge had dismissed the jury and demanded counsel meet her in her chambers immediately.

She was curious as to Billy's tactics in the courtroom, even wondered if he hadn't pulled off a brilliant defense in what she thought had been a foregone trial. The jury would have seen through the last witness, she thought.

You could go places, Counselor. Get a grip on your life. And put on a clean shirt the next time you stand before a judge.

But she didn't say any of it. She only expressed her dismay at his antics in her courtroom and demanded that prosecution and defense present closing arguments next. No more motions, no more surprise witnesses, this case was going to the jury room first thing Monday.

So agreed.

It no longer mattered. Billy wasn't going to be around Monday morning or any morning, for that matter.

"Can I help you?" A hand on his chest stopped him.

"Yes, counselor of Anthony Sacks. I have to see Ricardo Muness immediately."

"He knows you're coming?" The man was dressed in a blue pinstripe suit that looked completely out of place in the dingy hall.

"If he's as smart as I think he is, he does."

"Wait here." He stepped back in the shadows, spoke softly into a cell phone, then emerged.

"No."

"No? What do you mean, no?"

"It means you have about ten seconds before I break your face. Leave."

"Tell Muness that I have $526,000 dollars for him. If he refuses it, I will assume he intends for me to have it. The choice is his."

"You don't understand the word *no*, I take it."

"And I take it that you're about as stupid as a sack of air. Have it your way." Billy spun and headed back up the stairs.

He made it all the way into the main casino before the suited muscle caught him by the arm from behind.

"This way."

A single look in the man's eyes told him that the guy's head really was about as empty as a sack of air.

Ricardo Muness sat behind the pale desk that had become synonymous with Billy's image of the man. Bleached maple. Like bone. Otherwise everything about the man was dark. Boots, goatee, slicked hair, tanned skin. Even the dark glasses that covered his eyes.

"Sit," he said softly.

Billy sat in one of two black leather chairs and stared at Atlantic City's wealthiest underground financier.

Nothing. Not a whisper of the man's thoughts.

Glasses.

Okay, well, that was new. So he needed to actually see a person's eyeballs to hear their thoughts. Billy crossed his legs and nonchalantly dried his palms on his thighs. Over the last six hours his focus had been split between the keys into cyberspace that Sacks had given him, and the phenomenon that was opening his mind to the world's thoughts.

Between the two he'd discovered just how badly one could sweat when truly freaked out.

"I understand you have a death wish," Muness said.

"Is that what you heard? No, sir. I did what I knew you would want me to do given the information I was able to obtain."

"Never assume to know my mind."

The order struck Billy as a little too direct. Muness knew about his new talent?

"Then maybe I was mistaken," he said. "I could leave now if you wish."

"Or?"

"Or I could tell you about the money Anthony Sacks stole from you."

"And?"

"And show you how to retrieve it."

"How much?"

"Five hundred twenty-six thousand. And change."

"You missed some."

Billy felt his face flush. "What do you mean?"

"He's taken five hundred and thirty-seven thousand from me in the last twelve months. Eleven thousand of that was a loan he never paid back. The rest is in a bank in Belize, under my watch."

The fact that Sacks probably didn't consider the eleven thousand as stolen accounted for the disparity. But Muness knew about the money anyway

"So you've come all this way to return money that is already in my hands?" the man said.

"Evidently."

The man stared at him through the dark glasses. It was almost as if he really did know about Billy's gift and was playing him.

"We have a problem, my friend."

"We? Or me?"

"For the moment, we. There are those in my organization that know about our little arrangement. Which means I am obligated to follow through with the promises I made to you. If Tony goes down, so do you, it's that simple."

"That's my problem," Billy said. "What's yours?"

"The fact that you know about the money. I need to know how you found out."

Leverage. But not much.

"And you expect me to tell you when? After you remove my left arm?"

The man smiled. "The thought had occurred to me. If you don't tell me, I'll assume Sacks told you, in which case I'll have to kill both of you. The choice is yours. So much power in your hands, Billy boy. To give or take a man's life. Power."

"I tell you, you let me live but take my arms."

"Correct."

"I think I'd rather take a bullet in the head."

The man's hand came up, snugged around a stainless nine-millimeter pistol. "If you insist."

"You have to ask yourself, Ricardo, what else I might know about your organization. And whom I've told."

It was hard to tell in the dim light, but Billy thought the man's cheek had twitched, so he pressed on with the slight advantage.

"Do you really think I would be stupid enough to hang your man out to dry and then waltz into this gamble without an ace up my sleeve? You kill me and you'll be taken down within the week, my friend."

The fact that his voice held a slight tremor didn't help his cause, but he wasn't accustomed to looking death in the face.

"I think you're bluffing."

"I may be a gambling addict, but I'm not a complete idiot." He stood. "The real question is, are you willing to gamble your life on a hunch that I'm bluffing?"

Muness seemed at a loss for words.

Billy knew he had the man on his heels, if only for a moment. He moved then, forcing himself to ignore the black hole of the pistol.

"What I'm about to tell you will determine if you live out the week, Mr. Muness."

He slowly leaned forward, reached out his hand, and removed the man's glasses.

The room remained quiet. No gunshot.

He stared into Muness's eyes and let the man's thoughts stream into his mind.

"I hope you don't mind. It's important that we see things . . . eye to eye as it were." He set the glasses down. "You wonder whom I've told about the nine million dollars you've socked away in the Dominican Republic, don't you? Or if I've left instructions with my attorney to mail a letter to your wife in the event of my death, explaining why Angela has accompanied you on so many business trips."

He let the information settle in. Muness hadn't been wondering anything quite so detailed, naturally, but Billy had lifted enough information to make it clear he knew about both Angela and the money in the West Indies.

"Should I go on?"

"You've just sealed your fate."

"And now your fate is directly tied to mine. If I go, you go. If I get hurt, you get hurt."

Muness slammed a fist on the desk. "You have the audacity to even *think* you can blackmail me?"

"I do."

For a long time, the man just stared at him. And in that time, Billy learned precisely how a man as filthy rich as Ricardo Muness got to be so filthy rich.

A grin slowly split the man's mouth. "Well, well, well, I guess I underestimated you, didn't I?"

"So it seems. All I want is a week to prove to you that I will never use this information against you unless you exploit me. Just give me time."

"Time. Yes, of course. Isn't that what we all want? More time. But you're not the only one who knows things they have no business knowing, Billy."

Darcy.

The man's thoughts wrapped around the name with disturbing images that stopped Billy cold. He knew about Darcy? What possible connection could a loan secured in New Jersey have to Darcy, wherever she was?

Apart from scattered details, *Billy* didn't even know about Darcy. But now he did, because Muness knew where she lived, what she did for a living, other details that streamed into Billy's mind.

Clearly, Muness assumed that Billy cared.

"Only a fool loans a man three hundred thousand dollars without doing some homework," Muness said. "Insurance. Not everyone is as concerned about their own arms as they are someone else's arms."

"And you think that's me."

"Does the name Darcy ring a bell?"

Billy searched the man's thoughts for a few seconds, finding nothing useful.

"You've dug deep," he said.

Muness dipped his head. "You do anything I don't like, she pays."

"Fine."

"And your debt?"

Billy withdrew a slip of paper with the information he'd assembled on Sacks's theft and handed it to Muness. "My debt was three hundred thousand dollars. Now we're even."

Muness hesitated, then took the paper. His mind was running through ways to eliminate Billy along with the threat as efficiently as a college graduate might run through single-digit addition tables.

"I don't like to be blackmailed, Mr. Rediger. I can't live with the pressure hanging over my head, you understand. You want a week; I'll give you three days. Then we settle this, one way or another."

Billy took a deep breath, nodded once, and turned for the door. "Agreed."

But nothing could be further from the truth. Muness had already settled on his decision, one that made liberal use of force and torture within the hour of closing arguments in the case against Anthony Sacks.

Muness had no intention of allowing blackmail to rule his life. And Billy had no intention of allowing Muness to rule his.

He was going on the run. Tonight.

CHAPTER SIX

WATCHING A cloaked stranger nail her door shut in the middle of the night was enough to stop her lungs from inhaling. Staring into the stranger's shadowed eyes was enough to freeze her heart.

Darcy didn't know if he could see her eyeballs through the gap in the slats, but if he saw movement, he would know she was awake and watching him.

She had to get to the phone!

The man abruptly turned and walked along the wall, then disappeared around the corner. Going where? To seal the back door too?

Darcy released the blinds and ran toward the kitchen. White venetian blinds covered all of the windows in the family room adjacent to the kitchen. From her vantage point, the back door looked undisturbed.

She considered making a run for it now, into the garage, into her Chevy, into the night. But she hesitated—surely there was an explanation for all of this. Who'd ever heard of a woman being sealed in her own home by a man with a hammer? If he wanted in, he would have just shattered the door, not nailed it shut.

Run, Darcy! Get out now while you still can.

She ran for the garage door, thinking she should grab a knife just in case. But her urgency to escape, to get out now while she still could, over-powered the desire for a weapon. And she didn't want to alert the intruder by clattering through a drawer full of knives.

She slid her keys off the hook on the back wall and tried the door lead-ing to the garage. Locked. She eased the dead bolt back and shoved again.

No. *Locked.*

She checked the dead bolt again, thinking she'd turned it the wrong way, but the bolt was open. And the door handle twisted in her palm. The door was jammed from the outside.

Gooseflesh rippled on her arms. He'd gotten to the garage door?

Darcy spun around, breathing hard. Her mind was blank. She turned and slammed into the door, grunting, ignoring the pain in her shoulder.

It refused to budge.

The back door! She whirled, took one step, and slipped on the rug in front of the sink. Her arm caught her fall, but not without slapping into the metal sink. Loud.

She scrambled to her feet. The delay in her progress to the back door gave her time to recall her first impulse to call for help. Moving with less concern about stealth, she crossed the kitchen, snatched the phone off the counter, and pressed it to her ear.

It was programmed to engage upon contact with her fingers. But the familiar dial tone was gone. Instead, static.

Darcy punched the manual power button, tried again, and heard the same static.

Now, true panic collided with her mind. He'd cut her phone line! "Darcy . . ."

His voice came from the direction of her bedroom. Low and long, then again, tasting each syllable.

"Darcy . . ."

He was inside!

She ran for the back door, fumbled with the locks, and discovered exactly what she'd expected to find. A door that would not open. Which left only the windows and the attic.

All that banging from her dreams filled her ears. How long had he been building her house into a prison?

She tore for the nearest window, yanked the blinds up, and saw nothing but black. Black boards. He'd boarded up the windows too.

Darcy whispered frantically under her breath. "No, no, no, no, no!"

"Darcy, Darcy . . . Wanna play?"

She clamped a trembling hand over her mouth.

"There's no way out, honey. I know how to fix a house."

Access to the attic was in the master bath, and from the sound of it the intruder was between her and the bedroom. She had to let him enter the kitchen area and sneak past him if she hoped to make it.

The attic had a round vent she might be able to squeeze through if she could dislodge it before he found her. She knew this because she'd been up there with a cable repairman, tracking down a cable that a mouse had chewed through. The vent would put her on the roof, but from there she might stand a chance.

She eased to her knees and crawled toward the couch.

"You have to ask yourself if after going to all that trouble . . ."

He was in the kitchen already and she hadn't even heard him move.

". . . I would be stupid enough to give you a way out. Hmmm?"

Darcy lay flat, shivering. How had he come in? If there was a way in, there had to be a way out.

"You're wondering about the attic?"

Darcy inched forward on her knees again.

"Forget the attic, honey."

She went then, while the sound of his voice came from the garage area.

Sprinting through the doorway that led to the living room with her five-foot media screen. Scanning the walls for a window he'd left open. None.

She spun into the master bedroom and saw the opened miniblind beyond her bed. He'd crawled in through the window and shut it behind him. But he hadn't had the time to nail it, right?

"You want out so soon?" His voice was behind her, only feet, it seemed. She'd never make it!

Darcy dived forward, rolled across her bed, and came up airborne.

Behind her the lights came on.

She crashed against the wall next to the open window and fumbled with the latch. Opened it. Pulled the window open.

"Shh, shh, shh . . ." A hand grabbed her collar and jerked her back against his body. "Please, I just want to talk." Hot breath.

Darcy screamed, but his hand smothered her mouth. She bit into his flesh, felt warm blood rush between her teeth.

He withdrew his hand and slapped something else in its place. Around her head. Tape.

Her muffled cry filled her taped mouth, powerless now. She struggled hopelessly against his steel grip. Like a man who'd won his share of hog-tying contests, he secured her wrists behind her back, spun her around, and shoved her to the ground.

The black-clad man strode for the window, shut the blinds, and faced her. His hand was bleeding where she'd bitten him, but he didn't seem to notice.

"Well, well, well. So you would be Darcy, or, as you are so affectionately referred to back in the group, number thirty-five."

Her assailant stood over six feet, dressed in dark brown slacks and a black collared shirt, a day's stubble lining his jaw. Sweat glistened on his face, but otherwise he looked clean for a man who'd spent the night sealing her in her house.

"Now, just take a deep breath, Thirty-five. I've done this more times than I care to remember—gets old after a while. We'll be here for a while, a day, maybe more, depending on you."

He eyed her from head to toe. Grunted. "I really hope you're not the stubborn kind."

She told him what she thought of him in no uncertain terms, but it came out in a long "Uhummmmmmmm!"

"This doesn't have to be difficult," he said. "You're brimming with questions, and I don't blame you. We'll get to them. Where do you keep the bandages?"

She stared him in the eyes, refusing to clue him in.

"The bathroom, naturally. Just seeing if you were warming up." He walked to her, grabbed her by her hair, and tugged her to her feet. She stumbled beside him into the living room, where he shoved her onto the love seat.

Producing a pair of cuffs, he cinched one end to her ankle and the other to the sofa leg.

"Be right back. Can I get you anything? Coffee, lemonade, mint tea?"

The man left, banged about in the bathroom for a minute, then returned, hand bandaged in a strip of sterile cotton

"Problem with giving you a drink," he said, "is drinking it. If everything they tell me about your yapper is correct, I don't think I'll be taking the tape off any time soon."

He disappeared into the kitchen and returned with one of her wooden chairs. Spun it around and straddled it.

"You can call me Agent Smith. Not my real name, but it has a ring to it. You like old movies?" He pointed at her. "You, we'll call Darcy. Number thirty-five sounds a bit too clinical. Fair enough?"

She stared at him.

"Good. Now, the first thing you have to understand is that whether I kill you or not depends on how cooperative you are. If it were up to me, I would let you live. You're dangerous, I'm sure, but I think the world needs a bit of danger to make it interesting, and I'm not about to be the only one providing it. Follow?"

She didn't. She was about as dangerous as a mouse. He was mistaking her for someone else. This whole thing was a mistake! Which gave her some hope. If she could make him understand, he might let her go.

"But," he continued, "they disagree and they call the shots." He stared at the tape around her mouth. "If you really can do all they say you can, maybe it's best for everyone."

What was he talking about? She shook her head hard.

Agent Smith slowly smiled. "You really don't know, do you?"

"Hmmmm!" she shouted. *No!*

"We'll start with me and then move on to you. You're the prize here, after all."

Smith stood, withdrew a toothpick from his breast pocket, and began to pick his teeth. "I work for Rome. The Roman Catholic Church. Not as a priest, obviously, but I'm on the payroll. Evidently you have a history they aren't crazy about. A certain monastery in which you and thirty-six other children were sequestered for the first thirteen years of your lives. You remember?"

Long fingers of horror reached around Darcy's throat. Smith had the right girl, then. The nightmare she'd fled all these years had caught up to her. And this time it would finally kill her. Darcy felt hot tears leak down her cheek and drop onto her lap.

"One year ago, one of those children, a man now named Johnny Drake, demonstrated a rather remarkable set of powers that could ultimately embarrass the Catholic Church. Evidently, Johnny wasn't the only one who came into the possession of such powers."

Not me! You have the wrong person! But the words refused to form in her frozen throat.

"My mission is a simple one: find the grown children, find out what they really know, and then decide whether they should die."

She felt herself shiver with a deep-seated rage. Not only against this emissary but also at the institution that had reduced her to a shell of what most people were.

Smith drawled on. "The church is in a bit of a spot as you probably know. Everyone seems to hate her these days. Not without reason, mind you, but there it is. The only group of people more despised than Catholics are Protestants. Used to be Muslims and Hindus and all the Eastern freaks took the cake. Well that's all changed, and as a good Christian solider I feel compelled to do my part in cleaning things up."

He winked.

"Which brings me here. So then, let's begin. I need to know what you know." Agent Smith got off the wooden kitchen chair, settled into the leather recliner to the right of the sofa, crossed his legs, lay his head back, and closed his eyes.

"Go ahead, take some time. I'm in no hurry."

CHAPTER SEVEN

Day Two

BILLY REDIGER left his apartment at two in the morning, climbed into the old cobalt-blue Porsche 911 he'd won in a poker game a few months ago, ignited the engine, and left 2917 Atlantic Street behind for the last time.

At least that was the plan.

He'd made an emergency call to the judge and explained that, however inconvenient it might be for the court, health issues were forcing him to remove himself from the defense of Anthony Sacks. Unless, of course, she was willing to let him present his closing arguments *in absentia*, to be read by the clerk.

After five minutes of chastisement, she agreed to let the clerk read his closing arguments, only because the case against Sacks was so airtight that closing arguments were futile anyway, she claimed.

So much for Anthony Sacks's day in court.

Billy had typed up his closing argument—which took one last stab at confusing the jury by reminding them of their own sins—sent it to the judge via the Net, packed up his few belongings, and cleared out.

The night was cool and the traffic nearly nonexistent at such an early hour, so he lowered the top, turned up the stereo, and pretended that all was as fine as a sunny Sunday in June.

Truth was, he'd just hit bottom. And even now, the bottom felt like it was about to give way. Muness had long arms, and it would only take him a day at most to figure out that Billy had fled the city and done the only thing that made any sense.

Gone after Darcy. Which in Billy's mind didn't make much sense at all.

According to the online digital map index, Lewistown, Pennsylvania, was two hundred thirty miles from Atlantic City, up the 42 to the 76 to the 22. A good four hours without traffic. With any luck he'd beat the morning rush and arrive before she headed out for the Hyundai plant where she worked, information according to the thoughts of Ricardo Muness.

Billy tried to tap his hand to the beat crackling through the old speakers but couldn't get it right in such a ragged state of mind. He settled for chewing on his fingernail.

Darcy. He wasn't sure how he'd feel seeing her again. Depended if she attempted to bite his head off or not.

Butterflies fluttered in his belly. He'd sworn her off and gone his own way when they were still fourteen, but she'd been his first true love, if indeed love could be found in hell, which was the only way he could succinctly characterize the monastery they'd grown up in. But their experience had forged a bond between them that he could never deny. A part of Darcy had remained with him to this day. Though which part, he wasn't sure.

The thought made him swallow. What did she look like? Was she large, skinny? Had she become a socialite or retreated into a cocoon? Was she married, dating, an ax murderer, into sports? Did she think about him?

And above all, what would she say about what was happening? This new gift he'd suddenly found, out of thin air it seemed. It had to do with the monastery, didn't it? Strange things like this had occurred in the monastery, but not since, not till now.

The thought had drummed through his mind all day. Whatever was happening to him was tied directly to his childhood. Darcy had stood by his side then, and the fact that he was being driven to her side now felt more than a little ironic.

Muness said he'd dug into Billy's past and found out about Darcy, but how? The whole project had been buried, literally, if he'd heard it right. As far as the world was concerned, Project Showdown had never existed.

Most of the time *he* wasn't even sure it had all occurred. They'd only been thirteen, for Pete's sake. But it had happened, hadn't it?

He had conspired to do terrible evil.

He had persuaded Darcy to join him, then fallen in love with her.

He had opened a window into hell.

He now loathed all forms of religion, anything that reminded him of his abject failure as a child, because it wasn't really a failure at all. It was only doing what all thirteen-year-old boys do if given the chance.

And he now had this . . . he didn't even know what to call it . . . this gift. The ability to know thoughts.

Billy glanced at the speedometer, saw he was doing only seventy, and accelerated with renewed urgency to reach Darcy. Muness had threatened her, and that was reason enough to go to her after all these years.

But it wasn't really the threat that was driving him, was it? No, it was Darcy herself. The feisty girl who might very well be his only true friend now.

Assuming she didn't bite his head off.

DARCY SAT in near darkness, taped and bound as the minutes stretched into ten, at which time the man who'd boarded up her house stood and walked into the master bedroom.

The sound of his hammer pounding nails home fleshed out her fears of his intentions. Having rested from his work, Smith was putting the finishing touches on the job. He clearly had no intention of leaving any time soon.

Smith could have more easily broken into her house, tied her up, and threatened her. The fact that he'd gone to such trouble to seal her in could only mean he was the kind who preferred the weapon of terror and enjoyed taking the time to watch it work.

And it *was* working.

Par for the course, she thought. Religion had always used terror to wield power. Fear of hell, fear of getting your head blown off, your towers blown down, or just plain old fear for fear's sake. Thou shalt not, thou shalt not, thou shalt not. The church that Smith worked for had perfected terror.

She still wasn't sure she understood exactly what he intended her to confess, or how she should confess with her mouth sealed as tightly as her house. But his threat had accomplished what she assumed was his purpose: to throw her mind back into the monastery.

Problem was, she really couldn't remember. The names of a few, yes.

Billy. And she did know a few things about Billy.

Johnny.

Samuel.

The overseers. Paul. They were all orphans. And that was it. She'd spent thirteen years wiping her mind free of the experience. Going back now was digging around in the sewer to salvage a few coins.

Sewer. There was something about the sewers at the monastery that filled her throat with an urge to throw up. The worms from her nightmares.

He'd stopped hammering. His feet moved softly across the carpet behind her. Darcy stared at the dark screen on the wall and blinked away tears that had filled her eyes.

"Darcy . . ." His voice came breathy and low. He walked past her, picking his teeth again. "Thirty-five of thirty-six. I've found thirty-four of you. All dead now. The fact that most of you were given new surnames didn't help. I got your name from a pigheaded reporter named Paul Strang."

He turned to her.

"Ring any bells?"

Paul. The overseer? She shook her head anyway.

"Too bad. It usually takes them a few hours to start remembering. And then I start with the nails. Amazing what a few nails in one's thigh will do to jolt the memory."

Darcy glared at him, furious. At this Agent Smith. At the parents who'd abandoned her in the first place. At Billy, for clinging to her mind. At the monastery and the powers that had allowed such a careless project to be conducted in the first place. And if there was a God, at God. Above everything else she was *furious* at God.

"Take your time, Darcy. It's been a long night for both of us. And I have a feeling tomorrow will be even longer."

Agent Smith crossed to the recliner, eased his large body into the leather seat, and lay his head back again.

"I'm a light sleeper—anything more than breathing will wake me. Please don't try anything stupid. I suggest you get some sleep, you'll need it."

And that was it.

Darcy sat with her hands tied behind her back and her foot chained to the couch, expecting something, anything, to move the night forward.

But nothing happened. Smith looked like he'd fallen asleep within minutes of suggesting she do the same.

Her shoulders ached and her mind spun and her heart pumped hot blood through her veins—all reminders that she was definitely alive. But no other memories surfaced.

So she sat still, sweating and waiting and hating Smith and all those who pulled his strings. Terror frayed her nerves, numbed her mind. Fear, more fear than she'd ever felt, wore her thin, and in that thinness came exhaustion.

Darcy didn't know what time she slipped into a deep, peaceful sleep.

CHAPTER EIGHT

THE WARMTH of thick worms sliding over her face woke her.

She jerked upright and stared at the dark wall screen. She'd fallen asleep watching the Net in her pajamas and put an awful cramp in her shoulder from sleeping on her . . .

Agent Smith.

She turned her head to the leather chair on her left. No sign of the intruder. But a single tug from her arms confirmed her memory of being bound. And taped.

The harrowing events of the night flooded her mind. She craned her neck left, then right, searching for his form in the dim light. Gray seeped past the boards—it must be dawn or near dawn outside.

Darcy bolted from the sofa, caught her right foot on something and fell flat on her face, remembering too late that he'd cuffed her ankle to the furniture.

Unable to use her arms to push herself up, she lay still with her cheek pressed into the shaggy maroon area rug she'd bought online to brighten up the beige carpet. The whole thing had to be a bad nightmare.

It was then, as she recalled the name of the town where the monastery had been located, that she first heard the creaking from the direction of the kitchen.

Darcy lifted her head off the carpet and listened, eyes wide.

Creccccaaaak . . .

She knew that sound. A nail, not going into wood, but coming out of it. Someone was prying a plank from a window or the back door! The police had been called, perhaps. Should she call out?

If she heard it, then he'd hear it. Unless he was too far from the source of the sound to make sense of it.

It came again, and this time Darcy began to scream into her tape to cover the sound as much as to attract attention.

She half expected a boot to her side, but none came, so she screamed, muted by the tape.

A dark shape filled the doorway into the kitchen. Her scream caught in her throat. She could tell immediately that this wasn't Smith. Not large enough.

The form held a knife out. No gun, no flashlight. Not police? The thought embedded instantly.

This wasn't the police! Some idiot had stumbled upon the boarded up house and ventured in wielding only a knife. Which meant that they were both dead.

Darcy cried her warning too late. The visitor had already seen her and rushed to her side. Slid to his knees, whispering loud and harsh.

"Shh, shh, quiet, quiet!"

He snapped only two words, but they awakened such a conflict of emotion in her consciousness that she went rigid.

"It's Billy," he whispered. "I'm here. Oh man! Oh man! What have they done? Are you okay?"

His name triggered unwelcome emotions in her mind. She forced them aside and violently shook her head.

Still no reaction from Smith. He was there, though. He had to have heard!

Billy's fingers searched her face, found the edge of the tape, and pulled it from her mouth. She was whispering frantically before it was fully removed.

"He's here," she whispered, "be quiet, *quiet . . .*"

Breath.

"Get my wrists!"

Breath.

"I'm chained to the sofa! Hurry, hurry!"

Billy reached, found her wrists, elbows at her back, and sawed through the tape with his knife.

"My foot!" she whispered. "It's chained, get them off."

He shouldered the couch and tried to slip the cuffs off, but they were latched to a metal bar that ran perpendicular to the frame.

So close, they were so close to freedom! Darcy grabbed Billy by the collar with both hands and pulled him near so she could talk quietly. Came face-to-face with him.

"Billy." Her voice sounded panicked. She tried to calm herself. "Don't leave me, Billy! Don't let him do this to me! I need you, I'm sorry, I . . ."

His eyes stared wide, six inches from hers. Whether it was the panic speaking or some deep-seated bond, she didn't know, she didn't care. But she'd never been so grateful to see, to touch, to have another human so close.

"Promise me you'll never leave me, Billy, please, please . . ."

Her hands trembled on his collar.

"I won't leave you."

And then he went to work on the handcuffs.

"He's in here," Darcy whispered.

Billy spun back. "Where?"

"I don't know . . ." She looked around. "He boarded up the house and he's inside!"

"Who? Muness? From Atlantic City—"

"No, no, from the Vatican! He's after the survivors of the project back in Paradise. You have to get us out, Billy! He's planning to kill me—*us*."

Billy looked into her eyes, frozen by her words. *Survivors of Paradise.* But there was more than fear behind his eyes, she thought.

"I'm going to get you out of here, Darcy." His voice was strung tight. He took her head in one arm and pulled her close. "I promise, I swear, I'm not going to let you go."

Something more than fear was driving them together, Darcy thought. She clung to him. And all she could think to say was, "Thank you."

"Yes, thank you, Billy."

They both spun to Smith's deep voice. Lights blazed to life.

The bulky man from the Vatican stood by her bedroom door, legs spread, right arm cocked by his ear. In his left hand, he held a pistol and on his face he wore dark reflective glasses. Like desert goggles.

"What took you so long?"

Darcy screamed. She closed her eyes and screamed at the top of her lungs. A grunt from Billy stopped her.

When she opened her eyes, he was slumped to his side and Smith stood over him, big hand balled into a fist like a brick. The man withdrew a roll of gray tape, ripped off a two-foot piece, and held it up to her.

She tried to scramble out of the way, but his powerful grip pinned her to the floor. Agent Smith secured her hands behind her back again, then plastered another strip of tape over her lips.

She managed to squirm into a half-seated position against the couch, and she watched him work; he bound Billy—tape and chain—and shackled his ankle to the sofa like hers.

The boy she'd fallen in love with when she was barely a teen had grown into a man, but his hair still had the same red tones and his face didn't look a day older. Perhaps she was reacting out of sheer relief to have company in her misery, but she'd never felt such a powerful affinity with Billy as she did in this moment.

Why or how he'd found her and come at this precise moment was beyond her. But he had risked his life for her. He'd held her and sworn to save her.

When Smith was done securing Billy, he slapped him, hard. Billy groaned and struggled into a sitting position next to her on the floor.

Smith spun his pistol in his fingers and then shoved it into his belt. "That's better." He withdrew earplugs from both ears with his free hand and paced before them.

"Like two peas in the pod, Darcy and Billy. Rome is going to be pleased. Absolutely *ecstatic*. Two at one time? I'm outdoing myself, and that . . . that is hard to do. Now let's start from the top, shall we?

"The last two, thirty-five and thirty-six in the same shot. Two birds, one stone. You're going to tell what you know. Who else knows."

"You can tell Muness that my promise still stands," Billy said. "I'm going to burn him."

"Muness doesn't concern me," Smith said. "You think that your being here is a stroke of fortune, boy?" He chuckled. "What's the matter? You don't know what I'm thinking? Really?" His lips flattened. "Then let me tell you what: I'm thinking that your days of traipsing through the daisies are over. For both of you. You can help us by telling me what you know about Johnny Drake and Samuel Abraham, or you can lose your fingers and toes, tongues and eyes, eventually your lives. That's what I'm thinking."

Darcy's first thought was a simple one. *Do it, Billy! We'll do it! Make something up if you have to.*

But one look at Billy's twisted face and she doubted he was on the same page. And neither was she, not really. She might be panicked now, predisposed by her nightmares to turn against anyone who had anything to do with Paradise; but in truth, she couldn't betray another human to this beast.

"Go to hell," Billy said.

"I see we're not making progress here. Let me help." Smith knelt beside him, grabbed his hands behind his back, and reached around with a cigar cutter he'd withdrawn from his pocket.

Clink . . .

Billy started to scream. Blood squirted from his finger, now missing just the very tip.

"Shut *up!*"

Billy clamped his mouth shut and shook. Sweat vibrated from his forehead.

The man from the Vatican stepped over him, grabbed Darcy's foot, and clamped it under his arm. She felt his fingers spreading her toes and she cried out in horror. The tape muffled her voice. She kicked out.

Phffft! Phffft!

Agent Smith's head snapped back. His glasses exploded into shards of crimson glass. He dropped the cigar cutter and collapsed with one lip twitching and one finger squeezing a trigger that wasn't there anymore. After a moment, he didn't move at all.

"Billy Rediger and Darcy Lange?"

The man who'd killed Smith had appeared in similar fashion to Billy's entrance. With one exception.

He held a gun and he held it like he knew how to use it. And he, like Smith, wore dark glasses.

"Yes," Billy panted.

"Are there any more of them?"

"No."

"Thank goodness I made it in time."

CHAPTER NINE

BILLY SAT next to Darcy, nursing his bandaged finger. The man who saved them had cut them both free and suggested that Darcy tend to Billy's hand. When they emerged from the bathroom, the man had already hauled Smith's body into the garage.

He stood in front of them, sunglasses fixed in place, hands on hips like a platoon sergeant looking at two new recruits.

"Okay . . ." Darcy glanced from one to the other. "Will someone please tell me what's happening here?"

"More than meets the eyes," the man said. He removed one hand from his hip and tapped his chest. "My name is Brian Kinnard. A good guy, okay? The man I killed?" He jabbed at the garage doorway behind him. "Definitely a very bad guy."

"And what would that make us?" Billy asked.

"You two are the prize. Everyone wants you. Some prefer dead, some alive, but then you've probably already figured that out."

"No," Darcy said. "I haven't figured anything out. I was sleeping and this maniac boarded up my house and he . . ." She swallowed and faced Billy, eyes wide.

Thank you, Billy. You're like an angel. I could kiss you right now!

He felt heat in his face and looked back at Kinnard, whose mind he could not read, thanks to the glasses.

"Obviously you know more than we do," Billy said. "Tell us."

"How much do you know?"

"Just tell us everything," Billy said. "We need to know what you know."

Kinnard nodded and walked to his right. "Fair enough. You were both part of an experiment that went all wrong thirteen years ago. I'm sure you remember that much."

"I'm not sure I want to hear this," Darcy said, eyes misted with tears.

Billy nodded. "Like I said, tell us what you know. All of it."

"What I know was told to me by David Abraham, the director of the monastery, but then you both know that. What you may not know is that he's no longer with us."

"Dead?" Billy blinked.

"Long story I won't go into now. He told me about Project Showdown." Kinnard paced, face toward them. "An incredible story about a project sanctioned by the Roman Catholic Church that left Paradise, Colorado, in shambles and thirty-six orphans homeless. Damaged for life. The project was designed to study the effects of isolation and indoctrination on children. An attempt to create 'noble savages' destined to live lives pure enough to change the world. Three of you—you two and a boy from Paradise named Johnny Drake—came away not only damaged but gifted. Of course, I believed none of it. Until I met Johnny Drake."

"So you know him?" Darcy said. "If he's still alive, how could Billy and I be the last two?" She glanced at the carpet stain left by the assassin's head wound.

"Johnny wasn't technically from the monastery," Billy said. "We're the last two orphans from the monastery."

"Correct," Kinnard said. "And if Johnny is right, you're the only other two who have . . ." He left it there.

"This crazy power," Billy finished.

Kinnard's jaw flexed. "So it's real, then. The three of you received inhuman powers from the books you wrote in as children." He lifted a hand and ran it through his hair. "Your powers are the same as his?"

"You're wearing glasses," Billy said.

"I learned that from Johnny. The effectiveness of the power has something to do with eye contact. Johnny never subjected me to his . . . his gift, but I've seen it work."

"What in the world are you talking about?" Darcy demanded. "I don't know anything about Johnny or gifts. How did you happen to find me—us—anyway?"

"I made a vow to David Abraham. No contact until you came out, so to speak, but the minute I heard what happened to Billy in Atlantic City I left Washington."

"How did you know to come here?" Billy pushed.

"I've had a team keeping close tabs on both of you ever since my last meeting with Johnny, nearly a year ago. Your car is tagged with an electronic signal."

Kinnard turned to Darcy. "You think that the executive board at your plant doubles employees' salaries every day?"

She stared at him, confused.

"Just an educated guess at this point, but I think David was right. I think your powers have to do with your voices and ears and eyes. Johnny can make a man see; Billy can hear thoughts, can't you, Billy?"

So he did know. Billy's mind flashed back to the courtroom. A person who knew what to look for might easily suspect what Kinnard had just suggested.

"So it seems," he said.

Kinnard nodded. "And I doubt your voice is normal, Darcy. I suspect that you can be *very* persuasive."

"I *can*?"

"You can. And Smith somehow suspected it, which is why he taped your mouth shut before you had the opportunity to persuade him to kill himself or something." The intruder again, hammers and nails and duct tape and earplugs. Smith had been trying to *contain* Darcy?

Darcy arched an eyebrow at Billy. "You can't be serious. You can read thoughts?"

"Think something and look at me."

She stared into Billy's eyes.

"You're pleasantly surprised at how handsome I've turned out," he said. "You don't trust me because you don't trust anyone. But you *want* to trust me. And you just thought I might have been able to guess all of that so you switched your thinking to a candied apple being eaten by . . ." *Really? How odd.* ". . . by a vampire." Now it was his turn to cock an eyebrow.

"There you have it," Kinnard said. "A candied apple eaten by a vampire."

She looked at Billy, horrified.

"You don't remember?" he asked. "The ancient book we wrote in—you, me, Johnny Drake?"

"No. I don't remember much."

Billy faced Kinnard. "How did David Abraham know this?"

"Like I said, he didn't exactly know. The point is, he was right."

It was all incredible, but Billy found some comfort in any explanation. "Where's Johnny?"

"He's been allowed to remain in hiding. He was very adamant about that."

"So you don't know where he is."

"Like I said, he's been allowed to remain in hiding."

Which probably meant Kinnard knew more than he would admit.

"And what do you want from us?"

Kinnard took a deep breath. "To let me fulfill my obligation to David Abraham. To let me keep you alive." Kinnard looked at the bloodstained carpet. "There are others who will stop at nothing to see you both dead."

"Marsuvees Black?" Billy said.

Kinnard slowly nodded. "I hope you will agree."

"Agree to what?"

"To go with me to Washington, D.C. Under our full protection, naturally."

"Hold on . . ." Darcy stood. "Just slow down! You're saying all of this dates back to that experiment in Paradise . . ." She clenched her jaw, and Billy knew with a single glance into her eyes that she was fighting a flood.

It occurred to him again that he wouldn't leave her. And now he thought he understood why. She'd spoken to him, begged him to never leave her. Her words had cut deep into his heart, jerking long lost emotions to the surface. And this was her *gift*?

"I have a house here," she snapped. "I can't leave."

And she had a point, Billy thought. A very good one.

"You stay here and you die," Kinnard said. "It's as simple as that. Sure, you'll be able to work some of your magic and hold them off for a while, but eventually one of them will get in, tape your mouth shut, and slit your throat—I'm sorry to be so straightforward."

And he, too, had an excellent point.

"What about Muness?" Billy asked.

"And Muness too," Kinnard said. He glanced at the door. "For all we know, Muness is with them."

"He was wearing glasses," Billy said.

"Stop it!" Darcy looked at him.

"Glasses," Billy said, surprised that he was so unruffled about Kinnard's revelations. "He's right. I have to be able to see people in the eye to know what they're thinking. Muness was wearing glasses the last time I saw him. At night. It was almost as if he knew. And when I removed his glasses, he was thinking about you, Darcy. As if he wanted me to come after you."

"Smith . . ." she said.

Billy finished her thoughts. "Was expecting *me*. Exactly. A trap, set and baited."

"Which is why you need to make your decision," Kinnard said. "If you know anything about the Agent Smiths of the world, you know that they aren't the soft-and-sensitive type."

"So you're saying that there are more. How many?"

"Don't know. Only that they are efficient and experienced killers. Which brings us back to the question."

"You want us to go to D.C. and do what?" Billy asked.

"Help us."

"With what, your laundry?" Darcy snapped.

"Us?" Billy said. "Who else knows about this?"

"No one. Not really. Last year a small group of powerful leaders agreed to meet with me, should this day ever arrive. I will give you full protection, comfortable living quarters, transportation, and a healthy stipend."

"In exchange for?"

"Your agreement to meet with this council I'm pulling together and help us figure out how to best deal with your . . . with this situation. We may end up being the only friends you now have. I strongly suggest you take the offer."

"Please tell me it's not a religious group," Darcy said.

"No. If there are men or women of faith among us, they are fully tolerant and keep it to themselves."

"You?"

"Does it matter?" Kinnard said. "The man I killed worked for the Catholic Church; that should be enough."

Billy was at a loss for argument. Having just fled Atlantic City, the offer seemed perfectly reasonable to him. A godsend, in fact. He looked at Darcy, absorbed her with his eyes.

She had the same medium-length brunette hair, the same high cheekbones, same flashing eyes and aggressive spirit, same pouting lips. A woman now, roughly twenty-six, but how much had she really changed from the thirteen-year-old he'd fallen for at the monastery?

"Give us a moment," he said to Kinnard.

"We don't have a moment."

"Then leave and tell us where to find you."

Kinnard hesitated, then turned for the kitchen. "Please hurry."

For a moment neither of them spoke. Circumstances beyond their control had thrown them together, but a history of their own making weighed as heavily in Billy's mind as the predicament they now found themselves in.

She turned away and crossed her arms.

"Darcy . . ."

"You have no right to pry around my mind," she snapped.

"You're right. And I didn't ask to."

"This whole business is crazy."

"You don't think I know that? But we aren't exactly full of alternatives."

She turned, eyeing him. "I don't even know how you found me. Or what you do for a living. Or if you have a wife or children. I know nothing about you. And he wants me to leave my life here to run off with you?"

"No wife, no children. Hello, I'm an attorney. Now you know more than I know about you."

"No, you know my every thought. That's a disadvantage."

"I may know some of your thoughts, but by the sounds of it, you can create mine. Sounds to me like you're the one with the advantage."

She stared at him, wondering how this power she supposedly had actually worked. Wondering if she could get him to do what she suggested he do.

She was going to try it, he realized.

"Darcy—"

"Please be quiet, Billy. You're saying too much."

The suggestion was perfectly logical. There were a hundred things he could say, but none of them was necessary at the moment. He really had no reason to speak. In fact, speaking now would only make him look like a fool.

So he didn't.

She was wondering if she'd made him quiet. For several long seconds they faced each other in silence. And then the assailant named Agent Smith filled her thoughts and she blinked.

She glanced at the kitchen door, then back, thinking now that she needed Billy, wanted him to stay with her. Afraid of what might happen if they became separated. She'd forgotten that he could read her mind.

And in that moment she exposed her true feelings. *Please, Billy.*

Tears filled her eyes.

Please don't leave me. Promise me.

He felt his heart rise into his throat. She was a wounded child, caught up in a predicament that was far beyond the small world she'd constructed to protect herself here in Pennsylvania. But her world had collapsed around her today and she was afraid.

Finally she said it. "I'm afraid, Billy."

It was an invitation to speak. "I know. So am I."

There was a tremor in her voice. "What should we do?"

"I think we should go with him. I know it's all so sudden, but he's right. If you stay here . . ."

"Don't say it."

So he didn't.

Her fear was so great that Billy felt he would cry. But he refused. Someone had to be strong for Darcy.

"Come with me," he said and reached for her hand.

She hesitated, looked at his hand, then up into his eyes, taking his hand. *Please don't betray me, Billy. Please don't leave me.*

"I won't," he said.

CHAPTER TEN

ACCORDING TO the latest census, 89,213 people lived in Boulder City, Nevada, a scant twenty-nine miles south of Las Vegas, City of Sin. What was particularly interesting to the older residents was that much of the growth in the last two decades was within the Islamic community, a group that had been so vocal about the decadence of the Western world.

But the world had discovered a few things in the last twenty years, and chief among them was the realization that radical elements could tinge any group's image and trigger conflict where conflict could be easily avoided.

Most Muslims, like most Christians, like most Hindus, were moderate people who observed their faith as they might observe a high-school dance. The festivities could continue as long as there were no problems. And if a problem did surface, the adults would simply step in and either change it or cancel it.

In the realm of culture, religion in particular, the West had long ago embraced an all-inclusive disposition and called it *tolerance*. If a person did have a conviction of faith, which accounted for roughly 50 percent of the American populace, they learned to keep it to themselves in the name of tolerance. Common sense.

It was estimated that a full 30 percent of Boulder City residents were Muslims. Twenty-five percent Christian. Another 15 percent Hindu. Five percent miscellaneous, a blend of Buddhists and mystics. Only 25 percent were avowed atheists, which by national standards meant that this small city, nestled up against Las Vegas, was a hotbed of religious diversity.

Katrina Kivi, or Kat, as her friends and family called her, was a witch. Not the black-suited, spell-casting type that rode a broom or, for that matter, the Satan-worshipping die-hard type who believed that Lucifer would give them power if they cut themselves enough times or drank blood at one of the séances down by the river.

Kat was a witch because she wanted to be one, a choice that was as much a statement to herself as to the rest of the school. And the statement was unmistakable. *I am me, not any of you. Your rules and regulations are meaningless to me. And if I want to express my religion, I will; you can go to hell for all I care.*

A significant statement for a sixteen-year-old to make in the sea of adolescents who attended Boulder City High School, she thought.

Particularly an African American witch in a city that was mostly Anglo-Saxon Christian and Middle Eastern Muslim. Although she was not purely African American. Her grandfather had come from India and married an African American model from Los Angeles. They'd given birth to her father, who had married a Caucasian European, Helena, Kat's mother, then divorced her five years later. So what did that make Kat?

She wasn't sure, but she preferred to think of herself as African American. It had a desirable feel to it.

The negative consequences for such an admirable stand against the status quo came with the territory. Which was why she was on the city bus now, headed downtown to serve the first two of a hundred community service hours ordered by the judge for breaking Leila's jaw.

Leila, one of the Muslims who had overrun the school, had spit on the floor by Kat's feet and muttered something about burning in hell, and Kat had responded with a fist to the cheek.

Needless to say, Kat had never gotten along with the Muslims. Or the Christians. Or, for that matter, the Hindus. And she found those who walked around professing no faith to be the worst of the cattle, cowing to trends of the day to avoid disrupting the peace.

The school board put her before a local judge within the week, her second such appearance in the last two years. Among other things, the judge had made it painstakingly clear that this was the court's final expression of leniency. The next offense, and Kat would be subject to Nevada's adult criminal code. Any act of aggression or violence, regardless of the circumstance, would constitute a third strike and land her in jail for up to a year. No questions, no consideration.

The judge had then given Kat a choice—forty hours of anger-management classes, or a hundred hours of community service at one of the shelters. She'd taken anger classes twice before. At least the shelter would give her an opportunity to hang out downtown. The consensus between her friends Jay and Carla was that choosing a hundred hours over forty hours was stupid, but then they didn't *really* know Kat. They dressed the same, talked the same, dated the same types now and then, but deep down, Kat wasn't like any of them. Not the Christians, not the Muslims, not the Jews, not even the other witches.

The bus rocked down Adams Boulevard and slowed to a stop in front of the shelter. Kat walked to the rear door, watched an older man with pale blue eyes look her over. And what did he see? A dark-skinned teenager with long straight hair who looked part Indian, part Anglo, part black, all attitude. Jeans. Black flip-flops. If he looked closer he might see the scars on her arm from the period she and her friends had taken to cutting themselves before deciding it was a pointless expression of angst.

An object, not a person, that's what he saw.

His gaze shifted from hers when he saw that she was staring back at him. Same thing every time in this town. They looked because they disapproved, but they didn't have the guts to hold a stare. No one in this world did. How could they expect anyone to follow a certain path if they

weren't willing to hold eyes while giving directions? The world had lost
its willpower, she thought.

She swung onto the steps and exited the bus. Boulder City had grown
from the small-town tourist-trap at the entrance to Lake Mead. The
homeless and less fortunate had spread south from Las Vegas. Now it
was nothing more than a gray city without the bright lights that Vegas
offered at night.

Kat walked into Our Lady of the Desert Community Shelter and
looked around. No religious icons suggested it was run by the Catholics,
naturally; not if they accepted any government funding. Five or six
brown couches faced the walls. A television hung in one corner, playing
a twenty-four-hour news feed. Small groups of ragged-looking poor—
or scammers, as her friends called them—loitered.

Signs hung over several doors: Dining Room, Recreation Hall, Boarding,
Office.

Kat entered the office, signed in after speaking to a Miss Barbara
Collins (the Manager on Duty according to her badge), a large woman
with red hair who processed her court orders and handed her a blue volunteer badge.

"So what am I supposed to do?"

"You can start by mopping the bathroom floor. You think you can
handle that?"

"Do I have a choice?"

"You always got a choice. Next time you might want to wear sneakers.
Them flip-flops is liable to get wet working around here."

"I thought I was going to work in the kitchen."

"Cleaning up in the kitchen goes two hours past chowtime and com-
mences an hour prior. When that time comes, if you're here, you can do
all the work you want in the kitchen. We feed fifty hungry mouths every
night. Right now, you need to clean the bathroom. Mop's in the closet
next to the women's stalls."

The whole notion of completing a hundred hours of service in this building weighed like a mountain on her shoulders. But then she'd known it would be like this even as she took the swing that cracked Leila's jaw. *This is gonna hurt me more than it is you, and I already hate you for it.*

"We good?"

"Not really, no," Kat said. She turned without another word and left the office.

"I'm leaving, so check in with the kitchen when you have the floor clean," the MOD called after her. "And don't forget to put up them wet-floor cones."

It took her less than half an hour to do the floors, because from the moment water splashed on her flip-flops she began slipping like a fish. There was no way she could do a decent job, so she slapped the mop around enough to wet the floor and then put the bucket away.

When she poked her head into the office, she saw that Miss Barbara was gone, as promised. In fact, this whole end of the shelter looked vacant. The scammers had probably gone off for some handout or other. She decided to give the premises a quick once-over before reporting to the kitchen.

Kat walked through bunkrooms, wondering what it would be like to spend a night under one of the army-green blankets next to some stranger. She headed for the recreation hall.

Her father had long ago split, leaving her mother with an only child. Amazing they hadn't ended up in one of these places. Her mother, Helena, seemed to do well dealing nights at the casino tables at the new casino in Henderson. They shared a two-bedroom apartment on the north side of Boulder City and saw each other several times a week. It wasn't the lifestyle of the rich or famous, but at least they weren't forced to beg on the streets.

Kat entered the recreation hall—a gym actually, with a basketball court and a stage. These didn't concern her. The seven meatheads who stood in a line facing her, however, did.

They were from her school. Several from her grade, a few juniors and seniors, standing there like they were lined up for a game, staring her down.

"Hello, witch."

She turned around, surprised by the voice. The student standing in the doorway she'd entered through was an older student she'd seen around school—a Muslim who wore a black bandana over slicked hair, signifying his loyalty to his faith. Any such religious symbol was prohibited on school grounds, naturally, but it was still a free country off school property.

He grinned. "You know who I am?"

"A Muslim who knows I'm a witch," she said. "Why, are you lost?"

"Very funny, lady." The boy stepped a few steps closer. "Are all witches so funny?"

She'd walked into an ambush. These were friends of Leila, whose jaw she'd broken. They'd come to teach her a lesson.

One of the boys who stood abreast spoke in Arabic, thinking she didn't understand. But she'd learned enough around school to make out that he was saying they should do it quickly, whatever *it* was.

Kat backed onto the wood floor and scanned the walls for exits. Only two: one beyond the boys, and the door she'd entered.

"Asad," the boy said. "Asad bin Fadil. So that you will remember who has done this to you."

"Katrina Kivi," Kat said. "So that when you wake up blind, you'll know who took your eyes."

He wasn't sure what to do with her response; she knew by the way his eyes narrowed ever so slightly. *Easy, Kat, remember the judge's terms.* She should be running already.

But running felt like suicide to her, not because it was dangerous but because it was cowardly. There were some things she couldn't bring herself to do. Running from a person she hated was one of them.

And Katrina hated Asad. She knew this having only just made his acquaintance.

"You struck a Muslim," the older boy said.

"No, actually, I struck an idiot. The fact that she was also a Muslim was coincidental."

"She was also a very close friend of mine."

"I thought Muslim men kept their women in order. So why did you allow her to insult me?"

Asad let his grin fade. "Don't make the mistake of thinking that all Muslims are as tolerant as the millions of pretenders who call themselves Muslims. I would as soon insult any Muslim who mocks God by refusing to follow the Koran as insult an infidel who worships Satan."

"Then we have more in common than you think," she said. "I hate pretenders as well."

He stopped. "We have nothing in common but the ground we walk on, and I promise you that it will soon be covered with your blood."

"Or the fluid from your eyes."

One of the others chuckled, coaxing a smile from Asad. "A feisty one. You'd make a good wife for the cold nights."

"I think I'd probably throw up all over you," she said. The familiar calm before the storm settled over her.

Asad dipped his head. "And for that I would kill you."

"Didn't Muhammad preach peace?"

"Peace for the peaceful. Death to those who refuse to convert. How can you worship Satan? It's an abomination!"

"I'm not a Satanist. I'm a witch, for the fun of it. My way of protesting all world religions. Christianity, Islam, Judaism, and for that matter, Satanism. I find them all absurd. So I converted to my own religion. Witchery."

"Then you worship only yourself. Disgusting." Asad cast a glance at the others, who closed in slowly. He spit to one side. "Don't be fooled by the weak. God is great."

"Really? He's no longer willing to defend the helpless in this godforsaken place. I assumed it was because he is dead."

Asad's hands balled into fists.

She continued to goad him, seeking an advantage. "Your God, this so-called God of Abraham, Isaac, and Jesus that you Muslims live and kill for, is no more real than the God Christians have been killing for since the dawn of time. Muhammad was no more a prophet than Jesus was."

Asad's eyes flashed in the face of all of the terrible insults to his sacred faith.

"Muslims are as deluded as Christians. You're all a bunch of—"

"Stop!" he screamed. And Kat threw herself at him then, while his eyes were momentarily shut, midscream.

She reached his face before he could knock her away, cutting his jaw with two of her black nails.

Asad flailed with both arms, but the abruptness of her attack had taken him off guard. He swiped thin air as she ducked under and away.

She brought her knee up into his gut and shoved him toward his friends, who were diving in for the kill.

Run, Katrina!

Running from seven boys who had blood in their faces was no act of cowardice. But this realization came too late. She should have tried to outrun them instead of trying to infuriate their leader—a strategy that offered no advantage over the others.

She clawed at Asad's back, ripping his shirt and the skin beneath. And then she sprinted for the rear door.

A hand slammed into her back, shoving her forward. The flip-flops had dried, but they weren't made for running. She tripped over her own feet as she tried to catch herself, slammed to the floor, and rolled to avoid a vicious kick.

One of the boys fell on her—his mistake, because he could have just as easily kept her down with his boots. But Kat was best close in, where her claws and teeth became effective weapons.

Screaming, she grabbed the boy by his hair and jerked his head closer. She got her teeth on his chin and bit hard.

He howled and rolled off, leaving a chunk of his skin behind. Kat spat it out and rolled to her feet, energized by her small victory.

"Is that all the power your God gave you?" she cried. "You can't lick one stinking witch!"

Five of them descended on her at once, and she knew that she was in real trouble now. A fist smashed into her back. Another struck the side of her head.

She kicked hard, felt her heel connect with a bone. Heard it snap.

"Enough!"

The voice rang through the rafters from behind her attackers. As one, the Muslims spun to face it. In the doorway stood a white-collared priest dressed in jeans, black boots, and jacket. Tall, blond, and at first glance Kat could see that he was well built under his loose-fitting clothes. He wore dark sunglasses despite the dim light.

"Get away from the girl."

Asad clearly wasn't ready to release the woman who'd bloodied him, bitten off one friend's chin, and broken the bone of another, who was cradling his left arm.

"Trust me, son, you don't want me to tell you again. Get your hands off the girl and leave this building before I lose my patience."

Asad released her shoulder.

"Leave," the man said.

The boy nodded at his friends, then looked at Kat. "Hide behind his collar today. Tomorrow is a new day, witch."

They left reluctantly out the back door, wearing scowls.

Kat walked toward him, mind swelling with the judge's words. "I'm sorry, Father, I swear I didn't start that. We can keep this to ourselves. Right?"

The man pulled off his white collar, turned, and left the room. What kind of priest would do such thing? She'd just been assaulted, for heaven's sake! Kat walked after him.

"Hey! Did you see what happened in there? You saw it, right?"

He walked down the hall.

"Listen to me!" she shouted.

The man reached for the door that led into the main atrium and turned back. "The whole world is listening, Katrina Kivi."

Only then did she see the camera mounted in the corner above him. Of course, for legal reasons, every move in this publicly funded facility was captured on film. Including the violence she'd leveled at the Muslims, regardless of how justified.

"Then help me," she said. "You're a priest, please help me."

"I'm not a priest. But I do know your case, and I know that help is the last thing you want. A few months in prison might adjust your attitude."

Kat stood trembling with rage. She had the right to defend herself from extremists like Asad. For that matter she'd had the right to break Leila's jaw. She would be completely within her rights to slap this fellow for his arrogance.

Her anger was pointless, she realized, and as soon as she did, it was replaced by thoughts of prison.

"Then why did you save me?"

"Because you need saving. But the judge will see the video feed and she will stay true to her word."

"I had no choice!"

"You could have run."

"I don't run."

"No. You fight." The man stared at her through his dark glasses, hand still on the door handle. "It's a pity."

"You pity me standing up to them?"

"I pity you for standing up for your pitiful self." He opened the door and started to step through.

"Wait. What's your name?"

The man in dark glasses turned his head back to her and hesitated like a man trying to decide if he should answer.

"Johnny," he said.

"Then listen to me, Johnny, whoever you are. I'm begging you, I'll do anything. Please don't tell the judge."

"I don't think you understand. This institution is managed by the church, but it's state owned. We have protocol. I've read the file. The court has ordered your service monitored."

"Then you're saying that there's nothing you can do. Absolutely nothing, so help you God?"

He stared at her for a long moment.

"Please, Johnny. It's not like me to beg, surely you've gathered that much. But I'm begging you. Just give me one more chance. I'll do anything. Legal, that is."

He hadn't moved for over a minute now. Finally he pulled a pen and slip of paper from his shirt pocket, scribbled something on it, and offered it to her. She hurried forward and plucked it from his hand.

"Be at this address at six o'clock tonight. We'll talk to you."

She glanced at the address. "We?"

"Kelly and I."

"Talk to me about what?"

"About if there's any hope for you."

CHAPTER ELEVEN

WASHINGTON, D.C. Darcy rode in the back of the black Lexus sport utility vehicle, trying to adjust herself after five hours of dead sleep. Billy sat to her right, still sacked out. Prior to leaving, Brian Kinnard had given her fifteen minutes to pull together what belongings she needed and promised that his people would secure the house until she returned. Someone would come for the body he'd laid out on a tarp in the garage.

How long until she returned, Kinnard refused to speculate. But he insisted there was no need to take any personal belongings that could be replaced. Money would not be an issue.

She'd gathered the clothes she felt most comfortable wearing—mostly jeans and cotton dresses often pegging her as a hippie—her vampire novels, journal, more novels, iPod containing her entire collection of audiobooks and over a thousand albums. Her stuffed bunny, which she'd hugged every night for the last ten years, affectionately named . . . Bunny.

The rest of her life fit on one twenty-terabyte jump drive—large enough to fit a backup of her main drive and her entire HD3D movie collection.

When all was said and done, Darcy felt humbled by the fact that her whole world fit so easily inside two rolling duffel bags.

Kinnard had made Billy park the Porsche next to the electric Chevy in Darcy's garage. She watched him quickly transfer his possessions into the back of the Lexus, taking some comfort in the realization that his whole world fit into one duffel bag.

He shrugged. "I'm not big on things."

"Yeah," she said. "Me either."

They'd left Lewistown and headed south through Maryland toward Washington, the District of Columbia.

Kinnard spent the trip on the phone, setting up a meeting of what he was calling the council. It was clear that none of this so-called council was eager to drop whatever they had going tonight to meet about "something they couldn't afford to miss," as Kinnard was putting it. Not even "something that could change the landscape of American politics."

Darcy didn't share his conviction. She had no intention of changing anything but the current situation, which was dragging her away from a good life, thank you very much.

"Welcome to the Beltway," Kinnard said as they neared their destination. "The home of politics. Abandon all hope, ye who enter."

They drove along I-495, eighteen lanes of expressway that formed a loop around D.C., twenty miles across. "Falls Church is that way." Kinnard jabbed a thumb over his shoulder. "Bethesda is down south, and once we hit the Woodrow Wilson Bridge, you'll be over the Potomac and inside the Beltway proper. Make sure your soul is attached at all times—this town will steal it in a second, given the chance."

"God help us all," Billy said. Darcy turned to see that he was awake and staring at her. She had her glasses on, something she would be more careful about now.

"You're an attorney, I would think this town would sit well with you."

"Don't mistake the profession for the person," he said. "You mind clarifying a few things for me?" he asked Kinnard.

"Not at all. You're alive. Breathing. Is that clear enough?"

"Don't patronize us," Darcy said.

"Look around. Tell me what you see."

Darcy let her eyes wander over the traffic, the Potomac River ahead, the sea of towering office buildings in the skyline.

"A city," she said.

"A city of almost a million by the 2017 census. We're finally ahead of Wyoming. There's a lot more, though. D.C. isn't just a city. It's a *culture*. You're looking at the seat of the nation, a political representation of us all. What happens here affects every living person in the world. Each policy decision made here echoes into the jungles of Indonesia. You know what we call that?"

"Power," Billy said. "Absolute power."

The man adjusted his shades as if he suspected Billy had read his mind. "Power. This small piece of real estate is home to all three branches of government—not to mention the World Bank and the International Monetary Fund. Enough political power to flatten the earth again. Definitely a war zone too; a political battlefield mined with special interest groups, think tanks, some of the nation's most . . . um . . . *ambitious* minds."

"A good reason to stay away," Billy said.

"Also a good reason to come, apparently. There are as many paid consultants and lobbyists in Washington as there are homeless people on its streets. Almost as though they attract each other."

He merged onto George Washington Memorial Parkway, parallel to the Potomac.

"Here you can be homeless, and I mean hooked and doped, but you're never far from the political version of the same: a suit, a briefcase, and a congressional proposal. You can't politic if you can't beg. Washington is a collection of representatives who have learned to close the blinds and take the phone off the hook. Politically, the United States is bipolar. But then that's just my opinion."

"So how does any of this help Billy and me understand what we're doing here?" Darcy asked.

"I asked you what you saw outside, you said a city. What I see is a world of cutthroats, more than a few of whom are determined to cut yours. Patronizing or not, my observation that you're alive is recognizing a rather astonishing fact. I don't think you can see just how fortunate you are to be breathing any more than you can truly see just how dangerous Washington is, not without surviving it yourself."

Darcy glanced at Billy, who was trying to suppress a grin. Kinnard came across more like a seasoned litigator than a hired henchman.

Then again, he was from Washington. He was obviously more than he let on.

"Assuming, that is, you do survive it," Kinnard said. "They won't stop coming for you."

"But you can protect us," Darcy said. "Right?"

"If you play ball."

He was speaking in circles and Darcy was running out of patience. "And who exactly are you?"

"Me? I'm your best friend in the making, ma'am. I can be anything you need, anytime, for any reason. And that's a promise." He paused. "Or you can just think of me as one of those highly paid consultants I mentioned."

"And what does that make us?" Billy asked.

"Besides alive?"

"I think you've made your point."

"For now just think of yourselves as two more highly paid consult ants." And then he added, "Unless this all works out."

"In which case?"

"In which case you just might change the world."

IT TOOK them another half hour to pull up to the secure glass-paneled building on Wilson Boulevard that housed dignitaries visiting the capitol. Kinnard had saved them, brought them to Washington in one piece as promised, and by all accounts Billy knew he should be relieved.

But it wasn't until he looked into Kinnard's eyes for the first time that he gained confidence in the man. Kinnard exited the car, spoke into a radiophone, and exchanged quiet words with two plain guards who stood by the door.

Billy caught one of the guard's eyes through the tinted window and heard his thoughts. The man's concern lay in his rules of engagement. No secrets on the surface.

Kinnard removed his glasses absently. Rubbed the bridge of his nose. Glanced at the car's tinted window. And for the first time, Billy knew what he was thinking. Which was nothing more than how best to facilitate their safety.

Kinnard replaced his glasses.

"Do you trust him?" Darcy had seen the connection.

"Crazy, huh?" He shook his head.

"You do trust him, or you don't?"

"I do, I think. But this reading thoughts . . ."

"Yeah," she said. "Crazy."

Kinnard hurried them from the car into a small atrium featuring a waterfall and two large brass sculptures that could be considered flowers with a little imagination. A security station stood between the front rotating doors and a bank of elevators. Three guards dressed in maroon and gray watched them from their stations behind the counter.

No threatening thoughts.

Kinnard checked them in, ushered them into one of the elevators. A bellboy lugging their duffel bags stepped in last. The doors slid shut.

"You'll need elevator keys to get to the fortieth floor flat," Kinnard said and slid his card through a slot that read Penthouse Access. The elevator rose with enough acceleration to shove Billy's throat into his gut. He glanced at Darcy and saw that she'd kept her glasses on.

Double doors led to their flat. They spread open with a chirp, revealing an expansive glass room overlooking the city. Billy stood next to Darcy at the threshold, stunned by the view.

"Wow." Darcy took a step into the apartment. "This is where we're staying?"

"All yours." Kinnard stepped past them and paid the bellboy. "Thank you."

The bellboy nodded and left.

Billy entered the flat and looked at the white sofas, the ten-foot square Persian rug, the liquor decanter on the built-in bar by the door, the wall screen now showing ocean waves breaking.

But it was the outer wall that arrested his attention. Glass from floor to ceiling, side to side, forty feet of it. Beyond, Washington, D.C., in all of its glory.

"No kidding. Wow."

"The glass will stop anything short of a nuclear blast," Kinnard said. "Nice view, but our primary objective is to keep you safe." He handed them data cards.

"These will get you in and out. You need to go anywhere, you call the security desk and they contact me. A secure car will take you. Unfortunately, your access to the city will be limited due to safety concerns. The flat will have to do for now."

Darcy gazed about the room. "This place is incredible."

"Not bad," Kinnard agreed. He walked to the wall and hit a switch. Lights illuminated a kitchen that had been hidden by a dark wall until now. "Virtual wall," Kinnard said. "Lot of the upscale homes use them now. You'll find the refrigerator fully stocked with food and drinks. Call for anything you want. Anything."

Darcy ran her hands along the back of one of two white sofas facing a hand-carved, resin-coated coffee table inlaid with rivers of brass or gold. The large purple orchids in the vase were fresh, perfectly arranged except for one petal that was broken and browning along the break.

"Is this real?" Darcy asked, eyes on the sofa.

"No. That would be illegal, wouldn't it? Imitation lynx, bleached. Costs more than the real thing, but it's nice."

Billy walked past the couch, running his hand on the silken fabric. *Nice* was an understatement. Everything about the flat was extravagant. This was the kind of place that visiting heads of state paid dearly for.

He stood before the glass, where Darcy joined him, overlooking Washington. The Potomac River's gray-green waters were spanned by a bridge directly below them. Across the river, a wide swath of green parks, memorials, and pools ran a few miles or so, ending in the large domed Capitol. Stunning.

"I assume you know what you're looking at," Kinnard said.

Neither answered. Billy knew some, but not all.

Kinnard pointed with two fingers and dictated, working from the Potomac east. "Below us is West Potomac Park. Not actually part of the National Mall, but connected to it. Directly ahead and across the river is the Lincoln Memorial, and moving on to the reflecting pool, the Ulysses S. Grant Memorial, the Washington Monument, and the National Mall, all ending at the Capitol. In all, it's about three hundred acres of memorials, statues, and other reliquaries of American history."

He indicated a building to their left, which Billy recognized as the White House, and started clicking off buildings in rapid order. "Draw a line from the Jefferson directly northwest along Pennsylvania Avenue and you end up at the White House. Within ten minutes you can walk from the State Department to the Supreme Court. It's all here, Department of the Treasury, the World Bank, the IMF . . . all of it."

"That's it?" Darcy asked. "Somehow I was expecting it to be larger than life."

Kinnard chuckled. "No. Place hasn't been modified much since Congress restricted expansion in 2003." He turned from the window. "Bedrooms are on either side. I trust you'll find them satisfactory. I have more work to do. I'll pick you up at six. Get some rest."

They watched him close the door behind himself. For a long moment Billy stood still, unsure how they should proceed.

Twenty-four hours ago he'd been in the courtroom, facing a bitter end to his life. Now here he stood, forty floors above Washington, next to the girl he'd played God with when they were thirteen. It was all too fast. Too easy.

He walked to the bedroom on the right, peeked into a large room with a huge four-poster bed covered in white linens, and pulled his head back out.

"I don't like it," he said, turning.

Darcy was looking in the other bedroom. She closed the door. "Mine looks nice enough."

"Not the bed. The whole thing. It's way too fast." He crossed to the glass wall and paced in front of it. "Too easy."

"Maybe." She walked into the kitchen and began to inspect the appliances. "Do you have a theory to suggest?"

"Come on, Darcy. A few hours ago you were reluctant to leave your house. Don't tell me you're swallowing all of this like a good little baby."

She faced him, jaw firm. "Don't call me that."

Baby. Wanna trip, baby?

A shiver passed through his shoulders. "You remember writing in the books?"

"No." But her curiosity of the appliance had stalled. "And if I did, I wouldn't want to talk about it."

"We have to!" he said. "The fact is, we're here because of the monastery. Because we both embraced Black's ways. We wrote evil into this world and—"

"Evil existed long before we wrote!" she snapped. "Don't you saddle me with that."

"I'm not. But you have to admit that we're here because of those books we found in the monastery. The Books of History."

"I'm not willing to accept that!" She crossed her arms and walked to the window. "Please, don't do this. You of all people, Billy, should understand."

He nodded. Sat on the arm of the couch. "I know you're hurt, God only knows how much you're hurt. And I know that it was my fault. I practically forced you into the dungeons . . ."

"Please, Billy . . ."

"You have no idea how destroyed I felt when it was all over. I've gone to any lengths to stay clear of anyone even loosely tied to Project Showdown."

"Billy." A tear ran past her dark lenses. "Please."

"Fine." He stood and half lifted his right hand, turning away. The notion that they could continue pretending that none of it happened felt both ridiculous and obscene.

"Fine, we can pretend," he said, facing her again. "None of that really happened. I wasn't responsible for Marsuvees Black or the showdown he forced on Paradise. No one died, no damage done, and Black vanished forever. None of the books, not even a single page from the books, survived when they buried the monastery."

Emotion boiled to the surface, enough to make Billy's throat feel swollen.

"You weren't scarred for life, were you? No, life's been a rose garden. I haven't been looking over my shoulder for the last thirteen years, wondering what might come out of the night to cut me down. I haven't washed out my life with bourbon and poker."

"Stop it!"

But he'd smothered the words for too many years to hold them back now. "Black hasn't spawned any more monsters like himself. You didn't spend the night taped up by a man who sealed you into your own house. He didn't cut off my fingertip. I can't read minds and you can't speak into them! It's all a farce!"

"Okay!" she screamed. "Just stop it!"

She stood trembling in her jeans, on the verge of breaking. Her arms were white and frail, a homebody who rarely saw the sun, if ever. She'd lived in her bubble of protection, peering out at a world she hated. Retreating into those vampire novels of hers for comfort.

But she was strong, and she refused to turn away.

"Just because it happened doesn't mean you have to swim in it."

"I've run from it my whole life. Forgive the observation, but it seems to have caught *us*. I really don't think running's in the cards anymore."

She didn't have an answer to that.

Billy crossed to the window beside her and stared out at the city that hadn't changed in thirty years.

"I'm sorry. I'm afraid too, but I don't think I can run anymore, I just don't. We have these abilities because we defied the rules, found the ancient books, and wrote in them. We can't change that."

She had one elbow propped against her arm now, with her face in her hand. On one hand her reaction was understandable, on the other she was suffering far more than he had. Why? Six hours earlier she'd begged him never to leave her, and thinking about the words now, she knew he wouldn't dare.

"Why are you so afraid of the past?" he asked.

"Because," she said, "it's not the past. I feel like it's here, inside of me, waiting to raise its ugly head." She swallowed hard. "You ever feel like that? I think I have a snake inside."

Made sense.

"Then I need you to believe something," he said, reaching for her hand. "Look at me."

She lifted her face and looked at him through the dark glasses.

"I need you to believe that I'm not that snake. Can you do that?"

Darcy just looked at him.

"We're together again, Darcy; you and I. We're not in a dungeon, but for all we know it could be worse. Something tells me we're going to need each other. That means we have to trust each other."

She wiped her nose and nodded.

"Can you trust me?"

"Should I?"

"Yes," Billy said.

"How?"

"Take off your glasses," he said.

A soft smile played across her mouth. "Is that fair?"

"It's quid pro quo. When your eyes are covered, your own power isn't effective. Glasses blind us both, so to speak."

"You mean my words don't sweep you away?"

He grinned. "Not now. Remove your glasses and speak to me; it might be different."

"But then you'll be able to read my mind."

"Does that frighten you?"

She hesitated, then reached up and removed her glasses. Her light brown irises sparkled like crystals around a perfect black sphere. Billy felt himself pulled in the abyss beyond, where her thoughts echoed for him to hear.

I'm afraid, Billy. Please don't look at me like that. I'm afraid of what you will find.

I don't care what anyone thinks of me, but I care what you think about me, Billy.

"Can you . . . hear me?" she asked.

"Yes."

"They say the human mind can only store a handful of events or thoughts in the immediate, short-term memory. Are you going deeper?"

"I don't know. No, I'm just getting what you're thinking on the surface. Say something to me."

They were staring into each other's eyes like partners circling in an intimate dance.

"I am saying something."

"No. Tell me to do something. Persuade me. Don't you want to know how this gift of yours works? It might have some perks."

"Okay," she said. "Hop on one foot."

Billy felt nothing that compelled him to do so.

"I don't feel anything. Try something else."

"Stand on your head. Jump out the window."

"Isn't that a bit dangerous?"

"Clearly I don't have the authority to make you do anything of the sort."

"No, but if you did . . ."

"Then I would have seen you attempting to jump and stopped you with as much authority. So you can read minds and I can do nothing, is that it?"

"No, I felt your pull on my mind this morning. Try something else. Maybe something I'm predisposed to do. Or may want to do without realizing it."

She stared at him, thinking. A fire lit her eyes. "Could be a bit dangerous, don't you think?"

"Why is that? We're just trying—"

"Kiss me, Billy. Please shut up and kiss me."

The urge to step up to Darcy and gently kiss her lips pulled at him like an undertow. His fingers began to tremble. He couldn't kiss her, of course. That would be absurd, having just reconnected after so many years estranged from one another, never mind that they'd kissed before, in the dungeon.

"Kiss me, Billy," Darcy whispered.

Billy stepped in and kissed her lightly on the lips, pulled by her words. The moment his lips touched hers, his desire swelled until he could hardly resist her lure. And then he couldn't resist it at all.

He put his arms around her waist, pulled her against him, and kissed her deeply.

She returned the affection. His heart was pounding in his ears, flooding him with such a strong desire to love her, to protect her, to hold her that he thought he might do something rash.

Time seemed to stall.

He pulled back, disoriented.

"Well," she said, wearing a coy smile. "Was that me? Or was that you?"

"I . . . You. Both, maybe both. I'm sorry, I didn't mean to do that."

"I think you did."

"Maybe you should put your glasses back on," he said, turning away. "I don't know how much of that I can handle."

He felt himself blushing. He'd tipped his hand, hadn't he? Was that really how her voice worked? Persuading others to do what was really inside of them to do rather than something against their will?

It was all a bit dizzying.

"I like you too, Billy," Darcy said. "Just so you know."

He didn't know what to say. So he kept his mouth shut and walked back to the couch.

Darcy slid onto the seat opposite him. "Now what?"

They spent the afternoon catching up, respecting each other's boundaries, yet breaking down the past with a freedom Billy hadn't felt for a long time. That one kiss had melted thirteen years of ice that had barred him from realizing just how close he and Darcy really were.

They had been taken into a monastery as infants, two of thirty-six orphans who'd been rescued from various parts of the world and brought to Colorado, where a group of priests led by David Abraham had brought them up in the ways of virtue, protecting them from any form of evil. Noble savages, sequestered away as unknowing participants in an experiment between primitivism and morality. The overseers had known all along that a terrible kind of evil waited in the tunnels below the monastery.

Billy had been the first child lured into those tunnels where he'd discovered the ancient books responsible for these unique gifts. And Darcy had been right by his side. The consequences of writing in the pages had been disturbing enough for Billy to spend a lifetime hiding from, but the worst of it could still lie ahead.

"Marsuvees Black isn't dead," Billy said.

"You can't know that."

"You said you feel a snake in your gut, waiting to come out?"

"Something like that."

"So do I. And I think it's him. I think he's alive and after us."

"The Catholic Church is after us," she said.

"Could be. Or it could be Black, masquerading as the church."

She hesitated, not ready to abandon her conviction that the church was living up to its reputation by trying to squash them.

Billy glanced at the clock. "Six o'clock. Kinnard should be here."

The doorbell chimed.

CHAPTER TWELVE

KATRINA KIVI looked at the slip of paper the man named Johnny had written the address on: 1549 Inspiration Canyon Drive. The bus had dropped her off at the end of the street, a good ten-minute walk. Johnny whoever-he-was lived on the edge of the old district in one of the wood-frame houses that still stood.

Kat had finished her first day at the shelter and hit the road at five, but not before finding out more about the man who'd mysteriously appeared, broken up the fight with Asad, and then vanished.

Tobias, an Indian janitor at the shelter who liked to talk, had filled in a few blanks. Johnny wasn't a priest, not technically, no. But he often wore a collar and nobody seemed to mind. They called him Father Johnny or *Padre Juan.*

According to Tobias, Johnny was a quiet man who volunteered every other week, usually in the kitchen or cleaning up in the rec hall. Never to be seen without them glasses, said Tobias. Never.

Johnny had become somewhat of a legend around the halls of the shelter after subduing two armed men during a robbery a few months earlier. Bravest nut Tobias had ever seen. Spread his arms like he was some kind of savior, walked right up to them speaking in that low voice of his and then, *bang!*, he had both of them flipped over on their bellies, squealing like pigs. He shoved the guns into his belt like a man born with holsters in his skin and hog-tied them in ten seconds flat using an extension cord from one of the lamps.

Father Johnny.

Kat had spent the last five hours rehearsing every possible angle of her ostensibly simple predicament, and best as she could figure it, she was toast. The judge could reverse her previous order, but there was no reason for her to do so. Nevada's violence laws were some of the strictest in the nation. Three strikes and you're out. End of discussion.

This was Kat's third strike. She was out. There was a jail cell in Clark County with her name on it. Four to a cell. The idea had grown uglier as the hours ticked by. She'd never actually considered the possibility that it could come down to this. One lousy fight, a justified one at that, and here she was.

The idea made her palms sweaty.

Kat stopped on the porch and looked around. Streets were empty, large lawns, brown lawns. Not exactly your typical suburban neighborhood settled by rich Indians or Arabs like so much of the city. But not poor, either.

She lifted her hand and was about to knock on the door when a faint moan drifted to her on the wind. A sob. From behind the neighbor's house?

It came again, a cry and then a strange grunt that sounded angry. No one on the street that she could see.

Kat stepped off the porch and crept to the corner of the house. Then around and down the wall. A tall fence bordered the backyard, but the wooden gate was wide open. She stopped in the opening and studied a grassy lawn, at the end of which stood a white shed with a red roof.

The sob came again, from the direction of the shed, she thought. This time it was joined by a soft thump.

Three soft thumps, something hitting wood. Still no sign of anyone except for this one lonely voice crying softly on a slight breeze.

She almost returned to the front door, but the next cry was so sharp and laced with pain that she felt compelled to rush to the aid of whoever was in such trouble.

Kat hurried across the lawn toward the shed, one of those ready-made ones you could buy at Home Depot if she had to guess. She eased her head around the corner and blinked.

A blonde woman dressed in jeans and a sleeveless red blouse kneeled on the dirt, facing the shed's back wall, forehead pressed against the siding. A soft moan escaped her gaping mouth, though there were no tears that Kat could see.

This was the crying she'd heard. The woman was softly thumping her forehead on the shed in anguish.

The sight pulled at Kat's chords of empathy and terrified her at once. The woman looked clean and well groomed, not abused or hurt.

Kat pulled back, undecided about how to proceed. She could ask the woman if she needed any help, but anyone hiding like this obviously wanted privacy more than help.

The wail continued, and Kat thought she might start to cry herself. What kind of man was this Johnny? Maybe she'd gotten the wrong house.

She ran back to the gate and turned back to the shed. The afternoon seemed unnaturally quiet except for the sound of the woman's moaning.

"Hello, is there anyone back there?" she called out.

The crying stopped immediately.

"Hello? Is this Johnny's house?"

For a moment only the breeze blew, and then barely. The woman stepped from behind the shed. A genuine smile spread across her mouth.

"Hello, you must be Katrina Kivi. I was just getting some work done." The woman walked toward Kat, exhibiting no sign that she'd been crying and beating her head against the wall.

"My name's Kelly." The woman stuck out her hand and Kat took it.

She had blue eyes, the haunting kind that women who'd been around the block typically had, though she couldn't be older than thirty.

"Johnny told me all about you. Come on, he's been expecting you."

Kelly stepped past Kat and led her back around to the porch, through the front door, and into a living room filled with antique furniture.

The whole thing was downright freaky, Kat thought. But the woman had the right to her own privacy, she supposed. Kat had her own struggles that she wanted to keep to herself, and she wasn't interested in nosing about Kelly's business.

"Have a seat," Kelly said.

"No thanks, I'll stand."

Kelly's brow arched. "Really? You're not staying?"

"I don't even know why I'm here."

"Probably because you're in a jam, if I know Johnny. And I do."

Kelly smiled. The woman was pretty enough. Even confident, despite the shed incident. For all Kat knew, Johnny had taught *her* how to hogtie gunmen.

"You're his wife?"

"Not yet."

"I see you've met my fiancée," a voice said from behind. Johnny walked in, as blond as Kat remembered. He'd changed into khaki cargo pants and a loose black T-shirt. Still wore the same glasses, framed in black, like the glass itself. The expensive, stylish kind.

"Hello, Katrina." He took her hand like a gentleman and shook it once. "You hungry?"

"Not really."

"Eat anyway. You need some meat on those bones. You got tapeworm or something?"

"I'm not a pig," Kat said. "That a crime?"

"Not the last time I checked."

"You always so frank?" Kat asked.

"I speak my mind," he said. "That a crime?"

She was beginning to like him. "Not the last time I checked."

"Next time you check, it just might be. Kelly, could you get the pizza out of the warmer?"

"She didn't want to sit," Kelly said with a slight smile. Then she retreated into the kitchen.

"Sit," Johnny said, sitting on the sofa. He rested his feet on a large leather ottoman that doubled as the coffee table. "Mind the furniture, it's not mine. Came with the house."

Kat sat on the edge of a chair, elbows on her knees. "Would you mind telling me why I'm here?"

"I was under the impression you were in trouble. Something about a judge who plans to throw you in jail."

"Assuming that incident is—"

"Too late," Johnny said. "It's already on her desk."

Kat stood. "What? You said you could help me! You know very well that the moment she sees that footage, I go down."

"Yes, I do. Sit."

"Then why am I here?"

"I assume it's because you're toast. Please . . . sit."

Kat eased to her seat, confused as to his intentions. "Okay, stop being so cryptic here. Why did you give me your address?"

Kelly came in with a large Pied Piper Pizza box and three bottles of water.

"So that you could break some bread with my fiancée and me," Johnny said. "We'd like to know how serious you are about getting our help."

"I defended myself from a guy who was trying to beat me to a pulp," she snapped. "I wasn't knocking off a casino. You really think I deserve to go to jail for that?"

He took a slice of pepperoni pizza from the box, took a bite, wiped the corner of his mouth with the back of his hand, and then gestured toward her. "Have a piece."

But she was too frustrated to consider her hunger.

"I'm not the one who decides if you deserve to be locked up. We have judges for that. They look at all the evidence, your priors, and your attitude, put it all on their scales and make a judgment. In your case, I do believe the scales of justice will weigh in the favor of jail time." He took another bite.

"Why?"

"Because of your attitude," Johnny said. "Which is why you're here. To see if you really do want our help, Tell me, do you have something in particular against Indians?"

What kind of question was that? "No."

"Muslims?"

"No."

"How about Arabs?"

She hesitated. "No."

"So then that incident was race related?"

"I said no."

"But you do hate Arabs, don't you? You would never admit it in school, maybe not even to your friends. Everyone knows that anything less than tolerance isn't tolerated these days. I can see why you would lie about it."

He wasn't easily fooled. "You don't think the towel-heads have ruined our country? Talk to them about tolerance."

"As a matter of fact, no, I don't think Arabs have ruined our country And I think most of them are as tolerant as their neighbors. Perhaps more so. But you're being honest. You hate Arabs."

He left it at that, and Kat didn't see any need to confuse the issue.

"So let's say, just for the sake of argument, that I do really want your help," she said. "You said the judge already has the report. How would you propose to help me?"

"I'll tell you what: you have a piece of pizza, pretend you're grateful to be here sharing food with us, and then maybe I'll explain why I invited you."

Kelly sat down next to him, a slice of pizza in hand. She put her feet up on the ottoman, bit into her slice, and watched Kat while Johnny rubbed her back with his free hand.

Kat felt like a goldfish in a bowl, but she wasn't exactly in a position to turn her back on him yet. Her mother had often cursed her stubbornness, but she wasn't a complete fool.

Kat withdrew a piece of pizza, leaned back into the cushions, and crossed her legs, pretending to be interested in the oil paintings of lakes and mountains that hung on the walls.

They ate in what Kat found to be a very awkward silence for a few minutes. Johnny seemed content to stare out the window through those glasses of his, either lost in thought or busily manipulating her, tempting her to ask the one question that burned on her mind until she could no longer resist.

"Why the glasses?"

It was Kelly who answered. "I'm afraid that's just a bit too personal, Katrina."

"Kat," she snapped.

"Well, Kat, you're going to have to wake up to the fact that you're in a world of trouble here. Johnny can help you, trust me. But I have to agree with him, you don't seem to have a clue about how abrasive your attitude is. I'm not sure I'd blame the judge."

"You want me to pretend I'm someone I'm not?"

"No," Johnny said.

"And you? Are you allowed to pretend you're someone you're not?"

He stared at her, slowly smiling. "Now we're getting somewhere."

"Why the glasses?" she asked again.

"They're for your sake. I was involved in a bit of trouble and came out blind. But let's not talk about that."

"You're blind?" The revelation surprised her. "I'm . . . I mean, you don't seem blind."

"Tell me, Kat, do you believe in God?"

"God? What does God have to do with any of this?"

"Humor me."

"Seriously?"

He refused to answer.

"I'm a witch. Not the hocus-pocus kind or the Satan-worshipping kind, just the plain old love-the-earth-and-smoke-some-grass-when-you-get-the-chance variety. As for Allah"—she shrugged—"God, whatever . . . it all sickens me. Just being honest."

"Fair enough. Then where do you get your sense of right and wrong?"

"What's wrong today is right tomorrow," she said. "The world is full of hypocrites crying about what's right and wrong. I'll tell you what's wrong." She felt her temperature edge up. "God is wrong. Telling people to hate their neighbors because they don't have Jesus or Allah or Buddha."

"I see. And evil?"

"Like I said, I don't go for all the hocus-pocus."

"I see."

Johnny stood and walked to the kitchen, leaving Kelly with her legs curled under her on the sofa, smiling. That infuriating plastic smile.

"Okay? So now what?"

"Now you can go home, Katrina," Johnny said, washing his hands.

"You'll help me, then?"

"I'm afraid not."

She stood again. "What do you mean?"

"I mean I don't think you're very interested in being helped. I'm sorry you had to come all the way out here. Would you like a ride to the bus stop? Kelly?"

Kat's anger boiled to the surface. "What kind of nut are you? How the heck do you know what kind of help I'm interested in?"

"He knows," Kelly said quietly. "Trust me, he knows."

It was all Kat could do to keep from picking up a cushion and throwing it at the woman. *Easy, Kat. Don't do anything stupid.*

Johnny came back into the room, drying his hands on a towel. "I'm sorry, really, I am. Kelly?"

"I'll give you a ride," Kelly said, unfolding herself.

"No. Forget it. Where's your bathroom?"

"Down the hall," Kelly said, gesturing to it.

Kat walked across the brown carpet, dizzy with anger. She might have been tempted to think that the bait and switch had to do with her skin color, but she knew this false priest would never have invited her if he had any issue with blacks or Indians or whatever she was.

She walked down the hall, pushed her way into what she thought was the bathroom, and found herself in a bedroom instead. Queen-sized bed, overstuffed chair, drawn curtains. Looked unlived in. On the far side was a door that she thought might open to a bathroom.

Without a second thought she crossed to the door and pulled it open. But it wasn't a bathroom either. Rather, a very large walk-in closet. A dozen articles of clothing hanging neatly, several boxes piled on the right, each labeled with a month: January, February, March . . .

She saw all of this by the light filtering in from the door she'd opened. But the closet was deeper on her left, cloaked in darkness. She hit the switch on the wall and blinked.

A rack had been fixed to the wall. Seven or eight weapons sat in the rack, and next to each, several boxes of ammunition. Two rifles, an automatic weapon of some kind, three pistols, several knives . . . There was enough here to start a small war.

Whatever Father Johnny was, she doubted very much that he was blind. Unless this belonged to Kelly. But from what Kat could tell, Kelly didn't live in this house.

Kat took two steps toward the rack and stopped. Her right hand began to shake. She might not believe in God, but God may have just believed in her.

It was a crazy thought. The kind only a desperate person would even consider. But she was a desperate person, wasn't she? There was something about the mystery surrounding Johnny that could get her out of this fix. She hadn't come here to eat pizza before being sent to jail.

Kat moved up to the rack, ran trembling fingers over the pistols, and pulled one of them off the wall. Its black steel gleamed in her hand, cool to the touch. She'd fired several guns in the desert before, with boys showing off their toys. A tug on the slide revealed a round chambered. He was the kind who would leave his weapons loaded, she thought.

She stared up at the automatic weapon on the wall. Set the pistol down and reached for the larger gun. Held it gingerly.

Then she slid the pistol into her belt at her back, cradled the automatic weapon in both hands, and returned to the living room.

CHAPTER THIRTEEN

THE COUNCIL.

Kinnard led Darcy and Billy to the basement of Constitution Hall across Eighteenth Street from the U.S. Department of the Interior. They entered through a supply dock and made their way down a service elevator—all new over the last several years, Kinnard said—and into a large conference room.

Seated around one end of an oval cherry table, nursing drinks in crystal glasses, sat four men and two women, leaning back and talking in familiar tones. A couple of dozen high-backed chairs surrounded the table. Variable indirect lighting was set on low. The Hyundai plant in Lewistown had half a dozen similar conference rooms, all built to impress visitors and presumably to improve efficiency. Though with a full bar near at hand and such comfortable leather chairs, Darcy wondered how much of a priority efficiency really was here.

The conversation stalled, then stopped entirely. All eyes turned to them. All heads, to be more precise. Darcy couldn't see their eyes because they all wore dark glasses.

Yes, of course. She still had a hard time believing this ability she supposedly had was real. What had she really done to prove it? Talked Billy into kissing her. She was a girl, he was a guy, they'd shared a crush the last time they'd been together. Did it really take some kind of super-human power to talk him into kissing her?

"Ladies and gentlemen, I'd like for you to meet our guests," Kinnard announced with a knowing grin. "Billy Rediger and Darcy Lange." Then to Billy and Darcy, "Meet the Council of Seven."

"Council of Seven," Billy said. "I thought this was more of an informal group."

"Well, yes. But if I'm right, that will all change tonight." He pulled out two chairs. "Have a seat."

Darcy sat at the head next to Billy and crossed her legs under the table.

"Forgive the glasses. I took the liberty of insisting they all wear protection. We don't want all the Capitol Hill secrets bared to the world." A chuckle. "Not yet, at any rate."

There were six plus Kinnard. The four men all sported white shirts and ties; two wore navy blue jackets. The two women wore blouses, one pink silk and one white cotton, pants or skirts beneath the table, Darcy couldn't tell. At first glance she would place all but Kinnard and one of the women over fifty. All meticulously groomed and comfortable.

None of them had yet spoken. They simply stared from behind their protective lenses. David Abraham may have confided in Kinnard or another one of these power brokers, but that didn't necessarily make them all cozy bedfellows.

The room seemed robbed of air.

"Maybe introductions would be appropriate," Kinnard said. He went around the room clockwise using two fingers to point out each member.

Lyndsay Nadeau, attorney general, the older woman in white. Looked nearly anorexic.

Ben Manning, Democratic senator from Nevada. The only black man in the group.

Fred Hopkins, Democratic representative from New York. Overweight and short.

Annie Ruling, White House chief of staff, the younger woman in pink. The prettiest of the bunch by far.

Sanchez Dominquez, Republican senator from Illinois. Looked like a brother to the Hispanic president, Cesar Chavez.

Newton Lawhead, associate director of the FBI. Gray hair, pale face.

Brian Kinnard, with the CIA. And that's all he would share. Probably the only one here who could handle a gun with ease.

He smiled. "You're probably wondering how such a powerful and diverse group of leaders ever managed to agree on a meeting place. Let me assure you, it wasn't easy."

"Well, you got us here," the senator from Nevada, Ben Manning, said. "The question is, can you keep us?"

"I only have a few minutes," the chief of staff said. Annie. She kept her eyes on Billy. "Why don't we cut to the chase?"

They were a skeptical lot, and Darcy didn't blame them. She wondered what kind of favors Kinnard had called in to get them all here.

"Of course," Kinnard said. To Darcy and Billy: "Like I told you, this may take some convincing."

The attorney in Billy rose to the surface. "So, in essence, we rushed down here to meet with six highbrows who are a breath away from throwing us out on the street?"

"Close," Annie Ruling said.

"Then I'd have to advise my client to reserve her thoughts," Billy said.

"Client? Is that what you are, Miss Lange? I was led to believe you haven't seen each other for thirteen years." So Annie wasn't used to being handled by people who wore jeans.

"You think I would walk into this den of snakes without proper representation?" Darcy said.

The attorney general, Lyndsay Nadeau, smiled from the far side. "Feisty. That's a start. But can you bite, darling?"

Billy stood. "I think it would be best for us to leave."

"And go where?" Kinnard snapped. "Into the arms of Ricardo Muness?"

"He's got a point," Lyndsay said.

Darcy stood to show her solidarity with Billy.

"No," Billy said. "But once Muness understands what we can offer him, I think he'll be friendly enough. We appreciate your efforts in rescuing us this morning. The flat was a nice place to rest up. The food was excellent. But I'm afraid we're in the wrong room now. We really have to be going."

He started to turn. Posturing, Darcy thought. All posturing, and she loved Billy for how smoothly he did it.

"Sit down, son," the attorney general said. "None of us can say how Brian managed to pull this off, but you have the ear of seven of the most powerful people in the United States. Let's at least examine the reason for this rather unusual gathering, shall we?"

He looked at her. "To what end?"

"Well . . . If you can do what Brian says you can . . . Trust me, we'll be interested."

Billy looked at Darcy, who was feeling quite good about the way the meeting was going down. She'd never understood herself to enjoy conflict of this sort, but she certainly couldn't deny that at the moment she felt positively exhilarated.

She sat and Billy followed her lead. "So you want a show-and-tell, is that it?" she asked.

"Something like that."

Now Kinnard was smiling.

"Fine, then let's start with Annie," Darcy said. "Chief of staff, right? Do you mind taking your glasses off, Annie?"

She hesitated, then lifted her hand.

"I warn you, this could get embarrassing," Billy said.

Her hand stopped on her glasses. "Is that so?"

"Please try not to think about any . . . say, inappropriate relationship you might have engaged in during the last few years. Any derogatory thoughts about your neighbor's appearance, or any parts of your own body that you might find embarrassing. As long as you don't think about it, you should be fine."

The chief of staff sat speechless.

"You wanted a show-and-tell," Billy said. "You show, I tell. Unless, of course, I'm bluffing."

"Can he really do that?" Annie asked Kinnard.

He shrugged, but he was grinning.

"Think of a number, Annie. Do you mind if I call you Annie? Think of a number between one hundred and one million. Write it on the notepad in front—"

"Please, we didn't come here for parlor tricks. This is ridiculous."

Billy studied her for a moment. "You're right, it's been done, hasn't it? Then just remove your glasses, all of you, remove your glasses and let's see where this takes us."

No one did.

"How does it work?" FBI man Lawhead asked.

"You already know how it works. I see your eyes, I see the thoughts in your consciousness. Not the ones stored in memory banks, but those you are actually aware of at any given moment. Usually no more than five or six thoughts."

He'd explained his theories to Darcy earlier, and after a quick search on the Net and some testing she'd agreed to under the strictest conditions, they confirmed that those theories were at least likely.

Annie pulled her notepad forward, scribbled something under a cupped hand, and turned it over. "Okay, what number did I just write?"

"Think about it, remove your glasses for a second, and look at me."

Annie reached up and lifted her glasses. The moment they'd cleared her forehead, Billy spoke. "127,333," he said.

She froze, glasses hovering over her forehead.

"And now you're trying to figure out how I could have done that. You're efficiently running through a list of possibilities. Mirrors, no. Cameras, no. Other surveillance gadgets, but you know the room was swept before this meeting. No chance. And you're reminding yourself that you don't know me, never met me, besides, the number was completely random, not your birthday or something those who know you might be able to guess at. Should I go on?"

Annie lowered her glasses. Turned the notepad over for them to see.

127,333

Lawhead stared at the number. "So you're saying you can actually read thoughts as if they were in a book."

"The thoughts in your immediate consciousness," Billy said. "Care to try?"

Lawhead removed his glasses, stared at Billy for a few seconds, then replaced them.

"Your grandmother is in Saint Gabriel's Hospital, Columbia, Ohio. You're hoping the Vitamin B therapy they administer this afternoon will mitigate the adverse affects of the selective radiation administered last month."

"Anything else?"

"Fragments."

"What kind of fragments?"

"A hangman's noose. Doubts. Fear."

"You can read emotions?"

Billy shrugged. "I don't know. Thoughts about emotions maybe. I'm not exactly practiced yet."

"Does it come and go?"

"Not so far, no. I see your eyes, I pretty much know what you're thinking."

"This is absolutely incredible."

"Ladies and gentlemen," Kinnard said, "think of the implications."

Ben Manning, the black senator from Nevada, was frowning. "I am, and I'm not sure I like them. What about her?" Nodding at Darcy.

She glanced at Billy. Compared to him, her ability was virtually untested. Apart from the kiss, of course. She wasn't about to seduce anyone in this room.

Again, Billy came to the rescue. "Darcy can . . . what shall we say . . . help people do what they want to do. Or know they should do. Or what is logical to do. Or something like that."

"So you don't actually know what you can do?" Annie said.

"Well, evidently I can be persuasive. You'll have to ask Billy. He kissed me this morning." She dropped the admission in his lap and sat back to see how he would deal with it.

"Not exactly what I'd call a miracle," Lawhead said.

Billy's face had reddened a shade. "Trust me, sir, her ability to persuade isn't tied to any adolescent fantasies. Her words can be quite influential."

"You can persuade people to do what they're predisposed to do," Annie said. "As Newton said, that's not exactly a miracle."

"What do you want me to do, fly around the room for you? I'm not some freak on the Net. Please, take your glasses off. Just for one second."

The president's chief of staff plucked her dark lenses off and stared Darcy down with baby blues.

"Surely there's at least one person in this room you'd love to slap for the way they've conducted themselves lately. This is, after all, Washington. Slap them now."

At first there was no change in Annie's demeanor. "Don't be ridiculous."

"Just one slap, honey. He deserves it, you know he does."

Sweat beaded on Annie's forehead. She tapped a French manicured nail on a glass half filled with amber liquor. "This is ludicrous. What a juvenile suggestion." Her lips were trembling, just barely, but enough to betray her struggle. "The fact that you would even *think* of this shows just how immature you are. Yes, this *is* Washington—not some sorority house!"

Darcy leaned forward, speaking low, enunciating each word clearly.

"He deserves it, you know he does. And you know he would slap you if I asked him to. Under the plastic smiles in Washington, everyone wants to slap his neighbor. Do it now, Annie."

The war being waged in Annie's mind was now not only unmistakable but a bit frightening. No one rose to her position in this town without having extraordinary control of her faculties.

"This is ridiculous , ."

But that control was slipping.

"Okay, I think you've made your point," Ben Manning said.

"Slap him, Annie. Do it now."

"I can't! Don't . . ." She stopped, closed her eyes, trying to maintain the last threads of control. When her eyes snapped open, Darcy knew something had changed.

Annie reached over and struck Ben Manning on his shoulder with an open hand. "No!" She struck him again, unleashing a fit of anger directed at the Nevada senator. "No, no, no! How dare you threaten to expose the president's university binges over his stand on the health-care bill? He was just a kid!"

Annie stopped, stared at Darcy with wide eyes, slipped her glasses back on, and then lowered her head into her hands.

Okay. Awkward.

"Please tell me I didn't just do that," Annie mumbled, face red.

Ben Manning had paled. The rest didn't know how to react except to look between Darcy and Annie.

"Forgive me, Ben," Annie said, turning to the man. "I . . . I don't know what came over me. I didn't mean any of it . . ." She swallowed. "Well, yes, I did mean it, actually. Every word. But I had no right to act so unprofessionally. I'm sorry."

Lyndsay Nadeau smiled. "Well, well, well . . ." The attorney general looked like she was enjoying herself. "My deepest apologies, Brian. I'm impressed." She addressed Darcy. "Can you make people do things they don't want to?"

She was about to say no when Billy spoke. "It's too early to know."

"You may find all of this amusing, Miss Nadeau," Ben Manning said, "but I find it troubling. Setting these two loose in our nation's capital would be incredibly irresponsible!"

"Which is why we are here," Kinnard said.

"Ben's right," Annie said, arms crossed now. "This could be dangerous."

"Unless they work for us," the overweight senator from New York, Fred Hopkins, said.

"We're not guns for hire," Darcy snapped.

None of them seemed too interested in her comment.

"Imagine these two on the Senate floor," someone said.

"Heaven help us all."

"Whatever the advantage, two minds with these abilities would destroy Washington," Manning said. "We can't allow it."

The attorney general faced him. "What are you suggesting?"

For the first time, the full extent of their predicament settled over Darcy. She and Billy presented a real danger to the men and women in this room. One that might push them to extreme measures.

She turned to Billy and saw that a trail of sweat marked his temple.

"Yes, Ben, what are you suggesting?" he demanded. "That we should be suppressed somehow, knocked off?"

The senator just stared at them.

"Why don't you bolster my trust in you by removing your glasses so that I can see what you're really thinking?"

But Manning made no move to remove his glasses.

"Don't be foolish," Lawhead snapped. "We're looking at what might be this country's most valuable asset. I suggest we put our minds to protecting that asset!"

"Agreed," the attorney general said. Lyndsay Nadeau watched Darcy with a smile. "Don't you worry, dear. Argument is just part of the whole process."

"You're right," Annie said. "This could be good."

Manning shook his head. "If you're thinking we should use them to manipulate discussions made on the hill . . ."

"Come on, Ben, no one's suggesting we waltz Darcy into the White House to seduce the president," Lawhead said. "There are other ways to test the waters, so to speak."

"Assuming our two guests are in favor of working with us," Lyndsay said. "This is more about them than us."

They looked at Darcy and Billy.

"Yes, assuming," Lawhead said. "Brian?"

Kinnard had worn a perpetual grin. He might not hold the most power in this room, but he was clearly the mastermind.

"Our proposal is simple," Kinnard said to Darcy and Billy. "Commit to this council. Change Washington with us. Change the world. In exchange, we will provide for you without limitation. More importantly, we will guarantee your security. You are already in the crosshairs."

"That simple, huh?" Billy said.

"If you choose to go it alone, you're free to leave after this meeting."

"And if we stay? What would we do? Besides sit tight up in our glass box?"

Both Lyndsay and Lawhead spoke at once, then stopped. No shortage of ideas, naturally. The other members still sat in shock, trying to figure out if what they'd just witnessed was somehow rigged. But they were also reeling over the implications of the power, assuming it was real.

Lawhead looked around the table. "If I may?"

Lyndsay Nadeau nodded. She was the top authority here, Darcy thought. They would argue, but she would cast the final vote.

"I admit, this could . . . There's no telling what the repercussions of . . ." Lawhead shook his head. "It's hard to believe." He stood and walked to the bar. "We have to be cautious. See what we really have here. You've probably heard of these lynchings in Missouri. Homicide motivated by both race and religion with an intent to elicit revenge."

Darcy had heard it on the news just last night. Disturbing.

Lawhead poured himself a drink. "Two persons of color have been hanged in the last week, in and around Kansas City, one on Kansas soil, one on Missouri soil, making the case a federal one. Both victims were abducted immediately following the religious services they'd attended and found hung behind the church. Someone clearly has a beef with black Christians."

He faced Billy and Darcy, drink in hand. "What would you think about helping the FBI stop the killer?"

"No," Ben Manning snapped. "Not before we know more about these abilities."

Lyndsay Nadeau came to their defense. "Please, Mr. Manning, the suggestion seems reasonable to me."

"They should be locked up, not escorted around the country by the FBI."

They all turned to the senator from Nevada.

"Some respect for our guests," Kinnard demanded. "I don't think you appreciate—"

"I appreciate the fact that I was just slapped by Miss Ruling because of this woman. I appreciate that she has no business out in public. Even less business mixing with anyone who has any power in this country."

Darcy felt the blood drain from her face. She didn't know quite what to say.

Lawhead set his glass down. "You're overreacting, Mr. Manning."

But Manning wasn't easing up. "I insist you put them both under armed guard."

"They are," Kinnard said.

"And kept there."

"So now you want to incarcerate us?" Billy demanded. He faced Kinnard. "This is what you bring us to?"

"Actually . . ." Fred Hopkins, short and plump, wiped his beaded brow with a hankie. "Ben has a point. I realize this is awkward for all of us, but if the wrong party got their hands on Darcy in particular . . ." He didn't

SINNER 833

bother finishing the thought. "And she could do some major damage on her own."

The room fell silent. Darcy suspected that Billy was as taken aback as she over this assault.

Lyndsay Nadeau was the one who settled the issue.

"I appreciate your concern, and I'm sure that the FBI will take it under advisement. For the time being, let's keep you two under tabs, shall we? If you're not with Kinnard it would be best to stay in secure quarters."

"You're actually imprisoning us?"

"We are protecting you, just until we can figure this out."

"Nonsense!" Darcy cried.

Billy's hand on her arm immediately settled her.

"She's right, Darcy. It's for our protection."

But Senator Ben Manning's stern scowl spoke nothing of protection, she thought. He looked like a man who wanted their heads on a platter

CHAPTER FOURTEEN

THE AUTOMATIC weapon trembled in Katrina Kivi's hands as she walked down the hall toward the living room where Johnny and Kelly waited for her.

Jumbled thoughts pounded through her mind. Wrong, *wrong*, she was a fool to even think she could . . .

. . . do *what*? What did she think she would do?

. . . force them, force him, force anyone to just listen!

. . . she'd never aimed a gun at anyone. This wasn't her, not her, not Katrina Kivi, so why?

Because she had to do something, anything. She was only doing what he would do—pretend—because whoever Father Johnny was, he wasn't a priest.

Her hands felt slimy on the steel of the automatic. She nearly turned and ran back to the closet. She could still get back there and dump the weapons before they had any clue she'd gone this far.

But she kept on walking, ignoring her mother's voice in the back of her head mumbling that mantra about how her stubbornness would get her into real trouble one day. That one day was here. It was now.

Her eyes stung, blurring her vision, and she knew, she just *knew*, this was a bad, bad idea.

But she'd done it. It was too late.

A strange concoction of fear and rage screamed through Kat's head, and then she was around the corner, facing the back of Kelly's head on the couch. She stood behind Kelly, momentarily affixed to the carpet, gun extended.

". . . never know how it could turn out," Johnny was saying from the kitchen.

Again Kat nearly fled.

Again she forced her feet forward.

And then the gun was only three feet from the back of Kelly's head and Johnny was exiting the kitchen. "I think we . . ."

He saw her and stopped, bottle of water half raised to his mouth.

Kat stared at his black glasses. "Don't move, or she dies." Her words weren't hers, they couldn't be, because she wouldn't really say that, not really. She was a sixteen-year-old girl who had run into some bad luck with the Muslims; she was not a killer!

But she had said that. And now that she'd said it, her fear gave way to all the rage holed up for years.

Kelly turned her head.

"Don't move!" Kat screamed, gripping the gun more firmly. "Neither of you, don't—"

Kelly moved fast, whipping around, knocking the weapon aside with a brutal chop. The weapon flew from Kat's hands.

Kat may have been stalled by her lack of experience when it came to guns, but she'd been in her share of fights, and now on the defensive, her instincts returned.

She had the second gun out of her waistband before the automatic weapon hit the carpet. Fired one shot into the wall, surprised by the noise. The tremendous recoil forced her to take a step backward.

"I said don't move!"

Kelly now faced her, standing just beyond the couch with her hands half raised. Johnny still hadn't moved.

"Don't think I won't shoot," Kat cried. Her hands were still shaking, but now due to the adrenaline coursing through her veins.

Johnny slowly lowered the bottle in his right hand. She swiveled the gun to cover him, but then thought better of it and trained the barrel back on Kelly. Oddly enough, neither of them seemed too put off by her show of force, and this angered her more.

"I swear, I'll shoot."

"What do you want, Katrina?" Johnny asked in a soft voice.

Yes, what do you want, Katrina?

"Sit down. I want you to sit down."

"Why?"

"Be careful, Johnny," Kelly said. "This isn't why we are here."

"You think?"

She glanced at him, hands spread, but otherwise seemingly unconcerned. "She's nothing but a high-school student with a grudge."

"Is she? I don't know."

"You see something I don't?"

"Don't I always?" Johnny said.

"Yes or no?"

"I see a scared girl who was put into our path. I like her. She has a strong backbone. She needs some discipline, but I think she has a good heart."

Kelly faced Kat and studied her. They were obviously trying to distract her with all this nonsense. Kat took another step back, keeping the gun trained on the woman. "I just need your help," she said. "I . . . You have to listen to me!"

"I think we can trust her," Johnny said.

"Don't be foolish, Johnny!"

"They aren't after us—"

"You can't know that!" Kelly snapped.

"Stop it!" Kat shouted. "You think you can just talk nonsense and get me to drop my guard?"

"Please, Kat." Johnny set the bottle on the kitchen table and stepped into the living room, hands elevated by his sides. "You're far too intelligent to think shooting one of us might encourage the judge to extend you any leniency. It's the kind of thing dopers and pimps might try because they have a few burned circuits between the ears. You, on the other hand, know very well that harming either one of us will only ensure that your sentence is upgraded from months to years. And not jail, either. State prison."

He stopped by the couch in full view. "Am I wrong?"

"Then help me," she said.

"I offered you help, but you didn't want it."

"What are you talking about?" she cried. "You keep talking like that, but what did I do to make you hate me so much?"

"So you do want help in changing who you are?"

"What are you talking about? I am who I am! You can't tolerate who I am?"

"I can't tolerate your intolerance for Arabs, no. Or your hatred and fear of other people in general."

Here she stood, pointing a gun at a blind priest who wasn't really a priest and who couldn't possibly be blind, discussing *tolerance* of all things! The absurdity of it was as maddening as the fact that she no longer felt compelled to pull off this stunt.

But there was no way out now.

"You want me to stop hating Arabs? Fine, I swear to stop hating the towel-heads that've taken over Las Vegas and forced my mother to work long nights just to put macaroni and cheese on our table. Good enough? I'm a changed woman."

"You see? That's what I'm talking about. You want out of your predicament, but you don't want to change the person who got you into the predicament in the first place."

"Listen to me, honey," Kelly said. "If he's talking to you like this, you really should listen. Don't ask me why, but you've managed to get his attention. And trust me, it has nothing to do with the gun. He's faced far more than that toy in his days."

"Don't try to confuse me," Kat snapped. "I'm warning you . . ." But she stopped because even to her, her words sounded ridiculous.

"Kelly's talking about a time when I could make things do what they weren't supposed to do," Johnny said. "But it was temporary, a kind of surge, as best we can figure out."

"Don't let him fool you," Kelly said. To Johnny, "You sure you want to do this?"

If their intent was to distract her, they were succeeding with ease, Kat thought. They showed no fear, no real concern even. She might as well be holding a noodle. Their only dilemma was this business about whether Johnny should take her into his confidence.

"I don't know, Kat . . . What do you think? Are you willing to trust me on this?"

"Why should I?"

"Because you know it's the right thing to do. And because you have no other reasonable option."

"Okay. Fine. I'll trust you."

"Then lower the gun."

"Exactly!" she said. "You think I'm stupid?"

"No. Which is why you will lower the gun."

Her stubbornness had hit a wall. And Kat's curiosity had grown larger than her anger. So she lowered her gun, knowing that she could always lift it again.

"Give it to Kelly."

"That's not what you said."

"I'm saying it now."

Kelly held out her hand. Kat hesitated only a moment, then handed the weapon to her, relieved to be free from it. Kelly gathered up the automatic weapon and set both on the counter beside Johnny.

Kat felt weak in her knees, but she stood strong. Because that was what she'd always done. Stood strong.

"So who are you really, Father Johnny?"

"The real question, Kat, is who are you? If you can understand yourself, then you'll know where my journey started. Do you believe in God?"

"We already—"

"So then, I was once who you are today," he said. "If you want to understand me, you have to understand yourself. Why don't you believe?"

"For starters? Because everyone runs around killing in God's name."

"But that's a child's answer and you're already sixteen. You don't know much about religion, do you?"

"Should I?"

"Do you know the difference between Christianity and Islam?"

"Why are we talking about this? You're trying to get me to convert? There's a good reason why religion is not allowed in the schools. Because it brings out the kooks!"

"Please, humor me. The difference between Christianity and Islam?"

"How should I know? One prays in a mosque, one prays in a cathedral."

"So you know nothing. To you God is simply an extension of foolish religion. And if religion had much to do with God, I might agree with you. If you want to accept my help, the first thing you'll need to do is set any notion you have of religion aside. Put everything you think you know about Islam, Judaism, Christianity, Buddhism, all of it behind you. If you can do that, I may be able to help you."

"What are you trying to do? Convert me?"

"You've demonstrated that you have no true moral compass. No fundamental beliefs that guide what is right or wrong in this world. How can you hope to recognize good and evil for what they truly are if you have no belief in a moral authority greater than yourself?"

"Spoken like a true blood—"

"No!" Johnny snapped, cutting her off. "Please don't use that word in this house."

"Sorry. But you're saying that I'm going to jail because I don't believe in God."

Kelly stepped up beside him. He absently took her hand and kissed it.

"That's a bit simplistic, but yes. Because you haven't opened your eyes to see him. To love and be loved by him. 'For him who has eyes to see, let him see.' Jesus said that. Would you like to have your eyes opened?"

She had never heard such a preposterous line of argument. She knew the gist of God, naturally. Big guy in the sky who made it all and forgot to tell his subjects not to rape, kill, and destroy. But Johnny was right: she hadn't searched out the meaning behind any of the world's major religions.

The only religion she was truly familiar with was one called tolerance. Now the false priest was asking her if she wanted her eyes opened.

"How do you propose to do that?"

"I have a shortcut."

"Fine."

Johnny walked casually to the fireplace, something you wouldn't find in most homes in Nevada these days. But it was an old house. Kelly picked up a pair of sunglasses that sat on the kitchen counter and slid them onto the bridge of her nose.

"You're absolutely sure about this, Johnny?" Kelly asked.

"No."

He looked down at the floor, removed his own dark glasses, and stared straight down at the lenses.

Johnny lifted his head and stared at Kat with white eyes.

Not a speck of color, no retina, no pupil, just pure white eyes. The sight stopped her cold.

"You like?"

Like? She wasn't sure how she felt. He was blind after all.

"Can you see?"

"The question is, can you see? Really see?"

"Your . . ." Did she dare just blare it out? "Your eyes are white."

"That's their natural color, yes. And I can't see the world the way you see the world. It's more like heat signatures and geometrical shapes. But the power in these eyes of mine has more to do with you than me. They can help you see things differently."

On cue, his white eyes were gone, replaced by bright blue ones, as clear as sapphires.

Kat blinked, expecting them to change back, but they didn't. Johnny lifted his hand and snapped his fingers. An apple appeared in his palm.

"You like apples? If you try to eat this one, it will taste like air because it doesn't exist."

Impossible. Kat stepped up and put her hands on the back of the couch. "I . . ." She didn't know what to say.

"An illusion," Johnny said. "I can make you see what I want. I can either deceive you or let you see the truth."

He tossed the apple into the air and caught it, but now it was a snake, writhing in his fist. He struck the snake against his other palm and it became a wooden cross. He snapped his fingers and the cross vanished.

"That's incredible."

"No, it's commonplace. Half of what you think you know has been subjected to deception. You think you know so much about what matters: we all do. But we're blind to the real issue facing us. We've been sold a magic trick."

She was watching him, not six feet from him, when he vanished. She caught her breath. Kelly stood by the kitchen table, watching her, smiling.

"What happened?"

Kelly shrugged.

Kat studied the space that Johnny had occupied just a moment ago. "Is he . . . I mean, is he there?"

Johnny reappeared. "Exactly! Just because you didn't see me didn't mean I *wasn't* here, any more than seeing the apple meant it *was.*"

The simplicity of Johnny's point struck Kat broadside, like a locomotive on full steam.

"For him who has eyes to see . . ." she said.

Johnny finished the quote. "Let him see. Are you ready to see the truth, Kat?"

"Ummm . . ."

"It could change everything, I warn you."

"How do I know what it . . . What am I supposed to say to that? How could anyone say they don't want to see the truth?"

"You'd be surprised." He smiled. "Just say yes, Kat. Please say yes."

"Yes."

"Hold on to the couch."

She gripped the back of the couch, wondering what about the truth could possibly require her to hold on.

Johnny closed his blue eyes. When he opened them again they were white. But then they were black and then they weren't eyes at all.

They were a pool of darkness, drawing her deep, deep into hot black water, suffocating her. Pain ripped through her spine, and she heard herself—the self gripping the couch—gasp.

And then scream.

She was in a black lake, unable to breathe, smothered by the shock of it all. And yet she was screaming.

Kat doubled over and sucked at the blackness. Vile bitterness seared and flooded her lungs. Entered her capillaries. Seeped into her bloodstream.

And she knew then that she'd breathed evil. Raw, unfiltered evil.

From her own soul.

She felt herself falling, here by the couch. She was shaking from head to foot, unable to close her eyes, staring into Johnny's black eyeballs.

Screaming. Screaming.

From the corner of her eye she saw Kelly's mouth yelling at Johnny to stop, stop, stop, but Kat couldn't hear Kelly over her own screams.

And Johnny did not stop.

Kat wasn't sure how she knew, but she knew that she was seeing herself as she really was. Nothing more, nothing less. Just the truth of Katrina Kivi.

This evil within herself washed her mind with unrelenting waves of horror.

The water turned blood red. She was still screaming by the couch, but it occurred to her that she didn't need to scream any longer. The horror still clawed at her mind, but the pain and bitterness was soothed by the water.

A baby before birth.

Her voice caught in her throat. She stared around at the red water, stunned by the absence of pain. The change was so great, so overwhelming that she wanted to cry. To sob like a baby, safe, just safe in the belly of the . . .

A distant cry came to her ears.

The cry swelled to a scream that was not hers. The water around her was screaming. Oh the anguish, the pain, the remorse, the horror in the wail flogged her mind.

She rolled tight into a ball and began to scream with it, crying her remorse, her terror. She wanted to be out of this red lake, breathing new life, reborn.

And then Johnny closed his eyes and Kat was back in the room, behind the couch, screaming at the top of her lungs, shaking violently, standing only because her fingers had latched on to the cushion and refused to let her collapse.

But now she was here, just here, and she relaxed her grip. She fell to the carpet like a bag of rocks.

CHAPTER FIFTEEN

MARSUVEES BLACK stopped on the street curb, cracked his knuckles, and looked first to his right, then to his left. Twenty-ninth Street was quiet, too quiet, terrifyingly quiet for his own considerable tastes. He'd long ago discovered that he liked hanging out with people, particularly when their necks were doing the hanging. The small church across the street, however, was not quiet. Seventy or more parishioners were inside the converted watering hole being faithful, most of them were colored folk.

These seventy-or-more colored folk were about to help him change the course of history.

He had nothing against colored folk, no he did not. No sir. He himself was a colored folk, really. White skin, but his trench coat was black, his boots were black, his hat was black. If he'd had a choice, he himself would have been black because from his experience, most black folk were smarter than the white trash he'd run across. Take Arabs, take Indians, take Mexicans, take Africans, take whites, throw them all in a bowl and the dumbest of the bunch always came out as white as a pancake.

Another reason he wished he could have dark skin was because being white as a bowl of flour lumped him in with a group of people who were known to be more devious. He would be less likely to draw suspicion if he were black.

At one point in history, some had erroneously associated dark skin with certain negative, even criminal tendencies. The trend was now precisely the opposite. Being white was a distinct disadvantage. His timing was off by fifty years.

Hitler, now there was one fine white fellow who'd attempted to show the world the truth about whites. And despite being dead wrong in the end, he'd effectively demonstrated how to sweep away the sentiments of a whole country.

Marsuvees had no issue with skin color. Christianity, on the other hand, was a different matter altogether. He spat to one side. But the fact that these particular Christians were also colored was of the utmost importance. It was a two-for-one sale, and he intended on selling the whole lot to the world.

Satisfied that the quiet night was ready to accept him, Marsuvees Black stepped across the street.

Practice makes perfect, it was said. It was time to practice.

He stepped up to the entrance, cracked his neck, put his hand on the door, and entered the Holy Baptist Church of the Resurrection.

The crowd inside did not stop humming and swaying as a bass player and an organist filled the small, dimly lit, bar-turned church with a disturbing tune he'd heard a time or two in his life. None of the faithful turned to stare at the white guy who'd just entered. Indeed, no one seemed to have even noticed that Marsuvees Black was among them.

He suppressed a tinge of irritation—the briefest temptation to do some immediate and exquisitely painful damage to the lot of them. Although it was true that he found most colored folk more intelligent than pasty whites, his general hatred of all people by far superseded any respect he had for the people in the Holy Baptist Church of the Resurrection. And the fact that they had as of yet returned none of his respect only reinforced that hatred. He'd undoubtedly selected the right church for his deed.

One rather thin man with graying hair who might be considered an usher was smiling at Black from behind the bank of chairs set up on the right.

Black strode up to the man, black alligator-skin boots clunking upon the wood floor with each step. He stopped, keeping his eyes on the platform. "Christians," he said.

"Yes, that's right," the man returned.

Black again restrained himself, mission clearly in mind. He strode up the aisle, keeping his gaze on the bass player.

He spoke plainly but just loudly enough for those on either side to hear as he passed. "Shut up, shut up, you pathetic black bloodsuckers. Shut your black holes, every one of you stinking hatemongers. Die in hell, you filthy black bloody suckers."

The reaction was what he'd expected, stares and angry glares. They were obviously stunned by his choice of words, thinking perhaps that a lunatic had escaped from an institution and found himself in the wrong building. In this age of tolerance, walking around uttering such language was unthinkable to all but complete fools. He particularly liked the word *bloodsucker*, a useful slur popularized as of late that called into question the absurd habit Christians had of taking communion, of drinking Christ's blood to celebrate Christ's death.

Black held his tongue, having sown just enough bitterness to suit him, and stepped up on the stage. Four brothers were playing a bass, an electric guitar, a piano, and a set of drums. He mounted the stage and strode up to a microphone not in use.

The music went on as if he hardly mattered. But that would change.

He'd selected the church because it was located only blocks from Union Cemetery and was frequented by blacks, many of whom represented the city's key circles of influence. Judging by their dress, the place looked to be full of professionals tonight, though in a church it was always hard to tell.

He leaned into the mike, tapped it, and was rewarded with a loud *thunk*. The organ and bass were still in full swing, but he spoke over them.

"Thank you, Bill. Fantastic, fantastic. Let's give our well-groomed players a hand, shall we?" He applauded loudly and smiled at the organist, a proud-looking woman with high cheekbones whose fingers now stalled on the keys.

A smattering of applause spread among those who didn't yet realize that they were about to get more than they bargained for.

"Thank you. Not often do you get such superb playing from monkeys Bravo!"

The place fell quiet. Nice. Issue any similar statement directed to whites in a gathering of rednecks, and they would be hollering threats of retaliation. Here, Black would have to dig deeper.

"Thank you all for coming out tonight. In addition to the freak show on my left we have a very special treat for you tonight. Me. Here to set the record straight for all of you brothers and, uh . . . sisters."

A large, well-muscled man who might well be the preacher was approaching the stage. "Please, this isn't the place."

Black could have toyed with him, but he chose not to. He drew an old Smith & Wesson six-shooter he favored and shot into the air.

Boom!

"Actually, I do mind. Just hold your horses there, you fat pig," he drawled.

The man pulled up sharply. Somewhere a Bible or a hymnal thumped softly closed.

"Now, I realize that my words aren't the kind our society takes in stride, but you know as well as I do that plenty of people out there are thinking what I'm just saying. Not even ordinary types of people, but politicians and lawmen. Am I not right? The whole world hates you Christians."

Another man, whom Black now guessed was the pastor, stepped out, both hands stretched high in a plea for caution. "Sir, put the gun—"

"Shut up, gimpy. I'm here to help you, not hurt you. And don't bother calling the police. I'm leaving soon enough."

Now he had their fullest attention. The door banged as several scurried out the back. He let them go.

"Now, I'm not one of those who would put you back on the ship and send you back to Africa were it in my power to do so. I'm a man who realizes that blacks should probably run this country. All things being equal, they're smarter, they have more patience, they aren't as lazy, they are better lovers, they know how to entertain on the field, on the stage, you name it. Blacks rule, baby. But this Christianity bit . . . It's a bit much, don't you think?"

"Sir, I'm—"

"Please, sir, don't be so white. I'm trying to make a point. The time has come to deal with the race and religion issue once and for all. You've all heard about the lyncher."

Unless they were living under a mattress, they had, all of them. As had Black, who was, in fact, the very lyncher who had been making national headlines.

Marsuvees grinned. "You think this is the work of some lone psychopath? Not a chance. It's a calculated effort to enrage the black community, if not the community of believers. And if it doesn't work, you're not as intelligent as all the latest studies say you are. The first shots of a new cultural war have been fired. Pony up. Fire back. Or at the very least have your less restrained brothers fire back. For heaven's sake, don't be such wimps. The time has come for a cultural revolution. Black power!"

Black shoved his gun back into the holster under his arm.

"If my words haven't successfully enraged you, then I hope the lynchings will. They won't stop, not until riots turn the streets red."

He let them chew on that for several seconds.

"I have it on good authority that not one but two people in this room at this very moment will find themselves hung from a tree in Union Cemetery by morning."

He tipped his hat. "Thank you kindly for your attention."

Marsuvees Black stepped off the stage, exited through the side fire door, and receded into the dark. It was going to be a busy, busy night.

CHAPTER SIXTEEN

Day Three

DARCY WOKE to the annoying ring of the telephone. It was 7:00 a.m. by the clock on her wall. She assumed Billy had picked up from his suite after three rings, and rolled over for more sleep. They'd agreed on a nine o'clock pickup.

She was just beginning to slip away again when a rap on the door jerked her from sleep. "What is it?"

Billy poked his head in, eyes covered by dark glasses. "Kinnard's on his way."

He looked sophisticated in his white bathrobe. "What happened to nine?"

"Change of schedule. Lawhead has a plane fueled and waiting to take us to Kansas City. Kinnard wouldn't say, but something went down last night. He'll be here in half an hour."

"Nice of them to let us out of our cage early," she said bitterly.

He frowned, pulled his head out, and closed the door.

She rolled from the bed and dragged herself into the bathroom—an expansive living space with double doors, a large round Jacuzzi dead center, sinks on either side, a five-foot shower encased in clear glass, and a separate room, which housed the bidet. Fluffy white towels, slippers, bathrobe, all the bubble bath and body soaps she could possibly use.

The maid would clean the entire apartment once every day.

Billy's room had identical accommodations. This was how royalty lived, Darcy thought, the kind of lifestyle she'd railed against on more than one occasion. But standing in the middle of the bathroom this morning, she wasn't sure she entirely disapproved.

Billy sat at the breakfast bar scanning a Net feed on the wall monitor when she came out twenty minutes later. A silver tray rested on the table, neatly arranged with raspberry and vanilla Danishes, sliced apples, oranges, and a pot of something hot.

"That was quick. Coffee?"

She shook her messy mane. "Do I strike you as the kind who needs an hour to curl my locks? Coffee would be nice, thank you."

She watched him pour the steaming liquid from the white pot into a black porcelain mug. He gestured to the wall. "Another lynching in Kansas City last night. Front page."

She glanced at a headline: Two Dead from Kansas City Church.

"Someone's trying to make a point." She took a sip of coffee. "Pretty sick."

Billy stood, picked a black blazer off the back of the bar stool, and laid it on the sofa. Dressed in a pressed white shirt tucked smartly into black slacks, he undid his tie, pulled it free, and faced her. Her Billy, all grown up and dressed for success. She thought he looked handsome.

"You think I'm underdressed?" she asked. She'd chosen a stylish throwback to gothic dresses. Her standard fare. Charcoal.

"You're you. I think it may take them a day or two to get used to the idea, but anything different would be a mistake."

"Was that a yes or a no?"

"A no. Not at all. Not for my tastes anyway."

THEY FLEW to Kansas City in a government-leased supersonic Citation 25, one of the newer models that covered the thousand-mile flight in less than one hour.

Darcy sat next to Billy, arms and legs crossed, listening as he engaged Lawhead and Kinnard on all the pertinent facts regarding the Kansas City lyncher, as if this sort of thing came as naturally to him as tying his shoes.

How race could still be an issue with some people was beyond Darcy. There were some areas in which society had actually made progress over the years. Race was one. Surely those who thought race had any more to do with their value than the color of their underwear deserved to be locked up in a loony bin.

". . . which, as bad as it may seem, isn't our primary concern," Lawhead was saying.

"No?" Billy asked. "Then what is?"

"The potential spillover."

"Others jumping on the bandwagon," Billy said. "Copycat crimes, vigilante justice, revenge."

"Correct."

"Over race?" Darcy asked. "Last time I checked, we do live in the twenty-first century, *please*. I would think the religious tension would be greater than any racial divide."

Lawhead's brow arched. "Maybe. Hard to separate them at times. But race has *always* played a major role in any nation's evolution, including our own. Rwanda, Somalia, Sudan, Indonesia, Uganda, Croatia, Palestine, Germany—if history teaches anything about race it's that humans are hardwired to feel superior to their fellow men and women, and nowhere is that sentiment as easily expressed as in matters of race. It only takes a spark to provoke the minds of one race against another."

She'd never thought of it in those terms.

"We've had four sparks in the space of eight days," Lawhead continued. "The drums are beating already. Every Net feed in the country is featuring the story, top of the hour."

"Surely people have the sense to realize someone is purposefully stirring this up."

"That's not the point. A thousand editorials on the Net are ranting about the injustice—"

"As they should be," she said.

"As they should be. But the editorials take the rhetoric further, railing against any white supremacist who would dare stoop to this. In an issue as deep-rooted and tragic as race in America, passions are easily inflamed. More people have lost their lives over the race issue than any other issue in human history. Just counting our own Civil War and Hitler's extermination of Jews . . . well, I'm sure you get the point."

"I do. And religion?"

"Clearly someone hates Christians. But Christians aren't striking back, so the situation is stable. If there is any retaliation, however . . ."

"Then Christians will be as culpable as any race," she said. "Even if they aren't to blame, you'll have a true mess on your hands."

"God forbid," Lawhead said. "No pun intended."

"So, what exactly is the point of this?" she asked in a moment of silence. "Me and Billy, I mean. What exactly do you expect your two little lab rats to do? You really think we can solve this case for you?"

Perhaps she was just a bit harsh.

Lawhead glanced at Kinnard, then back to her, pushing the bridge on his sunglasses to snug them against his forehead.

"This trip is not about this case," Kinnard said. "It's about you. We would like to better understand exactly what you're capable of. In the field."

"You saw what we could do last night."

"If you can do in a group, under pressure, what you did last night . . ." He stopped there.

"We can take over the world," she finished.

Kinnard smiled. "Maybe not, but you get the picture."

They landed at nine and drove in an armored FBI Cadillac to the vicinity of Union Cemetery, just off Warwick Trafficway, two miles south of city central. The street was blockaded by several police cruisers, but onlookers were crossing into the large cemetery from the perimeter. Streams of people walked or ran toward a grove at the center of the burial grounds.

Lawhead swore and made a quick call on his cell. He snapped the phone closed. An officer who was trying his best to keep the road clear for authorized traffic waved them through the barricade.

"How long have they had the scene secured?" Billy asked.

"The bodies were discovered by a jogger at six thirty this morning. We were on-site with the local authorities shortly after. The crime scene is secured, but the cemetery is open access. They can't secure the whole thing."

The hanging had occurred among a group of large trees at the heart of the cemetery. Darcy saw the ropes hanging from two adjacent trees before they crossed the yellow tape that cordoned off the crime scene. Federal Bureau of Investigation—Crime Scene—Do Not Cross.

Two dangling ropes with nooses at the ends of each. The thick fiber ropes were twisted around themselves atop eighteen-inch loops, which were stained dark brown with blood. Her stomach turned. Whoever was behind this had chosen one of the most offensive symbols in American history to elicit precisely this kind of reaction. It was all far too sick for her tastes.

And as for those gathered . . . Gazing around, she wondered why they weren't rioting already.

"You really think it's wise to keep those up?" she asked. "Everyone can see the ropes. Even from the perimeter."

"Follow me," Lawhead said. He climbed from the car and walked to a white tent. Darcy and Billy followed with Kinnard, wearing glasses.

The two bodies had been laid out on white evidence mats in the center of the tent. A porous mesh cloth was tented over the bodies of each. A black woman in a purple dress who looked to be in her early twenties, and an older man who could have been her father. Their faces were bloated, eyes open, mouths gaping. Rope-burned wrists, bloodshot stares.

Darcy turned away, nauseated. She took one look around the tent, saw that the crime scene investigators had the situation covered, and stepped back outside.

A thousand stares met hers. People lined the perimeter, twenty, maybe thirty deep, set back fifty yards from the tent. If they weren't staring at her, they were looking up at the ropes. An eerie quiet gripped them all.

"You okay?" Billy took her elbow.

"Not really, no. I don't belong here."

"I know how you feel."

A fire truck was extending its ladder to remove the ropes.

"What kind of monster would do this?"

"The same kind of monster who was in your house two nights ago," Billy said.

Her head spun with the memory of the long night. So much had happened in such a short space of time. It was hard for her to wrap her mind around it all.

"Trust me, the world is full of people who would just as soon hang their neighbors as put up with them. I should know. I made my living defending some of those people."

Kinnard emerged from the tent with Lawhead. "You two okay?"

"Darcy was just making a good point," Billy said. "Remind us again exactly what it is you want us to do here."

Lawhead scanned the onlookers at the perimeter. "More than likely he's out there now, watching." His eyes settled on Billy. "You're looking for a white male, middle-aged."

Kinnard and Lawhead looked at him like scientists studying a new specimen. They both had worn glasses for the duration of the flight, unwilling to subject themselves to whatever forces probed Annie Ruling at the council meeting.

"You sure you're up to this?" Kinnard asked. "It's entirely up to you, as agreed. You say the word and we're gone."

"What about Darcy?" Billy asked.

"You're welcome to join us," Kinnard said to her.

Billy nodded. Plucked off his glasses, baring his green eyes. "Wait here for Darcy and me."

"No," Kinnard said. "I go with you. And I don't want you any closer to the perimeter than ten feet."

Yes, of course, their protector.

"Isn't this a bit dangerous? Seeing as there are people who might want us dead?"

"No one could possibly know you're here. Washington would be a different matter. Ready?"

"Go ahead," Lawhead said. "I have a call. I'll catch up with you."

Darcy followed Billy and Kinnard toward the perimeter, feeling even more out of sorts than she had earlier. Not because she was useless here, although she certainly felt like a third leg, but because they were now part of the spectacle. Three white goons walking around inside the perimeter, returning the stares of those gathered with hate in their hearts.

And she was the straggler, dressed like some kind of hippie behind the clean-cut attorney with his armed guard.

"Anything?" Kinnard asked.

Billy grunted and walked on, scanning the crowd, slowing at each white face. Darcy nearly turned and cut back for the tent several times but reminded herself there was nothing in the tent that was her business either.

"Anything?" Kinnard was impatient.

"Plenty. Frankly I'm not sure how much of this I can take."

"Meaning?"

"Meaning you have a problem here, my friend. Somebody better start talking to these people about why . . ." He stopped and stared at a man who held a noose in his right hand, twirling it in small circles, eyes fixed on them.

"You okay?" Kinnard asked.

Billy walked on. "Fine."

Darcy turned and headed back toward the tent. "I'll see you when you finish."

She stood by one of the ambulances and watched as Billy and Kinnard slowly made their full circuit before regrouping at the tent with Lawhead.

"Well?" the FBI man asked.

Billy slid his glasses over glazed eyes, hands trembling. He looked back at the crowd, as if testing the waters to see if the glasses were protecting him from their thoughts.

"Billy? You okay, son?"

"I'm fine."

But he wasn't, she thought.

"What did you get?" Lawhead pushed.

"More than I bargained for. How long are we going to be here?"

"They'll keep the scene secured for a few days. The heavy lifting will be done in a few hours. No reason to believe he's out there?"

"No. If he's out there, he's either not thinking about the crime or our eyes didn't meet."

"So it's working, then," Kinnard said.

"Working, yes."

Lawhead took Billy's elbow. "That's good. But before you go again, I want you to make a sweep inside the tent."

"Again?"

"You know as well as I do there's a good chance he's close by. You know how explosive the situation could get. Please, if there's even a small chance you can expose him . . ."

Billy hesitated. "Once more. That's all I think I can handle."

CHAPTER SEVENTEEN

DARCY DIDN'T think she was up to hanging out with two dead bodies or she would have followed them in. But she wasn't up to being the object of so many stares either.

She found her predicament positively absurd! Enraging even.

Without allowing herself another moment's hesitation, Darcy headed for the gap in the perimeter where two police cars controlled access to the crime scene.

She strode up to the barricade where an officer stepped in her path. "May I help you?"

"Yes, you can let me through. I need to get some air."

"I understand. Maybe I could get you an escort."

"No, I don't want an escort. I'm fine, these people have nothing against me."

"I really think you should wait for an escort, ma'am."

Darcy pulled off her glasses and stared him in the eyes. "You have no authority to keep me here. Let me pass."

He blinked. Twice. Then he stepped aside. "Of course, ma'am."

"If they ask, tell them I'm waiting in the trees over there."

"Yes, ma'am."

She stepped past him, wondering if she'd really done that. Of course she had! The power she held in this new voice of hers was a bit stunning. She put her glasses back on and headed for the public restrooms, eyes fixed ahead, refusing to be intimidated by a dozen angry stares.

There was no way she could know for certain that this ability of hers worked every time. In fact, of the three events thus far, only Annie's reaction to her suggestion she slap Manning was irrefutably linked to a power beyond her comprehension. Billy's kiss and this passing could be explained by other means.

Why are you so resistant to the idea, Darcy?

Because it was too much. Who'd ever heard of such a preposterous thing? The world turned on its axis, round and round without even the slightest pause, regardless of what anyone did. Some things did not change. Movies of superheroes who'd evolved, or vampires who fed on the living were one thing. This . . . this was another.

Then again, so was writing in the books below the monastery with Billy as a child.

The bulk of the crowd was gathered around the scene a hundred yards to her back now. Dozens, maybe hundreds, were still hopping the fences and pouring into the cemetery from all sides, coming to see what all the fuss was about. But the main entrance was guarded and lay directly behind the trees she walked to. Large gravestones rose from the ground like guards for the dead.

Darcy walked around a few of the monuments.

David Wilber

1999–2023

Who Loved Truth More Than Life

Rest in Peace

Another to Zephaniah Smith. Where did these names come from? America was a mishmash of a hundred cultures all thrown into one giant pot and stirred slowly over the fires of time. A delicious stew of harmonious humanity celebrating diversity and tolerance. Naming their children Zephaniah Smith.

"You lost?"

Darcy turned around, startled by the low voice. Five men stared at her from a distance of ten feet, two with their feet planted on headstones. She recognized the one who appeared to be their leader by the noose stuffed half into his jeans pocket. He'd stared at her from the crowd earlier.

"No, not really. You?" she asked.

"You look lost to me," the man said. They were blacks, gangbangers with red and blue bandanas wrapped around their upper arms. Silver chains with crosses hung heavy from their necks.

"Last I checked we were in Union Cemetery, close to downtown, Kansas City," she said. "You need directions somewhere?"

One of the others chuckled. "Man, she got it going, James."

"Shut up, fool." He jerked his chin at Darcy. "You think a smart mouth makes you any better?"

Darcy glanced at the rope. "What's the noose for?"

"They're used for hangings. Or did you think your kind were the only ones who knew how to have fun?"

It occurred to her that she might be in a bit of trouble here. She looked at them all, eyes fired for violence. Maybe she'd spoken too soon. There were times to fight back and times to walk away, and although she wasn't very good at the latter, this was shaping up to be a time for it.

"I'm sorry for your loss," she said with as much sincerity as she could. And she meant it.

James walked slowly up to her, grinning. He reached out for her chin, and although every bone in her body begged her to snap, she made no attempt to stop him. His finger traced a line down her cheek, down her neck, over her shoulder.

Darcy began to tremble.

"What's a lily-white party girl like you doing in our town? Hmmm?"

She swallowed. "I'm trying to help you out."

The one who'd chuckled earlier looked back at the crowd, then stepped up with the others. She took a step backward, then another, and ran into Zephaniah Smith's large tombstone. She thought about screaming Billy's name but knew he'd never hear her.

"All dressed up like a rock star," James said, plucking at the straps on her dress. "You came down here to rock out with the monkeys, celebrate the lynching. Huh?"

"Sing for us, rock star," one dressed in a red shirt said.

They pressed closer, forming a tight circle that prevented her from seeing past them. Her fear spiked and she began to sweat.

"You're mistaking me for someone else," she said. "I don't have a racist bone in my body."

"That so? How many times have I heard that? I saw the way you walked around all high and mighty."

"Come on, sing for us, lily-white," the one in the red shirt repeated.

"Disappointed by the turnout, party girl?" James said. His gleaming white teeth and wet lips were close, covered in the smell of tobacco. "I knew that girl you have in the tent back there. She was the valedictorian at my high school four years ago. You people never get it, do you?"

Darcy felt smothered. She could smell their deodorant, their breath, feel the heat from their bodies. Trapped. Boarded up, sealed tight, no way out.

"Please . . ." She felt her reserves of courage waning and closed her eyes. "Please, please . . ." Her own shift from defiance to dread sickened her, but she felt powerless to stop her sinking emotions.

"You heard him," James said. "Sing and we might let you walk away." She felt something touch her head, then slide down over her face. The noose, she saw with a glance. He'd slipped the noose over her head.

"How does it feel?"

She cowered against Zephaniah Smith's tombstone, hands flat against the surface on either side. She should sing, she thought. Just sing. How she'd found herself in such a predicament was no longer a relevant question. She had to get out, that was all that mattered now.

"Go on," James said, mouth hovering an inch from her face. "Sing like a bird."

"Please . . ."

"Sing!" he screamed.

She flinched and began to sing through a flood of tears. Random words unconnected to any tune she knew. "Please, don't hurt me, please save me, please, I beg you, I beg you, I beg you."

"What else, huh, baby? What else you beg us to do?"

She could barely think straight. Fury pushed her fear back—but then it returned, even more tangible than before.

"Sing for us that lily-white lullaby, baby," James said, lifting the glasses from her face.

Darcy clenched her eyes and tried to sing again, but the words refused to form any tune. "Please leave me alone. Please . . ."

She couldn't do this. Any moment and she would crack; she could feel the outrage coiled inside her mind, straining against good sense. When she snapped she would launch herself at them fingernails first, take some skin with her, and then be beaten to a pulp, she knew that. And she didn't want that. But she just couldn't cower here and sing for them.

"Please . . ." she whispered. "Billy, please. Please don't do this."

"Please don't do this," he mimicked. The noose tightened. "Don't do what? Make you sing or hang you by the neck? Isn't that what you people want us blacks to do for you? Perform like a bunch of monkeys?"

"No, no, that's not me."

Their leader leaned forward and licked her cheek. Her control broke then, while his tongue was still on her face.

"Don't!" She lowered her head, shoved both arms out, and pounded into his gut like a battering ram. "Don't. Don't you dare touch me! Don't, you sick beast!"

"Mother of . . ." Hands grabbed her and pinned her back against the tombstone, but she kicked out with both feet.

However noble and courageous her attack, it yielded nothing but rage from them. They smothered her, punched her in her gut. A hand slapped her face.

One of them got his arm around her throat and began to choke her so she couldn't breathe, much less beg for . . .

Then Darcy remembered her voice. A distant abstract detail floating on the edge of her mind. *Save yourself, Darcy! Look in their eyes and speak to them and save yourself!*

She snapped her eyes wide. James grabbed her face in one hand and squeezed her cheeks tight. "You're going to pay for that, lily-white."

Darcy tried to scream at him; nothing but rasping air came out.

"Back off, James. You can't kill her," one of them said.

"No?" His fist slammed into her gut and she jerked forward against the arm coiled around her throat. She tried to suck in some air, found none. Her oxygen-deprived head pounded; the world began to fade.

She was going to pass out! She wanted to look them in the eyes and use her voice, but now she was going to pass . . .

James grabbed her hair and jerked her head back so that she was forced to stare into his face. "It's nothing personal, lily-white, but we're going to send a message. And you're our messenger."

His eyes were only a few inches from hers when the arm around her throat relaxed.

She forced a single word from her lungs with her last reserve of air. "No," she breathed.

Then she sucked at the air. Her lungs filled with oxygen. James continued to drill her with his malignant stare. *It isn't going to work.* Tears blurred her vision. And then Darcy did the only thing left in her heart to do, knowing that they were going to kill her.

She screamed her rage. "No, no, no!" she screamed, each word growing in volume. "Let me go, you sick dog, you have no right to touch me,
no, no . . ."

The arm tightened, cutting off her voice.

James froze, breathing hard. His eyes were wide.

"Let her go," one of the others said.

The guy with his arm squeezing her neck wasn't getting the message.
James pulled back, confused, still fixed on her. "Let her go."

"What? What do—"

"Let her go!" he snapped.

The arm released its grip.

Darcy doubled over, gasping. Oxygen flooded her lungs, seeped into
her blood, swarmed her with life. She breathed deep and hard, and they
watched her.

"What's wrong with you fools?" the one who'd choked her said. "You
think this will bring Samantha back from the dead? We have this whore
dead to rights here and I'm be—"

"Shut up!" Darcy screamed, jerking her head around to face him.

He returned her stare, speechless.

She stood up, rubbing her throat. The anger she'd felt before dread had
set in returned with a vengeance. "You want me to sing? Is that what you
want? You want your pretty little rock star to sing for you? Huh?"

Darcy glanced over their shoulders. A few from the edge of the crowd
were looking their way, but no sign of the cavalry.

"Go ahead," she said, glaring at them again. "Beg me. Beg me! Beg me,
James. Beg the rocker girl you tried to kill for forgiveness."

His faced had lightened a shade. "Please . . ."

"You should be ashamed of yourselves, all of you!"

"I—"

"Shut up. Get on your knees."

They hesitated, so she put it another way. "You know you should grovel at my feet for what you've done. It's unforgivable! Get on your knees! Now!"

They sank to their knees, all five of them, and Darcy learned then that she didn't need to look at each one as long as they were looking at her eyes. They seemed to be more responsive than Annie Ruling. Why? Because of her own passion, perhaps.

She paced in front of them, breathing deeply. "You're petrified, aren't you? Well, you should be. You should feel terrified by yourselves."

Tears sprang to the eyes of the one in the red shirt "Please, oh please, we're so sorry."

They were like putty in her hands, she thought. Not robots who would do whatever she wanted them to do, but minds inclined to do what she could convince them was the right thing.

"I'm leaving," she said. "And I don't want you to tell anyone what happened here. You don't tell them you tried to lynch me, and you don't tell them you broke down like a bunch of babies. You hear?"

They all nodded except for James, who still looked like he'd been hit by a comet.

"James? You hear me?"

"Yeah."

"Good. Get up."

They stood.

"Now shake my hand, so anyone watching believes we were just messing around."

She shook their hands one by one, then left them standing by Zephaniah Smith's tombstone.

So . . . now she knew. She most certainly did have a gifted voice and it wasn't giving out. The power of it made her dizzy.

CHAPTER EIGHTEEN

BOULDER CITY High School had been flattened to the ground and rebuilt three years earlier to accommodate the swelling student body, a move that had sparked outrage from those who thought adding trailers to the old school would suffice in the face of rising taxes.

From the air, the academic halls looked like a plus sign, a Swiss cross, with a large circular atrium at the center. Directly to the west stood the gymnasium and lunchroom. All new, all beautifully furnished thanks to the taxpayers.

But the real beauty of the campus lay outside the buildings. Here the desert had been transformed into a lush greenway that could be mistaken for a golf course at first look. Twenty acres of manicured lawn, broken by small pockets of desert landscape and gazebos where students could escape the sun to study or loiter.

The greenway ended at a small concrete pond with a twenty-foot-high fountain that sprayed water behind a placard: From the Desert Rises a Fertile Mind, Never to Be Wasted.

As was so often the case, when the dust settled and the buildings stood proud, the tax-hike controversy had been long forgotten.

Other controversies among the 2,429 students that roamed the beautiful new campus, however, were new every morning.

Like every school in the United States, the race-religion controversy was more felt than spoken, because the public school system had long ago learned that some things were best left out of the classroom. Issues like freedom of religious expression, which had taken a brutal beating early in the century. Like politics, which was best discussed at home. Issues like racial prejudice, which had come full circle in its failure to be resolved. After all, whites, the historical perpetrators of most racial discrimination in the United States, were now a minority.

But the lynchings in Kansas City over the past week had sparked a flame among the students in most schools across the country, and Boulder City High was no exception. Principal Joseph Durst had used the public address system for a reasoned speech about the absurdity of racially motivated hate crimes. "Tolerance, students, is the pathway to harmony. Diversity should be celebrated, not snuffed out. Just remember we live in the twenty-first century, not the Dark Ages."

Although his intentions were undoubtedly sincere, the announcement only highlighted the news of the two latest lynchings in a Kansas City graveyard this morning.

Katrina Kivi walked down the covered walkway that led to the first set of gazebos in the yard, as they called it. The fountain rose majestically a hundred yards directly ahead. Carla walked beside her, noisily popping gum, rambling on about how Mexicans were worse than the whites and if there was anyone the cops should suspect, it should be a Chicano.

Katrina Kivi couldn't say that she didn't care, but compared to events that had forever altered her own world these past twenty-four hours, two hangings in a Kansas City graveyard, however tragic, seemed distant.

In fact, most of the day had felt disconnected from Kat. Like everything around her was actually part of a world to which she didn't belong. She'd awoken to discover that she was really an alien and had been sent here at birth by the mother ship as part of an experiment.

She dressed the same: blue jeans, black blouse. Still had the snake tat-
too on her shoulder blade that could just be seen slithering around her
neck when she wore a T-shirt. Same dark hair, same hazel eyes, same skull
ring on her left forefinger.

But she didn't feel like the same person who walked down this very
same outdoor walkway with Carla and Jay yesterday. Kat's friends had long
ago agreed they were three of the school's twenty-seven "true" witches,
who didn't dabble in the craft but lived by a respectable code.

It was the kind of hogwash Kat normally would have shot down in
flames, but she went along with this to be included. A person had to
belong somewhere. Today, though, she knew that she was a foreigner even
among her own clique.

"So you gonna tell me?" Carla asked.

"Hmmm?"

"C'mon, Kat. Don't you try to tell me nothing's wrong. Why you
being so quiet today? You sick?"

"No, I'm fine." She wasn't fine, of course. She was far better than fine.

"Okay . . . so what happened?"

The events of last night spun through her mind for the hundredth
time since leaving Johnny's house late last night. Her eyes had been
opened to another world. She'd seen herself as she truly was, but that
wasn't the main thing.

The main thing was that for the first time in her life she became
completely and utterly aware of a greater reality, of which she was a part.
Simple statements she'd once heard as distant, annoying barking dogs in
the night, yapping, yapping at the world, had thundered through her
mind. A huge monster had grabbed her by the hair, spun her around,
and roared in her face with enough power to rip her skin off.

Okay, that wasn't the way Johnny had put it, but it was what had happened. Only the huge monster had turned out to be God. Not in a million years would she have figured. How ludicrous.

God.

Walking next to Carla now, the word sounded so . . . strange.

"God," she whispered.

"What?"

"What?" She remembered that Carla was waiting for an explanation. "Never mind." But then Kat couldn't keep it back any longer.

She smiled, gripped her books tight against her chest. "Carla, what if I told you that everything you thought about life was wrong?"

Carla was looking at Charles Wright, who loitered with a group of football jocks. All blacks. "He thinks he's so hot." But the devilish grin on her face betrayed her infatuation with the running back, who was watching them.

He smiled and nodded. Carla lifted her fingers in a tempered acknowledgement, then turned back to Kat.

Carla feigned nonchalance, but her crush on Charles was well known to the group. "You see that look?" she said.

"I saw it." But Kat wasn't interested in it.

"Sorry. You were saying?"

Kat had thought through countless ways to spill the beans to her fellow witches, and none of them seemed particularly compelling.

"What if I told you that God was real?"

"Yeah? So what?" Carla glanced back at the group of jocks.

"I mean, really real? Like in Moses-in-the-ark real?" Or had she gotten that mixed up?

"Moses? I'd say you were starting to sound like a Muslim." Her friend grabbed her arm playfully. "Don't tell me you've decided to put aside your witchery and follow hard after Moses and Jesus! Oh, that's just wonderful news, Kat."

"Muslims? Do they follow Jesus?"

"'Course they do." Carla's voice was tinged with bitterness.

"Where'd you learn that?"

"Before my father converted to Islam, my family used to go to church. Trust me, I've had an earful. Muslims think Jesus was the only sinless person, prophet, whatever, to live. They worship the ground he walks on."

"They do?"

She shrugged and grinned. "What would I know? I'm just a witch."

After picking herself up off the floor last night, Kat had sat on the couch and wept in Kelly's arms for two hours as Johnny served them tea and talked about the truth of the matter, as he put it. But he hadn't spoken much about religion.

But what did that make her? She couldn't be a witch, surely. Was she a Christian? She supposed so. She was most definitely a follower of Jesus, because in the world that her eyes had been opened to last night, there was no difference between Jesus and God. Together they'd ruthlessly and yet so lovingly ruined her to this old world, with its cars and boyfriends and designer jeans.

How could she express all of that without sounding like a complete fool?

Carla punched her arm. "You're not serious, right?" They reached the gazebo and ducked out of the sun's hot rays.

"I . . ." *As a heart attack, honey.* But could she just say that? "As a heart attack, honey."

"Serious about what?" Carla asked. "Being a Muslim, or this bit about thinking God is real?"

"About God."

"Two black crows alone in their nest, eh?" Carla and Kat faced the familiar voice, surprised to see that Asad had appeared out of nowhere with twenty or more of his friends.

"Who you calling a crow, towel-head?" Carla snapped.

A square white bandage covered Asad's cheek where Kat had cut him with her fingernails yesterday. He hopped over the wall, joined by the others, mostly Arabs.

"I am calling you a crow, you black witch. In my father's court you would be nothing more than a slave for mopping the floor." His eyes moved to Kat. "And you, with your milky brown skin, might make for a good whore."

Some of them had straddled the wall, others hung behind. All watched expectantly. And Kat didn't have a clue what should be done.

"This coming from the desert donkeys who have nothing better to do than to hack each other to pieces over women and oil."

Had Carla lost her mind?

Asad's face darkened. "We are Muslims who follow the Koran and do only the will of Allah. If he commands us to kill the infidels, do you suggest we turn our backs on him? If he gives us the gift of a slave like you, do you suggest we throw his gift back in his face? You filthy crow."

"My father's a Muslim, you fool!" Carla shouted. "He'd come down here and twist your creamy little neck if he heard your militant, fundamentalist garbage."

The fact that Carla's father was a Muslim seemed to stall Asad.

"Not all Muslims follow the will of Allah," one of the others said.

"No, only those who blow themselves up for the virgins, I suppose," Carla shot back. "Your brand of extremism is dead!"

"What's going on here?" The black jocks had come up behind them. Seven of them, Kat saw. "You girls okay?" Charles asked, glancing at Carla. It didn't take Kat much to imagine that he could do as much damage off the football field as on.

"I don't know, are we?" Carla demanded, staring at Asad.

Asad was surrounded by his people, and he didn't back down easily. "From the beginning and in the end all your type will be good for is entertaining and serving the true followers of Allah."

"You got a death wish, boy?" Charles snapped.

Kat finally found herself. "Stop it! Both of you!"

She inched away from Carla, putting herself between the boys. "This isn't right, it can't be. And I'm to blame. So I'm going to fix it."

Carla stared at her as if she'd lost her marbles.

"That's where you're wrong," Asad said. "We're going to fix it for you."

"No, Asad, you can't, not like this. I'm sorry for cutting you. I'm sorry for hitting Leila." No sign of the girl in this group. "It was wrong of me."

No one seemed to know what to do with that, so Kat continued. "This isn't what God would want."

"What could a witch know about Allah?" the boy to Asad's right said.

So here it was, the moment of truth.

"I'm not a witch," she said, looking at Carla. "Not anymore. I met God yesterday and learned of his world."

"So now you expect us to believe that you're an expert on Allah's world?" Asad said. "What do you know about Allah? Christians and Hindus don't follow Allah!"

"*Allah* means *God*, right? I may not be familiar with who prays to which God yet, but I know that this isn't his way. If you were to see his world, you'd fall on your faces, crying out in fear and love!"

The words sounded idiotic here in the gazebo. Carla was still staring at her, dumbstruck. The jocks looked like they'd rather be slamming into a defensive line than facing off with a girl spouting Allah talk.

Johnny had introduced her to Jesus, so she dispensed with the God-Allah talk and spoke to the heart of the matter.

"You worship Jesus, right?"

"I worship no one but Allah."

"Okay, whatever, you worship the ground Jesus walks on if I remember correctly. You think he'd go for this?"

"Since when are you into Jesus?" Carla asked.

"I'm just saying, Carla, we got witches facing off Muslims and Arabs facing off blacks. Where does this end? Where's the room for love in that way of thinking? We should be loving each other, not trying to figure out how to cut each other's throats."

"Not if those throats refuse to pray to Allah," Asad said.

Kat whipped her head back to the boy. "Come on, you really think that's what Jesus taught? Don't Muslims believe he's the sinless prophet? Shouldn't we all follow his teachings?"

She was hardly the expert on Islam or Jesus, and undoubtedly she was full of mistakes that Johnny would help correct, but her reasoning sounded decent to her. And she knew that the love she'd felt last night after her initial meltdown was available to Asad and Carla as well.

"As Allah wills it," Asad said.

"And he does!"

They all just stared at her.

"Trust me, I saw him. Of myself as he sees me. My eyes were opened to the world the way God sees it, and it's changed me. I can't be the same ever again. I can't, because I believe in God."

"Even the demons believe in God and tremble," one of the Arabs said.

Now it was Kat's turn to be silenced.

"As to the infidels . . ." Asad said, regaining some confidence.

"Okay." Kat nodded. "Fair enough. I have a challenge for you. Rather than cut each other up, let's call a truce. On Monday we'll reconvene for a debate on the true will of Allah. If I lose, you may beat me to a pulp off school grounds without any retaliation from any of my friends."

When the idea had first presented itself to her it had sounded brilliant. But already she wondered just how brilliant. And all of this assumed that Johnny Drake could talk the judge out of a jail sentence for her.

Maybe the jail sentence was a better idea.

"A debate," Asad said.

"Yes. On Monday, after school."

Asad glanced at his line, seemed to receive no help either way. He evidently took this as a positive sign.

"Fine. On Monday." And then he added for good measure. "Infidel."

CHAPTER NINETEEN

Day Four

"I'M TELLING you, Billy . . ." Darcy turned from their apartment window with the Capitol's dome framed in the backdrop, folded her arms, and drilled him with a hard stare. "I've never felt anything like it."

"So you've told me," he said. She had woken him early, unable to sleep, all wound up. He tilted his shades down, stared past her to the graying Washington sky, then replaced them. He was losing interest in the prospect of living in the perpetual shade of sunglasses.

"This was different. Are you even listening to me?"

"Of course I am. I'm out of bed at six in the morning listening to you."

"Then *listen* to me. This was different. I had them in my hands." She made a fist. "I mean . . . I felt it this time."

"Okay, Darcy, I'm not being insensitive or anything, but both of us have had our worlds turned upside down this week. It's catching up to you, I get that. But it's not news." He paused. "Coffee?"

She uncrossed her arms, then crossed them again. "Well, it's news to me. And yes, coffee would be nice."

Billy left her standing by the window and retreated into the kitchen. She hadn't told him about her episode at Union Cemetery until they returned last night, and then she told him as if it should be a secret. It hardly sounded any different from her persuading Annie Ruling to slap the senator. But her perceptions of the cemetery event seemed to have shifted her understanding of her power. Maybe he should be more understanding.

"Look, I'm sorry if I sound impatient," he said, pouring the coffee. "But I'm starting to feel like a rat trapped in a glass cage. They whisked us off to Kansas City yesterday and what? Nothing. What are we, their sniffing dogs?"

"That's my point!"

But she'd made no such point. "It is?"

He placed her cup in her hands, but she set it down on the coffee table so she could use her hands to speak.

"Okay, so maybe I'm trying to make sense of this . . . these powers of ours, but I'm telling you, we have more power than either of us realizes, Billy. This ad hoc council of theirs may be scrambling around trying to figure out how to use us for their personal gain, but I don't think even they understand what kind of power we have."

"I think Kinnard knows exactly what we are capable of," Billy said. "He's been dreaming of this ever since he met Johnny. I think the council is over there plotting right now while we sit here like two rats trapped in this cage."

"Think of what we could do!"

"I have been. I've been thinking about it ever since I stood in the courtroom and—"

"I think I could have killed them, Billy," she said.

"Really?"

"I don't know. But I'm sure the power increases with my own emotion and forcefulness. No, I don't think I could have killed them, but I'll tell you what, this power is absolutely incredible."

So that's what this was about. The implications of her ability were finally sinking in. The only thing that had really changed was Darcy's perception of her gift.

"So, tell me again, why are we doing this?" she asked.

"Last I checked, there are people out there who want us both dead."

"And Kinnard and company can protect us?"

Billy arched an eyebrow. "They seem to be doing a decent job so far."

"So you're okay with being their sniffing dogs then?"

Billy sat on the couch and put his cup beside hers. "No, but that's not going to last."

"Oh?"

"They're just getting the feel of things themselves."

"And just who put them in charge?" she demanded.

For a moment she looked exactly like the thirteen-year-old Darcy he remembered from the monastery. She was showing her true feelings. And honestly, Billy preferred her this way.

"You find this funny?" she asked. "I'm trying to make a point here!"

"I was just remembering how beautiful you are when you get aggressive."

That stopped her.

"So tell me, Darcy, what exactly is your point?"

She thought about it, then turned to face the window and stared out at the rising sun.

"My point is that we should think about us, not them. We should use what we have for us. The gifts were given to us, not to them."

A bell went off in Billy's head. They'd been here before, only then it had been him trying to convince her. *Reach out, take the forbidden fruit.* And they had done it together.

He stood and walked up behind her. Put his hands on her shoulders and looked at the majestic buildings that housed Washington's power.

"Does that make sense?" she asked without turning.

Billy rubbed her shoulders gently. "Maybe more than you know."

"It's just that we should look out for ourselves, Billy. Not for the criminals in this town."

"We could do a few things, couldn't we?"

"We could become filthy rich."

He slid his hands around her belly and whispered into her ear, "Do you want to rule the world with me?"

She threw her head back and chuckled, exposing her neck to his lips. "Why not take over the universe while we're at it?"

Billy kissed the soft of her neck. "Become God."

She turned into him and traced his cheek with her finger. "Now there's an idea." Their lips met like two silk pillows, and Billy knew that he would follow Darcy to the grave for kisses like this.

The phone buzzed. Darcy bent for the receiver and spoke quietly into it, keeping her eyes on him.

"Hello?"

She listened for a moment, then hung up.

"What?"

"There's a car downstairs waiting for us."

"What is it?"

"Two more bodies were found lynched in the Union Cemetery last night. They were white."

"So they want their sniffing dogs in Kansas City again?"

"Kansas City is rioting."

"LISTEN AND observe," Kinnard said, marching Darcy and Billy through a sea of cubicles at FBI headquarters. They had taken a ride down the street, past the White House to the J. Edgar Hoover Building and been assigned visitors' passes upon arrival. "This is all seat of the pants, but Lawhead's eager to bring you inside."

So you can poke and prod your sniffing dogs some more, Darcy thought.

They passed a bank of computer stations manned by agents, most of them glued to their phones.

"Mind you, the others don't have a clue about you, and we'd like to keep it that way. Play along, be discrete. This way." Kinnard led them up a flight of stairs where glass walls overlooked a large conference room lined with large screens. She could see Newt Lawhead inside, bent over a conference table with a dozen other suits, intent in discussion. It looked like a war room from a movie set.

Kinnard stopped with his hand on the door and faced Billy and Darcy. "Keep your glasses on. I'm sure you understand. Lot of sensitive information floating around this building. Observe only. Speak only when you are addressed."

They entered the conference room and stood with him at the back, doing as instructed. Observing.

Now the sniffing dogs were muzzled, she thought wryly.

But she quickly lost herself in the scene on the large screens. All the news services were carrying live feeds of the riot in Union Cemetery. CNN, FOX, BBC, IRN . . . they all showed different views of the scene, some from the ground, others from the air.

She locked on to the footage taken from a helicopter high above it all. Smoke boiled skyward from at least five separate fires set to buildings around the cemetery. Dozens of fire trucks and police cars had formed a perimeter around what looked to be about a ten-block radius, but none were going into the battle zone.

Darcy stared at the scene, stunned by the destruction. All of America was seeing this? And over what? Race?

Several thousand rioters ran through the streets in gangs, smashing windows and overturning cars. The crime scene they visited yesterday had been overrun by several hundred rioters who looked to have set up a defensive position under assault from at least two fronts.

"Unbelievable," Billy muttered. "It looks like a war zone in Lebanon." Lawhead heard and looked up. He nodded.

"Gentlemen, if I may . . ." He motioned them forward as the others seated around the table turned. "Meet Billy Rediger and Darcy Lange. We've brought them in as consultants on the case. I wanted them here to observe in the event they might be of assistance. Thank you for coming."

"Observe in what capacity?" A stout man with bushy eyebrows watched her with pale blue eyes. One look and Darcy decided she didn't like him.

"None that concerns you," Darcy said. She had half a mind to tell the man where he could put his area of specialty.

Lawhead glanced between them. "Actually—"

"Then you can observe from the observation room in B wing. Let's get back to work, gentlemen. They're waiting for our—"

"I'd like a rundown," Darcy snapped, striding around the table. "Just the essentials. Starting with who's rioting, specifically."

"Blacks, presumably Christian—"

"I doubt it. Christians might not be completely right in the head, but they wouldn't attack law enforcement. The fact that the media is spinning this as a religious matter doesn't help. Maybe you should shut them down." A breath. "Why aren't the police evacuating the area?"

The room stilled to the sound of a buzz from the monitors. The FBI's upper echelon looked at Lawhead.

He nodded at a thin man with a bald head. "Pete?"

"Do you really think this is the time, Newt?" the man with bushy eyebrows demanded.

"Humor her."

Pete cleared his throat. He picked up a laser pen and directed the beam at a three-dimensional rendering of the riot zone. "First responders have set up a perimeter along Holmes Street to the east, Main Street to the east between Twenty-sixth and Thirty-first Streets. We have substantial gunfire from at least a dozen buildings along those lines. Fifteen dead that we know of so far, and that's just along the perimeter. No estimate from inside. They seem to be organized, well armed, and intentional. If there is a command center inside the perimeter, it's likely coming from this building and the original crime scene. The assault will have to come from the west—"

"Assault?" They'd brought her to observe, right? "You're considering waging war on the ground?"

The walrus wasn't liking her. "I really don't think you're in a position to question—"

"We're here to observe, sir," Billy interrupted. "Please let the sniffing dogs do their tricks."

Darcy took comfort in his support. "Well?"

Pete looked at Lawhead, who gave him a barely perceptible nod.

"The National Guard is on its way from Jefferson City," Pete continued. "Plans for an assault have been drawn up with consideration for collateral damage."

"So basically you're in a pickle either way," Billy said. "You let them fight it out and you have maybe a hundred dead. You roll in with tanks to stop the fighting and you end up with the same."

"Something like that, yes."

"We can't, as a matter of policy, allow rioters to take our streets hostage," one of the others said.

Billy was right, Darcy thought. She was staring at a scene on one of the small screens. A shaky camera operator had caught a man running for the perimeter with a child in his arms when a bullet blew off his hand. He dropped the child, who jumped up screaming. The man stared at his bloodied hand for a moment, then grabbed his child with his good hand and resumed his run.

"What about gas?" Billy asked.

"So you're a military expert as well?" the stout man asked. "That's not our call. Please, Newt. We really don't have time for this."

"I'm going in," Darcy said.

The statement was absurd; Darcy could hardly blame their silence.

Lawhead was the first to speak, asserting his authority. "I'm sorry, Ms. Lange, but I can't allow that."

She faced him. "Daylight's wasting. I need to know how to get to whoever in there has a say."

"Darcy . . ." This from Billy. "I'm not sure this is the wisest course of action here."

She could persuade him easily enough later. "I don't need this right now, Billy."

Lawhead wasn't buying it. "There's absolutely no way. This is not a good choice."

"You don't *have* a choice! Would you like me to prove my point?"

By the look in his eyes she knew that the truth of her statement had sunk in. She could remove her glasses and speak to them all, persuading them more pointedly. Maybe Lawhead had underestimated her. And maybe he'd begin to see her as a threat, the last thing she wanted.

So she quickly covered. "No disrespect. I really need to do this. If you'll allow me. Please."

"It's a war zone."

"I can see that. I insist."

CHAPTER TWENTY

THERE WAS good news and there was not-so-good news, Kat thought.

The good was that Johnny had talked to the judge and received a court order placing Kat under his supervision. As long as she bided by the terms of her six-month probation, which among other things strictly forbade any kind of violent behavior, she would remain a free woman.

She was required to stand before the judge first thing Monday to receive the instructions directly from the court.

The not-so-good news was that Johnny wasn't exactly thrilled about her challenge to debate Asad bin Salman.

Per their agreement, Kat hurried to Johnny's home at ten o'clock sharp Saturday morning, eager to share the details of her first day walking in the light, as he put it. She paced the carpet, a bundle of exuberance, overflowing with questions and opinions.

Kelly served them all iced tea and seated herself next to Johnny on the couch, where they watched Kat moving about the room like a kid who'd just discovered she won the lottery.

"Yes, of course it's all about the truth," Johnny said. "But the question is wrong. What exactly are you debating?"

"The true will of Allah, like they always say. God versus Allah. All of that."

"The question is Jesus."

"Perfect. Then the truth about Jesus."

"The truth isn't best shown with words. Particularly not when you're trying to determine God's will. Truth is an issue of the heart, not merely the mind."

"Of course it is. But you start with the mind, don't you?"

"You can."

"And on that note, why don't you just come with me, we'll get into it, and when the right time comes, you can just take off your glasses and get them all to see the truth. For that matter, why not just show the whole world, end all of this fighting over who knows what's right?"

Johnny frowned. "It doesn't work like that. Just because someone sees the truth doesn't mean they will accept it or allow that truth to change them. Fact is, most have seen the truth about themselves a thousand times, the truth about God even more often, and remain unchanged. Seeing that same truth in a more spectacular way didn't change the hearts of the crowds who saw Jesus feeding the five thousand. They still killed him."

"Sure, but you're showing them the truth all in one overwhelming shot. It nearly killed me! They'd fall to their faces, how could they not?"

"Maybe. It's not my habit to cast pearls before swine."

"Swine?"

"It's what Jesus said about not putting the truth in front of people who refuse to hear it."

"You showed me."

"I figured you would hear it and I was right. But the kingdom of light is foolishness to most, just remember that. Your friends . . . what did they think of this sudden change in you?"

"Carla?"

"Sure, Carla."

Kat shrugged. "She thinks I'm nuts."

"Exactly."

Kat walked to one of two chairs facing the couch, thought about sitting, then walked behind it and paced. "Exactly. I just can't get over how, two days ago"—she lifted her fingers at them in a peace sign—"just two days ago, I was as stupid as them."

"Stupid?"

"Whatever. I couldn't see it. There's this light all around us . . ." She smiled at the ceiling, unable to see it now but remembering what Johnny had shown her for a moment after she'd spent herself crying.

"It's here and I can feel it. I know it's here. This kingdom of heaven thing. The light." She glanced at him. "Can you show me again?"

"Maybe. Sometime. And how do you know it's not just another apple in my hand? An illusion?"

"Because I *felt* it! You showed me the apple and I thought, *Wow, that's incredible.* But when you showed me the light . . ." Tears sprang to her eyes.

Now she slipped into the chair, crossed her legs, and let the emotion come. A painful knot clogged her throat.

She looked at Kelly, the more mysterious one here, really. What did she know about Kelly, other than she smiled all the time?

Johnny, on the other hand, was crying. Tears ran from under his glasses, leaving thin trails down his cheeks.

Kelly followed Kat's eyes, and she rested her hand on his thigh when she saw his tears. She'd clearly been here before, supporting him. The image of Kelly crying behind the shed now seemed as unreal as a childhood nightmare.

"We'll have to work on your theology." Johnny smiled. "But I think your heart is doing just fine." He looked out the window and spoke in a soft voice. "The Book says that eternity is set in the hearts of men. But so is evil. That was Billy's problem; he let the evil get the best of his world. And it never seems to go away, not for good."

"Billy?"

"Billy," Kelly said. She'd remained quiet, but at the mention of Billy she'd come alive, eyes round. She blinked, catching herself, then offered an explanation. "Billy, a figure of speech as much as a real person. The common man who spawns evil and leaves it to roam through his life until it one day comes back to wreak havoc again. Billy."

Johnny looked at her, then nodded. "Yes, Billy. Question is, does the evil he created still walk among us? I think so."

Kat didn't know what he was talking about, and she said so.

Johnny sighed. "It doesn't matter right now. You know, when I was first given this gift it confused me. Of course, it was different then. The whole thing came on very strong, but then it all settled into this ability to help others see things. The truth about themselves. An apple. The light. But I myself can't look at a person and know the truth about him. I can't see God or see the evil. The light, yes, glimpses of the light, but that's all."

He faced her. "What I would give to be able to see what you saw again, Katrina Kivi. To feel what you felt."

"You don't feel it?"

"I do, yes, but not like a blind-born man seeing the world for the first time. The moment of freedom is mind blowing, isn't it?"

"It is."

"I'm a prophet to this world, though only God knows what my purpose is. I suppose one day it'll be clear. But now I live in the dark, knowing truth, frustrated by the inability of others to see what you and I have seen. Does that make sense?"

Kat was so taken aback by his admission that she couldn't answer. He was the most wonderful person in the world, living in this small house on the edge of Boulder City, Nevada, hidden from the world. He could change the world with his blind white eyes!

Instead, the man who'd saved her sat on his couch wearing glasses. Humbled.

Kat stood and crossed to him. She eased herself to one knee, leaned forward, and wrapped her arms around him, resting her head on his chest.

"You're a hero to me, Johnny. I love you. I love you with all of my heart."

Johnny put his hand on her head and they cried together for a few minutes. Kat eventually stood, wiped her eyes, and returned to her chair.

"It's infectious, isn't it?" Johnny said.

"I'm still trying to figure out what *it* is."

"Yes, well, we'll work on that. But it's your heart you have to guard, Kat. Most Christians have their facts cinched down pretty good. It's their hearts that are up for grabs. Really, most of the news about the kingdom of heaven can be summarized in a few words."

"Which are?"

"The kingdom of light is among us, and his name is Jesus. Follow him."

She felt a wry smile pull at her lips. "That's it?"

"It also helps to know what he taught."

"To love," she said.

"Yes, to love. Which is what we'll focus on today."

"So you'll help me prepare for the debate, then?"

Johnny smiled. "On the condition you promise that none of the knowledge we stuff into that brain of yours will make you cry any less."

She stood and raised her right hand. "I swear. On one condition."

"Which is?"

"That you cry with me."

He hesitated.

"Swear it," she said.

"I swear it."

CHAPTER TWENTY-ONE

THEY USED a QP-505 news helicopter borrowed from an ABC News affiliate for the flight in, so as to avoid any appearance of military aggression. Whoever controlled the whites, who were hunkered down in the center of Union Cemetery, would likely fire upon army green but be friendly toward news coverage that might spread their cause. No military personnel, no police, no one but her, she'd insisted. She had to go in flying friendly flags and she had to do it quickly.

At least that was the plan, and it sounded reasonable to Darcy. Maybe the only reasonable part of what she was about to attempt.

The blades chopped through the midday air above Kansas City as the helicopter moved closer to the green blotch of land spotted with a thousand graves. Billy sat beside her trying to hide his concern. One airman had accompanied them to operate the ladder.

"It's not too late," Billy said. "Please, Darcy, this can't go well."

She'd avoided speaking to him plainly without her glasses on, because she didn't want him to love her because of some spell she'd cast on him. At the moment his words seemed more convincing than her own.

"It is too late," she said. "Lawhead sold them on this attempt at negotiation. The governor and the commanding officer of the National Guard have acquiesced. They've held off the assault in hope that I can do something to prevent further bloodshed. I probably already have blood on my hands."

"No, that's not true! For all you know, delaying the assault has saved lives." He peered at the approaching cemetery from his side window. They tried to talk him out of accompanying her, but he'd been adamant to the point of belligerence.

"This is nuts."

"Please, Billy! You're not being helpful here!"

Billy saw the tremble in her hands and took them in his own. "Okay. I'm a nervous wreck. But you're right, this is precisely the kind of situation we can do some good in."

She nodded. "So much for looking out for just us."

"Beats being a sniffing dog." He brushed her hair back from her cheek. "You're not doing this for Washington. You're doing it for us, for them." He looked out the window. "Forget what I said—that's just me being me. The truth is, I couldn't be more proud of you."

They each wore one earpiece, which now crackled. "One minute." The pilot was from the Air National Guard, dressed in civilian clothes. "I'm going to drop like a rock right over the friendlies. Nick, you ready?"

The airman slid the door open, locked it into place, and readied a rolled aluminum ladder. The sound of the engine roared. The whole scenario felt horribly wrong out here in the air. She'd forgotten how much she hated heights until they climbed aboard the helicopter.

"Ready when you are." Nick faced her. "Just like we practiced. Let the ladder do the work. Just step off on the grass, easy." He tapped his palms. "Gloves on."

She could have hooked in but after some discussion decided that the risks of getting hung up outweighed any risk of falling. Looking through the open door, she wasn't so sure.

Darcy took the gloves from Billy and slid them over her hands.

He leaned over and spoke into her ear. "You can do this, Darcy. Just don't stop talking. Make them look into your eyes and talk. Just . . ."

"Here we go."

The helicopter dropped like a stone. Nick took her hand, ready to pull her into place as soon as they hovered over the clearing.

"Hold on , , ."

They fell for what seemed an eternity before the blades flared, slowing their descent like an elevator braking to a stop at the bottom floor Nick threw the first few feet of the ladder out.

"Go, go, go!"

She adjusted the flak jacket she'd donned, flung her glasses off, and slid off the seat with Nick's and Billy's help.

They're white, I'm white, they won't shoot. They won't shoot.

She grabbed the ladder, shoved first one, then her second foot into the third rung. "Okay."

The ladder began to uncoil and she swung into open air.

Darcy looked down, saw the grass twenty feet below. Bodies were scrambling to get out of her way. She kept telling herself that no one would shoot, that all she had to do was get her feet on the ground and everything would be okay. They were rioters armed with a few popguns and pipes, not an army with machine guns.

She kicked her feet out and dropped when she was still ten feet from the turf. Hit the ground hard and rolled as they'd shown her.

The helicopter's thumping deepened then faded as it climbed. Leaving Darcy on her belly in the grass, staring at a large tombstone ten feet from where she'd landed.

She shoved herself to her knees, looking for someone, anyone, who could do what she needed done. The clearing was roughly thirty yards across, encircled by the tombstones of those who had paid the most for the largest monuments to their loved ones. Perfect cover for a hundred or so rioters who'd taken up position on this side of them.

The tent that had housed the crime scene investigation just yesterday had been reduced to charred balls of plastic. A group of seven or eight men, at least two of whom were armed with rifles trained on her, hunkered down behind a row of gravestones.

A glance to her left showed another group with several handguns and three rifles, pointed in her direction.

She lifted her hands high above her head. "Don't shoot! I have critical information!" Her voice rang out above the sporadic popping of distant gunfire.

"Keep your hands high or we'll blow your head off."

"Just don't shoot! I'm unarmed. Just the messenger."

Based on her limited experience, her persuasive power seemed to work only in conjunction with a person's own intentions. She didn't think she could force a person to do something they knew to be wrong unless they harbored a deep-seated desire to do it.

She made eye contact with one of men who had a rifle trained on her. "I'm here to help—you don't want to shoot me! You hear me?"

She couldn't see his immediate response from this far away, but she felt exposed here, so she stood and went for the large group, hands lifted high.

"Look at me, all of you," she screamed. "Just look into my eyes, see if I'm not telling you the truth. You do *not* want to shoot me. You *will not* shoot me." She kept walking but turned her head to face the men behind the gravestones.

"You hear me? You don't want to harm me."

An unnatural stillness had gripped the clearing, and she knew that she was connecting with them. So she turned around, walking backward now. They looked to be a loose gang who'd taken advantage of the lynchings to express their own hatred or mistrust of blacks. Most if not all of the hundred or so gangsters were watching her.

"All of you listen to me," she cried out. "No one wants to harm me. No one will shoot. You all want to listen to every word I have to say. You hear me?"

Darcy stopped and looked around at the circle of men staring at her, dumbfounded. She couldn't tell who their leader was, or even if there *was* a leader, but learning this wouldn't be difficult.

"I have information that is going to change your day, my friends. You will want to do what I've come to suggest." Turning, she said it again. "I have information that is going to change your day, my friends. You will want to do what I've come to suggest. Show me who's in charge."

No one jumped to her wishes.

She turned, more angry than fearful now. "Show me, for heaven's sake! I need to speak to your leader now!"

A man armed with an automatic weapon stood and stepped out toward her. His pitted face frowned and his dark eyes seemed to sear her with hatred, but he came willingly.

"What's your name?"

"What do you want?"

"I want you to get everyone over by your position so I can address them."

"Are you nuts?"

"Don't be a fool." She threw the words at him in a flash of anger. "I'm here to save your rotten white skin and there's nothing more precious to you than your own skin. Now get everyone over here immediately."

He hesitated a moment, nodded once, and waved at the men across the clearing. "Get over here, all of you." When they hesitated, he cursed and raised his volume.

They hurried to his side, ducking behind the tombstones as they ran. An occasional bullet slapped into the tombstones surrounding them, but most of the firing came from the streets surrounding Union Cemetery. They had placed their command in the safest part of the field.

Darcy approached and stared at them all, tapping her cheek. "Look at me. Don't remove your eyes from mine. I know all hell is breaking loose out there, but you want to listen to what I have to say."

They watched her, attentive as dogs begging for a steak. She had them in her hands and the power was intoxicating.

"You're all going to lay down your weapons and leave this place. You're going to do that because you know in your gut that this is a dead-end fight. You don't want to die today. And you're not going to die today, because you're going to help me stop this standoff. Every one of you knows that's the right thing."

"Robby?" A skinny kid with one of the rifles was shaking, looking at the pitted-faced man for guidance. "Robby?"

"Shut up!"

"Listen to Robby," Darcy snapped. "Tell them how they can save themselves, Robby."

Their leader looked confounded and disturbed.

"Robby?"

"She's right," he said.

"Of course I'm right. You're going to leave this place now and run as fast as your legs can move."

How her words worked their effect she didn't know, but whatever power they carried had now fully engaged them. First a dozen and then twice as many dropped their weapons and began to run west, toward the warehouses and Main Street just beyond, the closest and safest line of exit.

"No, not that way," she cried.

They pulled up, disoriented. Others were dropping their guns and pipes. Standing, eager to be gone. But she needed more from them.

Darcy pointed east and north. "You're going to run that way, into the houses, spreading the word to everyone who will listen. You'll say, 'The riot's over, lay down your weapons, and run while the running is good.'"

"What?"

She didn't know who called the question and she didn't care. "If you go west, the National Guard will be waiting to clean you out. Go east, undo what you've done here, tell them all that it's over. Lay down your weapons and run, run, run! Go north and tell them to spread the word; get out now before it's too late."

The skinny kid who'd called out for Robby was the first to move. He threw his gun on the ground in a fit of panic, whimpering and swearing at once. And he ran pell-mell into the graveyard, headed due east.

Then they all ran. All except for Robby, who'd dropped his weapon and stood staring at her. It was as if his mind knew what to do, but his muscles were in shock and refused to move.

"Run, Robby," Darcy said, walking toward him. "You will yell the loudest."

He turned and jogged after the others.

BILLY PACED the street at the intersection of Main and Twenty-ninth, where Darcy would emerge. *If* she emerged.

He'd bitten his nails to stubs, pacing behind the line of police cars, waiting. If she'd succeeded, she would have been out by now. Unless she'd decided in all of this newfound confidence of hers to head farther into the war zone.

Her first plan had been to meet with both black and white leaders, but they'd talked her out of it. A white heading into a black zone couldn't turn out good. But what if she'd gone anyway?

A news van stood at the ready, filming the empty street. If Darcy managed to calm the storm, they would make sure the entire country knew. Already there were reports of vandalism in St. Louis, Miami, Detroit, and Los Angeles. Nooses with hangman's knots were found in half the universities across the country. Putting an end to the Kansas City riot was really about nipping a much larger problem in the bud.

Billy looked up to see Kinnard walking toward him with quick strides, phone plastered to his ear. Billy had removed his glasses, intent upon knowing the truth, however ugly it might be. Kinnard, however, still wore shades.

He covered the mouthpiece while he was still twenty feet off and called to Billy. "She did it," he said. "I think she actually did it!"

"What? Where is she?"

"Spotters are reporting a flood of rioters running east and north." Into the phone: "Say again . . . Let me know the moment you hear anything." He snapped the phone shut.

"Any word on Darcy . . ?"

"Look alive, people!" someone shouted. "We have incoming."

Billy ran up to the line of cars. A solitary figure was jogging toward them from around a warehouse a hundred yards out. There was no mistaking her long, dark brown hair, flowing in the breeze as she ran.

Darcy.

"You getting this?" someone said. The news crew.

Billy hopped over the barricade and sprinted toward her. An officer started to protest, but Kinnard shut him down. The rioters were headed east. Only Darcy was headed west.

He saw her beaming smile fifty yards off. And her wide brown eyes, glistening, uncovered in the sun.

"You made it," he said, slowing to a walk.

"And you were worried?"

"It's over?"

"I think so, Billy. I think they will do whatever I tell them to."

"You're alive," he said, stopping in front of her.

"Then kiss me."

She wasn't wearing any glasses, and looking into her intoxicating eyes, Billy realized that he desperately wanted to kiss her, more than he'd ever wanted to kiss anyone in his entire life.

"Do you love me?" he asked.

He heard her thoughts before she answered. *Of course I do, you silly boy. I never stopped loving you.*

"Yes," she said.

He took her into his arms, lifted her from her feet, and spun her around. Their mouths met and he kissed her deeply.

CHAPTER TWENTY-TWO

Day Five

THE COUNCIL sat around the same conference table, in the same order, wearing the same glasses the next morning. Oh yes, they would definitely wear the glasses now, wouldn't they? *Maybe they should consider getting the lenses surgically implanted*, Darcy thought.

Most of the rioters had vacated Union Cemetery and the surrounding area within an hour of Darcy's pep talk. Without an enemy to engage, the lingering hostiles slipped out during cover of darkness that night. Thirteen arrests were made, a fraction of the guilty, but by all accounts, the FBI's last-minute intervention was a smashing success.

Footage of Darcy jogging in from the war zone of Kansas City like some kind of Special Forces hero made the news, and that news spread fast and far, a byproduct of her feat that concerned Kinnard deeply, he said. Putting her to the test in the field where any potential enemy wouldn't likely see her was one thing, but exposing her to the nation was troublesome.

They covered her as best they could. She wasn't with the FBI or the SWAT team. She was a negotiator, a highly trained mediator who specialized in talking common sense to combative personalities in the most difficult situations.

Cued by "sources," talking heads throughout the Net extended Darcy's credit beyond this one situation. There was no telling how often the State Department dispatched negotiators to conduct secret meetings deep behind enemy lines. Or barter for trade policy, for human rights advocacy . . . the list was endless. And Darcy set an example for them all.

With just a little common sense and tolerance, any conflict could be avoided.

But the message fell on deaf ears. And the dawn brought unnerving news after a night of peace.

Sunday morning, three blacks hung from a tree behind a Pentecostal church in St. Louis.

Two whites hung in a graveyard next to a Catholic church twenty miles east of the first.

No rioting. Not yet. But the media was both stunned and expectant. The nation was a keg of gunpowder, silent and dormant.

"They're wrong," Lyndsay Nadeau said. The attorney general wore her perpetual smile. "It's not one spark, like the one in St. Louis, that will set off this keg. It's a thousand sparks. We all know that."

Darcy scanned the others for reaction: Ben Manning, the black Democratic senator from Nevada who had demanded they be kept locked up, stone faced.

Fred Hopkins. No better.

Annie Ruling, White House chief of staff. A slight amusement nudged the right side of her mouth northward.

Sanchez Dominquez. Might as well be a rock.

Associate director of the FBI, Newton Lawhead. Frowning, watching Darcy like a hawk.

Kinnard had excused himself after delivering them, explaining that he had someone else to pick up. Some mystery guest. For all she knew the president was coming.

She and Billy sat at one end, hands on the table, drumming their fingers lightly on the wood. She hadn't felt so alive in years and she decided to point this out.

"It's good to be alive," she said.

"Excuse me?"

"Nothing, just thinking aloud. We enjoy freedom in this country. That's a good thing. Hopefully we can all keep it that way."

"Random," Billy said.

"Ain't it great?" They were both smiling. Their moment of shared humor was lost on a few of them.

"I'm not sure you appreciate the gravity of the situation we're facing in this free country," Annie Ruling said. "So tell us—I'm curious—what was it like?"

"What was what like?"

"Doing your . . . thing in Kansas City yesterday."

"I spoke, they listened. They were persuaded."

"So you can just persuade anybody to do anything?" Ben Manning asked.

"Shall we test it with you?"

His flat lips curved downward. "It's that kind of ego that concerns me."

It had taken Darcy the better part of the week to wrap her own mind around her power. Manning and the members of the council were finally catching up. Perhaps she did owe them an explanation. The last thing she wanted was the council itself gunning for them.

The moment the thought occurred to her she knew that she'd hit on something. Kinnard feared that people like Ben Manning were as great a threat to them as the Catholic Church.

"To answer your question, no. I can't randomly persuade anyone to do anything. I'm not God."

"From what we can gather she can only persuade others to do what they know is right, or what they have a desire to do," Lawhead said.

She nodded once. "That's right. The rioters either realized that my suggestion to disband was the right thing to do, or deep in their minds where it counts, they wanted to disband."

"So what was it like?" Annie asked again. "I mean, having this kind of power must be quite exhilarating. Are you sure you can handle it?"

"Do we have a choice?" Billy asked. "We are what we are. The only question for this council is whether we will use our power to help you."

"This isn't an arbitration, Mr. Rediger," the attorney general said. "We're not a court of law. We're simply trying to determine if you can serve your country in a capacity never before appreciated."

"Are you?"

She removed her glasses and looked at him with sincere eyes. "I don't know, Billy. You tell me. Am I?"

"Yes. You at least believe you are."

"Thank you." She replaced her glasses. "This country is facing a crisis it hasn't faced since the Los Angeles riots or even the Civil War. We could use your help."

So at least the attorney general was being straight, Darcy thought. Maybe she'd been too quick to distrust this group.

She continued. "Annie, why don't you help our friends understand the scope of the crisis."

A knock sounded on the door behind Billy and Darcy. She turned as Brian Kinnard stepped through and a well-built man with blond hair, dressed in black slacks and a white button-down shirt filled the doorway. He wore glasses, no surprise.

Darcy didn't recognize him. Was she supposed to?

"My friends, please meet Johnny Drake."

Darcy's heart skipped a beat. A tremble overtook her fingers and spread to her hands. *Johnny?* This was Johnny from Paradise?

"Hello, Darcy. Billy." Johnny stretched out his hand. "Good to see you."

Billy stood and took the hand. "Johnny Drake . . . no kidding, is it really you?"

"In the flesh."

Darcy stood and he embraced her gently, then stepped back. They stood in an awkward moment of silence.

"Johnny heard the news, made contact with me yesterday, and agreed to come out. We consider Johnny to be a survivor of Project Showdown, though he was not a student there. As some of you know, Johnny is also quite . . ." He paused. "Special."

Darcy stood next to Billy, speechless.

Lyndsay Nadeau was the first to stand and take Johnny's hand. "Lyndsay Nadeau, attorney general. Good to meet you, Johnny. I've heard a few things here and there."

"Not too frightening, I hope." He smiled.

She grinned and turned to the others. "Our government has some classified history with Mr. Drake. Suffice it to say we can all be grateful for the sacrifice this man has paid on our behalf." She began pointing the others out, making personal introductions as they shook his hand.

"Okay, sit." Kinnard pulled out a chair next to Darcy's. "Like I said, you'll have time later."

Johnny looked at Darcy. "You okay? You look like you've seen a ghost."

"I'm sorry, I just never . . . Frankly, I'm a little speechless."

"Well, there's some hope for us all then," Annie laughed.

Johnny folded his hands on the table. Strong hands, but not rough like a bricklayer's. Certainly not the frail hands he'd had the last time she'd seen him as a boy. Darcy couldn't figure out how she felt about his dramatic reappearance.

"And what is your special gift, young man?" Ben Manning asked.

Kinnard spoke for him. "He can open the eyes, Mr. Manning. To see what the natural eye can't. Does that about cover it, Johnny?"

"Close enough."

They faced each other in an awkward stalemate. So Johnny had a backbone, Darcy thought. She liked that.

"Well then, can we continue?"

"Please," Kinnard said.

"Continue with what?" Billy asked. "Forgive my confusion here, but I still don't quite understand what you want from us."

Darcy pried her mind away from Johnny and glanced at Billy. True enough.

"You've seen what we can do," she said. "I think Billy's asking what your intentions are now. At the risk of imposing, of course."

Again Annie grinned, and Darcy grinned back. She liked the woman.

"Fair enough." The chief of staff slid her chair back and crossed one leg over the other. "Although I have to point out that forty-eight hours ago we didn't even know you existed. You can hardly blame our caution."

"Fine, Annie. But now we all know, so how are we going to help you change the world?"

Judging by the amusement on the faces of Annie Ruling and Lyndsay Nadeau, neither of them seemed to mind her boldness.

"President Chavez's primary concern extends beyond the recent hate crimes, however tragic they might be," Annie said. "Our real concern is in the news coming out of Los Angeles and Miami and a dozen other metropolitan cities. Racial and religious prejudice has been emboldened by the lynchings. We face a war of murderous words. Newton, what were those stats you had for us?"

Lawhead pulled a sheet out of the briefcase by his chair. "As you're well aware, both the CIA and the FBI track certain kinds of content on the Net. Over the past forty-eight hours, the incidents of racially and religiously motivated denigration have increased 437 percent."

He slid the paper onto the table. "A big number, and it's already outdated. That stat is from two hours ago. What's most disconcerting is the rate at which it continues to grow. The charts are all there; we can track it by the minute if we want. If our analysts are correct—and they are—as things stand, the rate of incidents will double again in the next twenty-four hours."

Johnny sat in silence. He struck Darcy as someone who'd seen far more than most men his age. And hadn't they all? But with Johnny, there was more. It was his statuesque stillness, his very slow breathing, the way his fingers were interlaced without so much as a slight twitch, the lean muscle on his bared forearms.

She was listening to the others, but behind her glasses she was watching him.

The attorney general continued. "Nothing less than racially and religiously motivated hate speech."

"Let's not forget the First Amendment," Manning interjected. "Free speech—"

"The president is the first to defend every citizen's right to free speech, Ben," Annie interrupted. "We're here to calm a storm, not generate one." She took a deep breath. "Wouldn't you agree, Mr. Drake?"

Johnny considered thoughtfully and answered in a soft voice. "Hatred is your enemy, Ms. Ruling, not racial insults."

"But hatred must find expression before it can affect daily life, isn't that right?"

"In a social arena, yes. But it can just as easily eat a man's heart out and leave him dead long before his pulse stops."

It was the simple truth, Darcy thought. Spoken by the man with hands that looked like they could strangle anyone in this room, perhaps with the exception of Kinnard, who'd proven he knew a thing or two about killing.

Annie smiled. "Well spoken. But we all know that this kind of hate mongering has to be stopped. Maybe these lynchings will allow us to finally change the law to curb certain kinds of speech. Someone has to muzzle the bloodsuckers."

All eyes turned to Annie. Darcy wasn't sure she'd heard correctly. *Bloodsuckers?* Meaning Christians, of course. It was strange to hear such an offensive word spoken in a place of such power. Clearly there was no love lost on Christians among this so-called council.

She could hear each breath.

Annie forced a smile to offer her apologies. "Pardon the French. The president is going on the air at six eastern tonight to address the nation, urging restraint. He will promise that any violation of our nation's laws will be prosecuted swiftly and with force."

"Messing with free speech will cause an uproar," Billy said.

"And what do you call the riots?"

"Do you know how long it's been illegal to display a Swastika in Germany?" Lyndsay Nadeau said. "Since Germany's constitution was changed at the end of the Second World War. A sensible restriction on free speech, I'm sure we would all agree."*

"Just a tad different, don't you think?"

She pressed on. "The United Kingdom's restriction of free speech has proven to be an effective deterrent to runaway bigotry in that country. Even here, speech is already restricted in some ways: perjury, contempt, treason, and sedition are all forms of spoken communication and are illegal in the United States, for good reason."

No one argued.

"We all know our history well enough to remember the highly debated so-called Noose Bill of 2008, which very nearly made the public display of any symbol offensive to race, religion, sexual orientation, and gender a hate crime.* The day is coming, ladies and gentlemen, when offensive remarks, gestures, and/or symbols will be—must be— considered hate crimes. Some freedoms must be sacrificed on the cross of social progress. Frankly I can't believe that this country still allows pundits to get licenses from the federal government to broadcast offensive hate speech."

Manning drummed his fingers on the table. "Offensive to whom? Hate crimes are nothing more than a nice tag for anything that offends anyone."

"Surely you can see the harm caused when a radio show host is allowed to get on public airwaves and berate a whole class of citizens for their religion. Or when they are allowed to rail against a class of people for their particular sexual orientation, going so far as to claim God hates their particular way of life and will send that whole class of citizens to hell. Our country should have put an end to this kind of overt discrimination a long time ago."

"That's the cost of freedom," Manning said. "That and the blood of those who've fought to protect those freedoms, or have you forgotten *your* history? Thank God for our Constitution."

"What does God have to do with it?" Annie said. "Common sense is what makes this a free country. Religion, on the other hand, has always fueled hatred. Isn't that right, Johnny?"

He looked at Billy and Darcy. "Did you know I was a chaplain in the army once?"

The revelation surprised her. "You're a religious man?"

"Not particularly. But I understand a few things about good and evil."

"And God?"

"Is good."

So there it was. Johnny didn't share her hatred of all things religious. But she wouldn't hold that against him. She was sure his reasoning was compelling enough, given his own experience.

"The crisis we're facing today is fueled in large part by hate speech," Annie said, pushing forward. "The keg that could explode isn't filled with gunpowder; it's filled with vocalized bigotry. The president's going to urge calm. The question is, Darcy, can you do the same?"

"That's it?" she asked. "You want me to calm the world one riot at a time?"

"I think what Annie's asking," Lawhead said, "is how good you are in front of a camera?"

Darcy had never considered the possibility that she could affect her listeners over the Net. But why not? Assuming they were watching her eyes.

The notion swept through her like a warm blast of wind. And all she could think to say was, "Wow."

"No," Billy said, standing. He stepped out and faced Kinnard. "It's too dangerous, you've made that clear."

"I agree, it's not what I had in mind," Kinnard said.

"We agreed to leave it up to Darcy," Annie was quick to say.

"Absolutely not," Manning snapped. "I can't stress the danger of this, not to her—although I take your point—but to the country. If it works, are we to turn over the minds of this land to this girl? It's irresponsible!"

"People are dying, Ben!" Annie cried. "Open your mind for once."

"How would this be dangerous to me?" Darcy asked.

Billy slid back into his seat. "Because being subjected to your voice is an unmistakable proposition. Your power is felt, not just heard."

"And just how exactly is that dangerous?"

"It would essentially 'out' you on a grand scale! Granted, most people would never realize *why* your words had such an impact on them, but some would begin asking questions. Once the questions start, your life is over, not only as a private citizen, but maybe quite literally."

"He does make a point," Lyndsay said. "Speaking to Congress might be one thing. But addressing the nation could change your life."

Darcy was concerned to realize she liked the idea.

"Johnny?" Annie asked. "You've lived with your gift for some time, I gather. Besides the obvious, any downsides?"

"There's always a price. But you'll both figure that out soon enough. I wouldn't do it if I were you. It could ruin you."

Ruin her? And who was he to judge?

"Assuming it works," Lawhead said. "It would be easy enough to find out. Let's put you in front of a closed-circuit camera."

And what if it didn't work?

"No," she said. "I think Billy and Johnny are right. I can't do it. Not now."

They just stared at her.

"No," she repeated. "I'm not some kind of mind-numbing ray gun you pull on whomever you want."

"I think you have a responsibility to your country," Annie said. "What did you expect to do here in Washington? You need to use your powers as much as we need you to use them."

"Don't patronize me."

"You want it, Darcy," Annie said softly. "You know you do."

How dare this woman speak to her like this?

"You love the power, I can see it in your eyes."

Johnny stood, looked at them for a moment, then dipped his head. "Excuse me, I'll have to be leaving." He faced Billy and Darcy. "Brian knows how to get in contact with me; please come out and visit."

"I take it you don't approve," Annie said.

"That's not for me to judge. I've just been reminded why I fled to the desert." To Billy and Darcy again: "Anytime you like, my house is open. Be careful, very careful."

"Just like that?" Darcy demanded. "You fly all the way out, stay for half an hour, and leave?"

"It was a mistake to come. Remember, the enemy is within. Don't think you're isolated from danger in these ivory towers of theirs."

He walked to the doors. "I'll take a cab." And then Johnny Drake was gone.

The room felt suffocating.

"So will I," Darcy said, standing.

Billy followed quickly. "And me."

Kinnard was already on his feet. "Not a chance. We'll take your no for now. I'll take you home."

ANNIE WATCHED the door close behind Brian Kinnard, unable to hide the amusement on her face. Simple fact: she liked them. Even without their gifts, she found Darcy in particular superbly suited for life in the capital. Not a career politician who thrived off the foggy landscape of compromises, but a real voice for change. The kind of person best suited for Washington was often the kind who hated it enough to suffer all that was required to effect change.

People like Darcy and Billy. So hard to attract, but oh so valuable if you could.

She kept her eyes on that sealed door. "Well, that went well. What do you think?"

"I think you're way out of line, even speaking about muzzling . . . Christians." Ben Manning spread his fingers out on the table and tapped a large gold ring on the wood. "Or any religion for that matter. And Darcy presents a significant problem. We have to end this."

The ice clinked in Deputy Director Newton Lawhead's glass. He took a sip, set the tumbler down, and slid his sunglasses into his pocket. But he offered no comment.

"I would say this is the beginning, not the ending," Lyndsay said.

Manning continued as if he hadn't heard. "I'm the last one to suggest extreme measures, but I hope all of you can appreciate the delicate nature of our problem here. We have to silence her."

Annie faced the senator, surprised by his bitter tone. "Silence her? What exactly are you suggesting?"

He pulled off his glasses and met her stare head-on. "I'm suggesting that all of this is horribly irresponsible. I can't be a party to it. That child could walk into any bank and leave the wealthiest woman in the world. Imagine what she could do in a war, or a presidential race, or . . . or . . ." Manning was too flustered to elaborate. "She could single-handedly bring this country to its knees in the worst of ways. She has to be stopped."

"No, Ben, she has to be guided. If she fell under the wrong influence, yes, then we'd have a problem. But she's not a child, and I don't see her as the kind who will easily fall under anyone's influence but her own. We work with her, not against her."

"Agreed," the attorney general said. "And for goodness' sake, we protect her."

Ben Manning stood abruptly, scowling. "You can't protect her. No prison can hold someone who has the power to seduce the first person who looks into her eyes. You're flirting with disaster. A vial of the deadliest virus. Drop it and we all die."

Lawhead cleared his throat. "You're suggesting we kill her, Ben?"

He didn't answer. He didn't have to. If they couldn't find a way to win Darcy and Billy's complete confidence, they could indeed have a very awkward problem on their hands.

But kill them? The very idea seemed ludicrous to Annie.

"We protect this country at all costs," Manning said. He walked around the table and strode for the door. "It's your job to figure out how to do that."

He turned back with his hand on the knob. "And if you don't, I will."

CHAPTER TWENTY-THREE

Day Six

KELLY DROVE the car down the street that wrapped around the school yard. Kat sat quietly beside her. Johnny was unexpectedly called out of town Saturday night, so Kelly had agreed to take her to the court-house and return her to Boulder City High during the lunch hour.

It had been four days since Kat's change, and those days had passed like a dream. She really did feel as though she'd been birthed into a new world. Everything was new to her.

The debate, however, had become a familiar fear. She'd imagined her face-off with Asad a hundred times, and each time it brought a tingle to her fingers. Who was she, to engage in such a debate? But she would do it anyway, in just a few hours when the bell rang at day's end.

During her time with Johnny Saturday, he'd shown her an account written by a prisoner named John the Apostle, who had actually been with Jesus while he was on earth, thousands of years ago. The basic truths of Jesus's teachings hurried through her mind like soft echoes in a deep canyon. Big words that sounded strange but right. Perfect.

Love the Lord your God with all your heart. Love your neighbor as your-self. Simple enough. Jesus was all about love.

The kingdom of God is among you. I am the Light of the World. The Truth, the Way. No one can go to the Father but through me. Again, simple enough. Truth was all about Jesus.

Others were less obvious. *The gate to heaven is narrow; only a few will pass through it. Unless you leave your mother and your father for my sake, you cannot enter the kingdom of heaven. Unless you eat my body and drink my blood, you cannot follow me.*

The world will hate you if you follow me.

Clearly, following Jesus wasn't a casual affair. She'd never imagined such startling, narrow-minded teaching could follow so easily in the path of love, love, love, all you need is love.

But it made perfect sense to her heart if not her mind. Jesus wasn't merely a good and wise prophet; he was God, and he was pointing the way *to* God. To himself. As it turned out, following that way came at a price few were willing to pay.

It cost their own pride, as Johnny put it. Their self-interest.

You won't make it through the narrow gate because your eyes are on yourself and your own endless arguments and you'll run into the wall, O blind one. That's how she had put it, and Johnny smiled.

So then, the debate. Johnny had been right in saying that truth was best shown, not simply argued. She had no idea what kind of words she could use to show Carla and Asad and the rest of them that Jesus was the Way.

It would be foolishness to them. Which, appropriately enough, was another one of Jesus's teachings.

The car rolled to a stop in the parking lot and Kat opened her door.

"So I can come over after school then?"

"Johnny will be back this afternoon. Why don't you come for dinner?"

"Really? I'll check with my mom, but that should work."

"What does your mother think of all this?"

"We haven't really talked about it. I mean, she knows something's up, but I wanted to wait until we actually have some time to talk it through. Not sure she would believe me, you know what I mean?"

"Cried wolf a few too many times?" Kelly said. "Don't worry, she'll see the change."

Kelly said it all with a smile, that perpetual smile, so constant that at times Kat wondered if it had been surgically affixed to her face.

She'd told Johnny about finding Kelly behind the shed, crying, but he only turned away. Kelly had been through hell in Hungary, he said. She had been caught up in an underground training camp for assassins hired out to the world's largest governments. Her mind had been stripped and forced into a mold that she'd since rejected.

She'd been his handler, he said. Forced to manipulate him before they'd fallen in love and gone on the run together. Without her, he'd be dead or worse, a vegetable. He owed his life to her. Johnny said it all with a knot in his throat and then dismissed the subject.

Kat wondered if whatever had happened hadn't blinded him just a bit. Not that she was jealous, but . . . just who *was* Kelly anyway? She never talked about Jesus. She never joined in the discussion. She never did anything but sit there with that flat smile, rubbing Johnny's back.

"That's what I was hoping," Kat said. "Okay, see you."

"Six?"

"Cool."

Kelly left Kat standing in the parking lot. The school grounds were quiet this time of day. A man on a riding mower was cutting the grass around the fountain pond, and two groundskeepers had weed cutters out, trimming the edges of the walkway around the concrete slab that surrounded the water.

Blue sky above, sun blazing hot. She headed for the lunch wing.

Tires squealed past her and she saw a news van brake to a hard stop. A camera crew spilled out and began to run toward her followed by a blonde woman dressed in a blue business suit.

They ran past.

"What's going on?"

"Stay outside," the blonde woman said.

Kat ran after them.

"Where is it?"

"In the lunchroom," the reporter said. "From what I've heard it's a mess in there. You need to stay back!"

Odd, here Kat was, basking in the light of this new kingdom, and all around her the world was coming apart at the seams.

The back entrance to the lunchroom was around the other side by the gym. She cut across the lawn, rounded the building, surprised to see no students on the greenway. The reason became immediately apparent: someone had rolled a large garbage bin in front of the cafeteria's fire door, blocking any exit.

Whatever was occurring inside had been planned.

She threw her weight against the bin, but it refused to budge. Fists were pounding on the other side of the door. She could hear screams.

"Does this door lead to the lunchroom?" the cameraman demanded, running up behind.

"Yes, push! We have to clear it."

With three of them pushing, the Dumpster rolled free. The door burst wide open with a bleat from the fire alarm, spilling a stream of students. The screams from the lunch hall weren't all cries of fear. There was as much anger in the voices as panic.

The cameras were already rolling behind her. "We're here at what appears to be an emergency exit at the Boulder City High School lunchroom, where students have been trapped for the last five minutes." The reporter spoke rapidly. "It appears that the exit was blocked before the riot began. No sources have come forward yet to reveal the nature of this conflict, purportedly a racially instigated conflict between Arab Americans and African Americans within the student body . . ."

Kat saw an opening in the flood of students and ducked inside. The sight that greeted her made her catch her breath.

The new lunchroom was set up food-court style, with hundreds of small round tables situated around a dozen stations that offered everything from pizzas to salads to sandwiches, some for a price, some as part of the school's free-lunch program.

Most of the tables were on their sides, a few broken. The food stations had been destroyed by thrown chairs, which appeared to be the weapon of choice.

A group of roughly fifty blacks were scattered along one end, facing off Hispanics who clutched chairs, shielding themselves from a fusillade of ketchup bottles, mustard tubes, glasses, and silverware. The floor was covered in condiments and bottles.

A line of Arabs headed by Asad and his gang stood along the wall to Kat's left, turned toward both the Hispanics and blacks on either end. It was a three-way face-off.

Of the seven hundred students in this lunch shift, only a hundred seemed to be directly involved. The rest had taken shelter behind stations or had taken up chairs to ward off flying objects.

She'd expected to see the Arabs and blacks going at it after last week's run-in. But Hispanics? Granted, there had always been some rivalry between black and Hispanic gangs, but that rivalry had been limited to a war of words.

She couldn't imagine what had pushed things to this level.

The principal's voice was screeching over the PA, demanding calm. It wasn't working. The camera crew piled in through the exit. The reporter was at her shoulder.

"Can you tell what's going on? You see anyone you know?"

Then Kat saw the fourth group on the far side, opposite the Muslims, mostly Indians huddled behind a makeshift fort made of overturned tables.

A four-way battle, and she could hardly tell who was against whom. Hispanics against blacks, Muslims against Hindus? Watching the projectiles, it looked more like all against all. Chaos.

An older Indian student she recognized as a Hindu was screaming at the Arabs. He cocked his arm back and hurled a bottle at the group.

"Death to Muslims!"

Two of his compatriots stood from behind their tables and hurled the same words, chasing them with a glass saltshaker and some cutlery.

The first projectile slammed into the wall behind Asad and shattered with a loud pop. A large blotch of ketchup splattered on the baby-blue wall, erasing *Is* from the large motto painted on the wall: Tolerance Is Beautiful.

Asad didn't bother ducking. No fewer than ten of the Arabs heaved a volley of condiments and silverware on the ducking Hindus.

"Death to the infidels! The Hindus are warmongers! *Allah akhbar!*"

Kat felt panic welling up in her chest. It didn't take much of an imagination to see how blacks against Hispanics versus Arabs could mutate into Christians against Muslims against Hindus, not when religion and race were so closely connected. Not when they all knew that they all secretly despised each other in spite of the tolerance preached in every classroom.

A small Indian girl suddenly stood from behind the tables, eyes fixed on the Arabs across the room. Kat had seen the dark-haired girl around a few times, a freshman who looked as green as a foreigner who'd just flown in from Calcutta. The wide-eyed girl looked at the open door behind Kat, stepped out from the makeshift fort, and scooted out into the open, angling across the open floor for the exit.

"Stop!" Kat cried, waving the girl back. "Get back, get back!"

The girl did not stop. Instead, she began to cry. She shuffled in fast, short steps with her arms by her sides. Crossfire whizzed past her and she began to run, white dress flapping around her thin tan legs.

Kat broke from her safe corner, holding her arm out to the Arabs. "Don't throw! Stop!"

A single glass ketchup bottle shot from the line to her left, covered the gap to the Indian girl in the space of one breath, and struck her on the side of her head.

The girl dropped to the ground.

Kat sprinted, screaming at the top of her lungs, "Stop! Stop!"

They weren't stopping—she could see that in her peripheral vision—but her eyes were on the young girl who hadn't moved.

She waved her arms over her head and raced into the cross fire. "Stop it, she's hurt, you're gonna kill someone! Stop this!"

A bottle flew past her head as she dropped to her knees beside the girl. The freshman was moaning now, rolling to one side. No sign of blood.

"You okay?"

A spoon struck her on the shoulder and clattered to the floor.

Kat stood up and faced the gang of blacks, knowing that they thought of her as one of their own.

"Stop this!" she screamed. She met their eyes and spun to the Arabs. "Just stop it!"

They seemed momentarily stalled by her boldness. The decibel level of the cacophony dropped. She seized the opportunity and cried out, facing the Hispanics. The Arabs had fired the ketchup bottle, but she knew that confronting them directly would only inflame Asad, who believed, as others once had, that a bloody crusade was the only way to convince people of anything.

"You've hurt a girl who only wants to be safe with her father!" she cried. "Is that what your mothers taught you?"

No bottles flew. All four sides stared at her. An older Indian girl raced out, weeping. "Hadas, Hadas!" She slid to the fallen girl's side and brushed her hair from her face. Touched the swelling bump on her head. "Speak to me, Hadas. What have they done, what have they done?"

The young girl tried to sit, and her friend helped her. "Are you okay? Are you sure you are okay?" She cradled her, and the young girl began to cry, soft moans.

By the door, the news camera rolled. Otherwise the room was still. She had to keep the focus on race rather than religion, Kat thought.

"Blacks and whites are lynching each other out there, is that what we're here on this earth to do? Hang each other because we're different? You're a black man in a Hispanic neighborhood, they rope you up, is that what you want? You're Hispanic in a black neighborhood, they lynch you, is that what you want?"

A single mustard bottle sailed out. She stepped aside and watched it bounce off the floor, unbroken. It slid to a stop at the feet of a Hispanic student, who picked it up.

"Go ahead, throw it back," she cried, pointing at the boy. "But throw it at me, not them. I'm black. Or am I Indian? For all you know I'm Hispanic! Go ahead, throw it."

The student looked at his people and received no encouragement.

Only now did Kat face Asad and his band. "We were made to love each other, not to fight. You think you're throwing ketchup bottles at the enemy, but you're not. You're just giving them more ammunition to throw back at you. Races have been doing that for centuries. The school teaches us to tolerate each other. But I say we should *love* each other! Tolerance is not enough! Blacks, Hispanics, Arabs, whites, Hindus, Muslims, Christians—love each other."

The Arab boy dropped his stare, and she decided to take her words a step further, right here in front of them all.

"This is my debate, Asad. *Love!* Love your neighbor as yourself; *that* is the teaching of Jesus. It's a narrow way, but it's a simple way and the whole world ought to listen."

For nearly twenty seconds, no one moved or threw a bottle.

"To hell with your debate," Asad finally said. "*Inshe'allah.* The will of Allah will be done."

Then he turned and walked toward the door, followed reluctantly by the others. The last few scrambled after.

A teacher came out from behind a salad kiosk. "Someone, call an ambulance."

Just like that, the riot at Boulder City High School was over.

And the news coverage of the girl named Katrina Kivi, who'd risked her neck to speak sense into a crowd of angry students, had just begun.

CHAPTER TWENTY-FOUR

Day Seven

DARCY FELT a bit lost. Powerless even. Which to her way of thinking was a bit terrifying. She'd gone from the highest peak of confidence and power to this miserable state of denial in the space of two days.

One day, God's gift to the world, the next day, scum of the earth.

She knew none of her feelings were justified. She hadn't lost any power, and even if she had, since when did she need this gift, this drug, to help her through the day? She'd made a perfectly good life for herself before all of this, thank you very much. And it didn't include performing for others at their whim.

And yet . . .

She'd fully expected the council to demand another meeting on Monday, but they left Billy and Darcy in their glass prison to stew and watch the Net.

Billy had spent Tuesday morning scanning the Net while she finished reading *Birthright*, the Frakes vampire novel. She eventually joined Billy on the couch, scanning the reports and blogs. Johnny's visit seemed to have stirred up fresh concerns about Marsuvees Black in him.

Interesting, yes, but something else had taken charge of Darcy's mind.

She simply could not dislodge the idea of speaking to a million people at once over the Net. A hundred thoughts, some of which might disturb Billy, buzzed through her mind, simple *what ifs* that she immediately rejected as preposterous.

But . . . what if?

It was one o'clock in the afternoon before the badgering thoughts became too much for her. She stood from the couch, intending to do something about it.

"I want to test it," she announced.

Billy tapped the remote and muted the Net. "Test what?"

"The Net. Me speaking over the Net."

They'd maintained a rule that at least one of them would wear glasses at all times unless both agreed to bare themselves to each other; at the moment she wore hers.

Billy retrieved his sunglasses from the table, slid them on, and sat back. "You mean your power, over the airwaves."

"We have to know, right? I'm not saying I would ever expose myself on the Net—it's dangerous, you've already established that." She walked toward the phone. "But it's stupid not to know."

"You sure you really *want* to know? I mean, even knowing that you have that kind of power could mess with your mind."

There, he'd said it. Darcy suppressed an urge to snap at him and picked up the phone.

"I have you to keep me in line, dear Billy." Maybe a little too much bite in her voice. She sighed. "I need to do this. It's driving me crazy."

He frowned and nodded. "It would be a trip, wouldn't it?"

There's my Billy. She smiled and dialed Kinnard.

IT WAS three o'clock before Kinnard broke free, set up a room at CIA headquarters for the test, and arranged secure transportation to Langley. They stood in a communications room, essentially a small television studio without the sets. A single camera faced a stool from a tripod ten feet away, blinking red. The technicians had been told that Kinnard wanted to do a simple camera test, which he would personally conduct. Billy would be in the adjacent room separated by a glass wall, watching a secured, closed-circuit image of her during the test. Both rooms and the adjacent corridor and technical offices were cleared of all other personnel.

"Okay, Darcy, you ready to do this?"

She'd reconsidered a dozen times since calling Kinnard, but not for the reason Billy had cited. She wasn't afraid of the possibility she had a power that could reach into every home in America. She was afraid the test would fail. Which is why she still wore her glasses and would wear them until Billy was safely out of the room.

They already knew that he couldn't read the thoughts of those on the Net. Which made sense: thoughts didn't travel thousands of miles or through wires, right? But her gift was different. Her voice could travel thousands of miles and be heard by millions. There was no reason she could see that it wouldn't work.

Still, her palms were moist and her heart was racing.

"Billy?"

"Okay." He headed for the door, then spoke over his shoulder, grinning. "Just don't make me do anything crazy. Like undress."

Darcy sat on the stool and chuckled nervously. "Scout's honor, dear Billy." She waited for him to enter the adjacent room, sit with his back to them, and face a black screen on the wall.

Kinnard stood behind the camera, sunglasses safely in place. "Okay, light goes green, you're live."

"Okay."

"Here we go."

The light changed from a red blink to a green blink. She looked to her right, saw the image of herself with her sunglasses fill the monitor. Billy had freed his eyes.

Now she did the same.

Darcy looked into the camera lens, silent for a few seconds. She hadn't considered what she would say. It had to be something definite. Unmistakable. Something that would get a physical reaction from him so that she wouldn't have to depend on his word.

"Billy . . . you're afraid of Black, aren't you? He terrifies you, because you know as well as I do that he's your brainchild. You created him. All of this is your fault. You're to blame. If Black is evil, then you are the father of that evil, isn't that right? You should be on your knees, weeping, begging the world for forgiveness."

Her own breathing had thickened as she slashed him with her words. She dared a glance but couldn't see if he was reacting, because his back was toward her.

She had to take him to his knees!

"Billy, you useless scum, get your lousy, worthless self off the chair and beg; beg like you deserve to!" She was shouting, letting herself go. "You did this to me! It was your idea—you went down first, you deceitful little runt!"

Darcy surprised even herself at the emotions that she'd put into those words. Is that how she really felt? She sat on the stool, breathing hard. Kinnard had turned and was watching Billy. She followed his gaze.

Billy sat upright, hands on his lap. Then he replaced his glasses, stood, and calmly exited the room.

He hadn't been affected? How could he not have been wounded by her words? They'd hurt even her, just saying them!

He stepped inside her room and stopped. Perhaps he had been too distraught to weep.

"Anything?"

"No."

"That's impossible."

"Did you mean what you said?"

But she wasn't listening to him. "Maybe the words mean nothing to you! Maybe I was wrong!" Only one solution presented itself to her. "Take off your glasses."

"Darcy, it didn't work."

"I have to know! Take off your glasses. Now!"

He slowly lifted his hand. Slid his glasses off.

"Now you listen to me, you beast, you are *terrified* of Black because you brought him to life, here in this world. This is all your fault; you did this to me! I've spent the last decade paying for your selfish ambitions, weeping like a child, running scared from my dreams, waking up drowned in sweat. Now, you get on your knees and weep like you have made me weep!"

Billy's shoulders had started to shake after the first sentence, and by the last he was falling. Not to his knees as she'd demanded, but to his side, where he curled up in a ball and began to sob.

"I'm sorry . . . Oh Darcy, I'm sorry. I'm so sorry . . ."

Tears flooded her eyes and she blinked them away. The test had failed, then. Her power was localized and therefore drastically inferior to what she'd hoped.

She'd accomplished nothing but to wound the one man she loved.

"Leave us," she snapped at Kinnard.

He stared at her for a long moment, then walked for the door. "Take your time. I'll be outside."

Darcy waited for him to leave, watching Billy writhing on the floor. What had she done? If there was a guilty soul in this room, it was her!

She rushed to him, fell to her knees, and threw herself over him. "No, Billy, no! I'm sorry, I didn't mean it. Please don't cry!"

But he didn't let up. So she held him tight and cried with him. What had she been thinking, leveling this kind of brutality at him? It had only been the truth, that much was now clear. Or at least, Billy believed it to be the truth.

She held him for a long time and begged him to be still. The test had failed. She'd destroyed Billy and the test had failed. Anger flushed her face.

It occurred to her that neither of them wore glasses. If she'd wounded him with her voice, she could heal him with it, couldn't she?

SINNER

She knelt beside him, hushing him gently. Took his head in her hands so that he faced her.

"No, Billy, listen to me, you don't have to do this. Look at me, look at me, baby. Please look at me."

But his eyes were clenched and he was still sobbing.

"Look at me!" she snapped.

His eyelids opened slowly and she stared into his tearful green eyes. "Don't cry, Billy. Please don't cry. I am as guilty as you are. This isn't your fault. You don't have to tear Black. It's true, you wrote him, but what you did, you can undo. And I love you, Billy, I love you. Hear my mind, hear my heart, do whatever you do, climb inside my head. You know that I love you! Stop crying, please stop crying."

She said it all so quickly, flooding him with her power. He stilled immediately.

"You see? I'm sorry, I didn't mean to hurt you." She quickly added, knowing he could read the truth in her mind, "And if I did, I was wrong. Please forgive me, tell me you forgive me."

He swallowed. "I forgive you. Tell me, Darcy. Tell me that you love me."

She did, washing him with her gift. "I love you, Billy. And you love me. You love me more than you've ever loved any woman."

Darcy brought her lips to his and they kissed deeply, smothered each other with comfort. She'd never been so direct with him, never presumed to tell him how he should feel. Only what he should do for her. Meddling with his mind was stepping on hallowed ground.

But the moment called for it.

Billy pushed himself to his knees and looked around, disoriented. "We're alone."

"I sent him out." Darcy stroked his hair.

"So the test failed."

And with those words Darcy felt her mood shift, subtly, but enough for her recognize it.

"Evidently." She looked away from him. "I really am sorry for this, Billy."

"Don't be. We both know there's plenty of truth in what you said."

He stood and walked out to the middle of the room, hands on hips.

"Have you ever wondered if this is all part of a much larger plan?"

"I think that maybe you've been talking to Johnny," she said pushing herself to her feet.

"No, really. What if we were actually drawn to Washington by forces we don't understand yet?"

"Maybe. So what?"

He turned around and faced her. They were still both bared to each other. "Maybe we should leave. Just pack up and run. We could—"

"No!"

"No?"

"Just because Johnny does his thing in anonymity without obligation doesn't mean we need to go chasing after him."

"That's not what I meant."

"We can't leave."

Billy looked into her eyes and read her mind, she could see it in him. So she countered quickly.

"Don't tell me you haven't thought about what our power could accomplish here, Billy." She stepped toward him. "Deep down inside, you feel it as much as I do. Who wouldn't? The desire to see just how far we can take this."

His eyes were wide, drinking in her words. She took his hand.

"I want us to do this, Billy. We're here for a purpose, we have these powers for a purpose. We have no reason to be their sniffing dogs any more."

"We could go a long way . . ."

"Think of the good we could do!" Darcy knew that she was exploiting him, but she did it because she knew he wanted it. She walked around him, turning him slowly, her hand over his.

"We've already skated on thin ice. Let's dance on it—with this power; what do you say?"

"We do have a lot of power," he said, grinning.

"So my powers don't work through the Net. There's more than enough good to be done locally."

"We couldn't be too obvious, you know," he said. "We don't need more enemies."

"That's right. But we could make more friends. We'd have to start with something very calculated. Something the council approves of. But something quiet."

"Work our way through this town like ghosts in the night."

"Exactly."

Billy grinned. "I can see you've given this a lot of thought." And he meant it literally. He'd taken the thought right out of her mind.

"I have." And then she said something she hoped he would forgive her for if the need ever arose.

"I need for you to go with me on this, Billy. I know you want to, but I want you to promise me that you'll trust me and do whatever it takes. Promise me. Whatever it takes."

He hesitated only a moment, and then answered with a coy grin.

"Whatever it takes. I swear it."

CHAPTER TWENTY-FIVE

Day Eight

ANY ILLUSION some may have fostered that the nation was not facing a crisis of monumental proportions was shattered Wednesday morning when the nation's capital woke to find six victims, all black, hanging from six consecutive streetlights on First Street, directly in front of the Capitol.

The victims: three males between the ages of thirty-five and sixty, two females in the same age bracket, and one older female in her sixties. They were discovered when security officer Joseph Custer arrived at his station at six. Three guards, whose names had been withheld from the press, were found dead in a Dumpster behind the National Gallery of Art, little more than a block away.

Five of the six bodies found hanging from the streetlights had not yet been identified to the press. But the identity of the sixth could not be hidden for the simple reason that most of those who lived in Washington and half of those who lived in Nevada knew him.

He was the well-heeled and occasionally outspoken Democratic senator from Nevada, Ben Manning.

By six thirty, footage of the lynched bodies taken just before dawn, presumably by those responsible, had been widely circulated on the Net. The victims looked unreal, like scarecrows floating against a gray Halloween sky, until the camera zoomed in on each face, each crooked neck, snapped by the heavy ropes from which they hung.

Darcy had woken, showered, dressed, and walked out into the living room to find Billy on the phone with the images frozen on the screen behind him.

He hung up. "Gotta go, come on."

"What's going on?" The images on the Net screen behind him answered her question in a matter of moments. Six had been lynched in front of the Capitol. She felt nauseated and turned from the pictures.

"Take a look."

He stared out the glass wall overlooking the corridor that extended from the Lincoln Memorial to the Capitol. A sea of people pushed in on a perimeter that had been established around the entire corridor, including the White House.

"What happened?"

"Over a hundred thousand. It hasn't turned violent yet, but nobody's holding their breath." Billy paused. "One of the victims was Senator Ben Manning."

"What?" She was stunned. "*The* Ben . . . ?"

"From the council. Yes."

She blinked, unable to come to grips with the idea that the man was actually dead. Had she had any part in that? Her thoughts refused to connect.

Fire trucks and police cars lined the streets along the Mall below, lights flashing. Several dozen military response vehicles, likely from the National Guard, D.C. Police, and monitored by the Secret Service, crept along Pennsylvania and Constitution Avenues. Several armored vehicles had been stationed around the White House.

"The keg of gunpowder is blowing up," Billy said. "I'll explain more along the way."

"Kinnard's here?"

"Downstairs. Annie Ruling is waiting for us at the White House."

Darcy's pulse spiked. "We're meeting the president?"

"I don't think so."

He hurried to the door, yanked it open, nodded at the armed guard stationed at the door, and quickly crossed to the elevator, followed closely by Darcy. She started again the moment the door slid shut.

"The council?"

"I don't know."

"Then who, just Annie?"

"I don't know, but she called us directly and insisted no one know that we were meeting."

"Other than Kinnard?"

"Other than Kinnard."

Darcy stared up at the floor lights as the elevator car dropped. "She's making an end run."

"Maybe."

The bell chimed, and they stepped out into the basement loading zone, where Kinnard waited, phone fixed to his ear. As dark as it was, she wondered how he could see anything with those glasses on. Then she remembered that her sight was darkened as well.

He rounded the truck's hood and climbed in behind the wheel as guards opened their doors for them.

Billy told her what he knew as Kinnard piloted the car up Arlington Boulevard, headed for Theodore Roosevelt Memorial Bridge. They were stopped at a checkpoint and quickly waved through when Kinnard flashed his ID.

He shut his phone and activated the bulletproof glass partition between the cab and the back. "Morning, kids. I'm sorry, it's just a tad busy out there."

"Why are we going to the White House?"

"Because that's where Annie Ruling and Lyndsay Nadeau want to meet you. But I'll let them speak for themselves, if you don't mind. Don't worry, our route is safe. The crowds are contained north of the White House. Just sit tight."

The glass partition rose, sealing them off.

They pulled onto Constitution in silence. No tour groups or crowds gazed upon the Lincoln Memorial or the reflecting pool on their right. Ahead, the Washington Monument pointed to the sky, tall and stately, like a lighthouse for the nation.

They took a left on Seventeenth before the monument Darcy had shrugged into a charcoal cotton dress with spaghetti straps and a lace hem—not exactly White House material. Her dark hair hung past her shoulders, slightly disordered by design, but if she was to become a regular in this town, she might want to consider a new style. She thought about sliding off the silver snake bracelet that coiled around three inches of her right wrist. And the silver choker chains around her neck

But then, who did she think she was? Miss Polyester Pantsuit?

Billy looked just as casual, dressed in jeans and a black polo shirt. His dark reddish hair was as ever, neatly ordered over his ears, the perfect gentleman. But too young to be anything more than an intern in this town.

Listen to you, Darcy, the Capitol is practically under siege and you're thinking about what you're wearing. This thing is getting to you.

As it turned out, Kinnard didn't take them to the White House proper, but into the Eisenhower Executive Office Building, just across the street from the White House's West Wing, and then into a back door that led into a basement.

Other than the guards, there was no indication that they had entered the halls of power in the world's most powerful nation. The protest was too far away to disturb the quiet, and she imagined that the staff had mostly stayed away this morning because of it.

"Watch your step."

They walked down a flight of steps into a dim white hall that needed a fresh coat of paint to cover the chips along the borders. Large framed photographs lined the walls, mostly old black-and-white images of people and buildings.

"This way." Kinnard led them down a second hall toward a white door with an old brass handle. "Don't let the lack of elegance fool you; more work gets done behind doors like this than you might realize." He smiled and twisted the knob.

They entered a large office, plainly decorated with several large paintings, a colonial-era wood desk, and a round conference table to one side. The attorney general, Lyndsay Nadeau, and Annie Ruling, the White House chief of staff, were both on their cell phones in different corners. They each glanced up and moved toward the conference table.

"Just keep a lid on their names," Annie was saying. "Promise me at least that much. Thank you, Charles."

She pocketed her phone and crossed to Billy and Darcy. Shook their hands. "Thank you for accommodating us on such short notice. As you can see, the world is falling down around our ears out there."

The attorney general offered her wizened smile. "Darcy. Billy."

Kinnard joined them at the table.

"Here we are," Darcy said.

"Here we are."

"Ben Manning . . ." She didn't know what do say.

"Tragic," Annie said. Her face was pale with concern. "It's gotten way out of hand."

"Why Manning?" Billy asked.

"Maybe you can tell us that, Billy. When we get to the bottom of this."

They looked at each other in silence. Both were out on a limb, Darcy thought. They all were.

"You're doing an end run?" Darcy said.

First Annie, then Lyndsay took off their glasses. "Let's just say we want to bring you in. No hidden agendas on our part. We need your complete confidence. No glasses."

Billy looked from one to the other. "All of us?"

"If you don't mind." Kinnard tapped his temple. "I have just a few sensitive details I can't expose."

"As do we all, Brian. Okay, all of us but the company man. Read our minds, speak carefully, do what you have to do. We aren't interested in playing any games. No more cloak-and-dagger among the four of us."

Billy pulled off his glasses and stared into their eyes for a moment. He set the shades on the table. "Fair enough. Go ahead, Darcy."

His was the more ominous power in some ways. Particularly in the town of a thousand secrets. Darcy bared her eyes.

The attorney general's light blue eyes smiled. "I hope you realize the significance of this gesture, Billy. You could walk out of this room with more classified information than even the president is privy to. And you will. But that only puts you in the crosshairs of more scopes than you can count. We will depend on each other. I for your confidence, you for my protection."

"I get it, ma'am. Really, I do."

"And we respectfully ask that you hear us out without any attempt to persuade, Darcy," Annie said. "None of us, not even you, knows just how long the effects of your persuasion last, but we have no interest in being at your whim, even for a few hours."

There was a veiled threat in there somewhere, Darcy thought. "You wouldn't do what's not in you to do. But I won't betray your trust, you have my word."

"Good. Lyndsay?"

The attorney general stood and walked around the table, arms crossed. Eyes on the walls. "You're probably wondering why the rest of our so-called council isn't here. Washington is all about arguing. Posturing. Frankly, knowing what we do about some of the others, we don't have the time to argue. Need I say more?"

"No," Darcy said.

"Good." Lyndsay faced Billy. "The only way to deal with hatred is to contain it through discipline. What do you tell a naughty child who has screamed at his sister over a toy? Used to be they would get a smack. Now we say, 'If you can't play nice, you can't play at all.' Put them in a time out. In this country we call that prison."

"What she's saying," Billy said, "is that the time has come to expose the hypocrisy of certain so-called freedoms and force adults to follow the same rules they impose on their own children."

Lyndsay smiled. "And what else am I thinking?"

"That you can't stop people from hating. But you can limit the freedom they have to express that hatred, just like we do with our children."

"And?"

"We're facing this crisis today because the children have been allowed to scream at each other for far too long. Everyone knows that screaming children eventually turn to sticks and stones. The only way to keep the sticks and stones on the ground is to end the screaming."

Her breathing thickened. "Bravo. My, that's a stunning gift you have."

"Thank you."

Won't you just listen to them, Darcy thought. *So taken with Billy.*

"And the solution is a constitutional amendment that would limit certain kinds of free speech," Darcy said. "Doesn't take a mind reader to guess that."

"That's right," Annie said. "Our current hate-crime laws only affect sentencing in racially motivated events. These laws used to be adequate for localized bigotry, but they don't and can't expand the definition of *what* those crimes are. Especially at the federal level. Our only option is to make certain kinds of *spoken* hate crimes illegal, punishable by law. And for that, we need to amend the Constitution."

The attorney general's eyes were on Billy again. "You know why we have to do this now?"

"That's a little more convoluted. One, the country needs a serious change to throw it off balance. A thundering shot across the bow to snap it out of all this racial idiocy. Martial law would likely inflame the country. Most protesters don't have the stomach for prison. Shut them down by making inflammatory racial remarks a prosecutable crime, and most of them would go home, unlikely to return."

"And the other reason?"

"The country's already reeling. Radical action like this is more easily digested in times of crisis."

"That's right."

It all made sense to Darcy. "When you say 'certain kinds of speech,' you mean racial slurs," Darcy said.

"And inflammatory expressions of faith."

So there it was. They were out to muzzle the religious as much as racial bigots. Considering how many citizens hated the faithful, it was only a matter of time. And that time was now. All things considered, it was a reasonable course of action, Darcy thought.

"Okay. When do we start?"

Kinnard spoke from his seat. "You do understand, Darcy, that what Annie and Lyndsay are suggesting constitutes a change of staggering proportions to the very fabric of this country."

"Of course she does," Billy said. "But the fact is, we've already discussed this, and we happen to be in agreement. Certain kinds of religious and racial speech should be subject to boundaries."

She and Billy hadn't so much discussed the particulars as they'd agreed to capitalize on something precisely like this.

"You realize that the opposition will be staggering," Kinnard said.

"Which is why Billy and I are here," Darcy said.

They fell silent.

"So. How do we go about this amending the Constitution thing?"

"Okay." Annie seemed skeptical that they'd been so easily convinced, but her small smile didn't say she was disappointed. "For starters, we do it quickly. I mean very quickly. And that, my friends, is where you come in."

"Quickly for two reasons," the attorney general interjected. "This crisis may be the only means we have to accomplish our objective; we also believe swiftness is the best way to end this crisis. Half a week, while the U.S. economy is still on level ground."

"Three days?" Billy said. "Both the House and the Senate have to repeal the applicable portions of the First Amendment with a two-thirds majority. And it has to then be ratified by three quarters of the states. That's a lot of representatives, a lot of senators, a lot of governors, and the president. Not to mention the inevitable judicial block at the Supreme Court. Laws typically take months, even years, and that's not even taking the enactment and enforcement into account. It's impossible."

Lyndsay confirmed the process. "And that's just repealing the amendment itself. We need a federal law that gives us the teeth to enforce the amendment."

"So you're thinking five days."

Annie held up her hand. "Please, this reading of the minds is cute, but for the rest of us, maybe we could revert to straight dialogue? Billy?"

"Okay. Why don't you just lay it all out in layman's terms so we can all understand, Lyndsay."

Was that a dig at Annie? Darcy glanced at him and winked.

The attorney general took her seat and pulled out a red folder. "Okay, from the start, then."

ERECTING THE framework for their carefully calculated plan took more than an hour with several interruptions for updates on the crisis surrounding the Capitol. The protesters, as they were now being called, had been mostly dispersed, but four smaller riots had broken out in California, Alabama, and Missouri again. The president had activated a nationwide order for National Guard units to respond at the first signs of any violence in any city, but the order did nothing to silence the war drums.

Darcy was surprised to see Annie Ruling pull out a pack of cigarettes and ask if they minded her smoking. The stress, she said. Legislators had all but banned smoking in the United States ten years earlier. But the fact that Annie smoked to relieve stress only endeared her to Darcy more.

And she was a smart one. The plan she and the attorney general laid out (assuming it was them and not Kinnard who'd engineered it) might be completely unthinkable without Billy and her to grease the wheels, but with them, the plan just might succeed.

They *needed* Billy and Darcy. The whole notion didn't merely energize Darcy, it thrilled her. Isn't this why she had this gift, to change history? Not to calm gangsters and seduce Billy, although that wasn't a bad thing. She hadn't asked for the power, unless you held a thirteen-year-old responsible for an impulsive decision to scratch a note in a book.

Fate had given her the power to be used for the good of all. And by *all* she meant herself as well.

Darcy looked at the notepaper strewn over the table, listing names and flowcharting the multipronged approach. She noticed that her fingers were trembling and she pulled them off the table.

Lying before them on a white sheet of paper were two versions of the First Amendment as adopted as part of the United States Bill of Rights, inspired by Thomas Jefferson and drafted by James Madison in 1791. At the top of the page, the original.

Amendment I

Congress shall make no law respecting an establishment of religion, or prohibiting the free exercise thereof; or abridging the freedom of speech, or of the press; or the right of the people peaceably to assemble, and to petition the government for a redress of grievances.

And below it, the amendment as proposed.

Amendment I (Amended)

Congress shall make no law respecting an establishment of religion, or prohibiting the free exercise thereof; or abridging the freedom of the

*press; or abridging the freedom of any speech that does not publicly
defame, slander, or libel another person's race, national origin, or religion; or the right of the people peaceably to assemble, and to petition
the government for a redress of grievances.*

The only material change was the addition of the clause that removed
defamation, slander, or libel in the context of race and religion as a form
of protected speech.

The media's rights were still protected; so long as they didn't slander
anyone's race or religion.

Religions were still protected, so long as they didn't preach inflammatory accusations against other ideologies or the faiths of their neighbors.

The right to assemble was still protected.

Honestly, the huge amount of effort required to make such a small,
long overdue change struck Darcy as a bit ridiculous. The ACLU would
have a cow, naturally, as would most religious institutions, fearing the
erosion of their rights to rail against whomever they wished to rail. But
in the end, they would bow to the winds of change, just as so many other
Western nations already had.

"So that's it, then?" Billy said. "What do you say, Darcy? You've been
quiet for the last ten minutes."

She cleared her throat. "Me? You know what I'm thinking, Billy."

"But do they?"

She looked at them. "I'm thinking we're going to change history."

Annie smiled. Then spoke carefully. "Tell us how, Darcy."

"You need convincing?"

"No. But I could use a little pick-me-up, and I can tell you have it."

Annie had felt her voice before and was now asking for it again. What,
she was Annie's personal drug now? But the idea appealed to her.

"All right. You're going to open all the doors we need, Annie, beginning
with the president and the Senate Judiciary, who will sponsor the bill. An
emergency session of Congress will be called and the bill will be presented

tomorrow for debate. I will address the House of Representatives, because you will see to it that I am allowed to. And I will also address the Senate. Once the bill is passed and signed by the president, the states will have forty-eight hours to ratify the amendment in compliance with a deadline passed in the House by common vote. Do you need more, Annie?"

"I do."

Her words were like a soothing balm, reinforcing what Annie already knew and desired. Like a preacher reassuring a choir shouting, "Amen, brother, preach it!"

"A new law based upon the amendment will be voted on and signed into law within forty-eight hours of the ratification. Yada, yada, yada . . ." Darcy leaned forward, drilling Annie with her stare, knowing that Lyndsay was watching her with as much interest. "I could go on and give you all the little twists and turns as you've outlined them, thrilling you with details that would bore an average person to tears."

She returned Lyndsay's stare. "But I won't. Instead I'll tell you what's really interesting here. It's the part you play. You've always dreamed of making a difference. Of being remembered as a figure that changed history. Which is what you're going to do, because you're going to make sure Billy stands in front of every single undecided politician so that he can find out exactly—and I do mean exactly—*all* those nasty secrets, which is what I need to persuade them to vote the right way. He's going to do that because of you. Do you need more, Lyndsay?"

"Yes."

"Do you need more, Annie?"

Sweat beaded her forehead. "I do, Darcy." She said it softly, without apparent emotions, but Darcy knew that she was only covering up a deep-seated pleasure that probably surprised even her.

"You're going to make sure I get to speak into the hearts and minds of each and every man or woman whose vote we need for a two-thirds majority. We're going to succeed, Annie, because Billy and I will know which buttons to push and how to push them. We'll try not to make enemies, but if we do, we'll protect ourselves by holding information about them that would be released in the event we were ever harmed. The kind of information that Billy will have in reams and reams. The kind he already has on both of you, or will have in the next few seconds now that I've brought it to the surface for you to think about."

She paused for that dose to work its bit, and then continued.

"In the end we will convince the House, the Senate, the president, all nine Supreme Court justices, and, maybe most importantly, the governors of those states who sit on the fence if we need their vote. And we will succeed, because of you. Because of us. Because of our commitment to each other."

She stopped, then pushed further. "This is your day, both of you. You will stop at nothing to accomplish the objectives you've laid out for us. Do you hear me? Nothing. And you will owe Billy and me a great debt for helping you achieve this plan. Wouldn't you both agree?"

"Yes," Annie said, struggling now to maintain an air of calm. "I would say that puts it accurately."

"Wouldn't you say, Lyndsay?"

"It think that's fair, yes." She looked like she'd been slapped.

"And if we help you achieve your objective—changing the first amendment in the Bill of Rights so that it limits protected speech—if we do this for you, you *will* agree to give us something in exchange, and you will be bound to that agreement in good faith."

Kinnard put his hands on the table. "Darcy—"

"No," Annie interrupted. "No, it's okay. She's right. What did you have in mind, Darcy?"

"Billy?"

He winked at her. "Anything permitted by law."

She nodded once. "There you go, then. Anything permitted by law. Is that fair?"

"I would say so."

"You don't have any resentment toward me for asking this while you

look in my eyes, do you? I don't want you to feel compelled unless it follows your true feelings. You do want to do this for us, right?"

Of course, the phrasing put Annie in a bit of a bind, unless she really
did think the request completely unreasonable, which Darcy knew she
would not.

"No." Annie looked at the attorney general, who was grinning. It was
the first time she'd felt Darcy's power personally. "Lyndsay?"

"No, not at all. Oh my, I think we might actually have a shot at this."

"Then you both swear to give us what we want, permitted by law?"

"Yes."

"Yes."

"Okay." Darcy looked at Billy and spread her hands. "Anything else?"

"No, not from me. I think I get the picture." He slid his glasses back
on, and Darcy followed his example.

"Where and when do we start?" she asked.

Annie took a deep breath, replaced her own glasses. "With the president. In fifteen minutes." She pushed her chair back and stood.

"I think history's going to like you, Billy and Darcy. I think I'm going
to like you very, very much."

The Books of History, Darcy thought. *She's thinking of the Books of
History.* And her heart skipped a beat.

II

WORDS OF POWER

The Apostle who saw the Light with his own two eyes said this:

*I came to you in weakness
and fear and with much trembling.*

*My message was not with wisdom
or persuasive words,
but with power . . .*

First-century letter written by
Paul to those in Corinth

CHAPTER TWENTY-SIX

Day Fourteen

THEY WERE calling the last week "the five days that changed America," but to Katrina Kivi, nothing had changed. Certainly not the kingdom of light that greeted her every morning, so to speak. In fact, nothing had changed except the newscasts on the Net, and for some reason the news never really felt very personal. Secondhand data from secondhand sources. Long before this so-called crisis, Kat had seen a thousand images of flag burnings, street violence, and Molotov cocktails exploding against cars, even if it was in other countries. And now it was coming to America, for real.

But it still didn't *feel* real, not next to her new real.

It had been all constitutional and civil liberties dialogue, all day, all night, all on the Net. Worse than a sci-fi marathon, only real.

Kat stood on the cliff's edge next to Johnny and Kelly, overlooking the valley before them. Except for the chirping of birds and the occasional rattle of lizards dislodging pebbles on the rocky surface beneath them, the day was quiet up here in the mountains.

Johnny stood still, breathing in the scent of pines and clean air, staring at the small Colorado town they'd come to see.

Paradise.

A large crow settled on a bare branch to Kat's right, eyed them with a beady eye, and cawed. Its head jerked a few times as it hopped down the branch, holding firm with long clawed feet. *Caw, caw.* Jet black. It leaped into the air and flapped away, calling out over the valley, as if announcing their presence to all who might be interested.

Kelly stood to one side, staring south, not looking terribly comfortable. But Kat hardly blamed her; it had been clear from the beginning that Johnny's hometown held a nearly mystical, very personal place in his mind.

"So, this is it, huh?" Kat said.

He didn't bother answering, because they all knew the question was rhetorical. Of course this was it. The real question was what *it* was.

Upon learning two days earlier about Johnny's occasional pilgrimage to this spot, Kat had talked her way into accompanying them. By helicopter.

"This is it," he said. "The place where I lost my sight. And saw for the first time."

Kat looked at the town. A single black strip of asphalt ran down the center, bordered by the kinds of buildings she would expect in any small town like this. A church complete with a steeple, surrounded by a huge lawn. A large community center. Gas station, odd shops, maybe a bar and a grocery store, though she couldn't actually see clearly enough from this distance.

Beyond the center of town, fruit farms filled the valley before it rose again to the mountains across the valley. Several green fields spotted the otherwise wooded landscape. A couple hundred homes dotted the valley, in rows around the town and like scattered seed beyond.

"And why are we here again?"

Johnny swiveled his head and faced her. "Because a very good friend of mine, Samuel, suggested that I have a date with destiny here."

"Now?"

"He seems to think so, yes."

"Samuel?" She waited for him to explain.

Johnny frowned. "A friend from Paradise a long time ago. I talked to him yesterday. He would have been here, but he seems to think I should face this alone."

"Face what?"

Johnny didn't seem eager to elaborate.

"Why can't you just tell me what happened here? You don't trust me?"

Johnny looked at her for several long seconds, then looked down the valley and told her about the birth and death of Project Showdown.

When he finished, Kat stared at him, stunned by his casual account of such improbable events. Who would believe that such books existed?

But then, who would believe that the kingdom of light existed unless they had seen it with their own eyes?

She cleared her throat. "What happened after that? The town doesn't look like it's on its knees any longer."

"No. No, the town pulled out, but at a high price. And Black escaped unscathed."

A crow cawed again, but Kat didn't know from where. She was fixed on the town below, mind lost on what must have happened here not so long ago.

"We're linked, Johnny. You know that, don't you?"

"Is that so?"

"You brought me into this kingdom."

"No, I don't think so . . ."

"And I'm not about to let you just drop me off at the nearest bus station now that we're here."

A slow grin twisted his lips. "I like the way you speak, Kat. I really do."

"That's a promise then?"

"It's a promise."

"What about you, Kelly? Did Johnny bring you into this kingdom?"

She chuckled. "Not exactly, no."

"But you do believe."

"Of course."

"You're with Johnny. I mean in heart and soul."

"Yes."

Kat scolded herself for asking such an obvious question that could only be interpreted by both of them as a kind of childish jealousy.

"Not to worry, you two," Kat said, gazing out. "I'm not suffering from a bout of youthful infatuation. Just to set your minds at ease."

"Infatuation? With whom?" Johnny asked.

The blind man was indeed quite blind when it came to matters of women, Kat thought.

Kelly was still smiling. "With you, dear," she said.

"Yes, with you," Kat said. "I'm sixteen, you know."

"My, you are a straight shooter," Johnny said.

It occurred to her that none of this was remotely necessary. She just felt so comfortable around him. Maybe she *was* developing a crush on him.

"Awkward," she said.

"Not at all," Johnny said, deadpan. "Thank you for setting my mind at ease." Then he offered her a smile. "Think of me as your spiritual father."

That was it, of course. The realization set her completely at ease. And if he was her spiritual father, then she had every right to look out for him as any daughter might. No question was out of bounds. Starting with why he was going to marry Kelly. Just to be sure.

"That's good, because I don't have a father, not one that I know anyway."

Kelly stepped up, arms crossed, and stared at the valley. "So then, it's begun."

"So it seems," Johnny said. "The supernatural reality that so many pretend to believe in has crossed over in physical form. The books did that for us. And now the stage is set for a new kind of conflict."

Kat's only experience with the kingdom of light revealed in Jesus had been quite physical, but she knew that very few had been exposed to such a dramatic unveiling as she had.

"You don't mean a physical conflict?" she said. "Or do you?"

Johnny nodded at the valley. "What do you see, Katrina?"

"The town that you grew up in. Paradise."

"But that's the same answer you would have given me two weeks ago. You know better now."

Realization dawned. "I see a valley filled with the struggle between good and evil. To be more precise, I *wish* I did, because I know it's there even though I can't see it. If you would just open my eyes again . . ."

"So much of what really happens in this world can't be seen with those round balls in our eye sockets. You could pluck them out and still see as bright as day. Or you could walk around with the prettiest blue eyes carved from the sky and be as blind as Black himself."

"Exactly."

"The valley is teeming with every sort of wraith from hell you can imagine, you just don't see it. Light defeated the darkness in this valley once, but I do believe that darkness is coming again."

Johnny frowned. "Samuel thinks the monastery existed for the sake of what will happen here. This final showdown."

"When?" Kelly asked.

Johnny's jaw muscles flexed. It was always hard to guess what he was thinking because of his dark shades, but that he was emotional about the prospect of returning to Paradise was obvious.

"Now," Johnny said.

Now? Alarm spread through Kat's chest. "You can't! There's the court order, you have to watch over me!"

"We'll have to speak to the judge."

"No. Just what's this all about anyway? Kelly, you can't just up and leave your home because he says it's time! What's so important about Paradise anyway?"

"It's not Paradise," Johnny said. "You may not realize it yet, but our lives changed when the Constitution changed."

"What are you talking about?" she demanded. "So you can't trash another person's race or religion. You yourself said the light is best shown, not just talked about. I don't see how our lives have changed, other than you think you have to come to Paradise to face this wraith of yours."

It was crucial he realize just how important he was in her life at this time. The thought of him abandoning her was terrifying.

"I'm not sure you understand, Kat," Johnny said. "This change in the Constitution allows Congress to create new laws that make it a crime to express your faith in public. What may seem like a good thing on the surface opens the doors to laws that could make following the teachings of Christ a hate crime."

What?

"Seriously? How could talking about the love of God be a hate crime?"

"Because saying that he is the only way to enter the kingdom implies that another's path is wrong. You're saying your faith is better than another's faith. They will say it's no different than a claim that black skin is better than white skin. Both will be interpreted as hate crimes."

She understood in a single flash that sent a buzz through her skull.

"So saying, 'Jesus is the only way, follow him,' is like calling those who don't follow him fools. An insult."

"Yes."

"But Jesus claimed he is the only way. The whole kingdom is based on teachings like that. Even by following him you could be judged as saying that others are fools for not following him the way he insisted the world follow him!"

"That would be an extreme interpretation, but yes, you get the point. What few Christians realize is that you can't follow Jesus without actually following his teachings—none of which include denying him with silence."

"Meaning what?"

"Meaning that we are in a bind, dear Kat. There will be challenges, but any public support for the narrow teachings of Jesus will likely be deemed by the courts as a personal attack on other religions. Take my word for it." And then he added under his breath, "This reeks of Marsuvees Black."

Kat's whole mind-set changed. Johnny's need to make a stand in Paradise, however that looked, had nothing to do with her. Her eyes had been opened to an incredible new world two weeks ago, a reality brimming with light and truth. The realization that Jesus was who he'd claimed to be. The Light of the World. The Truth. The only Way.

She would never abandon that light!

She'd only just learned that her whole life was oppressed by a great dark lie, and now some law was going to attempt to force her back into that darkness? How could she even consider not walking in the light?

She'd read about a dog named Rutt who was so severely beaten every time he left his cage that when he was finally set free he found his way back to the cage, entered it, and died of starvation.

Unlike Rutt, she would not return to the cage, not under any circumstances.

"We can't let that happen!" Kat paced along the cliff, mindless of where her feet landed. She spun back to Johnny.

"Someone has to tell them. This is what following Jesus means, they can't make following him a hate crime."

"Someone *is* going to tell them," Kelly said.

Kat hardly heard her. "And what about the Muslims or the Hindus? Are they going to take this, just . . . lying down? Doesn't this affect them?"

"The clerics will scream foul, but like nominal Christians, nominal Muslims don't actually follow their faith to the letter. In the face of this tide sweeping the West, most will argue for tolerance. As will most Christians."

"It's obscene!" Kat's voice rang out over the cliff so that a careful ear in Paradise might have wondered if they'd heard a hawk's cry. "Tolerance, yes, but tolerance for the darkness? Are we bats?"

They let the echo fade. Johnny faced Paradise. Kat recalled Kelly's last statement: *Someone is going to tell them.*

"Who's going to tell them?" she asked.

"Johnny is," Kelly said.

"Then so am I," Kat said, marching back to him. "I'm going to Paradise with you."

"I really don't—"

"I don't want to hear it. You promised me, you promised the judge."

"You're in the middle of a school term."

"There's no school in Paradise?"

"Your mother—"

"Will agree. And don't tell me about how dangerous standing up for my faith will be. I've done it."

They stood in silence once again, and Kat knew that the matter was settled. She suddenly felt quite emotional about going with him to stand up for all the world to see, because surely, knowing him, that's what would happen.

Johnny was this day's John the Baptist, a voice crying in the wilderness. Only this time John had himself an apprentice.

"Thank you, Johnny," she said.

"It could get very bad, Kat. You know that."

"No, thank you for showing me the light." Tears welled up in her eyes. "It's the kindest thing anyone has done for me."

He put his hand on her right shoulder and pulled her close. Kissed the top of her head. "You're welcome."

"When do we go?" Kelly asked.

CHAPTER TWENTY-SEVEN

DARCY STOOD at the podium in the United States Senate chamber staring out at ninety-seven senators, prepared to convince these men and women to pass the National Tolerance Act, the first federal law to be based on the amended Constitution. Ninety-seven—a full house, less three, compelled by Billy to abstain or have their abuses of power exposed: Brian Clawson (D-Utah), whom Billy had persuaded to either vote for the law, miss the vote entirely, or pay the fallout when the real purpose of his frequent trips to Thailand were made public; Nancy Truman (R-Texas), who was missing under similar pressure; and Rodney Walton, senior senator from Arkansas, who was in the hospital with a prostate flare-up. All other members were present, including two who had been escorted in by Capitol Hill police for a mandatory quorum call, the first time the Senate had enforced a quorum using compulsion since 1995.

Her mind flashed over the last five days. While she and Billy toiled around the clock, working their magic, the riots had spread, picking up steam over the weekend with nine separate national incidents that resulted in the death of at least one party.

Racial protests were joined by freedom-of-speech protests. It was all a bit jumbled. One image of a mob marching down Pennsylvania Avenue showed protesters carrying signs that read Stop the Hatred, No Tolerance for Bigots right next to signs that read Americans for Free Speech.

The outcry from all sides of the social and political spectrum was inevitable. Liberal social-progressives found themselves agreeing with archrivals, even though neither group shared any other common idea.

The Human Rights Watch, along with the Religious Action Center, attacked the constitutional amendment from both sides, one arguing that the legislation didn't do enough, the other that it was a step in the direction of national socialism.

The National Association for the Advancement of Colored People condemned the lynchings on one network and decried the constitutional amendment on another. A group calling itself the Nontheists of North America emerged from the political woodwork, hailing the amendment as a "bold new shift in social strategy."

Elliot Marshall, president of the National Association of Broadcasters, stated at a televised national conference that the government had just committed "the most flagrant act of legislative irresponsibility in U.S. history" by amending the Bill of Rights, which began with the specific phrasing "Congress shall make no law . . ." but that the American people deserved such severe repercussions. "Let us hope," he said, staring past bushy eyebrows into the camera, "that history forgives us."

The bottom line was that everybody wanted to be heard and nobody wanted to listen. But Darcy had changed all of that here in Washington. And now she would make them listen in the most sacred of all halls.

Located in the north wing of the Capitol building, the Senate chamber was a massive expanse that dwarfed the White House in both spaciousness and prestige. Royal blue carpet mapped the floor, surrounded by eggshell-white walls and populated with rich brown desks. A broad center aisle separated each political party, and three rows of chairs overlooked the room from the balustrade above.

She'd dressed in a blue business suit, one of seventeen of varying designs and fabrics that Annie had tailored for her five days ago, immediately following their successful meeting with the president. Darcy knew within ten minutes of sitting down across from President Chavez that as long as they could gain access to the right people over the next five days, they would succeed. He'd breathed in her words, converted wholeheartedly, and offered unlimited support in the initiative's passage.

Today, Billy sat behind and to her right, legs folded beneath a Queen Anne chair that had been given to the Senate as a gift by the Duchess of Wales before Darcy was born. His weapon was his mind, and he wielded it with a small PDA that transferred the notes he thumbed into the keypad to the prompter in front of her.

Hardin, D, 2 + 2. Religious Right concerns.

Which meant that Senator Hardin, a senior Democrat who sat two rows back and two seats over, was struggling under the excessive strain that had come from both his office and the House of Representatives.

The tension was a welcome advocate for Billy and Darcy. Together, they would motivate the Senate toward a resolution, like Mozart conducting an orchestra—every note and strain had to be perfect, he with his ears, she with her voice. There would be no second chances.

Darcy looked at the white-haired senator, who sat back frowning, tapping his pencil's eraser on the desk. "I realize that the Religious Right has come out of the woodwork regarding this resolution," she said. "The Christians and the Muslims are screaming bloody murder as we have expected. Try to muzzle a Doberman and he will try to bite your fingers off. Try to silence a bigot and he will turn his hatred on you. God himself understood this when he gave the Ten Commandments, restricting free speech. False witness in court was treated with stoning. This law we have before us today doesn't call for the stoning demanded in the biblical times, but it is critical we level appropriate punishment at those who spurn the Constitution of these United States as amended yesterday."

She watched his lips flatten, his throat bob as the conviction in her words resonated with some deep place of agreement in his psyche.

Darcy had spoken for less than ten minutes, and she already knew that they had the majority votes needed to pass the National Tolerance Act. It would provide federal provisions to enforce and prosecute the new terms of the Bill of Rights as a public bill, with the necessary appropriations included, to be voted on by the House of Representatives that very afternoon.

But she pressed them with her gift in this final push to change history, speaking in this language she now affectionately called *Washington lingo*.

"I have no doubt that each member of this Senate has been exposed to more hate mail and public contempt than ever before. With the power vested in each of you comes the responsibility to act, to engage in direct interdiction with these events. Yes, we've seen the vitriol on the news networks. Even out front of this building. There are rabid fanatics who have plagued your office lines with threats simply because you responded to the president's—no, the nation's—call to this session. I would ask you then, senators, delegates of our union—if the call to action has been heralded by civil unrest, social upheaval, and rampant crime, then when is the time more appropriate to call for a vote to stem the tide of recent violence and social distrust? When?"

The sensation of power had become her drug. Sweat veneered her face and cooled into ice from the air-conditioning and the wide-eyed stares of the Senate before her. Yes, it was her drug. She made no attempt to deny Billy's caution.

"Both houses have passed the resolution to amend the Bill of Rights. The president has signed it. Seven out of nine Supreme Court Justices have defined its interpretation as necessary and true to the durability of the Constitution. What we are asking of you, what *I* am asking of you today, is that this resolution, the National Tolerance Act, be acknowledged according to the urgency of the nation's need."

She paused and allowed a few breaths. Enough time to convey the exhaustion brought on by her passion, enough time to scan her prompter for an update from Billy.

She scanned the room slowly, seeking the strong to weaken, but she'd weakened so many over the past five days that only a few remained fixed to their convictions. Sixty-six men and thirty-one women, all dressed for business, watching her with glassy-eyed stares.

With great conviction comes great emotion. Perhaps more than anything it was this emotion that attracted Darcy to her undeniable power. Never had anger and contempt flared so hotheadedly than before she'd taken the stage when they'd gathered to vote four days earlier.

And then never so many tears.

"The power of the vote brings all of us into this chamber. The responsibility of legislation. As an American citizen today, I ask . . . even *demand* that you act to de-escalate the conflict. Make examples of yourselves as legislators by voting to support, enforce, and prosecute the National Tolerance Act. Sign it into law. History will remember you, but only if you act with definitive unity and decisive speed. A nation of hurt and disaffected people look to you to put your feet down and say 'This is enough.' It stops here. If you do not, thousands of municipal, state, and federal law-enforcement officers will be abandoned, without the support of the nation and the provisions and appropriations that this act supplies."

She loved the flow of words over her tongue.

"I realize that I'm only one voice, brought here to address you as a favor to the Senate Judiciary Committee; but when you look into my eyes you will *know* that I am the voice of the people," Darcy said. "This great country called the United States of America was founded because a few sought true freedom. They sailed for this land and endured terrible hardship for that freedom. They were the outcasts, the few who cried out for the right not to be trampled by oppressive beliefs. Now to preserve that freedom, not for a few who are black or white, Muslim or Christian, but for all, regardless of race or religion, you must pass this act"—she held up the sheaf of paper and shook it—"this law, which will deny any man the right to insult, defame, or degrade anyone's right to be black or white, Christian or Muslim!"

Her voice rose, and the truths mixed within her words washed over them with a conviction that they could not possibly understand.

"We are Americans, and that is enough for us to cling to. We *can* unite, as one body. As one voice. With one thing in common. We are states, united in freedom, and I say that our freedom comes from our unity, and *not* from our differences!"

Tears snaked down the cheeks of some. A few still retained set jaws, but not without a struggle.

"I say let no man be called unequal for the color of his skin! Let no woman be called a *witch* for her faith! Let no child be denied the sanctuary that this land offers their sacred beliefs."

She was almost yelling now.

"Stop the bigotry. End the violence. Break the impasse. Pass this law. Make history. Today!"

The chamber erupted in thundering applause. A senior senator from Connecticut was the first to stand to her feet and call out her support. "Hear, hear!"

She was joined by five, then fifty, then all but a dozen.

Brian Kinnard watched from the balustrade, emotionless, arms crossed, dark glasses affixed to his face.

Darcy lowered the transcript of the resolution and raised a hand to silence them. She read the summary at full volume, aware that the power behind her words was seeping into their minds like an addictive intoxicant.

"'This resolution, the National Tolerance Act, is a public bill, enveloping the national body of the United States and territories governed by the federacy. As by law, any occurrence of public expression that implicitly defames, denigrates, insults, or otherwise casts aspersion upon the race of persons of similar or dissimilar race shall be considered a personal attack of heinous nature upon that person's intrinsic value as a citizen as well as upon the moral character of that person, and as such, is to be considered a hate crime in that it brings into question the equality of all persons. The unalienable rights of all people are as protected as they are endowed, and each person is entitled to embody those things that are in their ethnic nature without harassment, molestation, denigration, or defamation.'"

A slight pause for effect, though she hardly needed it.

"'As by law, any public expression of religious faith that implicitly defames, denigrates, insults, or otherwise casts aspersion upon the beliefs of persons of any other religion shall be considered a personal attack of heinous nature upon that person's intrinsic value as a citizen as well as upon the moral character of that person, and as such, is to be considered a hate crime in that it brings into Issue the equality of all persons. Similar expressions of religious faith made in the privacy of individual places of worship or within the freedom of private domiciles are protected by the right to assemble and the right to free speech as provided by the First Amendment in the Bill of Rights of the U.S. Constitution. A place of worship shall be defined as a publicly recognized structure that has been licensed by each state in accordance with federal laws. A private domicile shall be defined as the private dwelling of any persons in accordance to each state's residential zoning requirements.'"

Darcy dropped the document on the podium.

"Give an example for the House of Representatives to follow. Give your country this law today, and history will smile on you all."

Then she left the stage, sweat standing out on her pores like dew. It had completely soaked her blouse.

Billy squeezed her elbow as they left. The drowning roar of the Senate followed them. "Congratulations," he whispered in her ear. "I think you just sealed the deal."

And she did, one hour and thirteen minutes later, with a vote of 83 to 17.

CHAPTER TWENTY-EIGHT

Day Seventeen

THE EPISCOPAL church on Main Street, Paradise, Colorado, was packed to the collar on Friday night, although there was only one liturgical collar in the building that Kat could see. That being worn by Father Stanley Yordon, who stood at the podium, trying to hush the excited crowd of three hundred who'd filed in over the past twenty minutes.

The auditorium's ceiling rose thirty feet to a single center beam, from which hung three huge bronze chandeliers. Pews padded in a maroon upholstery ran down both sides of a center aisle. A large wooden cross hung at the focal point in the center of the stained glass wall behind the platform. It was the first time Kat had actually been inside a church, and she found the environment rather moving. The church was at least symbolic of her new faith.

"Okay, ladies and gentlemen, please take your seats." The priest's voice boomed over the black speakers on either side of the platform. "No need to turn this into a barn. Please take your seats."

Kat sat between Kelly, who sat quietly with her hands folded, and Paula Smither, who'd taken it upon herself to introduce her around since their arrival earlier this morning. Her husband, Steve Smither, owned Smither's

Barbeque, the local gathering place for a closely knit community of Paradise's movers and shakers.

Before her trip to Paradise, Kat had never set foot outside of greater Las Vegas and Boulder City, but she'd seen enough movies and been exposed to enough U.S. history to imagine that Paradise was trapped in a thirty-year-old time capsule and had made no attempt at escape.

For example, although their lives were tied to the Net like the rest of the modern world, in the Smithers' home, where Kat was staying, the computer Paula used to do her shopping was wired to an old flat-panel monitor rather than the all-in-one wafer screens that had replaced the bulky boxes ages ago. She'd even seen a juke box in Smither's Barbeque.

More than the old technology that seemed prevalent in Paradise was the age of the people themselves. There were plenty of gray heads and plenty of children, but very few people between the ages of twenty and forty, which apparently was the popular age for locals to leave the time capsule for a taste of the new-fandangled world, as Paula put it, before they returned to settle down.

Mostly white. A few of mixed race like her, but even then, Kat stood out. Paula had spent the better part of the afternoon traipsing her around the town, meeting the neighbors, visiting the tiny grocery store, the salon, the recreation center, the few mom-and-pop shops. She'd advertised Kat as if she were a prize from the local fair. Kat had never felt so important in her life. She'd asked Paula why all the fuss.

"No fuss, they're just friendly." Paula paused. "And you have to understand that Johnny's a bit of a legend in this valley. You have to be something pretty special to come home with him."

There had been no helicopter, not this time. Johnny, Kelly, and Kat flew into Grand Junction and took an hour-long cab ride to Paradise. The street was deserted when they'd placed their bags on the boardwalk and walked into Smither's Barbeque unannounced. Steve Smither was there with half a dozen others, eating lunch. Johnny's mother, Sally, was there.

You'd have thought that Moses had just come home. The image of Sally flying across the room, chased by her own shriek, and throwing her arms around Johnny's neck was one Kat wouldn't forget.

Steve had his cell phone out and started a chain of calls that brought twenty people running to the bar and grill. In the space of five minutes, Paradise had come fully awake.

They made a tremendous fuss over Kelly, Johnny's fiancée, demanding to know all the arrangements and heaping him with suggestions when he said that there were no arrangements yet. They demanded it be a fall wedding on the church lawn. Kelly would be a beautiful, stunning bride. Johnny had really caught a fine woman.

Kelly took it all in, blushing, saying all the right things, but to Kat she looked out of place. Like a high-society type in Mayberry. Then again, that could be the instinctive protectiveness coming out in Kat. She was, after all, Johnny's spiritual daughter. He'd said so himself.

Guest accommodations were settled after a lot of back and forth over who got to host whom. Johnny would stay with his mother, naturally. Sleep in his old room.

Everyone else wanted *both* Kat and Kelly, but they divided themselves between Katie Bowers and Paula Smither. Katie would put Kelly up in her son's old room. He lived in Amarillo with his wife now, she was proud to point out.

Paula Smither staked a claim for Kat by hooking her hand around Kat's elbow and letting it remain there for a good ten minutes. She would put Katrina up in Roland's old room, she said.

Then Johnny left with his mother and Kat hadn't seen him since. That's what the meeting was for, to see Johnny. Hear his plan. The news had spread.

Father Yordon's call for quiet hadn't stilled the conversation between the pews.

"Never changes," Paula said to her, leaning so that Kat could hear. She swept her dark brown hair behind one ear. "You give people a little

SINNER 959

money and they lose all their manners, even the ones who had manners to begin with."

Most of the residents were farmers who grew exotic Paradise apples that were exported to Japan, where they sold for ten times the price of domestic Fuji apples. The valley's soil composition had changed thirty years earlier, resulting in an unusually sweet fruit unique to this single valley. Only so much land could support these trees farmed by these people. Their apples were rare; supply and demand dictated the rest.

When Kat had asked Steve why they sent the apples all the way to Japan, he'd winked and told her that no one in Paradise was beyond taking a healthy profit. The farmers might look dated, but they were by no means poor. Paradise was a small Eden, as rich as an oil field and much more beautiful.

Kat had no idea what they did with all their money. They all drove late-model cars, the only real sign of progress in the town, but not the flashy kind she would find on Las Vegas Boulevard any night of the week.

Johnny had managed to talk the judge and the school into granting her variances for a two-week sabbatical, which he claimed was critical to her progress and emotional stability—all true, because she wasn't sure she could have stayed in Boulder City, not knowing what she knew.

Which was what?

That the kingdom of light was buzzing all around them.

That the darkness she'd once walked in wasn't taking it without complaint.

That Johnny wasn't going to take it lying down, so neither would she.

"People!" Father Yordon kicked it up a notch. He probably faced the same unresponsive crowd every time he took the platform. There was no frustration on the gray-haired man's narrow face. This was only part of the ritual, and both he and the congregation had their roles to play.

"Now he yells at them, they'll listen," Paula said. But even her expression of disapproval included a wink and a nod.

Kat looked at the woman's twinkling eyes set in a comfortably round face. Steve sat by her side with arms and legs crossed, dressed in jeans and a black shirt. That was another thing—none of the farmers dressed much like what she imagined farmers would. Jeans, sure. But they likely shopped at Dillard's rather than Wal-Mart. Dresses, but not cheap ones. No flannel shirts. Lots of expensive leather jackets. No cowboy hats or even boots. But then, what did she know about rich farmers who sold exotic Paradise apples to the Japanese for a killing?

He caught her stare and winked. "She's right."

"People! I know this is a Friday night, but we have business here!"

Now they quieted.

A tall man built like a tree trunk remained standing. "Where is he, Father?"

"Well now, Claude, if you'd just have a seat I'll bring him on, won't I?"

Claude Bowers sat and put his arm behind his wife, Katie Bowers, who smiled back at Kat. She ran the beauty salon across the street, a pretty strawberry blonde who looked much younger than her sixty years, but Paula had been guessing on her age.

"Thank you, Claude."

The man dipped his head once, without showing a hint he'd understood the gentle rebuke.

Father Yordon sighed. "Thank you all for coming on such short notice. But I can promise you, you won't be disappointed. We've seen our days in here, haven't we?"

The place stilled to the sound of breathing.

"Well . . ." Father Yordon smiled at them, formed a teepee with his fingers. He didn't seem to know quite what to say. "So then . . ."

The back swinging door creaked, and as one, the congregation twisted in their seats. Sally Drake, Johnny's middle-aged mother, walked in with her son on her arm. She was a full foot smaller than he, but her smile was larger than both of them put together.

Johnny was dressed in the black slacks and knitted T-shirt he often wore, and with the dark glasses over his eyes he looked like some kind of misplaced superstar. But then he was, wasn't he? The white eyes behind those sunglasses said so.

He kissed his mother at the front pew, then hopped onto the stage. Took Father Yordon's hand. They shook too long, and Kat suspected it was the priest's doing.

"Folks." Yordon stepped up to the microphone. "Folks, I couldn't be more pleased to welcome Johnny home."

The congregation broke out in thundering applause, taking their feet, to the last man and woman

Paradise did indeed love Johnny.

He stepped up to the microphone and stared at them through the shades. "Thank you." But the applause drowned him out.

"Thank you . . ."

"Okay, let the man speak!" Claude Bowers thundered.

They settled and began to sit.

"Thank you, it's good to be . . . home."

He put his hands on the podium and looked down at them. For a long time he just stood there. He swallowed hard and a tear leaked past his black glasses. Silence smothered the room.

But he still didn't move, didn't apologize, didn't lift his hand to signal he needed a moment. He just stood there, hammered by emotion.

Somewhere a woman started to cry softly. Then another.

Kat glanced over at Paula and saw tears streaming from her eyes. There was a bond among the people in this room that Kat couldn't begin to understand.

But she could, she realized. She could! She'd stepped into the kingdom of light and been washed away with tears.

She wished he would take off his glasses and show all of them his eyes. Not the pain but the light. Show them the light!

Instead he just stood there, frozen by emotion.

There couldn't possibly be a dry eye in the room, and Kat was crying with them. Johnny had said he was blind, like Samson. She could only wonder at all the times this blind man had encountered the truth with those eyes of his. What memories were rushing through his mind.

Gradually he seemed to relax, and finally he lifted his head.

No apology. "The light came into the darkness, but the darkness did not understand it," he said. "It tried to crush the light. We've all seen the face of that darkness. We've all felt the horror."

Paula began to cry silently, shaking beside Kat. Kelly sat still, hands folded.

"But the light prevailed. It revealed to us the true reality that we now live in, a world crackling with power and light and more love than any one of us could dare ask for. Do you know this?"

"Yes! Yes, yes." The room filled with hushed yeses.

"Then you know why we can't now turn our backs on that love or deny that the light is our sole hope. Do you know this?"

"God, yes!" Father Yordon stood from his seat behind the podium that had blocked Kat's view of him. His face was wet and his eyes blurry. He stood there shaking. "Yes."

He seemed to come to himself, then eased back down out of her view.

"I've come back to Paradise to stand in the face of the darkness. They are telling us that we must hide our faces and our voices, that if we speak of the love that has rescued us from darkness we are guilty of hate and will be put in dark cells."

"Black!" someone in the back cried. A murmur rushed through the crowd. So they knew too.

Johnny let the statement stand.

"But I can't turn my back on the one who has saved me, nor on the kingdom of light, which he's led me into. For me, it is the source of life. I would have to die before I denied the truth, even with silence."

Johnny took a deep breath.

"I've come back to Paradise to ask you to stand with me, to stand in the face of the new law that our government has passed prohibiting us from following the teachings of Jesus. Will—"

Paula stood. "We will!"

"They're trying to do that?" Claude demanded.

"He's saying they've done it," Paula said. "And yes, we will stand with you, Johnny. We're not letting darkness back in this valley, never again!"

Father Yordon was out of his seat again, stepping forward. "What are you suggesting? Each denominational leader has posted Net bulletins, urging calm. They say the new act will be tested in the Supreme Court and overturned, And until then we should just worship in private."

"Well, you know where they can put that bulletin, and their new law," someone said.

"No!" Johnny stepped out from behind the podium. "No, Ben, this isn't about resistance or harsh words. This is *only* about staying faithful to the Way. The Truth. The Light that crushes darkness. I'm sure that millions of people of faith are screaming foul at this very moment, arming themselves to the teeth with legal briefs and signatures to force a repeal of the new law. Muslim clerics all over the world will condemn it, Mormons will march, Christians churches all over the country will denounce the law and work against their elected officials. And all of that will only satisfy the bitter while they *wait* for change."

He scanned the people. "But we will do none of that. We will simply hold up the light for all to see. And they will see it. The whole world will see the light shining out of this one small valley in the Colorado mountains. Paradise will be a beacon of truth, and they will see it above all others because they will see us, living in the light. And I will show it to them."

They weren't shouting their support, but at a glance Kat could see that to a man, woman, and child they were pinned to his every word, and the look in their eyes was resolute.

"We will use the Net and boldly announce our love of Jesus, our only hope. And they will know that Johnny Drake and the people of Paradise will not be muted."

His breathing had thickened.

"Our stand will grow beyond the Net. Others will come."

Dead silence filled the room.

"And then . . . then the darkness will come, like a torrent, to crush this light shining so brightly in the land."

Okay. That was the challenge, wasn't it? Kat wanted to jump up and tell them why they had to do what Johnny was suggesting. If they'd seen what she'd seen, felt what she'd seen.

"How?" Johnny's mother, Sally, asked in the small voice of one who'd faced too much suffering.

He faced her. "I don't know, Mother. But it could get bad."

What if they wouldn't support him? Kat couldn't sit a moment longer. She jumped to the stage next to Johnny and spun around.

"You can't let them shut us up! Two weeks ago I didn't know that this kingdom even existed, but then my eyes were opened and I saw it!"

The moment of her conversion swept through her again and she began to tremble. She hadn't been prepared for the emotion, and she couldn't stop the tears.

"It's like magic!" No, that wasn't quite right, but she couldn't think of a better way to put it. "The whole world has to see! How can we not scream out the truth from the tops of these mountains? We've found life! They have to know!"

Her voice rang out in the auditorium, greeted by silence.

Slowly, Sally stood, smiling. "But we will, Katrina. We wouldn't even consider turning our backs on the truth. We're in already."

Kat blinked. She'd misjudged them?

They began to stand, one by one, then in groups, then all.

Johnny reached out and placed his hand on her shoulder. By her, with her. To the congregation: "Remember the darkness and remember that it is dispelled by the light," he said to them. "Hold your children close. Love your wives. And pray, Paradise. Pray that the light will illuminate the world."

CHAPTER TWENTY-NINE

Day Eighteen

FOUR DAYS had spun by in a frantic buzz since their monumental victory in the Senate, and Darcy was feeling exceptionally pleased with herself. Pleased with Billy. With the power she'd used to bring justice to millions of people. Like a surgeon, she'd wielded a scalpel to cut out a life-threatening cancer. Not just any surgeon, but a specialist who alone could operate and alone could change history.

She couldn't have done it without Billy; he was the CAT scan, revealing layers of truth hidden beneath the skin so that she could apply her skill to rid the tissue of disease. To bring wholeness. However crucial he was, she had received most of the praise, as it had been her speech that convinced minds and secured votes.

Prior to the Senate vote, half of the lawmakers in Washington knew she could be very persuasive, flexing logic and leveling coercion in a kind of manipulation that they understood—they all practiced the same form of control, minus the uncanny gift. After the Senate vote, Washington knew without a doubt that Darcy Lange was also a supremely gifted orator. Maybe the best ever.

The notion that there was a supernatural component to the compulsion they felt to follow her suggestions was beyond the reach of most, but many surely sensed that there was more to her words than persuasive articulation. She'd given them all something to keep them awake at night.

She, on the other hand, was sleeping like a baby. The potential danger to their well-being had been drastically elevated in the last week—as Kinnard put it, "You don't coerce half the U.S. Capitol and then not expect these power-mongers to plot ways to eliminate you; you're a threat."

But Billy had done a good job identifying those whose minds were filled with nasty thoughts, and Kinnard was already working behind the scenes to discourage them from taking their thoughts too far.

The president signed the National Tolerance Act into law the day of the Senate resolution, before Congress had made its landslide vote to appropriate funds official.

The president addressed the country that night, promising instantaneous judicial response to any person, party, association, or denomination caught actively infringing upon the federal statute. Net-broadcasted sedition, even disguised as dissent or protest, would be subject to federal investigation by the U.S. Department of Justice and the FBI. Prison time would be administered; due process would be expedited from Maine to Maui. It wasn't just an amendment now, it was the law of the land, from the top down.

Knowledge that even ethnic slang could mean incarceration for a minimum of ninety days spread through the country like the ripples of a shockwave.

After sixteen days of social mayhem, the United States woke to an eerie calm on Wednesday morning.

In Darcy's mind the results were tantamount to liberating Poland at the end of World War II. The entire operation was a smashing success.

Even the Net was quiet as the talking heads took extra precautions not to violate the new laws with their blogs and editorials. There had been the rash of outcries and denouncements from the expected sources, naturally. Saber rattling that would eventually find its way into the courts.

But at least it was all off the streets. More importantly, Caucasians were no longer calling Arabs towel-heads, and if anyone was calling Christians bloodsuckers, they were doing it behind closed doors.

Peace had come to America.

Saturday Darcy rode the elevator to their penthouse suite, holding in both hands a box containing the $40,000 titanium Rolex she'd purchased for Billy. Her first major purchase. Kinnard had said no limit, and Darcy intended to test his words.

They'd celebrated late last night over a lobster dinner catered by Rosario's, an exclusive Italian restaurant that Annie insisted they try. Too dangerous to go into such a public place, Kinnard insisted, so they ate by candlelight, overlooking the city. It had been a perfect evening.

Better still, Billy didn't know she'd made arrangements with Kinnard to pick out the watch for him. With any luck, he was still asleep. She'd pounce on his bed, smother him with kisses, and pull him from under the covers before presenting him with her token of appreciation.

Just because Billy was Billy. And because she loved him, loved him desperately.

She nodded at the guard, slipped though the front door, and tiptoed through the vestibule.

"I will." Billy's voice sounded from the kitchen and she stopped. He was up. Change of plans. She'd slink in with the watch behind her back and kiss him hard before presenting it.

"This isn't good." A pause. "Right."

Darcy only half heard. She walked around the corner and saw that he had his back to her. He must have sensed her, because he turned and stared, eyes wide, and not because of the Rolex behind her back. Something was wrong.

"What?"

"Johnny called Kinnard an hour ago," he said.

"Johnny?"

"He's in Paradise."

"So? Good for him." She took another step, but there was more, wasn't there? Johnny going to Paradise wasn't the bad news.

"He's making a stand against the National Tolerance Act."

Her heart slogged through one heavy beat.

"Is that right?"

"He says the town has decided that they can't or won't deny their truth with silence."

Darcy's past came back to her at once, as if the monastery itself had been dropped from the sky to crush her. Johnny was defying them again. In Paradise.

"Making a stand, how?"

"By publicly claiming that Jesus is the only way to God."

She lowered the watch to her side and swallowed. "He can't do that. That defies the law. Right?"

"The attorney general thinks so. Hard not to interpret it that way." Billy's eyes dropped to the Rolex. "He posted a blog on the Net this morning—he's made his position very clear."

"His position?" She wagged her head. "Listen to him. *His position.* What position? And who cares? Just what does he think he's doing?"

But she knew that Johnny could make plenty of people care.

"Read it yourself."

Darcy saw that the large Net screen was open to a document. Not that it mattered; she already knew what he'd written. Light into darkness, blah, blah, blah. She could *kill* him for pulling a stunt like this!

She set the watch on the counter and crossed to the couch in spite of herself. Grabbed the remote and scrolled down the one-page statement, noting by the counter that the site had already been hit eight thousand times. After only a couple of hours, at most.

The blog was exactly what she'd expected, a run-on about the Way, the Truth, the Life, the Light of the World, Jesus, Jesus, Jesus.

"Jesus!" she snapped, slapping the remote down.

"Slow down, Darcy." Billy crossed the room. "He did go out of his way to make sure he didn't specifically deride any particular religion. He's only talking about his faith in Je—"

"Which is now legally the same as denigrating Muslims, Hindus, Buddhists, the lot of them! He knows very well that Christianity is exclusive. *Jesus* was an exclusivist!"

"Maybe, but he has some pretty direct words for all religions."

"Which is in itself a flagrant violation of our law."

"*Our* law?"

"You know what I mean," she said, standing and dismissing him with a wave of her hand. "The Tolerance Act."

"This kind of thing's going to happen all over the place for a while. We haven't exactly declared martial law. Let's give it some time to settle in."

"This isn't just any old place, Billy. This is Paradise. This is Johnny! And he's already got eight thousand hits; if this gets picked up—and knowing Johnny he'll make sure it does—it'll top the Net posts by the end of the day. How many people live in that town now?"

"About three hundred."

"You can bet they'll lap up whatever Johnny serves them."

"You're overreacting."

"And the fact that he called Kinnard makes it clear he's challenging us directly."

"We don't know that."

"He's breaking the law already! He's defying us. And he knows what he's doing. Johnny probably doesn't floss his teeth without a backup plan; do you think that this was just a *mistake*?" She was half tempted to take off her glasses and set Billy straight.

"You're right, he's defying the law. The attorney general agrees. I don't see how any court could interpret it differently. We crafted a pretty nasty little law. But we need to be thoughtful about how we proceed."

"Okay, that's more like it," she said. "So you agree we can't just leave this up to whatever local police they have up there? Does Paradise even have a sheriff? Do we have to wait for the state patrol to round him up?"

"What do you suggest?"

"Let's shut down the blog. Censure his statements and send in the FBI or whoever Kinnard has access to. We squash this before it has time to breathe!"

"Not that simple. We have jurisdictional considerations. The law would be enforced first by local authorities. The National Tolerance Act is still brand-new. It'll take time to work out the kinks."

Billy looked at the Rolex.

"I'm sorry." She walked up to him and they stared at the watch together. "I bought it for you. It's a Rolex. A kind of, you know, gift of appreciation. It was rude of me to get sidetracked."

"Thank you," he said. "I've always wanted a Rolex. That was kind of you."

"You're welcome."

But neither of them picked up the watch. Johnny had taken the air out of their celebratory mood.

"Kinnard had a suggestion."

"Let me guess," she said. "He wants us to go to Paradise."

"That's right."

Of course he would. Fly to Paradise, talk Johnny down, nip this whole thing in the bud before it grew out of local proportion. Wasn't that the skill she and Billy had perfected?

"I'm not sure I can go back to Paradise," Billy said.

She knew what he meant. The very idea of meeting Johnny in Paradise sent shivers down her spine. But the sound of fear in his voice betrayed something deeper than simple anxiety. Billy perhaps had more reason to fear Paradise than she; after all, he'd been the first to fall. The first to push the line between reality and terror. Black was his own evil progeny, and Black had been born in Paradise.

"He would agree to meet us outside of Paradise, don't you think?"

His eyes darted over to her. "Not the canyons."

"Of course not, no, not where the monastery was."

"I don't know why it makes me so nervous," he said. "It's just a place."

"A place that gave me nightmares for years," she said. "I understand perfectly well why you'd be terrified of it."

Darcy realized her mistake immediately. "I didn't mean to suggest that you're to blame any more than I am," she said, crossing quickly to him. She took his hand and lifted it to her lips. "We all made choices. Just because you were the first to defy the monks . . ."

Darcy stopped there, realizing that she'd already dug a hole of blame. She thought about using her eyes to comfort him, but they'd agreed not to manipulate each other without being invited. And she wasn't eager to have her mind read, though she had no apparent reason to fear it.

She brushed his hair from his forehead and spoke in a soothing tone. "Do you know what the best part of what we've done is, Billy?"

"We've stopped a string of lynchings."

"We've stopped priests from wandering around this country condemning people to hell."

Billy didn't share her resentment of the church, but neither did he lose any love on religion.

"Instead we have *Johnny* condemning people to hell," he said.

"Then let's go to Paradise and change that, once and for all."

"Talk him out."

"And if he doesn't talk out?"

Billy answered with fire in his eyes. "Then we burn him out."

JOSEPH HOUDE, a rail-thin, blond-cropped freelancer whose sudden rise in blog rankings a year earlier had led to significant demand for his stories on several larger Net feeds, was the first reporter to arrive in Paradise. His small yellow Volkswagen hybrid had quietly rolled into town at two on Friday afternoon after a four-hour drive from Denver.

He'd made the decision to cross the mountains after receiving an e-mail from one of his Washington sources, who had it on good faith that one of the many potential infractions of the new hate-crime law might bear a closer look. The e-mail had included a link to Johnny's blog, which in turn led Joseph to twenty-three similar blogs that had originated from the same geographical location.

Without coming right out and denouncing the National Tolerance Act, the blogs had unashamedly broken the law by doing precisely what many feared would test the law. Without naming any religion or group of people, the blogs asserted in a very public forum that when Jesus had repeatedly claimed to be the Way, the Truth, and the Life, who alone provided access to the Father, he meant precisely that.

It was a narrow-minded perception of the prophet's teaching, Joseph thought, but then the same prophet had also claimed that the path to God was indeed narrow, missed by most.

The legal conservatives were sure to wage full-scale war on the new law. The American public had choked it down in a time of crisis, but more than a few would vomit it back into the courts. The notion that people could not stand up and say whatever they pleased about their faith might make sense on paper, but two hundred fifty years of complete religious freedom would not be so easily squashed.

Indeed, similar positions were even now starting to pop up on the Net.

Then again, suppression of free speech in similar categories had been accepted with surprising calm in other countries already. Most European countries had put the brakes on freedom of expression years ago in an attempt to keep the peace between Christians and Muslims.

The Europeans had learned that it was one thing to say, "Starbucks makes the best coffee in the world." Such opinions, freely stated, had never been contested.

It was quite another thing to say, "White is by far the best color of skin in the world." Or, "Christianity is a better religion than Buddhism." Or even, "Islam." Or even, "Jesus is the only way."

Fighting words, all of them.

Regardless, as of today, running through Harlem screaming, "Whites rule!" was a crime. And so was holding up a sign in public claiming that Jesus was God. Which was what Johnny had done, albeit a virtual sign.

Hits on blogs were updated hourly, and on Johnny's blog they numbered eight thousand at 9:00 a.m. When the counter rolled over to seventy-six thousand at 10:00, Joseph threw his recorder, his computer, and a few clothes into a bag and scrambled down the stairs for the parking lot.

He'd been in the business long enough to recognize a story when he saw it, and this one had history in the making written all over it. Oddly enough, in dire need of a distraction the night before, he'd downloaded an old classic titled *300* off the Net and filled his mind with an hour and a half of raw heroism or foolishness, depending on how one viewed the movie. Either way it was a enjoyable flick, if a bit violent.

Although he knew it was purely coincidental, it amused Joseph that the current population of Paradise, the epicenter of this blog, was also three hundred.

The three hundred Spartans had taken their stand against impossible odds and been memorialized on film. Now the three hundred Paradisians were gathered in the valley, and if Joseph's nose told him anything, it was that the number would grow to three thousand. He wondered if a memorial would be built to honor them.

The town looked like a typical mountain community abandoned by progress and youth. One church, one grocery store, one bar and grill, one salon, four fruit stands. Nothing about his first drive down Main Street suggested that he was at the epicenter of any ideological struggle destined to be memorialized.

His research told him that the average income of Paradisians was nearly fifty times the average income of other American farmers, but only the expensive cars parked about town provided evidence of this.

There were no mobs standing around with pickets, no signs on the walls of the buildings denouncing the U.S. government, no prophets walking up and down the street with bullhorns, crying for the world to repent. In fact, there were no signs that anyone from this town had done anything to draw attention to themselves at all.

He spent the first hour speaking with residents, pretty much down-to-earth Americans eager to shake his hand, extraordinary only in their apparent simplicity and unapologetic appreciation for the light that had come to destroy darkness. It all sounded a bit kooky to him, although no one met his expectations of a kook.

Then Joseph met Katrina Kivi, the girl who'd hit the wires after her breakup of the Boulder City High School riot a week or so earlier, if he wasn't mistaken.

"You're a journalist?" she asked, eyes bright as the moon.

"I am."

"Really?" The news seemed to delight her. "What brings you here?"

"I was going to ask you the same question. Aren't you the girl from Boulder City—"

"In the flesh," she said. "Kat."

"And what brings you here, Kat?"

"I'm glad you asked. Do you want to meet him?"

"Who?"

"Johnny Drake. You're here because you read his blog, right? Is the word getting out?"

"Umm . . ." Her lack of guile was disarming, to say the least. "I would say yes. Are you sure you want that?"

"Of course. Why write a blog if you don't expect anyone to read it? Do you want to meet him?"

"Yes. I would."

"Come on."

She led him to a white house across from the church and informed him along the way that Johnny was staying with his mother for now.

Katrina bounded up the steps, rapped on the front door, and stepped back when a tall, well-built man wearing dark glasses answered the door.

"Hello, Kat."

She looked at Joseph, smiling coyly so that he couldn't help but to think he'd been set up for something.

"The press is here," she said.

"They are, huh?"

"His name is Joseph."

Johnny Drake studied him, then stepped to one side. "Come on in, Joseph."

Joseph Houde spent thirty minutes with Johnny, but he knew within the first three that he was sitting on top of a time bomb. The man had in mind an epic showdown between good and evil, and he held an utterly compelling conviction that he'd been born to make his stand here, in Paradise, Colorado, today, for all the world to see. There wasn't a breath of backdown in him.

Even worse, Joseph found himself strangely drawn to the man, wanting to believe his soft-spoken rhetoric.

He left the house thinking that if there was such a thing as a devil, Johnny could probably stand toe-to-toe with him and not bat an eye. He returned to his car, fired up his sat link, composed his first story for immediate release, and sent it to his clearing board.

Two minutes later he received a confirmation that Sapphire, the largest of the Net news services, had accepted the story at his regular rate.

When Joseph checked Johnny's blog, he discovered that the hits now numbered 989,498. Even more interesting, a few hundred bloggers outside of Paradise had picked up the cause and posted their own bold declarations of faith.

He looked out at the sleepy town before him. The Paradisians would indeed be immortalized.

CHAPTER THIRTY

Day Nineteen

IT HAD been a mistake to wait for all the arrangements before leaving Washington, Darcy thought, as they hovered far above the valley of Paradise. It had taken Kinnard four hours to reach Johnny by phone only to be told that he was unavailable before Sunday morning. Johnny was posturing. She had paced the carpet in the suite, telling herself that the bitterness she felt toward him was unreasonable, that this was just a simple misunderstanding, that even he had sat with the council and all but offered his support!

It was almost as if he wanted this showdown of his. But it would all work out. They'd all been through too much to let one little protest from one little man deny them now.

Billy sat beside her, staring out the window, brow beaded with sweat. At first glance, from three thousand feet above the town, Paradise looked deserted and untouched by time, still the same as she remembered.

But on closer inspection she could see one small difference. A dozen cars lined Main Street, more cars than she thought should be there. And now one of those cars was uploading information to the Sapphire News Network.

Darcy tapped the pilot on the shoulder. "How far?"

He fanned his fingers out: five minutes. Johnny had suggested a lunch at Smither's Barbeque, of all places. Billy refused, and they settled on the plateau above the canyons to the south, at noon. Johnny had the gall to offer to bring sandwiches.

Billy was still staring. His return to Paradise was beating him up more than he let on, she thought. She had expected to be the one slicked in cold sweat, but he seemed more deeply affected.

Darcy lowered her eyes to the red folder on her lap, flipped the file open, and stared at the first few lines from the Net report that Joseph Houde had filed from Paradise last night.

From the desert has come a voice crying in the wilderness, and his name is John. Johnny Drake to be more precise. But ask his disciples and they will tell you his mission is no less defined than the mission of John the Baptist, who first introduced the Light from heaven to the world over two thousand years ago. The multitudes listened to John, who told them that Jesus of Nazareth was the Way to God. Then Herod took John's head.

Now the question begs us: Will the world listen to Johnny Drake? And who will take his head?

It went on to characterize the town's stand as some kind of beachhead—yada, yada, yada.

How those sneaky reporter rats got around so quickly, she didn't know, but the story had spawned a flood of activity on the Net. It hadn't exactly become the media's focus, but it was enough to warrant a call from the attorney general first thing this morning seeking and receiving assurance that Darcy and Billy could handle Johnny.

Darcy was tempted to drop down there and tell this Joseph Houde exactly what he should do with his stories. And he would listen, wouldn't he?

Darcy put her hand on Billy's thigh. "You okay?"

He didn't answer, which was answer enough.

The helicopter gave the canyon ridges a wide berth, as Darcy had instructed, and homed in on the green plateaus to the south. Large groves of aspens interspersed with grassy fields covered the land. She picked out Johnny's helicopter sitting idly between two stands of trees that bordered one of the many small lakes on the high mesa. And not far from the helicopter, a white blotch.

A tent, she saw on closer inspection. Johnny had set up a tent. What did he think this was, a summit with Abraham, Isaac, and Jacob?

With some reluctance, Billy had agreed last night to the strategy she'd suggested. They had to handle Johnny on his terms, not theirs. They'd both learned a thing or two about negotiation over the past two weeks, and this was a time for seduction, not blackmail.

The helicopter settled on the ground forty yards from the tent, which turned out to be a canopy. Billy slid out, walked around, and helped her to the ground.

She took his hand. "You sure you're okay?"

"I'm fine." The chopper quickly wound down. "Perfectly fine."

"Then let's go."

Johnny had set up a table under the canopy, complete with a white table-cloth, a bowl of fruit, and a pitcher of water. Four chairs faced each other in pairs next to the table, and in one of these chairs sat a blonde woman.

So Johnny had brought his lover too. The woman could be anyone, for all Darcy knew, but she rather liked the idea that she had some competition. So to speak.

Johnny stood and waited for them at the edge of the canopy, dressed in what appeared to be the same black slacks and white shirt he'd worn on his visit to Washington. He wore his glasses, as did they all, even his lover or whoever she was.

Darcy dropped Billy's hand and walked up to him. "Hello, Johnny."

"Darcy. Billy." His hand was large and warm around her palm. "I'd like you to meet Kelly."

Darcy walked over to the pretty woman, who stood. "And who might Kelly be?"

"I'm a friend," she said. "Johnny and I go back a ways. It's good to finally meet you." Kelly turned to Billy and took his hand with both of hers. "And you, Billy. I've heard so much about you." She held his hand a bit too long, Darcy thought. "It really is such an honor to meet you, Billy."

No, this couldn't be Johnny's lover. If Darcy didn't know better, she would think the woman was attempting to seduce Billy right here in front of them all. But then again, Darcy's wary nature had always turned sparrows into hawks.

"And why exactly are you here?" Darcy asked.

"Because she's the only other person who knows everything," Johnny said. "I thought you'd want to meet her."

She thought about a clever retort, but then dismissed it. They were here to win Johnny, not threaten him.

"A drink?" Johnny asked, walking behind the table. "Fruit? The best apples in the world, they say."

Darcy took an apple and turned it in her hand. "Well, it's nice that something good has come out of Paradise," she said, eyeing him, then bit deeply. The apple's juice was surprisingly tasty. "Sweet."

"As sweet as the first time?" he asked.

What was he saying? They'd eaten apples together before?

"I'm sorry, I've put most of my memories of our childhood in a room and sealed the door." She smiled and took another bite. "Therapist's order, you know."

"Sometimes remembering isn't such a bad thing."

She glanced at Billy and saw that his jaw was fixed. Only then did the significance of the apples come to her. Billy had been the first to taste the proverbial forbidden fruit when he'd used the Books of History to write Marsuvees Black into flesh and blood. Johnny had brought the apples as some kind of cute object lesson, and the fact hadn't been lost on Billy who was now seething.

Darcy had to calm herself.

"So, what can I do for you?" Johnny asked.

"That's a low blow," Billy said softly.

"No, it's simply the truth. We've turned Paradise into the valley of truth and light, or hadn't you heard?"

"And we'll bury this valley!" Billy yelled.

"The truth isn't easily buried," Johnny said.

Billy's anger surprised even Darcy. This wasn't the right approach.

"Please, can we put the testosterone back in the bottle? Why don't we take a seat and discuss this reasonably. We're not children any longer."

Kelly eased into a chair, but neither Johnny nor Billy moved.

"Okay, then we can stand," Darcy said.

"I don't mean to be antagonistic," Johnny said. "But I've decided that I can't deny the truth we all know." He crossed to his chair, sat, and folded one leg over the other. "Until I saw Darcy on the Net, I was alone with this . . . gift. Finding you was like finding a long-lost brother and sister."

"And it was to us as well, Johnny," Darcy said, setting her apple down and sitting opposite him.

"I couldn't put my finger on what bothered me then—Kelly tells me that my ability to help others see makes me blind in more ways than I realize. But when I learned that you've been behind—"

"It doesn't have to be this way," Darcy interrupted. "You could join us. Imagine the good we three could do for this world. We'd be using our gifts to help millions!"

She looked back at Billy. "Come, Billy."

"This isn't going to work," Billy said, sitting. "Can't you see that, Darcy? He's here to reject any proposal before we even put it on the table."

"You're reading minds through glasses now? There are only three people in the world who have the gifts we have; surely we can see our way past fighting each other with them!"

"But you're wrong, Darcy," Johnny said. "We aren't the only three."

"No? Some of the other children also—"

"Black," Billy said. "You'll never let me live it down, will you?"

"It's not my intention to blame you for anything, Billy," Johnny said. "Only to help you remember the consequences of following the other path."

Darcy was having difficulty controlling her frustration.

"And just where has your path led you?" she asked as calmly as she could.

"To the same place yours has led you," he said. "Back to Paradise."

"But you see, that's where you're wrong! This is no paradise! The whole *idea* of a heaven was never based on reality, and it never will be."

"Not in this life, no."

She could feel the heat rise in her face. "If you think the message or manipulations of a man in a white collar can in any way lead to a paradise in this life or the next, then maybe your lover is right. Maybe you are as blind as a worm."

Then she thought twice about her haste to show her frustration.

"Speaking loosely, that is. So that you understand how *I've* been able to cope since being set free from the monastery."

"Your problem is that you've always blamed the monastery, Darcy. The monks weren't to blame. They gave you everything you needed and more. The *only* thing they forbade were the dungeons. They knew of the danger there. They tried to protect you from harm."

"They could have sealed it!" she snapped.

"But you couldn't stay away, could you? *You* went down into the dungeons, opened the ancient books, and brought the evil upon yourself. The priests weren't the sinners, *you* were the sinners. The books gave us three these gifts to be sure it never happens again, and all you want to do is crucify monks."

Billy stood, trembling. "Would you have done any different? Would you have stayed away?"

"I don't know. Maybe I'd have done the same as you. But I hope I would accept blame for what I'd done and learn from it."

It was too much for Darcy. "How dare you?" she screamed.

Birds took flight from the nearby scrub oaks.

"How dare you turn the pain we've suffered because of those monks against us, as if it's all *our* fault, as if we *chose* to be experiments, as if they aren't culpable, as if the dungeons had no blame! No child deserves to be put through that."

Johnny sat quietly for a moment.

"What have you come to say to me?" he finally said.

Billy was right, Darcy realized. Johnny had no intention of even considering any proposal from them. But they *had* to turn him away from his plan.

"We've come to say that what you're doing will end badly," she said. "Sit down, Billy."

Instead he turned to his left and headed toward the trees.

Darcy let him go.

She turned back to Johnny. "You really don't see the damage you're doing here, do you?"

He just looked at her from behind those glasses. She wondered what would happen if they both removed their lenses and spoke frankly.

Kelly stood. "Excuse me." So Johnny's trophy hadn't forgotten how to speak. She walked after Billy, but if she thought she could calm him down, she was even more foolish than Johnny.

"Maybe we could start over," Johnny said. "I think we know where we stand, but maybe there's a way we can understand each other better. I doubt you came all this way just to threaten me."

Now it was just the two of them.

Darcy took a deep breath. "No. No, that's not why we came. Tell me how we can work this out."

"The light came into the world, but the world did not understand it. Perhaps I could help you understand."

"You forget, I grew up having my head stuffed with all of that *understanding*."

"Then maybe I can help you remember."

"I've spent a lifetime trying to forget. Please, Johnny, you know as well as I do that this has nothing to do with understanding. I realize that you believe differently about the nature of things than I do. That doesn't give us the right to even attempt to change each other. Why can't we leave the world to believe what it wants to believe in peace without degradation or accusation? That's all this law does. It stops the finger-pointing. You have a problem with that?"

"Did you read my blog?"

"Half the world has probably read your blog by now."

"Did it call the Muslims *fools*?"

"Yes! Not in so many words, but by publicly claiming that your way is the *only* way, you're calling their way wrong. And in matters of race and religion, calling someone wrong is as inflammatory as calling them *fools*, or even worse. Can you imagine me walking around spouting off that all blacks are immoral or unequal because they are black? We'd have riots again!"

"You're making one mistake in equating the two."

Darcy held up a hand. "Stop. I know. Blacks aren't wrong because they're black any more than Hitler was wrong because he was white. Where you split hairs is that you believe that Muslims *are* wrong about some things, right? But that's *your* belief, Johnny! You have no right to force your morals down their throats."

"When did speaking your beliefs become synonymous with forcing them upon others?"

"When they involve explosive issues, like deciding who's going to hell!"

"Perhaps you're still misunderstanding. I'm condemning no one. I'm only saying that I will follow Jesus."

"But Jesus condemned all who refused to follow him!" Darcy cried. "His was a narrow, bigoted, exclusive faith that has no place in the world today."

"I'll let his words stand on their own," Johnny said. "He died for what he said two thousand years ago, and nothing in this world has changed

since then." He paused, then took a new approach. "Are you also denying the supernatural?"

"Of course not. I'm a living example of the extraordinary. Call it mystical, paranormal, whatever; that doesn't mean the church understands
it any better than the rest of us."

"I'm not speaking for any particular church. Only for the kingdom of
light that has reversed my understanding of reality."

"And you have to throw the *Jesus* element in there? He's the problem,
Johnny, not the light."

Johnny unfolded his legs and stood. He walked to the edge of the
canopy and stared out at the trees into which Billy had disappeared.

Darcy approached him from behind, struck by the broadness of his
shoulders. No telling what kind of hell he'd been through to make him
the man he was today. An intelligent man who understood the wisdom
of her words, with or without glasses.

She drew next to him and followed his gaze. No sign of Billy or Kelly.
"We can change the world, Johnny. I know we can. We could probably ban
war, stop global conflict, even eradicate poverty or disease—if we put our
minds to it."

"The scope of our power is an amazing thing," he said softly. "I would
love to see the Senate stare into my eyes."

She chuckled. "A sight to behold."

"We really do have the power to overcome evil, wherever it shows its
ugly head."

"To rid the world of poverty."

"And disease." He looked down at her, and she could smell his spicy
cologne. "You would use your gift to save the world at any cost,
wouldn't you?"

"I must!"

He turned and walked back into the tent. "And so must I. Which is why
I have to lift up the Light of the World by which *all* men can be saved.
Doing anything less would be like walking away from a dying leper."

He'd set her up.

Darcy decided then, as rage washed through her, that she would not let this man manipulate her again. Not ever.

He bit deeply into an apple and sat back down.

"You're assuming that the world has a disease, Johnny," she said, fuming. "You're also assuming you have the cure. And that, my friend, is the deadliest sickness to face humanity. Arrogance."

"You're forgetting again, Darcy," he said without a hint of reconsideration, "I have seen that disease with my own eyes, before I went blind. I've battled that disease. I've watched how this disease ravages life. And I've seen the cure to this disease. I would be a coward not to warn the world of the disease or to withhold the cure from the afflicted."

"So then that's that. You're flat refusing to listen to sense."

"I'm doing the only thing that makes any real sense."

"By defying this nation's laws? And make no mistake, the law will be held up and what you're doing will be judged by the courts as strictly illegal. Is that what your precious faith has taught you?"

"I'm simply refusing to dim the light that showed us both the way."

"Whatever happened to tolerance?"

"Tolerance of evil *is* evil. That's Black's new game." He faced her. "And I do believe that you, Darcy, have your tongue down his throat."

Her fingers shook.

He took another bite.

"This is going to end very, *very* badly, Johnny Drake."

UNTIL JOHNNY spoke, Billy wasn't sure why the idea of returning to Paradise had struck such a deep chord of horror in his mind or why the chorus rising out of that chord had refused to be silenced.

He long ago assumed he'd pretty much put his childhood to rest. Darcy was the one who still struggled. Sure, he had his bouts with nightmares, his flashbacks, his days of regret, his flogging sessions, but who didn't? Had he ever met a man or woman who did not have mistakes they wished they could take back?

How did it go? To err is to be human, be it a bite out of an apple, or a spilled cup of coffee. Error was a quintessentially human quality. Right?

He'd told himself that his fears were only of the unknown, and that once he returned to Paradise, he would put them to rest. The whole experience could be healing to them both. Put a lid on the past once and for all.

Seeing Paradise from the air had only made the fears perfectly real.

But not until Johnny recounted exactly what had happened in the monastery did Billy realize what that fear actually was.

Himself. He feared himself, because Johnny was right; he had been the one to first take a bite out of that apple. He'd been the one to drag Darcy down into the dungeons to join him.

He was the first sinner.

And he still was, wasn't he? He was afraid he would return to the vomit, like a hungry dog. That he, having once tasted, would want to taste again.

He wouldn't, of course, he'd learned his lesson. But the fear that he might, just maybe might, crushed him with more weight than he'd borne in many years.

The meeting with Johnny was a bust, he knew that already. All their efforts were coming down around them. They would have to enforce the law here in Paradise. Johnny had come here to make his stand, because he knew that more than poetic justice awaited them all here. A confrontation in Paradise would end it all for good.

But Johnny didn't realize that it was he who was going down this time.

Billy walked into a small clearing among the aspens, trying to clear his head. He'd walked away because he didn't trust himself to contain the rage that had welled up in him as Johnny reminded them all who had written Marsuvees Black into existence.

Which only confirmed how much Billy despised Black. He'd never doubted that.

Wanna trip, baby?

Billy shuddered.

"Billy?"

He spun, surprised to see that Kelly had followed him into the trees.

"Sorry, I didn't mean to startle you." She glanced back the way she'd come. "I just wanted to make sure you were okay."

"I'm fine." But it was just one of those meaningless rote statements. They both knew he wasn't within a radar's distance of fine.

"Billy . . ." She turned back to him and studied his eyes. "You sure you're okay?"

It was an awkward moment, he thought. Standing in a clearing with a friend of Johnny's while Johnny spoke to Darcy in dead-end negotiations.

"I think you should go back," he said.

"Yes. Yes, of course."

But she didn't leave. She stood there staring into his eyes with her blue ones. They misted and he realized that she was fighting back tears.

He hadn't considered what those surrounding Johnny must feel like, caught up in his predicament. Kelly realized that things couldn't turn out well here in Paradise, and she'd come to plead on Johnny's behalf. He hardly blamed her.

"Johnny's the one you should talk to," Billy said. "You realize that our hands are tied. We're here out of respect for an old friendship. But if we can't talk Johnny down, the authorities will step in. Laws that aren't enforced are worse than no laws at all."

A tear slipped from her right eye and broke down her cheek. At first glance he'd assumed Kelly was a confident woman, the way her blonde hair framed strong cheekbones. There was a firmness to her eyes suggesting anything but weakness.

But seeing her cry, he wondered if he'd misjudged her. Maybe she was fragile, vulnerable.

She looked away and wiped her cheek dry.

Billy didn't know what to say. "I'm sorry, really. This just isn't—"

"I love him so dearly, you know," she said.

"I'm sure you do. Unfortunately, there really is nothing I can do."

Kelly looked at him again. A slight grin crossed her face. She stepped closer. "You know that's not true, Billy." The grin flattened. "If there's anyone who can do something here, it's you."

"I'm not sure you understand."

"I understand better than you." Kelly lifted her hand and touched his face with a gentle finger, tracing his chin. "I understand him. We've been through hell together, Johnny and I. Do you know how many tears I've wept on his account?"

She walked slowly around him, brushing Billy's shoulder with her fingers.

"I know Johnny better than he knows himself, because in so many ways, I helped him become the man he is today. And I know how far he will go."

"Ma'am, I'm sure—"

"Call me Kelly." She looked into his face again. Tears rose to the rims of her eyes. "Johnny won't stop. I've seen him suffer through torture that would have even you screaming like a baby—he suffers without so much as flinching a muscle. He's a very, very powerful man, Billy. Did you know he was once known as the world's most dangerous assassin? They called him Saint."

He hadn't known, but then he knew very little about Johnny. An assassin named Saint. Go figure.

"What would that make me, Sinner?"

"My Johnny was put on this planet for a very special purpose."

Tears spilled from both eyes now. For a brief moment her resolve to keep from breaking down waned and her lips quivered. But then she drew air through her nostrils and regained what composure she could control.

"You can't stand in his way, Billy."

He wasn't sure what she was asking of him, but the conviction in her voice cut to his heart.

"And I mean that literally," she said. "You can't, because you, too, were put on this planet for a very special purpose."

"Forgive me for not—"

"Shh, shh." She placed a finger on his lips. Traced his mouth. "Don't pretend you don't know what I'm talking about. Don't try to say you don't believe in the power that swims all around us. Do you think your gift came from monkeys?"

What was he supposed to say to that?

"You're very special, Billy. Very, *very* special. Even more special than Johnny."

He was now at a complete loss. She knew something he did not, and it appealed to him like water to a fish.

Kelly leaned forward and kissed him lightly on his lips. "Promise me you'll remember that, Billy. For his sake, remember that."

Then Kelly turned and left him alone in the clearing.

CHAPTER THIRTY-ONE

THE TOWN'S inner circle gathered inside of Smither's Barbeque for their first ad hoc meeting as dusk grayed the western sky, twenty-two men and women by Kat's count, including Joseph Houde, who wasn't really an insider. But then neither was she.

Then again, Steve and Claude and Paula, all of them had a way of making even total strangers feel like insiders within minutes of arriving. Her understanding of friendship had been formed through cliques and alliances forged by kids of similar race and beliefs, and then only after a formal invitation to join the group.

Someone had forgotten to tell Paradise that the customs of society had become more complicated than theirs, which was simply: *Hello there, friend, how you doing this afternoon? Have a seat. Have a bite of my pie?*

The informal meeting had come about for two reasons: One, Johnny had headed out of town with Kelly for a meeting at ten o'clock this morning, and no one had heard a word from him since.

Two, people were coming.

Ben Ringwald, who had to be ninety if he was a day, chuckled. "Well, if we'd a'known this day was coming, we might have built us a few hotels with all that loot everyone's holdin' on to."

"I don't see it being a problem," Claude said. "We have over two hundred homes in this valley. And another hundred barns."

They hung around the bar and two round tables, half of them nursing drinks or popping the peanuts Steve had put out. The restaurant was once a proper bar before they'd converted it, and the old lights behind the counter still advertised Bud Light.

"We aren't putting visitors in barns," Paula said. "Not if I have anything to say about it. We can use the church if we have to, but we have plenty of room to house a hundred guests."

"A hundred? And what if no one turns this tap off? I'd say we already have fifty. Give it a couple of more days and we could have five hundred. You ready for that?"

"Well, it's not the housing I'd worry about. We can put ten to a house if we have to. It's food."

"Got ya covered there," Ben rattled with a twinkle in his eye. "Me and Charlie got us a few extras."

They looked at the old geezer. Richest in the valley on account he owned seven fields, Paula had told Kat. He glanced at their questioning gazes.

He shrugged. "You know Charlie. He's a bit of a survivalist. Trust me, food won't be a problem. Could prob'ly feed five thousand for a week out of that basement."

Kat spoke up. "Umm, excuse me?" They glanced at her. "I'm not sure you guys are getting the whole picture here." She thought Joseph Houde did, judging by his smile. "Any of you been on the Net in the last couple of hours?"

"Sure," Claude said.

"This thing's blowing up out there. I mean really, *actually* blowing up."

"That's just the Net, honey," Paula said.

"Just the Net? The Net is America. People live on the Net. And it's not just Johnny's blog, it's thousands of blogs. It's news stories. It's dialogue centers, chat rooms . . . Half the country is talking about Paradise."

They just looked at her, still not comprehending. To them, life was about getting a kick out of what junior did last night during supper. To the rest of the country, life was quick exchange over the Net about what Johnny did last night.

"Tell them, Joseph."

The reporter chuckled. "She's right. As of a half hour ago, Johnny's blog had over two hundred million hits worldwide and has been referenced over fifty thousand times on the news feeds. Today alone, his name has been viewed over a billion times if you include public chat rooms, unrestricted e-mail, and the rest of it."

"A billion?" Katie Bowers asked, as if she hadn't heard right. "How is that possible?"

"Think about it. One post on a bulletin board might use his name a half dozen times. Turn that into a hundred-page thread. Multiply it by a thousand threads. And that's just bulletin boards."

"Okay, so Johnny's gone and gotten famous on us."

"But it's not *just Johnny*," Joseph said. "There are threads cropping up suggesting that believers who support Johnny should join him in Paradise."

Kat watched realization settle over them.

"I'd say fifty people have rolled into town this afternoon, some of them press. It could be five hundred tomorrow. And it could be three thousand in three days."

"No, that's too much," Paula protested. "What in the world are we supposed to do with three thousand people?"

"Like I said," Claude replied, "We have plenty of barns."

"What do you expect them to sleep on, dirt?"

"The church won't hold that many either," someone said.

"We could set Johnny up on the old theater's roof and let him speak from there," Claude said.

The suggestion came from left field and had little to do with the point.

"I hate to point out the obvious," Joseph said, eyeing Kat as if only he and she were really in the know. She liked the man. "But accommodations are the least of your problems."

"Well, you can't just throw people into a barn and then expect them to live like human beings," Paula said. "What are we going to feed three thousand hungry mouths? Grain?"

"I think he means to say that these people will never arrive," Kat said.

"I thought you said three thousand people would arrive in a couple of days."

"Could," Steve said from behind the bar. "If they aren't stopped."

"Who would stop them?"

No one seemed to want to speak out the obvious, Kat thought. Were they really that naive?

"The law," she said. "The law's gonna come to Paradise."

"Claude's the law," Paula said. Paradise had no real law—they'd elected him as their "sheriff" two months earlier when the spot became vacant. But really, he was just the grocery store owner.

"She means the real law," Steve said.

Joseph stood and walked around the table, cracking his knuckles. "I still don't think you're getting the whole picture here. You do realize that you've broken the law. Not just a little law. Not like running a red light or being drunk in public. The law Congress just passed makes everything you're doing here illegal. A federal offense. They're not just going to sit by and let you keep doing it."

"Well, that's fine, Joseph," Paula said. "We know that. They'll try to keep us from saying what we know to be the truth, and we'll keep saying it, and then who knows what happens? Johnny will help us figure all that out. But in the meantime we have to figure what to do with all these people."

"And if they come in here tomorrow to arrest all of you? What will you do?" Joseph asked.

"Are you asking on the record?" Kat asked. "To publish, I mean?"

He shrugged. "Unless you don't want me to publish it."

Steve set his glass on the bar. "Publish what you want. Johnny will make the call, but I think if they come to arrest us, we'll lock ourselves in the church."

"You'd resist arrest?"

"Not with force, no. Call the church our prison."

"And if they demand that you surrender yourselves?"

"Then we'd have to go," Katie said.

Her husband shook his head. "Well, I ain't walking. If they want to throw me in prison, they's going to have to pick me off the floor."

"What good would that do? You're going. You're going one way or the other."

"Do you really think they would come in here and arrest the whole town?" Paula asked. "Three thousand people?"

"That's the whole point: they won't let it get to three thousand people because they know they can't deal with that many," Kat said. "Which is why they'll probably come in tomorrow and deal with five hundred."

"Even five hundred. They're going to arrest five hundred people?"

"They won't have to arrest five hundred." They all turned and stared at Sally, who sat quietly at the back with her cell phone on the table before her, waiting for a call from her son.

"They'll come for Johnny," she said.

"If they take Johnny, they take us all!" Claude said.

The screen door slammed behind Kat and she twisted around. Johnny faced them from the entry. Kelly followed to his right and slightly behind him.

Sally rushed past Kat and embraced her son. "You're back," she whispered.

"I'm fine, Mother," Johnny said, kissing on her cheek. And then he walked in, like a prophet, come to set his people straight.

"Hello, Johnny," Kat said.

"Hello, Kat. Claude." He scanned the rest. "Looks like the town's growing."

"The newsman thinks we'll have five hundred by tomorrow," Paula said. "We were just talking—"

"Five hundred isn't enough," Johnny said. "We need a gathering of three thousand by morning. Can you do that, Joseph? Tell them that Johnny Drake is calling for three thousand followers to drive through the night and join him in Paradise valley by sunrise."

"You might get more than three thousand."

He acknowledged Joseph with a single nod and faced the old geezer, Ben. "That food you told me about will feed them for a week?"

"Should."

Johnny looked at Steve. "There are still only two roads into this valley?"

"Only two."

"I want you and Claude to get a few men together and go house to house. Collect every weapon in this valley. Every gun, every hunting knife, all of it. Take them all up the road three miles and leave them in a pile, right in the middle of the road. You think you can do that?"

A thin smile crossed Steve's face. "Sure."

"We're going to have us a showdown," Johnny said.

"CRUSH IT!"

Darcy leaned forward in an overstuffed chair and faced Attorney General Lyndsay Nadeau across her dark wood desk. Darcy glanced at Billy, who sat beside her. He hadn't smiled once today that she could remember.

"She's right," Kinnard said, speaking from the couch next to FBI Deputy Director Lawhead. "Crush it. Question is, how? You're not suggesting we roll the National Guard in there."

"That's exactly what I'm suggesting. How else do you enforce the law, with threats? He's blatantly defying the laws of this country. If we don't respond now, send a clear message, we could face much worse than the Kansas City riots. Surely you see that."

Lyndsay watched them, perpetual smile fixed in place. The defiance on the Net was growing exponentially by the hour, but so far it had been contained to the Net. Except for Paradise.

"The president wants this shut down," the White House chief of staff said, turning from the window.

"Of course he does, Annie," Lyndsay said. "We expected something like this, maybe not in quite the same form, but we always knew the first challenges would come over the Net."

"And Johnny Drake's activities clearly break the new law, correct?"

"I've had a team of ten of the country's best attorneys on the case since this broke. There's a lot of noise out there, but the law the president signed isn't the most difficult to interpret. Trust me, what is happening in Colorado right now clearly defies the law in a most egregious manner. It's blatant and purposeful, done to make a very specific point."

"Johnny threatens to test our system in a way it's never been tested," Billy snapped. "This is spreading like fire out there. What are the stats?" He stood and waved off Kinnard. "Forget the stats, we know the problem. And it's going be almost impossible to shut down. You mess with people's faith and they tend to get just a bit lopsided on you. I've been there."

"Precisely why we wrote the laws," Annie said.

"If we don't shut Johnny down in the next twenty-four hours, it's going to be too late."

"I'm afraid I don't see the urgency," Lyndsay said.

"Think!" he snapped. Billy had indeed changed since his visit to Paradise, and Darcy liked him this way. "Today he was joined by roughly fifty people, so as of this moment the three hundred heroes standing in the gap number three hundred and fifty. I guarantee you that will swell to ten, even twenty times that number. Johnny isn't going to be talked down—he'd die first. That's what Darcy and I learned in Paradise today. We have two choices: either accommodate Johnny or silence him with force."

He took a breath.

"I know you won't accommodate him, so the question is whether you want to go in there with force tomorrow, when you only have to deal with a few hundred, or go in later and deal with thousands."

She nodded. "Point made."

Yes, point made, Darcy thought. But that wasn't Billy's true motivation. He'd always supported the new law, but not with the passion he wore on his sleeve now.

She'd tried to engage him on the flight home, but he stared out of the window most of the way, lost in thought. He said that Kelly had made a plea for Johnny, and at first she wondered if he was considering it. But Billy said that Johnny would get exactly what he had coming to him.

"The law will prevail," Darcy said. "We all know that getting the act passed was bound to happen anyway, just like similar laws have been passed in Canada and Europe. Billy and I just greased the wheels. The world can't afford certain freedoms any longer, and it just might take as much blood to purge them as it did to win them."

"And now Johnny is trying to put the brakes on it all," Annie said.

Billy waved his hand. "Keep this isolated to Paradise and Johnny won't be able to do a thing. Let Darcy and me handle this our way."

"Which is?"

"To roll in tomorrow and seal off the valley before we issue our ultimatum. Ignore the hundreds of thousands of voices joining Johnny on the Net and go after him now, before they actually join him on the ground."

"And then?"

"And then enforce the law using whatever force is necessary."

"And just how far do you suggest we take that force, Billy?"

Darcy answered for him, making her support clear.

"As far as it takes to silence Paradise. We want carte blanche from the governor of Colorado, the president, the Justice Department, and whoever orders the National Guard around in situations like this."

"Stop," Lawhead said. "Giving you that kind of authority could undo everything we've accomplished. First of all, activating the National Guard to do anything but assist the Justice Department will demonstrate to the American people that we are enforcing domestic laws with military force. We simply can't afford that for two reasons: One, engaging an American populace with military force is like trying to squash a bee with a sledge-hammer, which will take weeks of preparation and will effectively drive Americans toward insurrection at the national level. Enforcing change with troops will only convince people that they are no longer free *at all.* Secondly, because the National Tolerance Act is a federal statute, it needs to be handled by federal law enforcement."

"Which puts a quick response out of the picture?" Darcy snapped. "We can't afford to let this situation grow. We don't even have time to deliberate. We have to move *now.* Time is on Johnny's side, not ours."

"That's why we sent you two in first," Annie said. "And Johnny sent you both home."

"I'm not saying there isn't a solution," Lawhead said, glancing between them. He stood, clicked a remote, and began to highlight points on a digital map. "Paradise is in a valley, which is to our tactical advantage. Containment by the Colorado National Guard should be simple enough and shouldn't cause a PR disaster. Assuming that the governor will pro-vide us with support from the state patrol as well, we can cordon off the town within hours."

"He will," Darcy said.

Lawhead nodded, understanding her. "Fine." He clicked his remote and brought up another aerial image of Paradise Valley. "With medical and support troops in play, the FBI can begin a systematic sweep from both ends of the valley in coordinated tactical groups. We can fly them out from Quantico if necessary. A component of the Air National Guard can provide overwatch and strategic direction. The state patrol will put out descriptions, the guard will hold the line, and the FBI will prosecute the arrests while air support provides intel. It could work."

"It has to," Billy said. "What are the challenges?"

"Warrants and timing." Lawhead dropped his pencil on the table. "Justice won't arrest on suspicion alone. We need federal papers authorizing these arrests. And getting interagency cooperation will take twenty-four to seventy-two hours. In the meantime, the Net will be counting their score while we're still putting our pieces on the board."

Pause. "I didn't say it would be quick. But this is legal, and it could work: the FBI serves the warrants, the guard provides medical support and overwatch, and the DOJ and state get to preserve credibility."

Darcy removed her sunglasses, set them on the table for all to see. "Seventy-two hours is two days too long."

Lawhead planted his palms on the table and eyed her through his own spectacles. "I can't make miracles any more than you can talk Johnny Drake into a truce. You asked me for a legal solution that involved timing, force, and terrain. This is what I've got."

"Enough." Kinnard stared at them. "You have several points that I think could be refined for our purposes. One, the attorney general can supply—or demand—the warrants to make this legal. Two, the sedition currently growing in Paradise is still small enough to contain without diverting traffic. Three, because Paradise is in a valley, we can divert or block over 80 percent of the satellite-based communications, and simultaneously shield outgoing calls and uplinks."

Darcy bit into the idea. "No coverage means no media. No media means we can act without hesitation."

That settled them all.

"How far do we take this?" Billy asked.

Darcy frowned. "As far as we have to."

"Legally . . ." Lawhead dipped his head and thought a moment. "With the warrants and the timing . . . It could work. But we need the governor, the Justice Department, and a good window of timing. The public spin we can handle later."

"We can get all that," Kinnard said softly.

"Billy and I can," Darcy said, "make this happen."

"You're actually suggesting we place part of our national armed forces in your hands?" Lyndsay asked with a hint of incredulity.

None of this had been planned, but Darcy saw no reason to mince words. "Why not? We all know that using force on Paradise is the right thing to do given the laws of the nation. Would you prefer that I speak to you more directly, Lyndsay?"

The attorney general was quiet for a moment. "Be careful, Darcy. You're on very thin ice here."

"Get over yourself," Billy said. "Everything Darcy's suggesting is going to happen anyway. Tell me where we're wrong."

"You're not," Annie said, "unless you're actually hoping to spill blood in that valley."

Billy tipped his head back with exasperation. "I'm not suggesting you drop a bomb on Paradise. But Johnny has to believe that I could. *I* could. Not some commander who has no personal stake in the operation. Only then do we stand a frog's chance in the boiling pot of getting him to roll over."

"You're suggesting a bluff," Lawhead said. "Knowing that these people won't actually die for their position. And I tend to agree, Lyndsay. For all their talk, I can't imagine too many Americans willing to give their lives for the right to follow a guy who's been dead for two thousand years."

"They don't believe he's dead," Annie said.

"Yes, well, follow a ghost, then. Point is, they will capitulate if led to believe that the alternative is a prison sentence or a bomb."

"It only works if the bluff has teeth," Billy said.

"You'd do nothing without my personal approval," the attorney general said.

"Naturally."

We don't need you, you old prune, Darcy thought. *You don't think we could rip off those eyeglasses and make you do this anyway? I could probably make you commit suicide. Who doesn't believe, deep down inside, that they deserve to be dead?*

She'd never considered the possibility before. Maybe she should try it out on Johnny. Looking at Billy's set jaw, the dark circles under his eyes, the pale green eyes, she thought Billy just might approve. She was being influenced by his hatred. And honestly, it was all a bit exciting.

CHAPTER THIRTY-TWO

Day Twenty

"NOW, YOU get your pretty little head down when I say," old Ben said, eying Kat with a twinkle in his eyes.

"Got it."

He winked at her in the dawn light. "Time to go boom."

She winked back. "Boom, boom."

Steve placed his hand on her arm and pulled. "Down."

Kat gazed up the road one last time. It hadn't taken much to twist Steve into letting her tag along. She was from the city, she'd argued—used to much worse than any of this.

They'd laid out the plan with Johnny last night. There were only two roads leading into Paradise, this one heading west toward Delta, and the same one heading north out of Paradise. They would welcome visitors through the night, explain their plan, turn all weapons over as a symbolic gesture caught on film by Joseph and three other news crews, then blow both roads at daybreak. If anybody wanted out or in, a helicopter would be available.

Johnny was locking Paradise down and locking its artillery out.

As instructed, Steve and company had gone house to house, collecting two pickup loads of weapons, which now sat a hundred yards outside the blast zone with a large sign in the window that read: *Please don't lose. We'd like these back.*

Claude Bowers and Chris Ingles were blowing the northern road. Steve and Ben had selected this particular spot on the western road because of the cliffs on either side. Bring down all that rock and it would take heavy equipment at least a few days to clear the rubble, then another couple to rebuild the road.

It had taken them a couple of hours to rig the dynamite along the cliff walls and rig the detonator lines.

"You ready, Ben?"

He glanced at Jeremiah and Brodie, who'd been scurrying around like mountain goats for the last hour, setting charges.

"We're good. Let her rip."

"Cover your ears," Steve instructed.

Kat ducked low on her knees and pushed her palms against her ears. Beside her, Ben, who'd said plenty about how he preferred the old ways over all the fancy electronic wireless gizmos, gripped an ancient plunger with his wrinkled hand. "Fire in the hole."

He shoved the handle down.

Ka-boom!

The earth shook and the booms kept coming as huge slabs of rock tumbled from the cliff and slammed onto the road. Small pieces of gravel rained on them.

"Stay down!" Steve covered her back with his big arm. "Just stay down!"

But there was no need. The debris stopped falling and the show was over. Kat was the first on her feet, staring at the road.

Where the road *had been*, to be more precise. Now a mountain of rock at least fifty feet high filled the gap between the cliffs.

"Well now, that oughta discourage any pranksters," Ben cackled.

"You think the trucks got it?" Jeremiah asked.

"I guess we'll find out in a week."

They piled into Ben's new Lexus SUV and sped back into Paradise, a mile down the road.

As it turned out, 2,713 supporters had responded to the call to join Johnny in Paradise, mostly driving in from the Four Corners states but also as far as Los Angeles, California, to the west and Springfield, Missouri, to the east. (Jamie Peterson, the college kid who'd driven from Springfield, admitted to breaking every possible speed limit law on the way, just managing to fly past the checkpoint in his cobalt blue Corvette at dawn.)

Four people had elected to leave the valley, one of them pregnant, two more who'd just wandered in the day before to see what all the fuss was about, and one hitchhiker who was trying to get to Denver.

The gathering in Paradise stood at just over 3000, up from a population of just under three hundred twenty-four hours earlier. And despite all of her worrying, once Paula Smither settled for making do, she'd gotten them all situated just fine. The regulars opened their homes to as many as could sleep comfortably, seven or eight, which took care of two-thirds of the visitors. The rest preferred the church, the rec center, or the barns anyway. They were here because they'd been born into the kingdom of light, not because they wanted a five-star vacation getaway.

Ben and Charlie's food stash consisted mostly of dried soup packages. Pea soup, corn soup, tortilla soup without the tortillas, chicken noodle soup, turkey soup. And those were just the ones Kat could remember.

Looked like they would be eating soup and fruit for breakfast, lunch, and dinner. Which, again, was fine, Paula had decided. Wasn't no five-star resort, wasn't no five-star food.

Kat rode into Paradise at six thirty with Steve and Ben. The street was still quiet this early, but she immediately noticed two changes.

First change, the sheer number of cars. They were parked everywhere except for the town center, which they were keeping clear. Had to be a thousand cars strewn throughout all the alleys and surrounding fields.

Second change was the plywood platform Father Yordon and a team of a dozen men had built along the side of the old theater, looking out over the center of town and the church lawn. They'd built it tall, at least five feet, so that the whole town could see whoever was talking up there. They'd even set up a sound system with two black speakers balanced on top of crates.

Word had gone out: they would gather at eight.

Short on sleep, Kat slipped into the Smithers' house on Main Street, rolled onto her bed in the back bedroom, and was asleep before the first sounds of waking could mess with her mind.

She woke to a "Check, check, check," over an amplifier at 7:59 by the wall clock, and sat up with a start.

They'd started?

"Could I have your attention?" Yordon's voice rang out over the town. "Ladies and gentlemen, your attention up here please."

Kat splashed water on her face, dabbed it dry, ran out the front door, and pulled up sharply.

She gasped. The crowd started at the bottom of the Smithers' porch and stretched across the whole center of town to the field on the other side of the church lawn. No street that she could see, no lawn, nothing but people standing and looking up at Father Yordon on the platform.

Ordinary people dressed in everything from jeans to skirts, even a few business suits. A black boy of about ten stood beside the planter at the bottom of the porch steps, staring up at Kat. His closely shaven head was almost perfectly round.

Kat smiled and nodded. The boy grinned back, all gum except for one buck tooth.

Father Yordon was welcoming the people, giving them some basic instructions about keeping order. Sanitation. Food.

A helicopter chopped overhead, and Kat saw with a glance that there were two, actually, in army olive-drab green.

She returned her gaze to the crowd. It struck her that so many people had traveled so far at the drop of a hat to stand up for what was to them the essence of life. She remembered stumbling across a quote by George Washington saying that it was ". . . impossible to rightly govern a nation without God and the Bible," and she'd wondered what that meant about governing a school. And what about a town?

Johnny had made it clear in his blog that he wasn't as interested in politics as he was interested in matters of the heart. Faith in God. Following Jesus.

So all of these people had read that blog and come to follow Jesus with Johnny. To Kat, who'd only just stepped into the kingdom two weeks ago, the sight was an incredible thing.

The kingdom of truth wasn't just her alone in the high school.

It wasn't just her and Johnny.

It wasn't just a church full of old people in the Colorado mountains.

It was these 3,000 pilgrims who'd traveled hours to stand and be heard for Jesus. He'd been slain two thousand years ago, but he'd left the world with this.

Kat felt such a surge of gratitude that she didn't think she could contain it. Why the whole world didn't rush here and stand as one was beyond her.

Father Yordon was still going on about organization, which she knew was important. But she just couldn't bring herself to care. The helicopters were flying overhead, pilots' jaws probably dropped at the scene below. The Net was flooded, yes indeed, truly flooded with blogs and news from this very small town. The whole world had its eye on Paradise, and she was here because one blind man had shown her the light.

"Go, Johnny!" she screamed.

Her cry rang out over the crowd, which turned as one and stared at the dark-skinned girl standing on the porch next to Smither's Barbeque.

She'd actually screamed that?

"Go, Johnny!" The toothless black boy had seen fit to match her cry.

And then they all did, a dozen at first and swelling to three thousand voices calling for their leader.

"Johnny! Johnny! Johnny!"

But Johnny was nowhere to be seen.

Not yet.

CHAPTER THIRTY-THREE

"HOW LONG?" Billy demanded.

"Three days, four tops." Kinnard stood on a plateau high above Paradise, eyeing the wrecked roads through his glasses. "Assuming the Army Corps of Engineers can get their gear here before nightfall. You gotta hand it to Johnny—he knows what he's doing."

Darcy stood to one side watching Billy pace, white-faced.

"I don't care when they arrive, they can work by lights if they have to. We need those roads clear."

"And they will be. Three days," Kinnard said. "We'll have plans for an extraction long before that. We can't wait three days to deal with Johnny."

Darcy lifted her binoculars and stared at the valley again. They'd gotten the thumbs-up to bring in the National Guard late last night—no martyrs, not even one, Lyndsay warned—and immediately issued the orders to close the valley. But Johnny had beaten them to it. The first unit of the National Guard of the 947th Engineer Company arrived from Grand Junction to find both ends of the highway into the valley completely blown.

Apart from the single gathering earlier in the day, there had been no organized activity. Darcy wondered what they were eating. No sign of

Johnny, not even at the meeting. He was wisely staying out of the line of the snipers brought in by the FBI's Hostage Rescue Team and the Colorado National Guard, 5/19th Airborne Special Forces. They had the area mapped and scouted, but . . .

"Somehow I doubt extracting Johnny will be that easy," she said, lowering her binoculars.

Kinnard nodded. "Saint."

"You know about his days as an assassin?" Billy demanded.

"He was known as Saint. From what I can gather, Johnny was one formidable opponent, especially with a rifle."

"Johnny was an assassin?" Darcy asked. "So then what makes you think we can waltz in there and take him out?"

"No martyrs, remember?"

"Not take him out as in kill him," Billy snapped. "She means extract him. And that's not the point, Darcy. The point is to show him what he's up against, make him second-guess himself."

A large double-bladed helicopter thumped in from the north, settled to the ground behind them, and emptied its cargo onto the high mesa. Several large tents had already been erected in the guard's staging base, and this load brought another dozen with three times that many soldiers armed to the teeth.

A perimeter had already been established around the valley with seventeen carefully placed teams dug in and armed. Only two of these teams were responsible for the roads. The rest had taken up positions that protected any traffic in or out, on foot or by horse. They had enough rifles trained on Paradise to make the president pucker right up, no doubt about that.

"Yes, of course, give time for negotiations, we've all heard that," she said. "But we all also know that Johnny's not going to negotiate. Not without some juice."

"We'll force him to negotiate!"

The National Guard were being led on the ground by a Ranger battalion flown in from Fort Carson and commanded by a Colonel Eric Abernathy.

Kinnard took a call from the colonel, something about rules of engage-ment, civil response, and logistical support. Darcy eased over to Billy and took his arm, guiding him away from Kinnard.

"Is it really necessary to go through all these motions?" she whispered quickly. "I can change them all!"

"You don't know that. We can't change Johnny!"

"No? Maybe not, but his bringing all these people will work with him, I'm convinced of it."

"If you think you can change their minds—"

"I can! Drop me in the middle of that crowd down there and I'll show you."

"And if you can't? You expect them to revolt against their beloved Johnny?"

She was appalled by his lack of confidence in her.

"Did I or did I not convince the whole of Congress to revolt against their beloved Constitution?"

"Half of them already wanted to change it. I'm just saying"—he faced the town far below, scowling with bitterness—"Johnny wants a fight, and I swear, I'm going to give him his fight. And this time it won't just be with words."

"So you're just going to give up on me?" she demanded.

"I'm going to save you!" he cried. And she knew then that he was starting to lose it. His whole past had caught up to him in the last week, and he was starting to set reason aside to protect himself from it.

As are you, Darcy.

She ripped off her glasses. "Take off your glasses."

"Now?"

"Yes, now!" she screamed.

Kinnard spun around, ear still plastered to the phone, but he meant nothing to her now. She stepped forward and plucked Billy's glasses from his face.

Bore into his eyes with her own.

"You love me, Billy, but if you think you can save me you're not think-ing straight. I'm here to save *you*. What have you ever done to save me? It's not in your blood—accept it. You've always been an impetuous gam-bler, willing to throw yourself to the wolves for the chance to be crowned the wolf slayer. This time we will do things my way, you hear me? You're not taking me down with you again!"

Billy's face wrinkled with pain. She knew she'd been far too harsh, pushing him to the point where he might resent her words and obey her out of pure obligation.

But she was honestly afraid for him. He was beginning to lose himself in this whole affair.

"I want you to make them take me down there now, set me in the middle of the town down there"—she shoved a finger down toward the valley—"and let me deliver this ultimatum of yours in person."

Kinnard took a step toward them. "Are you two—"

"Shut up, Kinnard!" she snapped.

Billy's eyes leaked trails of tears. He looked both terrified and bitter at once, and Darcy felt a tinge of regret.

"Sorry to put it like that, Billy." She shoved her glasses back on. "I'm just a bit out of whack myself."

Billy spun to Kinnard. "Tell them we're going down."

"I'm not sure that's really a good idea."

Darcy drilled him with a glare. "Do you want an earful as well?"

"Just thinking of your safety."

"Johnny isn't going to guillotine us, you idiot. We're going to guillo-tine him!" she said. "It's time he learned what the stakes are."

THERE WERE only a couple hundred people milling about the center of town when the old Apache settled onto the church lawn and barely waited for Darcy and Billy to tumble out before screwing back into the sky.

She stood next to him beneath the pulsating air, long hair flying every which direction, calf-length black dress buffeted about, arms limp by her sides. She scanned the eyes that watched her from the perimeter.

"Take your glasses off and tell me what they're thinking," she instructed.

He did so, but must have gotten nothing, because he stepped closer to a group loitering by Smither's Barbeque. Used to be Smither's Saloon, if she remembered right.

Darcy followed by his side. "Anything?"

"They're wondering who we are. Some fear. Mostly curiosity."

"Who has the fear?"

"The one in the white shirt."

Darcy strode toward a woman in her forties, dressed in jeans and a white, sleeveless blouse and tennis shoes. No sunglasses, that was good. Hardly any of them wore sunglasses.

She plucked her own from her face. "You there in the white blouse, what's your name?"

The woman blinked, already aware of some subtle change in her own disposition. Darcy bore into her with her eyes and clearly annunciated each word.

"What is your name?"

"Holly."

"You're afraid, aren't you, Holly?"

Tears sprang to the woman's eyes, but she didn't respond.

"Fact is, you're all afraid," Darcy said, running her eyes over the group. "You're so afraid, that I think you'll demand to be taken out of here, to safety."

The woman in the white blouse had frozen, though confusion batted at her eyes.

Darcy had done this enough to know that her power was at its greatest when she exerted the full force of her own passion into each word. And at the moment, her passion was fueled by the frustration of Johnny having compelled her halfway across the United States not once, but quote.

twice now because he wanted men in clerical collars to be able to point their fingers at the world.

She ground her molars and looked into each of their eyes. "The National Guard is preparing to invade this valley. People will die. Innocent lives will be lost. But you've forced their hand, and so now you may die."

"No."

"Oh yes, Holly. Yes, *yes*." She'd exaggerated for effect, and Holly responded.

The woman was trembling head to foot, as were five others, hands to their mouths, shaking without being able to fully comprehend where the extreme emotion was coming from. Without realizing it, they were facing more than the simple fear of the National Guard.

"They're coming for you," Darcy said. "You're all terrified for good reason, and you're going to demand that Johnny take you out of here." She offered them a gentle smile and stopped ten feet from them. "Aren't you?"

"Leave?" one of them asked. A thin brunette.

"Yes, leave this valley."

"No," said Holly. She was crying earnestly now. "No, you don't understand, we can't leave."

Darcy blinked. "Oh? But you *will* leave!"

"No."

"Yes, yes, you *will* leave."

A moment of silent stalemate.

"No!" the woman screamed. "No, you can't make me leave. I will *not* be silenced! I will *not* deny the love of my Christ! Take my head, take my home, take my husband, but you will not take my heart!"

Darcy was too stunned to reply. The woman was resisting her? Her mind scrambled for better reasoning. Surely she could find and act on the morsel of doubt in this woman's mind. That sliver of fear. That spot that resented God, even.

"You've betrayed Christ before," she said.

"Yes!" The woman's hands flew to her face and she wept into them bitterly. "Yes! And I can't betray him again. Never!"

She was being defied? For the first time since Darcy had understood her gift, she feared that it might fail her. But she couldn't let that happen.

"You'll all leave!" she screamed at the women. "You're all whores who have no understanding of how dangerous your own betrayal really is, and you're terrified to stand here one more moment."

Holly began to wail through her hands, and the moment her volume rose, the rest of them began to weep with her.

"Run. Out! Get out of this valley. Don't be stupid, you hear me? Don't you dare be fools for the sake of a Christ you can't even see!"

She might have pulled the plug from their resolve. But instead of running from the town, screaming about their own foolishness, they fell to the ground, writhing in sobs, praying—*praying!*—begging to be forgiven.

"Have mercy on us sinners, Son of David! Have mercy on us sinners, Jesus Christ!"

She realized too late that she'd pushed them toward their beliefs, not away. Watching these women, she wasn't sure she *could* push them from their faith.

Darcy became aware of a murmur mixed with soft cries behind her. She spun, half expecting to see Johnny standing there. But it wasn't Johnny. Another five hundred at least had gathered and were watching the women on the ground, crying with them, some kneeling, some with their faces in their hands, some just staring with wet eyes.

The sight sliced through her chest like a white-hot blade. She didn't dare speak. Billy was beside her, eyes wide, truly afraid.

"Call the chopper," she managed. "Get us out of here."

"Darcy!"

There was no mistaking the sound of Johnny's voice. She turned back to Smither's Barbeque, where Holly and the others were now sobbing softly, and saw Johnny standing to the right of the building.

"I have something to show you."

"No," Billy shouted, but his voice sounded like a hoarse whisper.

"Take one look, Billy," Johnny challenged. "If you don't like what you see, then leave."

Billy thrust out his right arm and pointed at Johnny. "You have twenty-four hours from sunset today to surrender yourself before we use force." His fiery eyes scanned the crowd. "All of you, twenty-four hours, and then this game of yours comes to an end. You've been warned!"

"Then we have some time, Billy," Johnny said calmly. "Or would you prefer the camera told the world"—he indicated a newsman who was filming them—"that Billy and Darcy have forgotten how to negotiate?"

Darcy felt heat sting her face.

"We have to go with him," she said softly to Billy. "We're on. *Live.*"

"He's . . . he's . . ." Billy voice was laced with panic. "He's manipulating—"

"We have to give negotiation its due course." She turned and looked into his eyes. "I love you, Billy. I will be with you all the way. We're stronger than Johnny. You can do this. You can set aside your fear of Black and the memories that haunt you, because I am with you."

His face melted like snow under the heat of each word.

Darcy took his hand, at the risk of appearing juvenile in the camera's eye, and strode toward Johnny.

CHAPTER THIRTY-FOUR

THE SUN had sunk below the surrounding cliffs by the time Johnny's chopper settled into the old canyon above Paradise. Billy and Darcy had dutifully climbed aboard the helicopter behind the old theater. The flight to the upper canyon that had once housed the hidden monastery took seven wordless minutes.

It occurred to her that they had Johnny in their grasp. They could force the pilot to fly them to the staging plateau, where several hundred armed National Guardsmen awaited a command from the Special Forces within their indirect command.

But a single glance told her that Johnny was ahead of her. The pilot wore a helmet with a dark visor that shielded his eyes from the sun and, more importantly, from her. The helmet had been fixed to a strap that ran under his arms. There was no way they could get it off without brute force.

The chopper settled on the sand long enough for them to step out before being snatched back into the sky by blades that bit hard into the air.

"Follow me," Johnny said, heading up the canyon.

Darcy let her eyes follow the sheer rock walls on either side as silence replaced the chopper's whine. The white sand was littered with chunks of granite that had tumbled from the cliffs. The center of the canyon reminded her of a huge bowling lane strewn with broken balls. Larger boulders, taller than she, stood along the canyon walls.

"I don't like this," Billy said. "We shouldn't have gone down to the town in the first place, and we shouldn't have come up here."

"Yeah, well, sometimes you have to take the bull by the horns," she said.

He walked forward, face set. They followed Johnny up the canyon ten paces behind.

Around the bend.

The cliff on their left had been brought down in a landside and now covered the whole section of canyon that had once housed the monastery. A small cabin sat at the base of the slide.

Darcy was staring at her childhood, and the memories she'd worked so hard to bury now exploded to the surface.

Monks hurrying up and down the halls, gathering the children for dinner.

Classes with the others in an expansive library, learning of virtue, always virtue.

The dungeons that Billy had led her into. The worms. The Books of History from which all three had gotten their powers. All there, beneath the pile of boulders that had obliterated it.

"Doesn't look so bad," Billy said, stepping closer.

Johnny turned around and faced them, dark glasses in place. "Not so bad, Billy." He spread his arms wide. "The birthplace of unique evil never looked so innocuous."

"What evil? I see rocks and sand and a cabin. Your finger pointing won't change the fact that you have three thousand people trapped in a valley, facing their deaths." He flipped open his phone.

"I wouldn't do that," Johnny said, easing toward a boulder half his height.

"You don't think they know exactly where we are?"

Johnny suddenly had a pistol in his hand. "Problem is, so do I." He spun the weapon and caught it neatly in his palm. "I suggest you tell them to give us some space. We need to talk."

Billy hesitated. Judging by the way Johnny handled the gun, the rumors about him were true. Darcy had no doubt that he could kill them both before they had the time to notice.

"I could shoot the phone out of your hand, but you might lose a finger—it's been awhile. Please, Billy, tell Kinnard you're fine. We're just trying to understand some things."

Billy frowned and spoke into the phone. "Yes, we're fine. No, leave us here in the canyon."

"Pull back any observation posts," Johnny said.

"Pull back the spotter on the north face. I'll call for a chopper when we're ready." He snapped the phone closed.

Johnny tossed the gun into the sand and held up his hands in a sign of good faith. "Thank you."

Darcy clasped her hands behind her back and walked to her right, gazing at the piles of rock, trying to imagine the old entry to the monastery. "You really think dragging us back here will help you? I hate to disappoint you, Johnny, but we're here about our future. Clearly, our past is buried."

"On the contrary, this is all about the past," he said. "It's about what happened two thousand years ago. What happened twelve years ago. What happened last week. The truth doesn't change over time."

"Is that what lies under that pile of rocks? The truth? I think we were fed lies."

"Then why don't we put it to a test?"

She knew immediately what he had in mind.

"You want us to remove our glasses and see what happens, is that it?"

"I want you to use your gifts. They were given to you for good, not evil. Billy, search my mind, show me where my doubts hide. Darcy, persuade me of the errors in my way of thinking. I'll remove my glasses and let you speak to me clearly."

The notion put Darcy on guard. Why would he subject himself to such a baring of his soul?

Then she remembered Holly down in Paradise.

"If you don't see the sense of our way," she said, "you only prove that your deception runs all the way into your bones."

"Who cares about that?" Billy said. "He intends to make us look into *his* eyes." To Johnny: "Do we look like morons to you?"

"You do. But looks can be deceiving. My eyes are harmless. They will expose only truth, unless I decide to show you more."

"More?"

He hesitated. "Nothing that will hurt you. But I want you to see your souls, the way they really are, and that sometimes can be painful. You're not afraid of yourselves, are you?"

Darcy found the idea of staring into her own soul a bit esoteric but nonetheless unnerving.

"No," Billy said. "No, Darcy, I'm telling you this is a bad idea."

She looked at Johnny. "You heard him. It's a bad idea."

"Why?"

She faced Billy again. "Why, Billy?"

"Because he's not telling us something. He knows that his eyes can do something . . ." The tightness in his voice betrayed his fear.

"My eyes can show the truth. And only then if you are open to it."

Johnny lifted his hands and removed his glasses. His eyes were as blue as the sky. Nothing that looked threatening.

"You're not seeing my real eyes," he said. "I have the power to do a few tricks, like turn my eyes blue. Basic illusions. But that's not what we're interested in here, are we?"

"It doesn't matter what we see, then," Billy said. "How would you expect us to think that anything you show us isn't just an illusion? A hundred false faith healers have turned the world into cynics. So what are you, the ultimate miracle worker for the entire world to see? You're a fake!"

"Then you'll be fine, Billy. You'll know if what you see is just an illusion. Skeptics aren't easily won over."

Darcy stared at his blue eyes. Here it was then, three grown children with special powers facing off in the very canyon where they had been granted those powers. The world gathered on the Net for one of the largest global ideological battles it had yet faced, but this was the epicenter.

In the end there was Billy, Johnny, and Darcy.

Johnny took a step toward her, eyeing her with deep pools of impossible blue. "You've rejected the faith, but surely you remember your lessons. The account of the leader who swore to kill every follower of the Way, these so-called Christians, after they'd crucified Jesus. He rounded them up wherever they could be found, do you remember?"

"A story," she said.

"Verified by numerous historical documents. An accurate account."

"So what?"

"He took a journey to Damascus to bring followers of the Way to justice, just like you and Billy are doing here. But that journey changed his life dramatically. Instead of stomping out the Way, he vowed to spend his life speaking the truth about Jesus. What happened to bring about such a radical transformation from hatred to devotion, Darcy? Do you remember?"

"Of course she remembers," Billy snapped. "What are you now, an angel of light?"

Johnny kept his eyes on Darcy. "That's right, Billy, the apostle Paul saw a light on the road. A blinding shaft of truth that bared his soul and threw him to his knees."

Darcy reached up and snatched her glasses from her eyes. "Fine, Johnny. Show me your light. Do your tricks. The world's waiting."

He stared at her for a moment, then looked at Billy.

"And you?"

Billy's voice was laced with bitterness. "You think dragging us through the mud, shoving our pitiful failures in our faces, spitting on us when we're down will do anything more than prove what Darcy convinced me of a week ago?"

He meant that freedom from hate speech was grounded in hate, not love. But at the moment, Billy seemed to have cornered hate speech. He'd lost a bit of perspective, Darcy thought.

"Just because the truth disturbs someone doesn't make speaking that truth hate speech," Johnny said.

"It's nothing more than *your* version of the truth."

"Then take off your glasses, Billy, and see if it should be your version as well . . . or not."

Billy ripped his glasses off, and Johnny's thoughts flowed into his mind like a torrent. They locked eyes for a few long seconds that stretched into ten.

Darcy guessed by the deepening scowl on Billy's face that he was learning what they already knew: Johnny was indeed deceived by his own rhetoric. To the marrow of his bones he believed that he was speaking not only the truth but the only truth.

"Look at me, Johnny," Darcy said.

He blinked and turned his eyes to her.

She started to slowly walk toward him, light on the sand. "You will not use your eyes on me, Johnny. You respect me too much to force me against my will, and really, I don't want to hear any more of what you have to offer."

He took a step back, undoubtedly unprepared for the power in her voice. She pressed.

"Even if your version of truth has merit, you have to respect those who dislike it. Speaking of it in any arena where it is uninvited, such as in this country, is wrong."

Johnny's blue eyes did not blink. She wondered what it was like to see the way he saw, in lights and shapes rather than in color or texture.

"I do not want you to be rude to me, Johnny."

"Was Jesus rude to the money changers he drove from the temple?" Johnny asked.

"Yes. As a matter of fact, he was. And I don't want you to treat me that way. This is America, not ancient Palestine. We've grown up since then, don't you think?"

"The world has fallen into a dark pit. Is it rude or hateful to point the way to the light?"

She reached him and lifted her hand to his face. Rubbed her thumb on his cheek. His flesh was hot to her touch, closely shaven, smooth.

"I think the world likes this dark pit. So please shut up and let us all grope around in the dark if that's what we want to do."

He was feeling the full brunt of her words; she could see it in the sweat on his forehead. But she hadn't tested him yet, not really.

"I must follow that light," he said softly.

"You should join us, Johnny."

Why did she keep coming back to that? Because she liked Johnny, deep down where she had no business liking him. He was so wrong, so misguided, and so deceived, but she found his conviction nearly irresistible.

"Would you like to kiss me, Johnny?"

He didn't respond, so she turned back to Billy, smiling. "Does he want to kiss me, Billy?"

She realized in a flash that this tack was entirely inappropriate. Billy frowned bitterly and his eyes were dark with anger. But before she could backpedal, his frown morphed into a wide scream of raw terror.

It was as if a bucket of black fear had been thrown in his face, so sudden was the change. He stumbled back a step, threw his hands to his face, and shredded the air with a scream that made her hair stand on end.

She spun back to Johnny. His eyes were fixed over her shoulders on Billy. Black eyes, as black as polished coal.

She'd asked him not to use his eyes on her, but she'd said nothing about Billy, and now Billy was seeing whatever Johnny showed him.

"Stop it!" she cried. But he stared on, unaffected.

She slapped his face. "Stop it, I said!"

He blinked and looked at her, now with white eyes.

"It's just the truth, Darcy," he said, swallowing hard. "Please let me show you the truth. For their sakes, for the sake of those in Paradise. For all of our sakes!"

"Oh, God!" Billy wailed behind her. "Oh, my God, my God . . ." He sounded like a father who was helplessly watching his children being brutalized. Weeping uncontrollably.

"God, God, God!"

She whirled back and watched Billy fall to his knees, gripping his hair with both hands, eyes clenched.

"What did you do to him?"

"The truth . . ."

Darcy spun back. "If that's the truth, the world doesn't need it! Let him go!"

"I don't—"

She slapped him again. "Let him go, now!"

"I don't have him!" Johnny yelled. His eyes flashed blue.

"Oh, my God, my God," Billy sobbed. "What . . . what was . . ."

"Me, Billy." The voice came low, guttural like a rolling boulder from the direction of the cabin behind Johnny, flattening all other sound in the canyon.

Darcy's heart crashed into her throat at the sound of his voice. A voice she couldn't possibly forget. The one that had haunted her nightmares for thirteen years and made her weep on the therapist's couch so many times.

Black.

Johnny jerked around, and she saw Marsuvees Black over his shoulder even as he turned.

Black stood in the cabin's opened doorway, dressed in a black trench coat, black polyester pants, black Stetson hat. Silver-tipped black boots.

He stood there, leaning on the doorjamb with one ankle crossed over the other, chewing on a small twig. The left corner of his mouth suggested a grin, and his sparkling eyes confirmed it.

"You do remember me, don't you? Billy?"

He looked at Johnny and the grin faded.

"Keep your tricks, John-John. I've been staring at myself for thirteen years and I'm getting to like what I see. Granted, some of the older mes didn't cut the mustard, so to speak, but I do think I've hit upon the right ingredients this time. Don't you?"

"Tell him to tell you who he really is, Darcy," Johnny said. "At least give me that much."

"I know who he is."

"Pray, do tell," Black said, and stepped from the cabin, strutting toward them. "Who am I, Darcy?"

"You're something written from the books, words that have taken flesh."

"More, baby, more. Don't shortchange me now after all we've been through."

She said what was on the top of her mind. "You're an incarnation of evil." Then louder: "The demon in the dark, the ghost who whispers in the night. The bogeyman, if you want. One iteration of the figment of all our imaginations."

He stopped at that, as if disappointed, then walked on. "You reduce me to something that goes bump in the night? I expected more from you, Darcy. I'm not that plastic, not by a long shot."

"I want you to stop where you are," she said. But he continued as if he hadn't heard her, impervious to her voice. She began to fear him in earnest.

"Raw evil," he said. "Like a raw steak, just meat and blood. The devil incarnate. But there's more, baby, so much more. You've gone and saved the juiciest detail for last, you naughty little girl."

Darcy was struck by the undeniable fact that Black's very presence validated at least part of what Johnny had claimed.

"Tell me who I am!" Black snarled, lips twisted and wet. Darcy wanted to run. Her hands went cold and her breathing stopped.

Only then did she realize that he was staring past her at Billy. He was demanding that Billy confess the full truth.

"Tell me, you worthless brat. Tell me!"

"You're me!" Billy cried. He was on his knees and his arms were spread and his face was twisted in anguish. "I made you!"

Black strode past her and Johnny as if they didn't exist. His focus bore into Billy, who cowered on the ground, shaking.

"Almost. Let's be precise here. *You* are *me*, Billy. Say it."

"I am you!" Billy cried. "I am you!"

"You need me, Billy. Tell them."

He shook, robbed of breath.

"Leave him!" Johnny yelled. "You have no right to him."

Black halted midstride, slowly turned around, black eyes like holes in his face, head tilted to one side. "*Au contraire. I own* him."

He turned, grabbed Billy by the collar, and jerked him to his feet. But instead of verbally abusing him as Darcy expected, he wiped the tears from Billy's face, then pulled him close and hugged him.

"It's okay, Billy. You're okay now. I'm here."

Billy hung on Black's shoulder, limp like a rag doll and sobbing.

Darcy felt numb. She couldn't fathom the desperation that had brought Billy to this point, and seeing him reduced to such a pitiful state made her want to cry. She had to help him. But they'd come here to talk sense into Johnny, not face Billy's demons.

What if this was all just a trick played by Johnny's eyes to make a point?

As if he'd taken on Billy's gift and heard her thoughts, Johnny leapt to his right, snapped up the fallen gun, and spun to Black.

"Let him go."

Black whispered something into Billy's ear, and he immediately began to calm. The man appeared not to have heard Johnny's threat.

"Back away from him!"

But Black pulled back, gripped Billy's head in both of his hands, and then kissed him full on the lips.

Johnny cried in outrage and pulled the trigger. The gun bucked in his palm with a thunderclap. Black jerked once. Released Billy and turned slowly.

For a moment Darcy thought that Johnny just might have hit him.

Black's face twitched like a horse's hide, twitching at a fly. Billy stood with his head hung low, completely quieted.

Marsuvees Black strode back toward the cabin, black eyes fixed on Johnny. And as he passed them he spit something out of his mouth.

A copper-jacketed bullet plopped on the sand.

"Welcome to the real world," he said.

CHAPTER THIRTY-FIVE

Day Twenty-One

"NO, MA'AM, there's not a bit of bend in him," Billy said. "Do I need to explain to you how I know that?"

In the National Guard command center, Darcy watched Billy talk on the phone with the attorney general while eyeing a string of monitor panels he'd ordered set up for his personal surveillance. His eyes flickered from aerial surveillance to thermal images from one of the observation posts and back again. His transformation from wounded soul to enraged tyrant had become complete over the twenty-four hours since their encounter with Marsuvees Black, Darcy thought. And it frightened her.

But this is what they'd signed up for, and she wasn't about to backpedal now.

Brian Kinnard leaned over a backlit table on which the incursion plans had been drawn up, speaking quietly with the captain, who was dressed in camouflaged BDUs. The Ranger battalion's CO listened in but let them run with the conversation unless directly addressed.

Billy walked to the corner, and Darcy hung close. He'd taken the lead and she wasn't sure how she felt about that. Slightly resentful, but she couldn't very well reprimand him for doing exactly what she'd begged him to do when they were back in Washington. He was forcing Johnny's hand, and he was doing it with surprising command.

His face reddened momentarily, and then he spoke into the phone with black-ice calm. "Then Congress will just have to get used to the fact that laws are worthless unless they are enforced," he said. "Are you saying that you disagree with the use of force?"

He nodded at whatever she said.

"Exactly. My point. And as I've said, I've been inside his mind and I can tell you that this is going to get bloody. He has no intention of walking out of there with his hands up. The whole valley is drunk on his Kool-Aid. They'll die for their cause and they'll take down the first responders with much more than the pop guns they dumped outside the town for everyone to see."

Another pause.

"Don't worry about the Net. I know the movement is significant, but the backlash has already started. Over half the country thinks of Johnny and his cult as a band of lunatics. Darcy assures me that the sentiment will grow. If anything, this new hatred toward Johnny demands we take action before people start acting on their hate."

Billy faced Darcy and studied her with his green eyes. Glasses were a thing of the past for him: he wanted to know the thoughts of everyone in the command center at any given time. Only Kinnard and Darcy guarded themselves from his probing eyes, Kinnard because he insisted, Darcy because she didn't want to unfairly influence Billy, though she wasn't sure he cared any more. Maybe he thought he could resist her charm as Black had.

"That's fine, Lyndsay. But I'm asking you to expand our authority to the use of reasonable force. We gave them twenty-four hours from sunset, but we might as well have been speaking to the dirt. The Net feeds have the whole world glued to that valley, and they saw me issue the ultimatum. If we don't execute justice—"

Billy listened for a moment. "Hold on." He handed the phone to Darcy. "Talk sense to her, please."

She took the black cell and lifted it to her ear. "Hello, Miss Nadeau."

"Darcy," the attorney general acknowledged her politely.

"Why the hesitation?"

"No, dear, no hesitation. But I can't just turn over our police and military forces to two civilians, I'm sure you understand. I'm just establishing some ground rules."

"I think you're missing the point. It's time to make the president good on his word to deal swiftly with extreme prejudice. To do that, we must have certain authorities, surely you understand."

"Of course. Yes, but I want any decision you or Billy consider to pass through me. I, in turn, will need to get the president's—"

Darcy snapped at that. "How dare you throw the president in my face? He's indebted to *me*. We know his dirty little secrets, and don't think that we haven't put them in a very safe place. Are you already forgetting your promise to let Billy and me do what is necessary to effect this change?"

Her own anger surprised her, but the thought of smug Lyndsay Nadeau sitting in Washington, second-guessing them now, made Darcy want to fly back and forcibly remind the woman of her power.

"You're not suggesting that this is the favor I promised," the attorney general said. "You're asking for the head of Johnny Drake?"

Darcy had all but forgotten their agreement to be granted whatever they asked in exchange for their help. That had been a last-minute negotiation, thrown into the pot for good measure.

"No," she said. "Don't be stupid. I'm demanding that you give Billy the authority he's asking for. Tell Kinnard to pass the order. Neither of us has any intention of abusing that power; *please*, you know it's only a fraction of the power we already have. Or would you rather I rip Kinnard's glasses from his face and tell him myself?"

That brought silence.

"I'm not threatening you," Darcy said. "I'm just telling you that Billy and I are two people you have no choice but to trust."

Or kill, she didn't say. An unnerving thought. A very real thought.

Black's statement to Johnny spun through her mind. *Welcome to the real world*, he'd said. Meaning what? No amount of thinking brought clarity.

"Put Kinnard on," the attorney general said.

Darcy crossed the room. "Thank you, Lyndsay. We'll keep you up-to-date. I can promise you no force will be used except in the most extreme case."

"If you do use force, remember, Mr. Drake first," she said. "He's already used force to resist arrest by blowing up the road and refusing to turn himself in. There would be some fallout, but frankly I wouldn't mind. Someone has to take the fall for this."

"So you do agree, then."

"I never said I disagreed. The world has to accept the full enforcement of the law at some point. It might as well be now, before half the country gets swept up in this movement."

Hearing it like that, Darcy realized that the exchange wasn't just about Billy jockeying for position. Paradise was much closer to an escalation involving violence than any of them realized.

"Let's hope it doesn't get to that," she said, and handed the phone to Kinnard. "The attorney general."

Is that what she wanted? Johnny killed? Or worse?

Darcy returned to where Billy stood by the window, looking out over the tarmac, where six or seven helicopters waited in the dusk. The deadline was less than an hour away—they would go in under the cover of darkness.

"You okay?"

Billy's jaw muscles bunched. "Sure."

He'd refused to talk about his encounter with Black. The attack was nothing short of a rape, and Darcy had decided to give him space to deal with it on his own before interfering in any way. But she couldn't ignore the incident any longer, regardless of what wounds it would open.

"Walk with me."

She led him from the command center out onto the tarmac. A few army personnel carriers that had been used to transport guard forces to the perimeter around Paradise, roughly fifty miles south, now sat behind a barbed-wire fence, silent. Dozens more like them were parked along the two roads leading into the valley. Between the small operations base here and the staging area above the valley, the National Guard had the capacity to put a thousand soldiers on the streets of Paradise within thirty minutes of the order.

The plan was to arrest Johnny and the town council peaceably unless they resisted. The three thousand who'd entered Paradise would be released with a stern warning, only if they went peacefully.

But no one expected either Johnny or the three thousand to leave peacefully.

Darcy walked along the fence. "She's instructing them to give us the authority to use force. But we won't, Billy. Not yet."

"No, not yet."

"You're sure Johnny will resist? It doesn't seem like him."

"And if I'm not mistaken, you seem a little distracted by him."

His accusation surprised her "Don't be ridiculous. I'm just saying that he's had his chances to fight and hasn't, even though we know he has the skill."

"But he is resisting. He's defied us both!"

She couldn't deny that. And why did she even want to?

"Yes, he has. And Lyndsay Nadeau says we have full rights to use force if he doesn't comply in the next hour." She took a deep breath and let it seep out through her nostrils. "But you and I both know there's more to this story than what the rest of the world sees."

He didn't agree or disagree.

"So what really happened yesterday, Billy?"

"You tell me."

"I mean with Black."

"Ask Johnny."

"Why?"

Billy shrugged. "It was all his doing."

"You mean his eyes."

"That's right."

"So we didn't really see Black walk out of that cabin? It was just a figment of our imaginations?"

"That's what I'm saying."

She'd pondered the possibility all through the night.

"I'm not sure it adds up."

He stopped and turned, eyes fiery. "And your voice does add up? My
hearing? What about any of this adds up, Darcy? The way we got these
powers? The monastery? The fact that over half of this planet's population believes in some supernatural God or force that can bend spoons
and open a blind man's eyes and make another man blind with light? Does
any of that add up?"

"No. But the man we saw yesterday came from our own pens, Billy!
We saw him ruin Paradise once. He's haunted us ever since that day, and
now he's returned to destroy us!"

"You mean Johnny," Billy said. "Black's come to destroy Johnny."

She blinked. "So you acknowledge that he's real and he's really here."

He shrugged again. "You checked the cabin with Johnny after he walked
back in. You tell me where he disappeared to."

"Judging by the way you're acting, I might guess he crawled up inside
of you."

Billy's face paled. She might as well have gut-punched him.

"I didn't mean that. That was unfair. But you have to tell me what
happened, Billy. He . . . he kissed you, for heaven's sake!"

"Stop it!" he yelled. Tears sprang to his eyes.

His silence on the matter had been out of shame, and her speaking of it was like salt to the wound. But she had to know what Black's role was here.

"I'm sorry. But if Black's real and really here, in the flesh, then shouldn't we take that into account?"

Billy turned away. Walked a few feet and then back. He grabbed Darcy's hand and spoke quickly, eyes frantic.

"He's after us, Darcy. He's come back for the sinner. It's either Johnny or it's us."

"He said that?"

Billy didn't respond. "This is all Johnny's fault. I know I was the one who wrote Black into flesh, but now Johnny's using him to tear us down."

He wasn't speaking with any sense. "Listen to yourself, Billy. First you deny Black is real. Then you insist he's out to kill us. Which is it?"

Billy shook his fist. "Both!"

"How can it be both? You're not stable."

"Is the devil here, floating around us? Is he really here?"

She wasn't quite sure what to say.

"Is the devil out to kill us?"

"What's your point?"

"He's here, he's not here, he's out to kill us, it's all true, and it's all not true. That's Black for you, and I should know. I wrote him!"

Billy turned and strode for the door, both fists by his sides.

"Billy?"

He walked on.

"Be careful, Billy."

"Don't worry your sweet little backside, Darcy," he said without turning back. "I haven't lost my mind."

Watching the door close under the words Authorized Personnel Only stenciled in yellow, Darcy knew what she had to do. What she wanted to do.

She had just under an hour to get through to Johnny using every means at her disposal.

She spun and strode for a helicopter, where a pilot who'd just returned from a run was still filling out paperwork in the cockpit.

"Do you have enough fuel to take me to Paradise?"

The pilot glanced at her and grinned. "I'm sorry, do I look like a taxi to you?"

She snatched her glasses off and drilled him with a ruthless gaze. "You will fly me to Paradise or you will choke on your own vomit tonight in your sleep."

His eyes went round.

"And you'll do it without filing a report."

Three minutes later they were in the air.

CHAPTER THIRTY-SIX

BILLY LEANED over the light table, staring at the map of Paradise valley, which highlighted the location of the forces as currently deployed.

Small blue circles indicated the location of each of the thirteen snipers and scouts hiding in position around the hills and cliffs. Four larger green squares represented the units that waited inside the perimeter near the roads that had been blown.

The bulk of the forces waited on the plateau above Paradise and would be airlifted in if needed.

"I would strongly suggest we cut off their links now," said Ranger Captain Adams, speaking of the impulse generator they'd installed on the mesa. It would interfere with all conventional wireless communications within a ten-mile radius, cutting Paradise off from the world. The guard would rely exclusively on laser communications, a military-grade system that bounced beams off of satellites and back to receivers at specific GPS coordinates. Scrambler/transceivers gathered the signals and channeled them to tactical units within line of sight.

"For tactical reasons, but you might want to also consider the public relations side of things."

"Do it," Billy said.

Kinnard nodded, effectively under Billy's thumb.

"There's a call for you, sir." A staffer of some lower rank handed Billy a phone. He took it and walked from the table, grateful for the distraction. He couldn't just stand around and let his mind itch the way it had ever since Black had forced himself on him.

The clock was ticking. Forty-one minutes and counting.

"Hello?"

"Hello, Billy." A woman's voice. "How are you holding up?"

The voice was only vaguely familiar.

"Who is this?"

"I'm waiting for you in your room, Billy. We don't have much time."

He glanced over at the light table and saw that Kinnard was watching him through those annoying obsidian sunglasses.

"I'm sorry, who did you say this was?"

"I didn't." She paused. When she spoke again, her voice sent a chill through him. "You know me, Billy. You know me better than you know yourself."

The air left his lungs and the room seemed to tilt. Billy jerked the phone from his ear and disengaged the call.

"You okay, Billy?" Kinnard had walked over to him.

"I just need a minute."

"Who was that?"

"I . . . Nothing. Just Darcy. I'll be right back."

He took a breath, frozen by indecision. The compound comprised half a dozen buildings including the armory and officers' quarters, where they'd been put up for the last two nights—Darcy must have retreated to one of them. She wouldn't be standing outside where he'd left her twenty minutes earlier.

But the voice wasn't Darcy's, was it? This itching in his mind was clouding his thoughts.

"You're sure you're okay?"

He headed for the door and crashed through it without giving Kinnard an answer. An old barracks on the north side of the compound had been renovated to accommodate VIPs and visitors. Billy glanced around, saw that he was alone, and took off for his room.

It's you, Billy. You're the sinner.

Black's voice had washed into his body yesterday like a cool drink after a long hike through the desert.

I'm you and you're me, baby. And you know what we want, what we need.

Blackness had filled him from his mouth, chilling his body from the inside out. Billy didn't know if the man who'd shoved his mouth against his own was real or not—how could a person know that? But he did know that something had changed in that moment.

You know you wanna trip, baby. It's just you and me and we're going to slam this town.

A slight buzz had settled into the base of his mind with that voice, the cause of what he'd come to call the itch. The cold had reached down into his bones. But more than either of these had been the hatred of Johnny, the self-appointed prophet who'd forced Billy to face his past once again.

He thinks he's Johnny the Baptist, Billy Boy. He thinks he's come to introduce the world to salvation.

Billy shuddered and ducked into the dark hall that led to his room, number 105, on the left. He swiped his key card through the lock, pushed the handle down, and swung the door open.

"Hello?"

No answer.

He flipped the light on. Nothing. She'd lied to him. Billy felt a sting of bitter disappointment. There was no way anyone could have gotten in. He was hearing voices now. That buzz at the base of his brain wasn't only itching, it was whispering lies.

The clock on the nightstand glowed red. Thirty-three minutes till six.

Billy was about to turn when she stepped out of the corner shadows next to the curtains. He jumped back, startled, half expecting her to morph into Black and kiss him. Dump more of that cold blackness in his belly.

"I knew you would come," Kelly said.

Kelly. Yes, it was Kelly. She'd come with terms of surrender from Johnny.

The woman wore a sleeveless white dress that hung to her calves and swung evenly with each step. Her bare feet were white and her neck was pale even in the dim light.

"What are you doing here?" he asked.

"I think you know, Billy." She smiled. "I'm here to make sure you don't fall apart at the last minute."

"Johnny's surrendering?"

"No," she said. "But we both know that he isn't going to use force."

It occurred to him that he couldn't read her thoughts. She was staring at him with bright eyes, and he didn't have a clue what she was thinking. How was that possible?

"No we don't." But the likelihood that Johnny would not use any force had gnawed at him all day. Johnny himself had never suggested he would use force, which Billy suggested was an intentional omission for the attorney general's sake.

"He said it would get bloody. He didn't say that Johnny would draw that blood."

Billy felt the blackness creeping in. "Who said that?"

"*He* did."

"Black did? How do you know what Black said?"

"Because he and I go way back, honey. Not as far back as you do, but far enough."

"You're . . ."

Then Billy knew that he was looking at another person like Black who'd stepped into human form with the stroke of a pen. Kelly, Johnny's Kelly, was from the pages of Black's book.

She walked up to him and reached for his face, smiling. Her fingers were hot. Flesh. She leaned forward and kissed him with soft warm lips. Fleshy lips. She was more flesh than he'd ever known flesh.

"Johnny isn't going to cooperate, Billy. But he's destined to die. He needs to die. And you're going to kill him."

She kissed him again, longer this time, with more passion. Her lips smothered his. Once again he felt the chill pour into his belly and begin to fill him up. But this time he didn't resist. He welcomed it.

"You know why, Billy," she whispered into his mouth. Her arms reached around his back and she pulled him closer as she kissed his lips passionately, feeding on him. "You know why. Tell me why. Come on, baby, tell me why."

"Because I'm the sinner."

Sorrow engulfed him and he felt himself go.

"Because I was born to sin."

"That's right, baby. Say it again, tell me like you mean it. Tell me who you really are. Say his name." Her hands were in his hair, pulling him so hard against her lips that he could hardly speak.

He started to cry.

"Tell me! Tell me!" She pulled back just long enough to slap his face with an open palm. Then she gripped his cheeks in her fingers and kissed him again, biting his lip.

"Black," he whimpered.

"Say it like you mean it!"

"Black!" The full truth slammed into his mind, crushing him under its weight. Any self-pity weakening his resolve was rolled under by rage.

"I am Black! Black came from me. *We* are the sinner!"

"Yes! Say it again."

"It's me, I made him!"

"And you love him."

"I love him . . . I love him."

"You love me because I'm like Black. He made me. You made me. Tell me, tell me."

Billy felt it more than he could remember feeling anything. The authenticity of his confession brought such relief, such . . .

"I love you. I love you because I am Sinner."

Kelly immediately relaxed. Kissed him gently now, just barely touching his lips. "And so am I, Billy. I didn't even know he'd made me until just a few days ago. I didn't understand why I felt the conflict, the temptations, the inevitable pulling at my soul. Then he came to me, and I knew that he'd made me just like you made him."

He stepped back, panting. Trembling.

"Johnny—"

"I hate Johnny." Kelly ground out the words as if they were dirt. "Now that I know the truth, he makes me want to throw up. Black put me there to love him so that he would end up here—and that's all I knew until Marsuvees came to me. So I loved Johnny, and now I hate him for it. The Johnnys of this world have to die, Billy. They stand in the path of humanity. But we all know who will win."

Her words cut deep into his mind, cold steel penetrating flesh.

"You wrote Black because he was already in you." She flung her arm behind her, pointing at some imaginary enemy. "Now this kingdom of light, or whatever they insist on calling it, wants you to think that this is all your fault!"

Kelly was pulling at the air through her nostrils. He'd never seen a woman quite so enraged.

"That's why you have to kill him, Billy," she said. "You have to kill this Jesus freak or die with all those he condemns. I can't stand his bigoted, hateful nonsense about the narrow gates of heaven."

Kelly's hands trembled and her pale face had turned red.

"You made Black. Johnny's defying your creation. Now you kill him, you hear me?"

"Yes."

"Kill him!"

He felt his face screw up in hopeless acceptance. "I will."

"Kill him!" she yelled.

"I will, I'll kill him!"

"Kill them all, Billy. Do whatever it takes. Swear it to me!"

"I swear it." And he meant it with all of his heart. She was like a lover to him, and he would follow her to hell if he must. He didn't understand why he felt this way, but he embraced the sentiment and let the confusion fall away.

"I swear it on my life."

"Order a preemptive strike on the town. Kill them all."

"I will."

Kelly stared at him hard for a full ten seconds. Slowly the hard lines in her face softened. A smile tugged gently on one corner of her mouth.

She stepped forward, placed her mouth against his, and bit his lip hard enough to draw blood.

"I'm with you, lover. I'm with you all the way."

CHAPTER THIRTY-SEVEN

KATRINA KIVI stood on Main Street in the same spot she'd stood for the last half hour, facing the makeshift stage they'd built against the old theater, listening as first Father Yordon and then Paula Smithers spoke to the gathering about love.

The kind of love she'd seen with her own eyes when Johnny had opened them. She could feel it now, not like she had the first night three weeks—seemed more like a year to her—ago, but here, very much here, like static on the charged air.

She looked around, unable to wipe the slight grin from her face. Home, she thought. I've found my home. How else could she describe the feeling of knowing without the slightest shadow of a doubt that she had found what she'd been made for?

They'd called the meeting that morning because they all knew that the government had given them until sunset to throw up their hands and go home. Four people had already flown out by helicopter. But a strong resolve to stay here, where Holly and the others had fallen on their faces and cried out for mercy, had swept through the valley yesterday afternoon. News spread about what had gone down when Billy Rediger and

Darcy Lange delivered their ultimatum, and the town quietly prepared for whatever might come.

Now three thousand gathered in the town center, crowding the space between the stage on which Johnny stood and the trees that bordered the church lawn a hundred yards away. Kat sat on the Smithers' porch and watched those who hadn't taken a spot on the lawn earlier in the day trickle in. By four thirty the town center was a sea of people.

News came an hour ago that all wireless reception in the valley was gone. Joseph and the other crews were filming from both sides of the stage, but their footage was not going out live.

Her small friend with the toothless smile had taken up his spot next to the porch, grinning up at her. Paula kept busy, hemming and hawing about supper, but no one seemed interested in when or how dinner would be served. Claude paced the front of the stage, assuming the local-law role, which, as far as Kat could tell, was simply to assure those who asked that, yes, he supposed that they were breaking the law.

Steve had been tapped to handle sanitation, control the crowd, and make sure traffic didn't become a problem. Which meant he pretty much sat on the porch outside Smither's Barbeque, because apart from Mary Mae's clogged toilet, neither sanitation, crowd, nor traffic had presented anything remotely similar to a problem.

The town had remained hushed all afternoon as they gathered. Everyone knew something was going to go down. Something big.

This was the gathering. This was the 3000, as the reporters called it.

Now the crowd stood in complete silence, fixed on the stage, staring at Johnny, who stared back through his sunglasses, feeling with them.

Feeling what Kat felt. The electrical charge of expectancy. But she felt more than that. She knew because she'd *seen* this feeling before.

They were feeling the kingdom of light, which raged bright around them, just past their eyesight.

Beside Kat, a thin, gray-haired woman was crying silently from eyes that said she'd been here before. It was about time.

Kat swallowed and looked back at the platform. The two towers of speakers stood to either side, silent now. Two spotlights had been rigged to shine on center stage, and someone had set a potted fruit tree with some apples on it to the back.

Otherwise it was just Johnny. And those sunglasses, which everyone attributed to some kind of affliction that made his eyes sensitive to light. But Kat knew the truth.

Johnny could see best in the dark.

"Take them off," she whispered to herself. "Show them the light, Johnny."

The gray-haired woman glanced down, then faced forward again.

Johnny had already spoken for ten minutes, calmly explaining that if the authorities came, no one should lift a finger against them. If police wanted to take them to prison, they should go. Even in prison they could speak the truth.

He told them that the beacon of light that had been ignited in this valley had been seen by the whole world—it was all he could ask for. The rest was out of his hands. Most people would vow to stomp out the light, and they would not stop until they believed they were successful. But a few would follow the light and step into the kingdom.

Then he fell silent.

And so did the crowd.

Someone whispered, "Thank you, thank you, Father," nearby. The gentle sound of sniffing could be heard here and there. But otherwise even the children had been trapped in Johnny's silence. No squabbling, no crying, just . . .

. . . silence. Beautiful, sweet silence.

Kat wanted to scream at the top of her lungs. Raise her fists and just scream because she felt like she might burst if she didn't.

Instead she stood there and let her fingers tingle.

And let the silence work deeper.

Then Johnny spoke.

"Who has believed our message, and to whom has the arm of the Lord been revealed?"

Kat knew these words penned by a prophet several thousand years ago! Johnny had poured over them with her like an excited child. He had a copy of the scrolls found near the Dead Sea dating back to the time before Christ. The book of Isaiah, chapter fifty-three.

She knew the words and had become as addicted to them as Johnny was.

Kat gripped both fists before her chest and raised up on her toes in her excitement. *Show them, Johnny. Show them the light!*

"He grew up before the world like a tender shoot out of dry ground." Johnny's voice was soft and low, so that she had to lean into the words. They should have been screamed.

But in his softness, Johnny was screaming. Not a single soul could hear this and not know: Johnny was indeed screaming.

"He had no beauty, nothing in his appearance that would make man desire him. He was despised and rejected and hated by men. A man of sorrows, acquainted with grief. They hid their faces from him. Who was this man?"

No one dared answer. It was Johnny's prerogative, Johnny's honor. His voice trembled with each word, as if by uttering them he sowed magic in the air.

The sound of weeping began to wax through the valley, softly, like the hushed sniffs of a mother remembering the long-past death of her son.

Johnny lifted one hand and spread his fingers. "He was pierced for our transgressions. He was crushed for the evil in our hearts. He was smitten and afflicted, and his brutal punishment brought us peace."

A single tear leaked down from behind his dark glasses. *Show them, Johnny. Show them!*

"Who was this man?"

Still not a soul dared speak. Not yet. Who could dare interrupt?

"He was led like a lamb to the slaughter, cut off from the land of the living. He bore the sin of many and his name was Jesus."

A roar erupted. From humming silence to ground-shaking thunder, these three thousand followers who'd entered the kingdom of light could hold back their agreement with the words of magic no longer.

They tilted their heads and opened their throats and filled the air with a cry that drew tears from Kat's eyes in rivers.

It was so dramatic, so over the top, so unearthly, yet so, so, so real. And Kat could hardly stand it.

"Show them!" she cried, eyes clenched, hardly aware that she was yelling aloud. "Show them. Show them, Johnny!" In this moment there was nothing she wanted so desperately as to see that light again.

"Show them, Johnny!"

The crowd's roar had peaked, and that last cry screamed above them all in its high pitch. *Show them, Johnny.*

He slowly turned his head and looked down at her. A tortured smile spread over his face. He continued to speak but kept his eyes on her.

"He taught that he was the only way, and that following him made for a light burden, open to all: the poor, the disadvantaged, the sick, the lepers, the widows, the lost and hurting and wounded. And he taught that the path was narrow, missed by most. For that teaching they hated him, and he warned any who dared follow him that they, too, would be hated."

Johnny took his eyes off Kat and scanned the people who stood in the lights of the surrounding porches and three overhead streetlights. The sun had vanished behind the western mountains, leaving behind a gray sky. The evening was cool, but Kat's skin tingled with heat.

Show them, Johnny.

"They will come for us because they hate us. Not because we are Christians or Muslims or Hindus, but because we would rather follow the teachings of Jesus and die than deny them and live."

Kat had been so fixated on Johnny that she hadn't seen the woman who approached the right of the stage, staring up at Johnny. It was the woman who'd spoken to Holly yesterday. The government's agent, Darcy Lange, who'd come wearing sunglasses like Johnny, despite the dark.

Had he seen her?

"But I'm not asking you to die," Johnny said. "I'm only asking you to follow the light that first rescued you from the darkness."

"Is this the same light that I followed?" Darcy's voice rang out for all to hear. She walked toward the stage as Johnny turned.

"When I was a child, was this the truth that the priests shoved down my throat, Johnny?"

She stepped up the two crates that led to the platform.

"Are all my nightmares and my cold sweats the result of this light from heaven that has miraculously come to save the lost?"

They've come, Kat thought.

"When all of this is over, will all your faithful disciples be left with the same fears that have haunted me for the last thirteen years?"

She faced the people and snatched her glasses from her face. Kat stared into her bright eyes.

"When they kill your daughters and sons who blindly followed you here, will you clap for joy and sing praises to the light?"

Kat wasn't sure what kind of power the woman possessed, but her voice sliced through her heart like a razor.

"Do you really want blood on your hands?" she cried.

The words might as well have been kicked from a mule. Kat caught her breath.

"You're fools! All of you, complete fools for believing all this nonsense about the sweet little baby Jesus!"

Kat wanted to scream again, this time in fear. How dare she say this? *Show her, Johnny. Show her!*

But Johnny only smiled.

"Hello, Darcy."

The woman spun back to him, jaw set.

"Welcome to the kingdom of light."

BILLY BOILED with hatred but he was no longer confused, and that alone was worth any price he might pay for the evil roiling through him.

He burst into the command center with Kelly at his side and eyed Kinnard, who still wore his glasses. "I need to speak to you."

Kinnard closed his phone. "Of course."

Billy glanced around. "Where's Darcy?"

"She's not with you?"

Billy had offended Darcy. The thought that he should discuss all of this with her before he pulled the trigger crossed his mind, but Kelly touched his elbow and he pulled back from the thought.

"This is Kelly. You'll recognize her from the photographs on the wall." He nodded at a corkboard that held a dozen pictures of the featured conspirators in Paradise. Hers was next to Johnny's and had a question mark under it.

"We have some information. Outside."

Kinnard exchanged glances with the others and followed them outside. "We're ordering the evacuation of Johnny in fifteen minutes," he said, closing the door behind him. "Does this—"

"Change of plans," Billy interrupted. A shaft of fear crashed through his mind and was gone. "We need to take them out."

Kinnard hesitated before speaking. "Take them out."

"Make an example of them. Before this becomes contagious. Meaning kill them. Drop a bomb down their throats. Take them out!"

He hadn't meant to hurl the words at Kinnard, but they came from a place of dark hatred that had fermented in his belly for a very long time.

"I'm not sure you have the authority—"

"You know very well that I have the authority to do whatever I think is reasonable to remedy this flagrant disregard for our nation's laws," Billy snapped. "We have inside information that confirms the town is planning an all-out assault on any force that enters the town. They will let us enter and then slaughter us. Knowing this, I'm ordering a preemptive strike on Paradise. I want you to bomb them. I want you to kill them all."

"Do you have any idea what kind of fallout we would be facing?"

"What did I tell you?" Kelly mumbled under her breath. She faced the mysterious CIA man who'd first saved Billy and Darcy from the killer in Pennsylvania. "Don't tell me the idea of cutting them down doesn't draw your blood to the surface. Their betrayal is unpardonable. One strike and this is all over. Just do it!"

Billy glanced from one to the other, surprised at the frankness of Kelly's demand, as if she were the true leader here.

But she was right. One strike would end it all, including Johnny's life.

Billy pressed. "Truth be told, I don't care one iota what you think we should do here, Kinnard. I want you to order the strike, and I want you to do it now. This is my responsibility, my call."

"The snipers are in place, we could take out Johnny."

"And create a full-scale revolt? Make a martyr out of a felon? Aren't you listening? They're armed to the teeth down there! The guns they dumped on the road were nothing but a lie. We need to end it. Now!"

For a few moments they stood in the night air, the woman born of Black and two men, deciding the fate of the world. At the least a very significant part of the world.

"You're sure?" Kinnard said

But the right corner of his mouth twitched, unsuccessfully betraying a grin of approval.

"Absolutely."

Kinnard dipped his head once. "Okay. Okay, then. I hope you know what you're doing. The bomber is fueled. We can get it airborne in minutes."

"Just do it."

Billy glanced around. Where was Darcy?

He needed Darcy.

CHAPTER THIRTY-EIGHT

"WELCOME TO the kingdom of light."

He was smiling, not a big grin plastered on his face, but a whisper of a smile that reached deep into Darcy's chest and filled her with rage.

The world was gathered and would peer in on this stage through the camera's eye. Enough military force to wipe out every living creature in this valley was gathered on the cliffs above them, waiting the order. Three thousand believers stood to her right, most probably willing to live or die for this so-called kingdom of light.

But all of them were truly at the mercy of two people now, facing each other on the stage. Johnny and Darcy. Two childhood acquaintances who'd grown up on opposite sides of the question that the whole world wanted answered, even if they long ago stopped asking.

Is it real?

Is there really another "kingdom" unseen by human eyes?

And what, please tell us, what does the here and now have to do with this ancient prophet named Jesus?

Darcy knew the answers. No. No. Nothing.

True, she acknowledged there was more to the way the world worked than what we can see with our eyes. Her own gift was proof enough. But reality, in its purest form, surely had nothing to do with a solitary rebel who'd been put to death two thousand years ago!

But Johnny . . . he stood there with that gimpy grin because he actually, truly, completely believed all that hooey.

She took a deep breath, stilling the fury building in her chest. "Johnny, please. You have to listen to me. They don't know I'm here."

"Why did you come, Darcy?"

She glanced at the people, expecting more participation from them. How had three thousand strangers fallen into lockstep so quickly? Well, she'd affected them with her one outburst, and she wasn't done with them yet, not by a long shot.

But Johnny first.

She looked into his glasses. "Maybe I shouldn't have come. Do you realize what's about to go down here? How many snipers have us in their sights at this very moment? They're going to use force if you so much as lift a finger, I thought you should know that."

"Force?" Johnny looked at the people. "My friends, this is Darcy Lange, a representative of the United States government, and she says they're going to use force."

"Please, I'm begging you, Johnny," Darcy said, keeping her eyes on him. "It doesn't have to be this way. You've taken this too far." Those who were looking at her eyes shifted uneasily under the power of her words.

Johnny swung around and faced her. "But we haven't taken it anywhere yet. This is only the beginning, surely you know that."

Her anger seeped out. She shoved a finger at the mountains. "The monastery was the beginning!" she cried, leaning into her words. "The beginning of a lie! We can end it here, tonight." She stomped one boot. "Give this up!"

"How can you ask us to deny the truth?"

"And just what is that truth, Johnny?"

"That Jesus is the Light of the World."

"Jesus? Only Jesus? Do you even know how foolish that sounds? You're spitting in the face of the world!"

She was still focused on Johnny, but her words reached into the crowd. A well-rounded woman standing at the front was shaking, bug-eyed eyes on Darcy. She looked too frightened to cry.

The whole western half of the crowd had been smothered by her accusation of foolishness and was already staggering under the weight of doubt her words had awakened in them.

Johnny looked out over the people again. "We are not here to itemize the rights or wrongs of Christianity or Islam or Buddhism or any religion. We are here because we believe the Light that came into the darkness is hated by that darkness. I believe Jesus is the Word made flesh. Despised and rejected by all but a few. He said you would call us fools."

Darcy leapt to the edge of the stage and faced them all. "It's a lie!" she screamed.

The effect was immediate. As if her words had physical power, they hit the nearest people like a gale. But it wasn't enough. They should be *falling* under the force of their doubt, Darcy thought.

"It is all a big mistake," she cried, "taught to you by your parents and their parents, all this nonsense about light! Think for yourselves! How dare you insult the American people by defying our laws and dying for a faith in what you can't prove!"

The round woman in the front was on her knees, eyes clenched tight, begging some unseen force to rescue her. Darcy's words reached all the way to the back of the dimly lit town square, filling it with the sound of whimpering and shifting feet.

Darcy pushed before anyone could form an argument against her.

"You're giving up your lives as zealots for a truth that is based on a lie!"

"No!"

The scream came from Darcy's left. A young, dark-skinned teenager with hair past her shoulders stood at the front, glaring at her.

She knew this girl from the Net reports. It was Katrina Kivi, the one who'd stopped the school riot in Boulder City, Nevada.

"No, that's not true!" the girl cried. "I was a witch full of hate until I saw the kingdom of light. It filled me with love, although I can say that loving you at this moment isn't easy. How dare you step on our stage and tell us that we are foolish!"

Darcy was at a loss. The girl stood firmly against the full weight of Darcy's words. She'd swayed all of Washington to embrace constitutional change but she couldn't sway the mind of one teenager?

"I was once a true believer too," she finally said. "I've earned the right to question."

"Then question," Johnny said from her left.

She watched Katrina Kivi's eyes shift to where he stood. They widened and the girl's mouth parted slightly.

Darcy turned. Johnny had removed his glasses and stared at her with bright blue eyes

"Show her, Johnny," Katrina said. "Show us all."

"I've heard your words, Darcy. I've listened to you explain the world and remain unconvinced. The question is, are you willing to look into my world and see the light?"

"There is no light but what your trickery shows," she said. "You are a trickster." But she felt inexorably drawn to see what all the fuss was about. Her breathing thickened at the mystery of it all.

"No, I won't use any illusion. I'll simply open your eyes. What you see is beyond my ability to control."

"Show her, Johnny." There was a desperation in Katrina's voice now. Darcy glanced over and saw that she was walking slowly toward them with her hands clasped in front of her. Tears wet her cheeks.

"Please, Johnny, show us."

"Why, Kat?" Johnny asked.

"Because I want to be reminded."

"You have eyes of faith."

"But you're here, and she's here, and we're all here. Isn't that why he gave you your eyes?"

Johnny gave her a slight nod and looked at Darcy.

"I've listened to you. Will you look at me?"

"I am looking at you."

BILLY PACED in the command center's lounge, ignoring Kelly, who stood with her arms crossed watching him. Looking into her eyes did nothing but fill him with more hate, and he already hated the hate seeping from his pores like a sour sweat.

He'd ordered the room closed to all but them and Kinnard, who was making the final arrangements now. The clock on the wall read five minutes past six o'clock.

They were looking for Darcy. She'd gone off sulking, and not having her with him at this time was making him sweat.

"Stop it, please," Kelly said.

Billy absently lifted his hand and trimmed the nail on his index finger with his teeth. "Stop what?"

"Pacing. You're making me think that you're full of second thoughts."

She lowered her arms and walked up to him. Placed her hand on his cheek and brushed his hair back.

"Are you?"

"How could I have second thoughts about killing Johnny?" he snapped. "He's ruined me!"

"Not Johnny. I know how much you hate him. I'm talking about the others."

The three thousand or so conspirators who'd joined Johnny in his stand against the law.

Billy turned away from her, fighting back a fresh wave of fury.

At Johnny.

At Paradise.

At the three thousand.

At Black.

At Kelly.

At himself.

Where was Darcy?

"They've made their own choice," he said. "Three thousand fewer bloggers to clog up the Net next week."

His eyes stung and he blinked away blurred vision.

Kelly turned his face back to hers. Her eyes watched his lips, then rose to his. "Accept it, Billy. This is what you were born to do. It's a great honor."

She kissed his lips where she'd bitten him and pulled back, fighting to control some unnamed emotion. "I would give anything to be you. To be flesh, real flesh. Human. You're the king of the world."

He felt a moment of pity for the beautiful woman who walked because he'd written Black into flesh. Black had written Kelly for the sole purpose of delivering Johnny to this night.

And all of it was because of him. Billy.

The door opened and Kinnard entered. He stopped at the sight of Kelly's hand on Billy's face, but she didn't remove it until he reached them.

"Well?" she demanded.

"In the air now. One air-fuel bomb. Over the target in fifteen minutes."

"Air fuel?" Billy asked. "What will that do?"

"It's twenty thousand pounds of high-explosive, designed to spread as it burns. It will detonate two hundred feet above the ground and has a blast radius of 1.2 kilometers. Basically? It will incinerate the whole town, including the buildings, the media, the cars—all of it will burn. We'll be able to say whatever we want about how this went down. There won't be any evidence to the contrary."

"Good," Kelly said.

Billy nodded. "Good."

KAT STOOD in front of the stage, looking up at Johnny and Darcy squaring off.

"I *am* looking at you," Darcy said, and Kat knew by her tone of voice that she was saying yes.

Her hands were trembling and her heart was racing because she wanted to see the light on the road to Damascus the way the apostle Paul had seen it.

"The problem, Johnny," Darcy said, placing both hands on her hips, "is that you just don't—"

But that's all she could say, because Johnny's eyes went black and she sucked at the air as if a huge boot had landed in her belly.

Johnny was showing Darcy herself.

Kat felt fear's familiar fingers lock on to her heart as she fell into the twin holes where Johnny's eyes had been. She ripped her stare away and threw her hand up to block the image. She'd been here before and the image had been much stronger then, but she couldn't bear to face it again, weak or not.

A terrible groan swelled behind her. She leaped to the stage and spun to face the crowd. Looks of horror had rounded their eyes in shock. Most stared at Johnny, unable to tear themselves from the striking sight of blackened eyes, from the very real, albeit forgiven, evil that haunted them all.

The light, they needed to see the light!

"Look away!" she cried, sweeping her hands to one side. "Don't look yet!"

They threw up their arms and buried their heads in their hands, but most were weeping already.

Kat whirled back and faced Johnny, whose eyes were fixed, coal black. She clenched her jaw against the terror that lapped at her mind and turned to the woman.

Darcy had fallen to her knees and allowed her arms to go limp as the darkness flowed into her. Her body shook with terrible sobs and her face was twisted in such anguish that Kat couldn't help but feel her pain.

Still, Johnny refused to remove his gaze. Darcy's eyes were held captive. The woman's mouth went wide in a silent cry.

"Johnny?" Kat cried.

Still he would not let her go. Darcy clamped her jaws shut and bared her teeth as if trying to keep her head from shaking off.

Kat had stared into those eyes for only a couple of seconds and nearly died. Darcy had endured thirty seconds, and Kat wondered if it just might kill her.

"Johnny!"

But he kept it up. Deeper, harder. Her eyes began to roll back into her head. That she was reacting meant she'd opened herself to the truth, which was a good thing, but not if it ended her life!

"Stop it!" Kat jumped in front of Darcy, blocking her from Johnny's eyes. "You're going to kill her!"

He closed his eyes and opened them again. Blue.

For a moment he looked at her, dazed. She could hear Darcy breathing hard through a soft whimper behind her, the only sound on the night air.

Then Johnny blinked and his eyes became white, and Kat caught her breath.

"SIR, WE'VE located Darcy Lange."

Billy swiveled to the door and looked at the staffer who'd intruded. They were now less than two minutes from the strike and Darcy had finally come out of hiding. Lovely.

Kelly stepped up behind him and placed a supportive hand on his elbow. He had no idea what Darcy would think of Kelly, who wasn't really vying for his affection as much as returning to him. She presented no real threat to Darcy, not in a romantic way.

Darcy was flesh and blood. Kelly was flesh and words. She was here to help them take down the traitor who would destroy them all.

"Is she coming?" he asked.

"She's not on the base, sir."

"At the armory then, whatever. Why isn't she coming?" Heat flared up his neck.

"She's in Paradise, sir."

Billy's blood ran cold. "Paradise? She's in the town of Paradise?"

"That is our understanding, yes, sir."

There had to be a mistake.

"*The* Paradise?"

"A helicopter pilot just called in reporting that she forced him to fly her to Paradise almost an hour ago. He left her there and is on his way back now."

Billy was too stunned to speak.

"I knew she would betray you," Kelly said in a low voice. "It was the way she was looking at him that first day in the tent. She's—"

"No!" He shook her arm off and ran forward, then pulled up and paced back, gripping his hair. "No, no, that's not right, she would never do that."

The staffer watched them with big eyes.

"She's there, isn't she?" Kelly snapped.

"She isn't there for Johnny."

"Then why?"

Billy didn't know why. Nothing else made any sense. Darcy had crossed over to Johnny? No, this wasn't right.

"Should we call off the strike, sir?"

"No," Kelly whispered. "Johnny has to die."

DARCY DIDN'T have the thoughts, much less the words, to describe what had happened to her in those eternal thirty seconds, but she knew that everything she had known for the past ten years was in fact wrong.

Not just wrong. Dreadfully, horribly incorrect.

She'd looked at the world and seen dark gray, when all along it was a brilliant red.

She'd walked through life looking for nice, neat squares to protect her from her past when in reality there wasn't a straight line to be found.

Tonight she'd come face-to-face with the rawest kind of evil and this feeling, this terror . . . it had made a mockery of her worst nightmare.

Then she'd become perfectly aware that this evil resided in her. Was a part of her nature. Was a disease that she had contracted and protected like a deep pit might protect the fungus growing on its walls. She drowned in the black lake of her own soul.

She was drowning in that lake, unable to scream, when the water had turned red. And for a moment she thought she had died.

Now someone was standing in front of her, the young girl, Katrina Kivi, yelling out for Johnny to stop. It occurred to Darcy that she was trembling on her knees, not drowning in a lake.

The girl gasped and stepped away.

Johnny stood where she'd seen him last. But his eyes weren't black any longer; they were white.

And then the world erupted with white-hot light. The brightness rushed her, slammed into her chest, and knocked her back on her seat.

For the briefest of moments, she wondered if a massive explosive had been detonated right here on the stage. But she wasn't dead. Was she?

No. Two realizations crashed through her mind with equal force. The first was that she was shaking again, but this time with pleasure.

The second was that she was more alive than she had ever been. And at this moment she was seeing the kingdom of light.

Darcy began to weep.

CHAPTER THIRTY-NINE

HOW MUCH time passed was difficult to tell, because the minutes had either slowed or sped up and Darcy couldn't tell which.

It seemed as though the sum of all Darcy's awareness had been concentrated into a drug and administered to her intravenously. Every synapse, every nerve ending, every sense she possessed was stretched to the limit of its capacity.

There was light, yes, but this particular light wasn't just white beams floating around the town square. It was a warm charge of energy that she could breathe and feel on her skin. It was the complete absence of darkness here in Paradise, Colorado.

Darcy stood and turned slowly, gazing at the town square. Johnny faced the people, frozen in time, eyes blazing white. But it wasn't just his eyes, it was the whole town square, swimming in light. He wasn't the source of the brightness, he'd simply opened their eyes to what was already here—a prophet showing them the chariots of heaven.

Slow motion. Perfectly ethereal, perfectly real. And silent.

The people were moving, heads turning, tilting, eyes wide as they gazed in wonder at the change. But slow, very slow, at one tenth the normal speed of things.

An older gentleman on the front row had his arms spread wide, his head tilted back, and his mouth wide open in what could only be a scream of pure delight. A silent scream.

Next to him, a gray-haired woman dressed in the brightest yellow dress Darcy had ever seen stood with both hands over her mouth, looking up. Tears streamed from her wrinkled eyes that seemed to cry out on their own. *I knew it. What did I tell you? I knew it!*

Darcy looked over the three thousand. To a man, woman, and child they breathed the light, some jumping, some trembling, all gripped in this force that had slowed time and was filling their mouths, their throats, their bones with raw power and pleasure.

Joseph Houde, the newsman who'd first broken the story about Paradise, stood next to two other reporters apart from the crowd, filming, but they were anything but steady. One of them had dropped his camera and was on his knees, face in hands.

But of them all, young Katrina Kivi stood out. She was leaping two feet off the ground in slow motion, flinging her arms over her head and grabbing at the light. Silent words cried from her mouth, like a delighted child who was finally allowed on that ride, the big one that she'd stared at for so many years until she was tall enough to buckle in.

They were all swept up in one overpowering sentiment, Darcy thought: *It's here. It's really here. It's really, really here.*

And it was. So real and vibrant, so heavy with power that she wondered if this was heaven.

Darcy saw all of this at once, maybe in the span of a few seconds, maybe an hour. But there was no transition for her. She knew the moment that the light slammed into her that she'd been wrong about Johnny and the three thousand. About Jesus and the kingdom he'd insistently talked about over two thousand years ago.

And about preventing any human being from placing this light on the top of the tallest mountain for all the world to see.

Darcy wept.

For joy, for sorrow, for regret, for desire of whatever was now coursing through her veins.

And then the light collapsed into itself and vanished, as if someone had pulled the plug. Slow motion fell into real time and the silence was pulled away like a blanket.

Her own scream was the first to reach her ears, and she hadn't even been aware that she was screaming. Then Katrina Kivi's high-pitched cry of delight, several feet away. Then the whole crowd's, a roar of approval and cries, the sound of weeping and moaning, all rolled into one symphony of fascination and bliss.

It only took a few seconds for everyone to realize that it was gone. The only sound came from their weeping, and then even that softened.

They stared around in wonder, stunned by the change. Breathing hard.

Darcy ran her hand through the air, half expecting to hit something. A wisp of light trailed off her fingers and then even that was gone. She faced Johnny, who watched her, eyes now blue.

"None of that was me," he said.

She knew, but she couldn't manage an answer.

A smile curved his mouth. "Tell them, Darcy."

Tell them?

"Tell them what you know. Use your voice for them."

Then she knew, Johnny had his eyes; she had her voice.

She was facing Johnny with her side to the crowd, so she twisted to see them again. They were still shell-shocked, looking around. A murmur was growing.

Darcy looked at Johnny. "Tell them?"

He chuckled. "Tell them, sing to them, scream to them, do your thing, Darcy. I think they deserve it, don't you?"

She strode to the edge of the stage, captured by the idea. "Listen to me," she said, but her voice came out hoarse from all her screaming.

"Listen! Listen to her!" Katrina Kivi shouted.

They looked up at Darcy.

"I . . . I was . . ."

The floodgates of her soul broke open, and she could not hold back her emotion. She couldn't say *wrong* because her throat wasn't cooperating. Her heart was lodged firmly there.

She began to sob again. Staring through tears at the three thousand, sobbing and sobbing.

Darcy thrust two fingers into the air and spoke as clearly as she could. "The kingdom of heaven actually *is* among us." The words from the priests who'd raised her filled her mind for the first time in thirteen years. As did the opening from the Gospel of John, the apostle who gave his life for the words he penned.

"In the beginning was the Word, and the Word was with God, and the Word was God."

Any unbelieving soul could have heard the words from her and stared back dumbly, because her voice could only excite what already was hidden in a person's mind. But Paradise was not filled with unbelieving souls.

These were the three thousand who had crossed the country to stand for the truth they believed and now saw. And now the Word reached into their hearts and minds as it never had.

Katrina Kivi shoved her hands in the air. "Tell us, Darcy!" she screamed. "Tell us more!"

Darcy gained strength. "Through him all things were made; without him nothing was made that has been made. In him was life and that life was the light of men."

They began to cry out in agreement, white knuckles gripping the air high over their heads.

Darcy screamed the words.

"The light . . ." She grabbed some breath. "The light shines in the darkness, but . . ."

Their roar drowned out her words, but not their power. They bent their heads back like birds desperate for food, and they screamed at the black sky. The roar ran long, and even though she could hardly hear herself, Darcy hurled her words into it.

Because she couldn't wait for them. She was as impatient to speak as they were to hear. So she drilled them with her eyes and spoke the truth, knowing that they could hear with their hearts if not their ears.

"But the darkness has not understood it. He came to his own, but his own did not recognize him or receive him. Yet to all who received him, to those who believed in his name, he gave the right to become children of God."

She took a deep breath.

"The Word became flesh and made his dwelling among us. We have seen his glory, the glory of the One and the Only, who came from the Father, full of grace and truth."

She wanted to sing this. To cry it out with more than just words. The power that flowed from her mouth begged to be carried by music.

Trembling, Darcy began to sing the only words that came to mind, but she sang the song in a new melody, not the one the priests used to sing on occasion. A melody she'd heard on the radio once, sung by an artist called Agnew who had a deep, rich voice that had made her chest shake as her hand hovered over the dial.

The voice that sang the words now was hers, soft and light in a high, pure tone. But a thousand times more powerful than any voice that had ever sung the words before.

Amazing grace, how sweet the sound;
That saved a wretch like me.

The words, however thin, slammed into the audience as if God's breath were visiting Paradise and had come with the force of a hurricane. They were his words, but they were her story—and she could barely stand under the weight of their truth.

I once was lost, but now am found,
Was blind but now I see.

The song thundered from three thousand voices and shook the ground in Paradise.

"HOW LONG has she been on that stage?" Billy demanded, staring at the image Kinnard handed him as the National Guard helicopter homed in on the dark valley.

"Nearly an hour."

His hands were shaking, and despite Kelly's reassuring hand on his knee, he felt torn apart by the growing realization that Darcy had defected.

"I don't understand."

"And that's the problem," Kelly said. "Not that you don't understand, but that Johnny has this kind of power even over someone as strong as Darcy." She looked out the window. "He's a dangerous man."

Kinnard sat with arms crossed, stoic in this moment of crisis. "So that's it, then?" Billy said.

He dipped his head once. "So it seems."

"She's the one who demanded all of this," he snapped. "Begged me to follow her. Spoke of ruling the world, all that nonsense. Darcy changed the Constitution, for heaven's sake! Now she's joined the enemy?"

"She didn't start this," Kinnard said. "You did."

A chill washed down Billy's spine. Yes he did, when he wrote Black, although Kinnard was probably thinking about the decision to destroy Johnny.

"And she didn't change anything," Kinnard continued. "She just helped things along. It was always only a matter of time."

An air force sergeant leaned out of the cockpit. "Sir, where do you want me to drop it?"

"As close as you can."

"I can put it right on top of them if you want."

"Then put it on top of them!" Billy snapped.

The helicopter wound for the ground. Kelly's insistence that he take out Johnny personally rode up his throat like a black acid. Killing him outright in front of the three thousand would only result in the kind of upheaval that followed a martyr's death.

There was a kind of poetic justice to the plan Kelly had suggested.

What she couldn't know was that the hatred she'd dumped into him left Billy with more than this crawling desire to end the life of Johnny Drake once and for all.

It had also left him feeling the same about himself. And if it was true that Darcy had betrayed him, then more so. It had all started with him and it would all end with him.

But not before he ended Johnny.

CHAPTER FORTY

THE HELICOPTER seemed to come out of nowhere. Low from the north, thumping just above the trees that surrounded the town square.

Kat jerked her head skyward and shielded her eyes from gusts of wind. It was a green army chopper. Maybe the authorities had seen the change in Darcy and decided to think things over before enforcing their twenty-four-hour ultimatum.

But Darcy evidently didn't think so. She ran to the edge of the stage and cried out to the audience, "Leave!" Johnny was frozen in place, center stage, but Darcy ran to the right, waving the crowd away.

"Get out now, hide, back behind the buildings!"

They might not have followed the demands of any other person, but this was Darcy, and the crowd was running before she finished.

All but Steve, Claude, and Kat.

The helicopter hovered above the lawn, then began to sink, scattering the crowd into the corners of the town like windblown dust bunnies. The microphone on the platform toppled over, and one of the wooden chairs caught a gust and tumbled along the back of the stage before dropping from sight. The chopper settled on the lawn, smack-dab in the middle of Paradise, surrounded by boiling wisps of dust from the street.

Darcy's dress whipped around her calves, but she stood firm beside Johnny, hands now clenched into fists by her side. Kat jumped onto the stage and took a position beside them.

"Johnny?" Claude Bowers had his eyes on the helicopter's door, now swinging open.

"Keep everyone back, Claude. Go with him, Steve. Just keep them back, out of sight."

"You're sure you—"

"Go, Steve. Go now."

They both hurried off, yelling at onlookers who hung close, ordering them back, out of the way, inside.

Now only Kat and Darcy remained with Johnny, and that place of honor wasn't lost on her. Kat and Johnny.

Kelly stumbled out of the helicopter and sprawled face-first onto the lawn, followed immediately by the redheaded man who'd delivered the ultimatum. Billy Rediger. Wearing glasses. A taller man who also wore sunglasses strode around from the other side of the helicopter, looking like a Las Vegas hit man in his black sports jacket.

Billy scowled, grabbed the back of Kelly's collar, and jerked her to her feet. He lifted a gun and pressed it against her temple, drilling Kelly, then Johnny, with a dark glare.

The helicopter's blades roared and lifted the chopper into the night sky.

"Johnny!" Billy cried, frantic. "This is *your* doing, Johnny!"

Kelly had been quiet these last few days, staying clear of the limelight, helping out where needed without propping herself up as Johnny's trophy. And he'd seemed content to allow her to play that role. When Kat hadn't seen her near the stage at the outset of tonight's meeting, she'd thought nothing of it, assuming she was helping behind the scenes.

And judging by Johnny's wide blue eyes, he'd assumed the same.

The beating blades of the chopper faded. The wind settled.

"Get your hands off of her." Johnny's voice came low and with a bite that surprised Kat. He was often stern, but always gentle. But the man who stared at Billy now might cause any stranger to cross the street rather than meet him on the same sidewalk.

"Or what, Johnny? Or you'll kill me? With your bare hands? Wring my neck? I don't think so. I think this time you've ruined enough lives."

Kat stood with Johnny and Darcy, but the fact that she was the smallest, weakest voice in this particular gathering began to assert itself. She'd never feared much, but the bitterness on Billy's face qualified.

The helicopter was hovering in the distance, waiting.

"I think this time you'll come with me, away from the valley, where you and I can talk through this like reasonable men," Billy said. "If you refuse, I'll kill her."

A fresh cut marked Kelly's right cheek. She shut her eyes and bit a trembling lip. "Johnny, please."

Johnny seemed to be at a loss. He could kill Billy with the flip of a knife. With a pistol he could shoot the redhead right through his forehead before Billy had time to blink.

But Johnny had left his guns at home. He was now a man of peace.

"I'm sorry," Kelly cried. "I thought I could talk to them. I'm sorry, Johnny."

"No." Johnny walked to the platform's edge, palm extended to urge calm. "You did the right thing." He dropped to the ground and walked forward.

Darcy broke from Kat's side and ran to the front of the stage. "Stop, Johnny! What is wrong with you, Billy?"

"You are!" he screamed, shaking with rage. "You're what's wrong with me, Darcy." She thought he might start to cry. "I . . . I can't stop it now."

Kelly looked like a rag doll in Billy's grip. "Don't listen to him," she said, but she didn't sound convinced.

It was odd, Kat thought. Kelly had been Johnny's handler, not the kind who would show such weakness. She was in obvious pain. Johnny was staring at her, either so distraught that he didn't know what to do or confused.

Something wasn't right. The realization hit Kat squarely, and she shifted her right foot forward. Something about all of this was terribly wrong, but she couldn't put her finger on it.

"Johnny, be careful."

Billy looked up at Kat as if she were nothing but a nuisance, then glared at Johnny again.

"I'm going to call the helicopter back, and we're going to go now, all of us. Up to the plateau. And we'll end it there, once and for all."

"He's going to kill you, Johnny." Darcy dropped off the stage and strode forward. "Who put you up to this, Billy? What's gotten into you?"

"You did," he said.

She measured him with a skeptical eye. "Take your glasses off."

"I'll go," Johnny said, putting his hand out to back Darcy down.

But she stepped closer to him. "Take them off, Billy. You swore to love me. You swore to follow me, and I'm ordering you to take your glasses off now."

"No," the man in the jacket said, as if he were the final authority here. "I spoke to the attorney general before we left, and she made it clear that we can't leave this valley without Johnny. Not this time, Darcy."

"You heard Kinnard, Billy," she said. "He's using you. We have the power, not him or the bureaucrats back in Washington. But he thinks he can just step in and make the final call. He doesn't want you to remove your glasses because he's afraid I'll talk you out of this madness. And what about you, Kinnard? Why don't you ever show your cards to us? Are you afraid?"

A grin tempted the man's mouth, but he said nothing.

"Take them off, Billy."

Billy scowled. "You heard Kinnard. Johnny goes with us or Kelly dies. You can stay, but Johnny goes with us."

"No," Kinnard said again. "Darcy comes. She's now a liability."

"I said I'll go!" Johnny said, pushing past Darcy.

But Darcy wasn't ready to give in. "What is it, Billy?" she demanded, circling to her left. "What's not right here? What's wrong, Kelly?"

She was right, Kat thought again. Something wasn't right. Something about Kelly. What was missing?

"You don't need to cry, honey," Darcy said. "This is exactly what you need now, to throw your life on the line for the man who you once tortured—"

"No!" Johnny cried. "Call your helicopter, Billy. We'll settle this away from here. Call it in!"

Kinnard lifted his phone and spoke quietly into it.

Her glasses, Kat thought. Kelly's eyes were bare!

She spoke from behind them. "She isn't wearing glasses, Johnny."

This time she'd proven more than a nuisance to Billy. He turned his eyes up and stared, and his face immediately registered concern.

"Why isn't she responding?" Kat asked. There had to be an explanation.

"I've seen his eyes, Kat!" Kelly cried.

But in that cry Kat knew that something was very wrong with Kelly. There was no reason for her to defend herself, but she had.

"But have you seen mine?" Darcy demanded. "Why aren't you responding to my voice?"

"You think you own the world?" Billy cried.

But Darcy fixed on Kelly. "Fall to the ground and beg forgiveness for the horror you caused Johnny!"

Kelly's face remained stricken, but she did not react as Kat had seen others react to the voice. She didn't weep or sag at the accusation.

The helicopter started to approach.

"This is completely absurd!" Johnny snapped.

Kelly isn't who Johnny thinks she is, Kat thought. Her heart was pounding with the certainty of it, spinning back to the times she spent in Johnny's house. She more than anyone here had spent time with both of them, and all along she'd wondered why Kelly remained so distant, so mysterious.

If so, her jealousy had been partly justified.

Kat leaped off the platform, landed on light feet, and ran forward, eyes fixed on Kelly. She sprinted past Johnny right up to Billy, who held

Kelly like a puppet with one hand and had the gun pressed to her head with the other.

She was counting on the fact that she was young to save her, but as she neared Billy's crazed stance, she wondered if it would be enough.

"Johnny will help you, Billy. There's no threat here, he just needs to know the truth about Kelly so that he can go with you peacefully. They just want to know if you're being tricked by this man and Kelly and . . ."

She reached up, jerked his sunglasses from his face, and hurled them to one side.

"They just want to know the truth!"

The thumping of the helicopter grew.

"Tell me who she is, Billy," Darcy said, staring at his frenzied eyes. "You cannot lie to me. Tell me who she is now."

A look of terrible anguish gripped Billy's face and distorted it.

Kinnard turned his back and paced away, speaking softly into his phone again. The helicopter's descent stopped.

Tears ran down Darcy's face. "Are you betraying me, Billy?"

Kelly jerked away from Billy with a swing of her arm. She spun back and slapped his face. *Whack!*

"You pitiful worm, you can't even be *you* without messing it up!"

"Stop it!" Billy screamed, leveling the gun at her face. Flecks of spittle flew from his mouth and wet his lips. "Don't say that!"

"Go ahead, Billy, kill me. Crucify me. Put a bullet in my head." She breathed hard. "Be who you are!"

Johnny's face had gone white with shock.

"But you can't kill your own children, can you?" A crooked grin snaked over her mouth. "It would be like killing yourself."

"Kelly?" Johnny's voice was hardly more than a whisper. Kat wanted to stand up for him, to protect him. But the sickening turn terrified her as much as it did him.

Kelly looked over at Johnny. "You. I should have killed you in the pit." Then she faced the barrel of Billy's gun.

She reached up and took the weapon out of his hand as if he were a child. Spit to one side. Flipped the gun on end and lifted it into his face.

"I hate you, Billy."

Billy's shoulders began to shake. He lowered his arms and went limp.

"Should I kill him, Johnny? Should I put Black's author out of his misery?"

Johnny's mouth parted, but his throat was frozen.

"No," Darcy said. "We'll go. We'll go with you, please just let Billy go."

Kelly wasn't listening. "I really, really hate you, Billy."

The detonation sounded like a thunderclap, there on the lawn in Paradise. Kat flinched.

But Billy's head did not move, did not snap back, did not blow into a dozen pieces.

Kelly's, on the other hand, did.

Her chin jerked skyward, exposing her neck as the bullet slammed through her forehead. She collapsed in a heap with her head twisted at an odd angle and her lifeless eyes staring up at the night.

The round hole in her head started to smoke, and as Kat watched, still too stunned to move, Kelly's eyes turned as black as the deepest, darkest pit.

"No." Johnny sank to his knees, blue eyes leaking tears.

"Hello, ladies and gentlemen."

Kat jerked her head in Kinnard's direction. But Kinnard was nowhere to be seen.

In his place, twenty yards off, stood a man dressed in a black trench coat, two guns cocked up by his cheeks, grinning wickedly. A thin trail of smoke rose from one gun's barrel and coiled around the rim of a broad black hat.

"Welcome to Paradise," Marsuvees Black said.

CHAPTER FORTY-ONE

WHEN MARSUVEES Black spoke those so distant but familiar words, a sense of déjà vu swept through Darcy with enough force to knock her back a step.

"Welcome to Paradise."

With sudden clarity she knew the sum of it all.

However clever Black thought himself, he was proving now—by orchestrating the events over the last thirteen years, by forcing this showdown tonight in Paradise—that evil was utterly predictable.

His very presence proved that the evil spawned from the hearts of men did not walk into the sunset never to return for another go.

Billy had never rid himself of Black, so Black was back, facing him down in the same way, in the same place, wearing the same cocky-gunslinger grin.

But Darcy had also learned tonight that things would not end Black's way. Because the light did exist, and it was swimming around them with more power and brilliance than even Jonathan Frakes, vampire word-smith extraordinaire, could possibly conjure.

Nevertheless, Darcy felt powerless to stop the sharp fingers of fear that raked her spine as she stared at Kinnard, who'd become Black.

Billy hadn't yet turned. He sagged with his arms limp at his sides, eyes closed, tears silently sliding down his cheeks.

She wanted to hold him and tell him that this mess wasn't his fault, even though it was. She wanted to tell him that she was as guilty as he was, but that she'd seen the light and so could he.

And you are the key, Billy. The end of this story is all about you. You have to shine the light on this man of darkness that you breathed life into when you were a child.

Black strutted forward in the same black boots Billy had dressed him with thirteen years ago. Pleased with himself. He'd used the pages from a stolen Book of History to write himself as he saw fit, and to write more like himself into existence. For all Darcy knew, Agent Smith was one of Black's characters. He and Muness, who'd manipulated Billy, had been part of the larger plot to draw Billy and her to Washington.

Where they'd been guided by Kinnard.

Who was none other than Black himself.

It had all been perfectly set up, perfectly executed.

"Ain't it great?" he said, spinning two six-shooters in his hands. "Just like old times. We should make us a campfire. A big one like the last time. Have a little song and dance before we cook the goose."

Katrina Kivi had stepped aside and was staring at Black with huge eyes. Johnny was still on his knees, powerless in the wake of Kelly's betrayal. Both he and Billy had been reduced to shells of themselves.

Darcy could see the similarity between Black's grinning mug and Kinnard's, and how he'd worked his magic to change it. Like a wolf in sheep's clothing, the monks used to say.

"I know," he said, pacing around them slowly, guns now up by his ears. "You're wondering how deep it all goes. How much of it was actually my doing."

She refused to engage him with more than her eyes.

"How long I've walked the halls in Washington. How many people I hung from the neck until dead to make this all happen so smoothly. Why I didn't just have Kelly shove a needle through Johnny's eyes while he was asleep in his bed."

He took a deep breath and sighed long. "So many opportunities to put all three of you in the dirt."

Billy. It's all about Billy.

Darcy eased closer to Billy, whose eyes were still shut as if he couldn't bear to look at his own creation. This was why he'd been so terrified of coming back to Paradise.

She faced Black. "You could have killed us, but that wouldn't extinguish the light, would it? You can only make what's already dark darker. You need us to extinguish the light. You need him."

She'd asked it to test Black, and she knew by his slight hesitation that she was right. Billy was indeed the key.

"There is no light in him," Black said. "And for the record, speaking about the light is now illegal, thanks to you." He winked.

From the corner of her eye, Darcy saw that some of the three thousand had stepped out from their refuge and were watching. She recognized some who lived in the town. Steve and Paula.

Black still didn't seem to have any idea of the trap he'd walked into. He was too enamored with his own darkness to understand the power of the light, and up until an hour ago, she'd been in lockstep with him.

"You think you can really play all the way to the end?" Darcy said, moving closer, closer to Billy. "We were given the power to fight evil, which I now understand means to dispel the darkness."

"Is that so?" Black's eyes darkened to onyx. He exhaled hot air and it came out like charcoal smoke from a stovepipe. "Do I look like Billy's maker? I think not. I came from him, baby. So go on, dispel him. God knows he deserves it. My precious little sinner."

This was his play: to accuse Billy, who'd breathed life into him.

SINNER 1077

But there was more to that fact. It meant that Black was *dependent* on Billy. She didn't see how evil could exist without the humans who chose it.

Steve and Paula had been joined by dozens of others. Perhaps as many as a hundred, stepping out on all sides. The original citizens of Paradise were coming out to see Black again.

He glanced around and chuckled. "It's a happy, happy day."

"What do you hope to accomplish?"

"Not me, Darcy. Billy. Billy's going to kill Johnny the Baptist."

Katrina Kivi stepped in front of Johnny and faced Black, shaking but courageous. "I don't know who you think you are, but if you think anyone can just kill Johnny, you obviously don't know him."

Black grinned wide. "I know. I trained him. Do you want to die as well, little lady?"

She hesitated, then spoke in a very plain voice. "I don't think you're thinking straight."

They were coming out of the woodwork now, a couple of hundred at least, maybe three. Walking in from all sides in a large collapsing circle.

Johnny took one last look at Kelly, then stood and slowly turned his head, judging what he saw. Suddenly nervous.

"Step back, Katrina."

"Yes," Black said. "Move your skinny backside back, Kat, kitty cat. You don't want to get burned."

She did as she was told, stopping ten paces out, where the first of the circle now stood, watching. Paula, Claude, Steve, Katie—Darcy recognized them all from when she was a child, writing.

Black turned to the circle, arms spread with the six-shooters in each hand. "Thank you. Thank you all for coming. I had hoped for some, but this is too much. Have you all played nicely in my absence?"

"You shouldn't have come back," Paula said in a tone that could have frozen milk. "We have Johnny."

"But Johnny isn't who you need," Black said. "You need Billy, lover. He's the one who gave me life, you know that. And now I'm in his belly."

Darcy moved then, while Black had his back turned. She took the last two steps up to Billy, put her arms around his waist, and kissed him lightly on his lips. "I'm here, Billy," she whispered. "It's okay. I'm here, and Johnny's here, and we don't blame you. I love you more now than I did then, you hear me, Billy?"

"No, but I do," Black said. "How about a kiss for the inner child?"

Darcy ignored him. "Billy, he needs you. You're the one who feeds him and gives him life. I've seen the light and now I know it can wash away all that darkness he put inside of you. Take it, Billy. Let it fill you."

"Too late, peaches," Black chuckled. "You've just gotten reacquainted. I've been with him all along. You really think your pathetic kisses will do the trick?"

She kissed him again, deeply this time.

"Take the light, Billy."

She knew that there was nothing in her display of affection that did any more to heal him than rubbing mud in a blind man's eyes. But she wanted to comfort him and let him feel her love.

"I love you. I will always love you."

His eyes opened, and she spoke while she had his attention.

"Kill him," she whispered.

He swallowed.

"In the kingdom of light there is no darkness," she whispered under her breath so that he could feel the words as much as hear them. "I know that now."

"Step back . . ." No chuckle from Black this time.

Darcy spoke quickly. "He doesn't know it, because the darkness doesn't understand the light, but if you accept the light, he can't exist."

It was that simple. She'd spent countless hours fighting her nightmares and all along, victory was as simple as the Word, which was the Light.

"Yours wasn't the only word that became flesh, Billy. Another came and it was the Light."

He blinked.

"Step back!"

She did when she saw that Black had trained his gun on her. But she spoke loudly now, so that they could all hear her.

"Put an end to him, Billy. Once and for all, put this snake in the grave where he belongs!"

Billy's eyes turned to Black and he began to tremble again. His vocal cords sounded as if they might snap when he spoke, frantic. "Can I write him out like I wrote him in?"

"No more books!" Black said. "Gone. Good while they lasted, but gone."

"You don't need books of paper! You need the book that's in your heart! Write it!"

"Don't be a fool, boy!" Black snapped. "This is all so much nonsense. All this light-and-darkness brouhaha, please."

"She's right, Billy," Johnny said. "You can end this."

"He can end nothing," Black screamed, face red and twisted. "You think I'm stupid? This isn't just about our dandy little reunion here, it's about a whole world out there that hates your kind!"

"Because they hated him first," Johnny said.

"Don't throw that at me! I either take Johnny's head to them or they come in here with bazookas blazing like Billy ordered. I told them to give me fifteen minutes. They know that Darcy crossed over, and I've just informed them that Billy has as well. His last order to level this valley stands. From where I'm sitting, Billy can either kill Johnny like a reasonable little sinner, or he can let the whole valley go up in smoke."

Darcy's eyes darted to Billy's and she saw they were misted again. "Is that true?"

"Darcy . . ." He began to cry.

"No, shh, no more." She took his face in her hands and forced him to look at her. "Billy, I need you to listen to me. End Black's life."

"Kill me," Johnny said.

"No!" Darcy cried.

Johnny glanced down at Kelly, dead on the ground. Darcy couldn't imagine what kind of emotions must be tearing him up. He looked up.

"Take my life, it's the only way."

"Don't be ridiculous!"

Johnny eyes darted around at the circle of onlookers. But they remained silent—it wasn't their fight, not this time. The ultimate showdown had started with Billy, and it would end with him.

"There are three thousand people in this valley," Johnny cried. "I can't have their deaths on my hands! Kill me and he'll call it off."

But Darcy was ahead of him.

She spun to the three hundred. "Get out!" she screamed, turning to look at them all. "Into the mountains. Run! In that day, flee to the mountains! Run, run."

Her voice struck them like a battering ram and they ran, like mice for their holes when the lights go bright.

"Run!"

Darcy whirled back to Billy. "*Now*, Billy! Or he'll hunt us down."

Black was smiling, but a tremble had overtaken his fingers. "It's a big bomb," he said.

Johnny paced, wringing his fingers. "He's right, they'll never make it out!" He shook his head. "We don't have a choice, Darcy. This is my fate. It's my time." To Billy: "You have to kill me!"

But Billy was staring at Black, face wrinkled, breathing heavy now. Darcy couldn't tell if he was terrified or enraged. Either way, he was rooted to the ground like a tree rattled by the wind.

"No!"

The cry had come from Kat.

Tears brimmed her eyes. "I can't believe you're arguing over Johnny's life!" She marched up to Billy and stared at him, jaw set. "Now you listen to me. Three weeks ago Johnny showed me the light and it turned my world upside down. I don't know what happened when you were all kids to make this happen, but I don't care. It doesn't matter any more. What does matter is that if you can get rid of the black thing back there, you should!"

She breathed through her nostrils deliberately.

"And you can, just like they told you. Why are you still standing here? Finish him!"

Billy slowly shifted his gaze down to her. Where Darcy had failed to penetrate him using her gift, this one young woman was reaching him.

"Can I?" He sounded not even slightly confident.

"Yes!" she said. "I did!"

"Shut up, you little runt." The order from Black came out like a bitter growl. "Shut your little hole."

She spun to the man, fists by her side. "I've seen the opposite of you and now there's nothing you can do to me, so why should I shut up? Why should any of us shut up about the light?"

"Stand back, Kat," Johnny said, taking a step forward. "This isn't your—"

"It is my battle, Johnny. I won't stand by while some monster threatens the truth."

Johnny spoke quickly, sensing danger. "Of course, but you don't know what he's capable of. Stand back. This is mine!"

"He can't hurt me, Johnny," she said, looking at him. "Not really. That's why he wants me to shut up."

"Johnny's right." This from Billy, who seemed to have been awakened by Kat. He glanced at Black, whose jaw muscles worked slowly, crushing molars. His eyes darted back to Kat. "Please, this isn't your problem."

A small smile twisted her mouth. "It is now, Billy." And then, drilling him with a bright stare, "Kill Black."

Black's left hand flashed. His gun bucked in a big fist. *Boom!*

Kat flew backward a full ten feet and landed on her backside, bright stare and smile still on her face. But she was facing the dark sky now, and blood seeped into her white shirt over her heart.

It took three full seconds for Darcy to get her mind going. When she did, it told her that Black had just killed Katrina Kivi.

"No . . ." Johnny stood in a crouch, frozen by horror. His face was wrinkled in the awful realization that Kat was dead. "No . . ." He stumbled over to her and sank to his knees. "Noooooo . . ."

"I'll hunt you down and kill every last one of you," Black said in his gravelly voice.

"Do it, Billy," Darcy whispered, trembling with it all. "Kill him!"

Billy tore his stricken eyes from Kat's body and began to cry. He reminded Darcy of a man forced to kill one child to save the rest of the family. Was he so deceived? Even now?

But there was fire in his eyes. The look of rage was so sharp, so visceral, that Darcy shied back a step.

"Do it, Billy," she said, softly now. Then again: "Do it."

"Yes, Billy, do me. Please, Papa, do me in. Put a gun to my head and shoot me dead." Black grinned, but sweat had beaded his upper lip.

"Ahhhhhh!" Billy's mouth gaped, then clamped shut. He growled again through clenched teeth. His whole body was shaking badly, from his head to his knees. But he didn't move. Didn't embrace the light. Didn't finish Black.

"You abused me . . ." he breathed.

"Did I?"

Now in a cry of agony. "You violated me! You kissed me . . . You came in . . ."

Black's grin spread wide. "Yes. And you made me, baby. How about another one?"

With those words, Billy froze. Darcy had never seen the look of such anguish on a face before. She was tempted to run to him and tell him it was okay, he didn't have to do this now.

Johnny jumped to his feet. He leaned into his words, red-faced. "Kill him!"

Billy's body was coiled like a large spring about to break.

Darcy opened her mouth to stop him.

Billy wrenched his feet from the earth and rushed forward. Right at Black. Before the man whom Billy had spawned could react with more than a blink, Billy grabbed him by his hair with both hands, thrust his head forward, and slammed his mouth onto Black's.

He screamed, a blood-freezing shriek of fury and regret and torment.

Black's lips peeled back as if the force of the scream itself had pushed them off his teeth like a blast of wind. His mouth was open so that Billy's teeth appeared to have locked onto Black's pearly white enamel.

Screaming into his mouth.

And then the scream took shape. Light, beaming from the gaps between their teeth.

Darcy's throat had locked tight. Light was streaming from Billy into Black's mouth, carried by that scream. Which could only mean that Billy himself had embraced the light.

Black dropped the six-shooters in either hand and flung his arms up to break Billy's grip on his hair.

But Billy's grip was iron, and his rage only intensified as he raged against the evil that he himself had given breath to.

Still the light flowed, rushing into Black's mouth, blasting into his throat and his lungs and his belly.

Black began to flail his arms, frantically jerking and pulling to get away from the light. Like a rat desperate to pull away from the trap whose metal jaws had clamped on its head in the middle of the night.

Black was a bigger man by a head, but now that head was locked in Billy's vice, and his legs began to thrash. The light streamed out from the corners of Black's eyeballs first. Then his eyeballs were gone, replaced by cords of light that shot into the night sky. His fingernails cracked, spilling white. Then his skin, cracking to reveal the light that had ravaged the darkness beneath his flesh.

The blazing hot light burned Black to a crisp from the inside out, reducing him to ash that fell away in clumps, leaving only the man's head in Billy's hands.

Still he screamed into Black's gaping teeth.

The head—skull, hair, and flesh—imploded, became black powder, and drifted to the ground. Only Black's teeth stubbornly remained, as if trying to bite back at Billy's teeth in retribution.

Then the demon's clackers fell as well, and the scream died in Billy's throat.

The teeth landed in the pile of ash, one at a time, *plop-plop-plop-plop.* Like bullets. A muted drum roll that announced the end of Marsuvees Black.

He was finished.

Dead by Billy.

Dead by the light.

Darcy was sure that this time he was gone forever.

Billy opened his eyes and faced them all. Johnny looked slowly over the forms that lay around their feet. Kelly, his lover. Kat, this young disciple who'd given her life to save theirs. Surely the pain in his chest would tear any lesser man in two.

They stared at each other, all three of them, stunned by the light's display of power, broken by the price paid.

"The bomb," Darcy said.

Johnny moved fast, scooping up Katrina Kivi's body in both arms. "Run for the overlook."

Darcy could hear the roar of engines high above. For all they knew the bomb was already in the air . . .

"Run!" she cried.

And they ran.

CHAPTER FORTY-TWO

Day Twenty-Two

DARCY STOOD between two large pine trees at the cliff's edge staring down at what had been Paradise, Colorado, just last evening. The blast had gutted half of the town, smashing everything from the Episcopal church to Smither's Barbeque into blackened splinters. Most of the wreckage was still on fire, and the orchards were incinerated from the edge of the blast radius to the ridge line. The concussion from the detonation had stripped the trees above them.

And when they'd climbed high enough to clear the trees that blocked their vantage, the town was nothing but raging fires in the night.

Paradise was lost.

Johnny, Billy, and Darcy had spent the night in the cabin, where young Katrina's body still lay on an old bed covered by a blanket. Johnny had lain beside her and cried himself to sleep.

They woke early and worked their way down to this white cliff edged by stubborn pines overlooking the entire valley.

The burnt-out husks of several vehicles lay on their sides like tossed toy cars. Flames had swept through the houses that surrounded the main town before finally petering out near the trees. Some of the buildings still stood at the extremities of the town, and some walls had survived the blast, but nothing was worthy of more than a bulldozer.

Three large green army helicopters sat on the black lawn where Marsuvees Black had killed Kelly last night. Twenty or thirty troops were picking through the smoldering ruins, presumably looking for bodies.

It's a nightmare, Darcy thought. *I'm going to wake up now because this is all just a nightmare.*

"It's my doing," Billy said next to her.

She looked at him, reminded that this was not a nightmare. "No, Billy, it's our doing. Yours and mine."

"No," Johnny said. "Black did this. And you killed him, Billy."

They stared in silence for a long minute. They'd already decided what to do, but standing over the scene now, their plans felt pointless. What was done was done.

"Do you think anyone was hurt?" Billy asked.

Yes, of course, that was the question on all of their minds.

Darcy took out her cell phone. Flipped it open. "We'll know soon enough."

"The Net will ultimately say the government did what it had to do," Johnny said. "And the world will remember Paradise as a tragic but unavoidable step on the path to global harmony."

Darcy turned away from the valley. "All in the name of tolerance."

"When you enforce tolerance it's natural to be intolerant of those who stand against you," Johnny said. "Someone has to be intolerant of the Hitlers and Stalins of the world. I don't blame them for that. They're just doing what they think is right."

Darcy cringed at the words. *They* had been her and Billy, not some faceless government.

"So. Christians are now criminals . . ."

"It's not about a religion." Johnny looked at Darcy. "Is it?"

Despite an initial backlash against the National Tolerance Act from all the expected quarters, it was supported on the Net by a strong majority. And that was the Pandora's box Darcy and Billy had now opened.

She swallowed. "No. It's about Jesus, who had the audacity to stand on a hill and say, 'I am the Way, and no one will find their way into the kingdom without me, and without me you will be condemned to hell.' The majority of the world now believes that's hate speech."

Darcy hit the speed dial on her phone. "But he's love, not hate."

The phone rang twice before Annie Ruling answered.

"Darcy?" Annie sounded surprised.

"Hello, Annie."

"Hold on." Darcy could hear her tell someone that she needed to take this call, and then she was back.

"You're alive."

"More than you know," Darcy said. "You thought I was dead?"

"Well . . . we had our doubts. Where in the world have you been? Do you have any idea what kind of mess this has all become?"

"Actually I was hoping you could tell me."

"What do you know?"

"I know that Paradise was incinerated last night. What I don't know is if anyone was hurt in the blast."

"One dead that we know of. They were apparently warned. By you?"

"By Billy and me."

The phone felt heavy in Darcy's hand.

"So . . ."

"So," Darcy agreed.

"You're not telling me that the reports are accurate."

"If they're saying that Billy and I have seen the light and joined Johnny, then yes, the reports are accurate. We all survived the blast. Brian Kinnard—or should I say Marsuvees Black?—killed Katrina Kivi. We have her body with us."

Annie Ruling remained silent. Her world had just become rather more complicated. She had to choose her words carefully, Darcy knew. What

Johnny, Darcy, and Billy could do as a team was hardy thinkable. Clearly
Annie didn't want them as enemies.

"And Kinnard?"

"He's dead," Darcy said.

"We haven't recovered a body."

"You won't. Is any word of the attack on the Net?"

"A few images, nothing except for some footage that appears to be the
faithful whipped up into a frenzy. Some footage taken during the detonation, nothing that changes anything if that's what you're asking. The
spin is all in our favor."

As they'd predicted.

"I was wrong, Annie. Just so you know, I was wrong."

"I don't think so, but it's moot at this point, isn't it?"

"We have a deal for you."

"I'm listening."

"You owe Billy and me a favor. You may not feel obligated to honor
your promise to me, but I did deliver what you asked, and you do owe me."

"Go on."

"No one knows if Johnny, Billy, or I survived the attack. Let the world
think we're dead. And don't come after us. It's better that way for now."

"For now?"

"Paradise," Johnny said, as a reminder.

She nodded at Johnny, who was watching her from behind his sunglasses. "Rebuild Paradise from the ground. Pay damages to the tune of
a million dollars to each resident."

A pause. "And in exchange?"

"I'm not finished. Drop any case against anyone who participated in
this debacle. The three thousand go home peacefully. If any lost their
cars, buy them new ones."

"And?"

"And in exchange we will consider your obligation to us met, and
we will agree not to undermine this administration or any of those on

the council. You do realize that we could bring any individual down quite easily."

"Is that a threat?"

"No, just making sure you realize we aren't powerless. Does this work, or do I have to come out there and speak more frankly with you?"

Annie chuckled on the other end.

"I'll have to make some calls—"

"No, I want this agreed to now. You promised me far more."

"You step foot back in Washington and the deal is off."

"Agreed," Darcy said. "And Katrina Kivi's mother gets a federal stipend of five hundred thousand dollars to help with her daughter's funeral."

Annie was silent.

"Agreed?"

"Fine."

"I want to verify all of this."

"You're sure you want to do this, Darcy? We could have done so much together, you and I."

"We could have. But I'm seeing things differently today. It was fine working with you, Annie."

"And you, Darcy."

"I hope we don't cross paths again. It could be a problem."

"I understand."

"Good-bye, Annie." She hung up.

"So she agreed, I take it?" Billy asked.

Darcy took his hand in hers. He was the sinner but then so was she, and no less guilty than he. She would love him and cover a multitude of his sins, because she liked Billy very much.

No, she loved him.

Darcy squeezed his hand. "She agreed."

"How many do you think there are?" Billy asked, facing the burnt-out valley.

"How many of what?"

"Kinnards. Kellys. Makes you wonder if one of them has a 666 stamped on the crown of his head."

"There are three fewer than yesterday," Johnny said, turning with him. They let the statement stand.

Darcy sighed. "Now what?"

"Now we run for the hills," Johnny said. "We run for the hills and we pray that the end will come quickly."

THE END

Then you will be handed over to be persecuted and put to death, and you will be hated by all people because of me.

At that time many will turn away from the faith and will betray and hate each other, and many false prophets will appear and deceive many people.

The love of most will grow cold, but he who stands firm to the end will be saved. And this good news of the kingdom of light will be declared in the whole world as a testimony to all.

And then the end will come.

MATTHEW 24:9–14

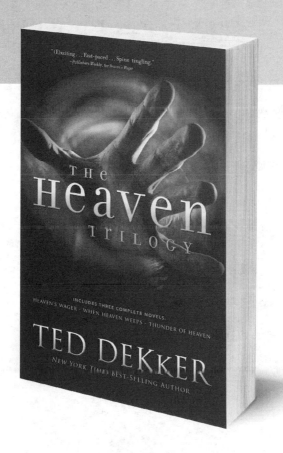

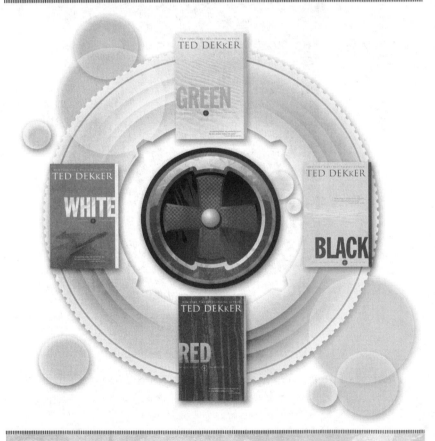

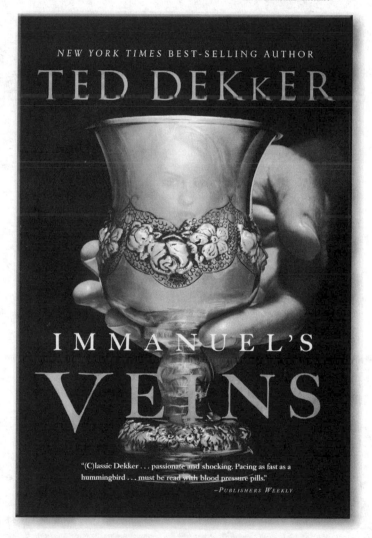

"A FULL-FORCE CLASH BETWEEN GOOD
AND EVIL. A TORNADO OF ACTION . . .

THE BEST-SELLING

Cheryl Muhr

Ted Dekker is the *New York Times* best-selling author of more than 25 novels. He is known for stories that combine adrenaline-laced plots with incredible confrontations between good and evil. He lives in Texas with his wife and children.